BITTER FRUIT

PRAISE FOR SAADAT HASAN MANTO

'What is characteristic of [Manto's] best work is a wry, sardonic refusal to be shocked. His attitude is that of a man who can no longer be surprised by the things people do to each other, but who nevertheless retains his humanity and compassion'
—*Times Literary Supplement*

'There is still no literary rival to Manto'
—*Independent*, London

'Manto is a master storyteller'
—Khushwant Singh

'A powerful exponent of man's essential freedom in a world which has forgotten its own soul, Manto stands for the spirit of man in a world surrounded by a callous materialism'
—Gilani Kamran

'Manto's irony and humanity raise him on par with Gogol'
—Anita Desai in *The Spectator*

BITTER FRUIT

The Very Best of Saadat Hasan Manto

EDITED AND TRANSLATED BY
KHALID HASAN

PENGUIN BOOKS

PENGUIN BOOKS

USA | Canada | UK | Ireland | Australia
New Zealand | India | South Africa | China

Penguin Books is part of the Penguin Random House group of companies whose addresses can be found at global.penguinrandomhouse.com

Published by Penguin Random House India Pvt. Ltd
7th Floor, Infinity Tower C, DLF Cyber City,
Gurgaon 122 002, Haryana, India

First published by Penguin Books India 2008

15 14 13 12 11 10

ISBN 9780143102175

www.penguinbooksindia.com

This book is dedicated to the memory of Saadat Hasan Manto and his wife, Safia, who stayed by his side through good times and bad. And to his favourite nephew and literary executor, the late Hamid Jalal, and his wife Zakia Jalal. But, above all, this book is for Manto's three daughters, Nighat, Nuzhat and Nusrat.

CONTENTS

PORTRAITS

LETTERS TO UNCLE SAM

MANTO ON MANTO

APPENDIXES

INTRODUCTION

This collection brings together in English translation Saadat Hasan Manto's best works. It includes stories from several of my collections published since 1987 in London, New York, New Delhi and Lahore, and twenty or so stories that I had left out for one reason or another and which have now been translated for this volume. No other Urdu writer's work has been so extensively translated into English as that of Manto, though the quality of some translations has tended to be less than satisfactory. A collection of his stories has been published in a Japanese translation; and here and there in anthologies, the odd Manto story, almost always his classic 1947 tale 'Toba Tek Singh', continues to appear. Manto has also been translated into many languages spoken in the subcontinent.

I have also translated for this collection the only stage play—'In This Vortex'—that, to my knowledge, Manto ever wrote. It is a powerful work and it is the first time it has been translated into English. I have also translated a short and amusing piece Manto wrote, not long before his death, on himself, as well as a moving letter he once wrote to his readers. He also put into that document his views on ideologically motivated literature, accusing members of the Progressive Writers' Association of trying to turn a machine into a poem and a poem into a machine. This volume also carries Manto's nine letters to Uncle Sam, which reflect Manto's sharp understanding of power politics. Translations of two conversations about Manto, one among his daughters, his sister (who has since passed on) and his wife's sister, and one among his friends are included in the appendix.

I have revised several of my earlier translations, some in order to deal with the charge made by one Indian critic that I had 'summarized' certain passages in certain stories, instead of translating them literally, word for word. I hope no fault will be found on that count—for now at least—with what this book contains. However, a translation is a translation is a translation.

In presenting Manto, I have tried to retain the bite and sharpness, no less than the infrequent but moving lyricism of his style. Manto was one of the great writers of Urdu prose and I have attempted to retain the essence of his style—or perhaps I should call it the sound of his voice—in translation. However, like all translators, I am painfully aware of the fact that translations are approximations of the original, at best. My only aim, if not my ambition, was and has been to bring Manto's work to the attention of as large an audience beyond the subcontinent as possible. This he deserves, more than any other writer of his generation. Perhaps I have had some success in that direction, though of a limited nature, because of the reluctance of western publishers to print translations from the subcontinent's writers, especially short fiction. This has meant that Manto's name and reputation outside India and Pakistan remain confined to a small though select readership, mostly in universities.

Born in Sambrala, now in the Indian state of Punjab, on 11 May 1912, Saadat Hasan Manto died in Lahore, Pakistan, on 18 January 1955. He was not even forty-three. In a literary and journalistic career spanning more than twenty years, he wrote over 250 stories and a large number of plays and essays, but it is on his stories that his reputation rests.

Coming from a middle-class Kashmiri family of Amritsar, Manto showed little enthusiasm for formal education. He failed his school-leaving examination twice in a row; ironically, one of the subjects he was unable to pass was Urdu, in which he was to produce such a powerful and original body of work in the years to come. He was also to bloom into one of the language's great stylists.

Manto entered college in Amritsar in 1931, failed his first-year examination twice, and dropped out. Those were turbulent years in the history of India. The horrific Jallianwala Bagh massacre in Amritsar had taken place in 1919, when Manto was a boy of seven; one of his most poignant stories, 'It Happened in 1919', is based on that event. Punjab, and Amritsar in particular, was in constant turmoil throughout the 1920s. Political life was characterized by civil disobedience, often turning into open and militant defiance of British authority. Manto, restless and rebellious by nature, found the situation and atmosphere intensely exciting. It was during these impressionable years that he fell under the influence of a man who was to push him towards literature and politics. That man, Bari Alig, now mainly remembered as the author of a history of the East India Company, was then a footloose writer, journalist and armchair revolutionary, devoted to 'revolution' but mortally afraid of the police. He was a man who had read extensively and was the first to sense Manto's talent, and help transform his vague fascination with revolution into strong literary commitment. Bari introduced him to Russian and French literature, ultimately persuading him to undertake an Urdu translation of Victor Hugo's *The Last Days of a Condemned Man*, a task the young Manto completed in two weeks. The book was accepted by a small publishing house in the neighbouring city of Lahore and printed.

Thrilled by his first success, Manto undertook a translation of Oscar Wilde's *Vera*, published in 1934. He was greatly inspired by the florid style of the original. As he later wrote, he and his friends, walking the streets of Amritsar, would pretend that they were in Moscow launching a revolution. Manto was also much taken with the firebrand Punjabi revolutionary and Indian nationalist Bhagat Singh, who was hanged in Lahore in 1931 for the murder of a British police officer. Those were heady times. There was a smell of revolt and revolution in the air and, for the first time, it appeared possible to force the British to quit India. Bari now began to urge his protégé to write original stories in Urdu. Manto wrote at amazing speed and never took a second look at what he had written. For example, one of his longest stories, 'Mummy' (included in this collection), was written in one or two marathon sittings. Among the first of Manto's Urdu stories, 'Tamasha', published in a small literary magazine from Lahore, was built around the Jallianwala Bagh massacre. He was to return to the subject in his later years in a powerfully evocative tale ('It Happened in 1919').

In 1934, under the influence of a school friend from Amritsar, Manto decided to enter the famous Aligarh Muslim University. Predictably, he did not do well as a student, but he used the time to write and publish more original stories for magazines. Unfortunately, his stay at the university lasted only nine months. He was diagnosed with tuberculosis—falsely as it turned out—and sent to recover at the small hill town of Batot in Kashmir (he wrote a number of stories of his time there and may have had a brief romantic fling while recuperating). He returned to Amritsar, and then moved to Lahore to take up his first regular job with a magazine called *Paras*.

But he soon tired of what he described as 'yellow journalism' and in 1936 arrived in Bombay to edit a film weekly, *Mussawar*. By this time, Bari had moved to Rangoon in search of employment. The two were never to be close associates again, though Manto, who was generally too vain to acknowledge a debt, always considered Bari the most important literary and political influence of his life. He wrote once that had he not met Bari in Amritsar he might have become a criminal instead of a writer.

Manto loved Bombay, which was not only India's film capital, but also its most vibrant and stylish city. His love affair with Bombay was to last throughout his life, though he left the city twice, once only briefly in 1941 but for good the second time, after Partition in 1947. In his powerful memoir about his friend, the actor Shyam ('Krishna's Flute', included here), he summed up his feelings about Bombay and the trauma of Partition and his departure for Pakistan. 'I found it impossible to decide which of the two countries was now my homeland—India or Pakistan?' In the summer of 1952, in an appendix to one of his finest collections of stories, *Yazid*, he recalled his days in Bombay and wrote about the city he considered to be the best thing that ever happened to him.

In a poignant piece, in the form of a letter to his readers, he wrote:

> My heart is steeped in sorrow today. A strange melancholy has descended on me. Four and a half years ago, when I said goodbye to my second home, Bombay, I had felt the same way. I was sad at leaving a place where I had spent so many days of a hard-working life. That piece of land had offered shelter to a family reject and it had said to me, 'You can be happy here on two pennies a day or on ten thousand rupees a day, if you wish. You can also spend your life here as the unhappiest man in the world. You can do what you want. No one will find fault with you. Nor will anyone subject you to moralizing. You alone will have to accomplish the most difficult of tasks and you alone will have to make every important decision of your life. You may live on the footpath or in a magnificent palace; it will not matter in the least to me. You may leave or you may stay, it will make no difference to me. I am where I am and that is where I will remain.'

> . . . I am a Bombay on the move. Wherever I happen to be, that is where I will make a world of my own.

Manto would have felt sad, were he alive today, to know that Bombay has been renamed Mumbai by an intolerant, revivalist party of religious zealots, the kind of people he hated passionately all his life. The ultimate reason for his leaving Bombay was the hate mail that was being sent to Filmistan, the studio where he worked with such close friends as Ashok Kumar, accusing Manto of infiltrating the studio with Muslims. It was shattering for a humanist like Manto, and for a man who was above the religious divide that had set India on fire, to be branded a Muslim communalist. He stopped going to the studio and would stay in his flat all day long in a somnambulist state. And then one day, he packed his bags and left for Karachi by ship.

His last years in Lahore were years of intense creativity, extreme poverty and ill health caused by heavy drinking; he felt inconsolably nostalgic for Bombay and regretted ever having left it.

But to return to his time in Bombay, he was engaged as a staff writer by Imperial Film Company from where he moved to Film City after one of the films he had written crashed at the box office. At the urging of friends, he returned to Imperial some time later. He was both fascinated and disgusted by the world of movies. As he wrote to a friend in Lahore, 'The people who have the most influence in film companies are those whose ideas are old and useless, who are completely ignorant.' At one point, he was not only writing for films, but also editing two magazines. In between, he was contributing to All India Radio. His first collection of stories was published in 1940, followed by a volume of essays in 1942, a year after he left Bombay for the first time to move to Delhi to join All India Radio as a staff writer. He was going through a period of depression because of the death of his son and his mother, to whom he was deeply attached in contrast to his relationship with his father, a harsh and stern disciplinarian who scoffed at the writing of his youngest son, whom he wanted to become a lawyer like his half-brothers, who were settled in East Africa and Fiji.

Manto lived in Delhi less than two years before returning to Bombay, the city he felt was his real home. He took his old job at *Mussawar* and began to freelance for the movies. In 1943, he joined

Filmistan, a company set up by a group of his friends from the famous Bombay Talkies. Manto wrote a number of successful films for Filmistan, including *Eight Days*, the story of a shell-shocked soldier in the Second World War.

On the eve of Independence, communal tension in Bombay, as elsewhere, was high. Then came Partition and the emergence of the free dominions of India and Pakistan. Hundreds of thousands of refugees had begun to move from one country to the other and some of history's worst carnages and bloodletting was in progress in Punjab and several other areas. Manto's wife and children and some other members of his family had already migrated to Pakistan. He was in two minds as to what he should do. His wife and others were sending him messages to get out of Bombay and come to Lahore. A new era had begun, but no one was sure what lay ahead. What decided the issue for Manto was a string of threats to the Bombay Talkies management that unless it sacked all its Muslim employees its studio would be burnt down.

Manto himself has not written about it but his wife, Safia, wrote to one of Manto's Indian biographers, Brij Premi, on 6 April 1968:

> He was always treated unjustly by everyone. The truth is that he had no intention of leaving India, but a few months before Partition, Filmistan handed him a notice of termination and that, believe me, broke his heart. For a long time, he kept it hidden from me because he was proud of his friendship with Mr Mukerjee and Ashok Kumar. So how could he tell me that he had been served with a notice? That was when he started drinking heavily, which in the end claimed his life. I had come over earlier; he came in January 1948. While he was alone in Bombay, his drinking got completely out of hand. Here his life was full of worries. You can yourself imagine the state he was in and if it was conducive in any sense. His health had also become poor. But one thing he did. He wrote prodigiously, almost a story a day, until the day he died. That is all I know.

Whether Manto was sacked or whether he left on his own, one day in January 1948, he packed his bags and took a ship to Karachi, the first capital of the new Muslim homeland of Pakistan.

Manto wrote about his last days in Bombay in his moving tribute to his friend, the debonair actor Shyam who died in a tragic accident during the shooting of a movie a couple of years before Manto's own death.

It seems such a long time ago. The Muslims and Hindus were engaged in a bloody fratricidal war. Thousands died every day from both sides. One day, Shyam and I went to visit a Sikh family from Rawalpindi—Shyam's hometown—and sat there listening in shocked silence to their horrifying account of the killing and rioting they had witnessed and survived. I could see that Shyam was deeply moved. I could well understand what was passing through his mind. When we left, I said to him, 'I am a Muslim, don't you want to kill me?' 'Not now,' he replied gravely, 'but while I was listening to them and they were telling me about the atrocities committed by the Muslims, I could have killed you.' His answer shocked me deeply. Perhaps I could have killed him too when he spoke those words. When I thought about it later, I suddenly understood the psychological background of India's religiously motivated bloodbath. Shyam had said he could have killed me 'then' but not 'now'. Therein lay the key to the holocaust of Partition.

In Bombay Talkies religious tension was rising every day. Since Ashok Kumar and Savak Vacha had taken over Bombay Talkies, most senior positions had gone to Muslims, but it was pure coincidence. This had caused much resentment among the Hindu staff. Vacha had begun to receive a steady stream of hate mail containing threats of arson and murder. Not that he or Ashok gave a damn about this sort of thing; however, being sensitive by temperament, I could not help but feel deeply disturbed by the atmosphere. A number of times, I expressed this unease to Ashok and Vacha and even suggested that they should sack me because some Hindu employees believed that the Muslim influx in Bombay Talkies was entirely due to me. Both said I had taken leave of my senses.

Indeed I had. My wife and children were in Pakistan, but they had gone there when it was still the India that I knew. I was familiar with the occasional riot which broke out between Hindus and Muslims, but now that piece of land that I had once known as India had a new name. Would that change everything? I did not know. What self-government was going to be like, I had no idea, though I thought long and hard about it.

In *Siyah Hashye*, Manto's collection of vignettes and sketches about the 1947 killings (included in entirety in this volume), none of the bloody participants is identified by religion because to Manto what mattered was not what religion people professed, what rituals they followed or which gods they worshipped, but where they stood on a human level. If a man killed, it did not matter whether he killed in the name of his gods or for the glory of his country or his way of life. To Manto, he was a killer. In his book, nothing could justify inhumanity, cruelty or the taking of life. In the holocaust of 1947, he found no heroes, except those whose humanity occasionally and at the most unexpected moments caught up with them as they pillaged, raped and killed those who had done them no personal harm and whom they did not even know. Manto saw the vast tragedy of 1947 with detachment, but not with indifference because he cared deeply.

The sketches, some of them no longer than a line or two, bring out the enormity of the tragedy set in motion by the great divide. They are deeply ironic and often profoundly moving. A Kashmiri labourer finds himself in the middle of a street riot and as the crowd breaks into stores and begins to loot the goods, he too picks up a sack of rice, but is pursued by the police and shot in the leg. He falls to the ground and is made to carry the bag he has stolen to the police station. After he fails to persuade them to let him keep it, he stutters, 'Exalted sirs, you keep the rice, all poor me ask is my wages for carrying the bag, just four annas.'

In another sketch, a husband and wife save themselves by hiding in the basement of their home, but emerge two days later to get some food and are caught by the new occupants who happen to be members of a faith that forbids the killing of any living thing. They refuse to let the couple leave and instead send for 'help' from a neighbouring village whose inhabitants have no compunction about taking life. The fugitives perish but the religious obligations of the pacifists stand duly fulfilled.

The greatest of Manto's Partition stories is 'Toba Tek Singh', now an acknowledged masterpiece. The madness that has gripped the subcontinent at the time of Independence has permeated even the lunatic asylums and the great decision-makers in the two countries decide that since there has been a transfer of populations and assets, it is only logical that non-Muslim lunatics should be repatriated to India and Muslim lunatics in India to Pakistan. On the day of the great exchange, there is only one man, Bishan Singh, who refuses to leave because he wants to stay where he was born and where his family lived, in the town of Toba Tek Singh in Pakistani Punjab. The exchange takes place at the line that divides the two new states which, until a few days ago, were one state. The guards try to push Bishan Singh into India but he refuses to move because he says he wants to live neither in India nor in Pakistan, but in Toba Tek Singh. They leave him alone because he is known as a harmless old man who talks gibberish that nobody can understand. As the morning breaks, Bishan Singh screams just once, falls and dies. This is how Manto ends this classic parable: 'There, behind barbed wire, on one side, lay India and behind more barbed wire, on the other side, lay Pakistan. In between, on a bit of earth which had no name, lay Toba Tek Singh.'

'Colder Than Ice', another masterpiece that earned Manto an obscenity charge and a trial, is the story of Isher Singh, a Sikh who abducts a Muslim girl during the riots and rapes her, only to realize later that she has been dead all along. Another story, 'The Assignment', is set in Amritsar in 1947. A dying Muslim judge who is alone with his teenage daughter, is visited by the son of an old Sikh whom he had once done a favour, in acknowledgement of which he sends him a gift of food every year on the occasion of the festival of Id. The old Sikh has died but has instructed his son from his deathbed never to discontinue the giving of the annual gift. The son comes to Amritsar from his village, finds the city in flames, with bands of crazed killers roaming the streets. Some of them are about to attack the Muslim judge's house, but delay their assault at the young Sikh's urging. What happens next chillingly illustrates the savage irony of those times.

'The Dog of Titwal' and 'The Last Salute' relate to the war in Kashmir in the wake of independence. In the first story, bored soldiers whose one link with normalcy is a dog that keeps shuttling between the two positions decide one day to have some fun by firing at the animal while he tries to seek the safety that the players are unwilling to give him. Their sport ends in tragedy. In the second story, two men fighting on opposing sides in Kashmir, discover that they had fought together during the Second World War and were the best of friends. They shout across the dividing line to each other, recall old times, crack jokes and call each other by their regimental nicknames. But their reunion ends tragically, underscoring the ironic dilemma of yesterday's comrades having become today's enemies because of a line drawn across a map.

After arriving in Lahore in 1948, Manto wrote just one film but it flopped badly. After that he did not get any work. Actually, there was very little work around as the Pakistan movie industry had started from scratch and, there being no ban on the import of movies from India at the time, the meagre output from Lahore with its ageing production facilities offered little competition to the fare from across the border. There was hardly any money to be made from writing. Most writers subsisted on what they could make out of Radio Pakistan. Ironically, every frontline writer was on the government's banned list, Manto being one of them. The list's existence was never officially acknowledged but it was common knowledge that it not only existed, but was scrupulously adhered to. Even today, sixty years into independence, the government-run media maintains a distinction between those who will be invited to contribute and those who will be ignored. Manto would have been amused but not surprised.

What money Manto made in Lahore was either through token royalties, meagre advances from publishers or through newspaper and magazine writings. He was a prodigious writer and he wrote at amazing speed. Many times, he would walk into the office of a newspaper or magazine, demand money and, on being told that it could only be given in exchange for a contribution, seat himself in a corner and produce a piece in less than an hour. Some of these pieces were pure potboilers, but amazingly most have survived the test of time. Starved of cash, he began to write his reminiscences of the Bombay cinema and its personalities for two Lahore publications: the newspaper *Afaq* and the monthly movie journal *Director* edited by Chaudhri Fazle Haq.

In the early years of independence, there were not too many taxis in Lahore, the tonga still being the most commonly used mode of transport. Manto liked to ride in smartly turned-out tongas and would commandeer one and keep it all day as he made the rounds of publishers' offices and the last port of call, the liquor store. Many of the tongawalas of Lahore knew Manto well enough to sometimes provide him service on credit. When he had money, he was generous with it.

Lack of work and ill health notwithstanding, it was in Lahore in the last seven years of his life that Manto produced some of the greatest short stories written in any language. He pined for Bombay and wrote to his friend, the Urdu writer Ismat Chughtai a number of times that she should get him to India, and preferably Bombay, after speaking to Mukerjee at Bombay Talkies. That was not to be. Certain things in life are irreversible; this was one such. Manto felt neglected by officialdom (he remains neglected till today as no posthumous honour has been conferred on him, no road or institution named after him, no acknowledgement of his ever having lived or written made, barring a one-time issue postage stamp).

In a postscript to one of his collections he wrote, addressing his readers:

> You know me as a story writer and the courts of this country know me as a pornographer. The government sometimes calls me a communist, at other times a great writer. Most of the time, I am denied all means of making a living, only to be offered opportunities of gainful work on other occasions. I have been called an unnecessary appendage to society and expelled accordingly. And sometimes I have been told that I am on the list of those the state considers desirable. As in the past, so today, I have tried to understand what I am. I want to know what my place in this country that is called the largest Islamic state in the world is. What use am I here?
>
> You may call it my imagination, but for me it is the bitter truth that so far I have failed to find a place for myself in this country called Pakistan, which I love greatly. That is why I am always restless. That is why sometimes I am to be found in a lunatic asylum and sometimes in a hospital. I have yet to find a niche for myself in Pakistan, though as far as I am concerned, I think of myself as an important person. I believe that I have a name and a place in Urdu literature because, frankly, if I did not have that delusion, life would become quite unbearable.

In all, six of his stories were considered 'obscene' by the state, three of them before Independence ('The Gift', 'A Wet Afternoon' and 'Odour') and two in Pakistan ('Colder Than Ice' and 'The Return'). The Punjab government declared 'Colder Than Ice' obscene and harmful for public morality. Manto was tried and convicted, but the judgement of the lower court was set aside in appeal, only to be reconfirmed by a Lahore High Court judge. Manto recalled that episode and his state of mind in a note appended to his book *Ganjay Frishtay*:

> I felt utterly lost. I wasn't sure what I should do. Should I stop writing altogether or should I write recklessly, unconcerned with consequences? I felt utterly listless. Sometimes I wished they would give me a lucrative piece of property so I could be free for a few years not only of financial worry but this entire business of reading and writing. I dreamt of becoming a different person who would no longer think, preferring to make a living selling contraband stuff for profit or producing illicit liquor. The last possibility I eventually crossed out from my list of alternative lifestyles because I was afraid I would drink half my produce myself. Contraband stuff I could not trade in because that needed capital and I had none.

While everyone with the slightest influence was engaged in grabbing properties abandoned by the non-Muslims who had moved to India, Manto really got nothing because the authorities saw him as a dangerous and undesirable 'progressive' and possibly a crypto-communist plotting to overthrow established authority. Ironically, the Progressive Writers' Movement had some time earlier declared that Saadat Hasan Manto was a 'reactionary'. In the end, Manto decided to write so that he could pull himself out of the depression in which he had fallen. He began by writing about the Bombay film world that he had known and the stars with whom he had worked and formed such close friendships. His first piece, 'Naseem: The Fairy Queen', was published in the Lahore newspaper *Afaq*.

This is how he recalled that time:

> I was happy that I had found a way out and would be safe from the government's displeasure and those who declare that all writing should be 'clean'. But I was wrong. The moment my first piece appeared, there was an uproar. The newspaper received piles of mail denouncing the author . . . And when my piece on Shyam ['Krishna's Flute'] was published, a certain lady, Nayyar Bano from Sialkot, wrote a long letter to the

editor that made me feel very sorry for her. Here are some excerpts from her letter: 'Now please read "Krishna's Flute" yourself once again and decide what it is. Can a person, no matter how far removed from the virtuous life and how low of character, ever wish to sit at home, surrounded by his wife and children, and narrate the experiences you have written about? It doesn't matter how much drinking he has done, or how fond he is of being in his cups. He may even talk nothing but filth or treat women as mere condiments that are to be used to spice his daily meal. Can he ever call a woman something other than a "sali" or set his bed on fire when he finds it without a woman inside.

'Please tell me in what way are you serving humanity or public morals when you splash this sort of thing across the pages of newspapers? There are others out there who have homes and families and children whom you should think of as you think of your own home, family and children. Or does this world belong only to men who are free to do what their fancy dictates, who are free to spread dirt and soil themselves and others with that dirt, even infect the innocent? Are these men not accountable to anyone? Where should people like us find refuge? How should we shelter ourselves? Perhaps the only thing parents can do, considering the evil being spread by newspapers, magazines and literature, is to join the perpetrators. Fathers should teach their sons how to drown themselves in drink and how these "sali" women should be dragged into the pit of infamy. Mothers should instruct their daughters in the latest methods of seduction. God forbid, just think of the kind of world it would be. Just think about it. I smoulder when I think about it.'

When I read this letter, by God I felt greatly affected. I experienced great pity for Nayyar Bano's condition and it occurred to me that I may have done this lady a great injustice and I must do something to make it up to her. But then I thought that if, to the best of my ability and understanding, I tried to make it up to a woman who feels herself lowered in her own eyes when she looks at pictures printed in a magazine and feels as if she had invaded someone's privacy, she may not be able to bear the shock. She may even fall unconscious. She may even die of shock. I am in no doubt that Nayyar

> Bano is among those mentally sick people who deserve our pity. Their only treatment, as far as I can diagnose, is that entire pools should be filled with liquor with corks flying out of bottles in every direction, while they are forced to watch the Bacchanal proceedings. The worst filth in the world should be kicked up for their benefit. One should throw dust on one's head and if one is unable to perform these acts oneself, one should hire people who should shout every obscenity there exists in their ears. The advertisements that appear in rags such as *Shama*, *Bisween Sadi* and *Roman* [a reference to advertisements for aphrodisiacs and 'secret' sexual ailments] should be repeatedly hurled at them loudly. And if this recipe fails to cure them, then Saadat Hasan Manto should be made to pick up Nayyar Bano's old sandal and hit himself in the head till he is completely bald.

Another correspondent claimed that Manto had shown disrespect to the dead by exposing their sexual peccadilloes and exposing their moral frailties instead of drawing a veil over their failings and saying something nice about them. The morally outraged correspondent also complained that Manto's writings were so depraved that no 'lady of the house' or young girls and children should be exposed to them. Manto dealt with this gentleman characteristically, in the process outlining his literary credo. He wrote:

> If I have committed a sin, then I have committed it in the full knowledge that it was a sin. The correspondent assures me that in every civilized society and every civilized country, only good words are used to remember those who have passed on, even if they were enemies in life. Only their virtues are highlighted; their failings are overlooked and ignored. If that indeed is what happens, then I pronounce a thousand curses on that civilized society and that civilized country where every dead person's character and personality are carted off to a laundry so that they can come back scrubbed clean and white, ready to be hanged under a sign saying 'Of Blessed Memory'.
>
> In my reform house, I keep no combs, curlers or shampoos because I do not know how to apply make-up to human beings. If Agha Hashr [celebrated playwright known as 'the Indian Shakespeare'] was cross-eyed, I have no device that can

> straighten his crooked eye, nor can I make him shed flowers from his mouth in place of the four-letter words that were his forte. I am also unable to purify the deviant character of Meeraji [Urdu poet who had some strange and peculiar personal characteristics], as I have been unable to make my friend Shyam not describe self-important women as 'salis'. Every angel admitted to the facility I operate has been barbered thoroughly and in style so that not a single hair may be left standing on his head.

Manto wrote his own epitaph, though ironically, it does not appear on his grave because his family was afraid that, if it did, there were enough mad mullahs in the country, one or more of whom would immediately declare the act heretical and the author 'outside the pale of Islam'. Instead, the family chose a couplet from Manto's favourite nineteenth-century poet, Ghalib, to whom one of his books is dedicated; and about whom he had once said that after Ghalib the right to compose poetry stood forfeited. The couplet from Ghalib reads: 'Dear God, why does time erase my name off from the tablet of the living? I am, after all, not one of those words that is mistakenly calligraphed twice and, on detection, removed.'

Here in Manto's own hand are the words that he wanted to mark his grave with:

> In the name of God, the Compassionate, the Merciful
> Here lies Saadat Hasan Manto and with him lie buried all the secrets and mysteries of the art of short-story writing . . . Under tons of earth he lies, still wondering who among the two is the greater short-story writer: God or he.
>
> Saadat Hasan Manto
> 18 August 1954

And while Manto lies there wondering, there can be no two opinions about his greatness. His stories have stood the test of time, the only test that establishes greatness or the lack of it.

May 2008 KHALID HASAN
Washington

Dear God, master of the universe, compassionate and merciful: we who are steeped in sin, kneel in supplication before your throne and beseech you to recall from this world Saadat Hasan Manto, son of Ghulam Hasan Manto, who was a man of great piety.

Take him away, Lord, for he runs away from fragrance and chases after filth. He hates the bright sun, preferring dark labyrinths. He has nothing but contempt for modesty but is fascinated by the naked and the shameless. He hates sweetness, but will give his life to taste bitter fruit. He will not so much as look at housewives but is in seventh heaven in the company of whores. He will not go near running waters, but loves to wade through dirt. Where others weep, he laughs; and where others laugh, he weeps. Faces blackened by evil, he loves to wash with tender care to make visible their real features.

He never thinks about you but follows Satan everywhere, the same fallen angel who once disobeyed you.

SAADAT HASAN MANTO

SHORT STORIES

A WET AFTERNOON

On his way to school, Masood walked past a butcher carrying a huge basket on his head that contained two recently slaughtered sheep. Their skins had been removed and from the bare flesh rose a misty vapour. The carcasses were so fresh that they were still throbbing. He saw it and his body trembled, bringing a glow to his cold cheeks and reminding him of the way one of his eyelids sometimes throbbed.

It was a quarter past nine but, because of a dull, low cloud, it felt like the early hours of the morning. There was no bite in the cold but he could see the breath coming out of people's mouths as they went their way. It was like puffs of steam pouring forth from the nozzle of a samovar. There was a heaviness in the air, as if it was weighted down by the overhanging clouds. This weather gave him the same feeling that walking in rubber shoes did. And while there were many people up and about in the bazaar, and the shops were beginning to show signs of life, the level of noise was low, like a whispered conversation. People were moving slowly as if they were afraid of having their footsteps heard.

Masood moved lazily; his satchel was under his arm. When he had seen the vapour rising from the freshly slaughtered sheep, he had experienced a strange pleasure, experienced a certain warmth rise in his body. It felt good and he wished he could experience the same comforting sensation when, on cold days, he was caned on his outstretched hands by the teacher.

The light of the day was not clear but diffuse. Everything seemed to be coated with a thin layer of mist, making the atmosphere heavy, but it did not strain the eyes because the contours of everything were indistinct.

When Masood arrived at the school, his classmates told him there would be no classes because of the death of the school secretary. They looked happy; in fact, they had already begun to play in the school yard, having flung their satchels to the ground. Some had gone home, while others were gathered at the school noticeboard, reading the school closure announcement over and over again.

The news brought Masood no joy. He felt no emotion at all. He was not the least bit sorry that the school secretary had died. He thought of the time the year before when his grandfather had died and there had been much difficulty with the burial because of rain. He had accompanied the body to the graveyard and almost slipped into the open pit because the ground was so muddy. He remembered it distinctly. It was very cold and there were red blotches of mud all over his white clothes. His hands were blue with cold and, when he pressed them for warmth, whitish spots appeared under the skin. His nose felt like an icicle. He remembered coming home, washing his hands and changing into fresh clothes. The school secretary's death had brought all that back. He was sure when they carried him for burial, it would begin to rain and the graveyard would get muddy. Many people would slip and suffer painful injury. He made straight for the classroom, unlocked his desk, took out the books he was going to bring in the next day and left them in. Then he picked up his satchel and began to walk home.

On the way, he again came upon those two freshly slaughtered sheep. One of them was now hanging by a hook in the butcher's shop and the other was lying across a large cutting board. Masood had an urge to touch the flesh from which he had seen vapour rising. He stopped and touched the still throbbing part with his cold finger. It felt good. The butcher was busy sharpening his knives, which encouraged him to touch the flesh again before walking off.

When he told his mother about the school secretary's death, she said that his father had gone for the funeral. That left only two people in the house, his mother, who was cooking in the kitchen, and his sister Kalsoom who, her hands placed for warmth over a small fire, was trying to memorize the musical scale of the raag Darbari.

Since his friends from the neighbourhood all went to Government School, the death of the secretary of Islamia School had earned them no holiday. That meant there was no one to play with, nor any homework to do. In any case, whatever there was to be learnt in the sixth form, his father had already taught him at home. He had no particular game to play with either, except a dirty pack of cards lying in the alcove. Masood was not interested. The board games that his sister played with her friends were beyond his comprehension. Since he was simply not interested in them, he had never even tried to learn the rules.

He placed his satchel in its customary niche, took off his jacket and went to the kitchen to sit next to his mother. He could hear his sister intoning the scale of the raag with its repetition of *sa*, *ga* and *ma*. His mother was chopping spinach, which she now threw into a saucepan and, as the heat reached the wet and finely cut green leaves, a whitish vapour began to rise from them. This reminded Masood of the two slaughtered sheep.

'Ammi jan,' he said, 'I saw two sheep at the butcher's shop today. They had been skinned and the flesh was sending up a misty vapour just like my breath on cold mornings.'

'Oh yes!' his mother said absent-mindedly, as she tried to stoke the fire.

'And I touched the flesh with my finger. It was warm.'

'Oh yes!' she said, moving the saucepan in which she had washed the spinach, before leaving the kitchen.

'And this flesh throbbed at so many spots.'

'Oh yes!' This was Masood's sister who, forgetting her exercise, was suddenly attentive. 'How did it throb?'

'Like this . . . like this,' Masood said, snapping his fingers.

'What happened then?'

Masood thought for a moment. 'What then? Nothing, I just told you what I saw at the butcher's shop. I even touched it. It was warm.'

'It was warm . . . now come here and do something for me.'

'What?'

'Come with me first.'

'No, first tell me what.'

'Come with me first.'

'No, first tell me.'

'All right, my back is hurting badly . . . I will lie on the bed and you press the sore areas with your feet . . . Aren't you my darling brother! I swear it really hurts.' Then she began to pound her back with clenched fists.

'What is wrong with your back? It is always hurting. And I am the one you always pick on to press it. Why don't you ask your friends to do that? They are always hanging around here.'

He stood up. 'All right, I will do it but no more than ten minutes.'

'Good boy, good boy!' she said, and put away the exercise book from which she was trying to memorize her musical scales and went into the room where both of them slept.

To get to the room, they had to walk across a small open courtyard. Kalsoom paused there for a moment, stretched herself, looked up at the sky which was overcast and said, 'Masood, it will definitely rain today.' But Masood was already in the room, sprawled on his bed.

Kalsoom came in and threw herself on her bed, face down. Masood stood up and looked at the clock which said ten minutes to eleven. 'At exactly eleven, I will stop,' he announced.

'All right, but get on with it. And do it well; otherwise I will pull your ears.' Resting his hands against the wall along which the bed lay, Masood climbed on Kalsoom's back and began to work her waist rhythmically with his feet, pressing the flesh in, then relieving the pressure, like construction workers mixing clay with their feet. Kalsoom began to moan softly.

Whenever Masood's feet happened to fall on Kalsoom's buttocks, he felt as if he was gently pounding the butchered sheep's flesh that he had touched that morning. He felt somewhat confused, not quite sure what was passing through his mind.

Once or twice, it seemed to him that Kalsoom's flesh was throbbing under his feet, just like the sheep's that morning at the butcher's shop. Having started half-heartedly, he now was beginning to enjoy what he had earlier seen as a chore. Under his weight, Kalsoom was moaning softly, her oohs and ahs keeping time with the movement of his feet and making him feel good.

The clock said it was past eleven but Masood kept on. After some time, she turned around and lying flat on her back said, 'Now Masood, nice brother, do the same up front.'

Balancing himself against the wall, he placed his feet on her thighs but, every time he did that, he slipped. She began to giggle, almost making him lose his balance. Resting his hands against the wall once again, he placed his feet on her thighs firmly and began to work his feet, under which he could feel her flesh throbbing. 'Why do you keep giggling? Lie still,' he said.

Kalsoom straightened herself and said, 'I feel funny. You kick in like a savage.'

'I promise, I will not put my full weight on you this time . . . I will be careful so that you don't feel any discomfort,' he said.

Once again, balancing himself against the wall with his hands, he placed his feet carefully on Kalsoom's thighs so that she should only feel half his body weight. He began to press her thighs dexterously as the flesh under his feet rippled from side to side. Masood thought of the tightrope walker who had once come to perform at his school. He felt like one himself.

It was not the first time he had pressed Kalsoom's legs but never before had he felt this way. His mind kept going back to the butcher's shop with that misty vapour rising from the slaughtered sheep's bare flesh. What if Kalsoom was slaughtered and skinned? Would the same kind of vapour rise from her flesh, he wondered. But he immediately wiped off this thought from his mind just as he wiped off the writing on his slate with a sponge.

'That's enough, that's enough,' Kalsoom said, sounding exhausted.

Masood thought of teasing her a little and, as he stepped down from the bed, he began to tickle her in her armpits, sending her into convulsions. She was so weak with laughter that she did not have the strength to push him away. She tried to kick him once but he was quicker and jumped off. Then he picked up his slippers and ran out of the room.

When he walked into the courtyard, a gentle rain had begun to fall, the raindrops disappearing in the brick floor as soon as they touched it. The clouds had come even lower. Masood's body felt warm and the wind felt good on his cheeks. The raindrops sent a shudder through his body. On the roof of the house across the street, a pair of pigeons sat, their feathers fluffed up. He was sure they were warm like a clay pot that has been on a low fire all night. The chrysanthemums in the courtyard looked clean and washed. A strange drowsiness hung in the air, wrapping him up like a warm woollen shawl.

Masood felt overwrought but he could not understand his thoughts. Whatever it was, it felt nice.

He stood in the rain till his hands went cold. When he pressed them, he saw whitish spots that disappeared just as quickly. He clenched his fists and began to blow on them. He felt warmer though wet. Then he walked into the kitchen. The food was ready and he began to eat. His father returned from the burial. They did not talk. Masood's mother rose and went into her room, followed by her husband. He heard the two of them talking in low voices.

After he had eaten, Masood went to the living room, opened the window and lay down on the carpeted floor. Because of the rain, it had become colder. A wind had also risen. But Masood did not find it unpleasant, though his muscles hurt slightly. Once or twice, he stretched himself and it felt good. It seemed to him that there was some strange presence in his body, but where exactly it was, he couldn't tell. A feeling of restlessness washed over him. His body seemed to be getting longer.

After tossing and turning on the floor for some time, he stood up, went to the kitchen and from there walked into the courtyard. Nobody was around. The rain had stopped. Masood pulled out his hockey stick and ball from where he always kept them and began to play. Once when the ball hit a door with a loud bang, his father screamed, 'Who is that?'

'It is I, Masood.'

'What are you doing?' his father asked.

'Playing.'

'All right, play,' then after some time, 'your mother is pressing my head so don't make a noise.'

Masood let the ball rest where it was and, hockey stick in hand, walked towards the bedroom. One door was shut while the other was half open. On tiptoe, Masood moved forward and threw the doors ajar. Kalsoom and her friend Bimla screamed, then covered themselves with a quilt. But he had seen what they were doing.

Bimla's blouse was unbuttoned and Kalsoom was staring at her breasts.

Masood could not quite understand. His brain felt foggy. He returned to the living room and sat down. A surge of power rose in his body, paralysing his ability to think.

He picked up the hockey stick, placed it across his thighs and wondered if it would snap if he were to push it down at both ends with all his strength. He began to do that but could only manage to bend it slightly. He wrestled with it for some time and, finally, in frustration, he chucked it away.

TOBA TEK SINGH

A couple of years after the partition of the country, it occurred to the respective governments of India and Pakistan that inmates of lunatic asylums, like prisoners, should also be exchanged. Muslim lunatics in India should be transferred to Pakistan and Hindu and Sikh lunatics in Pakistani asylums should be sent to India.

Whether this was a reasonable or an unreasonable idea is difficult to say. One thing, however, is clear. It took many conferences of important officials from the two sides to come to the decision. Final details, like the date of actual exchange, were carefully worked out. Muslim lunatics whose families were still residing in India were to be left undisturbed, the rest moved to the border for the exchange. The situation in Pakistan was slightly different, since almost the entire population of Hindus and Sikhs had already migrated to India. The question of keeping non-Muslim lunatics in Pakistan did not, therefore, arise.

While it is not known what the reaction in India was, when the news reached the Lahore lunatic asylum, it immediately became the subject of heated discussion. One Muslim lunatic, a regular reader of the fire-eating daily newspaper *Zamindar*, when asked what Pakistan was, replied after deep reflection, 'The name of a place in India where cut-throat razors are manufactured.'

This profound observation was received with visible satisfaction.

A Sikh lunatic asked another Sikh, 'Sardarji, why are we being sent to India? We don't even know the language they speak in that country.'

The man smiled. 'I know the language of the Hindostoras. These devils always strut about as if they were the lords of the earth.'

One day a Muslim lunatic, while taking his bath, raised the slogan 'Pakistan Zindabad' with such enthusiasm that he lost his balance and was later found lying on the floor unconscious.

Not all inmates were mad. Some were perfectly normal, except that they were murderers. To spare them the hangman's noose, their families had managed to get them committed after bribing officials down the line. They probably had a vague idea why India was being divided and what Pakistan was, but, as for the present situation, they were equally clueless.

Newspapers were no help either, and the asylum guards were ignorant, if not illiterate. Nor was there anything to be learnt by eavesdropping on their conversations. Some said there was this man by the name Muhammad Ali Jinnah, or the Quaid-e-Azam, who had set up a separate country for Muslims, called Pakistan.

As to where Pakistan was located, the inmates knew nothing. That was why both the mad and the partially mad were unable to decide whether they were now in India or in Pakistan. If they were in India, where on earth was Pakistan? And if they were in Pakistan, then how come that until only the other day it was India?

One inmate had got so badly caught up in this India–Pakistan–Pakistan–India rigmarole that one day, while sweeping the floor, he dropped everything, climbed the nearest tree and installed himself on a branch, from which vantage point he spoke for two hours on the delicate problem of India and Pakistan. The guards asked him to get down; instead he went a branch higher, and when threatened with punishment, declared, 'I wish to live neither in India nor in Pakistan. I wish to live in this tree.'

When he was finally persuaded to come down, he began embracing his Sikh and Hindu friends, tears running down his cheeks, fully convinced that they were about to leave him and go to India.

A Muslim radio engineer, who had an MSc degree, and never mixed with anyone, given as he was to taking long walks by himself all day, was so affected by the current debate that one day he took off all his clothes, gave the bundle to one of the attendants and ran into the garden stark naked.

A Muslim lunatic from Chaniot, who used to be one of the most devoted workers of the All India Muslim League, and obsessed with bathing himself fifteen or sixteen times a day, had suddenly stopped doing that and announced his name was Muhammad Ali—that he was Quaid-e-Azam Muhammad Ali Jinnah. This had led a Sikh inmate to declare himself Master Tara Singh, the leader of the Sikhs. Apprehending serious communal trouble, the authorities declared them dangerous, and shut them up in separate cells.

There was a young Hindu lawyer from Lahore who had gone off

his head after an unhappy love affair. When told that Amritsar was to become a part of India, he went into a depression because his beloved lived in Amritsar, something he had not forgotten even in his madness. That day he abused every major and minor Hindu and Muslim leader who had cut India into two, turning his beloved into an Indian and him into a Pakistani.

When news of the exchange reached the asylum, his friends offered him congratulations, because he was now to be sent to India, the country of his beloved. However, he declared that he had no intention of leaving Lahore, because his practice would not flourish in Amritsar.

There were two Anglo-Indian lunatics in the European ward. When told that the British had decided to go home after granting independence to India, they went into a state of deep shock and were seen conferring with each other in whispers the entire afternoon. They were worried about their changed status after independence. Would there be a European ward or would it be abolished? Would breakfast continue to be served or would they have to subsist on bloody Indian chapatti?

There was another inmate, a Sikh, who had been confined for the last fifteen years. Whenever he spoke, it was the same mysterious gibberish: *'Uper the gur gur the annexe the bay dhayana the mung the dal of the laltain.'* Guards said he had not slept a wink in fifteen years. Occasionally, he could be observed leaning against a wall, but the rest of the time, he was always to be found standing. Because of this, his legs were permanently swollen, something that did not appear to bother him. Recently, he had started to listen carefully to discussions about the forthcoming exchange of Indian and Pakistani lunatics. When asked his opinion, he observed solemnly, *'Uper the gur gur the annexe the bay dhayana the mung the dal of the Government of Pakistan.'*

Of late, however, the Government of Pakistan had been replaced by the government of Toba Tek Singh, a small town in the Punjab which was his home. He had also begun inquiring where Toba Tek Singh was to go. However, nobody was quite sure whether it was in India or Pakistan.

Those who had tried to solve this mystery had become utterly confused when told that Sialkot, which used to be in India, was now in Pakistan. It was anybody's guess what was going to happen to Lahore, which was currently in Pakistan, but could slide into

India any moment. It was also possible that the entire subcontinent of India might become Pakistan. And who could say if both India and Pakistan might not entirely vanish from the map of the world one day?

The old man's hair was almost gone and what little was left had become a part of the beard, giving him a strange, even frightening, appearance. However, he was a harmless fellow and had never been known to get into fights. Older attendants at the asylum said that he was a fairly prosperous landlord from Toba Tek Singh, who had quite suddenly gone mad. His family had brought him in, bound and fettered. That was fifteen years ago.

Once a month, he used to have visitors but, since the start of communal troubles in the Punjab, they had stopped coming. His real name was Bishen Singh, but everybody called him Toba Tek Singh. He lived in a kind of limbo, having no idea what day of the week it was, or month, or how many years had passed since his confinement. However, he had developed a sixth sense about the day of the visit, when he used to bathe himself, soap his body, oil and comb his hair and put on clean clothes. He never said a word during these meetings, except occasional outbursts of, *'Uper the gur gur the annexe the bay dhayana the mung the dal of the laltain.'*

When he was first confined, he had left an infant daughter behind, now a pretty, young girl of fifteen. She would come occasionally, and sit in front of him with tears rolling down her cheeks. In the strange world that he inhabited, hers was just another face.

Since the start of this India–Pakistan caboodle, he had got into the habit of asking fellow inmates where exactly Toba Tek Singh was, without receiving a satisfactory answer, because nobody knew. The visits had also suddenly stopped. He was increasingly restless, but, more than that, curious. The sixth sense, which used to alert him to the day of the visit, had also atrophied.

He missed his family, the gifts they used to bring and the concern with which they used to speak to him. He was sure they would have told him whether Toba Tek Singh was in India or Pakistan. He also had a feeling that they came from Toba Tek Singh, where he used to have his home.

One of the inmates had declared himself God. Bishen Singh asked him one day if Toba Tek Singh was in India or Pakistan. The man chuckled. 'Neither in India nor in Pakistan, because, so far, we have issued no orders in this respect.'

Bishen Singh begged 'God' to issue the necessary orders so that his problem could be solved, but he was disappointed, as 'God' appeared to be preoccupied with more pressing matters. Finally, he told him angrily, *'Uper the gur gur the annexe the mung the dal of Guruji da Khalsa and Guruji ki fateh . . . jo boley so nihal sat sri akal.'*

What he wanted to say was, 'You don't answer my prayers because you are a Muslim god. Had you been a Sikh god, you would have been more of a sport.'

A few days before the exchange was to take place, one of Bishen Singh's Muslim friends from Toba Tek Singh came to see him—the first time in fifteen years. Bishen Singh looked at him once and turned away, until a guard said to him, 'This is your old friend Fazal Din. He has come all the way to meet you.'

Bishen Singh looked at Fazal Din and began to mumble something. Fazal Din placed his hand on his friend's shoulder and said, 'I have been meaning to come for some time to bring you news. All your family is well and has gone to India safely. I did what I could to help. Your daughter Roop Kaur . . .'—he hesitated—'She is safe too . . . in India.'

Bishen Singh kept quiet; Fazal Din continued, 'Your family wanted me to make sure you were well. Soon you will be moving to India. What can I say, except that you should remember me to bhai Balbir Singh, bhai Vadhawa Singh and bahain Amrit Kaur. Tell bhai Balbir Singh that Fazal Din is well by the grace of God. The two brown buffaloes he left behind are well too. Both of them gave birth to calves, but, unfortunately, one of them died after six days. Say I think of them often and to write to me if there is anything I can do.'

Then he added, 'Here, I brought you a nice treat from home.'

Bishen Singh took the gift and handed it to one of the guards. 'Where is Toba Tek Singh?' he asked.

'Where? Why, it is where it has always been.'

'In India or in Pakistan?'

'In India . . . no, in Pakistan.'

Without saying another word, Bishen Singh walked away, murmuring, *'Uper the gur gur the annexe the bay dhayana the mung the dal of the Pakistan and Hindustan dur fittay moun.'*

Meanwhile, the exchange arrangements were rapidly being finalized. Lists of lunatics from the two sides had been exchanged between the governments, and the date of transfer fixed.

On a cold winter evening, buses full of Hindu and Sikh lunatics, accompanied by armed police and officials, began moving out of the Lahore asylum towards Wagha, the dividing line between India and Pakistan. Senior officials from the two sides in charge of exchange arrangements met, signed documents and the transfer got under way.

It was quite a job getting the men out of the buses and handing them over to officials. Some just refused to leave. Those who were persuaded to do so began to run pell-mell in every direction. Some were stark naked. All efforts to get them to cover themselves had failed because they couldn't be kept from tearing off their garments. Some were shouting abuse or singing. Others were weeping bitterly. Many fights broke out.

In short, complete confusion prevailed. Female lunatics were also being exchanged and they were even noisier. It was bitterly cold.

Most of the inmates appeared to be dead set against the entire operation. They simply could not understand why they were being forcibly removed, thrown into buses and driven to this strange place. There were slogans of 'Pakistan Zindabad' and 'Pakistan Murdabad', followed by fights.

When Bishen Singh was brought out and asked to give his name so that it could be recorded in a register, he asked the official behind the desk, 'Where is Toba Tek Singh? In India or Pakistan?'

'Pakistan,' he answered with a vulgar laugh.

Bishen Singh tried to run, but was overpowered by the Pakistani guards who tried to push him across the dividing line towards India. However, he wouldn't move. 'This is Toba Tek Singh,' he announced. *'Uper the gur gur the annexe the bay dhayana mung the dal of Toba Tek Singh and Pakistan.'*

Many efforts were made to explain to him that Toba Tek Singh had already been moved to India, or would be moved immediately, but it had no effect on Bishen Singh. The guards even tried force, but soon gave up.

There he stood in no-man's-land on his swollen legs like a colossus.

Since he was a harmless old man, no further attempt was made to push him into India. He was allowed to stand where he wanted, while the exchange continued. The night wore on.

Just before sunrise, Bishen Singh, the man who had stood on his legs for fifteen years, screamed and as officials from the two sides rushed towards him, he collapsed to the ground.

There, behind barbed wire, on one side, lay India and behind more barbed wire, on the other side, lay Pakistan. In between, on a bit of earth, which had no name, lay Toba Tek Singh.

COLDER THAN ICE

As Ishwar Singh entered the room, Kalwant Kaur rose from the bed and locked the door from the inside. It was past midnight. A strange and ominous silence seemed to have descended on the city.

Kalwant Kaur returned to the bed, crossed her legs and sat down in the middle. Ishwar Singh stood quietly in a corner, holding his kirpan absent-mindedly. Anxiety and confusion were writ large on his handsome face.

Kalwant Kaur, apparently dissatisfied with her defiant posture, moved to the edge and sat down, swinging her legs suggestively. Ishwar Singh still had not spoken.

Kalwant Kaur was a big woman with generous hips, fleshy thighs and unusually high breasts. Her eyes were sharp and bright and over her upper lip there was faint bluish down. Her chin suggested great strength and resolution.

Ishwar Singh had not moved from his corner. His turban, which he always kept smartly in place, was loose and his hands trembled from time to time. However, from his strapping, manly figure, it was apparent that he had just what it took to be Kalwant Kaur's lover.

More time passed. Kalwant Kaur was getting restive. 'Ishr Sian,' she said in a sharp voice.

Ishwar Singh raised his head, then turned it away, unable to deal with Kalwant Kaur's fiery gaze.

This time she screamed, 'Ishr Sian.' Then she lowered her voice and added, 'Where have you been all this time?'

Ishwar Singh moistened his parched lips and said, 'I don't know.'

Kalwant Kaur lost her temper. 'What sort of a motherfucking answer is that!'

Ishwar Singh threw his kirpan aside and slumped on the bed. He looked unwell. She stared at him and her anger seemed to have left her. Putting her hand on his forehead, she asked gently, 'Jani, what's wrong?'

'Kalwant.' He turned his gaze from the ceiling and looked at her. There was pain in his voice and it melted all of Kalwant Kaur. She bit her lower lip. 'Yes jani.'

Ishwar Singh took off his turban. He slapped her thigh and said, more to himself than to her, 'I feel strange.'

His long hair came undone and Kalwant Kaur began to run her fingers through it playfully. 'Ishr Sian, where have you been all this time?'

'In the bed of my enemy's mother,' he said jocularly. Then he pulled Kalwant Kaur towards him and began to knead her breasts with both hands. 'I swear by the Guru, there's no other woman like you.'

Flirtatiously, she pushed him aside. 'Swear over my head. Did you go to the city?'

He gathered his hair in a bun and replied, 'No.'

Kalwant Kaur was irritated. 'Yes, you did go to the city and you looted a lot more money and you don't want to tell me about it.'

'May I not be my father's son if I lie to you,' he said.

She was silent for a while, then she exploded, 'Tell me what happened to you the last night you were here. You were lying next to me and you had made me wear all those gold ornaments you had looted from the houses of the Muslims in the city and you were kissing me all over and then, suddenly, God only knows what came over you, you put on your clothes and walked out.'

Ishwar Singh went pale. 'See how your face has fallen,' Kalwant Kaur snapped. 'Ishr Sian,' she said, emphasizing every word, 'you're not the man you were eight days ago. Something has happened.'

Ishwar Singh did not answer, but he was stung. He suddenly took Kalwant Kaur in his arms and began to hug and kiss her ferociously. 'Jani, I'm what I always was. Squeeze me tighter so that the heat in your bones cools off.'

Kalwant Kaur did not resist him, but she kept asking, 'What went wrong that night?'

'Nothing.'

'Why don't you tell me?'

'There's nothing to tell.'

'Ishr Sian, may you cremate my body with your own hands if you lie to me!'

Ishwar Singh did not reply. He dug his lips into hers. His moustache tickled her nostrils and she sneezed. They burst out laughing.

Ishwar Singh began to take off his clothes, ogling Kalwant Kaur lasciviously. 'It's time for a game of cards.'

Beads of perspiration appeared over her upper lip. She rolled her eyes coquettishly and said, 'Get lost.'

Ishwar Singh pinched her lip and she leapt aside. 'Ishr Sian, don't do that. It hurts.'

Ishwar Singh began to suck her lower lip and Kalwant Kaur melted. He took off the rest of his clothes. 'Time for a round of trumps,' he said.

Kalwant Kaur's upper lip began to quiver. He peeled her shirt off, as if he was skinning a banana. He fondled her naked body and pinched her arm. 'Kalwant, I swear by the Guru, you're not a woman, you're a delicacy,' he said between kisses.

Kalwant Kaur examined the skin he had pinched. It was red. 'Ishr Sian, you're a brute.'

Ishwar Singh smiled through his thick moustache. 'Then let there be a lot of brutality tonight.' And he began to prove what he had said.

He bit her lower lip, nibbled at her earlobes, kneaded her breasts, slapped her glowing hip resoundingly and planted big, wet kisses on her cheeks.

Kalwant Kaur began to boil with passion like a kettle on high fire.

But there was something wrong.

Ishwar Singh, despite his vigorous efforts at foreplay, could not feel the fire which leads to the final and inevitable act of love. Like a wrestler who is being had the better of, he employed every trick he knew to ignite the fire in his loins, but it eluded him. He felt cold.

Kalwant Kaur was now like an overtuned instrument. 'Ishr Sian,' she whispered languidly, 'you have shuffled me enough, it is time to produce your trump.'

Ishwar Singh felt as if the entire deck of cards had slipped from his hands on to the floor.

He laid himself against her, breathing irregularly. Drops of cold perspiration appeared on his brow. Kalwant Kaur made frantic efforts to arouse him, but in the end she gave up.

In a fury, she sprang out of bed and covered herself with a sheet. 'Ishr Sian, tell me the name of the bitch you have been with who has squeezed you dry.'

Ishwar Singh just lay there panting.

'Who was that bitch?' she screamed.

'No one, Kalwant, no one,' he replied in a barely audible voice.

Kalwant Kaur placed her hands on her hips. 'Ishr Sian, I'm going to get to the bottom of this. Swear to me on the Guru's sacred name, is there a woman?'

She did not let him speak. 'Before you swear by the Guru, don't forget who I am. I am Sardar Nihal Singh's daughter. I will cut you to pieces. Is there a woman in this?'

He nodded his head in assent, his pain obvious from his face.

Like a wild and demented creature, Kalwant Kaur picked up Ishwar Singh's kirpan, unsheathed it and plunged it in his neck. Blood spluttered out of the deep gash like water out of a fountain. Then she began to pull at his hair and scratch his face, cursing her unknown rival as she continued tearing at him.

'Let go, Kalwant, let go now,' Ishwar Singh begged.

She paused. His beard and chest were drenched in blood. 'You acted impetuously,' he said, 'but what you did I deserved.'

'Tell me the name of that woman of yours,' she screamed.

A thin line of blood ran into his mouth. He shivered as he felt its taste.

'Kalwant, with this kirpan I have killed six men . . . with this kirpan with which you . . .'

'Who was the bitch, I ask you?' she repeated.

Ishwar Singh's dimming eyes sparked into momentary life. 'Don't call her a bitch,' he implored.

'Who was she?' she screamed.

Ishwar Singh's voice was failing. 'I'll tell you.' He ran his hand over his throat, then looked at it, smiling wanly. 'What a motherfucking creature man is!'

'Ishr Sian, answer my question,' Kalwant Kaur said.

He began to speak, very slowly, his face coated with cold sweat.

'Kalwant, jani, you can have no idea what happened to me. When they began to loot Muslim shops and houses in the city, I joined one of the gangs. All the cash and ornaments that fell to my share, I brought back to you. There was only one thing I hid from you.'

He began to groan. His pain was becoming unbearable, but she was unconcerned. 'Go on,' she said in a merciless voice.

'There was this house I broke into . . . there were seven people in there, six of them men whom I killed with my kirpan one by one

. . . and there was one girl . . . she was so beautiful . . . I didn't kill her . . . I took her away.'

She sat on the edge of the bed, listening to him.

'Kalwant jani, I can't even begin to describe to you how beautiful she was . . . I could have slashed her throat but I didn't . . . I said to myself . . . Ishr Sian, you gorge yourself on Kalwant Kaur every day . . . how about a mouthful of this luscious fruit!

'I thought she had gone into a faint, so I carried her over my shoulder all the way to the canal which runs outside the city . . . then I laid her down on the grass, behind some bushes and . . . first I thought I would shuffle her a bit . . . but then I decided to trump her right away . . .'

'What happened?' she asked.

'I threw the trump . . . but, but . . .'

His voice sank.

Kalwant Kaur shook him violently. 'What happened?'

Ishwar Singh opened his eyes. 'She was dead . . . I had carried a dead body . . . a heap of cold flesh . . . jani, give me your hand.'

Kalwant Kaur placed her hand on his. It was colder than ice.

THE ASSIGNMENT

Beginning with isolated incidents of stabbing, it had now developed into full-scale communal violence, with no holds barred. Even home-made bombs were being used.

The general view in Amritsar was that the riots could not last long. They were seen as no more than a manifestation of temporarily inflamed political passions which were bound to cool down before long. After all, these were not the first communal riots the city had known. There had been so many of them in the past. They never lasted long. The pattern was familiar. Two weeks or so of unrest and then business as usual. On the basis of experience, therefore, the people were quite justified in believing that the current troubles would also run their course in a few days. But this did not happen. They not only continued, but grew in intensity.

Muslims living in Hindu localities began to leave for safer places, and Hindus in Muslim majority areas followed suit. However, everyone saw these adjustments as strictly temporary. The atmosphere would soon be clear of this communal madness, they told themselves.

Retired judge Mian Abdul Hai was absolutely confident that things would return to normal soon, which was why he wasn't worried. He had two children, a boy of eleven and a girl of seventeen. In addition, there was an old servant who was now pushing seventy. It was a small family. When the troubles started, Mian sahib, being an extra cautious man, had stocked up on food . . . just in case. So on one count, at least, there were no worries.

His daughter, Sughra, was less sure of things. They lived in a three-storey house with a view of almost the entire city. Sughra could not help noticing that, whenever she went on the roof, there were fires raging everywhere. In the beginning, she could hear fire engines rushing past, their bells ringing, but this had now stopped. There were too many fires in too many places.

The nights had become particularly frightening. The sky was

always lit by conflagrations like giants spitting out flames. Then there were the slogans which rent the air with terrifying frequency—'Allaho Akbar', 'Har Har Mahadev'.

Sughra never expressed her fears to her father, because he had declared confidently that there was no cause for anxiety. Everything was going to be fine. Since he was generally always right, she had initially felt reassured.

However, when the power and water supplies were suddenly cut off, she expressed her unease to her father and suggested apologetically that, for a few days at least, they should move to Sharifpura, a Muslim locality, where many of the old residents had already moved to. Mian sahib was adamant. 'You're imagining things. Everything is going to be normal very soon.'

He was wrong. Things went from bad to worse. Before long there was not a single Muslim family to be found in Mian Abdul Hai's locality. Then one day Mian sahib suffered a stroke and was laid up. His son, Basharat, who used to spend most of his time playing self-devised games, now stayed glued to his father's bed.

All the shops in the area had been permanently boarded up. Dr Ghulam Hussain's dispensary had been shut for weeks and Sughra had noticed from the rooftop one day that the adjoining clinic of Dr Goranditta Mal was also closed. Mian sahib's condition was getting worse day by day. Sughra was almost at her wits' end. One day she took Basharat aside and said to him, 'You've got to do something. I know it's not safe to go out, but we must get some help. Our father is very ill.'

The boy went, but came back almost immediately. His face was pale with fear. He had seen a blood-drenched body lying in the street and a group of wild-looking men looting shops. Sughra took the terrified boy in her arms and said a silent prayer, thanking God for his safe return. However, she could not bear her father's suffering. His left side was now completely lifeless. His speech had been impaired and he mostly communicated through gestures, all designed to reassure Sughra that soon all would be well.

It was the month of Ramadan and only two days to Id. Mian sahib was quite confident that the troubles would be over by then. He was again wrong. A canopy of smoke hung over the city, with fires burning everywhere. At night the silence was shattered by deafening explosions. Sughra and Basharat hadn't slept for days.

Sughra in any case couldn't because of her father's deteriorating condition. Helplessly, she would look at him, then at her young, frightened brother and the seventy-year-old servant Akbar, who was useless for all practical purposes. He mostly kept to his bed, coughing and fighting for breath. One day Sughra told him angrily, 'What good are you? Do you realize how ill Mian sahib is? Perhaps you are too lazy to want to help, pretending that you are suffering from acute asthma. There was a time when servants used to sacrifice their lives for their masters.'

Sughra felt very bad afterwards. She had been unnecessarily harsh on the old man. In the evening, when she took his food to him in his small room, he was not there. Basharat looked for him all over the house, but he was nowhere to be found. The front door was unlatched. He was gone, perhaps to get some help for Mian sahib. Sughra prayed for his return, but two days passed and he hadn't come back.

It was evening and the festival of Id was now only a day away. She remembered the excitement which used to grip the family on this occasion. She remembered standing on the rooftop, peering into the sky, looking for the Id moon and praying for the clouds to clear. But how different everything was today. The sky was covered in smoke and on distant roofs one could see people looking upwards. Were they trying to catch sight of the new moon or were they watching the fires, she wondered.

She looked up and saw the thin sliver of the moon peeping through a small patch in the sky. She raised her hands in prayer, begging God to make her father well. Basharat, however, was upset that there would be no Id this year.

The night hadn't yet fallen. Sughra had moved her father's bed out of the room on to the veranda. She was sprinkling water on the floor to make it cool. Mian sahib was lying there quietly, looking with vacant eyes at the sky where she had seen the moon. Sughra came and sat next to him. He motioned her to get closer. Then he raised his right arm slowly and put it on her head. Tears began to run from Sughra's eyes. Even Mian sahib looked moved. Then with great difficulty he said to her, 'God is merciful. All will be well.'

Suddenly there was a knock on the door. Sughra's heart began to beat violently. She looked at Basharat, whose face had turned white like a sheet of paper. There was another knock. Mian sahib gestured to Sughra to answer it. It must be old Akbar who had come back, she thought. She said to Basharat, 'Answer the door. I'm sure it's

Akbar.' Her father shook his head, as if to signal disagreement.

'Then who can it be?' Sughra asked him.

Mian Abdul Hai tried to speak, but before he could do so Basharat came running in. He was breathless. Taking Sughra aside, he whispered, 'It's a Sikh.'

Sughra screamed, 'A Sikh! What does he want?'

'He wants me to open the door.'

Sughra took Basharat in her arms and went and sat on her father's bed, looking at him desolately.

On Mian Abdul Hai's thin, lifeless lips, a faint smile appeared. 'Go and open the door. It is Gurmukh Singh.'

'No, it's someone else,' Basharat said.

Mian sahib turned to Sughra. 'Open the door. It's him.'

Sughra rose. She knew Gurmukh Singh. Her father had once done him a favour. He had been involved in a false legal suit and Mian sahib had acquitted him. That was a long time ago, but every year, on the occasion of Id, he would come all the way from his village with a bag of sawwaiyaan. Mian sahib had told him several times, 'Sardar sahib, you really are too kind. You shouldn't inconvenience yourself every year.' But Gurmukh Singh would always reply, 'Mian sahib, God has given you everything. This is only a small gift which I bring every year in humble acknowledgement of the kindness you did me once. Even a hundred generations of mine would not be able to repay your favour. May God keep you happy.'

Sughra was reassured. Why hadn't she thought of it in the first place? But why had Basharat said it was someone else? After all, he knew Gurmukh Singh's face from his annual visit.

Sughra went to the front door. There was another knock. Her heart missed a beat. 'Who is it?' she asked in a faint voice.

Basharat whispered to her to look through a small hole in the door.

It wasn't Gurmukh Singh, who was a very old man. This was a young fellow. He knocked again. He was holding a bag in his hand of the same kind Gurmukh Singh used to bring.

'Who are you?' she asked, a little more confident now.

'I am Sardar Gurmukh Singh's son Santokh.'

Sughra's fear had suddenly gone. 'What brings you here today?' she asked politely.

'Where is Judge sahib?' he asked.

'He is not well,' Sughra answered.

'Oh, I'm sorry,' Santokh Singh said. Then he shifted his bag from one hand to the other. 'Here is some sawwaiyaan.' Then after a pause, 'Sardarji is dead.'

'Dead!'

'Yes, a month ago, but one of the last things he said to me was, "For the last ten years, on the occasion of Id, I have always taken my small gift to Judge sahib. After I am gone, it will become your duty." I gave him my word that I would not fail him. I am here today to honour the promise made to my father on his deathbed.'

Sughra was so moved that tears came to her eyes. She opened the door a little. The young man pushed the bag towards her. 'May God rest his soul,' she said.

'Is Judge sahib not well?' he asked.

'No.'

'What's wrong?'

'He had a stroke.'

'Had my father been alive, it would have grieved him deeply. He never forgot Judge sahib's kindness until his last breath. He used to say, "He is not a man, but a god." May God keep him under his care. Please convey my respects to him.'

He left before Sughra could make up her mind whether or not to ask him to get a doctor.

As Santokh Singh turned the corner, four men, their faces covered with their turbans, moved towards him. Two of them held burning oil torches; the others carried cans of kerosene oil and explosives. One of them asked Santokh, 'Sardarji, have you completed your assignment?'

The young man nodded.

'Should we then proceed with ours?' he asked.

'If you like,' he replied and walked away.

MOZAIL

Tarlochan looked up at the night sky for the first time in four years, and only because he felt tired and listless. That was what had brought him out on the terrace of Advani Chambers to take the open air and think.

The sky was absolutely clear, free of cloud, stretched over the entire city of Bombay like a huge dust-coloured tent. As far as the eye could see, there were lights. Tarlochan felt as if a lot of stars had fallen from the sky and lodged themselves in tall buildings that looked like huge trees in the dark of the night. The lights shimmered like glow-worms.

This was a new experience for Tarlochan, a new feeling, his being under the open night sky. He felt that he had been imprisoned in his flat for four years and thus deprived of one of nature's great blessings. It was close to three and the breeze was light and pleasant after the heavy, mechanically stirred air of the fan under which he always slept. In the morning when he got up, he always felt as if he had been beaten up all night. But in the natural morning breeze, he felt every pore in his body happily sucking in the air's freshness. When he had come up, he was restless and agitated but now, half an hour later, he felt relaxed. He could think clearly.

He began to think of Kirpal Kaur. She and her entire family lived in a mohalla, which was predominantly and ferociously Muslim. Many houses had been set on fire there and several lives had been lost. Tarlochan would have evacuated the entire family except that a curfew had been clamped down—probably a forty-eight-hour one—and Tarlochan was helpless. There were Muslims all around, and pretty bloodthirsty Muslims they were. News was pouring in from the Punjab about atrocities being committed on Muslims by Sikhs. Any hand—easily a Muslim hand—could grab hold of the soft and delicate wrist of Kirpal Kaur and push her into the well of death.

Kirpal Kaur's mother was blind and her father was a cripple.

There was a brother, who lived in Deolali, where he took care of the contract he had recently won.

Tarlochan was really annoyed with Kirpal's brother, Naranjan, who read about the riots every day in the newspaper. In fact, a week ago, he had been told of the rapidity and intensity with which the riots were spreading. He was warned in clear words: 'Forget about your business for the time being. We are passing through difficult times. You should stay with your family or, better still, move to my flat. I know there isn't enough space, but these are not normal times. We'll manage somehow.'

Naranjan had merely smiled through his thick moustache. 'Yaar, you are unduly worried. I have seen many such riots here. This is not Amritsar or Lahore: it is Bombay. You have only been here four years; I have lived here for twelve, a full twelve years.'

God knows what Naranjan thought Bombay was. To him it was a city which would recover from the effects of riots by itself, in case they ever were to take place. He behaved as if he had some magic formula, or a fairy-tale castle that could come to no harm. As for Tarlochan, he could see quite clearly in the cool morning air that this mohalla was not safe. He was even mentally prepared to read in the morning papers that Kirpal Kaur and her parents had been killed.

He did not care much for Kirpal Kaur's crippled father or her blind mother. If they were killed and Kirpal survived, it would be good for Tarlochan. If her brother, Naranjan, was killed in Deolali, it would be even better, as the coast would be clear for Tarlochan. Naranjan was not only a hindrance in his way, but a huge, big boulder blocking his path. Whenever his name came up in a conversation with Kirpal Kaur, he would call him Khingar Singh—Punjabi for 'boulder'—instead of Naranjan Singh.

The breeze was blowing gently, imparting a cool, pleasant sensation to Tarlochan's head, shorn of its long hair, religiously ordained. But his heart was full of apprehensions. Kirpal Kaur had newly entered his life. Although she was the sister of the rough and ruddy Khingar Singh, she was soft, delicate and willowy. She had grown up in the village, lived through its summers and winters, but she did not have that hard, tough, masculine quality that is common to average Sikh village girls, who have to do hard, physical work. She had delicate features as if they were still in the making and her breasts were small, still in need of a few more layers of creamy fat.

She was fairer than most Sikh village girls are, fair as unblemished white cotton cloth. Her body was smooth like printed linen. She was very shy.

Tarlochan belonged to the same village but he had not lived there very long. After primary school, he had gone to the city to attend high school and never went back. High school done, he began his life at college and, although during those years he went to his village numerous times, he had never even heard of this girl called Kirpal Kaur. But that may have been because he was always in a hurry to get back to the city.

The building he lived in was called Advani Chambers and, as he stood on the balcony looking at the pre-morning sky, he thought of Mozail, the Jewish girl who had a flat here. There was a time when he was in love with her 'up to his knees', as he liked to say. Never in his thirty-five years had he felt that way about any woman.

But those college days were long in the past. Between the college campus and the terrace of the Advani Chambers lay ten years, a period full of strange incidents in Tarlochan's life: Burma, Singapore, Hong Kong—and Bombay, where he had now lived for four years. And it was for the first time in those four years that he had seen the sky at night, which was not a bad sight. In its dust-coloured canopy twinkled thousands of clay lamps while a cool breeze blew his way gently.

While thinking of Kirpal Kaur, he began to think about Mozail, the Jewish girl who lived in Advani Chambers and with whom he had fallen in love 'right up to the knees'. It was a love the like of which he had not known before. He had run into Mozail the very day he had moved into a second-floor flat at Advani Chambers, which a Christian friend of his had helped him rent. His first impression of her was that she was really quite mad. Her brown hair was cut short and looked dishevelled. She wore thick, unevenly laid lipstick that sat on her lips like congealed blood. She wore a loose white dress, cut so low at the neck that you could see three-quarters of her big breasts with their faint blue veins. Her thin arms were covered with a fine down. She seemed to have just stepped out of a hairdresser's after a haircut. Her lips were not as thick as they looked, but it was the liberal quantities of crimson-red lipstick she plastered on them that gave them the appearance of thick beefsteaks.

Tarlochan's flat faced hers, divided by a narrow passage. When he stepped forward to go into his flat, she stepped out of hers in wooden sandals. He heard their clatter and stopped. She looked at him with her big eyes through her dishevelled hair and laughed. This made Tarlochan nervous and he pulled out his key from the pocket and moved towards his door. One of Mozail's wooden sandals slipped from her foot and came skidding across the floor towards him. Before he could recover, he was on the floor and Mozail was over him, pinning him down. Her trussed-up dress revealed two bare, strong legs which had him in a scissors-like grip. He tried to get up and, in so doing, brushed against her entire body as if soaping it. Breathless now, he apologized to her in very proper words. Mozail straightened her dress and smiled. 'These wooden sandals *ek-dum kandam*, just no good.' Then she carefully re-threaded her big toe in her sandal and walked out of the corridor.

Tarlochan was afraid it might not be easy to get to befriend her, but she became quite close to him before long. She was headstrong and she did not take Tarlochan too seriously. She would make him take her out to dinner, the cinema or Juhu beach, where she would spend the entire day with him, but whenever he tried to go beyond hands and lips she would tell him to lay off. She would do it in such a way that all his resolve would get entangled in his beard and moustache.

Tarlochan had never been in love before. In Lahore, Burma, Singapore, he would pick up girls and pay for the service. It would never have occurred to him that one day he would find himself plunged 'up to the knees' in love with a wild Jewish girl in Bombay. She treated him with strange indifference, although she would dress up and get ready whenever he asked her to go to the movies with him. Often they would hardly have taken their seats when she would start looking around and, if she found someone she knew, she would wave to him and go sit next to him without asking Tarlochan if he minded.

The same thing would happen in restaurants. He would order an elaborate meal and she would abruptly rise in the middle of it to join an old friend who had caught her eye. Tarlochan would get terribly jealous. And when he protested, she would stop meeting him for days on end and, when he insisted, she would pretend that she had a headache or her stomach was upset. Or she would say, 'You are a Sikh. You are incapable of understanding anything subtle.'

'Such as your lovers?' he would taunt her.

She would put her hands on her hips, spread out her legs and say, 'Yes, my lovers, but why does it burn you up?'

'We cannot carry on like this,' Tarlochan would say.

And Mozail would laugh. 'You're not only a real Sikh, you're also an idiot. In any case, who asked you to carry on with me? I have a suggestion. Go back to your Punjab and marry a Sikhni.' In the end Tarlochan would always give in because Mozail had become his weakness and he wanted to be around her all the time. Often she would humiliate him in front of some young 'Kristan' lout she had picked up that day from somewhere. He would get angry, but not for long.

This cat-and-mouse game with Mozail continued for two years, but he was steadfast. One day when she was in one of her high and happy moods, he took her in his arms and asked, 'Mozail, don't you love me?'

Mozail freed herself, sat down in a chair, gazed intently at her dress, then raised her big Jewish eyes, batted her thick eyelashes and said, 'I cannot love a Sikh.'

'You always make fun of me. You make fun of my love,' he said in an angry voice.

She got up, swung her brown head of hair from side to side and said coquettishly, 'If you shave off your beard and let down your long hair which you keep under your turban, I promise you many men will wink at you suggestively, because you are very dishy.'

Tarlochan felt as if his hair was on fire. He dragged Mozail towards him, squeezed her in his arms and put his bearded lips on hers.

She pushed him away. 'Phew!' she said, 'I brushed my teeth this morning. You don't have to bother.'

'Mozail!' Tarlochan screamed.

She paid no attention, but took out her lipstick from the bag she always carried and began to touch up her lips which looked havoc-stricken after contact with Tarlochan's beard and moustache.

'Let me tell you something,' she said without looking up. 'You have no idea how to use your hirsute assets properly. They would be perfect for brushing dust off my navy-blue skirt.'

She came and sat next to him and began to unpin his beard. It was true he was very good-looking, but being a practising Sikh he had never shaved a single hair off his body and, consequently, he had come to assume a look which was not natural. He respected his religion and its customs and he did not wish to change any of its ritual formalities.

'What are you doing?' he asked Mozail. By now his beard, freed of its shackles, was hanging over his chest in waves.

'You have such soft hair, so I don't think I would use it to brush my navy-blue skirt. Perhaps a nice, soft woven handbag,' she said, smiling flirtatiously.

'I have never made fun of your religion. Why do you always mock mine? It's not fair. But I have suffered these insults silently because I love you. Did you know I love you?'

'I know,' she said, letting go of his beard.

'I want to marry you,' he declared, while trying to repin his beard.

'I know,' she said with a slight shake of her head. 'In fact, I have nearly decided to marry you.'

'You don't say!' Tarlochan nearly jumped.

'I do,' she said.

He forgot his half-folded beard and embraced her passionately. 'When . . . when?'

She pushed him aside. 'When you get rid of your hair.'

'It will be gone tomorrow,' he said without thinking.

She began to do a tap dance around the room. 'You're talking rubbish, Tarloch. I don't think you have the courage.'

'You will see,' he said defiantly.

'So I will,' she said, kissing him on the lips, followed by her usual 'Phew!'

He could hardly sleep that night. It was not a small decision. However, the next day he went out to a barber in the Fort area and had him cut his hair and shave off his beard. While this operation was in progress, he kept his eyes closed. When it was finished, he looked at his new face in the mirror. It looked good. Any girl in Bombay would have found it difficult not to take a long, second look at him.

He did not leave his flat on his first hairless day, but sent word to Mozail that he was not well and would she mind dropping in for a minute. She stopped dead in her tracks when she saw him. 'My darling Tarloch,' she cried and fell into his arms. She ran her hands over his smooth cheeks and combed his short hair with her fingers. She laughed so much that her nose began to run. She had no handkerchief and calmly she lifted her skirt and wiped it. Tarlochan blushed. 'You should wear something underneath.'

'Gives me a funny feeling. That's how it is,' she replied.

'Let's get married tomorrow,' he said.

'Of course,' she replied, rubbing his chin.

They decided to get married in Poona, where Tarlochan had many friends.

Mozail worked as a salesgirl in one of the big department stores in the Fort area. She told Tarlochan to wait for her at a taxi stand in front of the store the next day, but she never turned up. He later learnt that she had gone off with an old lover of hers who had recently bought a new car. They had moved to Deolali and were not expected to return to Bombay 'for some time'.

Tarlochan was shattered, but in a few weeks he had got over it. And it was at this point that he had met Kirpal Kaur and fallen in love with her.

He now realized what a vulgar girl Mozail was and how totally heartless. He thanked his stars that he hadn't married her.

But there were days when he missed her. He remembered that once he had decided to buy her some gold earrings and had taken her to a jeweller's, but all she wanted was some cheap baubles. That was the way she was.

She used to lie in bed with him for hours and let him kiss and fondle her as much as he wanted, but she would never let him make love. 'You're a Sikh,' she would laugh, 'and I hate Sikhs.'

One argument they always had was over her habit of not wearing any underclothes. Once she said to him, 'You're a Sikh and I know that you wear some ridiculous shorts under your trousers because that is the Sikh religious requirement, but I think it's rubbish that religion should be kept tucked under one's trousers.'

Tarlochan looked at the gradually brightening sky.

'The hell with her,' he said loudly and decided not to think about her at all. He was worried about Kirpal Kaur and the danger which loomed over her.

A number of communal incidents had already taken place in the locality. The place was full of orthodox Muslims and, curfew or no curfew, they could easily enter her house and massacre everyone.

Since Mozail had left him, he had decided to grow his hair. His beard had flourished again, but he had come to a compromise. He would not let it grow too long. He knew a barber who could trim it so skilfully that it would not appear trimmed.

The curfew was still in force, but you could walk about in the street, as long as you did not stray too far. He decided to do so. There was a public tap in front of the building. He sat down under it and began to wash his hair and freshen up his face.

Suddenly he heard the sound of wooden sandals on the cobblestones. There were other Jewish women in that building, all of whom for some reason wore the same kind of sandals. He thought it was one of them.

But it was Mozail. She was wearing her usual loose gown under which he could see her breasts dancing. It disturbed him. He coughed to attract her attention, because he had a feeling she might just pass him by. She came towards him, examined his beard and said, 'What do we have here, a twice-born Sikh?'

She touched his beard. 'Still good enough to brush my navy-blue skirt with, except that I left it in that other place in Deolali.'

Tarlochan said nothing. She pinched his arm. 'Why don't you say something, Sardar sahib?'

He looked at her. She had lost weight. 'Have you been ill?' he asked.

'No.'

'But you look run down.'

'I am dieting. So you are once again a Sikh?' She sat down next to him, squatting on the ground.

'Yes,' he replied.

'Congratulations. Are you in love with some other girl?'

'Yes.'

'Congratulations. Does she live here, I mean, in our building?'

'No.'

'Isn't that awful?'

She pulled at his beard. 'Is this grown on her advice?'

'No.'

'Well, I promise you that if you get this beard of yours shaved off, I'll marry you. I swear.'

'Mozail,' he said, 'I have decided to marry this simple girl from my village. She is a good, observing Sikh, which is why I am growing my hair again.'

Mozail got up, swung herself in a semi-circle on her heel and said, 'If she's a good Sikh, why should she marry you? Doesn't she know that you once broke all the rules and shaved your hair off?'

'No, she doesn't. I started growing a beard the very day you left me—as a gesture of revenge, if you like. I met her some time later, but the way I tie my turban, you can hardly tell that I don't have a full head of hair.'

She lifted her dress to scratch her thigh. 'Damn these mosquitoes,' she said. Then she added, 'When are you getting married?'

'I don't know.' The anxiety in his voice showed.

'What are you thinking, Tarlochan?' she asked. He told her.

'You are a first-class idiot. What's the problem? Just go and get her here where she would be safe.'

'Mozail, you can't understand these things. It's not that simple. You don't really give a damn and that is why we broke up. I'm sorry,' he said.

'Sorry? Come off it, you silly idiot. What you should be thinking of now is how we can get . . . whatever her name is . . . to your flat. And here you go talking about your sorrow at losing me. It could never have worked. Your problem is that you are both stupid and cautious. I like my men to be reckless. OK, forget about that, let's go and get your whatever Kaur from wherever she is.'

Tarlochan looked at her nervously. 'But there's a curfew in the area,' he said.

'There's no curfew for Mozail. Let's go,' she said, almost dragging him.

She looked at him and paused. 'What's the matter?' he asked.

'Your beard, but it's not that long. However, take that turban off, then nobody will take you for a Sikh.'

'I won't go bareheaded,' he said.

'Why not?'

'You don't understand? It is not proper for me to go to their house without my turban.'

'And why not?'

'Why don't you understand? She has never seen me except in a turban. She thinks I am a proper Sikh. I daren't let her think otherwise.'

Mozail rattled her wooden sandals on the floor. 'You are not only a first-class idiot, you are also an ass. It is a question of saving her life, whatever that Kaur of yours is called.'

Tarlochan was not going to give up. 'Mozail, you've no idea how religious she is. Once she sees me bareheaded, she'll start hating me.'

'Your love be damned. Tell me, are all Sikhs as stupid as you? On the one hand, you want to save her life and at the same time you insist on wearing your turban, and perhaps even those funny knickers you are never supposed to be without.'

'I do wear my knickers—as you call them—all the time,' he said.

'Good for you,' she said. 'But think, you're going to go to that awful area full of those bloodthirsty Muslims and their big maulanas. If you go in a turban, I promise you they will take one look at you and run a big, sharp knife across your throat.'

'I don't care, but I must wear my turban. I can risk my life, but not my love.'

'You're an ass,' she said exasperatedly. 'Tell me, if you're bombed off, what use will that Kaur be to you? I swear, you're not only a Sikh, you are an idiot of a Sikh.'

'Don't talk rot,' Tarlochan snapped.

She laughed, then she put her arms around his neck and swung her body slightly. 'Darling,' she said, 'then it will be the way you want it. Go put on your turban. I will be waiting for you in the street.'

'You should put on some clothes,' Tarlochan said.

'I'm fine the way I am,' she replied.

When he joined her, she was standing in the middle of the street. Her legs apart like a man, and smoking. When he came close, she blew the smoke in his face. 'You're the most terrible human being I've ever met in my life,' Tarlochan said. 'You know we Sikhs are not allowed to smoke.'

'Let's go,' she said.

The bazaar was deserted. The curfew seemed to have affected even the usually brisk Bombay breeze. It was hardly noticeable. Some lights were on but their glow was sickly. Normally at this hour the trains would start running and shops begin to open. There was absolutely no sign of life anywhere.

Mozail walked in front of him. The only sound came from the impact of her wooden sandals on the road. He almost asked her to take the stupid things off and go barefoot, but he didn't. She wouldn't have agreed.

Tarlochan felt scared, but Mozail was walking ahead of him nonchalantly, puffing merrily at her cigarette. They came to a square and were challenged by a policeman. 'Where are you going?' Tarlochan fell back, but Mozail moved towards the policeman, gave her head a playful shake and said, 'It's you! Don't you know me? I'm Mozail. I'm going to my sister's in the next street because she's sick. That man there is a doctor.'

While the policeman was still trying to make up his mind, she pulled out a packet of cigarettes from her bag and offered him one. 'Have a smoke,' she said.

The policeman took the cigarette. Mozail helped him light it with hers. He inhaled deeply. Mozail winked at him with her left eye and at Tarlochan with her right and they moved on.

Tarlochan was still very scared. He looked left and right as he walked behind her, expecting to be stabbed any moment. Suddenly she stopped. 'Tarloch dear, it is not good to be afraid. If you're afraid, then something awful always happens. That's my experience.'

He didn't reply.

They came to the street which led to the mohalla where Kirpal Kaur lived. A shop was being looted. 'Nothing to worry about,' she told him. One of the rioters who was carrying something on his head ran into Tarlochan and the object fell to the ground. The man stared at Tarlochan and he knew he was a Sikh. He slipped his hand under his shirt to pull out his knife.

Mozail pushed him away as if she was drunk. 'Are you mad, trying to kill your own brother? This is the man I'm going to marry.' Then she said to Tarlochan, 'Karim, pick this thing up and help put it back on his head.'

The man gave Mozail a lecherous look and touched her breasts with his elbow. 'Have a good time, sali,' he said.

They kept walking and were soon in Kirpal Kaur's mohalla. 'Which street?' she asked.

'The third on the left. That building in the corner,' he whispered.

When they came to the building, they saw a man run out of it into another across the street. After a few minutes, three men emerged from that building, and rushed into the one where Kirpal Kaur lived. Mozail stopped. 'Tarloch dear, take off your turban,' she said.

'That I'll never do,' he replied.

'Just as you please, but I hope you do notice what's going on.'

Something terrible was going on. The three men had re-emerged, carrying gunny bags with blood dripping from them. Mozail had an idea. 'Look, I'm going to run across the street and go into that building. You should pretend that you're trying to catch me. But don't think. Just do it.'

Without waiting for his response, she rushed across the street and ran into Kirpal Kaur's building, with Tarlochan in hot pursuit. He was panting when he found her in the front courtyard.

'Which floor?' she asked.

'Second.'

'Let's go.' And she began to climb the stairs, her wooden sandals clattering on each step. There were large bloodstains everywhere.

They came to the second floor, walked down a narrow corridor and Tarlochan stopped in front of a door. He knocked. Then he called in a low voice, 'Mehnga Singhji, Mehnga Singhji.'

A girl's voice answered, 'Who is it?'

'Tarlochan.'

The door opened slightly. Tarlochan asked Mozail to follow him in. Mozail saw a very young and very pretty girl standing behind the door trembling. She also seemed to have a cold. Mozail said to her, 'Don't be afraid. Tarlochan has come to take you away.'

Tarlochan said, 'Ask Sardar sahib to get ready, but quickly.'

There was a shriek from the flat upstairs. 'They must have got him,' Kirpal Kaur said, her voice hoarse with terror.

'Whom?' Tarlochan asked.

Kirpal Kaur was about to say something, when Mozail pushed her in a corner and said, 'Just as well they got him. Now take off your clothes.'

Kirpal Kaur was taken aback, but Mozail gave her no time to think. In one moment, she divested her of her loose shirt. The young girl frantically put her arms in front of her breasts. She was terrified. Tarlochan turned his face. Then Mozail took off the kaftan-like gown she always wore and asked Kirpal Kaur to put it on. She was now stark naked herself.

'Take her away,' she told Tarlochan. She untied the girl's hair so that it hung over her shoulders. 'Go.'

Tarlochan pushed the girl towards the door, then turned back. Mozail stood there, shivering slightly because of the cold.

'Why don't you go?' she asked.

'What about her parents?' he said.

'They can go to hell. You take her.'

'And you?'

'Don't worry about me.'

They heard men running down the stairs. Soon they were banging at the door with their fists. Kirpal Kaur's parents were moaning in the other room. 'There's only one thing to do now. I'm going to open the door,' Mozail said.

She addressed Tarlochan, 'When I open the door, I'll rush out and run upstairs. You follow me. These men will be so flabbergasted that they will forget everything and come after us.'

'And then?' Tarlochan asked.

'Then, this one here, whatever her name is, can slip out. The way she's dressed, she'll be safe. They'll take her for a Jew.'

Mozail threw the door open and rushed out. The men had no time to react. Involuntarily, they made way for her. Tarlochan ran after her. She was storming up the stairs in her wooden sandals with Tarlochan behind her.

She slipped and came crashing down, head first. Tarlochan stopped and turned. Blood was pouring out of her mouth and nose and ears. The men who were trying to break into the flat had also gathered round her in a circle, forgetting temporarily what they were there for. They were staring at her naked, bruised body.

Tarlochan bent over her. 'Mozail, Mozail.'

She opened her eyes and smiled. Tarlochan undid his turban and covered her with it.

'This is my lover. He's a bloody Muslim, but he's so crazy that I always call him a Sikh,' she said to the men.

More blood poured out of her mouth. 'Damn it!' she said.

Then she looked at Tarlochan and pushed aside the turban with which he had tried to cover her nakedness.

'Take away this rag of your religion. I don't need it.'

Her arm fell limply on her bare breasts and she said no more.

THE RETURN

The special train left Amritsar at two in the afternoon, arriving at Mughalpura, Lahore, eight hours later. Many had been killed on the way, a lot more injured and countless lost.

It was at ten o'clock the next morning that Sirajuddin regained consciousness. He was lying on bare ground, surrounded by screaming men, women and children. It did not make sense.

He lay very still, gazing at the dusty sky. He appeared not to notice the confusion or the noise. To a stranger, he might have looked like an old man in deep thought, though this was not the case. He was in shock, suspended, as it were, over a bottomless pit.

Then his eyes moved and, suddenly, caught the sun. The shock brought him back to the world of living men and women. A succession of images raced through his mind. Attack . . . fire . . . escape . . . railway station . . . night . . . Sakina. He rose abruptly and began searching through the milling crowd in the refugee camp.

He spent hours looking, all the time shouting his daughter's name . . . Sakina, Sakina . . . but she was nowhere to be found.

Total confusion prevailed, with people looking for lost sons, daughters, mothers, wives. In the end Sirajuddin gave up. He sat down, away from the crowd, and tried to think clearly. Where did he part from Sakina and her mother? Then it came to him in a flash—the dead body of his wife, her stomach ripped open. It was an image that wouldn't go away.

Sakina's mother was dead. That much was certain. She had died in front of his eyes. He could hear her voice: 'Leave me where I am. Take the girl away.'

The two of them had begun to run. Sakina's dupatta had slipped to the ground and he had stopped to pick it up and she had said, 'Father, leave it.'

He could feel a bulge in his pocket. It was a length of cloth. Yes, he recognized it. It was Sakina's dupatta, but where was she?

Other details were missing. Had he brought her as far as the railway station? Had she got into the carriage with him? When the rioters had stopped the train, had they taken her with them?

All questions. There were no answers. He wished he could weep, but tears wouldn't come. He knew then that he needed help.

A few days later, he had a break. There were eight of them, young men armed with guns. They also had a truck. They said they brought back women and children left behind on the other side.

He gave them a description of his daughter. 'She is fair, very pretty. No, she doesn't look like me, but her mother. About seventeen. Big eyes, black hair, a mole on the left cheek. Find my daughter. May God bless you.'

The young men had said to Sirajuddin, 'If your daughter is alive we will find her.'

And they had tried. At the risk of their lives, they had driven to Amritsar, recovered many women and children and brought them back to the camp, but they had not found Sakina.

On their next trip out, they had found a girl on the roadside. They seemed to have scared her and she had started running. They had stopped the truck, jumped out and run after her. Finally, they had caught up with her in a field. She was very pretty and she had a mole on her left cheek. One of the men had said to her, 'Don't be frightened. Is your name Sakina?' Her face had gone pale, but when they told her who they were she had confessed that she was Sakina, daughter of Sirajuddin.

The young men were very kind to her. They had fed her, given her milk to drink and put her in their truck. One of them had given her his jacket so that she could cover herself. It was obvious that she was ill at ease without her dupatta, trying nervously to cover her breasts with her arms.

Many days had gone by and Sirajuddin had still not had any news of his daughter. All his time was spent running from camp to camp, looking for her. At night, he would pray for the success of the young men who were looking for his daughter. Their words would ring in his ear: 'If your daughter is alive, we will find her.'

Then one day he saw them in the camp. They were about to drive away. 'Son,' he shouted after one of them, 'have you found Sakina, my daughter?'

'We will, we will,' they replied all together.

The old man again prayed for them. It made him feel better.

That evening there was sudden activity in the camp. He saw four men carrying the body of a young girl found unconscious near the railway tracks. They were taking her to the camp hospital. He began to follow them.

He stood outside the hospital for some time, then went in. In one of the rooms, he found a stretcher with someone lying on it.

A light was switched on. It was a young woman with a mole on her left cheek. 'Sakina,' Sirajuddin screamed.

The doctor, who had switched on the light, stared at Sirajuddin.

'I am her father,' he stammered.

The doctor looked at the prostrate body and felt for the pulse. Then he said to the old man, pointing at the window, 'Open it.'

The young woman on the stretcher moved slightly. Her hands groped for the cord which kept her shalwar tied round her waist. With painful slowness, she unfastened it, pulled the garment down and opened her thighs.

'She is alive. My daughter is alive,' Sirajuddin shouted with joy.

The doctor broke into a cold sweat.

A BELIEVER'S VERSION

I swear by Allah . . . recite the Kalima . . . There is no God but Allah and Mohammed is His Prophet. You are all believers. You must believe what I tell you . . . I speak nothing but the truth . . . This has nothing to do with Pakistan . . . I can lay down my life for my beloved Quaid-e-Azam, the Great Leader, Muhammad Ali Jinnah, but this has nothing to do with Pakistan . . . I swear by God.

Please let's not be in a hurry . . . I know there are riots on the streets and you have little time for me, but in the name of God, I beseech you to hear me out . . . You've got to listen to my story . . . I have never denied murdering Tuka Ram. Yes, I ripped him open with a knife but I didn't kill him because he was a Hindu. Why did I kill him then? You have the right to know . . . but you must let me tell you the entire story.

I'll speak the truth and nothing but the truth . . . recite the Kalima . . . there is no God but Allah and Mohammed is His Prophet. May I die in sin, an infidel, if I did what I did knowing it would lead to this. The last time we had Hindu–Muslim trouble, I killed three Hindus but that was different. This Tuka Ram business was something else.

You are men of learning . . . You know all about women . . . The wise have said . . . beware of their wiles and, by God, they are right . . . If you don't hang me, I promise you I'll never go near a woman as long as I live . . . Oh God! What a fool I've been! Show me a woman and I get all worked up. Yes, yes, I know we all have to go one day to the Maker and He is going to be asking questions . . . well, well, Inspector sahib, I'll be straight with you . . . The moment I set eyes on Rukma, I knew I was in for it. What a woman!

You'd be perfectly right to tell me that someone who earns thirty-five rupees a month has absolutely no business running after women. I suppose I should have been doing my job, collecting rent, and keeping my nose clean. You see, I am a rent collector. But you should know how it all began. Flat 16 was where she lived. I had merely gone to collect the rent—all part of my monthly round. So I knock at the door and who opens it but Rukma Bai herself. I had seen her several times before but that day she looked ravishing. She had something flimsy on and her body shimmered. I think she had rubbed herself all over with oil. Oh God! I went crazy! I wanted to whip off that silly piece of cloth she had around her middle and start massaging her body—furiously. That was how it all began and before I knew it I was her slave.

What a woman! Her body was solid as a rock . . . I used to bruise myself making love to her . . . And she! Ah! She would say, 'A little harder, a little harder!'

Married? Yes, Inspector, the bitch was married. She even had another lover on the side, or so she claimed. Khan, the night watchman. Oh! I am going to spill the beans on her.

I was crazy about her . . . and she knew it because she would sometimes look at me sideways and smile . . . and when she did that, I swear to God, a chill ran down my spine . . . Oh! How I pined for her! Let me start at the beginning, shall I?

I was obsessed with her. All I wanted was that woman. I couldn't think of anything else. I was trapped and I knew it. My problem was that blasted toy-maker husband of hers. He was always in that one-room flat of theirs with those silly wooden toys of his. I just couldn't find the opportunity to sneak in with her.

And then I got a break. I was bumming around in the bazaar when I saw that man . . . What was he called? Yes, Girdhari. He was sitting on the pavement selling those wooden toys of his. And before you could blink your eyes, I was standing in front of Flat 16, my heart beating in my mouth. I knocked and she opened the door. I didn't know what to say. I almost turned and walked off but she smiled and called me in.

She closed the door, then asked me to sit down. 'I know what you are after but as long as Girdhari, my husband, is alive you can forget about it,' she said, the witch!

I stood up. She was so close to me, wearing the same flimsy excuse for a dress, her body glistening. Oh! I couldn't resist it any longer. I threw my arms around her. I was wild with excitement. 'I don't know what you are talking about,' I said. She embraced me right back. God, what a body that woman had, Inspector! But let me tell you my story.

'Girdhari can burn in hell,' I whispered, 'I want you.'

Rukma pushed me away. 'You don't want your nice clothes soiled by the oil on my body, do you?'

'I don't care what I soil,' I said as I grabbed her once again.

Inspector sahib, if you had lashed my back with a whip, I wouldn't have let go of her. 'Sit down,' she purred. 'Don't stand there. Come, I want to talk to you,' she told me. I was like putty in her hands. So there I was sitting, not saying a word. What was she planning? That sala, Girdhari, was in the bazaar selling toys, so what was she afraid of?

'Rukma,' I said breathlessly, 'There never will be an opportunity as good as this.'

She ran her fingers through my hair. 'There'll be better ones but you'll have to do something for me. Will you?'

Inspector sahib, I was not myself at the time. I didn't know what I was doing. Oh, the devil had taken hold of me. I told her, 'I'll kill fifteen men if you want me to.'

She smiled, the witch, and said, 'I believe you.'

I spent some more time with her. She fed me something she had cooked. We talked of this, that and the other, you know. Finally, she asked me to leave.

Ten days passed. On the eleventh, at two in the morning, someone woke me up gently. I sleep on the landing; yes, in the same building where Rukma lives. It was she. My heart leapt with excitement. 'Come with me,' she said softly. I followed her on tiptoe. She pushed her door open and I slipped in after her. I lunged for her; I just couldn't wait. 'Not yet,' she said, as she switched on the light. Someone was asleep on the floor, face covered. 'Who's that?' I asked in sign language. 'Sit down,' she answered. She ran her fingers lovingly through my hair but what she said next so casually made me break out in a cold sweat. And you know what she said?

Recite the Kalima . . . There is no God but Allah and Mohammed is His Prophet . . . I speak the truth and nothing but the truth . . . a woman like Rukma, I've never met in my entire life. You know what she told me with a smirk? 'I've killed Girdhari.' Just like that! With her bare hands she had killed a strong, well-built man like her husband. Some woman she was! As God is my witness, Inspector sahib, when I think of that night, I break out in goosebumps. She had garrotted him to death with wire rope. She had squeezed the last breath out of his body by twisting the wire rope around his neck with the aid of a small stick. The poor man's tongue was hanging out and his eyes had nearly popped out of their sockets. She said it hadn't taken long.

She insisted that I should see Girdhari's face. My blood froze when I looked at him but Rukma, she didn't bat an eye. Then she lay down only a few feet from the body and told me to lie next to her. I felt dead myself but then she did something to me, something very unexpected, and I was suddenly on fire. I'll never forget that night! There lay Girdhari and there lay the two of us, one on top of the other. What a night that was!

In the morning, quite methodically, Rukma and I cut Girdhari into three pieces with his very own tools. We must have made a bit of noise but the neighbours were used to Girdhari making his usual racket every morning as he got down to work. You may well ask, Inspector sahib, why I went along with this grisly business, why I didn't rush to the police and rat on her. I'll tell you why. That one night with her had me eating out of her hand. If she had asked me to go kill fifteen men, I would have gone right out and done that.

There was the question of getting rid of the body. All said and done, she was a woman and needed a hand there. 'Not to worry, darling,' I told her. 'We'll put Girdhari in a trunk and, as night falls, I'll take it out and dump it somewhere.' But God moves in strange ways. That day, Hindu–Muslim killings erupted in the city and a thirty-six-hour curfew was clamped on the worst-affected neighbourhoods. 'Abdul Karim,' I said to myself, 'you've got to do it tonight.' At two in the morning, I heaved that trunk down. God, it was heavy, but I didn't let that worry me. There I was, with that dead weight on my back, walking briskly, praying all the time. Please, God, no police, not tonight. And God heard me. I crossed the street and was walking past a mosque when I had an inspiration. I put the trunk down, took Girdhari out, I mean all three pieces of him, and chucked them over the low protective wall right inside the mosque.

Truly God is great and moves in strange ways. Next morning I heard that the Hindus had burnt the mosque down. 'There goes poor Girdhari,' I said to myself, 'cremated like a good Hindu.' I advised Rukma to spread word that Girdhari had gone on a trip and hadn't come back as he should have. 'And, sweetheart, I'll be with you nights doing what I like best,' I added. 'Not so soon,' Rukma said. 'We must not see each other for at least fifteen days.'

Seventeen days passed and nothing happened. I had nightmares about Girdhari but I told him, 'You are dead Girdhari, so don't try to scare me. There is nothing you can do to me because you are no longer around. Ha, ha!'

A day later, I was sleeping in my usual place when Rukma woke me up around midnight. She asked me to follow her to her room. Then she lay down on that mattress of hers, naked as on the day she was born. 'I ache all over, darling, rub some oil on my body to soothe the pain,' she whispered in a husky voice. Quite happily I began to massage her all over. In an hour I was exhausted, with sweat dripping out of every pore in my body on to hers, but she did not say, 'That was nice, Abdul Karim, but you must be worn out yourself. That's enough.'

'I am done for, Rukma darling,' I finally said. She gave me one of those smiles. Then she pulled me down next to her and before I knew it I was sound asleep, one of my hands on her breasts.

I woke up with a start because there was something sharp and metallic around my throat but before I could do anything, Rukma had jumped on my chest and was tightening the noose. That was how she had killed Girdhari. I couldn't scream, though I tried to. Then everything went black.

When I came to, it was about four in the morning and I ached all over. Suddenly, there were voices. I lay without daring to breathe, so scared was I. I couldn't see anything but then I realized what was going on only a few feet from me. A man and a woman, locked in each other's arms, breathing heavily and making love. I heard Rukma's voice. 'Tuka Ram, switch on the light.' And his frightened voice, 'No, no, Rukma, please!' 'You big coward!' Rukma replied angrily. 'How are you going to chop him up in three pieces and carry him out for disposal?'

I must have fainted briefly, for the next thing I remember is the light coming in. That made me sit up. Tuka Ram shrieked with fright and ran out of the room. Rukma bolted the door calmly. This Tuka Ram character I knew. He was a mango seller, the kind who went from house to house.

Rukma was looking at me as if she did not believe her eyes. She was sure she had killed me but there I was, sitting bolt upright. I didn't know what she was going to do to me because there was a knock at the door and I heard several voices. Rukma pushed me into the bathroom, telling me to stay there.

It was the neighbours wanting to know if everything was all right because they had heard strange noises. 'I must have been walking in my sleep,' she told them and they left. Then she bolted the door. I was very frightened. I knew she was going to kill me, but strangely, this conviction brought back my physical strength. I stepped out of the bathroom. She didn't hear me. She was leaning out of the window. I rushed forward, put my hands on her buttocks and, with all my strength, heaved her up and pushed her out. There was a loud thud and that was that. I stalked out of her room unobserved.

I lay low for the better part of the morning. My throat was marked because the wire had cut into it. I put a handkerchief around it after massaging it with oil. I was sure that when Rukma was discovered in the morning everyone would think she had fallen out of the window because had she not told the neighbours she walked in her sleep? By midday nothing had happened. Had they found Rukma? She must have fallen into the dead-end street at the back of two buildings, mostly used as a huge refuse bin by the residents, but it was swept every morning. So why hadn't they found Rukma? Maybe it hadn't been cleaned today.

Even by the afternoon nothing had happened. There was only one thing to do. Check out that back street myself. I steeled myself for the shock of discovering her broken body lying on flat stone but there was nothing, no sign of her at all. What could have happened? I swear on the Holy Book if I escape from this mess I have got myself into, Inspector sahib, I'll not be half as surprised as I am about the disappearance of that woman's body. After all, she fell from the third floor and it is logical that the impact should have killed her. That being so, why didn't I find her? Perhaps she is alive, the witch. The neighbours think she has either been abducted by a Muslim or been killed in the riots. If she is dead, well that is the best that could have happened, and if she has been abducted, then God help the man who took her. I know what lies in store for him.

Yes, sir, I must tell you about Tuka Ram. About three weeks after that night I ran into him in the street. 'Where is she?' he demanded. 'I don't know where she is,' I replied. 'You know bloody well where she is,' he snarled. 'I swear by the Holy Book I do not know,' I said sincerely but he didn't seem to believe me. 'You liar! You killed her! I am going to the police! You first killed Girdhari, then you killed her!' he hissed.

After he left, I reviewed my situation. There were no two ways about it. I had to kill him. So, Inspector sahib, what was I to do? I put my knife into my pocket and went out looking for Tuka Ram. I finally found him in the evening at, of all places, the public urinal. He was about to answer the call of nature when I got him. 'Tuka Ram,' I said, 'this is curtains for you.' And I plunged my knife into him. He put both hands on his stomach and fell forward. What a fool I am, Inspector sahib! I should have run but what did I do? I waited around, the knife still in my hand. I even bent down to feel his pulse, just to be sure he was dead. And you know, I have no idea where the pulse is—somewhere about the wrist but where exactly, well, I wasn't quite sure.

And just then, as I was fooling around with his wrist, in walks this burly policeman, looking rather keen to do something which nobody else could do for him and he sees me, knife in hand and the rest of it, and I am nabbed, what else!

Read out the Kalima, the word of God, in a loud voice. There is no God but Allah and Mohammed is His Prophet . . . and what I have told you was the truth, nothing but the truth.

A WOMAN'S LIFE

She had had a long day and she fell asleep as soon as she hit the bed. The city sanitary inspector, whom she always called Seth, had just gone home, very drunk. His love-making had been aggressive as usual and he had left her feeling bone-weary. He would have stayed longer but for his wife who, he always said, loved him very much.

The silver coins, which she had earned, were safely tucked inside her bra. Her breasts still bore the traces of the inspector's wet kisses. Occasionally the coins would clink as she took a particularly deep breath.

Her chest had felt on fire, partly because of the pint of brandy which she had drunk followed by the home-made brew they had downed with tap water after the brandy had run out.

She was sprawled face down on her wide, wooden bed. Her bare arms, stretched out on either side, looked like the frame of a kite which has come unstuck from the paper.

It was a small room and her things were everywhere. Three or four ragged pairs of sandals lay under the bed; a mangy dog lay sleeping with his head resting on them. There were bald patches on its skin and, from a distance, one could have mistaken it for a worn doormat.

On a small shelf lay her make-up things: face powder, a single lipstick, rouge, a comb, hairpins.

Swinging from a hook in the ceiling was a cage with a green parrot. The bird was asleep, its beak tucked under one of its wings. The cage was littered with pieces of raw guava and orange peels, with some black moths and mosquitoes hovering over them.

A wicker chair stood next to the bed, its back grimy with use. To its left was a small table with an antiquated His Master's Voice gramophone resting on it. On the wall were four pictures.

It was her habit, after being paid, to rub the money against the picture she had of the Hindu elephant god Ganesha, for good luck, before putting it away. However, whenever Madhu was expected from Poona, she hid most of the money under her bed. This had first been suggested by Ram Lal, who knew that every visit by Madhu was like a raid on Saugandhi's savings. One day he said to her, 'Where'd you pick up this sala? What kind of a lover boy is he? He never parts with a penny and he is back every other week having a good time at your expense. What's more, he cheats you out of your hard-earned money. Saugandhi, what is it about this sala that you find so irresistible? I've been in this business for seven years and I know you chhokris well but this one beats me, I have to admit.'

Ram Lal, who scouted around for men looking for a good time, had a range of girls worth anything from ten to a hundred rupees for the night. He said to her one day, 'Saugandhi, don't ruin your business; I warn you this scoundrel will take the shirt off your back if you don't watch out. Tell you what, keep your money hidden under your bed and the next time he is here tell him something like, "I swear on your head, Madhu, for days I haven't set eyes on so much as a penny. I haven't even eaten today. Can you get me something to eat and a cup of tea from that Iranian cafe across the street?"'

Ram Lal went on, 'Sweetheart, these are bad times. By bringing in prohibition, this sali Congress government has taken the life out of the bazaar. But how would you know? You get your drop somehow or the other. As God is my witness, whenever I see an empty liquor bottle in your room, I almost want to change places with you.'

Saugandhi liked to offer advice too. She had once said to her friend Jamuna, 'Let me give you some advice. For ten rupees, you let men pluck you like a chicken. Let someone so much as touch me in the wrong place and he will come to grief. You know what happened last night? Ram Lal brought a Punjabi man at about two in the morning. When we went to bed, I put out the light. I swear to you, Jamuna, he was scared! He couldn't do anything! "Come on," I said to him. "Don't you want it? It is nearly morning." But all he wanted was for the light to be switched on. I couldn't hold back my laughter. "No light," I teased him. Then I pinched him and he jumped out of bed and the first thing he did was to put the light back on. "Are you crazy?" I screamed, then I put out the light. He was scared. I tell you, it was such fun. No light, then light again. When he heard the first tram car rattle past in the morning, he hurriedly put on his clothes and ran. The sala must have won that money in gambling. Jamuna, you are still very naive. I know how to deal with men. I have my ways.'

This was true. She had her ways, which she often told her friends about. 'If the customer is nice, the quiet type, flirt with him, talk, tease him, touch him playfully. If he has a beard, comb it with your fingers and pull out a hair or two just for fun. If he is fat, then tease him about it. But never give them enough time to do what they really want; keep them occupied and they'll leave happily and you'll be spared possible misadventure. The quiet types are always dangerous. Watch them because they are often very rough.'

Actually, Saugandhi was not as clever as she pretended. She didn't have a great number of clients either. She liked men, which was why all her clever methods would desert her when it was time to use them. It only took a few sweet words, softly cooed into her ear, to make her melt. Although she was convinced that physical relations were basically pointless, her body felt otherwise. It seemed to want to be overpowered and left exhausted.

When she was a little girl, she used to hide herself in the big wooden chest which sat in a corner of her parents' home while the other children looked for her. The fear of being caught, mixed with a sense of excitement, would make her heart beat very fast. Sometimes she wanted to spend her entire life in a box, hidden from view yet dying to be found. The last five years had been like a game of hide-and-seek. She was either seeking or being sought. When a man said to her, 'I love you, Saugandhi,' she would go weak in the knees, although she knew he was lying. Love, what a beautiful word, she would think. Oh, if only one could rub love like a balm into one's body! However, she did like four of her regulars enough to have their framed pictures hanging on her wall.

She had lived intensely in the last five years. True, she hadn't had the happiness she would have wished but she had managed. Money had never interested her much. She charged ten rupees for what she did, out of which one-fourth went to Ram Lal. What she was left with was enough for her needs. In fact, when Madhu came from Poona, she spent ten to fifteen rupees on him quite happily. This was perhaps the price she paid for that certain feeling that Ram Lal had once said existed between the two of them.

He was right. There was something about Madhu which Saugandhi liked. When they met, the first thing Madhu had said to her was, 'Aren't you ashamed of selling yourself, putting a price on your body? Ten rupees you take with one-fourth going to that man, Ram Lal, which leaves you with seven rupees and eight annas, doesn't it? And for that you promise to give something which you can't love. And what about me? I have come looking for something which really cannot be had. I need a woman but do you need a man? I could do with any woman but could you do with any man? There is nothing between us except this sum of ten rupees, one-fourth of which is to go to Ram Lal and the rest to you. But I know we like each other. Shouldn't we do something about it? Perhaps we could fulfil our separate needs that way. Now listen. I am a sergeant in the police at Poona. I'll come once a month for three or four days. You don't have to be doing anything from now on. I'll look after all your expenses. What is the rent for this kholi of yours?'

Madhu had made her feel like the police sergeant's chosen woman. He had also rearranged everything in the room. There were posters showing half-clad women that she had stuck on the wall. He had removed them without her permission and then torn them up. 'Saugandhi, my dear, I won't have these. And look at this slimy earthen pitcher of yours. It needs to be scrubbed and cleaned. And what are those smelly rags lying around? Throw them out. And look at your hair. It is matted and in need of a wash. And . . . and . . .'

After three hours of conversation, mostly Madhu's, Saugandhi had felt as if she had known him for many years. Never before had anyone spoken to her like that, nor made her feel that her kholi was home. The men who came to her did not even notice that her bed sheets were soiled. Nobody had ever said to her, 'I think you are catching a cold; let me run along and get you something for it.' But Madhu was different; he told her things nobody ever had and she knew she needed him.

He would come once a month from Poona and before going back he would say, 'Saugandhi, if you resume that old business of yours, you'll never see me again. Yes, about this month's household expenses, the money will be on its way as soon as I get to Poona . . . so what did you say the monthly rent for this place was?'

Madhu had never sent her any money from Poona or elsewhere and Saugandhi had continued her business as usual. They both knew it but she never said, 'What rubbish you are talking! You have never given me so much as a bum penny.' And Madhu had never asked her how she was managing to survive. They were living a pretension and they were quite happy with it. Saugandhi had argued to herself that, if one was unable to buy real gold, one might as well settle for what looked like gold.

But now she was sound asleep. She was too tired to even bother to switch off the harsh, unshaded light over her bed.

There was a knock at the door. She only heard it as a faint, faraway sound. This was followed by a succession of knocks, which woke her up. She first wiped her mouth, still sodden with the aftertaste of bad liquor, and her eyes, then looked under the bed where the dog was still asleep, its head resting on her old sandals. The parrot was also in its cage, its beak tucked under its wing.

There was another impatient knock. She rose from her bed and realized that she had a splitting headache. She poured herself some water from the earthen pitcher and rinsed her mouth, then filled another glass and drank it down in one gulp. Carefully, she opened the door and whispered, 'Ram Lal?'

Ram Lal, who had almost given up, replied caustically, 'I thought you had been bitten by a snake. I have been out here for an hour. Didn't you hear me?' Then in his discreet voice he asked, 'Is anybody with you?' She told him no and let him in. 'If it is going to take me an hour getting you chhokris out of bed, I might as well change my line of work. What are you looking at me like that for? Put on that nice flower-print sari of yours and dust your face with powder, and a bit of lipstick too. Out there in a car I have a rich Seth waiting for you.'

Instead, Saugandhi fell into her armchair, picked up a jar of rubbing balm from the table, eased off its lid and said, 'Ram Lal, I don't feel well.'

'Why didn't you say so right away?'

Saugandhi, who was now rubbing her forehead with the balm, replied, 'I just don't feel good; maybe I had too much to drink.'

Ram Lal's expression changed. 'Is there some left? I'd love a drop.'

Saugandhi returned the balm to the table. 'If I had saved some, I would have done something about this awful headache. Look, Ram Lal, bring that man in.'

'I can't,' Ram Lal answered. 'He is an important man. He was even reluctant to park on the street. Look, sweetheart, put on those nice clothes and off we go. You won't be sorry.'

It was the usual deal: seven rupees eight annas. Had Saugandhi not been in need of money, she would have sent Ram Lal packing. In the next kholi lived a Madrasi woman whose husband had recently died in an accident. She had a grown-up daughter and they wanted to go back to Madras but didn't have the train fare. Saugandhi had said to her, 'Don't you worry, sister, my man is expected from Poona any day. He'll give me some money and you'll be on your way.' While Madhu was indeed expected, the money, of course, was to be earned by Saugandhi herself. So she rose reluctantly from her chair and began to change. She put on the flower-print sari and a bit of make-up, and then drank another glass of water from the pitcher.

The street was very still. The lights had been dimmed because of the war. In the distance, she could see the outline of a car. They walked up to it and stopped.

Ram Lal stepped forward and said, 'Here she is, a sweet-tempered girl, very new to the business.' Then to her, 'Saugandhi, the Seth sahib is waiting.'

She moved closer, feeling nervous. A flashlight suddenly lit her face, blinding her. 'Ugh!' grunted the man in the car, then revved up his engine and drove off without another word.

Saugandhi had had no time to react because of the torch in her face. She hadn't been able to see the man; she had only heard him say, 'Ugh!' What did he mean by that?

Ram Lal was muttering to himself. 'You didn't like her; that's two hours of mine gone waste.' He left without speaking to her. Saugandhi was trembling, trying hard to deal with the situation. 'What did he mean by "Ugh"? That he did not like me? The son of a . . .'

The car was gone, the red glow from its fading tail-lights barely visible now. She wanted to scream, 'Come back . . . Stop . . . Come back!'

She was alone in the deserted bazaar wearing her grey flower-print sari which fluttered in the night air.

She began to walk back slowly but then she thought of Ram Lal and the man in the car and she stopped. Ram Lal had said the Seth didn't like her; he hadn't said it was because of her looks. Well, so what? There were people she did not like. There were men who came to her that she did not care for. Only the other night she had one who was so ugly that when he was lying next to her she had felt nauseated. But she hadn't shown it.

But the man in the car? He had practically spat in her face. 'Ram Lal,' he had implied, 'from what hole have you pulled out this scented reptile? And you want ten rupees for her? For her? Ugh!'

She was angry with herself and with Ram Lal who had woken her up at two in the morning, though he had meant well. It wasn't his fault and it wasn't hers but she wanted the whole scene replayed just one more time. Slowly, very slowly, she would move towards the car, then the torchlight would be flashed in her face to be followed by a grunt, and she, Saugandhi, would scratch that Seth's face with her long nails, pull him out of that car by his hair and hit him till she broke down exhausted.

Saugandhi, she said to herself, you are not ugly. While it was true that the bloom of her early youth was gone, nobody had ever said she was ugly. In fact, she was one of those women men always steal a second look at. She knew she had everything a man expects in a woman. She was young and she had a good body. She was nice to people. She couldn't remember a single man in the last five years who hadn't enjoyed himself with her.

She was soft-hearted. Last year at Christmas time when she was living in the Golpitha area, this young fellow from Hyderabad who had spent the night with her had found his wallet missing in the morning. Obviously, the servant boy, who was a rogue, had nicked it and disappeared. He was extremely upset because he had come all the way to Bombay to spend his holidays and he hadn't the fare to go back. She had simply returned him the money he had given her the night before.

She wanted to go home, take a long, cool drink, lie on her bed and go to sleep. She began to walk back.

However, once she was outside her kholi, the pain and humiliation came back. She just couldn't forget what had happened. She had been called out to the street and a man had slapped her across the face. She had been looked at as they look at sheep in a farmers' market. A torch had been shone on her face to see if she had any flesh on her or whether she was just skin and bones. And then she had been rejected.

If that man came back, she would stand in front of him, tear up her clothes and shout, 'This is what you came to buy! Well, here it is. You can have it free, but you'll never be able to reach the woman who is inside this body!'

The key was where she always kept it, inside her bra, but the lock on the door had been released. She pushed gently and it creaked on its hinges. Then it was unlatched from the inside and she went in.

She heard Madhu laugh through his thick moustache as he carefully closed the door. 'At last you have done what I've always suggested,' he said. 'Taken an early morning walk. There is nothing like that for good health. If you do it regularly, all your lassitude will disappear, also that back pain you are always going on about. Did you walk as far as the Victoria Gardens?'

Saugandhi said nothing, nor did Madhu appear to expect an answer. His remarks were generally supposed to be heard, not answered.

Madhu sat in the cane chair, which bore much oily evidence of earlier contact with his greasy hair. He swung one leg on top of the other and began to play with his moustache.

Saugandhi sat on the bed. 'I was waiting for you today,' she said.

'Waiting?' he asked, a bit puzzled. 'How did you know I was coming today?'

Saugandhi smiled. 'Because last night I dreamt about you and that woke me up but you weren't there so I went for a walk.'

'And there I was when you came back,' Madhu said happily. 'Haven't the wise said that lovers' hearts beat together? When did you dream about me?'

'A few hours ago,' Saugandhi answered.

'Ah!' said Madhu. 'And I dreamt about you not too many hours earlier. You were wearing your flower-print sari. Yes, the same one you have on now. And there was something in your hands. Yes, a little bag full of money. And you said to me, "Madhu, why do you worry so much about money? Take it. What is mine is yours." And I swear on your head, Saugandhi, the next thing I knew I was out of Poona and on my way to Bombay. There is bad news though. I am in trouble. There was this police investigation I botched up and, unless I can get twenty or thirty rupees together and bribe my inspector, I can say goodbye to my job. But never mind that. You look tired. Lie down, darling, and I'll press your feet. If you are not used to taking walks, you get tired. Now lie down and turn your feet towards me.'

Saugandhi lay down, cradling her head in her arms. Then in a voice which wasn't really hers, she asked, 'Madhu, who's this person who has put you in trouble? If you are afraid of losing your job and going to jail, just let me know. In such situations, the higher the bribe, the better off you are. Since you gave me the bad news about your job, my heart has been jumping up and down. By the way, when are you going back?'

Madhu could smell liquor in Saugandhi's breath and thought this was a good time to make his pitch. 'I must take the afternoon train. By this evening, I should slip around a hundred rupees in my inspector's pocket; on second thoughts, perhaps fifty will do.'

'Fifty,' Saugandhi said. Then she rose from the bed and stood facing the four pictures on the wall. The third was Madhu's. He was sitting in a chair, his hands on his thighs and a black curtain with painted flowers forming the background. There was a rose in his lapel and two thick books lay on a small table next to his chair. He sat there, looking very conscious of being photographed. He was staring at the camera with an almost painful expression.

Saugandhi began to laugh. 'Is it the picture you find so amusing?' he asked.

Saugandhi touched the first, the sanitary inspector's. 'Look at that face. Once he told me that a rani had fallen in love with him. With him!' She pulled down the frame from the wall with such violence that some of the plaster came off; then she smashed it to the floor. 'When my sweeperess Rani comes in the morning, she will take away this raja with the rest of the rubbish,' Saugandhi said. Then she began to laugh, a light laugh like the first rain of summer. Madhu managed a smile with some difficulty and followed it with a forced guffaw.

By then Saugandhi had pulled down the second picture and thrown it out of the window. 'What's this sala doing here? No one with a mug like his is allowed on this wall, is he Madhu?' she asked. Madhu laughed but the sound was unnatural.

She pulled down the fourth picture, a man in a turban, and then, as Madhu watched apprehensively, his own, throwing them out together through the window. They heard them fall on the street, the glass breaking. Madhu somehow managed to say, 'Well done! I didn't like that one of mine either.'

Saugandhi moved slowly towards him. 'You didn't like that one, yeah? Well, let me ask you, is there anything about you which you should like? This bulb of a nose of yours! This small, hairy forehead! Your swollen nostrils! Your twisted ears! And that awful breath!

Your filthy, unwashed body! This oil that you coat yourself with! So you didn't like your picture, eh?'

Madhu was flinching away from her, his back against the wall. He tried to put some authority into his voice. 'Look, Saugandhi, it seems to me you have gone back to that dirty old profession of yours. I am telling you for the last time . . .'

Saugandhi mimicked him, 'If you return to that dirty old profession of yours, that'll be the end. And if I find out that another man has been in your bed, I'll drag you out by your hair and throw you out on the street. As for your monthly expenses, a money order will be on its way as soon as I return to Poona. And what is the monthly rent of this kholi of yours?'

Madhu listened in total disbelief.

Saugandhi had not finished with him yet. 'Let me tell you what it costs me every month—fifteen rupees. And you know what my own rental is? Ten rupees. Out of that two rupees and eight annas go to Ram Lal, which leaves me with seven rupees and eight annas exactly, in return for which I sleep with men. What was our relationship anyway? Nothing! Ten rupees, perhaps. Every time you came you took away what you wanted—and the money too. It used to be ten rupees; now it is fifty.' She flicked away his cap with one finger and it fell to the floor.

'Saugandhi!' Madhu yelled.

She ignored him. Then she pulled out his handkerchief from his pocket, raised it to her nose, made a face and said with disgust, 'It stinks! Look at yourself, at your filthy cap and these rags that you call clothes. They all smell! Get out!'

'Saugandhi!' Madhu screamed again.

But she screamed right back. 'You creep! Why do you come here? Am I your mother, who will give you money to spend? Or are you such a ravishing man that I'd fall in love with you? You dog, you wretch, don't you dare raise your voice at me! I am nothing to you! You miserable beggar, who do you think you are? Tell me, are you a thief or a pickpocket? What are you doing in my house at this hour anyway? Should I call the police? There may or may not be a case against you in Poona but there will be a case against you here in Bombay!'

Madhu was scared. 'What has come over you, Saugandhi?'

'Who are you to put such questions to me? Get out of here . . . this instant!' The mangy dog, who had so far slept undisturbed, suddenly woke up and began to bark at Madhu, which made Saugandhi laugh hysterically.

Madhu bent down to pick up his cap from the floor but Saugandhi shouted, 'Leave it there! As soon as you get to Poona, I'll money-order it to you.' She began to laugh again as she fell into the chair. The dog, in the meanwhile, had chased Madhu out of the room and down the stairs.

He came back wagging his short, ugly tail and flapping his ears and sat down at Saugandhi's feet. Everything was very still and for a minute she was terrified. She also felt empty, like a train which having discharged its passengers is shunted into the yard and left there.

For a long time she sat in the chair. Then she rose, picked up her dog from the floor, put it carefully on the bed, laid herself next to him, threw an arm across his wasted body and went to sleep.

PERIN

I was in Bombay and living in what I can only call utter poverty. At night I slept in a kholi, a tiny room, for which I was charged nine rupees every month. It had neither water nor electricity and it was abominably filthy. At night, every variety of bug fell from the ceiling on to my body and there was no shortage of rats; larger rats than those I have yet to see.

Our chawl—Bombaiya for building—had only one bathroom but the door did not lock. Early every morning, the women would gather outside, waiting their turn to get the day's drinking water. They were all kinds: Jews, Marathis, Gujaratis, Christians, you name it.

It was my custom to beat the women to the bathroom every morning, shut the door and take a bath. One morning I was late and as I rushed in to snatch a hurried wash, the door was flung open and one of my neighbours, a woman, walked in with a pitcher under her arm. She took one look at me and turned, and her pitcher fell to the floor. As it began to roll, she ran as if a tiger was chasing her. I could not stop laughing but I finished my bath.

The next time the door opened, it was Brij Mohan, but I was done and was putting on my clothes. 'It is Sunday,' he said.

Then I remembered that every Sunday Brij Mohan travelled to Bandra to meet his friend Perin, a rather plain-looking Parsi girl with whom he had been having an affair of sorts for the last three years. Every Sunday, he would borrow eight annas for his train fare to Bandra where he would spend some time with her, helping her solve crossword puzzles published in the *Illustrated Weekly of India*. He had no work and, at home during the day, I would see him bent over Perin's puzzles. He had won many small prizes for her but she had never given him a penny for his labours.

Brij Mohan was a photographer and had a large collection of Perin's pictures that he had taken. There you could see her in every pose and all sorts of clothes. Here was Perin in a tight shirt and shalwar, and here she was in a sari; and if you preferred western dresses, she had posed in quite a few of them; and if you liked bathing suits, she had been photographed in those things too. She was by no means beautiful; in fact, as far as I was concerned, she was nothing much to look at. However, I had never revealed this to Brij Mohan. Come to think of it, I had never shown any curiosity about her, such as who she was, what she did, when she had first met him, how their friendship had begun or whether he planned to marry her. Brij Mohan had never volunteered anything himself either. The routine was that every Sunday, after breakfast, he asked me for eight annas so that he could go to Bandra to meet her. He was back by noon.

One Sunday, after he came back, contrary to our established practice, he said to me, 'It's all over.'

'What's all over?' I asked, because, frankly, I did not know what he meant.

I seemed to have taken a weight off his chest. 'I am through with Perin. I told her she is like a bird of ill omen for me because whenever I start meeting her regularly, I find myself out of work. So she said, "Then stop meeting me and let's see if you find work or not. You think I bring you bad luck, but the fact is it is all your fault. You are a good-for-nothing idler who doesn't wish to work."'

Then he paused, 'In any case, good riddance, I have little doubt that I will find something tomorrow. If you donate four annas to me in the morning I will go meet Seth Nanoo Bhai who, I am sure, will hire me as his assistant.'

Seth Nanoo Bhai was a film director who had more than once refused to hire Brij Mohan because, like Perin, he did not hold too high an opinion of his enthusiasm for work. But that notwithstanding, next morning, I gave Brij Mohan the bus fare and when he returned in the afternoon he brought the good news that he had been hired on a year's contract at two hundred and fifty rupees a month by Seth Nanoo Bhai. Then he produced a hundred rupees from his pocket, 'This is my advance. I have a wild desire to go to Bandra and tell Perin but I am afraid if I do that I will be sacked tomorrow. I mean this is the way it has always been. Not once but several times. Brij Mohan gets hired; Brij Mohan meets Perin; Brij Mohan gets fired. God alone knows what sort of star she was born under. Not a good one, I can tell you. I am determined to stay away from her for at least a year. You know I have nothing to wear. In a year, I would have earned enough to get some decent clothes for myself.'

Six months passed. Brij Mohan still had his job and new clothes too, including a dozen cambric handkerchiefs. In fact, by now he was a fully equipped bachelor living in comfort. One day a letter arrived for him in the mail, but when he returned in the evening, somehow I forgot to give it to him. Next morning, as we sat down at breakfast, I handed it to him. He took one look at it and screamed, 'Damn!'

'What's the matter?' I asked.

'It is Perin and to think that I had begun to enjoy life,' he replied as he retrieved the note from the envelope with the aid of a spoon. 'It is she. I can tell her handwriting from a mile.'

'What has she written?' I asked.

'Says I must meet her Sunday; there is something she needs to tell me.' He put the letter in his pocket and added, 'There you are, my friend, no question I will be shown the door tomorrow.'

'What nonsense!'

'You mark my words. I have no doubt when I see Seth Nanoo Bhai on Monday, he will have found something wrong with my work and I will be sacked,' he declared confidently.

'If you are so sure of it, then don't meet her,' I suggested.

'That I can't do; if she wants me to see her, I have to go,' he said.

'Why?'

'Maybe I am a bit tired of holding on to this steady job; after all, it's been over six months now.' He smiled and left.

The next day he was off to Bandra after breakfast. He met Perin but said nothing about the meeting. In the end, I had to ask him, 'So you have seen the bird of ill omen?'

'Yes, and I have told her I am unlikely to remain employed much longer. But let's go out and eat.'

We walked over to Haji's Hotel and ate but carefully avoided any mention of Perin. All that Brij Mohan said when we left was, 'Let's see what happens tomorrow.'

I was sure nothing would happen but to my surprise Brij Mohan was back earlier than usual. He laughed when he saw me. 'She's done it again.'

'Come off it,' I said.

'How can I come off it when the studio has been sealed and everyone asked to go home. I am sorry it was I who triggered it.

Had it not been for me, Seth Nanoo Bhai would have lived happily ever after.' Brij Mohan began to laugh.

'This is getting very strange,' I said.

'Don't say you hadn't been told,' he said before picking up his camera and walking out of the door.

Brij Mohan was out of work again. He soon ran out of the money he had saved and our old routine took over. Every Sunday, he would ask me for eight annas after breakfast, travel to Bandra, spend a couple of hours with Perin and return straight home. What he talked to her, I had no idea. I only knew that he made great conversation, but what sort of conversation he made to this girl about whose baleful stellar influence he was in no doubt about, I was unable to guess. One day, I asked him, 'Brij, does Perin love you?'

'No, she loves someone else.'

'Why does she see you then?'

'Maybe because I am interesting, maybe because I make her look more beautiful in the pictures I take than she is, maybe because I solve her crosswords for which she occasionally picks up a prize. Manto, you don't know these girls as I do. She loves someone else and what he lacks she probably finds in me and thus she has it all nicely sewn up. She is a fraud,' he smiled.

'Then why do you meet her?'

'I enjoy it,' Brij Mohan replied, adjusting his sunglasses.

'Enjoy what?'

'Well, her ill influence. I am experimenting as to how much bad luck she brings and, I must say, she has passed the test with flying colours. Whenever I have renewed contact with her, I have been fired from whatever job I had. I have only one wish: I want to cheat this bird of ill omen.'

'How?'

'By resigning before I am fired. Tell the boss I am resigning because I knew he was going to fire me and I did not wish him to have to perform that unpleasant task. I would also tell him that it is not he who is firing me but my friend Perin, who has a nose so long that when I photograph her it almost touches my lens.' He smiled, then added, 'This is my little wish, so let's see if it gets fulfilled or not.'

'It is a strange wish,' I said.

'Everything about me is a little strange. Last Sunday, I took a photograph which will be entered in a competition by Perin's friend in his name and I am sure he will win a prize,' he said, looking amused.

Brij Mohan was indeed strange. This was not the first photograph he was going to gift to Perin's friend. He had done it several times and the pictures had appeared in the *Illustrated Weekly of India*, pleasing Perin no end. Brij Mohan had never set eyes on this friend of hers and had no idea what he looked like. He was supposed to have some sort of a job in a mill and was reportedly very good-looking.

One Sunday when Brij Mohan returned from Bandra, he announced, 'It is all over.'

'The Perin business?' I asked.

'Yes. I was running out of clothes to wear so I said the hell with it. I have no doubt in a matter of days I will get a job. I'm going to see Seth Niaz Ali who has announced a new movie. Can you find out for me where his office is.'

I phoned a friend, got the address and told Brij Mohan. He went the next day and came back wearing a most contented look. 'Look Manto,' he said, producing a typed paper from his pocket which he pushed towards me. 'A contract for the new movie—salary two hundred rupees a month but Seth Niaz Ali says he will raise it. Good?'

'So when are you going to see Perin?' It was my turn to smile.

'When will I see her? The thought has crossed my mind. But I don't think I should hurry although I am still keen on my little wish being fulfilled. But let me earn enough to get some decent clothes. Here, I have an advance of fifty rupees; you keep twenty-five.'

I took the money to pay the roadside hotel where I owed. Life kept bobbing along and we were both quite pleased with the way things were going. I would bring home a hundred rupees and Brij Mohan twice that amount, so money was one thing that was not in short supply. After five months, there arrived a letter from Perin. Brij Mohan took one look at it and said, 'Well, here is the angel of death.'

Frankly, the sight of the letter sent a shiver down my spine but Brij Mohan opened it with a smile. It was a short letter. All I asked was, 'And what does Her Ladyship wish this time?'

'Her Ladyship wishes that I see her Sunday as the business at hand is important.' He put the letter back in its envelope.

'Will you go?'

'Will have to,' he replied, as he began to sing a recent movie hit about the inevitability of travel.

'For God's sake, Brij, don't go. Life has been good to us. You have no idea how I used to manage those eight annas I gave you every Sunday,' I begged.

He smiled. 'I know but I am afraid those days are going to return when God knows how you will manage those eight annas every Sunday.'

The next day he was off early to meet Perin. When he returned, all he said was, 'I told her it would be the twelfth time I would have been sacked because of her, may the blessings of Zarathustra be on her!'

'Did she say anything?'

'All she said was, "You're a silly idiot."'

'There she was right,' I added.

'One hundred per cent,' Brij laughed. 'Tomorrow I will go to work and put in my resignation first thing. In fact, I wrote it out at Perin's place.' He showed it to me.

He left unusually early the next day and when he returned in the evening, he looked depressed. He said nothing, so I had to ask, 'Brij, what happened?'

'Nothing, the whole thing is over.'

'Meaning?'

'When I handed in my papers to Seth Niaz Ali, he smiled and placed a typed, official-looking letter in my hand which said my salary had been raised from two hundred to three hundred rupees a month.'

From that day on, Brij Mohan lost all interest in Perin. Once he said to me, 'With the nullification of the Perin curse, Perin herself has been nullified. And thus has ended one of my most interesting hobbies. The question is, who will keep me out of work now?'

ODOUR

It was about this time of year. The monsoons had come and, outside his window, the leaves of the peepal tree danced as the raindrops fell on them. On the mahogany bed with the spring mattress that had now been pushed away from the window, a girl lay next to Randhir, their bodies clinging. Outside, in the milky dankness of the evening, the leaves of the peepal tree swung in the breeze like a golden ornament on a woman's forehead.

This was how it had happened. Having already read everything in the day's paper, including the advertisements, he had stepped out on the balcony. That was when he had seen her. She stood under the tamarind tree to stay dry. She must have been one of the workers in the sweatshop next door that made rope. To attract her attention, he coughed a couple of times and, when she looked up, he waved to her to come to him.

He was tired of being lonely because, since the war, most of the young Anglo-Indian girls of Bombay had joined the army's women's auxiliary corps, while some had opened private dance places in the Fort area to which only whites were admitted.

Randhir felt bored and a little sorry for himself. His ego hurt because he was far more cultured, far better educated and much better looking than those British tommies who were welcome in these clubs while he wasn't because of his colour. Before the war, Randhir had had several flings with the better-known hookers from the Nagpara area and the Taj Hotel. He always thought those Christian chhokras who ran after them, sometimes ending up marrying them, offered no competition.

He wanted the girl who stood under the tree as his revenge on Hazel, who lived on the ground floor and left every morning for work in her new, crisp uniform with a khaki cap sitting at a jaunty angle on her fashionably coiffeured hair. She was proud and flirtatious, expecting any man she came across to pay court to her. She had also decided to ignore Randhir.

When Randhir made a sign to the girl who stood under the tree to come upstairs, he wasn't sure if he wanted her. But she had come anyway. He noticed that her clothes were wet and he was afraid she might catch a chill, so he said to her, 'Take your wet clothes off unless you want to catch something.' He could see from her eyes that she knew why she was there. He gave her a dry towel to wrap herself in. She hesitated but only for a second. Then she took off her lehnga that was tied around her waist with a cord, placed it aside, hurriedly covered her thighs with the towel he had handed her and tried to wriggle out of her choli which was knotted in the front. She couldn't undo it because it was wet. She worked at the knot that was half embedded in her deep cleavage but it didn't yield. Finally she gave up. 'I can't; it won't give.'

Randhir made her sit next to him on the bed and began to struggle with the knot. In exasperation, he tugged at it and it snapped, revealing a pair of throbbing breasts like new clay cups from a potter's wheel: soft, round, cool, fragile and sensual. Dusky and virginal, they glowed like two floating lamps in a muddy pond.

It was the same time of year as it is now. The monsoons had come, and the leaves of the peepal tree danced as the raindrops fell on them. The wet clothes of the girl lay in a heap on the floor as she clung to Randhir, her naked body radiating a strange heat, a feeling of goodness and warmth that one gets in a steam bath. She never let go of him as long as she stayed. They said no more than a few words. There was no need to because their breath, their lips, their bodies had made that unnecessary. Randhir's hands moved over her breasts like breeze over open land. Her nipples were small and there were dark circles around them. They pressed their throbbing bodies together and he felt as if he was engulfed by fire.

Randhir was no novice to such encounters. He had slept with scores of girls and he knew the ecstasy of fulfilled desire. He had spent many nights lying next to beautiful women, his hard chest pressed against their tender breasts. He had known women who had no experience of men and who told him things one doesn't tell strangers. Then there were those who asked him to just lie back while they did all the work. But this girl who only a few minutes ago was standing under the tamarind tree trying to stay dry was different.

All through the night, Randhir remained aware of the odour that her body emitted, a smell both pleasant and unpleasant, a smell he drank all night. The odour that came out of her armpits, her breasts, her hair, her belly, in fact, from every part of her body, was overwhelming. Had she smelt different, he would have felt nothing for her. But this odour had penetrated the inner recesses of his being and gone beyond anything he had ever experienced. It was the odour that had welded their two bodies together. He felt as if he were drowning in a bottomless sea of desire, the closest a man can come to total physical satisfaction, a state both transitory and timeless. At moments he felt as if the two of them were flying high in an indescribably blue sky.

The odour cascaded out of every pore of her body and every pore of Randhir's body opened up to drink it in, but there was nothing he could compare it with. Perhaps it was closest to the smell of dry earth when sprinkled with water. Perhaps it wasn't. Her odour was not artificial like perfume: it was strong and earthy, like the physical union between man and woman that is both sacred and eternal.

Randhir had always hated the smell of perspiration and after a shower he would rub his body with talcum powder and put deodorant in his armpits. But wasn't it strange that he had kissed her repeatedly in her armpits and felt no nausea? In fact, a deep sense of satisfaction had washed over him. He was profoundly aware of the powerful smell of her body, something impossible to explain.

The monsoons had come as they had come that year. He looked out of the window. The peepal tree was where it had been that day. The raindrops fell over its leaves and the breeze blew over them gently as they fluttered. The sky was dark, yet there was a glow everywhere as if the rain had brought down starlight with it.

The rains had come as they had come that day, except that there were now two beds in the room, lying next to each other. There was also a new dressing table in one corner. One bed was empty and on the other lay Randhir, watching the rain fall on the leaves of the peepal tree. A fair-complexioned girl was stretched out next to him. She had fallen asleep while trying to cover her naked body with a bed sheet but had only half succeeded. Her red shalwar lay heaped at the foot of the bed, its silken cord dangling. Her other clothes also lay on the bed: the gold-coloured flowered jumper, the brassiere, the panties, the dupatta. Her clothes were bridal red and they were perfumed. There were bits of glitter in her black hair that, off and on, caught the light. Her face was rouged and made-up, and her brassiere had left a faint red imprint on her white, slightly bluish breasts. Her armpits were shaved and the skin was steel grey.

Randhir looked at the girl who lay next to him. She could have been sent to him in a wooden crate and he would have pulled out the nails to examine the contents. She had fine lines on her skin like old porcelain. Randhir had relieved her of her brassiere and seen its faint red imprint on her skin. Around her waist, the tight cord of her red shalwar had also left an imprint. There were also marks on her skin left by the heavy necklace she had been wearing.

It was the same time of year as it was then. He could hear the rain coming down on the leaves of the peepal tree, the same sound he had heard that night. He felt a cool breeze rise and carry the girl's perfume with it. Randhir fondled her breasts gently and a current ran through her body. He was conscious of the excitement embedded in her limbs. He lay next to her, their breasts touching. He heard her body hum but no odour leapt out of it. He remembered that dark girl to whom he had made love all night. Her odour had called out to him, as had her body, the same way a child calls out to its mother when hungry for her milk.

Randhir looked out of the window. The leaves of the peepal tree, now wet and washed, danced in the breeze. Beyond the trees he could see clouds in the sky that glowed as the breasts of the dark girl he had made love to all night had glowed. Their bodies had bonded.

He looked at the girl lying next to him. Her body was soft as if it were made of milk and melted butter, but the perfume she wore had a tired smell now, even a sour smell, a sad, colourless smell. He looked at her again. Her white skin with scratch marks reminded him of milk gone bad. He recoiled from the perfume she exuded. His mind went back to that night when that dark girl had lain next to him, her odour overwhelming his senses. It was something that leapt out of her body at him with a primeval force, far sweeter than the perfume his bride wore. The dark girl's odour had penetrated his body like an arrow, he remembered.

Randhir ran his hands over her white body but felt nothing. There was no sense of gathering excitement under his skin. His bride was the daughter of a judge, a college graduate and the heart-throb of her fellow students, but for Randhir she may as well not have been there. He had sought in her perfumed body that lost, remembered odour that had cascaded out of the unwashed body of that dark girl on a certain evening when the rain had begun to fall gently on the wet and dancing leaves of the peepal tree outside his window.

KINGDOM'S END

The phone rang. Manmohan picked it up.'Hello, 44457.'

'Sorry, wrong number,' said a woman's voice.

Manmohan put the receiver down and returned to his book. He had read it about twenty times, not because it was anything extraordinary, but because it was the only book in this room.

For one week now, Manmohan had been the sole occupant of this office room. It belonged to a friend of his who had gone out of town to raise a business loan. Since Manmohan was one of this big city's thousands of homeless people who slept nights on its footpaths, his friend had invited him to stay here in his absence to keep a watch on things.

He hardly ever went out. He was permanently out of work because he hated all employment. Had he really tried, he could easily have got himself hired as director with some film company, which is what he once was when he had decided to drop out. However, he had no desire to be enslaved again. He was a nice, quite harmless man. He had almost no personal expenses. All he required was a cup of tea in the morning with two slices of toast, a little bit of curry and chapatti in the afternoon and a packet of cigarettes. That was all. Luckily, he had enough friends who were quite happy to provide for these simple needs.

Manmohan had no family or close relations. He could go without food for days on end if the going got hard. His friends didn't know much about him except that he had run away from home as a boy and had lived on the broad footpaths of Bombay for many years. There was only one thing missing in his life—women. He used to say, 'If a woman were to fall in love with me, my life would change.' Friends would retort, 'But even then you wouldn't work.'

'It would be nothing but work from then on,' he would answer.

'Why not have an affair then?'

'What good is an affair when the initiative comes from the man?'

It was afternoon now, almost time for lunch. Suddenly, the phone rang.

He picked it up. 'Hello, 44457.'

'44457?' a woman's voice asked.

'That's right,' Manmohan answered.

'Who are you?' the voice asked.

'I am Manmohan.'

There was no response. 'Who do you wish to speak to?' he asked.

'You,' the voice said.

'Me?'

'Unless you object.'

'No . . . not at all.'

'Did you say your name was Madan Mohan?'

'No. Manmohan.'

'Manmohan?'

There was a silence. 'I thought you wanted to talk to me,' he said.

'Yes.'

'Then go ahead.'

'I don't know what to say. Why don't you say something?'

'Very well,' Manmohan said. 'I have already told you my name. Temporarily, this office is my headquarters. I used to sleep on the city's footpaths, but for the last one week I have been sleeping on a big office table.'

'What did you do to keep the mosquitoes away at night? Use a net on your footpath?'

Manmohan laughed. 'Before I answer this, let me make it clear that I don't tell lies. I have slept on footpaths for years. Since this office came under my occupation, I have been living it up.'

'How are you living it up?'

'Well, there's this book I have. The last pages are missing, but I've read it twenty times. One day, when I can lay my hand on the missing pages, I will finally know what end the two lovers met.'

'You sound like a very interesting man,' the voice said.

'You are only being kind.'

'What do you do?'

'Do?'

'I mean, what is your occupation?'

'Occupation? None at all. What occupation can a man have when he doesn't work? But to answer your question, I loaf around during the day and sleep at night.'

'Do you like your life?'

'Wait,' Manmohan said. 'That is one question I have never asked myself. And now that you have put it to me, I'm going to put it to myself for the first time. Do I like the way I live my life?'

'And what is the answer?'

'Well, there is no answer, but I suppose if I've lived my life the way I've lived it for so long, then it's reasonable to assume that I like it.'

There was laughter. 'You laugh so beautifully,' Manmohan said.

'Thank you.' The voice was shy. The call was disconnected. For a long time, he kept holding the receiver, smiling to himself.

The next day at about eight in the morning, the phone rang again. He was fast asleep, but the noise woke him up. He yawned and picked it up.

'Hello, this is 44457.'

'Good morning, Manmohan sahib.'

'Good morning . . . oh it's you. Good morning.'

'Were you asleep?'

'I was. You know I have become spoilt since I moved here. When I return to the footpath, I'm going to run into difficulties.'

'Why?'

'Because if you sleep on the footpath, you have to get up before five in the morning.'

There was laughter.

'You rang off abruptly yesterday,' he said.

'Well, why did you say I laugh beautifully?'

'What a question! If something is beautiful, it should be praised, shouldn't it?'

'Not at all.'

'You are not to impose conditions. I have never accepted conditions. If you laugh, I'm going to say that you laugh beautifully.'

'In that case, I'll hang up.'

'Please yourself.'

'Don't you really care if I get upset?'

'Well, to begin with, I don't wish to upset myself, which means that if you laugh and I don't say that you laugh beautifully, I would be doing an injustice to my good taste.'

There was a brief silence. Then the voice came back: 'I'm sorry, I was having a word with our maid. So you were saying that you were partial to your good taste. What else is your good taste partial to?'

'What do you mean?'

'I mean . . . what hobby or work . . . or, shall I ask, what can you do?'

Manmohan laughed. 'Nothing much except that I am fond of photography—just a bit.'

'That's a very good hobby.'

'I have never thought of it in terms of its being good or bad.'

'You must have a very nice camera.'

'I have no camera. Off and on, I borrow one from a friend. Anyway, if I'm ever able to earn some money, there is a certain camera I am going to buy.'

'What camera?'

'Exacta. It's a reflex camera. I like it very much.'

There was silence. 'I was thinking of something.'

'What?'

'You have neither asked me my name nor my phone number.'

'I haven't felt the need.'

'Why not?'

'What does it matter what your name is? You have my number. That's enough. When you want me to phone you, I'm sure you will give me your name and number.'

'No, I won't.'

'Please yourself. I'm not going to ask.'

'You're a strange man.'

'That's true, I am.'

There was another silence.

'Were you thinking again?' he asked.

'I was, but I just can't think of anything to think about.'

'Then why don't you hang up? Another time.'

There was a touch of annoyance in the voice. 'You're a very rude man. I am hanging up.'

Manmohan smiled and put the phone down. He washed his face, put on his clothes and was about to leave, when the phone rang. He picked it up. '44457.'

'Mr Manmohan?' asked the voice.

'What can I do for you?'

'Well, I wanted to tell you that I'm not annoyed any more.'

'That's very nice.'

'You know while I was having breakfast, it occurred to me that I shouldn't be annoyed with you. Have you had breakfast?'

'No, I was just about to go out when you phoned.'

'Oh, then I won't keep you.'

'I'm in no particular hurry today, because I have no money. I don't think there'll be any breakfast this morning.'

'Why do you say such things? Do you enjoy hurting yourself?'

'No, I'm quite used to the way I am and the way I live.'

'Should I send you some money?'

'If you want to. That will be one more name on the list of my financiers.'

'Then I won't.'

'Do what you like.'

'I am going to hang up.'

'Hang up then.'

Manmohan put down the phone and walked out of the office. He came back very late in the evening. He had been wondering about his caller all day. She sounded young and educated and she laughed beautifully. At eleven o'clock the phone rang.

'Hello.'

'Mr Manmohan.'

'That's him.'

'I've been phoning all day. Could you please explain where you were?'

'Although I don't have a job, I still have things to do.'

'What things?'

'Loafing about.'

'When did you come back?'

'An hour ago.'

'What were you doing when I called?'

'I was lying on the table and trying to imagine what you looked like, but I have nothing to go on except your voice.'

'Did you succeed?'

'No.'

'Well, don't try. I'm very ugly.'

'If you are ugly, then kindly hang up. I hate ugliness.'

'Well, if that's the case, I am beautiful. I don't want you to nurture hatred.'

They didn't speak for some time. Then Manmohan asked, 'Were you thinking?'

'No, but I was going to ask you . . .'

'Think before you ask.'

'Do you want me to sing for you?'

'Yes.'

'All right, wait.'

He heard her clear her throat, then in a very soft, low voice she sang him a song.

'That was lovely.'

'Thank you.' She rang off.

All night long he dreamt about her voice. He rose earlier than usual and waited for her call, but the phone never rang. He began to pace around the room restlessly. Then he lay down on the table and picked up the book he had read twenty times. He read it once again. The whole day passed. At about seven in the evening, the phone rang. Hurriedly, he picked it up.

'Who's that?'

'It's me.'

'Where were you all day?' he asked sharply.

'Why?' the voice trembled.

'I've been waiting. I haven't had anything to eat, although I had money.'

'I'll phone when I want to . . .'

Manmohan cut her short. 'Look, either put an end to this business or let me know when you will call. I can't stand waiting.'

'I apologize for today. From tomorrow I promise to phone both morning and evening.'

'That's wonderful.'

'I didn't know you were . . .'

'Well, the thing is that I simply can't bear to wait and, when I can't bear something, I begin to punish myself.'

'How do you do that?'

'You didn't phone this morning. I should have gone out, but I didn't. I sat here all day fretting.'

'I didn't phone you deliberately.'

'Why?'

'To find out if you miss my call.'

'You are very naughty. Now hang up. I must go out and eat.'

'How long will you be?'

'Half an hour.'

He returned after an hour. She phoned. They talked for a long time. He asked her to sing him the same song. She laughed and sang it.

She would now ring regularly, morning and evening. Sometimes they would talk for hours. But, so far, Manmohan had neither asked her her name nor her phone number. In the beginning he had tried to imagine what she looked like, but that had now become unnecessary. Her voice was everything—her face, her soul, her body. One day she asked him, 'Mohan, why don't you ask me my name?'

'Because your voice is your name.'

Another day she said, 'Mohan, have you ever been in love?'

'No.'

'Why?'

He grew sad. 'To answer this question, I'll have to clear away the entire debris of my life and I would be very unhappy if I found nothing there.'

'Then don't.'

A month passed. One day Mohan had a letter from his friend. He said he had raised the money and would be returning to Bombay in a week. When she phoned that evening, he said to her, 'This is my kingdom's end.'

'Why?'

'Because my friend is coming back.'

'You must have friends who have phones?'

'Yes, I have friends who have phones, but I can't give you the numbers.'

'Why?'

'I don't want anyone else to hear your voice.'

'Why?'

'Let's say I'm jealous.'

'What should we do?'

'Tell me.'

'On the day your kingdom ends, I'll give you my number.'

The sadness he had felt was suddenly gone. He again tried to picture her, but there was no image, just her voice. It was only a matter of days now, he said to himself, before he would see her. He could not imagine the immensity of that moment.

When she called next day, he said to her, 'I'm curious to see you.'

'Why?'

'You said you would give me your phone number on the day my kingdom ends.'

'Yes.'

'Does that also mean you'll tell me where you live? I want to see you.'

'You can see me whenever you like. Even today.'

'Not today. No, I want to see you when I am wearing nice clothes. I have asked a friend of mine to get me some.'

'You're like a child. When we meet, I'll give you a present.'

'There can be no greater present in the world than meeting you.'

'I have bought you an Exacta camera.'

'Oh!'

'But there's a condition. You'll have to take my picture.'

'That I'll decide when we meet.'

'I shan't be phoning you for the next two days.'

'Why?'

'I'm going to be away with my family. It's only two days.'

Manmohan did not leave the office that day. The next morning he felt feverish. At first he thought it was boredom because she hadn't phoned. By the afternoon, his fever was high. His body felt on fire. His eyes were burning. He lay down on the table. He was very thirsty. He kept drinking water all day. There was heaviness in his chest. By the next morning, he felt completely exhausted. He had trouble in breathing. His chest hurt.

His fever was so high that he went into a delirium. He was talking to her on the phone, listening to her voice. By the evening, his condition had deteriorated. There were voices in his head and strange sounds as if thousands of phones were ringing at the same time. He couldn't breathe.

When the phone rang, he did not hear it. It kept ringing for a long time. Then suddenly there was a moment of clarity. He could hear it. He rose, stumbling uncertainly on his feet. He almost fell but, steadying himself against the wall, he picked it up with trembling hands. He ran his tongue over his lips. They were dry like wood.

'Hello.'

'Hello, Mohan,' she said.

'It is Mohan,' his voice fluttered.

'I can't hear you.'

He tried to say something, but his voice dried up in his throat.

She said, 'We came back earlier than I thought. I've been trying to call you for hours. Where were you?'

Manmohan's head began to spin.

'What is wrong?' she asked.

With great difficulty he said, 'My kingdom has come to an end today.'

Blood spilled out of his mouth, making a thin red line down his chin, then along his neck.

She said, 'Take my number down. 50314 . . . 50314. Call me in the morning. I have to go now.'

She hung up. Manmohan collapsed over the phone, blood bubbling out of his mouth.

BRIBING THE ALMIGHTY

Ahmed Din came from a well-off family and everyone acknowledged that from among his friends and playmates he was the most neatly turned out.

But things changed.

He completed college, scoring high grades, and his father, Khan Bahadur Ataullah, announced to everyone that he was going to send his son to England for a higher degree. A passport was applied for and obtained, and new clothes were ordered and stitched for the young man. About this time, on the advice of a friend of his, Khan Bahadur Ataullah took to playing the stock market. In the beginning, he made a great deal of money, which was good because it meant his son's English education was all but paid for. However, he became greedy. He also became convinced that he would always be on a winning streak. The friend who had induced him to play the market would say things like, 'Khan Bahadur, you are one of those who are born lucky. I am sure if you touched dust it would turn into gold.' Such flattery always earned him gifts in cash, which was no burden on Khan Bahadur, who was rolling in the stuff.

Ahmed Din was wise for his years and one day he said to his father, 'Father, playing the market is not a good thing. It never leads to any good.'

Khan Bahadur was not amused. 'Son, how dare you interfere in my business! Whatever I am doing is what I need to do. The money I make is not going with me to my grave: it will all come to you.'

Ahmed Din, not about to give up, asked innocently, 'Father, how long can the money keep coming in? Suppose it were to start going the other way one day?'

'Shut up, it has to keep coming in,' Khan Bahadur said angrily.

And he seemed to have got it right. His winning streak continued.

One day, he invested a large amount in certain stocks. They sank without a trace. He redoubled the stakes the next day and lost again. And the next day the same thing happened. Confident that his luck would turn, he placed all the cash he had on a single position, only to learn from the following day's newspaper that he had lost. Not one to give up easily, he mortgaged his house and placed the entire proceeds on silver, 'all in God's name', as he put it.

While there could be no two opinions about God, it was questionable whether He also found time to manage the stock market. Next day, Khan Bahadur found that the silver market had crashed. That was when he had his first heart attack.

Ahmed Din said to his father, 'Give it up, even now.'

'Shut up, I am doing the right thing,' was the reply he received.

In a respectful voice, Ahmed Din ventured, 'But, father, what do you think has brought on your heart trouble?'

'How should I know? Human beings fall sick, don't they; God alone knows why,' he said.

Ahmed Din was lost in thought for a couple of minutes; then he said, 'That is true, human beings do get stricken by disease but there is always a reason. For instance, were you to eat something which carried cholera germs . . .'

Khan Bahadur was uneasy with this conversation. 'Get out of my room and don't bother me with your nonsense . . . I know exactly what I am doing.'

'That's what you think, but no human being should make such a boastful claim,' Ahmed Din replied as he walked out of the room.

The fact was that Khan Bahadur Ataullah was beginning to have doubts about the advisability of his actions, but he did not want his son to know he was assailed by self-doubt.

So he said to himself, while lying on his bed, 'Khan Bahadur Ataullah, you prance around thinking you are God knows who or what, but the fact is that you are an ass. Why don't you listen to your son, especially when you know he is right? Whatever money you won in the beginning, you have lost twice that figure. Is that wise?' Then in order to console himself, he added, 'Maybe what others say is correct and maybe I am wrong, but I am sure things are going to change.'

After two weeks of bed rest, when Khan Bahadur Ataullah was well enough to move about, he sold a second house that he had and threw the money into another venture in the hope that he would recover his losses. It was not to be. He lost again.

Ahmed Din watched his father ruin himself, but did not know how to make him see the folly of his ways because he was impervious to advice. But he decided to make one last effort.

One day, as his father sat in his room smoking and looking lost, Ahmed Din came in, and in an apprehensive voice began, 'Father . . .'

So engrossed in his thoughts was Khan Bahadur that he had not heard his son enter or speak.

Ahmed Din called more loudly, 'Father, father . . .'

Khan Bahadur came out of his reverie. 'What is it?'

Ahmed Din trembled. 'Nothing, father. There was something I wanted to say to you.'

'Out with it then.'

'I wanted to beg you, father, to stop playing the stock market.'

Khan Bahadur inhaled on his hubble-bubble deeply once and screamed, 'Who are you to lecture me? I am the one who decides what I want to do. Do you think I have run my life so far on your advice? I am warning you, never again poke your nose into my affairs. I will tolerate no such impertinence. Do you understand?'

With head bent, Ahmed Din replied, 'I understand.'

Then he left his father's room.

Gambling is a far more difficult habit to shake off than drinking. Khan Bahadur Ataullah was now beyond redemption. He lost whatever he owned, even the ornaments of his late wife. A day after that happened, he collapsed in his bathroom and was dead within seconds.

Ahmed Din was shattered. When he could muster some strength to recover, he took stock of his situation. All he had was a college degree. The houses had been sold and his father had left him not a penny. He had to vacate the house, which he did after selling off what little it contained; then he rented himself a single room in a filthy city neighbourhood but how long could his meagre capital last? Before long, he was utterly penniless.

He began to look for a job, any job, even if it earned him next to nothing. He often thought of his mother and cried although she had died in his infancy. He did not remember her but he knew that she had suckled him.

Ahmed Din did everything he could to land a job but without luck. The few jobs that were on offer were being chased by far too many hopefuls like him. He felt like a drop of water in an ocean of unemployment.

But he did not give up. He kept trying.

Finally, he came to the conclusion that you could only get a job if you had the money to bribe an official. But where was he going to get the money to do so?

One day when he walked into an office, the head clerk said to him in an affectionate voice, 'Look, son, empty-handed you will gain nothing. The position you have applied for has over two hundred and fifty contenders. I speak plainly. If you can come up with five hundred rupees, the job is yours.'

But all Ahmed Din had was thirty rupees, so he said to the head clerk, 'Sir, I do not have that kind of money, but if you get me the job, half my salary will go to you.'

The head clerk burst out laughing. 'You take me for a fool! Get lost.'

Ahmed Din continued looking but wherever he went he ran into the same wall. Perhaps the world was created so that people could offer and accept bribes, he said to himself one day. Maybe someone bribed God to create the world.

In the end, he became a labourer, earning around two rupees for a full day's work. Times were bad and money did not go very far. All he could manage to save, despite his best efforts, were a few pennies a day, no more.

And all the while that he worked at those back-breaking jobs, he thought of bribery and what a great curse it was. How could it be wiped out? He hated physical work and wished he could find himself a desk job, something in keeping with his college education. After all he had a bachelor's degree, first class first.

Then it occurred to him that he should start praying regularly. He decided to ask God to help him. However, despite his ardent prayers, five times a day, nothing came his way. So one day, after his morning prayers, he went to the post office, bought a postal order for the thirty rupees he had saved, put it in an envelope, along with a note, and mailed it.

The note said, 'Dear Allah Mian, I am convinced you expect a bribe before helping anyone. All I have is thirty rupees, which I am enclosing herewith. Please get me a nice job. I can no longer carry heavy loads. My back is killing me.'

On the envelope he wrote, 'Allah Mian, Proprietor of the Universe.'

After a few days, he received a reply from one Muhammad Mian, editor of a newspaper called *The Universe*. He had been summoned for an interview. Ahmed Din went and was hired as a translator at one hundred rupees a month.

'It did work, did it not?' he said to himself.

THE SEVEN MAGIC FLOWERS

From the moment we met, we were friends. All I knew about him was that he was a Syed and even a distant relation, although it seemed illogical, he being a Syed and I a mere Kashmiri.

In any case, that hardly seemed important. He was fond of reading and, when he learnt that I wrote stories, he asked if he could borrow some of my books. I was surprised that not only did he read them but he praised the very stories that had gained much popularity. He was also my neighbour. He had a large family and, as his flat was not large enough, he had commandeered a garage attached to the building, turning it into a sort of reception room. The flat proper was for the exclusive use of the women of the house. Shah Sahib, which was what they called him, had a large number of friends and the garage was the perfect place to receive and entertain them.

One day as we were talking about short-story writing, he said to me, 'There are many things in my life that you could turn into short stories.' Since I was always on the lookout for story ideas, I became interested. 'Well, I hope you can provide me with good material.'

Shah Sahib replied, 'I am not a writer but there is a certain incident in my life that is worth your serious attention. I say serious attention because since you are a great short-story writer, you are bound to find what I am about to narrate most extraordinary.'

'How extraordinary can it be!' I said, then quickly amended it by adding, 'But maybe it was extraordinary for you.'

Shah Sahib said, 'Well, I am not claiming that what I am about to narrate will surprise everyone. I was only speaking for myself, but the fact is that what you are about to hear has no rational explanation.'

Shah Sahib was clipping his nails as he talked and, after finishing that dexterously conducted operation, put the clipper on the table, lit a cigarette and began, 'I used to live in Kabul where I owned an expensive, well-stocked general store, the biggest in the city, which was also a special haunt of the city's women shoppers. On days when I had more men than women customers, the other store owners would tease me in Persian, "Agha, what is the matter today! Have the women and girls of Kabul all died or is it that your good fortune is no longer smiling on you?"

'My response was always a smile. I mean what could I say? I knew that most of my customers were women and I also knew why. They came because I was a very good conversationalist. I am a very good salesman, Manto sahib, especially when it comes to women. I tell you there is not a shopkeeper in this city of Lahore who can excel me in salesmanship. I not only have a college education but I am also a student of human psychology. I know how to deal with women. That was the only reason for the success of my store in Kabul.'

'I don't doubt that. I can gather that from the way you talk,' I said, somewhat sarcastically because he was blowing his own trumpet.

Shah Sahib smiled. 'But I am afraid I will not be able to tell my story like a good salesman.'

'I think you should begin the story,' I suggested.

Shah Sahib seemed to be searching his memory, which I let him. Then he began to talk. 'Manto sahib, this was about ten years ago. I was younger and far stronger than I am today. I was a health freak, working out vigorously every day. I neither drank nor smoked; my only weakness was good Indian, not Afghani, food. From Amritsar, I had brought along a Kashmiri cook who was a magician. Life was good and the money was great. I had a fair amount of cash stashed away in the bank.'

Shah Sahib stopped talking suddenly. 'You have fallen silent; does it mean, despite all you had, you were not really happy?' I asked.

'That's true. Despite all I had, I was not happy because I was single. Had so many women not made my store their favourite haunt, I may not have experienced the loneliness that often assailed me. But it was the other way around. There was hardly a rich or well-known family in Kabul whose women did not shop at my store. The first thing they did as they walked in was to rid themselves of their burqa, veil or chaddar. If you think they were austerely dressed, you couldn't be more wrong. Purdah they all observed, but they were highly westernized: skirts, styled hair, painted nails, bare legs. And they were not in the least self-conscious, so absorbed were they in their shopping.'

Shah Sahib paused. 'Surely, you developed a crush on one of them,' I said.

He became grave. 'Yes, on a certain girl who never took off her veil.'

'Who was she?'

'She came from an old family, daughter of a stern army general. I fell in love with her because of her hands, the only part of her body she made visible.'

'Why?'

'That I can't say, nor have I ever tried to analyse it. I imagined her as being very beautiful, young and nubile with a perfect body. She never stayed for more than a few minutes. She would buy what she had to buy and leave.'

'How long did that continue?' I asked.

'Almost six months. I did not have the courage to tell her how I felt about her. She was quite different from others and her personality fascinated me. She carried herself with great dignity. I just couldn't take my eyes off her, though I knew it was a rude thing to do, but I could not help myself. One day, as I was sitting in the store thinking about her, the phone rang. My assistant picked it up and said there was a woman on the line who wished to speak to me. I thought it must be a customer inquiring about new arrivals. "Yes, madam, how can I help you?" I asked as I took the call. It was she. I knew her voice. "You're Syed Muzaffar Ali?" she asked. "I am," I replied nervously. "Look," she said, "whenever I visit your store, you keep staring at me. Such behaviour is intolerable. I warn you to mend your ways." Before I could say anything, she had hung up. I could not put the phone down, wondering what she had meant by her threat.'

'Was it really a threat?' I asked.

'It was, because she came to the store four days later and, as always, I looked at her veiled face longingly, and you know what she said angrily in front of my assistants—"Aren't you ashamed of the way you stare at me!" I was petrified. Then she bought a few things, paid for them and drove away in her chauffeured car.'

'What a strange girl! She seemed to hate you and yet she continued to visit your store,' I said.

'Manto sahib, I began to believe that it was her way of reacting to the love she saw in my eyes. However, one day she spoke to me so harshly that I decided to forget all about her, but no matter how hard I tried, I just could not stop thinking about her. I felt foolish, considering that I had never even seen her face and that I had received nothing from her but reprimands. But love is a strange thing. No matter what I did, I just could not overcome my infatuation. I used to argue with myself. "Look," I would say, "you have a fine business running and a good name in the entire country, so what is this foolishness!" But Manto sahib, this thing called love is a strange monster. I had no control over my feelings.'

'Your story is getting longer,' I said, 'let's get to the end.'

Shah Sahib rose from his chair. 'My friend, these stories are always long. Love is an ailment and it always takes time before becoming an affliction. But I will try to make my story brief. My love for her had now become an obsession. I could think of nothing but her. I would get so depressed sometimes that I would weep. And that was the point when Sardar Balwant Singh Majeethia enters the picture. Like me, he came from Amritsar and worked for a Kabul engineering firm. Off and on, he would come to me and ask for a small loan. It was for the same reason that he walked into my store one day. He took one look at me and said, "My friend, something is troubling you." "No, no, it's nothing," I replied. He smiled through his thick, overhanging moustache. "You are lying. Tell me, are you in love?" I kept quiet. "Look, if that is what it is, I can make everything work out," he said. In the end, I told him my story.'

'So what did he suggest?' I asked.

'He gave me a spell to recite.'

'Spell!'

'Yes.'

'You are a Syed; do you believe in such mumbo-jumbo?'

'Well, I know our religion forbids this, but lovesick that I was, I had to try it. He told me to get seven flowers of different colours, recite the spell and then blow on each flower, one by one. On a Tuesday, I was to somehow make that girl smell the seven flowers. I still remember the spell.'

'How did it go?'

'This is how: *Phul khilay, phul hassey; phul chugay Nahir Singh pyare; jo koi lay phulon ki baas; kabhi na chhoray hamara sath; hamain chhor kisi aur par maray; pait bhasam ho maray; duhai Sulaiman Pir Paighambar ki.'* Flowers bloom, flowers laugh; dear Nahir Singh picks up the flowers; he who smells the flowers will never leave us. If he leaves us to fall in love with someone else, fire will consume his body and he will die. We seek the protection of Sulaiman, pir and prophet.'

I was reminded of a spell I had learnt from a book of magic when I was in school. One of them was supposed to guarantee success in school examinations. It went like this: *Oong numa kameshri utma dey bhraing pra swa*. However, the result was that I failed my ninth grade examination. I did not tell Shah Sahib my story but asked him, 'Did you recite the spell and blow on the seven flowers?'

'Yes, on a Monday, then I sent her word that I had just received fresh goods from Czechoslovakia and, if she came on Tuesday, she could take a look at them.'

'Did she?'

'Yes, she came at five minutes to five in the evening and asked about my Czech imports. I told her that the consignment had yet to be opened. She was offended. Then she noticed me looking at those flowers on my table. "Flowers?" she asked. "I bought them for you. If you like them, I mean their fragrance, I hope you'll accept them," I answered. She picked up the flowers and smelled them.'

'And what was her reaction?' I asked.

'She pulled a face and said, "You call these flowers! They have no smell at all." Then she made a few purchases and left. Later that evening, Sardar Balwant Singh Majeethia dropped in and asked if I had followed his instructions. I told him I had, but wasn't sure anything would change. He laughed. "Friend, consider it done, almost."

'I was sceptical, but Manto sahib, believe me, she called the next morning to say she was on her way. She came but I could see that she was not interested in buying anything. She kept going up and down the aisle for a long time, then she came to me and said, "How many times have I told you not to stare at me! And what did you mean by making me smell those flowers?"

'"Those flowers . . . I . . . I . . . got them for you because my assistants had forgotten to open the Czech consignment . . . hence those flowers," I stammered. She was restless behind her impenetrable veil. "Why did you make me smell those flowers?" she asked. "Did that cause a problem?" I asked in turn. "Yes, all night long, I have been dreaming of those seven flowers. I would see them, and when I would reach out to grab them, they would slip away. What sort of flowers were they?" she asked. "They came from my country, which was why I gave them to you. I am surprised you dreamt about them all night," I replied.'

'And where did you get those flowers?' I asked Shah Sahib.

'Where did I get them! Why, they were local flowers, and not very nice either. For one thing, they had no fragrance,' Shah Sahib answered.

Then he continued with his story. 'In the evening, Balwant Singh Majeethia came to borrow more money and asked if there had been any development. I told him. He forgot about the money, slapped me across the back with his hairy hand and shouted, "Shah Sahib, that does it. Order a bottle of whisky because it calls for a celebration." A bottle of whisky was sent for, as well as a tin of cigarettes. Balwant Singh Majeethia smoked several cigarettes, the diehard smoker that he was, and before leaving, advised me, "The thing needs a slight push. Repeat the ritual next Tuesday and you will have your heart's desire." I wasn't sure how I was going to make her smell my flowers again when she had already expressed her suspicions about the first episode. But I was in love and when you are in love you are ready to do anything. This time I sent for flowers from Peshawar, chose seven of the prettiest, read out the spell and blew on them one by one, as instructed, and placed them in a vase on my table. On Monday, I phoned her to say that the Czech goods were at last in the store and would she come the next day? She came but found that there were no Czech goods. I sent for the assistants and screamed at them for being lazy and irresponsible. This time she had brought her mother with her who was more interested in toiletries. The girl noticed the flowers and looked both surprised and disturbed. She walked up to the table, bent and smelled the flowers, "These flowers are not from Afghanistan," she said. "That's right, they are from my country and I had them sent for, specially for you." And there for the first time I told her that I was in love with her. She looked annoyed and left with her mother.

'In the evening, Balwant Singh Majeethia appeared. I told him of the day's events and also lent him ten rupees which he pocketed. Then he slapped his hairy hand on mine and said, "Shah Sahib, it is now more than done. A bottle of whisky is called for." I sent for the whisky, half of which he drank sitting there, while taking the rest with him.'

'And what result did the second bunch produce?' I asked.

'She came the next day and told me she was terribly confused and restless. She was not only seeing flowers at night but also during the day. Then she removed her veil, which she had never done before, and said, "You have cast a spell on me." Manto sahib, I took one look at her face and nearly had a heart attack. I had not seen a more beautiful girl in my life. I just kept looking at her. "Why did you make me smell those flowers?" she asked angrily. "I am losing my mind; they dance in front of my eyes day and night. I know you are in love with me but you should know that I am about to be married. What have you done to me?" Then she turned to the vase that was still on the table, pulled out the flowers, threw them on the floor and trampled them under her feet. She looked annoyed but I had a feeling that it wasn't really so and that she wanted to stay and have me talk to her. However, still feeling uncertain of myself, I kept quiet and after a few minutes, she put her veil back on and stormed out of the store.'

'So Sardar Balwant Singh Majeethia's spell worked in the end?' I asked.

'Yes, it did . . . all she could see was flowers. My rational mind was still sceptical but in my heart of hearts I knew that the spell had worked. Odd, isn't it, considering that the words were so absurd. Next time, she came to my store, she took off her veil and threw her arms around me. I kissed her several times without encountering any resistance. Then she snatched the flowers that were in the vase, threw them on the floor and stamped on them before veiling herself and walking out.'

'But what happened in the end? Did you get her?' I asked.

'No, she got married as arranged, and on her wedding night, the moment she entered the bridal chamber, she collapsed to the floor and died. In her hand they found seven flowers of seven different colours.'

At that time precisely, I noticed that in the brass vase on the table next to Shah Sahib's chair there were seven flowers of seven different colours.

UPSTAIRS DOWNSTAIRS

Husband: 'It is after ages that we are sitting down like this, together and alone.'

Wife: 'Yes.'

Husband: 'Engagements . . . as much as I try to avoid them, there is no let-up. Being aware of the incompetents with whom we are surrounded and conscious of my responsibilities to the nation, I have to keep working.'

Wife: 'Actually, you just happen to be far too tender-hearted, when it comes to these things. Just like me.'

Husband: 'Yes, I keep myself abreast of your social activities. When you find a minute, do let me read the speeches you have been making on several recent occasions. I would like to go through them when I find time.'

Wife: 'Very well.'

Husband: 'Yes, Begum, you recall my mentioning that business to you the other day.'

Wife: 'What business?'

Husband: 'Perhaps I did not. Yesterday, by chance I happened to find myself in our middle son's room and found him reading *Lady Chatterley's Lover*.'

Wife: 'You mean that scandalous book!'

Husband: 'Yes, Begum.'

Wife: 'What did you do?'

Husband: 'I snatched the book from him and hid it.'

Wife: 'You did the right thing.'

Husband: 'I am going to consult a doctor and ask him to suggest a different diet for him.'

Wife: 'That would be absolutely the right thing to do.'

Husband: 'And how are you feeling?'

Wife: 'Fine.'

Husband: 'I was playing with the idea of . . . requesting you today . . .'

Wife: 'Oh, you are getting too bold.'

Husband: 'And all because of your winning ways.'

Wife: 'But . . . your health?'

Husband: 'Health? . . . I feel well . . . but unless I consult the doctor, I won't make any move . . . and I should be fully satisfied about that being all right from your side.'

Wife: 'I will have a word with Miss Saldhana today.'

Husband: 'And I will speak to Dr Jalal.'

Wife: 'That's the way it should be.'

Husband: 'If Dr Jalal permits.'

Wife: 'And if Miss Saldhana has no objection . . . Do wrap your scarf around your neck carefully. It is cold outside.'

Husband: 'Thank you.'

Dr Jalal: 'Did you say yes?'

Miss Saldhana: 'Yes.'

Dr Jalal: 'So did I . . . but out of mischief.'

Miss Saldhana: 'Out of mischief, I almost said no.'

Dr Jalal: 'But then I took pity.'

Miss Saldhana: 'So did I.'

Dr Jalal: 'After one full year.'

Miss Saldhana: 'Yes, after one full year.'

Dr Jalal: 'When I said yes, his pulse quickened.'

Miss Saldhana: 'She was the same way.'

Dr Jalal: 'He said to me, the fear showing in his voice, "Doctor, it seems to me my heart is not going to keep up with me. Please take a cardiogram."'

Miss Saldhana: 'That is exactly what she said to me.'

Dr Jalal: 'I gave him an injection.'

Miss Saldhana: 'I too, except that it was simple distilled water.'

Dr Jalal: 'Water is the best thing in the world.'

Miss Saldhana: 'Jalal, if you were married to that woman?'

Dr Jalal: 'And if you were married to that man?'

Miss Saldhana: 'I would have become a nymphomaniac.'

Dr Jalal: 'And I would have met my Maker by now.'

Miss Saldhana: 'You don't say.'

Dr Jalal: 'When we examine these high society idiots, they put some funny ideas in our heads.'

Miss Saldhana: 'Today as well?'

Dr Jalal: 'Today of all days.'

Miss Saldhana: 'The trouble with these people is that these funny ideas come to them after year-long intervals.'

Wife: '*Lady Chatterley's Lover*? Why is that book under your pillow?'

Husband: 'I wanted to see for myself how obscene it is.'

Wife: 'Let me take a peek also.'

Husband: 'No, I will read out from it; you do the listening.'

Wife: 'That would be very nice.'

Husband: 'I have had our son's diet changed as recommended by the doctor after I spoke to him.'

Wife: 'I was sure you would not let this matter go unattended.'

Husband: 'I have never put off till the next day what needed to be done today.'

Wife: 'I know that . . . And what is to be done today, I am sure you will not . . .'

Husband: 'You seem to be in a very pleasant mood.'

Wife: 'All because of you.'

Husband: 'I am obliged. And now if you permit . . .'

Wife: 'Have you brushed your teeth?'

Husband: 'Yes, not only have I brushed my teeth, I have also gargled with Dettol.'

Wife: 'So have I.'

Husband: 'The two of us were made for each other.'

Wife: 'That goes without saying.'

Husband: 'I will now slowly read from this infamous book.'

Wife: 'But wait, please take my pulse.'

Husband: 'It is fast . . . feel mine.'

Wife: 'Yours is racing too.'

Husband: 'Reason?'

Wife: 'A weak heart?'

Husband: 'Has to be that . . . but Dr Jalal had said there was nothing the matter.'

Wife: 'That was what Miss Saldhana also told me.'

Husband: 'He examined me thoroughly before giving his permission.'

Wife: 'I was examined thoroughly too.'

Husband: 'Then I suppose there is no harm . . .'

Wife: 'You know better . . . but your health . . .'
Husband: 'And yours?'
Wife: 'We should exercise the greatest care before . . .'
Husband: 'Did Miss Saldhana take care of that thing?'
Wife: 'What thing? . . . Oh, yes. She took care of that.'
Husband: 'So there should be no worry on that score?'
Wife: 'None.'
Husband: 'Feel my pulse now.'
Wife: 'Feels normal . . . and mine?'
Husband: 'Yours feels normal too.'
Wife: 'Read something out of that scandalous volume.'
Husband: 'Very well, but I can feel my heart racing.'
Wife: 'So is mine.'
Husband: 'Do we have all we need?'
Wife: 'Yes, everything.'
Husband: 'If you don't mind, could you take my temperature?'
Wife: 'There is a stopwatch around . . . the pulse rate should be measured.'
Husband: 'I agree.'
Wife: 'Where are the smelling salts?'
Husband: 'Should be with the other things.'
Wife: 'Yes, on the side table.'
Husband: 'I think we should raise the room thermostat as well.'
Wife: 'I agree.'
Husband: 'If I am overcome by weakness, don't forget my medicine.'
Wife: 'I will try, if . . .'
Husband: 'Yes . . . but only if necessary.'
Wife: 'Read out the whole page.'
Husband: 'Get ready to listen then.'
Wife: 'You sneezed.'
Husband: 'I don't know why.'
Wife: 'Strange.'
Husband: 'I find that strange also.'
Wife: 'Oh, I know what happened. Instead of raising the thermostat, I lowered it by mistake.'
Husband: 'I am glad I sneezed. That way we just found out in time.'
Wife: 'I am sorry.'
Husband: 'Not to worry, a dozen drops of brandy will do the needful.'

Wife: 'Let me measure the brandy; you are prone to get the count wrong.'

Husband: 'You are right there . . . why don't you then?'

Wife: 'Please swallow it very slowly.'

Husband: 'Can't do it any slower.'

Wife: 'Do you feel restored?'

Husband: 'I am coming round.'

Wife: 'Take some rest.'

Husband: 'Yes, I feel that I need to rest.'

Servant: 'What is the matter with the mistress today? Haven't seen her.'

Maid: 'Not feeling well.'

Servant: 'The master is not feeling well either.'

Maid: 'We knew that would happen.'

Servant: 'Yes . . . but can't understand.'

Maid: 'What?'

Servant: 'Nature plays tricks . . . both of us should be on our deathbeds, considering . . .'

Maid: 'Don't say such things . . . let the deathbed be theirs.'

Servant: 'Their deathbed would be rather grand. I would want to move it to the tiny hovel they have put us in.'

Maid: 'Where are you going?'

Servant: 'To look for a cabinetmaker. Our bed is practically broken down.'

Maid: 'And tell him to use more hardy wood this time.'

A MAN OF GOD

Chaudhry Maujoo sat on a string cot under a leafy peepal tree, smoking his hookah. The afternoon was hot, but a gentle breeze blew across the fields, wafting the blue smoke away.

He had been ploughing his field since early morning, but was quite tired now. The sun was harsh, but it did not seem to bother him. He was enjoying his well-earned rest.

He sat there waiting for his only daughter, Jeena, to bring him his midday meal—tandoori roti and buttermilk. She was always on time, though there was nobody to help her with the housework. He had divorced her mother in a fit of temper about two years ago after a bitter domestic fight.

Jeena was a very obedient daughter who took good care of her father. She was never idle. When household chores were done, she would occupy herself with her spinning wheel. Only occasionally would she gossip with her friends.

Chaudhry Maujoo did not have much land, but it was enough to take care of his modest needs. The village was small and the nearest railway station was miles away. A mud road linked it to another village to which Chaudhry Maujoo rode twice a month to buy provisions.

He used to be a happy man, but since his divorce it had often troubled him that he had no other children. However, being a very religious man, he had managed to console himself with the thought that it was God's will.

His faith was deep, but he knew very little about religion, except that there was no God but God and He must be worshipped, and Mohammed was His Prophet and the Quran was God's word revealed to Mohammed. That was all.

He had never fasted or prayed. In fact, the village was so small that it did not even have a mosque. The people prayed at home and were generally God-fearing. Every household had a copy of the Quran but nobody knew how to read. It was kept wrapped up on the top shelf, to be used only when someone was required to take an oath.

A maulvi would be invited to the village to solemnize marriages. Funeral prayers were offered by the villagers themselves, not in Arabic, but in their own language, Punjabi.

Chaudhry Maujoo was much in demand on such occasions. He had developed a style of his own for funeral orations.

For instance, the year before when his friend Dinoo had lost his son, Chaudhry Maujoo had addressed the villagers after the body had been lowered into the grave.

'What a strong, handsome young man he was! When he spat, it landed at a distance of twenty yards and he had such strength in his abdomen that he could urinate farther than any other young man in the village. He never lost an arm-wrestling competition. He could fight free of a hold as easily as you unbutton a shirt.

'Dinoo my friend, for you, judgement day is already here. I doubt if you will survive it. I think you should die, because how are you going to live through this great shock! Oh, what a handsome young man your son was! I know for a fact that Neeti, the goldsmith's daughter, cast many spells on him to win his love but he spurned her. He was not tempted by her youth and beauty. May God grant him a houri in paradise and may he remain as untempted by her as he was by Neeti, the goldsmith's daughter. God bless his soul.'

This brief address was so effectively delivered that everyone broke down, including Chaudhry Maujoo himself.

When Maujoo decided to divorce his wife, he did not bother to send for a maulvi. He had heard from his elders that all it required was for the man to say thrice: I divorce you. And that was exactly what he had done. He had felt sorry the next day and even a bit ashamed of himself. It was no more serious than everyday quarrels between husband and wife and should not have ended in divorce.

It was not that he wasn't fond of Phatan, his wife. He liked her, and though she was no longer young her body was still well preserved. What was more, she was the mother of his daughter. But he had made no effort to get her back and life had gone on.

Jeena was beautiful like her mother had been in her youth, and in two years she had grown from a little girl into a young and luscious woman. He often worried about her marriage and on such occasions he particularly missed his wife.

He was still reclining on his string cot, enjoying his smoke, when he heard a voice: 'May the blessings and peace of God be upon you.'

He turned round and found an old man with a flowing beard and shoulder-length hair, all dressed in white, standing there. Maujoo greeted him, wondering where he had materialized from.

The man was tall and his eyes were the most striking feature of his face—large and tinged with kajal. He wore a big white turban on his head and a yellow silk scarf was thrown over one of his shoulders. He held a silver-headed staff in his hand. His shoes were made of soft leather.

Chaudhry Maujoo was immediately impressed. In fact, he felt a deep respect bordering on awe for this imposing elderly figure. He rose from his cot and said, 'Where did you come from and when?'

The man smiled. 'We men of God come from nowhere and have no home to go to. No particular moment is ordained for our arrival and none for our departure. It is the Lord who directs us to move in fulfilment of His will and it is the Lord who orders us to break our journey at a particular point.'

Chaudhry Maujoo was deeply affected by these words. He took the holy man's hand, kissed it with great reverence and put it to his eyes. 'My humble house is yours,' he said.

The holy man smiled and sat down on the cot. He held his silver-tipped staff in both hands, and resting his head against it said, 'Who can say what particular deed of yours found approval in the eyes of the Lord that he directed this sinner to come to you?'

Chaudhry Maujoo asked, 'Maulvi sahib, have you come to me on orders from the Lord?'

The holy man raised his head and said in an angry tone, 'And do you think we came at your orders? Do we obey you or that supreme being whom we have humbly worshipped for forty years and can at last count ourselves among those He has chosen to favour?'

Chaudhry Maujoo was terrified. In his simple, rustic manner he whimpered, 'Maulvi sahib, we illiterate people know nothing about these matters. We do not even know how to say our prayers. Were it not for men of God like you, we would never find forgiveness in His eyes.'

'And that's why we are here,' the holy man said, his eyes half-shut.

Chaudhry Maujoo sat down on the ground and began to press his visitor's legs. Presently, Jeena appeared with his food. When she saw the stranger, she covered her face.

'Who is that, Chaudhry Maujoo?'

'My daughter, Jeena, Maulvi sahib.'

Maulvi sahib glanced at Jeena through slanted eyes. 'Ask her why she is hiding her face from holy mendicants like us.'

'Jeena,' he said to his daughter, 'Maulvi sahib is God's special emissary. Uncover your face.'

Jeena did what she was told. Maulvi sahib sized her up and said, 'Your daughter is beautiful, Chaudhry Maujoo.'

Jeena blushed. 'She takes after her mother,' Maujoo said.

'Where is her mother?' Maulvi sahib asked, surveying Jeena's young and virginal body.

Chaudhry Maujoo hesitated, not knowing how to answer that.

'Where is her mother?' Maulvi sahib asked again.

'She is dead,' Maujoo replied hurriedly.

Maulvi sahib looked at Jeena, carefully noting her startled reaction. Then he thundered, 'You are lying.'

Maujoo fell at his feet and said in a guilty voice, 'Yes, I told you a lie. Please forgive me. I am a liar. The truth is that I divorced her, Maulvi sahib.'

'You are a great sinner. What was the fault of that poor woman?'

'I don't know, Maulvi sahib. It was really nothing, but it ended up in my divorcing her. I am indeed a very sinful man. I realized my error the very next day, but by then it was too late. She had already returned to her parents.'

Maulvi sahib touched Maujoo's shoulder with his silver-tipped staff and said, 'God is great and He is merciful and kind. All wrongs can be righted if He wishes. And if that is His command, perhaps this servant of His will be empowered to lead you to your salvation and find you forgiveness.'

A grateful and totally humiliated Chaudhry Maujoo threw himself at Maulvi sahib's feet and began to weep. Maulvi sahib looked at Jeena and found tears rolling down her cheeks as well.

'Come here, girl,' he ordered.

There was such authority in his voice that she found it impossible not to obey. She placed the food aside and walked up to him. Maulvi sahib grabbed her arm and said, 'Sit down.'

She was about to sit on the ground, but Maulvi sahib pulled her up. 'Sit next to me here,' he commanded.

Jeena sat down. Maulvi sahib put his arm around her waist

and, pressing her close, asked, 'And what have you brought for us?'

Jeena wanted to move away, but Maulvi sahib's hold was vice-like. 'I have some tandoori roti and buttermilk and some greens,' she said in a low voice.

Maulvi sahib squeezed her slim waist once again and said, 'Then go get it and feed us.'

As Jeena rose, Maulvi sahib struck Maujoo gently on the shoulder with his staff and said, 'Maujoo, help us wash our hands.'

Maujoo went to the well, which was nearby and came back with a bucket of fresh water. He helped Maulvi sahib wash his hands like a true disciple. Jeena put the food in front of him.

Maulvi sahib ate everything. Then he ordered Jeena to pour water on his hands. She obeyed, such was the authority of his manner.

Maulvi sahib belched loudly, thanked God even more loudly, ran his wet hand over his beard and lay down on the cot. With one eye he watched Jeena, and with the other her father. She picked up the utensils she had brought the food in and left. Maulvi sahib said to Maujoo, 'Chaudhry, we are going to take a nap.'

Chaudhry Maujoo pressed his legs and feet for some time and when he was sure he had fallen asleep he stepped aside and warmed up his hookah. He was very happy. He felt as if a great weight had been lifted off his chest. In his heart, he thanked God in his simple words for having sent to him in the form of Maulvi sahib one of His angels of mercy.

He sat there for some time watching Maulvi sahib resting, then he returned to his field and got down to work. He hadn't even noticed his hunger. In fact, he was thrilled that the honour of feeding Maulvi sahib with food meant for him had fallen to his lot.

When he returned in the evening, he was gravely disappointed to see Maulvi sahib gone. He cursed himself. By walking off, he had offended that man of God. Perhaps he had put a curse on him before leaving. He trembled with fear and tears welled up in his eyes.

He looked for Maulvi sahib around the village but did not find him. The evening deepened into night, but there was no trace of Maulvi sahib. He was walking back to his house, his head down, feeling the weight of the world on his shoulders, when he came upon two boys from the village. They looked scared. First they wouldn't tell him what was wrong, but when he insisted they told him their story.

Some time earlier, they had brewed strong country liquor, put it in an earthen pitcher and buried it under a tree. That evening they had gone to the spot, unearthed their forbidden treasure and were about to imbibe it when an old man, whose face radiated a strange light, had suddenly appeared and asked them what they were doing.

He had admonished them for the evil deed they were about to commit. He had asked them how they could even think of drinking something which God Himself had forbidden men to touch. They had been so terrified that they had run away, leaving the earthen pitcher behind.

Chaudhry Maujoo told them that the old man with the radiant face was a holy man of God and, since he had been offended, he was likely to put a curse on the entire village.

'May God save us my sons, may God save us my sons,' he murmured and began to walk back to his house. Jeena was home, but he did not speak to her. He was convinced that the village would not escape Maulvi sahib's wrath.

Jeena had prepared extra food for Maulvi sahib. 'Where is Maulvi sahib, father?' she asked. 'Gone . . . he is gone. How could a man of God abide along with sinners like us?' he told her in a grief-stricken voice.

Jeena was sorry too because Maulvi sahib had promised he would find a way to have her mother come back. And now that he was gone, who was going to reunite her with her mother? Jeena sat down on a low stool. The food kept getting cold.

There was a sound of approaching feet at the door. Both father and daughter sprang up. Suddenly Maulvi sahib entered. In the dim light of the earthen lamp, Jeena noticed that he was staggering. In his hands he held a small pitcher.

Maujoo helped him to a cot. Handing over the pitcher to him, Maulvi sahib said, 'God put us through a severe test today. We chanced upon two youngsters from your village who were about to commit the grave sin of drinking liquor. When we admonished them, they ran away. We were deeply grieved. So young, and in such deep mortal error. But we felt that their youth was to blame for what they were about to do. So we prayed in the heavenly court of the Lord that they be forgiven. And do you know what reply we received?'

'No,' Chaudhry Maujoo said, greatly moved.

'The reply was: are you prepared to face the consequences of their sin? And we said: yes, Almighty God. And then we heard a voice: you are commanded to drink this entire pitcher of liquor. We forgive the boys.'

Maujoo's hair stood on end. 'Did you then drink it?'

Maulvi sahib's tongue became even thicker. 'Yes, we drank to save the souls of those two young sinners and to gain merit in the eyes of God, who alone is to be honoured. There is still some left and that too we have been commanded to drink. Now put it away carefully and make sure that not a drop is wasted.'

Maujoo picked up the pitcher, secured its top with a clean length of cloth and took it into one of the small, dark rooms of his modest house. When he returned, Maulvi sahib was sprawled on the cot and Jeena was massaging his head. He was telling her, 'He who helps others wins the Lord's favour. He is pleased with you at this moment . . . and we are pleased with you too.'

Then Maulvi sahib made her sit next to him and planted a generous kiss on her forehead. She tried to get up, but was unable to wrest herself free. Maulvi sahib then embraced her and said to Maujoo, 'Chaudhry, I have awakened your daughter's sleeping destiny.'

Maujoo was so overwhelmed that he couldn't even express his gratitude properly. All he managed to say was, 'It is all a result of your prayers and your kindness.'

Maulvi sahib squeezed Jeena against his chest once again and said, 'Truly, God has touched you with His grace. Jeena, tomorrow we will teach you a holy prayer and if you recite it regularly you will forever find acceptance in the eyes of the Lord.'

Maulvi sahib rose late the next day. Maujoo had not gone to the fields, afraid he might be needed. Dutifully, he waited and, when Maulvi sahib was ready, he helped him wash his face and hands and, in accordance with his wishes, brought out the earthen pitcher.

Maulvi sahib mumbled a prayer, then he untied the cloth which covered its top and blew into it three times. He drank three large cups, mumbled another prayer, looked up at the sky and declaimed, 'God, You will not find us wanting in the test You have put us through.'

Then he addressed Maujoo, 'Chaudhry, we have just received divine orders that you should proceed to your wife's village and bring her back. The signal we were seeking has come through.'

Maujoo was thrilled. He saddled his horse and promised to be back by the next day. He instructed Jeena to leave no stone unturned to keep Maulvi sahib happy and comfortable.

After her father had left, Jeena got busy with housework. Maulvi sahib kept drinking steadily. Then he produced a thick rosary from his pocket and began to run it through his fingers. When Jeena was through, he ordered her to perform her ablutions.

Jeena replied innocently, 'Maulvi sahib, I don't know how to.'

Maulvi sahib reprimanded her gently on her lack of knowledge of essential religious practices. Then he began to teach her how to do her ablutions. This intricate exercise was performed with the help of close physical contact.

After the ablutions, Maulvi sahib asked for a prayer mat. There was none in the house. Maulvi sahib was not pleased. He told her to get him a clean bed sheet. He spread it on the floor of the inside room, summoned Jeena in and instructed her to bring the pitcher and cup with her.

Maulvi sahib poured out a large quantity and drank half of it. Then he started to run his rosary through his fingers, while Jeena watched in silence.

For a long time, Maulvi sahib was busy with his rosary. His eyes were closed. Then he blew into the cup three times and ordered Jeena to drink it.

Jeena took it with trembling hands. Maulvi sahib said in a thundering voice, 'We order you to drink it. All your pain and suffering will come to an end.'

Jeena lifted the cup to her lips and drank it down in one go. Maulvi sahib smiled. 'We are going to resume our special prayers, but when we raise our index finger pour out half a cup from the pitcher and drink it.'

He did not allow her to react and went into a deep reverie. There was an awful taste in Jeena's mouth and a fire blazing in her chest. She wanted to get up and drink buckets of cold water, but she did not dare. Suddenly Maulvi sahib's index finger rose. Hypnotized, she poured herself the ordained quantity and drank it in one gulp.

Maulvi sahib kept praying. She could hear the rosary beads rubbing against each other. Her head was spinning and she felt very sleepy. She had a vague, almost unconscious feeling that she was in the lap of a young, clean-shaven man who was telling her that he was taking her on a trip through paradise.

When she came to, she was lying on the floor inside the room.

Bleary-eyed, she looked around. Why was she lying here and since when? Everything was in a mist. She wanted to go back to sleep, but she got up. Where was Maulvi sahib? And where had that paradise vanished to?

She walked into the open courtyard and was surprised to see that it was almost evening. Maulvi sahib was performing ablutions. He heard her and turned with a smile on his face. She went back to the room, sat down on the floor and began to think about her mother, who was going to come home. There was only one night left. She was very hungry but she didn't want to cook. Her mind was full of strange and unanswered questions.

Suddenly, Maulvi sahib appeared at the door. 'We have to offer special prayers for your father. We will pray in a graveyard all night and return in the morning. We will be praying for you too.'

He appeared next morning. His eyes were very red and he stammered a little when he spoke. He wasn't steady on his feet either. He walked into the courtyard and hugged and kissed Jeena with great warmth. Jeena sat on a low stool in a corner trying to untangle the strange, half-remembered events of the last twenty-four hours. She wanted her father to return . . . and her mother, who had been gone for two years. And then there was that paradise . . . what sort of paradise was it she had been taken to . . . and the Maulvi sahib . . . was it he who had taken her? It couldn't be because she remembered a young man who had no beard.

Maulvi sahib addressed her, 'Jeena, your father has not returned yet.'

She said nothing.

He spoke again, 'All night long he has been in our prayers. He should have returned by now . . . with your mother.'

All Jeena could say was, 'I don't know. He should be on his way . . . and mother too. I really don't know.'

The front door opened. Jeena rose. It was her mother. The two fell into each other's arms, weeping profusely. Maujoo followed his wife. With great respect, he greeted Maulvi sahib and then said to his wife, 'Phatan, you haven't greeted Maulvi sahib.'

Phatan disengaged herself from her daughter, wiped her eyes and greeted Maulvi sahib, who examined her through bloodshot eyes. 'We have been praying all night for you and have just returned. God has answered our prayers. All will be well.'

Chaudhry Maujoo sat down on the ground and began to press

Maulvi sahib's feet. With a lump in his throat, he said to his wife, 'Phatan, come here and express your gratitude to Maulvi sahib. I don't know how to.'

Phatan came forward. 'We are poor and humble folk. There is nothing we can do for you, holy man of God.'

Maulvi sahib looked at her penetratingly. 'Maujoo Chaudhry, you were right. Your wife is beautiful and even at this age she looks young. She is another Jeena, even better. We will set everything right, Phatan. God has decided to be kind and merciful to you.'

Chaudhry Maujoo kept pressing Maulvi sahib's feet, while Jeena got busy with cooking.

After a while, Maulvi sahib rose, patted Phatan's head affectionately and said to Maujoo, 'It is the Almighty's law that when a man divorces his wife and then wants to bring her back he may not do so unless the woman first marries another man and is divorced by him to be reunited with her first husband.'

Maujoo said in a low voice, 'That I've heard, Maulvi sahib.'

Maulvi sahib asked him to rise, put his hand on his shoulder and said, 'Last night, we begged of the Almighty to spare you the punishment due to you because of your error. And the voice from beyond said, "How long are we going to accept your intercession on behalf of others? Ask something for yourself and it shall be granted." We begged again, "King of the universe, sovereign of all the lands and seas, we ask nothing for ourselves. You have given us enough. Maujoo Chaudhry is in love with his wife." And the voice said, "We are going to put his love and your faith to the test. You are to wed her for one day and divorce her the next and return her to Maujoo. That's all we can grant you, because for forty long years you have worshipped us faithfully."'

Maujoo was ecstatic. 'I accept, Maulvi sahib . . . I accept.' Then he looked at Phatan, his eyes shining with inner happiness. 'Right, Phatan?' He didn't wait for her answer. 'We both accept.'

Maulvi sahib closed his eyes, recited a prayer, blew it in their faces and raised his eyes heavenwards. 'God of all the skies, grant us the strength not to fail the test You are putting us through.'

Then he said to Maujoo, 'We are leaving now, but we want you and Jeena to go away somewhere for the night. We shall return later.'

When he came back in the evening, Jeena and Maujoo were ready to leave. Maulvi sahib was reciting something under his breath. He didn't speak to them, but made a sign that they were to leave. They left.

Maulvi sahib bolted the door and said to Phatan, 'For one night you are our wife. Go inside, get the bedding and spread it on this cot. We wish to take a nap.'

Phatan went inside, brought out the bedding and spread it neatly on the string cot. Maulvi sahib asked her to wait for him. He went inside.

An earthen lamp cast a shadowy light around the little room. The pitcher stood in a corner. Maulvi sahib shook it to see if there was anything left in it. There was. He raised the pitcher to his lips and took a few quick swigs. He wiped his mouth with his yellow silk scarf and went out.

Phatan sat on the cot. Maulvi sahib carried a cup in his hand. He blew some holy words on it thrice and offered it to Phatan. 'Drink it down.'

She drank and was almost immediately sick, but Maulvi sahib patted her on the back vigorously and said, 'You will be all right.' Then he lay down.

Next morning, when Jeena and Maujoo returned, they found Phatan sleeping on the cot in the courtyard. Maulvi sahib was not around. Maujoo thought he had gone for a walk in the fields. He woke up his wife, who opened her eyes and mumbled, 'Paradise . . . paradise.' When she saw Maujoo, she sat up.

'Where is Maulvi sahib?' he asked.

Phatan was still a little groggy. 'Maulvi sahib, which Maulvi sahib . . . I don't know where he is . . . he is not here.'

'No,' Maujoo exclaimed, 'I'll go and look for him.'

He was at the door when he heard Phatan scream. She was fumbling with something she had found under the pillow.

'What is it?' she asked.

'Looks like hair,' Maujoo said.

Phatan threw away the black bunch on the floor. Maujoo picked it up, examined it and said, 'Looks like human hair.'

'Maulvi sahib's beard and shoulder-length hair,' Jeena exclaimed.

Maujoo was confused. 'And where is Maulvi sahib?' he asked. Then his simple and believing heart provided him with the answer. 'Jeena, Phatan you don't understand. He was a man of God who could perform miracles. He brought us what our hearts desired and he has left us something of his person to remember him by.'

He kissed the false beard and hairpiece, touched his eyes with them reverently and handed them to Jeena. 'Go and wrap them up in a clean piece of cloth and place them on top of the big wooden chest. The grace of God shall never abandon our house.'

Jeena went in. Maujoo sat down next to Phatan and said, 'I am going to learn how to pray and I will remember that saint in my prayers every day.'

Phatan remained silent.

THE GIFT

Before Sultana moved to Delhi, she lived in the Ambala cantonment, where many of her regulars were British goras. She had, consequently, picked up bits of English but she used the language most sparingly, and never in day-to-day conversation. When she realized that business in the new city was almost non-existent—at least her sort of business—she said to her friend and neighbour, Tamancha Jan, in English one day, 'This laif very bad,' which meant that this was no way to live when there was no work and you weren't even sure where your next meal was coming from.

Ambala cantonment had been different; she had more business than she could handle. The goras, all British tommies, would hit her place roaring drunk most evenings and, in a matter of three to four hours, she would have them on their way to the barracks, lighter in the pocket by twenty to thirty rupees. She preferred the goras to her own countrymen though she had some visiting her off and on. While it was true that she did not understand the language the Brits spoke, in a way it suited her fine. For instance, when one of them was keen to bargain to bring down the price, she would pretend she didn't understand. She would shake her head and tell him in Urdu, 'Sahib, I don't know what you are saying.' And if they tried to take more liberties than she normally allowed, she would start cursing them in Urdu. They would look at her, quite puzzled as to what she was going on about, and she would say, 'Sahib, you are *ek-dum, ulloo ka patha*, an owl's offspring, and a *haramzada*, of illegitimate birth. Understand?' The goras would laugh and Sultana would chuckle, 'Oh! They do look like the owl's offspring when they laugh.'

However, not one gora had been to visit her in the three months she had lived in Delhi. All the stories she had been told about this big city when she was in Ambala had turned out to be false. Where were all the big laat sahibs who lived here, who reportedly moved to Simla in the summer where it was cool? All she had had here by way of business were six men in three months. Just six, which came to two a month. What was funny was that even these six had told her the same old story about Delhi being the city of the burra sahibs and the rich, who moved to Simla in the summer. From these six visits she had made a total sum of eighteen rupees and eight annas. Not one of them was willing to fork out a penny more than three rupees, which appeared to be the upper limit here. From the first five, she had initially demanded ten rupees but it was strange that they had all insisted that three rupees was what she was going to get and no more.

Why they considered her worth visiting she couldn't say. Anyway, by the time the sixth man turned up, she had decided to save her breath. 'Look,' she had told him in her no-nonsense voice, 'three rupees is what I charge and not a penny less. Take it or leave it.' The man had said nothing and stepped into her room. When he was taking off his jacket, Sultana had said, 'Let's have an extra rupee, shall we?' Instead, he had given her a newly minted eight anna coin with the Emperor of India's head on it. Sultana had accepted it on the sound principle that something was better than nothing.

The arithmetic is all wrong, Sultana thought. Only eighteen rupees and eight annas in three months. And against that she had to pay twenty rupees for her kotha, this hovel of a place that the landlord insisted on describing as a flat. It had one of those modern WCs with a chain. Sultana had never seen, much less used, one before. The first time she did, she thought the chain was meant to help heave you up. She had a backache that day and as she reached for the chain there was a tremendous explosion. She screamed.

Khuda Bux was in the next room sorting out his photographic paraphernalia. He rushed out to see what had happened. 'Sultana,' he shouted, 'was that you?' Her heart was beating rapidly. 'My God,' she said. 'Is this a lavatory or a railway station? I thought I would die!' Khuda Bux began to laugh. 'Silly, this is a big city vilayati bathroom. Understand?'

How Sultana and Khuda Bux met was interesting. He came from Rawalpindi. After passing high school, he became a lorry driver and took a job with a bus company, which operated a fleet between Rawalpindi and the Kashmir Valley. In Kashmir he met a woman who ran away with him to Lahore. However, he failed to find any work in the new city and decided to enrol her in the world's oldest profession for the sake of survival. This arrangement lasted for a couple of years till one day she left him for another man. Somebody had told him she was in Ambala and he had gone there looking for her. Instead, he had found Sultana, who took an immediate fancy to him.

Khuda Bux's arrival brought Sultana luck. Business started booming. Since she was a superstitious woman, she attributed her good fortune to Khuda Bux.

Khuda Bux was hard-working. He hated to be idle. There was a street photographer outside the local railway station whom he befriended. In a few months, he managed to learn to take pictures. Sultana gave him sixty rupees and he bought an old camera, an ornate backdrop, a couple of chairs and some basic chemicals. Then he launched a business of his own. One day he told Sultana that he was going to move from the city to the cantonment area. Within a month, he had got to know most of the goras stationed there, and his business began to flourish. Soon he had persuaded Sultana to leave the city and they found themselves a nice place to live in the cantonment. Many of Khuda Bux's gora customers became Sultana's clients as well.

Sultana had by now saved enough money to buy herself a pair of silver earrings and eight gold bracelets. She had also built up a wardrobe of fifteen nice saris. She also bought some decent furniture for the house. Everything was going well till one day Khuda Bux decided on a whim that they should move to Delhi. Sultana had agreed enthusiastically because she really had come to believe that he brought her good luck.

Sultana was well aware that it took time before a business got going. During the first month, she had not worried but, by the end of the second month, she was beginning to. Not one customer had materialized so far. 'What do you think is going on? It is two months now and not one man has come to the kotha. I know things are tough these days but are they that tough?' she said to Khuda Bux.

Although he hadn't spoken to her about it, Khuda Bux too had been feeling the strain. 'I have been thinking about it myself and I have come to the conclusion that because of the war our business has ceased to interest people. It is also possible that . . .' He did not finish the sentence. They heard footsteps. Then there was a knock at the door. Khuda Bux leapt up and undid the latch. Sultana's first customer had arrived but all he paid was three rupees. The other five had done the same. So there she was, richer in three months by no more than eighteen rupees and eight annas.

The situation had become difficult. The rent on the flat was twenty rupees a month. Then there were the water and electricity bills, followed by food, clothes and odds and ends. And there was no income. You couldn't call eighteen rupees and eight annas income, could you? The eight gold bangles she had bought herself in Ambala had been sold one by one. When she was selling the last one, she had said to Khuda Bux, 'Let's return to Ambala. There's nothing for us in this city. It hasn't been good to us. What we have lost is lost. Let's just convince ourselves that we gave it to charity. Go sell this last bangle; I'll pack in the meanwhile and we'll take the night train to Ambala.'

Khuda Bux had taken the bangle. 'No, sweetheart, we won't go to Ambala. We'll stay in Delhi and earn money. All your gold bangles will be bought back. Just have trust in God. He will show us the way.' Sultana had not argued and only stared disconsolately at her bare wrists.

Two more months went by with earnings covering only a tiny percentage of expenses. Sultana just didn't know what to do. Khuda Bux would spend most of his time away from home, which was an added reason for her unhappiness. In the beginning, she used to spend her day gossiping with friends but after a while she had begun to feel uneasy in their company and stopped seeing them almost altogether. All day long she would sit alone in her flat, trying to while away her time by preparing betel leaf condiments or darning and adjusting her old clothes. Sometimes she would stand on her balcony staring for hours at the railway yard across the street with its stationary and shunting engines and wagons.

The railway goods godown was also part of the yard. Hundreds of bales and crates of different sizes lay scattered around under a huge shed with a tin roof. To its left was an open space with a criss-crossing railway track. The noonday sun would make the blue steel shimmer, reminding Sultana of her hands with their increasingly protuberant blue veins. There was always something going on there: an engine being shunted about or a goods train moving slowly towards the yard to unload its cargo, only to chug away later.

There were always engines blowing their steam hooters, their rhythmic chug chug fading in the distance. When she came out on the balcony very early in the morning, she was always struck by the sight. Through the hazy light, she would see an engine belching smoke, then she would look up at the sky and watch it rise in a thick column. Sometimes she would see a long wagon just disconnected from an engine, which would be sent rolling down the track, and would think of herself. Had she too not been pushed on the track of life? She was moving, but not of her own volition. The levers were in the hands of others and one day the momentum would begin to weaken and, at some unknown point at an unknown place, she would slowly come to a stop, never to move again.

Her time was now increasingly spent standing on the balcony, looking at the railway track, the stillness frequently broken by an engine chugging past. Strange thoughts would crowd her head. In the Ambala cantonment, her house was not too far from the station but she had never noticed trains or anything of the sort. There were times now when she felt that the railway yard was like a vast, smoky, steamy brothel, its fat engines much like the rich traders who would occasionally visit her in Ambala.

Sometimes an engine, all by itself, slowly shunting past stationary wagons, would look to her like a man walking past women sitting at their windows waiting for customers. Such sensations were disturbing in the extreme and she had stopped going out on the balcony altogether because it distracted her.

Not once, not twice, but several times she had tried to talk to Khuda Bux. 'Look, have pity on me. What do you think I do here all day? Like a bedridden patient I am confined indoors from morning to night. Please!' But every time, he would say, 'Sweetheart, I am trying to work out something. God willing, it is only a matter of time; our days are going to change.'

Five months had passed and nothing had changed. Khuda Bux was still out there all day, trying to work out something and she was still cooped up in the flat. The month of Muharram was only a few days away. That was one time of the year when Sultana observed every sombre ritual commemorating the martyrdom of Hussain, the Prophet's grandson, and his companions at Karbala fourteen hundred years ago. She always wore black, the colour of mourning.

But what was she going to do this year? She had no money for new clothes. Mukhtar, the girl across the street who was in the same line of work as herself, had got herself a black Lady Hamilton shirt stitched, and very elegant it was too, with the sleeves fashioned out of georgette. She also had a matching black silk shalwar which shimmered. Another girl, Anwari, had bought herself a georgette sari. She had also told Sultana that she would have a white silk petticoat to go with it as that was the latest fashion. Anwari had even found herself a new pair of very delicate-looking black velvet shoes. Sultana had never felt more depressed. For the first time in her life, she had nothing to wear for Muharram.

She came home after visiting Mukhtar and Anwari that morning and just stretched herself out on the floor, which was covered with a coarse cotton carpet, feeling very sorry for herself. The house was empty. Khuda Bux was out as usual. She had kept lying there for a long time, her head propped up against a large pillow. Then she had felt her neck stiffen and stepped out on the balcony involuntarily. She was very sad.

The railway yard wore a desolate look. There was no movement at all, just a few old bogies without any engines. They had sprinkled the street with water, as on most evenings, and there was no dust hanging in the air. A few men were walking past but they all looked like the kind who liked to ogle women like Sultana and then went straight home to their wives. One of them looked up at her and she gave him a smile. Then she turned her eyes towards the yard, but she had a feeling he was still there, looking at her, which he was. Sultana waved to him to come up, pointing to the stairs which led to the flat.

He walked up looking diffident. 'Were you afraid to come?' Sultana asked. 'Why do you say that?' he replied with a smile. 'Well, you have probably been in the street for some time wondering if you should make a move,' she said. He smiled again. 'Not at all. I was actually watching a woman in the flat above yours using body language to communicate with a man in the flat across. Then you switched on the green light in your room and came out on the balcony. I love green; it is so soothing to the eyes.' He began to look around the room. 'Are you leaving?' Sultana asked. 'No, no, I just wanted to see the flat. Would you like to show me around?'

Sultana showed him around the flat, which had just three rooms. Then they came back to the main room with the cushions on the floor. 'My name is Shanker,' the man said.

For the first time, Sultana really looked at him. He was a man of average height with average looks but his eyes were extraordinarily clear and bright. His temples had a touch of grey and he was wearing a pair of beige trousers and a white shirt with a raised collar.

Shanker sat down on the floor, which was covered by a simple cotton rug. He was so much at home that it seemed to Sultana as if their roles had been reversed—she the client and he the one dispensing the service. 'And what can I do for you?' she asked him at last. He stretched himself on the floor. 'What can I say? I leave it to you. Didn't you ask me over?' When Sultana did not answer, he got up. 'All right, since you ask, I'll tell you. What you thought I was, I am not. I am not one of those who leave money or what have you. I am like a doctor; I have a fee. When I am asked over, the fee has to be paid.'

Sultana began to laugh. 'What is your line of work?'

'The same as yours,' Shanker replied.

'What?'

'What do you do?' he asked.

'I . . . I . . . I don't do anything.'

'I don't do anything either.'

'That doesn't make sense!' she said sharply. 'There must be something you do.'

'So do you, I am sure,' Shanker retorted calmly.

'I fritter myself away,' she said.

'So do I.'

'Then let's do some frittering together.'

'I am willing but I must tell you I never pay for it.'

'Are you out of your mind! This is not a soup kitchen for the homeless!'

'Neither am I a volunteer.'

'What's a volunteer?' she asked.

'A volunteer is an owl's offspring,' Shanker answered.

'Well, I'm not an owl's offspring.'

'But that man Khuda Bux who lives with you is.'

'Why?'

'Because for several weeks now he has been spending his time in the company of a fake holy man, begging him to make fortune smile on him, not realizing that he whose own fortune is like a permanently rusted lock cannot help others.'

'Because you are a Hindu, you can't understand these things. You can only make fun of our Muslim fakirs,' she said.

Shanker smiled. 'It is not a Hindu–Muslim thing at all.'

'God knows what nonsense you talk,' she said, then added, 'Would you like to . . .'

'Yes, but on my terms.'

Sultana stood up. 'Then let me show you to the door.'

Shanker rose, put his hands in his pockets and said, 'I pass this way off and on. Whenever you need me, just say so . . . I am a very useful man.'

Shanker left and Sultana, Muharram's black clothes momentarily forgotten, kept thinking about him. She felt somehow better. She thought if he had come to her in Ambala, she would have had him thrown out but Delhi was different. She felt lonely and Shanker's strange and amusing conversation had made her feel quite good.

When Khuda Bux returned in the evening, Sultana asked him where he had been all day. He looked totally exhausted. 'I was in the city's old fort area. For some days past, a holy man has taken up residence there. I go to him every day so that our luck will change,' he said.

'Has he said anything so far?'

'No, not yet. He hasn't made up his mind about me but I tell you, Sultana, my devotion to him will never go waste. By the grace of God, times are about to change.'

Sultana's mind went back to Muharram. In a tearful voice she said to him, 'You are out all day, leaving me alone to fend for myself in this cage. I can't even go anywhere. Muharram is round the corner. Has it occurred to you that I would need new black clothes? There is not a penny in the house. The last gold bangle is also gone. Tell me, what is going to happen to us? As for you, all day long you keep chasing these beggars and that fake holy man. It seems in Delhi even God has turned His face away from us. Why don't you start your old street photo business again? It'll bring in something at least.'

Khuda Bux lay down on the floor. 'But to start I'd need some capital. Maybe it was a mistake to leave Ambala, but it was God's will and I am sure it was all for the best. Who knows? He may be testing us . . .'

Sultana cut him short. 'I beg you, get me a length of black cloth for a shalwar. I have a white satin shirt which I'll have dyed black. I also still have the white chiffon dupatta you brought me in Ambala at Diwali. That can be dyed too. All I am missing is a black shalwar. I don't care whether you steal it; I want that shalwar. Swear on my head that you'll get it for me, and if you don't, may I die.'

Khuda Bux stood up abruptly. 'Stop that, please! Where do you think I am going to get the money? I don't have a single penny.'

'I don't care as long as I get four and a half yards of black satin,' Sultana said with finality.

'Let's pray to God to send three or four customers tonight,' Khuda Bux suggested.

'What about you? Won't you do anything yourself? If you tried, you could easily make enough to buy the cloth. It used to cost twelve to fourteen annas a yard before the war. I don't think it is more than a rupee and a quarter now. Look, how much can four and a half yards cost?'

'Well, since you insist, I will think of something. Now let me run down to that food stand across the street and get us something to eat,' Khuda Bux said. They ate the bazaar food quietly and went to bed. In the morning Khuda Bux was off to see the holy man, leaving Sultana to herself again. She slept for a while, then rose, and walked about from room to room to stretch her legs and kill time. She ate around noon, then pulled out her white chiffon dupatta and white satin shirt from the old box and took them to the laundry which also dyed clothes. She came back to read for a while from one of her books which contained scripts with the dialogue and lyrics of her favourite films. At some point she must have dozed off, because when she woke up it was nearly four. She bathed, put on fresh clothes, threw a light woollen stole over her shoulders and stepped out on the balcony. She stood there for an hour. The street had begun to show early signs of evening life and it had become a bit chilly. Suddenly she saw Shanker, who smiled at her. Without quite meaning to, she asked him to come up.

When Shanker came, she was somewhat embarrassed, not knowing what to say to him. However, he was totally relaxed, as if he were in his own home. Without much formality, he stretched himself on the floor, a cushion under his head. Sultana still hadn't said a single word to him. 'Look, you can invite me to come up a hundred times and ask me to leave each time. I'll not mind at all.'

'No one is asking you to leave,' Sultana answered.

'So it is on my terms then,' Shanker said with a smile.

'What terms? Are you going to marry me?' Sultana asked with a laugh.

'Marriage? You and I won't be involved in that sort of nonsense as long as we live. Such things are not for people like us.'

'Cut out this rubbish. Say something useful,' Sultana suggested.

'What do you want me to say? You are the woman. Say something which should help us while away the time nicely. There is more to life than talking shop.'

'Tell me frankly what you want,' Sultana asked.

'The same as other men,' he said, sitting up.

'Then what's the difference between you and them?'

'Between you and me there is no difference but between me and them, well, we are worlds apart. Not everything should be reduced to a question. There is much one can try to comprehend oneself,' Shanker said.

'I understand,' Sultana said after a pause.

'Well then?'

'You win, but I very much doubt if this sort of thing ever takes place,' Sultana remarked.

'You are wrong there. In this very neighbourhood, there must be thousands of families who will never believe that a woman will accept the sort of degradation of her body that you do without even thinking. But despite that, there are thousands of women in your profession in this city alone. Your name is Sultana, isn't it?'

'Sultana it is.'

Shanker laughed. 'And mine is Shanker. Names are rubbish. Let's go to the next room.'

When they returned, they were both laughing. When he was leaving, Sultana said, 'Will you do something for me?'

'Say it first,' he replied.

Sultana hesitated, 'You might think I was trying to charge for what we just did.'

'Come on, say it,' he encouraged her.

Sultana plucked up her courage. 'Muharram is not too far and I do not have any money to get a new black shalwar stitched. Well, what can I say? I have the dupatta and the shirt, which are now at the dyer's.'

'Do you want me to give some money for the black shalwar?' Shanker asked.

'I didn't mean that,' she answered. 'You could get me a black shalwar.'

Shanker smiled. 'It is rare for me to have any money. However, I promise you will have the shalwar on the first day of Muharram. Cheer up now.' He looked at Sultana's earrings. 'Can you give me those?'

'What'd you want with them?' Sultana said with a smile. 'They are ordinary silver, worth no more than five rupees.'

'I asked you for the earrings. I did not ask what they cost.'

'Here you are then,' Sultana said. After he was gone she felt sorry she had parted with the earrings but it was too late.

Sultana was quite sure Shanker would not keep his word. On the morning of the first day of Muharram, there was a knock at the door. It was Shanker. He had something in his hand, wrapped in a newspaper. 'The black satin shalwar. Could be a bit long—see you later.'

He looked a bit dishevelled. It seemed he had just hopped out of bed. They didn't talk.

When he was gone, Sultana unwrapped the package. It was a lovely black silk shalwar, much like the one her friend Mukhtar had shown her. She forgot about her earrings.

In the afternoon, she went down to pick up her dyed dupatta and shirt from the laundry. Then she put on her new clothes. There was a knock at the door. It was Mukhtar. After sizing up Sultana carefully, she said, 'The dupatta and shirt appear to be dyed but the shalwar looks new. Did you have it stitched?'

'Only today. The tailor brought it first thing this morning,' Sultana lied. Suddenly she noticed Mukhtar's ears. 'When did you get those earrings?'

'This very morning,' Mukhtar said.

For a long time neither of them spoke.

THE ROOM WITH THE BRIGHT LIGHT

He stood quietly by a lamp post off the Qaiser Gardens, thinking how desolate everything looked. A few tongas waited for customers who were nowhere in evidence.

A few years ago, this used to be such a gay place, full of bright, happy, carefree men and women, but everything seemed to have gone to seed. The area was now full of louts and vagabonds with nowhere to go. The bazaar still had its crowds, but it had lost its colour. The shops and buildings looked derelict and unwashed, staring at each other like empty-eyed widows.

He stood there wondering what had turned the once fashionable Qaiser Gardens into a slum. Where had all the life and excitement gone? It reminded him of a woman who had been scrubbed clean of all her make-up.

He remembered that many years ago when he had moved to Bombay from Calcutta to take up a job, he had tried in vain for weeks to find a room in this area. There was nothing going.

How times had changed. Judging by the kind of people in the streets, just anybody could rent a place here now—weavers, cobblers, grocers.

He looked around again. What used to be film company offices were now bed-sitters with cooking stoves, and where the elegant people of the city used to gather in the evenings were now washermen's backyards.

It was nothing short of a revolution, but a revolution which had brought decay. In between, he had left the city, but knew through newspaper reports and friends who had stayed back what had happened to Qaiser Gardens in his absence.

There had been riots, accompanied by massacres and rapes. The violence Qaiser Gardens had witnessed had left its ugly mark on everything. The once splendid commercial buildings and residential houses looked sordid and unclean.

He was told that during the riots women had been stripped naked and their breasts chopped off. Was it then surprising that everything looked naked and ravaged?

He was here this evening to meet a friend who had promised to find him a place to live.

Qaiser Gardens used to have some of the city's best restaurants and hotels. And if one was that way inclined, the best girls in Bombay could be obtained through the good offices of the city's high-class pimps who used to hang out here.

He recalled the good times he had had here in those days. He thought nostalgically of the women, the drinking, the elegant hotel rooms. Because of the war, it was almost impossible to obtain Scotch whisky, but he had never had to spend a dry evening. Any amount of expensive Scotch was yours for the asking, as long as you were able to pay for it.

He looked at his watch. It was going on five. The shadows of the February evening had begun to lengthen. He cursed his friend who had kept him waiting. He was about to slip into a roadside place for a cup of tea when a shabbily dressed man came up to him.

'Do you want something?' he asked the stranger.

'Yes,' he replied in a conspiratorial voice.

He took him for a refugee who had fallen on bad times and wanted some money. 'What do you want?' he asked.

'I don't want anything.' He paused, then drew closer and said, 'Do you need something?'

'What?'

'A girl, for instance?'

'Where is she?'

His tone was none too encouraging for the stranger, who began to walk away. 'It seems you are not really interested.'

He stopped him. 'How do you know? What you can provide is something men are always in need of, even on the gallows. So look, my friend, if it is not too far, I am prepared to come with you. You see, I was waiting for someone who hasn't turned up.'

The man whispered, 'It is close, very close, I assure you.'

'Where?'

'That building across from us.'

'You mean that one?' he asked.

'Yes.'

'Should I come with you?'

'Yes, but please walk behind me.' They crossed the road. It was a run-down building with the plaster peeling off the walls and rubbish heaps littering the entrance.

They went through a courtyard and then through a dark corridor. It seemed that construction had been abandoned at some point before completion. The bricks in the walls were unplastered and there were piles of lime mixed with cement on the floor.

The man began to ascend a flight of dilapidated stairs. 'Please wait here. I'll be back in a minute,' he said.

He looked up and saw a bright light at the end of the landing.

He waited for a couple of minutes and then began to climb the stairs. When he reached the landing, he heard the man who had brought him screaming, 'Are you going to get up or not?'

A woman's voice answered, 'Just let me sleep.'

The man screamed again, 'You heard me, are you getting up or not? Or you know what I'll do to you.'

The woman's voice again: 'You can kill me but I won't get up. For God's sake, have mercy on me.'

The man changed his tone. 'Darling, don't be obstinate. How are we going to make a living if you don't get up?'

'Living be damned. I'll starve to death, but for God's sake, don't drag me out of bed. I'm sleepy,' answered the woman.

The man began to roar with anger, 'So you're not going to leave your bed, you bitch, you filthy bitch . . . !'

The woman shouted back, 'I won't, I won't, I won't!'

The man changed his tone again. 'Don't shout like that. The whole world can hear you. Come on now, get up. We could make thirty, even forty rupees.'

The woman began to whimper, 'I beg of you, don't make me go. You know how many days and nights I have gone without sleep. Have pity on me, please.'

'It won't be long,' the man said, 'just a couple of hours and then you can sleep as long as you like. Look, don't make me use other methods to persuade you.'

There was a brief silence. He crossed the landing on tiptoe and peeped into the room where the very bright light was coming from. It was not much of a room. There were a few empty cooking pots on the floor and a woman stretched out in the middle with the man he had come with crouching over her. He was pressing her legs and saying, 'Be a good girl now. I promise you, we'll be back in two hours and then you can sleep to your heart's content.'

He saw the woman suddenly get up like a firecracker which has been shown a match. 'All right,' she said, 'I'll come.'

He was suddenly afraid and ran down the stairs. He wanted to put as much distance between this place and himself as he could, between himself and this city.

He thought of the woman who wanted to sleep. Who was she? Why was she being treated with such inhumanity?

And who was that man? Why was the room so unremittingly bright? Did they both live there? Why did they live there?

His eyes were still partly blinded by the dazzling light bulb in that terrible room upstairs. He couldn't see very well. Couldn't they have hung a softer light in the room? Why was it so nakedly, pitilessly bright?

There was a noise in the dark and a movement. All he could see were two silhouettes, one of them obviously that of the man whom he had followed to this awful place.

'Take a look,' he said.

'I have,' he replied.

'Is she all right?'

'She is all right.'

'That will be forty rupees.'

'All right.'

'Can I have the money?'

He could no longer think clearly. He put his hand in his pocket, pulled out a fistful of bank notes and handed them over. 'Count them,' he said.

'There's fifty there.'

'Keep it.'

'Thank you.'

He had an urge to pick up a big stone and smash his head.

'Please take her, but be nice to her and bring her back in a couple of hours.'

'OK.'

He walked out of the building with the woman, and found a tonga waiting outside. He jumped quickly in the front. The woman took the back seat.

The tonga began to move. He asked him to stop in front of a ramshackle, customerless hotel. They went in. He took his first look at the woman. Her eyes were red and swollen. She looked so tired that he was afraid she would fall to the floor in a heap.

'Raise your head,' he said to her.

'What?' She was startled.

'Nothing, all I said was raise your head.'

She looked up. Her eyes were like empty holes topped up with ground chilli.

'What is your name?' he asked.

'Never mind.' Her tone was like acid.

'Where are you from?'

'What does it matter?'

'Why are you so unfriendly?'

The woman was now wide awake. She stared at him with her blood-red eyes and said, 'You finish your business because I have to go.'

'Where?'

'Where you picked me up from,' she answered indifferently.

'You are free to go.'

'Why don't you finish your business? Why are you trying to ridicule me?'

'I'm not trying to ridicule you. I feel sorry for you,' he said in a sympathetic voice.

'I want no sympathizers. You do whatever you brought me here for and then let me go,' she almost screamed.

He tried to put his hand on her shoulder, but she shook it off rudely.

'Leave me alone. I haven't slept for days. I've been awake ever since I came to that place.'

'You can sleep here.'

'I didn't come here to sleep. This isn't my home.'

'Is that room your home?'

This seemed to infuriate her even more.

'Cut out the rubbish. I have no home. You do your job or take me back. You can have your money returned by that . . .'

'All right, I'll take you back,' he said.

And he took her back to that big building and left her there.

The next day, sitting in a desolate hotel in Qaiser Park, he told the story of that woman to a friend, who was greatly moved by it. Expressing sorrow, he asked, 'Was she young?'

'I don't know,' he replied. 'The fact is that I didn't really look at her. I only had this savage desire to pick up a rock and smash the head of the man who had brought me there.'

His friend said, 'That would have been a most worthy deed.'

He did not stay with his friend for very long in that hotel. He felt greatly depressed by the events of the day before. They finished their tea and left.

He quietly walked to the tonga stand, his eyes searching for that procurer, who was nowhere to be found. It was now six o'clock and the big building was right across, just a few yards from him. He began to walk towards it and, once there, went in.

There were people walking in. Quite calmly, taking steps through the dark, he came to the stairway and noticed a light at the top. He looked up and began to climb very quietly. For a while, he stood at the landing. A bright light was coming out of the room, but there was no sound, not even a stir. He approached the wide open doors and, standing aside, peeped in. The first thing he saw was a bulb whose light dazzled his eyes. He abruptly moved aside and turned towards the dark to get the dazzle out of his eyes.

Then he advanced towards the doors but in a way that his eyes should not meet that blinding light. He looked in. On the bit of floor he could see, there was a woman lying on a mat. He looked at her carefully. She was asleep, her face covered with her dupatta. Her bosom rose and fell with her rhythmic breathing. He moved deeper into the room and screamed but he quickly stifled it. Next to that woman, on the bare floor, lay a man, his head smashed into a pulp. A bloodied brick lay close by. He saw all this in one rapid sequence, then he leapt towards the stairs but lost his foothold and fell down. Without caring for his injuries, while trying to keep his sanity intact, he managed to get home with great difficulty. All night, he kept seeing terrifying dreams.

SIRAJ

There was a small park facing the Nagpara police post and an Iranian teahouse next to it. Dhondoo was always to be found in this area, leaning against a lamp post, waiting for custom. He would come here around sunset and remain busy with his work until four in the morning.

Nobody knew his real name, but everyone called him Dhondoo—the one who searches and finds—which was most appropriate because his business consisted of procuring women of every type and description for his clients.

He had been in the trade for the last ten years and during this period hundreds of women had passed through his hands, women of every religion, race and temperament.

This had always been his hangout, the lamp post facing the Iranian teahouse which stood in front of the Nagpara police headquarters. The lamp post had become his trademark. Often, when I passed that way and saw the lamp post, I felt as if I was actually looking at Dhondoo, besmeared like him with betel juice and much the worse for wear.

The lamp post was tall, and so was Dhondoo. A number of power lines ran in various directions from the top of this ugly steel column into adjoining buildings, shops and even other lamp posts.

The telephone department had tagged on a small terminal to the post and technicians could be seen checking it out from time to time. Sometimes I felt that Dhondoo was also a kind of terminal, attached to the lamp post to verify the sexual signals of his customers. He not only knew the locals, but even some of the big seths of the city who would come to him for an evening to get their sexual cables straightened out.

He knew almost all the women in the profession. He had intimate knowledge of their bodies, since they constituted the wares he transacted, and he was familiar with their temperaments. He knew exactly which woman would please which customer. But there was one exception—Siraj. He just had not been able to fathom her out.

Dhondoo had often said to me, 'Manto sahib, this one is off her rocker. I just cannot make her out. Never seen a chhokri like her. She is so changeable. When you think she is happy and laughing her head off, just as suddenly she bursts into tears. She simply cannot get along with anyone. Fights with every "passenger". I have told her a million times to sort herself out, but it has had absolutely no effect on her. Many times I have had to tell her to go back to wherever she first came from to Bombay. Have you seen her? She has practically nothing to wear and not a penny to her name, and yet she simply will not play ball with the men I bring her. What an obstinate, mixed-up piece of work!'

I had seen Siraj a few times. She was slim and rather pretty. Her eyes were like outsize windows in her oval face. You simply could not get away from them. When I saw her for the first time on Clare Road, I felt like saying to her eyes, 'Would you please step aside for a minute so that I can see this girl?'

She was slight and yet there was so much of her. She reminded me of a glass goblet, which had been filled to the brim with strong, underdiluted spirits, and the restlessness showed. I say strong spirits because there was something sharp and tangy about her personality. And yet I felt that in this heady mixture someone had added a bit of water to soften the fire. Her femininity was strong, despite her somewhat irate manner. Her hair was thick and her nose was aquiline. Her fingers reminded me of the sharpened pencils draughtsmen use. She gave the impression of being slightly annoyed with everything, with Dhondoo and the lamp post he always stood against, with the gifts he brought her and even with her big eyes which ran away with her face.

But these are the impressions of a storyteller. Dhondoo had his own views. One day he said to me, 'Manto sahib, guess what that sali Siraj did today? Boy, am I lucky! Had it not been for God's mercy and the fact that the Nagpara police are always kind to me, I would have found myself in the jug. And that could have been one big, blooming disaster.'

'What happened?'

'The usual. I don't know what the matter with me is. I must be off my head. It is not the first time she has got me in a spot and yet I continue to carry her along. I should just wash my hands off her. She is neither my sister nor my mother that I should be running around trying to get her a living. Seriously, Manto sahib, I no longer know what to do.'

We were both sitting in the Iranian teahouse, sipping tea. Dhondoo poured from his cup into the saucer and began slurping up the special mixture he always blended with coffee. 'The fact is that I feel sorry for this sali Siraj.'

'Why?'

'God knows why. I wish I did.' He finished his tea and put the cup back on the saucer, upside down. 'Did you know she is still a virgin?'

'No, I didn't, Dhondoo.'

Dhondoo felt the scepticism in my voice and he didn't like it. 'I am not lying to you, Manto sahib. She is a hundred per cent virgin. You want to bet on that?'

'How's that possible?' I asked.

'Why not? A girl like Siraj. I tell you she could stay in this profession the rest of her life and still be a virgin. The thing is she simply does not let anyone so much as touch her. I know her whole bloody history. I know that she comes from the Punjab. She used to be on Lymington Road in the private house run by that memsahib, but was thrown out because of her endless bickerings with the passengers. I am surprised she lasted three months there, but that was because madam had about twenty girls at the time. But Manto sahib, how long can people feed you? One day madam pushed her out of the house with nothing on her except the clothes she was wearing. Then she moved to that other madam on Faras Road. She did not change her ways and one day she actually bit a passenger.

'She lasted no more than a couple of months there. I don't know what is wrong with her. She is full of life and nobody can cool it. From Faras Road she found her way into a hotel in Khetwari and created the usual trouble. One day the manager gave her marching orders. What can I say, Manto sahib, the sali doesn't seem to be interested in anything—clothes, food, ornaments, you name it. Doesn't bathe for months until lice start crawling over her clothes. If someone gives her hash, she smokes a couple of joints happily. Sometimes I see her standing outside a hotel, listening to music.'

'Why don't you send her back? I mean it's obvious she's not interested in the business. I'll pay her fare if you like,' I suggested.

Dhondoo didn't like it. 'Manto sahib, it's not a question of paying the sali's fare. I can do that. Won't kill me.'

'Then why don't you send her back?'

He lit a cigarette, which he had tucked above his ear, drew on it deeply, exhaled the smoke through his nose and said, 'I don't want her to go.'

'Do you love her?' I asked.

'What are you talking about, Manto sahib!' He touched both his ears. 'I swear by the Quran that such a vile thought has never entered my head. It is just . . . just that I like her a bit.'

'Why?'

'Because she's not like the others who are only interested in money—the whole damn lot of them. This one is different. When I make a deal on her behalf, she goes most willingly. I put her in a taxi with the passenger and off they go.

'Manto sahib, passengers come for a good time. They spend money. They want to see what they are getting and like to feel it with their hands. And that's when the trouble starts. She doesn't let anyone even touch her. Starts hitting them. If it's a gentleman, he slinks away quietly. If it's the other kind, then there's hell to pay. I have to return the money and go down on my hands and knees. I swear on the Quran. And why do I do it? Only for Siraj's sake. Manto sahib, I swear on your head that because of this sali my business has been reduced by half.'

One day I decided to see Siraj without Dhondoo's good offices. She lived in a no-good locality near the Byculla station, dumping ground for garbage and other refuse. The city corporation had built a large number of tin huts here for the poor. I do not want to write here about those tall buildings which stood not too far from this dump of filth because that has nothing to do with this story. This world after all is but another name for the high and the low. I knew roughly through Dhondoo where her hut was located. I went there—feeling apologetic about the good clothes I was wearing—but then this is not a story about me.

Outside her door a goat was tethered. It bleated when I approached. An old woman hobbled out, bent over her stick. I was about to leave when, through a hole in the coarse length of tattered cloth which hung over the door and served as a curtain, I saw large eyes in an oblong face.

She had recognized me. She must have been doing something, but she came out. 'What are you doing here?' she asked.

'I wanted to meet you.'

'Come in.'

'No, I want you to come with me.'

The old woman said, 'That'll cost you ten rupees.'

I pulled out my wallet and gave her the money. 'Come,' I said to Siraj.

She looked at me with those big window-like eyes of hers. It once again occurred to me that she was pretty, but in a withdrawn, frozen kind of way, like a mummified but perfectly preserved queen.

I took her to a hotel. There she sat in front of me in her not-quite-clean clothes, staring at the world through eyes which were so big that her entire personality had become secondary to them.

I gave Siraj forty rupees.

She was quiet and, to make a pass at her, I had to drink something quickly. After four large whiskies, I put my hands on her like passengers are expected to, but she showed me no resistance. Then I did something quite lewd and was sure she would go up like a keg of gunpowder but, surprisingly, she did not react at all. She just looked at me with her big eyes. 'Get me a joint,' she said.

'Take a drink,' I suggested.

'No, I want a joint.'

I sent for one. It was easy to get. She began to drag on it like experienced hash smokers. Her eyes had somehow lost their overpowering presence. Her face looked like a ravaged city. Every line, every feature suggested devastation. But what was this devastation? Had she been ravaged before even becoming whole? Had her world been destroyed long before the foundations could be raised?

Whether she was a virgin or not, I didn't care. But I wanted to talk to her, and she did not seem interested. I wanted her to fight with me, but she was simply indifferent.

In the end, I took her home.

When Dhondoo came to learn of my secret foray, he was upset. His feelings, both as a friend and as a man of business, had been hurt. He never gave me an opportunity to explain. All he said was, 'Manto sahib, this I did not expect of you.' And he walked away.

I didn't see him the next day. I thought he was ill, but he did not appear the day after either. One week passed. Twice a day I used to go to work past Dhondoo's headquarters and whenever I saw the lamp post I thought of him.

I even went looking for Siraj one day, only to be greeted by the old woman there. When I asked her about Siraj, she smiled the million-year-old smile of the procuress and said, 'That one's gone, but I can always get you another.'

The question was: Where was she? Had she run away with Dhondoo? But that was quite impossible. They were not in love and Dhondoo was not that sort of person. He had a wife and children whom he loved. But the question was: Where had they disappeared to?

I thought that maybe Dhondoo had finally decided that Siraj should go home, a decision he had always been ambivalent about. One month passed.

Then one evening, as I was passing by the Iranian teahouse, I saw him leaning against his lamp post. When he saw me, he smiled.

We went into the teahouse. I did not ask him anything. He sent for his special tea, mixed with coffee, and ordered plain tea for me. He turned around in his chair and it seemed as if he was going to make some dramatic disclosure, but all he said was, 'And how are things, Manto sahib?'

'Life goes on, Dhondoo,' I replied.

'You are right, life goes on,' he smiled. 'It's a strange world, isn't it?'

'You can say that again.'

We kept drinking tea. Dhondoo poured his into the saucer, took a sip and said, 'Manto sahib, she told me the whole story. She said to me that that friend of yours, meaning you, was crazy.'

I laughed. 'Why?'

'She told me that you took her to a hotel, gave her a lot of money and didn't do what she thought you would do.'

'That was the way it was, Dhondoo,' I said.

He laughed. 'I know. I'm sorry if I showed annoyance that day. In any case, that whole business is now over.'

'What business?'

'That Siraj business, what else?'

'What happened?'

'You remember the day you took her out? Well, she came to me later and said that she had forty rupees on her and would I take her to Lahore. I said to her, "Sali, what has come over you?" She said, "Come on Dhondoo, for my sake, take me." And Manto sahib, you know I could never say no to her. I liked her. So I said, "OK, if that's what you want."

'We bought train tickets and arrived in Lahore. She knew what hotel we were going to stay in.

'The next day she says to me, "Dhondoo, get me a burqa." I went out and got her one. And then our rounds began. She would leave in the morning and spend the entire day on the streets of Lahore in a tonga, with me keeping company. She wouldn't tell me what she was looking for.

'I said to myself, "Dhondoo, have you gone bananas? Why did you have to come with this crazy girl all the way from Bombay?"

'Then, Manto sahib, one day, she asked me to stop the tonga in the middle of the street. "Do you see that man there? Can you bring him to me? I am going to the hotel. Now."

'I was confused but I stepped down from the tonga and began to follow the man she had pointed out. Well, by the grace of God, I am a good judge of men. I began to talk to him and it did not take me long to find out that he was game for a good time.

'I said to him, "I have a very special brand of goods from Bombay." He wanted me to take him with me right away, but I said, "Not that fast, friend, show me the colour of your money." He brandished a thick wad of bank notes in my face. What I couldn't understand was why, of all the men in Lahore, Siraj had picked this one out. In any case, I said to myself, "Dhondoo, everything goes." We took a tonga to the hotel.

'I went in and told Siraj I had the man waiting outside. She said, "Bring him in but don't go away." When I brought him in and he saw her, he wanted to run away, but Siraj grabbed hold of him.'

'She grabbed hold of him?'

'That's right. She grabbed hold of the sala and said to him, "Where are you going? Why did you make me run away from home? You knew I loved you. And remember you had said to me that you loved me too. But when I left my home and my parents and my brothers and my sisters and came with you from Amritsar to Lahore and stayed in this very hotel, you abandoned me the same night. You left while I was asleep. Why did you bring me here? Why did you make me run away from home? You know, I was prepared for everything and you let me down. But I have come back and found you. I still love you. Nothing has changed."

'And Manto sahib, she threw her arms around him. That sala began to cry. He was asking her to forgive him. He was saying he had done her wrong. He had got cold feet. He was saying he would never leave her again. He kept repeating he would never leave her again. God knows what rot he was talking.

'Then Siraj asked me to leave the room. I lay on a bare cot outside and went to sleep at some point. When she woke me up, it was morning. "Dhondoo," she said, "let's go." "Where?" I asked. She said, "Let's go back to Bombay." I said, "Where is that sala?" "He is sleeping, I have covered his face with my burqa," she replied.'

Dhondoo ordered himself another cup of tea mixed with coffee. I looked up and saw Siraj enter the hotel. Her oval face was glowing, but her two big eyes looked like fallen train signals.

AN OLD-FASHIONED MAN

Khan Bahadur Muhammad Aslam Khan presided over a happy household. He had two daughters and one son. The older girl was around thirteen, the younger about eleven. The son was the last born but had grown taller than his sisters. All three were yet to cross the line that stands between childhood and adolescence. Their entire world revolved around their toys, games and amusements.

Khan Bahadur's greatest joy was these three children, Farida, Saeeda and Najeeb, all schoolgoing. Every morning they went to their classes as if they were going out to play. When they returned home, they looked even happier. At examination time, they excelled one another, taking the top position turn by turn.

Khan Bahadur was content with his children and even more content with his life in retirement, having served the department of agriculture for thirty-two years. Starting out at the bottom, he had reached the top through hard work. Of him it could be truly said that he had earned the leisurely life he was now leading. Most of the time he spent in his room reading. Off and on, one of the children would drop in to relay a message from their mother, get a reply and leave. After retirement, his reading room and bedroom had become one. He spent his days in peace, oblivious of the hustle and bustle of life outside his sanctuary. Sometimes his wife would come, obviously wanting to talk, but he would soon send her on her way, using one excuse or another. Normally, it was the still largely hypothetical question of the dowry of their two daughters. He would say to her, 'It's your daughters you should be worrying about. One day, they have to be married. Gold prices are going up by the day. Why not buy some now? I don't want you complaining later about the expense.'

Sometimes he would say to her, 'Farkhanda Khanum, my love, we have grown old and it is time for us to be concerned about each other, as one shows concern for a child. Have you noticed that all my turbans are in tatters? It hasn't occurred to you to buy some muslin to replace my turbans, and in the bargain get yourself and the girls a couple of new dupattas. And yes, I have run out of miswaks. You know every morning I must clean my teeth and freshen my breath with these green twigs full of nature's own cleansing juices.'

Farkhanda would find herself a perch on her husband's bed and say, 'Everyone these days uses a toothbrush but you are so old-fashioned that you continue to insist upon a miswak.'

Khan Bahadur's voice would become tender. 'Farkhanda, my love, these new-fangled brushes and toothpastes are no use whatsoever.'

Farkhanda's face would light up but only for a moment because Khan Bahadur, his ear cocked to the racket in the courtyard, would say, 'Farkhanda, send for the muslin tomorrow and a length of cotton cloth too.' He would pause, then add as an afterthought, 'No, not the cotton. It is not needed yet.' White cotton cloth was what the dead were wrapped in.

Out in the courtyard, the children had found a new playmate in recent days. Her name was Shadaan, the new house help. The girls were particularly fond of her and would wait eagerly for her every morning. They loved to play hide-and-seek with her.

Shadaan's parents were Christian. Her real name was not Shadaan but it was the name Khan Bahadur's wife had chosen for her on the first day. She was a good-tempered girl and she had become immediately popular. She would come early while the children were getting ready for school. 'Look sharp, children, time for school,' their mother would say, as they gathered around Shadaan hoping to play. However, they would be sent packing by their mother, and they would leave waving their goodbyes to Shadaan.

In the late afternoon, after having finished her household chores, as well as run a few errands for other families in the neighbourhood, Shadaan would start playing with the three children. Sometimes they would get so noisy that Khan Bahadur would scream at them to be quiet. This would frighten Shadaan but Saeeda and Farida would calm her down. 'This is nothing at all; even if we make more noise, he will not admonish us. He only does it once.' And they would resume playing.

Shadaan loved Ludo, the new board game that Najeeb had received as a present. That was the game she always wanted to play, but none of the three children was much fond of it. 'This is no game, you put the dice in this tiny container, shake it and throw it down. Next you keep moving your pieces up and down. You call that a game!' one of them would say.

Shadaan was the same age as Farida but there was a different air to her. Her cheeks glowed red as if she had coloured them with a pencil. It wasn't that Farida and Saeeda were lacking in the physical signs of approaching womanhood that Shadaan displayed; all those lines and half-formed curves were there. What was different about Shadaan was that her pubescence practically leapt out of her body.

She was a fair complexioned girl with dishevelled hair, her dupatta tightly wrapped across her chest and waist as she ran around and played. She was nimble on her feet, attentive to every sound and sensitive to every odour in the air. None of her features was extraordinary and if someone were to look for faults, he would have found many. It was not her face but her physical presence that was so utterly striking. It was not possible to isolate her face for what it lacked and ignore her body. You couldn't separate one from the other because they combined perfectly.

Shadaan was hyperactive. Anything given to her was done quickly and in time. She would come in the morning, do some work and leave, then return in the afternoon to play for an hour or so with the children and do the rest, but only after Khan Bahadur's wife had shouted, 'Shadaan, for God's sake, get on with it now.' She would run up the stairs, a basket under her arm, do the daily cleaning, rush down and sweep the courtyard. She was neat and quick because both Khan Bahadur and his wife were fussy people who wanted things kept tidy. Shadaan had never given them cause for complaint and they never grudged her her playtime. They treated her well because, being liberal in outlook, they did not discriminate against her because of her religion or the fact that she was only a household help.

In the beginning, Farkhanda, in keeping with the common prejudice that household help and maidservants are unclean, had instructed her daughters to avoid physical contact with Shadaan, but after some time this restriction had been lifted. All she had been asked to do was wash her hands with soap when she came in. While Shadaan's mother was still not permitted to touch anything in Khan Bahadur's room, there was no such restriction on the daughter. She could touch what she liked while dusting and mopping the master's sanctuary.

The first room Shadaan swept and cleaned in the morning was

Khan Bahadur's. He would be bent over his newspaper when Shadaan entered with a mop in hand and announced, 'Khan Bahadur sahib, please move to the veranda for a minute.' Khan Bahadur would lift his eyes from the paper while Shadaan would pull out his slippers from under the bed for him to leave the room. When she was done, she would stand at the door, leaning at an angle, and say, 'Come in, Khan Bahadur sahib.' He would walk in, newspaper in hand and Shadaan would get busy with other work.

She had been working in the house for nearly two months when Khan Bahadur's wife felt that in some way she couldn't quite put her finger on that the girl had changed. After giving it some thought, she came to the conclusion that Shadaan had got something going with one of the young men from the street. She had also noticed that Shadaan had begun to take greater care of her appearance. No longer were her clothes plain. They were now well stitched and in keeping with the day's fashion. Once she came in wearing a spotless white cotton shalwar and a shirt made of silk georgette. Farida noticed that clearly outlined under the fabric were two round cup-like things. Later, when the children were playing hide-and-seek, and Shadaan, eyes tight shut, was standing against the wall, waiting for the others to hide before setting out to find them, Farida, who had been unable to forget what she had seen that morning, dragged Saeeda by the arm into a room and whispered, 'Saeeda, did you notice what she was wearing?'

'Who?' Saeeda asked.

'Shadaan,' Farida whispered in her ear.

'What was she wearing?'

When Farida whispered something in her ear, Saeeda put her hand on her heart and gasped, 'What!'

The two sisters kept whispering to each other for some time, then the door swung open and Shadaan came running in. Normally, when one of the players was caught there was much screaming and laughter, but this time there was none. Even Shadaan, who was on the verge of shouting with joy at having caught her quarries, was quiet. The two sisters stayed in the dark, looking scared. 'What is the matter?' Shadaan asked in a whisper, in keeping with the atmosphere. Farida said something to Saeeda, who whispered something right back to her. They both elbowed each other in the ribs before Farida asked in a tremulous voice, 'What is it that you are wearing under your shirt?'

Shadaan burst out laughing.

'Where did you get it?' Saeeda asked.

'From the bazaar,' Shadaan replied.

'How much?' Fareeda asked.

'Ten rupees.'

'So expensive!' the two sisters almost screamed.

All Shadaan said in reply was, 'Can't we poor people sometimes buy something nice that we like?'

There were no further questions. After a few minutes' silence, they resumed playing.

Khan Bahadur's wife was sure something very odd was going on. Shadaan had begun to put scented oil in her hair and no longer was she barefooted but in sandals. There was one thing Khan Bahadur's wife had no illusions about. The game that was in progress would soon manifest itself through Shadaan's body. However, so far the only thing that could be seen on her body was new clothes. In the end, Khan Bahadur's wife decided not to bother about it any more. Such girls always ended up that way. It won't be the first time. The streets of the city were full of such cases, she said to herself.

Some time passed.

Then came the wedding of the daughter of one of Farkhanda's closest friends, almost a sister. The entire family was invited; only Khan Bahadur was staying home. It was winter time and getting cold. Some time after Farkhanda arrived at the bride's home, she remembered that she had forgotten to wear her woollen shawl. She first thought of sending a servant to fetch it but then it occurred to her that it was stored in one of her wooden chests where she had also hidden some money. It would be best to go herself, the house not being too far. With Najeeb in tow, she came home and found the door closed, as it should have been. She knocked, but when Najeeb pushed it a little, it fell open.

She made straight for the storeroom, found her shawl and said to Najeeb, 'Go see what your father is doing. Tell him that while you will return home shortly the rest of us will spend the night at my friend's place and be back in the morning. Now run along son.'

She rearranged the clothes in the chest and was about to lock it when Najeeb returned. 'Father is not in his room,' he announced.

'Where is he if he is not in his room?' his mother asked, locking the chest. Then she put the key in her handbag and said, 'You stay right here; I will go and find out.'

She went into her husband's room, which was empty, but the light was on. There were no sheets on the bed. The floor looked freshly washed. There was a strange smell in the air. She peeped under the bed. Nothing there. She looked again and found Khan Bahadur's miswak with which he insisted on cleaning his teeth and freshening his breath every morning.

The door creaked open and Khan Bahadur entered the room, bringing with him a strong smell of kerosene oil. She hid the miswak behind her back. He looked deathly pale. 'What are you doing here?' he asked, his voice unsteady.

'I came to get my shawl and thought I would see how you were doing while I was here.'

'Please leave,' he said.

She walked out and heard the door close behind her. She went to her room, sat there for some time, then rose and with Najeeb by her side returned to her friend's house.

The next morning she learnt that Khan Bahadur had been picked up by the police. The story was that Shadaan had returned home that evening, her clothes all bloodied. She had fallen unconscious as soon as she had stepped across the threshold. Her parents had taken her to the hospital and the police had been called. She had come to for a few minutes but all she had managed to say was, 'Khan Bahadur.' Then she had gone into a coma and died.

There was a trial but the only witnesses were the girl's blood-drenched clothes and her dying words. The prosecution had no doubt that it was Khan Bahadur who had killed her. There was one witness who had seen Shadaan entering the Khan Bahadur residence that evening. There were only two defence witnesses: Khan Bahadur's wife and a doctor who had testified that Khan Bahadur was incapable of sexual relations with a woman, least of all a minor. Khan Bahadur's wife had said that the doctor was right.

Khan Bahadur Muhammad Aslam Khan was acquitted after a long trial. He resumed his old life, but with one difference. He no longer used a miswak.

THE ANGEL

A rough red blanket covered Ataullah as he slowly opened his eyes and turned on his side. All around him, there was a thick fog that covered every object so that they could only be seen in a hazy outline. The room where he lay, but it could also be a veranda, was long and appeared to stretch into infinity. The light was dim and in places discoloured.

At the far end stood a huge statue whose head he could not see as it had obviously gone through the ceiling. Still, it was an awesome sight. Perhaps it was the god of death who was deliberately hiding his face. Ataullah whistled at the statue as one whistles for a dog. The moment the sound left his lips, thousands of wagging dog tails materialized in the room. Then they disappeared into a huge glass jar that contained methylated spirit. The jar rose slowly in the air, floated across the room and came to a standstill in front of him. It had shrunk in size and he could see his heart floating inside, trying to beat but not very successfully.

A stifled scream escaped Ataullah's throat; then with a trembling hand he touched the spot where his heart used to be and fainted.

He lay unconscious for a long time and when he opened his eyes the fog in the room had lifted and the awesome statue had disappeared. He was drenched in perspiration and his body felt like a slab of ice, except the spot where his heart should have been. All he could feel there was the intense heat of a fire. He looked up and was horrified to discover that many objects were burning in that fire, including his wife and children, their bones crackling, but his own flesh and bones were intact. Except for the spot where his heart used to be, the rest of his body was cold.

Then with his frozen hands, he picked up his pale, emaciated wife and skeletal children and flung them aside. He also noticed that hundreds of job applications, written in different languages, all bearing his signatures, were burning in the fire without making a sound.

On the other side of the flames, he could see his own face, dripping with cold sweat. He reached out, grabbed a flame and wiped his forehead with it; then he threw it back into the fire where it landed like a wet sponge. Ataullah felt sorry for it.

The applications kept burning as Ataullah watched. After a few minutes, his pale wife appeared with a pan that held fresh dough. She rolled the dough into round pellets that she threw into the fire, one by one. They all turned into red cinders, a sight that caused Ataullah a violent pain in the stomach. He pounced on the one remaining ball of dough and put it in his mouth. It was dry like sand and he began to choke. Then he fainted.

He was having a disjointed dream. There was an arched gateway with an inscribed Persian couplet that said: On Judgement Day when the final reckoning is done, the first question asked would be: did you always pray five times a day?

He flung himself on the floor, wanting to ask God to forgive him because he had never offered his prayers, but all he could feel was an unbearable hunger. He heard someone call his name in a loud and authoritative voice.

'Ataullah!'

He stood up with the arched gateway behind him. There in front of him against a pulpit stood a naked man. His lips were not moving, yet he could hear him.

'Ataullah, why are you alive? One only remains alive so long as one has help. Tell us, do you have any help or can you offer help to anyone? You are sick. Your wife will fall sick too, if she is not already sick. Those who have nobody to help them fall sick. They are the living dead. You are also losing your children. What a pity you have not terminated your life, or the lives of your wife and children! Do you need help even here? You are looking for pity. You fool, nobody is going to take pity on you. And why should death itself rescue you from life? It is bad enough for death that it is death. It cannot oblige everyone. You are not the only Ataullah; there are millions of Ataullahs in this world. Go, find a way out of your troubles yourself. It is not, after all, so difficult to send two half-starved children and that weakling of a wife of yours to their deaths! If you lighten yourself of this burden, death will come to you because it will otherwise feel embarrassed.'

Ataullah felt angry and began to tremble. 'You, you are cruel. Who are you? Before I kill my wife and children, I want to kill you.'

The naked man laughed. 'I am Ataullah. Look carefully, don't you even recognize yourself?'

Ataullah looked at the naked man and bent his head because he had seen himself, stark naked. Beside himself with rage, he picked up a stone, taking advantage of his sharp, overgrown nails, and flung it at the pulpit. His head began to reel and to steady himself he put his hand to his forehead and felt blood gushing out. He ran across the stone courtyard and found himself surrounded by a crowd. Everyone in that crowd was Ataullah, bleeding from the forehead.

He freed himself from them with some difficulty and next found himself on a dark and narrow road on which he walked for a long time. On both sides he could see cacti and marijuana bushes and, here and there, grew poisonous weeds. Ataullah took out a bottle from his pocket and filled it with cacti milk; then he plucked some leaves from the poisonous weeds and pushed them into the bottle, shaking it as he walked. Finally he arrived home, a crumbling structure of broken bricks with a dirty jute curtain hanging across the front door. He pulled the curtain aside and found a clay lamp burning in an alcove and his two emaciated children lying on a bare cot. They were moving under the dirty sheet that covered them, so at least they were alive. He pulled out the bottle from his pocket and sat down on the bare floor.

They were both boys, five and four, and they were hungry. He pulled off the sheet and looked at their skeletal bodies. It was amazing they were still alive. Putting the bottle to one side, he grabbed one of them by his neck and twisted it. He heard a crack and the boy's head rolled to one side lifelessly. Ataullah was delighted; it had been easy. He called out to his wife, 'Jeena, Jeena, come here, look how neatly I have killed Rahim. He felt no pain.'

He looked around the house. 'Where is Zainab? Where has she disappeared? Maybe she has gone to cadge some food for the children, or perhaps she is at the hospital to look someone up,' he thought. Then he chuckled as the other boy turned in the bed and began to shake his dead brother by the arm. 'Rahim, Rahim.'

There was no response from Rahim. The boy turned towards his father and his tiny black eyes lit up for a moment. 'O! You are home.'

'Yes, Karim, I am home,' Ataullah replied gently.

With a bony hand, the boy shook his brother again. 'Get up, Rahim, father is back from the hospital.'

Ataullah put his hand on his mouth, 'Keep quiet, he is asleep.'

Karim shook it off. 'How can he be asleep . . . we haven't eaten anything . . .'

'Were you awake?'

'Yes, father.'

'You will also fall asleep.'

'How?'

'I'll put you to sleep,' Ataullah lunged for his son's neck and tried to twist it, but there was no snapping sound.

'What are you doing?'

'Nothing,' Ataullah replied, wondering what had made his son so tough. 'Don't you want to sleep?'

Karim rubbed his neck and said, 'I want to sleep but you have to give me something to eat first.'

Ataullah picked up the bottle of poison. 'First drink this medicine.'

'All right.' Karim opened his mouth.

Ataullah poured the entire bottle down Karim's throat and said in a relieved voice, 'You will soon go into a deep sleep.'

Karim grabbed his father's hand. 'Father, now give me something to eat.'

Ataullah was annoyed. 'Why don't you die?'

'What, father?' Karim asked.

'Why don't you die? I mean if you die, you will also go to sleep.'

Karim did not understand. 'But only God can make people die.'

'He used to, but He has stopped doing that now. Get up.'

Ataullah didn't wait for him to get out of bed; he picked him up while trying to decide how best he could do God's work. When he stepped into the street, it looked as if the sky had come close and instead of stars it was lit by clay lamps. As to where God was, God alone knew. And where was Zainab? She must have gone out to beg for food. Ataullah laughed but became sombre when he remembered that he was playing God. There were large boulders on the ground. He thought of smashing Karim against them, but did not have the strength to do so. Once or twice, he tried to lift Karim so that he could throw him against the rocks but failed. 'Jeena, Jeena,' he called.

There was no response. Where was she? Had she gone off with that doctor who always spoke to her in such a sympathetic manner? She must have fallen in his trap. Or had she sold herself to him for his sake?

The thought made him so angry that he threw away Karim's

frail body in a drain and began to run towards the hospital.

It was past midnight and everything was totally still. He walked towards the patients' ward and while he was still in the corridor he heard voices. One was his wife's who was saying, 'You are a cheat. You betrayed me . . . whatever money he gave you, you have pocketed yourself.' A man's voice replied, 'You are wrong. He did not fancy you, that is why he left.'

His wife screamed in an insane voice, 'What are you talking about! It's true I am the mother of two children and my looks have faded, but had it not been for you, he would have found me acceptable. You are a very cruel man.' She sounded on the verge of tears. 'I would never have humiliated myself like this if my husband was not sick and my children were not hungry. Why did you do this to me?'

The man's voice came again, 'There was no third person. All the time, it was I. When you agreed to go with me, I realized what sort of a human being I was and I lied to you when I said that the man you were going to spend time with was already gone. Your husband, let me tell you, is going to die, as will your children and as will you, but . . .'

'But?'

'I will remain alive because you saved me from a life which would have been worse than death. Come, Ataullah is calling to us.'

'Ataullah is right here,' Ataullah said in a tense voice.

Two shadows moved. One of them was the doctor's who used to express so much sympathy for Zainab, but all he could manage to say to Ataullah was, 'It's you?'

'Yes, and I have heard everything.' Then Ataullah turned to his wife. 'Jeena, I have killed Rahim and Karim. That only leaves us.'

Zainab screamed, 'You killed the children!'

'Yes, they died painlessly. I am sure you will feel no pain either. We have a doctor around,' he answered confidently.

The doctor began to tremble as Ataullah moved towards him. 'Give her an injection that will kill her immediately.'

The doctor opened his bag, pulled out a syringe full of poison and plunged it into Zainab's arm. She fell to the floor and died. Her last words were, 'My children, my children.' Ataullah said in a relieved voice, 'Good, so that's done, which leaves me.'

'But I have no more poison,' the doctor stammered.

'That's all right, I will go lie on this bed and you run out and get the poison,' Ataullah told him.

He lay down on the bed and, adjusting the rough red blanket he had found there, he turned on his side and opened his eyes. There was a thick fog in the room, making every object look indistinct. He was also conscious of a long, unending, dimly lit corridor, unless it was a room, some of it in the dark.

In the distance, stood an angel who began to move towards him but as he moved he appeared to shrink in size. When he approached Ataullah's bed, he turned into the doctor who used to be so solicitous of his wife. Ataullah tried to get up. 'You're here, doctor,' he said.

But the man disappeared. The fog had also lifted.

Ataullah felt clear-headed. Suddenly, there was a commotion in the room. He could hear Zainab's voice but he could not understand what she was saying. Ataullah tried to rise from his bed once again. He also tried to call out to Zainab but could not do so. The fog returned and the other end of the room or the ward where he was began to recede into the distance.

He heard Zainab walk in. Like someone crazed, she began to shake him by the shoulder. 'I have killed him. I have killed that bastard.'

'Whom have you killed?'

'The man who used to show me such sympathy. He had promised to save you . . . he was a liar . . . a cheat. He was a black-hearted person. To me, to me . . .' she was unable to finish her sentence.

'But did he not kill you?' Ataullah asked, feeling confused.

'No, I killed him,' Zainab screamed.

Ataullah gazed in the distance, then said, 'Get aside, he is coming.' He pushed Zainab away.

'Who?'

'The same doctor . . . the angel.'

The angel approached his bed slowly. He was carrying a syringe full of poison. Ataullah smiled. 'You have it?'

'Yes, I have it.' The angel shook his head affirmatively.

Ataullah extended a trembling arm towards him. 'Then give it to me.'

The angel pushed the needle in.

Ataullah died.

Zainab began to shake his shoulder violently. 'Get up, get up, Karim and Rahim's father. This hospital is a horrible place. Let's go home.'

Then the police arrived, pulled Zainab away from Ataullah's prostrate body and took her away.

BY THE ROADSIDE

Yes, it was this time of the year. The sky had a washed blue look like his eyes. The sun was mild like a joyous dream. The fragrance from the earth had risen to my heart, enveloping my being. And, lying next to him, I had made him the offering of my throbbing soul.

He had said to me, 'You have given me what my life had always lacked. These magic moments that you have allowed me to share have filled a void in my being. My life would have remained an emptiness without your love, something incomplete. I do not know what to say to you and how, but today I have been made whole. I am fulfilled. Perhaps I no longer need you.'

And he had left, never to come back.

I had wept. I had begged him to answer me. 'Why do you no longer need me, when my whole being is on fire with longing and love? The moments you say have filled the emptiness in your soul have created an emptiness in mine.'

He had said, 'These moments we have shared have filled my emptiness. The atoms of your being have made me complete. Our relationship has come to its preordained end.'

These were cruel words, like being stoned alive. I had wept. I had cried, but his mind was made up. I had said to him, 'These atoms of my being that you speak about, these atoms which have made you whole, were a part of my body. I gave them to you, but is it where our relationship ceases? Can what is left of me ever sever itself from what I have given you? You have become complete, but by leaving me incomplete. Haven't I worshipped you like a god?'

He had said, 'The honey which bees suck from half-opened flowers can never adorn the flowers or sweeten their bitterness. God is to be worshipped, but He is not the worshipper. In the great void, He created being through union with non-being, but then the void ceased to be, because He did not need it. The mother died after giving birth.'

A woman can weep. She cannot argue. Her supreme arguments are the tears that spring from her eyes. I had said to him, 'Look at me. I am crying. If you must leave, I cannot hold you back, but wrap these tears in the shroud of your handkerchief and take them away and bury them somewhere, because when I cry again I would know that you once performed the last rites of love. Do this small thing for me, for my happiness.'

He had said, 'I have made you happy. I have brought you that supreme joy which, until I came, was like a mirage in your life. Can you not live the rest of your life in remembrance of that joy which I conferred on you? You can say that my completion has rendered you incomplete, but is incompletion not what life needs if it is to continue? I am a man. Today, you have brought completion to my life. Tomorrow, it will be another woman. I am fashioned out of elements that are destined to experience the same moment of supreme joy many, many times. The emptiness that you filled today will appear again and there will be others to fill it.'

I had kept crying.

I had thought, 'These few moments which I held in my hand so briefly are gone. Why did I let myself be swept away by their magic? Why did I put my restless, throbbing soul into the cage of life? Yes, it was ecstasy beyond words. Yes, it was like a dream when the two of us held each other. Yes, it was an accident, but he walked away from it, whole and undamaged, leaving me broken. Why does he no longer need me, while the intensity of my desire for him sets my body and soul on fire? I have given my power to him. We were like two clouds in the sky, one heavy with rain, the other a flash of wild lightning, which moved away. What kind of law decrees it to be so? The law of the skies, of the earth, or of their Creator?'

Yes, I had thought about these things.

Two souls meet and one acquires the vastness of eternity and moves away. Is it all poetry? When two souls meet, they must converge on that tiny dot, which is the embryo of the universe itself. But why is it ordained that, of the two, one should be broken on the rack and abandoned? Is it punishment for helping the other discover that tiny dot which is the embryo of the universe itself?

Yes, it was this time of the year. The sky was a wash of blue like his eyes, as it is today. The sun was mild like a joyous dream. And lying next to him, I had made him the offering of my throbbing soul.

He is not here. He is a flash of lightning playing with other clouds in other skies. He left because he had found his completion. He was a snake that bit me and is gone, but what is this strange restlessness in my belly where he had once moved? Is this the beginning of my completion?

No, it cannot be. This is my undoing, my end. But why are the empty spaces in my body filling up? What debris is being used to feed these gaping holes? What are these strange sensations in my veins? Why do I want my entire being to contract and become one with that tiny presence in my belly? In what vast seas will this sinking paper boat, which is my heart, re-emerge?

In the fires of my body I feel milk being boiled. Who is the expected guest? For whom is my heart pumping blood to weave soft eiderdowns? In my mind are a million silken threads of splendid hues being joined together to fashion tiny clothes.

For whom is my complexion turning gold?

It was this time of the year. The sky was a wash of blue like his eyes, as it is today. But why has the sky come down to form a blue canopy over my belly? Why do I feel the blue of his eyes running wild in my blood?

Why have my rounding breasts acquired the sanctity of marble domes adorning mosques?

No, there is no sanctity in what is happening. I will demolish these domes. I will put out the fires in my body, which are preparing repasts for the uninvited guest. I will tangle up those silken threads of a million hues.

It was this time of the year. The sky was a wash of blue like his eyes, as it is today. But why am I trying to recapture the memory of days which no longer bear his footprints? But what is it that I feel in the depths of my belly? Is it a tiny footprint? Do I know it?

I will obliterate it. It is like a cancer, a carbuncle, a terrible affliction.

But why does it feel like a balm, which soothes? If it is a balm, what wound is it meant to heal? The wound that he left?

No, this is a wound I have carried with me since the day I was born. A wound that was always in my womb, dormant and unseen.

What is my womb? A useless pot of clay, a child's toy, which I will smash into pieces.

But a voice whispers in my ear: this world is a crossroads. Smash not your clay pot in the middle of it. Accusing fingers will be pointed at you.

This world is a crossroads, but he left me in the middle of two roads, both leading to incompletion. And tears.

A tear has slipped into my oyster to produce a pearl. Whom will it adorn?

Accusing fingers will be raised when the oyster opens to reveal its pearl and disgorge it on the crossroads. The fingers will turn into snakes and bite the oyster and the pearl and turn them blue with venom.

The sky was a wash of blue like his eyes, as it is today. Why does it not fall? What pillars are keeping it in place? Will the earthquake that is to come shake the foundations of this immense edifice? Why is the sky like a canopy over my head?

I am drenched in perspiration.

All my pores are open. There is fire blazing everywhere. In my crucible, gold is being melted. Flames are leaping. The gold is seething like molten lava. The blue of his eyes is streaming through my veins. I hear bells ringing. Someone is coming. Board up the doors.

The crucible has been turned over. The molten gold is flowing. The bells are ringing.

It is on its way.

My eyes are heavy with sleep. The blue sky has become soiled. Soon it will come crashing down.

Whose cries are these that I hear? Make them stop. They are like hammer blows on my heart.

Make it stop. Make it stop. Make it stop.

I am a waiting lap. My arms are reaching out to hold it. The milk is boiling on the blazing fires of my body. My rounded breasts have turned into cups. Bring it to me. Lay it gently in my arms.

No, don't snatch it from me. Don't take it away, I beg you in the name of God.

Fingers . . . fingers . . . let them raise their fingers. I no longer care. The world is a crossroads. Let my clay pot be shattered in the middle of it.

My life will be in ruins. So be it. Give me back my flesh. Don't snatch my soul from me. You do not know how precious it is. It is the supreme fruit of those moments in my life when my body made someone whole. Is this the moment of my completion?

Ask the gaping vacuum in my belly, if you don't believe me. Ask my breasts full of milk. Ask the lullabies which are rising from every pore of my body. Ask my arms, which have turned into gentle swings.

Accusing fingers. Let them be raised. I will chop them off and pick them up and stuff my ears with them. I will go dumb. I will go deaf. I will go blind, but this tiny thing which is a part of me will know me and I will know it by running my hands over it.

I beg of you. Don't take it away.

Don't overturn my overflowing cups of milk. Don't set fire to the eiderdown I wove with my blood. Don't sever the swings that are my arms. Don't deprive my ears of the music that are its cries. Don't take it away from me.

Lahore, 21 January: The police have found a newborn baby by the roadside. Its naked body had been wrapped in wet linen with the obvious intention that it should die of cold and exposure. However, the baby was alive and has been taken to hospital. It has pretty blue eyes.

THE WILD CACTUS

The name of the town is unimportant. Let us say it was in the suburbs of the city of Peshawar, not far from the frontier, where that woman lived in a small mud house, half hidden from the dusty, unmetalled, forlorn road by a hedge of wild cactus.

The cactus was quite dry but it had grown with such profusion that it had become like a curtain shielding the house from the gaze of passers-by. It is not clear if it had always been there or whether it was the woman who had planted it.

The house was more like a hut with three small rooms, all kept very spick and span. There wasn't much in it by way of furniture, but what there was was nice. In the back room was a big bed, and beside it an alcove where an earthen lamp burned all night. It was all very orderly.

Let me now tell you about the woman who lived there with her young daughter.

There were various stories. Some people said the young girl was not really her daughter, but an orphan whom she had taken in and raised. Others said she was her illegitimate child, while there were some who believed her to be her real daughter. One does not know the truth.

I forgot to tell you the woman's name, not that it matters. It could be Sakina, Mehtab, Gulshan or something else, but let's call her Sardar for the sake of convenience.

She was in her middle years, and must have been beautiful in her time. Her face had now begun to wrinkle, though she still looked years younger than she was.

Her daughter—if she was her daughter—was extremely beautiful. There was nothing about her to suggest that she was a woman of pleasure, which is what she was. Business was brisk. The girl, whom I will call Nawab, was not unhappy with her life. She had grown up in an atmosphere where no concept of marital relations existed.

When Sardar had brought her her first man in the big bed in the back room, it had seemed to her quite a natural thing to have happened to a girl who had just crossed the threshold of puberty. Since then it had become the pattern of her life and she was happy with it.

And although, according to popular definition, she was a prostitute, she had no knowledge or consciousness of sin. It simply did not exist in her world.

There was a physical sincerity about her. She used to give herself completely, without reservations, to the men who were brought to her. She had come to believe that it was a woman's duty to make love to men, tenderly and without inhibitions.

She knew almost nothing about life as it was lived in the big cities, but through her men she had come to learn something of their city habits, like the brushing of teeth in the morning, drinking a cup of tea in bed and taking a quick bath before dressing up and driving off.

Not all men were alike. Some only wanted to smoke a cigarette in the morning, while others wanted nothing but a hot cup of tea. Some were bad sleepers; others slept soundly and left at the crack of dawn.

Sardar was a woman without a worry in the world. She had faith in the ability of her daughter—or whoever she was—to look after the clients. She generally used to go to bed early herself happily drugged on opium. It was only in emergencies that she was woken up. Often customers had to be revived after they had had too much to drink. Sardar would say philosophically, 'Give him some pickled mango or make him drink a glass of salt water so that he can vomit. Then send him to sleep.'

Sardar was a careful woman. Customers were required to pay in advance. After collecting the money she would say, 'Now you two go and have a good time.'

While the money always stayed in Sardar's custody, presents, when received, were Nawab's. Many of the clients were rich and gifts of cloth, fruit and sweets were frequent.

Nawab was a happy girl. In the little three-bed mud house, life was smooth and predictable. Not long ago, an army officer had brought her a gramophone and some records, which she used to play when alone. She even used to try to sing along, but she had no talent for music, not that she was aware of it. The fact was that she was aware of very little, and not interested in knowing more. She might have been ignorant, but she was happy.

What the world beyond the cactus hedge was like, she had no idea. All she knew was the rough, dusty road and the men who drove up in cars, honked once or twice to announce their arrival and when told by Sardar to park at a more discreet distance, did so, then walked into the house to join Nawab in the big bed.

The regulars numbered not more than five or six, but Sardar had arranged things with such tact that never had two visitors been known to run into each other. Since every customer had his fixed day, no problems were ever encountered.

Sardar was also careful to ensure that Nawab did not become pregnant. It was an ever-present possibility. However, two and a half years had passed without any mishap. The police were unaware of Sardar's establishment and the men were discreet.

One day, a big Dodge drove up to the house. The driver honked once and Sardar stepped out. It was no one she knew, nor did the stranger say who he was. He parked the car and walked in as if he was one of the old regulars.

Sardar was a bit confused, but Nawab greeted the stranger with a smile and took him into the back room. When Sardar followed them in, they were sitting on the bed, next to each other, talking. One look was enough to assure her that the visitor was rich and, apart from that, handsome. 'Who showed you the way?' she asked, nevertheless.

The stranger smiled, then put his arm amorously around Nawab and said, 'This one here.' Nawab sprung up flirtatiously and said, 'Why, I never saw you in my life!' 'But I have,' the stranger answered, grinning.

Surprised, Nawab asked, 'When and where?' The stranger took her hand in his and said, 'You won't understand; ask your mother.' 'Have I met this man before?' Nawab asked Sardar like a child. By now Sardar had come to the conclusion that the tip had come from one of her regulars. 'Don't worry about it. I'll tell you later,' she said to Nawab.

Then she left the room, took some opium and lay on her bed, satisfied. The stranger did not look the kind to make trouble.

His name was Haibat Khan, the biggest landlord in the neighbouring district of Hazara. 'I want no men visiting Nawab in future,' he said to Sardar on his way to his car after a few hours. 'How's that possible, Khan sahib? Can you afford to pay for all of them?' Sardar asked, being the woman of the world she was.

Haibat Khan did not answer her. Instead, he pulled out a lot of money from his pocket and threw it on the floor. He also removed a diamond ring from his finger and slipped it on Nawab. Then he walked out hurriedly, past the cactus hedge.

Nawab did not even look at the money, but she kept gazing at the ring with the big resplendent diamond. She heard the car start and move away, leaving clouds of dust in its wake.

When she returned, Sardar had picked up the money and counted it. There were nineteen hundred rupees in bank notes. One more, and it would have been two thousand, she thought, but it didn't worry her. She put the money away, took some opium and went to bed.

Nawab was thrilled. She just couldn't take her eyes off the diamond ring. A few days passed. In between, an old client came to the house, but Sardar sent him packing, saying she anticipated a police raid and had therefore decided to discontinue business.

Sardar's logic was simple. She knew Haibat Khan was rich and money would keep coming in, as before, with the added advantage that there would be only one man to deal with. In the next few days she was able to get rid of all her old clients, one by one.

A week later, Haibat Khan made his second appearance, but he did not speak to Sardar. The two of them went to the back room, leaving Sardar with her opium and her bed.

Haibat Khan was now a regular visitor. He was totally enamoured of Nawab. He liked her artless approach to love-making, untinged by the hard-baked professionalism common to prostitutes. Nor was there anything housewifely about her. She would lie in bed next to him as a child lies next to its mother, playing with her breasts, sticking his little finger in her nose and then quietly going off to sleep.

It was something entirely new in Haibat Khan's experience. Nawab was different, she was interesting and she gave pleasure. His visits became more frequent.

Sardar was happy. She had never had so much money coming in with such regularity. Nawab, however, sometimes felt troubled. Haibat Khan always seemed to be vaguely apprehensive of something. It showed in little things. A slight shiver always seemed to run through his body when a car or bus went speeding past the house. He would jump out of bed and run out, trying to read the number plate.

One night, a passing bus startled Haibat Khan so much that he suddenly wrested himself free from her arms and sat up. Nawab was a light sleeper and woke up too. He looked terrified. She was frightened. 'What happened?' she screamed.

By now, Haibat Khan had composed himself. 'It was nothing. I think I had a nightmare,' he said. The bus had gone, though it could still be heard in the distance.

Nawab said, 'No, Khan, there is something. Whenever you hear a noise, you get into a state.'

Haibat Khan's vanity was stung. 'Don't talk rubbish,' he said sharply. 'Why should anyone be afraid of cars and buses?'

Nawab began to cry, but Haibat Khan took her in his arms and she stopped sobbing.

He was a handsome man, strong of limb and a passionate lover, who ignited the fires in Nawab's young body every time he touched her. It was really he who had initiated her into the intricacies of love-making. For the first time in her life, she was experiencing the state called love. She used to pine for him when he was gone, and would play her records endlessly.

Many months went by, deepening Nawab's love for Haibat Khan, and also her anxiety. His visits had of late become somewhat erratic. He would come for a few hours, look extremely ill at ease and leave suddenly. It was clear he was under some pressure. He never seemed willing or happy to leave, but he always left.

Nawab tried to get to the truth many times, only to be given evasive answers.

One morning his Dodge drove up to the house, stopping at the usual place. Nawab was asleep but she woke up when she heard him honk the horn. She rushed out and ran into Haibat Khan at the door. He embraced her passionately, picked her up and carried her inside.

They kept talking to each other for a long time about things lovers talk about. For the first time in her life, Nawab said to him, 'Khan, bring me some gold bangles.'

Haibat Khan kissed her fleshy arms many times and said, 'You will have them tomorrow. For you I can even give my life.'

Nawab squirmed coquettishly. 'Oh no Khan, it is poor me who'll have to give her life.'

Haibat Khan kissed her and said, 'I'll return tomorrow with your gold bangles and I'll put them on you myself.'

Nawab was ecstatic. She wanted to dance with joy. Sardar watched her contentedly, then reached for her opium and went to bed.

Nawab rose the next morning, still in a state of high excitement. This is the day he will bring me my gold bangles, she said to herself, but she felt uneasy. That night she couldn't sleep.

She said to her mother, 'Khan hasn't come. He promised and he hasn't come.' Her heart was full of foreboding.

Had he had an accident? Had he been suddenly taken ill? Had he been waylaid? She heard cars passing and thought of Haibat Khan and how these noises used to terrify him.

One week passed. The house behind the cactus hedge continued to remain without visitors. Off and on, a car would go by, leaving clouds of dust behind. In her mind, passing cars and buses were now associated with Haibat Khan. They had something to do with his absence.

One afternoon, while both women were about to take a nap after lunch, they heard a car stop outside. It honked, but it was not Haibat Khan's car. Who was it then?

Sardar went outside to make sure it was not one of the old customers, in which case she would send him on his way. It was Haibat Khan. He sat in the driver's seat but it was not his car. With him was a well-dressed, rather beautiful woman.

Haibat Khan stepped out, followed by the woman. Sardar was confused. What was this woman doing with him? Who was she? Why had he brought her here?

They entered the house without taking any notice of her. She followed them inside after a while and found all three of them sitting next to one another on the bed. There was a strange silence about everything. The woman, who was wearing heavy gold ornaments, appeared to be somewhat nervous.

Sardar stood at the door and when Haibat Khan looked up she greeted him, but he made no acknowledgement. He was in a state of great and visible agitation.

The woman said to Sardar, 'Well, we are here; why don't you get us something to eat?'

'I'll have it ready in no time, whatever you wish,' Sardar replied, suddenly the hostess.

There was something about the woman which suggested authority. 'Go to the kitchen,' she ordered Sardar. 'Get the fire going.

Do you have a big cooking pot?'

'Yes.' Sardar nodded.

'Rinse it well. I'll join you later,' she said. Then she rose from the bed and began examining the gramophone.

Apologetically, Sardar said, 'One cannot buy meat around here.'

'It'll be provided,' the woman said. 'And look, I want a big fire. Now, go and do what you have been told.'

Sardar left. The woman smiled and addressed Nawab, 'Nawab, we have brought you gold bangles.'

She opened her handbag and produced heavy, ornate gold bangles, wrapped in red tissue paper.

Nawab looked at Haibat Khan, who sat next to her, very still. 'Who is this woman, Khan?' she asked in a frightened voice.

Playing with the gold bangles, the woman said, 'Who am I? I am Haibat Khan's sister.' Then she looked at Haibat Khan, who seemed to have suddenly shrunk. 'My name is Halakat,' she said, addressing Nawab.

Nawab could not understand what was going on, but she felt terrified.

The woman moved towards Nawab, took her hands and began to slip the gold bangles on them. Then she said to Haibat Khan, 'I want you to leave the room. Let me dress her up nicely and bring her to you.'

Haibat Khan looked mesmerized. He did not move. 'Leave the room. Didn't you hear me?' she told him sharply.

He left the room, looking at Nawab as he walked out.

The kitchen was outside the house. Sardar had got the fire going. He did not speak to her, but walked past the cactus hedge, out on the road. He looked half-demented.

A bus approached. He had an urge to flag it down, get on board and disappear. But he did no such thing. The bus sped by, coating him with dust. He tried to shout after it, but his voice seemed to have gone.

He wanted to rush back into the house where he had spent so many nights of pleasure, but his feet seemed to be embedded in the ground.

He just stood there, trying to take stock of the situation. The woman who was now in the house, he had known a long time. He used to be a friend of her husband, who was dead. He remembered their first encounter many years ago. He had gone to console her after her husband's death and had ended up being her lover. It was very sudden. She had simply commanded him to take her, as if he was a servant being asked to perform a simple task.

Haibat Khan had not been very experienced with women. When Shahina, who had told Nawab her name was Halakat, or death, had become his lover, he had felt as if he had accomplished something in his life. She was rich in her own right and now had her husband's money. However, he was not interested in that. She was the first real woman in his life and he had let her seduce him.

For a long time he stood on the road. Finally, he went back to the house. The front door was closed and Sardar was cooking something in the kitchen.

He knocked and it was opened. All he could see was blood on the floor and Shahina leaning against the wall. 'I have dressed up your Nawab for you very nicely,' she said.

'Where is she?' he asked, his throat dry with terror.

'Some of her is on the bed, but most of her is in the kitchen,' she replied.

Haibat Khan began to tremble. He could now see that there was blood on the floor and a long knife. There was someone on the bed, covered with a bloodstained sheet.

Shahina smiled. 'Do you want me to lift the sheet and show you what I have there? It is your Nawab. I have made her up with great care. But perhaps you should eat first. You must be hungry. Sardar is cooking the most delicious meat in the world. I prepared it myself.'

'What have you done?' Haibat Khan screamed.

Shahina smiled again. 'Darling, this is not the first time. My husband, like you, was also faithless. I had to kill him and then throw his severed limbs for wild birds to feast on. Since I love you, instead of you, I have . . .'

She did not complete the sentence, but removed the sheet from the heap on the bed. Haibat Khan fainted and fell to the floor.

When he came to, he was in a car. Shahina was driving. They seemed to be in a wild country.

IT HAPPENED IN 1919

'It happened in 1919. The whole of Punjab was up in arms against the Rowlatt Act. Sir Michael O'Dwyer had banned Gandhiji's entry into the province under the Defence of India rules. He had been stopped at Pulwal, taken into custody and sent to Bombay. I believe if the British had not made this blunder, the Jallianwala Bagh incident would not have added a bloody page to the black history of their rule in India.'

I was on a train and the man sitting next to me had begun talking to me, just like that. I hadn't interrupted him and so he had gone on.

'Gandhiji was loved and respected by the people, Muslims, Hindus and Sikhs alike. When news of the arrest reached Lahore, the entire city went on strike. Amritsar, where the story I am going to narrate happened, followed suit.

'It is said that by the evening of 9 April, the deputy commissioner had received orders for the expulsion from Amritsar of the two leaders, Dr Satyapal and Dr Kitchlew, but was unwilling to implement them because, in his view, there was no likelihood of a breach of the peace. Protest meetings were being organized and no one was in favour of using violent methods.

'I was a witness to a procession taken out to celebrate a Hindu festival, and I can assure you it was the most peaceful thing I ever saw. It faithfully kept to the route marked out by the officials, but this Sir Michael was half-mad. They said he refused to follow the deputy commissioner's advice because he was convinced that Kitchlew and Satyapal were in Amritsar waiting for a signal from Gandhiji before proceeding to topple the government. In his view the protest meetings and processions were all part of this grand conspiracy.

'The news of the expulsion of the two leaders spread like wildfire through the city, creating an atmosphere of uncertainty and fear. One could sense that disaster was about to strike. But, my friend, I can tell you that there was also a great deal of enthusiasm among the people. All businesses were closed. The city was quiet like a graveyard and there was a feeling of impending doom in the air.

'After the first shock of the expulsions had died down, thousands of people gathered spontaneously to go in a procession to the deputy commissioner and call for the withdrawal of the orders. But, my friend, believe me, the times were out of joint. That this extremely reasonable request would be even heard was out of the question. Sir Michael was like a pharaoh and we were not surprised when he declared the gathering itself unlawful.

'Amritsar, which was one of the greatest centres of the liberation struggle and which still proudly carries the wound of Jallianwala Bagh, is now of course changed . . . but that is another story. Some people say that what happened in that great city in 1947 was also the fault of the British. But if you want my opinion, we ourselves are responsible for the bloodshed there in 1947. Anyway.

'The deputy commissioner's house was in the Civil Lines. In fact, all senior officers and the big toadies of the Raj lived in that exclusive area. If you know your Amritsar, you will recall that bridge which links the city with the Civil Lines. You cross the bridge from the city and you are on the Mall, that paradise on earth created by the British rulers.

'The protest procession began to move towards the Civil Lines. When I reached Hall Gate, word went round that British mounted troops were on guard at the bridge, but the crowd was undeterred and kept moving. I was also among them. We were all unarmed. I mean there wasn't even a stick on any of us. The whole idea was to get to the deputy commissioner's house and protest to him about the expulsion of the two leaders and demand their release. All peacefully.

'When the crowd reached the bridge, the tommies opened fire, causing utter pandemonium. People began to run in all directions. There were no more than twenty to twenty-five soldiers, but they were armed and they were firing. I have never seen anything like it. Some were wounded by gunshot; others were trampled.

'I stood well away from the fray at the edge of a big open gutter and someone pushed me into it. When the firing stopped, I crawled out. The crowd had dispersed. Many of the injured were lying on the road and the tommies on the bridge were having a good laugh. I'm not sure what my state of mind at the time was, but I think it couldn't have been normal. In fact, I think I fainted when I fell in. It was only later that I was able to reconstruct the events.

'I could hear angry slogans being chanted in the distance. I began to walk. Going past the shrine of Zahra Pir, I was in Hall Gate in no time, where I found about thirty or forty boys throwing stones at the big clock which sits on top of the gate. They finally shattered its protective glass and the pieces fell on the road.

'"Let's go and smash the queen's statue," someone shouted.

'"No, let's set fire to the police headquarters."

'"And all the banks too."

'"What would be the point of that? Let's go to the bridge and fight the tommy soldiers," suggested another.

'I recognized the author of the last proposal. He was Thaila kanjar—kanjar, because he was the son of a prostitute—otherwise Mohammad Tufail. He was quite notorious in Amritsar. He had got into the habit of drinking and gambling while still a boy. He had two sisters, Shamshad and Almas, who were considered the city's most beautiful singing and dancing girls.

'Shamshad was an accomplished singer and big landlords and the like used to travel from great distances to hear her perform. The sisters were not exactly enamoured of the doings of their brother, Thaila, and it was said that they had practically disowned him. However, through one excuse or the other, he was always able to get enough money from them to live in style. He liked to dress and eat well and drink to his heart's content. He was a great storyteller, but unlike other people of his type he was never vulgar. He was tall, athletic and quite handsome, come to think of it.

'However, the boys did not show much enthusiasm for his suggestion of taking on the tommies. Instead, they began to move towards the queen's statue. Thaila was not the kind to give up so easily. He said to them, "Why are you wasting your energy? Why don't you follow me? We'll go and kill those tommies who have shot and killed so many innocent people. I swear by God, if we're together, we can wring their necks with our bare hands."

'Some were already well on their way to the queen's statue, but there were still some stragglers who began to follow Thaila in the direction of the bridge where the tommies stood guard. I thought the whole thing was suicidal and I had no desire to be part of it. I even shouted at Thaila, "Don't do it, yaar, why are you bent upon getting yourself killed?"

'He laughed. "Thaila just wants to demonstrate that he's not afraid of their bullets," he said cavalierly. Then he told the few who were willing to follow him, "Those among you who are afraid can leave now."

'No one left, which is understandable in such situations. Thaila started to walk briskly, setting the pace for his companions. There seemed to be no question of turning back now.

'The distance between Hall Gate and the bridge is negligible, maybe less than a hundred yards. The approach to the bridge was being guarded by two mounted tommies. I heard the sound of fire as Thaila closed in, shouting revolutionary slogans. I thought he'd been hit, but no, he was still moving forward with great resolution. Some of the boys began to run in different directions. He turned and shouted, "Don't run away . . . Let's go get them."

'I heard more gunfire. Thaila's back was momentarily towards the tommies, since he was trying to infuse some life into his retreating entourage. I saw him veer towards the soldiers and there were big red spots of blood on his silk shirt. He had been hit, but he kept advancing, like a wounded lion. There was more gunfire and he staggered, but then he regained his foothold and leapt at the mounted tommy, bringing him down to the ground.

'The other tommy became panic-stricken and began to fire his revolver recklessly. What happened afterwards is not clear, because I fainted.

'When I came to, I found myself home. Some men who knew me had picked me up and brought me back. I heard from them that angry crowds had ransacked the town. The queen's statue had been smashed and the town hall and three of the city bands had been set on fire. Five or six Europeans had been killed and the crowd had gone on a rampage.

'The British officers were not bothered about damage to property, but the fact that European blood had been shed. And as you know, it was avenged at Jallianwala Bagh. The deputy commissioner handed the city over to General Dyer, so on 12 April the general marched through the streets at the head of columns of armed soldiers. Dozens of innocent people were arrested. On 13 April a protest meeting was organized in Jallianwala Bagh which General Dyer "dispersed" by ordering his Gurkha and Sikh soldiers to open fire on the unarmed crowed.

'However, I was telling you about Thaila and what I saw with my own eyes. Only God is without blemish and Thaila was, let's not forget, the son of a prostitute and he used to practise every evil in the book. But he was brave. I tell you he had already been hit when he exhorted his companions not to run away but to move forward. He was so intoxicated with enthusiasm at the time that he did not realize he had been hit. He was shot twice more, once in the back and then in the chest. They pumped his young body full of molten lead.

'I didn't see it, but I'm told that when Thaila's bullet-ridden body was pulled away both his hands were dug into the tommy's throat. They just couldn't get his grip to loosen. The tommy had of course been well and truly dispatched to hell.

'Thaila's bullet-torn body was handed over to his family the next day. It seemed the other tommy had emptied the entire magazine of his revolver into him. He must have been dead by then, but the devil had nevertheless gone on.

'It is said that when Thaila's body was brought to his mohalla it was a shattering scene. It's true he wasn't exactly the apple of his family's eye, but when they saw his minced-up remains, there wasn't a dry eye to be seen anywhere. His sisters, Shamshad and Almas, fainted.

'My friend, I have heard that in the French Revolution, it was a prostitute who was the first to fall. Mohammad Tufail was also a prostitute's son, so whether it was the first bullet of the revolution which hit him or the tenth or the fiftieth, nobody really bothered to find out because socially he did not matter. I have a feeling that when they finally make a list of those who died in this bloodbath in Punjab, Thaila kanjar's name won't be included. As a matter of fact, I don't think anyone would even bother about a list.

'Those were terrible days. The monster they call martial law held the city in its grip. Thaila was buried amid great hurry and confusion, as if his death was a grave crime which his family should obliterate from the record. What can I say except that Thaila died and Thaila was buried.'

My companion stopped speaking. The train was moving at breakneck speed. Suddenly I felt as if the clickety-clack of its powerful wheels was intoning the words 'Thaila died, Thaila buried . . . Thaila died, Thaila buried . . . Thaila died, Thaila buried.' There was no dividing line between his death and his burial. He had died and in the next instant he had been buried. 'You were going to say something,' I said to my companion.

'Yes,' he replied, 'yes . . . there is a sad part of the story which I haven't yet come to.'

'And what's that?'

'As I have already told you, he had two sisters, Shamshad and Almas, both very beautiful. Shamshad was tall, with fine features, big eyes, and she was a superb thumri singer. They say she had taken music lessons from the great Khan Sahib Fateh Ali Khan. Almas, the other one, was unmusical, but she was a fantastic dancer. When she danced it seemed as if every cell of her body was undulating with the music. Oh! They say there was a magic in her eyes which nobody could resist . . .

'Well, my friend, it is said that someone who was trying to make his number with the British told them about Thaila's sisters and how beautiful and gifted they were. So it was decided that to avenge the death of that Englishwoman . . . what was the name of that witch? Miss Sherwood I think . . . the two girls should be summoned for an evening of pleasure. You know what I mean.'

'Yes.'

'These are delicate matters, but I would say that when it comes to something like this, even dancing girls and prostitutes are like our sisters and mothers. But I tell you, our people have no concept of national honour. So, you can guess what happened.

'The police received orders from the powers that be and an inspector personally went to the house of the girls and said that the sahib log had expressed a desire to be entertained by them.

'And to think that the earth on the grave of their brother was still fresh. He hadn't even been dead two days and there were these orders: come and dance in our imperial presence. No greater torture could have been devised! Do you think that it even occurred to those who issued these orders that even women like Shamshad and Almas could have a sense of honour? What do you think?'

But he was speaking more to himself than to me. Nevertheless, I ventured, 'Yes, surely they too have a sense of honour.'

'Quite right. After all, Thaila was their brother. He hadn't lost his life in a gambling brawl or a fit of drunkenness. He had volunteered to drink the cup of martyrdom like a valiant national hero.

'Yes, it's true he was born of a prostitute, but a prostitute is also a mother and Shamshad and Almas were his sisters first and dancing girls later. They had fainted when they had brought Thaila's bullet-ridden body home, and it was heart-breaking to hear them bewail the martyrdom of their brother.'

'Did they go?' I asked.

My companion answered after a pause, 'Yes, yes, they went all right. They were dressed to kill.' There was a note of bitterness in his voice.

'They went to their hosts of the evening and they looked stunning. They say it was quite an orgy. The two sisters displayed their art with fascinating skill. In their silks and brocades they looked like Caucasian fairy queens. There was much drinking and merrymaking and they danced and sang all night.

'And it is said that at two in the morning the guest of honour indicated that the party was over.'

'The party was over, the party was over' the wheels intoned as the train ran headlong along the tracks. I cleared my mind of this intrusion and asked my companion, 'What happened then?'

Taking his eyes away from the passing phantasmagoria of trees and power lines, he said in a determined voice, 'They tore off their silks and brocades and stood there naked and they said . . . look at us . . . we are Thaila's sisters . . . that martyr whose beautiful body you peppered with your bullets because inside that body dwelt a spirit which was in love with this land . . . yes, we are his beautiful sisters . . . come, burn our fragrant bodies with the red-hot irons of your lust . . . but before you do that, allow us to spit in your faces once.' He fell silent as if he did not wish to say any more.

'What happened then?'

Tears welled up in his eyes. 'They . . . they were shot dead.'

I did not say anything. The train stopped. He sent for a porter and asked him to pick up his bags. As he was about to leave, I said to him, 'I have a feeling that the story you have just told me has a false ending.'

He was startled. 'How do you know?'

'Because there was indescribable agony in your voice when you reached the end.'

He swallowed. 'Yes, those bitches . . .' he paused, 'they dishonoured their martyred brother's name.'

He stepped on the platform and was gone.

THE PRICE OF FREEDOM

The year I do not remember, but there was great revolutionary fervour in Amritsar. 'Inqilab Zindabad'—long live revolution—was the slogan of the day. There was excitement in the air and a feeling of restlessness and youthful abandon. We were living through heady times. Even the fearful memories of the Jallianwala Bagh massacre had disappeared, at least on the surface. One felt intensely alive and on the threshold of something great and final.

People marched through the streets every day raising slogans against the Raj. Hundreds were arrested for breaking the law. In fact, courting arrest had become something of a popular diversion. You were picked up in the morning and quite often released by the evening. A case would be registered, a hearing held and a short sentence awarded. You came out, raised a few more slogans and were put in gaol again.

There was so much to live for in those days. The slightest incident sometimes led to the most violent upheaval. One man would stand on a podium in one of the city squares and call for a strike. A strike would follow. There was of course the movement to wear only Indian-spun cotton with the object of putting the Lancashire textile mills out of business. There was a boycott of all imported cloth in effect. Every street had its own bonfire. People would walk up, take off every imported piece of clothing they were wearing and chuck it into the fire. Sometimes a woman would stand on her balcony and throw down her imported silk sari into the bonfire. The crowd would cheer.

I remember this huge bonfire the boys had lit in front of the town hall and the police headquarters, where in a wild moment my classmate Sheikhoo had taken off his silk jacket and thrown it into the flames. A big cheer had gone up because it was well known that he was the son of one of the richest men of the city, who also had the dubious distinction of being the most infamous 'toady', as government sympathizers were popularly called. Inspired by the applause, Sheikhoo had also taken off his silk shirt and sent it the way of his jacket. It was only later that he remembered the gold cufflinks that had gone with it.

I don't want to make fun of my friend, because in those days I too was in the same turbulent frame of mind. I used to dream about getting hold of guns and setting up a secret terrorist organization. That my father was a government servant did not bother me. I was restless and did not even understand what I was restless about.

I was never much interested in school, but during those days I had completely gone off my books. I would spend the entire day at Jallianwala Bagh. Sitting under a tree, I would watch the windows of the houses bordering the park and dream about the girls who lived behind them. I was sure one of these days one of them would fall in love with me.

Jallianwala Bagh had become the hub of the movement of civil disobedience launched by the Congress. There were small and big tents and colourful awnings everywhere. The largest tent was the political headquarters of the city. Once or twice a week, a 'dictator'—for that was what he was called—would be nominated by the people to 'lead the struggle'. He would be ceremoniously placed in the large tent; volunteers would provide him with a ragtag guard of honour, and for the next few days he would receive delegations of young political workers, all wearing homespun cotton. It was also the 'dictator's' duty to get donations of food and money from the city's big shopkeepers and businessmen. And so it would continue until one day the police came and picked him up.

I had a friend called Ghulam Ali. Our intimacy can be judged from the fact that both of us had failed our school leaving examination twice in a row. Once we had run away from home and were on our way to Bombay—from where we planned to sail for the Soviet Union—when our money ran out. After sleeping for a few nights on footpaths, we had written to our parents and promised not to do such a thing again. We were reprieved.

Shahzada Ghulam Ali, as he later came to be called, was a handsome young man, tall and fair as Kashmiris tend to be. He always walked with a certain swagger that one generally associates with 'tough guys'. Actually, he was no Shahzada—which means prince—when we were at school. However, after having become active in the civil disobedience movement and run the gamut of revolutionary speeches, public processions, social intercourse with pretty female volunteer workers, garlands, slogans and patriotic songs, he had for some reason come to be known as Shahzada.

His fame spread like wildfire in the city of Amritsar. It was a small place where it did not take you long to become famous or infamous. The natives of Amritsar, though by nature critical of the general run of humanity, were rather indulgent when it came to religious and political leaders. They always seemed to have this peculiar need for fiery sermons and revolutionary speeches. Leaders had always had a long tenure in our city. The times were advantageous because the established leadership was in gaol and there were quite a few empty chairs waiting to be occupied. The movement needed people like Ghulam Ali who would be seen for a few days in Jallianwala Bagh, make a speech or two and then duly get arrested.

In those days, the German and Italian dictatorships were the new thing in Europe, which is what had perhaps inspired the Indian National Congress to designate certain party workers as 'dictators'. When Shahzada Ghulam Ali's turn came to go to gaol, as many as forty 'dictators' had already been put inside.

When I learnt that Ghulam Ali had been named the current 'dictator', I made my way to Jallianwala Bagh. There were volunteers outside the big tent. However, since Ghulam Ali had seen me, I was permitted to go in. A white cotton carpet had been laid on the ground and there sat Ghulam Ali, propped up against cushions. He was talking to a group of cotton-clad city shopkeepers about the vegetable trade, I think. After having got rid of them he issued a few instructions to his volunteers and turned to me. He looked too serious, which I thought was funny. When we were alone, I asked him, 'And how is our prince?'

I also realized that he had changed. To my attempt at treating the whole thing as a farce, he said, 'No, Saadat, don't make fun of it. The great honour which has been bestowed on me, I do not deserve. But from now on the movement is going to be my life.'

I promised to return in the evening as he told me that he would be making a speech. When I arrived, there was a large crowd of people around a podium they had set up for the occasion. Then I heard loud applause and there was Shahzada Ghulam Ali. He looked very handsome in his spotless white and his swagger seemed to add to his appeal.

He spoke for an hour or so. It was an emotional speech. Even I was overcome. There were moments when I wished nothing more than to turn into a human bomb and explode for the glory of the freedom of India.

This happened many years ago and memory always plays tricks with detail, but as I write this I can see Ghulam Ali addressing that turbulent crowd. It was not politics I was conscious of while he spoke, but youth and the promise of revolution. He had the sincere recklessness of a young man who might stop a woman on the street and say to her without any preliminaries, 'Look, I love you.'

Such were the times. I think both the British Raj and the people it ruled were still inexperienced and quite unaware of the consequences of their actions. The government, without really fully comprehending the implications, was putting people in gaol by the thousands, and those who were going to gaol were not quite sure what they were doing and what the results would be.

There was much disorder. I think you could liken the general atmosphere to a spreading fire which leaps out into the air and then just as suddenly goes out, only to ignite again. These sudden eruptions that died just as suddenly, only to burst into flame once again, had created much heat and agitation in the lacklustre, melancholy state of slavery.

As Shahzada Ghulam Ali finished speaking, the entire Jallianwala Bagh came to its feet. I stepped forward to congratulate him, but his eyes were elsewhere. My curiosity was soon satisfied. It was a girl in a white cotton sari, standing behind a flowering bush.

The next day I learnt that Shahzada Ghulam Ali was in love with the girl I had seen the previous evening. And so was she with him, and just as much. She was a Muslim, an orphan, who worked as a nurse at the local women's hospital. I think she was the first Muslim girl in Amritsar to join the Congress movement against the Raj.

Her white cotton saris, her association with the Congress and the fact that she worked in a hospital had all combined to soften that slight stiffness one finds in Muslim girls. She was not beautiful, but she was very feminine. She had acquired that hard-to-describe quality so characteristic of Hindu girls—a mixture of humility, self-assurance and the urge to worship. In her, the beauty of ritualistic Muslim prayer and Hindu devotion to temple gods had been alchemized.

She worshipped Shahzada Ghulam Ali and he loved her to distraction. They had met during a protest march and fallen for each other almost immediately.

Ghulam Ali wanted to marry Nigar before his inevitable and almost eagerly awaited arrest. Why he wanted to do that I am unable to say as he could just as well have married her after his release. Gaol terms in those days varied between three months and a year. There were some who were let out after ten or fifteen days in order to make way for fresh entrants.

All that was really needed was the blessing of Babaji.

Babaji was one of the great figures of the time. He was camped at the splendid house of the richest jeweller in the city, Hari Ram. Normally, Babaji used to live in his village ashram, but whenever he came to Amritsar he would put up with Hari Ram, and the palatial residence, located outside the city, would turn into a sort of shrine, since the number of Babaji's followers was legion. You could see them standing in line, waiting to be admitted briefly to the great man's presence for what was called darshan, or a mere look at him. The old man would receive them sitting cross-legged on a specially constructed platform in a grove of mango trees, accepting donations and gifts for his ashram. In the evening, he would have young women volunteers sing him Hindu devotional songs.

Babaji was known for his piety and scholarship, and his followers included men and women of every faith—Hindus, Muslims, Sikhs and untouchables.

Although on the face of it Babaji had nothing to do with politics, it was an open secret that no political movement in the Punjab could begin or end without his clearance. To the government machinery, he was an unsolved puzzle. There was always a smile on his face, which could be interpreted in a thousand ways.

The civil disobedience movement in Amritsar with its daily arrests and processions was quite clearly being conducted with Babaji's blessing, if not his direct guidance. He was in the habit of dropping hints about the tactics to be followed and the next day every major political leader in the Punjab would be wearing Babaji's wisdom as a kind of amulet around his neck.

There was a magnetic quality about him and his voice was soft, persuasive and full of nuances. Not even the most trenchant criticism could ruffle his composure. To his enemies he was an enigma because he always kept them guessing.

Babaji was a frequent visitor to Amritsar, but somehow I had never seen him. Therefore, when Ghulam Ali told me one day that he planned to call on the great man to obtain his blessing for his intended marriage to Nigar, I asked him to take me along. The next day, Ghulam Ali arranged for a tonga, and the three of us—Ghulam Ali, Nigar and I—found ourselves at Hari Ram's magnificent house.

Babaji had already had his ritualistic morning bath—ashnan—and his devotions were done. He now sat in the mango grove listening to a stirring patriotic song, courtesy of a young, beautiful Kashmiri Pandit girl. He sat cross-legged on a mat made from date-palm leaves, and though there were plenty of cushions around, he did not seem to want any. He was in his seventies but his skin was without blemish. I wondered if it was the result of his famous olive oil massage every morning.

He smiled at Ghulam Ali and asked us to join him on the floor. It was obvious to me that Ghulam Ali and Nigar were less interested in the revolutionary refrain of the song, which seemed to have Babaji in a kind of trance, than their own symphony of young love. At last the girl finished, winning in the bargain Babaji's affectionate approval, indicated with a subtle nod of his head, and he turned to us.

Ghulam Ali was about to introduce Nigar and himself, but he never got an opportunity, thanks to Babaji's exceptional memory for names and faces. In his low, soothing voice he inquired, 'Prince, so you have not yet been arrested?'

'No sir,' Ghulam Ali replied, his hands folded as a mark of respect.

Playing with a pencil, which he had pulled out from somewhere, Babaji said, 'But I think you have already been arrested.' He looked meaningfully at Nigar. 'She has already arrested our prince.'

Babaji's next remark was addressed to the girl who had earlier been singing. 'These children have come to seek my blessing. Tell me, when are you going to get married, Kamal?'

Her pink face turned even pinker. 'But how can I? I am already at the ashram.'

Babaji sighed, turned to Ghulam Ali and said, 'So you two have made up your minds.'

'Yes,' they answered together. Babaji smiled.

'Decisions can sometimes be changed,' he said.

And despite the reverence-laden atmosphere, Ghulam Ali answered, 'This decision can be put off, but it can never be changed.'

Babaji closed his eyes and asked in a lawyer's voice, 'Why?'

Ghulam Ali did not hesitate. 'Because we are committed to it as we are committed to the freedom of India, and while circumstances may change the timing of that event, it is final and immutable.'

Babaji smiled. 'Nigar,' he said, 'why don't you join our ashram because Shahzada is going to gaol in a few days anyway?'

'I will,' she whispered.

Babaji changed the subject and began to ask us about political activities in Jallianwala Bagh. For the next hour or so, the conversation revolved around arrests, processions and even the price of vegetables. I did not join in these pleasantries, but I did wonder why Babaji had been so reluctant to accord his blessing to the young couple. Was he not quite sure that they were in love? Why had he asked Nigar to join the ashram? Was it to help her not to think of Ghulam Ali being in gaol, or did it mean that if she joined the ashram she would not be allowed to marry?

And what was going to happen to Nigar once she was admitted to the rarefied surroundings of the ashram? Would she spend her time intoning devotional and patriotic songs for the spiritual and political enlightenment of Babaji? Would she be happy? I had seen many ashram inmates in my time. There was something lifeless and pallid about them, despite their early morning cold baths and long walks. With their pale faces and sunken eyes, they somehow always reminded me of cows' udders. I couldn't see Nigar living among them, she who was so young and fresh, made up entirely, it seemed to me, of honey, milk and saffron. What had ashrams got to do with India's freedom?

I had always hated ashrams, seminaries, saints' shrines and orphanages. There was something unnatural about these places. I had often seen young boys walking in single file on the street, led by men who administered these institutions. I had visited religious seminaries and schools with their pious inmates. The older ones always wore long beards and the adolescents walked around with sparse, ugly hair sprouting out of their chins. Despite their five prayers a day, their faces never showed any trace of that inner light prayer is supposed to bring about.

Nigar was a woman, not a Muslim, Hindu, Sikh or Christian, but a woman. I simply could not see her praying like a machine every morning at the ashram. Why should she, who was herself pure as a prayer, raise her hands to heaven?

When we were about to leave, Babaji told Ghulam Ali and Nigar that they had his blessing and he would perform the marriage the next day in (where else?) Jallianwala Bagh. He arrived as promised. He was accompanied by his usual entourage of volunteers, with Hari Ram the jeweller in tow. A much-bedecked podium had been put up for the ceremony. The girls had taken charge of Nigar and she made a lovely bride. Ghulam Ali had made no special arrangements. All day long, he had been doing his usual chores, raising donations for the movement and the like. Both of them had decided to hoist the Congress flag after it was all over.

Just before Babaji's arrival, I had been telling Ghulam Ali that we must never forget what had happened in Jallianwala Bagh a few years earlier, in 1919 to be exact. There was a well in the park, which people say was full of dead bodies after General Dyer had ordered his soldiers to stop firing at the crowd. Today, I had told him, the well was used for drinking water, which was still sweet. It bore no trace of the blood which had been spilt so wantonly by the British general and his Gurkha soldiers. The flowers still bloomed and were just as beautiful as they had been on that day.

I had pointed out to Ghulam Ali a house which overlooked the park. It was said that a young girl, who was standing at her window watching the massacre, had been shot through the heart. Her blood had left a mark on the wall below. If you looked carefully, you could still perhaps see it. I remember that six months after the massacre, our teacher had taken the entire class to Jallianwala Bagh and, picking up a piece of earth from the ground, had said to us, 'Children, never forget that the blood of our martyrs is part of this earth.'

Babaji was given a military-style salute by the volunteers. He and Ghulam Ali were taken around the camp, and as the evening was falling the girls began to sing a devotional song and Babaji sat there listening to it with his eyes closed.

The song ended, and Babaji opened his eyes and said, 'Children, I am here to join these two freedom lovers in holy wedlock.' A cheer went up from the crowd. Nigar was in a sari, which bore the three colours of the flag of the Indian National Congress—saffron, green and white. The ceremony was a combination of Hindu and Muslim rituals.

Then Babaji stood up and began to speak. 'These two children will now be able to serve the nation with even greater enthusiasm.

The true purpose of marriage is comradeship. What is being sanctified today will serve the cause of India's freedom. A true marriage should be free of lust and those who are able to exorcize this evil from their lives deserve our respect.'

Babaji spoke for a long time about his concept of marriage. According to him, the true bliss of marriage could only be experienced if the relationship between man and wife was something more than the physical enjoyment of each other's bodies. He did not think the sexual link was as important as it was made out to be. It was like eating. There were those who ate out of indulgence and there were those who ate to stay alive. The sanctity of marriage was more important than the gratification of the sexual instinct.

Ghulam Ali was listening to Babaji's rambling speech as if in a trance. He whispered something to Nigar as soon as Babaji had finished. Then, standing up on the podium, he said in a voice trembling with emotion, 'I have a declaration to make. As long as India does not win freedom, Nigar and I will live not as husband and wife but as friends.' He looked at his wife. 'Nigar, would you like to mother a child who would be a slave at the moment of his birth? No, you wouldn't.'

Ghulam Ali then began to ramble, going from subject to subject, but basically confining his emotional remarks to the freedom of India from the British Raj. At one point, he looked at Nigar and stopped speaking. To me he looked like a drunken man who realizes too late that he has no money left in his wallet. But he recovered his composure and said to Babaji, 'Both of us need your blessing. You have our solemn word of honour that the vow made today shall be kept.'

The next morning Ghulam Ali was taken in because he had threatened to overthrow the Raj and had declared publicly that he would father no children as long as India was ruled by a foreign power. He was given eight months and sent to the distant Multan gaol. He was Amritsar's fortieth 'dictator' to be gaoled and the forty thousandth prisoner of the civil disobedience movement against the Raj.

At that time most of us were convinced that the ousting of the British from India was a matter of days away. However, the Raj was cleverer than we were prepared to give it credit for. It let the movement come to a boil, then made a deal with the leaders, and everything simmered down.

When the workers began to come out of gaol, they realized that the atmosphere had changed. Wisely, most of them decided to resume their normal, humdrum lives. Shahzada Ghulam Ali was let out after seven months, and while it is true the old popular enthusiasm had gone, he was received by a large crowd at the Amritsar railway station from where he was taken out in a procession through the city. A number of public meetings were also held in his honour, but it was evident that the fire and passion had died out. There was a sense of fatigue among the people. It was as if they were runners in a marathon who had been told by the organizers to stop running, return to the starting point, and begin again.

Years went by, but that heady feeling never returned. In my own life, a number of small and big revolutions came and went. I joined college, but failed my exams twice. My father died and I had to run from pillar to post looking for a job. I finally found a translator's position with a third-class newspaper, but I soon became restless and left. For a time, I joined the Aligarh Muslim University, but fell ill and was sent to the more salubrious climate of Kashmir to recover. After three months there, I moved to Bombay. Disgusted with its frequent Hindu–Muslim riots, I made my way to Delhi, but found it too slow and dull and returned to Bombay, despite its impersonal inhabitants who seemed to have no time for strangers.

It was now eight years since I had left Amritsar. I had no idea what had happened to my old friend or the streets and squares of my early youth. I had never written to anyone and the fact was that I was not interested in the past or the future. I was living in the present. The past, it seemed to me, was like a sum of money you had already spent, and to think about it was like drawing up a ledger account of money you no longer had.

One afternoon—I had both time and some money—I decided to go looking for a pair of shoes. Once, while passing by the Army & Navy Store, I had noticed a small shop, which had a very attractive display window. I didn't find that shop, but I noticed another, which looked quite reasonable.

'Show me a pair of shoes with rubber soles,' I told the shop assistant.

'We don't stock them,' he replied.

Since the monsoons were expected any time, I asked him if he could sell me rubber ankle-boots.

'We don't stock those either,' he said. 'Why don't you try the store at the corner? We don't carry rubber or part-rubber footwear at all.'

'Why?' I asked, surprised.

'It's the boss's orders,' he answered.

As I stepped out of this strange place which did not sell rubber shoes, I saw a man carrying a small child. He was trying to buy oranges from a vendor.

'Ghulam Ali,' I screamed excitedly.

'Saadat,' he shouted, embracing me. The child didn't like it and began to cry. He went into the shop and told the assistant with whom I had just been talking to take the child home.

'It's been years, hasn't it?' he said.

He had changed. He was no longer the cotton-clad revolutionary who used to make fiery speeches in Jallianwala Bagh. He looked like a normal, homely man.

My mind went back to his last speech. 'Nigar, would you like to mother a child who would be a slave at birth?'

'Whose child was that?' I asked.

'Mine. I have another one who is older. How many children do you have?' he answered without hesitation.

What had happened? Had he forgotten the vow he had taken that day? Was politics no longer a part of his life? What had happened to his passion for the freedom of India? Where was that firebrand revolutionary I used to know? What had happened to Nigar? What had induced her to beget slave children? Had Ghulam Ali married a second time?

'Let us talk,' he said. 'We haven't seen each other for ages.'

I didn't know where to begin, but he didn't put me to the test.

'This shop belongs to me. I've been living in Bombay for the last two years. I'm told you are a big-time story writer now. Do you remember the old days? How we ran away from home to come to Bombay? God, how time flies!'

We went into the shop. A customer who wanted a pair of tennis shoes was told that he would have to go to the shop at the corner.

'Why don't you stock them? You know I also came here looking for a pair,' I asked.

Ghulam Ali's face fell. 'Let's say I just don't like those things,' he replied.

'What things?'

'Those horrible rubber things. But I'll tell you why,' he said.

The anxious look, which had clouded his handsome face suddenly, cleared. 'That life was rubbish. Believe me, Saadat, I have forgotten about those days when the demon of politics was in my head. I'm very happy. I have a wife and two children and my business is doing well.'

He took me to a room at the back of the store. The assistant had come back. Then he began to talk. I will let him tell his story.

'You know how my political life began. You also know what sort of person I was. I mean we grew up together and we were no angels. I wasn't a strong person and yet I wanted to accomplish something in my life. I swear upon God that I was prepared then, as I am prepared today, to sacrifice even my life for the freedom of India. However, after much reflection, I've come to the conclusion that both the politics of India and its political leadership are immature. There are sudden storms and then all is quiet. There is no spontaneity.

'Look, man may be good or evil, but he should remain the way God made him. You can be virtuous without having your head shaved, without donning saffron robes or covering yourself with ash. Those who advocate such things forget that these external manifestations of virtue, if that be indeed what they are, will only get lost on those who follow them. Only ritual will survive, what led to the ritual will be overlooked. Look at all the great prophets. Their teachings are no longer remembered, but we still have their legacy of crosses, holy threads and unshaven armpit hair. They tell you to kill your baser self. Well, if everyone went ahead and did it, what sort of a world would it be?

'You have no idea what hell I went through because I decided to violate human nature. I made a pledge that I would not produce children. It was made in a moment of euphoria. As time passed, I began to feel that the most vital part of my being was paralysed. What was more, it was my own doing. There were moments when I felt proud of my great vow, but they passed. As the pores of my consciousness began to open, reality seemed to want to defeat my resolve. When I met Nigar after my release, I felt that she had changed. We lived together for one year and we kept our promise to Babaji. It was hell. We were being consumed by the futility of our married life.

'The world outside had changed too. Spun cotton, tricolour flags and revolutionary slogans had lost their power. The tents had disappeared from Jallianwala Bagh. There were only holes in the ground where those grand gatherings used to take place. Politics no longer sent the blood cruising through my veins as it used to.

'I spent most of my time at home and we never spoke our minds to each other. I was afraid of touching her. I did not trust myself. One day, as we sat next to each other, I had a mad urge to take her in my arms and kiss her. I let myself go, but I stopped just in time. It was a tremendous feeling while it lasted. However, in the days that followed, I couldn't get rid of a feeling of guilt.

'There had to be a way out of this absurd situation. One day we hit upon a compromise. We would not produce children. We would take the necessary steps, but we would live like husband and wife.

'Thus began a new chapter in our lives. It was as if a blind man had been given back the sight of one eye. But our happiness did not last. We wanted our full vision restored. We felt unhappy and it seemed that everything in our lives had turned into rubber. Even my body felt blubbery and unnatural. Nigar's agony was even more evident. She wanted to be a mother and she couldn't be. Whenever a child was born in the neighbourhood, she would shut herself in a room.

'I wasn't so keen on children myself because, come to think of it, one did not really have to have them. There were millions of people in the world who seemed to be able to get by without them. I could well be one of them. However, what I could no longer stand was this clammy sensation in my hands. When I ate, it felt as if I was eating rubber. My hands always felt as if they had been soaped and then left unrinsed.

'I began to hate myself. All my sensations had atrophied except this weird, unreal sense of touch, which made everything feel like rubber. All I needed to do was to peel off my terrible affliction with the help of two fingers and throw it as far as possible. But I didn't have the courage.

'I was like a drowning man who clutches at straws. And one day I found the straw I was looking for. I was reading a religious text and there it was. I almost jumped. It said, "If a man and woman are joined in wedlock, it is obligatory for them to procreate." And that day I peeled off my curse and have never looked back.'

At this moment, a servant entered the room. He was carrying a child who was holding a balloon. There was a bang and all the child was left with was a piece of string with a shrivelled piece of ugly rubber dangling at the other end.

With two fingers, Ghulam Ali carefully picked up the deflated balloon and threw it away as if it were a particularly disgusting piece of filth.

THE WOMAN IN THE RED RAINCOAT

This dates back to the time when both east and west Punjab were being ravaged by bloody communal riots between Hindus and Muslims. It had been raining hard for many days and the fire which men had been unable to put out had been extinguished by nature. However, there was no let-up in the murderous attacks on the innocent, nor was the honour of young women safe. Gangs of young men were still on the prowl and abductions of helpless and terrified girls were common.

On the face of it, murder, arson and looting are really not so difficult to commit as some people think. However, my friend 'S' had not found the going so easy.

But before I tell you his story, let me introduce 'S'. He's a man of ordinary looks and build and is as much interested in getting something for nothing as most of us are. But he isn't cruel by nature. It is another matter that he became the perpetrator of a strange tragedy, though he did not quite realize at the time what was happening.

He was just an ordinary student when we were in school, fond of games, but not very sporting. He was always the first to get into a fight when an argument developed during a game. Although he never quite played fair, he was an honest fighter.

He was interested in painting, but he had to leave college after only one year. Next we knew, he had opened a bicycle shop in the city.

When the riots began, his was one of the first shops to be burnt down. Having nothing else to do, he joined the roaming bands of looters and arsonists, nothing extraordinary at the time. It was really more by way of entertainment and diversion than out of a feeling of communal revenge, I would say. Those were strange times. This is his story and it is in his own words.

'It was really pouring down. It seemed as if the skies would burst. In my entire life, I had never seen such rain. I was at home, sitting on my balcony, smoking a cigarette. In front of me lay a large pile of goods I had looted from various shops and houses with the rest of the gang. However, I was not interested in them. They had burnt down my shop but, believe me, it did not really seem to matter, mainly because I had seen so much looting and destruction that nothing made any sense any longer. The noise of the rain was difficult to ignore but, strangely enough, all I was conscious of was a dry and barren silence. There was a stench in the air. Even my cigarette smelt unpleasant. I'm not sure I was thinking even. I was in a kind of daze. Very difficult to explain. Suddenly a shiver ran down my spine and a powerful desire to run out and pick up a girl took hold of me. The rain had become even heavier. I got up, put on my raincoat and, fortifying myself with a fresh tin of cigarettes from the pile of loot, went out in the rain.

'The roads were dark and deserted. Not even soldiers—a common sight in those days—were around. I kept walking about aimlessly for hours. There were many dead bodies lying on the streets, but they seemed to have no effect on me. After some time, I found myself in the Civil Lines area. The roads were without any sign of life. Suddenly I heard the sound of an approaching car. I turned. It was a small Austin being driven at breakneck speed. I don't know what came over me, but I placed myself in the middle of the road and began to wave frantically for the driver to stop.

'The car did not slow down. However, I was not going to move. When it was only a few yards away, it suddenly swerved to the left. In trying to run after it, I fell down, but got up immediately. I hadn't hurt myself. The car braked, then skidded and went off the road. It finally came to a stop, resting against a tree. I began to move towards it. The door was thrown open and a woman in a red raincoat jumped out. I couldn't see her face, but her shimmering raincoat was visible in the murky light. A wave of heat gripped my body.

'When she saw me moving towards her, she broke into a run. However, I caught up with her after a few yards. "Help me," she screamed as my arms enveloped her tightly, more her slippery raincoat than her, come to think of it.

'"Are you a Englishwoman?" I asked her in English, realizing too late that I should have said 'an', not 'a'.

'"No," she replied.

'I hated Englishwomen, so I said to her, "Then it's all right."

'She began to scream in Urdu, "You're going to kill me. You're going to kill me."

'I said nothing. I was only trying to guess her age and what she looked like. The hood of her raincoat covered her face. When I tried to remove it, she put both her hands in front of her face. I didn't force her. Instead, I walked towards the car, opened the rear door and pushed her in. I started the car and the engine caught. I put it in reverse and it responded. I steered it carefully back on to the road and took off.

'I switched off the engine when we were in front of my house. My first thought was to take her to the balcony, but I changed my mind, not being sure if she would willingly walk up all those stairs. I shouted for the houseboy. "Open the living room door," I told him. After he had done that, I pushed her into the room. In the dark, I caught hold of her and gently pushed her on to the sofa.

'"Don't kill me. Don't kill me please," she began to scream.

'It sounded funny. In a mock-heroic voice I said, "I won't kill you. I won't kill you, darling."

'She began to cry. I sent the servant, who was still hanging around, out of the house. I pulled out a box of matches from my pocket, but the rain had made it damp. There hadn't been any power for weeks. I had a torch upstairs but I didn't really want to bother. "I'm not exactly going to take pictures that I should need a light," I said to myself. I took off my raincoat and threw it on the floor. "Let me take yours," I suggested to her.

'I fumbled for her on the sofa but she wasn't there. However, I wasn't worried. She had to be in the room somewhere. Methodically, I began to comb the place and in a few minutes I found her. In fact, we had a near collision on the floor. I touched her on the throat by accident. She screamed. "Stop that," I said. "I'm not going to kill you."

'I ignored her sobbing and began to unbutton her raincoat, which was made of some plastic material and was very slippery. She kept wailing and trying to struggle free, but I managed to get her free of that silly coat of hers. I realized that she was wearing a sari underneath. I touched her knee and it felt solid. A violent electric current went through my entire body. But I didn't want to rush things.

'I tried to calm her down. "Darling, I didn't bring you here to murder you. Don't be afraid. You are safer here than you would be outside. If you want to leave, you are free to do so. However, I would suggest that as long as these riots last, you should stay here with me. You're an educated girl. Out there, people have become like wild beasts. I don't want you to fall into the hands of those savages."

'"You won't kill me?" she sobbed.

'"No sir," I said.

'She burst out laughing because I had called her sir. However, her laughter encouraged me. "Darling, my English is rather weak," I said with a laugh.

'She did not speak for some time. Then she said, "If you don't want to kill me, why have you brought me here?"

'It was an awkward question. I couldn't think of an answer, but I heard myself saying, "Of course I don't want to kill you for the simple reason that I don't like killing people. So why have I brought you here? Well, I suppose because I'm lonely."

'"But you have your live-in servant."

'"He is only a servant. He doesn't matter."

'She fell silent. I began to experience a sense of guilt, so I got up and said, "Let's forget about it. If you want to leave, I won't stop you."

'I caught hold of her hand, then I thought of her knee which I had touched. Violently, I pressed her against my chest. I could feel her warm breath under my chin. I put my lips on hers. She began to tremble. "Don't be afraid, darling. I won't kill you," I whispered.

'"Please let me go," she said in a tremulous voice.

'I gently pulled my arms away, but then on an impulse I lifted her off the ground. The flesh on her hips was extremely soft, I noticed. I also found that she was carrying a small handbag. I laid her down on the sofa and took her bag away. "Believe me, if it contains valuables, they will be quite safe. In fact, if you like, there are things I can give you," I told her by way of reassurance.

'"I don't need anything," she said.

'"But there is something I need," I replied.

'"What?" she asked.

'"You," I answered.

'She didn't say anything. I began to rub her knee. She offered no resistance. Feeling that she might think I was taking advantage of her helplessness, I said, "I don't want to force you. If you don't want it, you can leave, really."

'I was about to get up, when she grabbed my hand and put it on her breast. Her heart was beating violently. I became excited.

"Darling," I whispered, taking her into my arms again.

'We began to kiss each other with reckless abandon. She kept cooing "darling" and God knows what nonsense I myself spoke during that mad interlude.

'"You should take those things off," I suggested.

'"Why don't you take them off yourself?" she answered in an emotional voice.

'I began to caress her. "Who are you?" she asked.

'I was in no mood to tell her, so I said, "I am yours, darling."

'"You're a naughty boy," she said coquettishly, while pressing me close to her. I was now trying to take off her blouse, but she said to me, "Please don't make me naked."

'"What does it matter? It's dark," I said.

'"No, no!"

'She lifted my hands and began to kiss them. "No, please no. I just feel shy."

'"Forget about the blouse," I said. "It's all going to be fine."

'There was a silence, which she broke. "You're not annoyed, are you?"

'"No, why should I be? You don't want to take off your blouse, so that's fine, but . . ." I couldn't complete the sentence, but then with some effort, I said, "But anyway something should happen. I mean, take off your sari."

'"I am afraid." Her throat seemed to have gone dry.

'"Who are you afraid of?" I asked flirtatiously.

'"I am afraid," she replied and began to weep.

'"There is nothing to be afraid of," I said in a consoling voice. '"I won't hurt you, but if you are really afraid, then let's forget about it. You stay here for a few days and, when you begin to feel at home and are not afraid of me any longer, then we'll see."

'"No, no," she said, putting her head on my thighs. I began to comb her hair with my fingers. After some time, she calmed down, then suddenly she pulled me to her with such force that I was taken aback. She was also trembling violently.

'There was a knock at the door and streaks of light began to filter into the dark room from outside.

'It was the servant. "I have brought a lantern. Would you please take it?"

'"All right," I answered.

'"No, no," she said in a terrified, muffled voice.

'"Look, what's the harm? I will lower the wick and place it in a corner," I said.

'I went to the door, brought the lantern in and placed it in a corner of the room. Since my eyes were not yet accustomed to the light, for a few seconds I could see nothing. Meanwhile, she had moved into the farthest corner.

'"Come on now," I said, "we can sit in the light and chat for a few minutes. Whenever you wish, I will put the lantern out."

'Picking up the lantern, I took a few steps towards her. She had covered her face with her sari. "You're a strange girl," I said, "after all, I'm like your bridegroom."

'Suddenly there was a loud explosion outside. She rushed forward and fell into my arms. "It's only a bomb," I said. "Don't be afraid. It's nothing these days."

'"My eyes were now beginning to get used to the light. Her face began to come into focus. I had a feeling that I had seen it before, but I still couldn't see it clearly.

'I put my hands on her shoulders and pulled her closer. God, I can't explain to you what I saw. It was the face of an old woman, deeply painted and yet lined with creases. Because of the rain, her make-up had become patchy. Her hair was coloured, but you could see the roots, which were white. She had a band of plastic flowers across her forehead. I stared at her in a state bordering on shock. Then I put the lantern down and said, "You may leave if you wish."

'She wanted to say something, but when she saw me picking up her raincoat and handbag, she decided not to. Without looking at her, I handed her things to her. She stood for a few minutes staring at her feet, then opened the door and walked out.'

After my friend had finished his story, I asked him, 'Did you know who that woman was?'

'No,' he answered.

'She was the famous artist Miss "M",' I told him.

'Miss "M",' he screamed, 'the woman whose paintings I used to try to copy at school?'

'Yes. She was the principal of the art college and she used to teach her women students still-life painting. She hated men.'

'Where is she now?' he asked suddenly.

'In heaven,' I replied.

'What do you mean?' he asked.

'That night when you let her out of your house, she died in a car accident. You are her murderer. In fact, you are the murderer of two women. One, who is known as a great artist, and the other who was born from the body of the first woman in your living room that night and whom you alone know.'

My friend said nothing.

THE DUTIFUL DAUGHTER

The country had been divided. Hundreds of thousands of Muslims and Hindus were moving from India to Pakistan and from Pakistan to India in search of refuge. Camps had been set up to give them temporary shelter, but they were so overcrowded that it seemed quite impossible to push another human being into them, and yet more refugees were being brought in every day. There wasn't enough food to go round and basic facilities were almost non-existent. Epidemics and infections were common, but it didn't bother anybody. Such were the times.

The year 1948 had begun. Hundreds of volunteers had been assigned the task of recovering abducted women and children and restoring them to their families. They would go in groups to India from Pakistan and from Pakistan to India to make their recoveries.

It always amused me to see that such enthusiastic efforts were being made to undo the effects of something that had been perpetrated by more or less the same people. Why were they trying to rehabilitate the women who had been raped and taken away when they had let them be raped and taken away in the first place?

It was all very confusing, but one still admired the devotion of these volunteers.

It was not a simple task. The difficulties were enormous. The abductors were not easy to trace. To avoid discovery, they had devised various means of eluding their pursuers. They were constantly on the move, from this locality to that, from one city to another. One followed a tip and often found nothing at the end of the trail.

One heard strange stories. One liaison officer told me that in Saharanpur, two abducted Muslim girls had refused to return to their parents who were in Pakistan. Then there was this Muslim girl in Jullandar who was given a touching farewell by the abductor's family as if she was a daughter-in-law leaving on a long journey. Some girls had committed suicide on the way, afraid of facing their parents. Some had lost their mental balance as a result of their traumatic experiences. Others had become alcoholics and retorted with abusive and vulgar language when spoken to.

When I thought about these abducted girls, I only saw their protruding bellies. What was going to happen to them and what they contained? Who would claim the end result? Pakistan or India?

And who would pay the women the wages for carrying those children in their wombs for nine months? Pakistan or India? Or would it all be put down in God's great ledger, that is, if there were still any pages left?

Why were they being described as 'abducted women'? I had always thought that when a woman ran away from home with her lover—the police always called it 'abduction'—it was the most romantic act in the world. But these women had been taken against their will and violated.

They were strange, illogical times. I had boarded up all the doors and windows of my mind, shuttered them up. It was difficult to think straight.

Sometimes it seemed to me that the entire operation was being conducted like import-export trade.

One liaison officer asked me, 'Why do you look lost?'

I didn't answer his question.

Then he told me a story.

'We were looking for abducted women from town to town, village to village, street to street, and sometimes days would go by before we would have any success.

'And almost every time I went across to what is now India, I would notice an old woman, the same old woman. The first time it was in the suburbs of Jullandar. She looked distracted, almost unaware of her surroundings. Her eyes had a desolate look, her clothes had turned to rags and her hair was coated with dust. The only thing that struck me about her was that she was looking for someone.

'I was told by one of the women volunteers that she had lost her mind because her only daughter had been abducted during the riots in Patiala. She said they had tried for months to find the girl but had failed. In all probability, she had been killed, but that was something the old woman was not prepared to believe.

'The next time I ran into her at Saharanpur. She was at the bus stop and she looked much worse than she had the first time I had seen her. Her lips were cracked and her hair looked matted. I spoke to her. I said she should abandon her futile search; and to induce her to follow my advice, I told her—it was brutal—that her daughter had probably been murdered.

'She looked at me. "Murdered? No. No one can murder my daughter. No one can murder my daughter."

'And she walked away.

'It set me thinking. Why was this crazy woman so confident that no one would murder her daughter, that no sharp, deadly knife could slash her throat? Did she think her daughter was immortal or was it her motherhood that would not admit defeat nor entertain the possibility of death?

'On my third visit, I saw her again in another town. She looked very old and ragged. Her clothes were now so threadbare that they hardly covered her frail body. I gave her a change of dress, but she didn't want it. I said to her, "Old woman, I swear to you that your daughter was killed in Patiala."

'"You are lying," she said. There was steely conviction in her voice.

'To convince her, I said, "I assure you I'm telling the truth. You've suffered enough. It's time to go to Pakistan. I'll take you."

'She paid no attention to what I had said and began muttering to herself. "No one can murder my daughter," she suddenly declared in a strong, confident voice.

'"Why?" I asked.

'"Because she's beautiful. She's so beautiful that no one can kill her. No one can even dream of hurting her," she said in a low whisper.

'I wondered if her daughter was really as beautiful as that. I thought it was just a matter of all children being beautiful to their mother. But it was also possible that the old woman was right. Who knew? But in this holocaust nothing had survived. This mad old woman was deceiving herself. There are so many ways of escape from unpleasant reality. Grief is like a roundabout, which one intersects with an infinite number of roads.

'I made many other trips across the border to India and almost every time I somehow ran into the old woman. She was no more than a bag of bones now. She could hardly see and tottered about like a blind person, a step at a time. Only one thing hadn't changed—her faith that her daughter was alive and that no one could kill her.

'One of the women volunteers said to me, "Don't waste your

time over her. She's raving mad. It would be good if you could take her to Pakistan with you and put her in an asylum."

'Suddenly, I didn't want to do that. I didn't want to divest her of her only reason for living. As it was, she was in a vast asylum where nothing made any sense. I didn't wish to confine her within the four walls of a regular one.

'The last time I met her was in Amritsar. She looked so broken that it almost brought tears to my eyes. I decided that I would make one last effort to take her to Pakistan.

'There she stood in Farid Chowk, peering around with her half-blind eyes. I was talking to a shopkeeper about an abducted Muslim girl, who, we had been informed, was being kept in the house of a Hindu moneylender.

'After my exchange with the shopkeeper, I crossed the street, determined to persuade the old woman to come with me to Pakistan.

'I noticed a couple. The woman's face was partly covered by her white chaddar. The man was young and handsome—a Sikh.

'As they went past the old woman, the man suddenly stopped. He even fell back a step or two. Nervously, he caught hold of the woman's hand. I couldn't see her full face, but one glimpse was enough to know that she was beautiful beyond words.

'"Your mother," he said to her.

'The girl looked up, but only for a second. Then, covering her face with her chaddar, she grabbed her companion's arm and said, "Let's get away from here."

'They crossed the road, taking long, brisk steps.

'The old woman shouted, "Bhagbari, Bhagbari."

'I rushed towards her. "What is the matter?" I asked.

'She was trembling. "I have seen her . . . I have seen her."

'"Whom have you seen?" I asked.

'"I have seen my daughter . . . I have seen Bhagbari." Her eyes were like burnt-out lights.

'"Your daughter is dead," I said.

'"You're lying," she screamed.

'"I swear on God your daughter is dead."

'The old woman fell in a heap on the road.'

THREE SIMPLE STATEMENTS

Not far from Congress House and Jinnah Hall in Bombay is a urinal, called mootri by the locals, who also have made a habit of dumping all their rubbish outside this facility. The stink it produces is so revolting that you cannot walk past it without covering your nose with your handkerchief.

He was once constrained to go into this hellhole, his nose protected by a handkerchief, while trying all the time not to breathe. The floor was wet and filthy. The walls were covered with crude representations of human genitalia and in one corner someone had scribbled in charcoal the words: 'ram Pakistan up the you-know-what of the Muslims'.

He felt revolted and stepped out as quickly as he could.

Both Congress House and Jinnah Hall were under the control of the government, but the mootri was free, free to spread its stink far and wide, free to receive the garbage of the local community at its doorstep.

A few days later, he found himself visiting the mootri once again to answer the call of nature. He had his face covered and his breath held in his lungs. There was more filth on the floor than the last time and more murals on the wall depicting the engines of human procreation.

Under the words 'ram Pakistan up the you-know-what of the Muslims' someone had scrawled with a thick pencil: 'ram Akhand Bharat up the you-know-what of the Hindus'. He left hurriedly, feeling as if he had been sprayed with acid.

Some time later, Mahatma Gandhi was granted unconditional release by the British Indian government. Mr Jinnah was defeated in the Punjab. As for Congress House and Jinnah Hall, they were neither defeated nor released. And the mootri, which was only a short distance from these imposing buildings, continued to remain under the occupation of malodorous filth. Only the pile of garbage outside had grown larger.

He went for the third time to the mootri—but not to answer the call of nature.

He covered his nose and held his breath as he entered. The floor was crawling with vermin. No further space was left on the wall to draw more human genitalia.

The words 'ram Pakistan up the you-know-what of the Muslims' and 'ram Akhand Bharat up the you-know-what of the Hindus' had somewhat faded.

When he left, a new line had appeared under the two declarations: 'ram Mother India up the you-know-what of both Muslims and Hindus'.

For a moment these words seemed to dispel the stink of the mootri like a light fragrance dancing in the wind—but only for a moment.

THE DOG OF TITWAL

The soldiers had been entrenched in their positions for several weeks, but there was little, if any, fighting, except for the dozen rounds they ritually exchanged every day. The weather was extremely pleasant. The air was heavy with the scent of wild flowers and nature seemed to be following its course, quite unmindful of the soldiers hiding behind rocks and camouflaged by mountain shrubbery. The birds sang as they always had and the flowers were in bloom. Bees buzzed about lazily.

Only when a shot rang out, the birds got startled and took flight, as if a musician had struck a jarring note on his instrument. It was almost the end of September, neither hot nor cold. It seemed as if summer and winter had made their peace. In the blue skies, cotton clouds floated all day like barges on a lake.

The soldiers seemed to be getting tired of this indecisive war where nothing much ever happened. Their positions were quite impregnable. The two hills on which they were placed faced each other and were about the same height, so no one side had an advantage. Down below in the valley, a stream zigzagged furiously on its stony bed like a snake.

The air force was not involved in the combat and neither of the adversaries had heavy guns or mortars. At night, they would light huge fires and hear each others' voices echoing through the hills.

The last round of tea had just been taken. The fire had gone cold. The sky was clear and there was a chill in the air and a sharp, though not unpleasant, smell of pine cones. Most of the soldiers were already asleep, except Jamadar Harnam Singh, who was on night watch. At two o'clock, he woke up Ganda Singh to take over. Then he lay down, but sleep was as far away from his eyes as the stars in the sky. He began to hum a Punjabi folk song:

Buy me a pair of shoes, my lover
A pair of shoes with stars on them

Sell your buffalo, if you have to
But buy me a pair of shoes
With stars on them.

It made him feel good and a bit sentimental. He woke up the others one by one. Banta Singh, the youngest of the soldiers, who had a sweet voice, began to sing a lovelorn verse from 'Heer Ranjha', that timeless Punjabi epic of love and tragedy. A deep sadness fell over them. Even the grey hills seemed to have been affected by the melancholy of the songs.

This mood was shattered by the barking of a dog. Jamadar Harnam Singh said, 'Where has this son of a bitch materialized from?'

The dog barked again. He sounded closer. There was a rustle in the bushes. Banta Singh got up to investigate and came back with an ordinary mongrel in tow. He was wagging his tail. 'I found him behind the bushes and he told me his name was Jhun Jhun,' Banta Singh announced. Everybody burst out laughing.

The dog went to Harnam Singh, who produced a cracker from his kitbag and threw it on the ground. The dog sniffed at it and was about to eat it, when Harnam Singh snatched it away . . . 'Wait, you could be a Pakistani dog.'

They laughed. Banta Singh patted the animal and said to Harnam Singh, 'Jamadar sahib, Jhun Jhun is an Indian dog.'

'Prove your identity,' Harnam Singh ordered the dog, who began to wag his tail.

'This is no proof of identity. All dogs can wag their tails,' Harnam Singh said.

'He is only a poor refugee,' Banta Singh said, playing with his tail.

Harnam Singh threw the dog a cracker, which he caught in mid-air. 'Even dogs will now have to decide if they are Indian or Pakistani,' one of the soldiers observed.

Harnam Singh produced another cracker from his kitbag. 'And all Pakistanis, including dogs, will be shot.'

A soldier shouted, 'India Zindabad!'

The dog, who was about to munch his cracker, stopped dead in his tracks, put his tail between his legs and looked scared. Harnam Singh laughed. 'Why are you afraid of your own country? Here, Jhun Jhun, have another cracker.'

The morning broke very suddenly, as if someone had switched on a light in a dark room. It spread across the hills and valleys of Titwal, which is what the area was called.

The war had been going on for months but nobody could be quite sure who was winning it.

Jamadar Harnam Singh surveyed the area with his binoculars. He could see smoke rising from the opposite hill, which meant that, like them, the enemy was busy preparing breakfast.

Subedar Himmat Khan of the Pakistan army gave his huge moustache a twirl and began to study the map of the Titwal sector. Next to him sat his wireless operator, who was trying to establish contact with the platoon commander to obtain instructions. A few feet away, the soldier Bashir sat on the ground, his back against a rock and his rifle in front of him. He was humming:

Where did you spend the night, my love, my moon?
Where did you spend the night?

Enjoying himself, he began to sing more loudly, savouring the words. Suddenly he heard Subedar Himmat Khan scream, 'Where did *you* spend the night?'

But this was not addressed to Bashir. It was a dog he was shouting at. He had come to them from nowhere a few days ago, stayed in the camp quite happily and then suddenly disappeared last night. However, he had now returned like a bad coin.

Bashir smiled and began to sing to the dog. 'Where did *you* spend the night, where did you spend the night?' But he only wagged his tail. Subedar Himmat Khan threw a pebble at him. 'All he can do is wag his tail, the idiot.'

'What has he got around his neck?' Bashir asked.

One of the soldiers grabbed the dog and undid his makeshift rope collar. There was a small piece of cardboard tied to it. 'What does it say?' the soldier, who could not read, asked.

Bashir stepped forward and with some difficulty was able to decipher the writing. 'It says Jhun Jhun.'

Subedar Himmat Khan gave his famous moustache another mighty twirl and said, 'Perhaps it is a code. Does it say anything else, Bashirey?'

'Yes sir, it says it is an Indian dog.'

'What does that mean?' Subedar Himmat Khan asked.

'Perhaps it is a secret,' Bashir answered seriously.

'If there is a secret, it is in the word Jhun Jhun,' another soldier ventured in a wise guess.

'You may have something there,' Subedar Himmat Khan observed.

Dutifully, Bashir read the whole thing again. 'Jhun Jhun. This is an Indian dog.'

Subedar Himmat Khan picked up the wireless set and spoke to his platoon commander, providing him with a detailed account of the dog's sudden appearance in their position, his equally sudden disappearance the night before and his return that morning. 'What are you talking about?' the platoon commander asked.

Subedar Himmat Khan studied the map again. Then he tore up a packet of cigarettes, cut a small piece from it and gave it to Bashir. 'Now write on it in Gurmukhi, the language of those Sikhs . . .'

'What should I write?'

'Well . . .'

Bashir had an inspiration. 'Shun Shun, yes, that's right. We counter Jhun Jhun with Shun Shun.'

'Good,' Subedar Himmat Khan said approvingly. 'And add: This is a Pakistani dog.'

Subedar Himmat Khan personally threaded the piece of paper through the dog's collar and said, 'Now go join your family.'

He gave him something to eat and then said, 'Look here, my friend, no treachery. The punishment for treachery is death.'

The dog kept eating his food and wagging his tail. Then Subedar Himmat Khan turned him round to face the Indian position and said, 'Go and take this message to the enemy, but come back. These are the orders of your commander.'

The dog wagged his tail and moved down the winding hilly track that led into the valley dividing the two hills. Subedar Himmat Khan picked up his rifle and fired in the air.

The Indians were a bit puzzled, as it was somewhat early in the day for that sort of thing. Jamadar Harnam Singh, who in any case was feeling bored, shouted, 'Let's give it to them.'

The two sides exchanged fire for half an hour, which of course was a complete waste of time. Finally, Jamadar Harnam Singh ordered that enough was enough. He combed his long hair, looked at himself in the mirror and asked Banta Singh, 'Where has that dog Jhun Jhun gone?'

'Dogs can never digest butter, goes the famous saying,' Banta Singh observed philosophically.

Suddenly the soldier on lookout duty shouted, 'There he comes.'

'Who?' Jamadar Harnam Singh asked.

'What was his name? Jhun Jhun,' the soldier answered.

'What is he doing?' Harnam Singh asked.

'Just coming our way,' the soldier replied, peering through his binoculars.

Subedar Harnam Singh snatched them from him. 'That's him all right and there's something around his neck. But, wait, that's the Pakistani hill he's coming from, the motherfucker.'

He picked up his rifle, aimed and fired. The bullet hit some rocks close to where the dog was. He stopped.

Subedar Himmat Khan heard the report and looked through his binoculars. The dog had turned round and was running back. 'The brave never run away from battle. Go forward and complete your mission,' he shouted at the dog. To scare him, he fired at the same time. The bullet passed within inches of the dog, who leapt in the air, flapping his ears. Subedar Himmat Khan fired again, hitting some stones.

It soon became a game between the two soldiers, with the dog running round in circles in a state of great terror. Both Himmat Khan and Harnam Singh were laughing boisterously. The dog began to run towards Harnam Singh, who abused him loudly and fired. The bullet caught him in the leg. He yelped, turned around and began to run towards Himmat Khan, only to meet more fire, which was only meant to scare him. 'Be a brave boy. If you are injured, don't let that stand between you and your duty. Go, go, go,' the Pakistani shouted.

The dog turned. One of his legs was now quite useless. He began to drag himself towards Harnam Singh, who picked up his rifle, aimed carefully and shot him dead.

Subedar Himmat Khan sighed, 'The poor bugger has been martyred.'

Jamadar Harnam Singh ran his hand over the still-hot barrel of his rifle and muttered, 'He died a dog's death.'

THE LAST SALUTE

This Kashmir war was a very odd affair. Subedar Rab nawaz often felt as if his brain had turned into a rifle with a faulty safety catch.

He had fought with distinction on many major fronts in the Second World War. He was respected by both his seniors and his juniors because of his intelligence and valour. He was always given the most difficult and dangerous assignments and he had never failed the trust placed in him.

But he had never been in a war like this one. He had come to it full of enthusiasm and with the itch to fight and liquidate the enemy. However, the first encounter had shown that the men arrayed against them on the other side were mostly old friends and comrades with whom he had fought in the old British Indian army against the Germans and the Italians. The friends of yesterday had been transformed into the enemies of today.

At times, the whole thing felt like a dream to Subedar Rab Nawaz. He could remember the day the Second World War was declared. He had enlisted immediately. They had been given some basic training and then packed off to the front. He had been moved from one theatre of war to another and, one day, the war had ended. Then had come Pakistan and the new war he was now fighting. So much had happened in these last few years at such breakneck speed. Often it made no sense at all. Those who had planned and executed these great events had perhaps deliberately maintained a dizzying pace so that the participants should get no time to think. How else could one explain one revolution followed by another and then another?

One thing Subedar Rab Nawaz could understand. They were fighting this war to win Kashmir. Why did they want to win Kashmir? Because it was crucial to Pakistan's security and survival. However, sometimes when he sat behind a gun emplacement and caught sight of a familiar face on the other side, for a moment he forgot why they were fighting. He forgot why he was carrying a gun and killing people. At such times, he would remind himself that he was not fighting to win medals or earn a salary, but to secure the survival of his country.

This was his country before the establishment of Pakistan and it was his country now. This was his land. But now he was fighting against men who were his countrymen until only the other day. Men who had grown up in the same village, whose families had been known to his family for generations. These men had now been turned into citizens of a country to which they were complete strangers. They had been told: we are placing a gun in your hands so that you can go and fight for a country which you have yet to know, where you do not even have a roof over your head, where even the air and water are strange to you. Go and fight for it against Pakistan, the land where you were born and grew up.

Rab Nawaz would think of those Muslim soldiers who had moved to Pakistan, leaving their ancestral homes behind, and come to this new country with empty hands. They had been given nothing, except the guns that had been put in their hands. The same guns they had always used, the same make, the same bore, guns to fight their new enemy with.

Before the Partition of the country, they used to fight one common enemy who was not really their enemy perhaps but whom they had accepted as their enemy for the sake of employment and rewards and medals. Formerly, all of them were Indian soldiers, but now some were Indian and others were Pakistani soldiers. Rab Nawaz could not unravel this puzzle. And when he thought about Kashmir, he became even more confused. Were the Pakistani soldiers fighting for Kashmir or for the Muslims of Kashmir? If they were being asked to fight in defence of the Muslims of Kashmir, why had they not been asked to fight for the Muslims of the princely states of Junagarh and Hyderabad? And if this was an Islamic war, then why were other Muslim countries of the world not fighting shoulder to shoulder with them?

Rab Nawaz had finally come to the conclusion that such intricate and subtle matters were beyond the comprehension of a simple soldier. A soldier should be thick in the head. Only the thick-headed made good soldiers, but despite this resolution, he couldn't help wondering sometimes about the war he was now in.

The fighting in what was called the Titwal sector was spread across the Kishan Ganga river and along the road which led from

Muzaffarabad to Kiran. It was a strange war. Often at night, instead of gunfire, one heard abuse being exchanged in loud voices.

One late evening, while Subedar Rab Nawaz was preparing his platoon for a foray into enemy territory, he heard loud voices from across the hill the enemy was supposed to be on. He could not believe his ears. There was loud laughter followed by abuse. 'Pig's trotters,' he murmured, 'what on earth is going on?'

One of his men returned the abuse in as loud a voice as he could muster, then complained to him, 'Subedar sahib, they are abusing us again, the motherfuckers.'

Rab Nawaz's first instinct was to join the slanging match, but he thought better of it. The men fell silent too, following his example. However, after a while, the torrent of abuse from the other side became so intolerable that his men lost control and began to match abuse with abuse. A couple of times he ordered them to keep quiet, but did not insist because, frankly, it was difficult for a human being not to react violently.

They couldn't of course see the enemy at night, and hardly did so during the day because of the hilly country which provided perfect cover. All they heard was abuse, which echoed across the hills and valleys and then evaporated in the air.

Some of the hills were barren, while others were covered with tall pine trees. It was very difficult terrain. Subedar Rab Nawaz's platoon was on a bare, treeless hill which provided no cover. His men were itching to go into attack to avenge the abuse, which had been hurled at them without respite for several weeks. An attack was planned and executed with success, though they lost two men and suffered four injuries. The enemy lost three and abandoned the position, leaving behind food and provisions.

Subedar Rab Nawaz and his men were sorry they had not been able to capture an enemy soldier. They could then have avenged the abuse face to face. However, they had captured an important and difficult feature. Rab Nawaz relayed the news of the victory to his commander, Major Aslam, and was commended for gallantry.

On top of most hills one found ponds. There was a large one on the hill they had captured. The water was clear and sweet and, although it was cold, they took off their clothes and jumped in. Suddenly they heard firing. They jumped out of the pond and hit the ground—naked. Subedar Rab Nawaz crawled towards his binoculars, picked them up and surveyed the area carefully. He could see no one. There was more firing. This time he was able to determine its origin. It was coming from a small hill, lying a few hundred feet below their perch. He ordered his men to open up.

The enemy troops did not have very good cover and Rab Nawaz was confident they could not stay there much longer. The moment they decided to move, they would come in direct range of their guns. Sporadic firing kept getting exchanged. Finally, Rab Nawaz ordered that no more ammunition should be wasted. They should just wait for the enemy to break cover. Then he looked at his still naked body and murmured, 'Pig's trotters. Man does look silly without clothes.'

For two whole days, this game continued. Occasional fire was exchanged, but the enemy had obviously decided to lie low. Then suddenly the temperature dropped several degrees. To keep his men warm, Subedar Rab Nawaz ordered that the tea kettle should be kept on the boil all the time. It was like an unending tea party.

On the third day—it was unbearably cold—the soldier on the lookout reported that some movement could be detected around the enemy position. Subedar Rab Nawaz looked through his binoculars. Yes, something was going on. Rab Nawaz raised his rifle and fired. Someone called his name, or so he thought. It echoed through the valley. 'Pig's trotters,' Rab Nawaz shouted, 'what do you want?'

The distance that separated their two positions was not great; the voice came back, 'Don't hurl abuse, brother.'

Rab Nawaz looked at his men. The word 'brother' seemed to hang in the air. He raised his hands to his mouth and shouted, 'Brother! There are no brothers here, only your mother's lovers.'

'Rab Nawaz,' the voice shouted.

He trembled. The words reverberated around the hills and then faded into the atmosphere.

'Pig's trotters,' he whispered, 'who was that?'

He knew that the troops in the Titwal sector were mostly from the old 6/9 Jat Regiment, his own regiment. But who was this joker shouting his name? He had many friends in the regiment, and some enemies too. But who was this man who had called him brother?

Rab Nawaz looked through his binoculars again, but could see nothing. He shouted, 'Who was that? This is Rab Nawaz. Rab Nawaz. Rab Nawaz.'

'It is me . . . Ram Singh,' the same voice answered.

Rab Nawaz nearly jumped. 'Ram Singh, oh, Ram Singha, Ram Singha, you pig's trotters.'

'Shut your trap, you potter's ass,' came the reply.

Rab Nawaz looked at his men, who appeared startled at this strange exchange in the middle of battle. 'He's talking rot, pig's trotters.' Then he shouted, 'You slaughtered swine, watch your tongue.'

Ram Singh began to laugh. Rab Nawaz could not contain himself either. His men watched him in silence.

'Look, my friend, we want to drink tea,' Ram Singh said.

'Go ahead then. Have a good time,' Rab Nawaz replied.

'We can't. The tea things are lying elsewhere.'

'Where's elsewhere?'

'Let me put it this way. If we tried to get them, you could blow us to bits. We'd have to break cover.'

'So what do you want, pig's trotters?' Rab Nawaz laughed.

'That you hold your fire until we get our things.'

'Go ahead,' Rab Nawaz said.

'You will blow us up, you potter's ass,' Ram Singh shouted.

'Shut your mouth, you crawly Sikh tortoise,' Rab Nawaz said.

'Take an oath on something that you won't open fire.'

'On what?'

'Anything you like.'

Rab Nawaz laughed. 'You have my word. Now go get your things.'

Nothing happened for a few minutes. One of the men was watching the small hill through his binoculars. He pointed at his gun and asked Rab Nawaz in gestures if he should open fire. 'No, no, no shooting,' Rab Nawaz said.

Suddenly, a man darted forward, running low towards some bushes. A few minutes later he ran back, carrying an armful of things. Then he disappeared. Rab Nawaz picked up his rifle and fired. 'Thank you,' Ram Singh's voice came.

'No mention,' Rab Nawaz answered. 'OK, boys, let's give the buggers one round.'

More by way of entertainment than war, this exchange of fire continued for some time. Rab Nawaz could see smoke going up in a thin blue spiral where the enemy was. 'Is your tea ready, Ram Singha?' he shouted.

'Not yet, you potter's ass.'

Rab Nawaz was a potter by caste and any reference to his origins always enraged him. Ram Singh was the one person who could get away with calling him a potter's ass. They had grown up together in the same village in the Punjab. They were the same age, had gone to the same primary school, and their fathers had been childhood friends. They had joined the army the same day. In the last war, they had fought together on the same fronts.

'Pig's trotters, he never gives up, that one,' Rab Nawaz said to his men. 'Shut up, lice-infested donkey Ram Singha,' he shouted.

He saw a man stand up. Rab Nawaz raised his rifle and fired in his direction. He heard a scream. He looked through his binoculars. It was Ram Singh. He was doubled up, holding his stomach. Then he fell to the ground.

Rab Nawaz shouted, 'Ram Singh' and stood up. There was rapid gunfire from the other side. One bullet brushed past his left arm. He fell to the ground. Some enemy soldiers, taking advantage of this confusion, began to run across open ground to securer positions. Rab Nawaz ordered his platoon to attack the hill. Three were killed, but the others managed to capture the position with Rab Nawaz in the lead.

He found Ram Singh lying on the bare ground. He had been shot in the stomach. His eyes lit up when he saw Rab Nawaz. 'You potter's ass, whatever did you do that for?' he asked.

Rab Nawaz felt as if it was he who had been shot. But he smiled, bent over Ram Singh and began to undo his belt. 'Pig's trotters, who told you to stand up?'

'I was only trying to show myself to you, but you shot me,' Ram Singh said with difficulty. Rab Nawaz unfastened his belt. It was a very bad wound and bleeding profusely.

Rab Nawaz's voice choked, 'I swear upon God, I only fired out of fun. How could I know it was you? You were always an ass, Ram Singha.'

Ram Singh was rapidly losing blood. Rab Nawaz was surprised he was still alive. He did not want to move him. He spoke to his platoon commander, Major Aslam, on the wireless, requesting urgent medical help.

He was sure it would take a long time to arrive. He had a feeling Ram Singh wouldn't last that long. But he laughed. 'Don't you worry. The doctor is on his way.'

Ram Singh said in a weak voice, 'I am not worried, but tell me, how many of my men did you kill?'

'Just one,' Rab Nawaz said.

'And how many did you lose?'

'Six,' Rab Nawaz lied.

'Six,' Ram Singh said. 'When I fell, they were disheartened, but I told them to fight on, give it everything they'd got. Six, yes.' Then his mind began to wander.

He began to talk of their village, their childhood, stories from school, the 6/9 Jat Regiment, its commanding officers, affairs with strange women in strange cities. He was in excruciating pain, but he carried on. 'Do you remember that madam, you pig?'

'Which one?' Rab Nawaz asked.

'That one in Italy. You remember what we used to call her? Man-eater.'

Rab Nawaz remembered her. 'Yes, yes. She was called Madam Minitafanto or some such thing. And she used to say: no money, no action. But she had a soft spot for you, that daughter of Mussolini.'

Ram Singh laughed loudly, causing blood to gush out of his wound. Rab Nawaz dressed it with a makeshift bandage. 'Now keep quiet,' he admonished him gently.

Ram Singh's body was burning. He did not have the strength to speak, but he was talking nineteen to the dozen. At times he would stop, as if to see how much petrol was still left in his tank.

After some time, he went into a sort of delirium. Briefly, he would come out of it, only to sink again. During one brief moment of clarity, he said to Rab Nawaz, 'Tell me truthfully, do you people really want Kashmir?'

'Yes, Ram Singha,' Rab Nawaz said passionately.

'I don't believe that. You have been misled,' Ram Singh said.

'No, you have been misled, I swear by the Holy Prophet and his family,' Rab Nawaz said.

'Don't take that oath . . . you must be right.' But there was a strange look on his face, as if he didn't really believe Rab Nawaz.

A little before sunset, Major Aslam arrived with some soldiers. There was no doctor. Ram Singh was hovering between consciousness and delirium. He was muttering, but his voice was so weak that it was difficult to follow him.

Major Aslam was an old 6/9 Jat Regiment officer. Ram Singh had served under him for years. He bent over the dying soldier and called his name, 'Ram Singh, Ram Singh.'

Ram Singh opened his eyes and stiffened his body as if he was coming to attention. With one great effort, he raised his arm and saluted. A strange look of incomprehension suddenly suffused his face. His arm fell limply to his side and he murmured, 'Ram Singh, you ass, you forgot this was a war, a war . . .' He could not complete the sentence. With half-open eyes, he looked at Rab Nawaz, took one last breath and died.

THE NEW CONSTITUTION

Mangu the tongawala was considered a man of great wisdom among his friends. He had never seen the inside of a school, and in strictly academic terms was no more than a cipher, but there was nothing under the sun he did not know something about. All his fellow tongawalas at the adda, or tonga stand, were well aware of his versatility in worldly matters. He was always able to satisfy their curiosity about what was going on.

Recently, when he had learnt from one of his fares about a rumour that war was about to break out in Spain, he had patted Gama Chaudhry across his broad shoulder and predicted in a statesmanlike manner, 'You will see, Chaudhry, a war is going to break out in Spain in a few days.' And when Gama Chaudhry had asked him where Spain was, Ustad Mangu had replied very soberly: 'In Vilayat, where else?'

When war finally broke out in Spain and everybody came to know of it, every tonga driver at the Station adda, smoking his hookah, became convinced in his heart of Ustad Mangu's greatness. At that hour, Ustad Mangu was driving his tonga on the dazzling surface of the Mall, exchanging views with his fare about the latest Hindu–Muslim rioting.

That evening when he returned to the adda, his face looked visibly perturbed. He sat down with his friends, took a long drag on the hookah, removed his khaki turban and said in a worried voice, 'It is no doubt the result of a holy man's curse that Hindus and Muslims keep slashing each other up every other day. I have heard it said by my elders that Akbar Badshah once showed disrespect to a saint, who angrily cursed him in these words: "Get out of my sight! And, yes, your Hindustan will always be plagued by riots and disorder." And you can see for yourselves. Ever since the end of Akbar's raj, what else has India known but riot after riot!'

He took a deep breath, drew on his hookah reflectively and said, 'These Congressites want to win India its freedom. Well, you take my word, they will get nowhere even if they keep bashing their heads against the wall for a thousand years. At the most, the Angrez will leave, but then you will get maybe the Italywala or the Russiawala. I have heard that the Russiawala is one tough fellow. But Hindustan will always remain enslaved. Yes, I forgot to tell you that part of the saint's curse on Akbar which said that India will always be ruled by foreigners.'

Ustad Mangu had intense hatred for the British. He used to tell his friends that he hated them because they were ruling Hindustan against the will of the Indians and missed no opportunity to commit atrocities. However, the fact was that it was the gora soldiers of the cantonment who were responsible for Ustad Mangu's rather low opinion of the British. They used to treat him like some lower creation of God, even worse than a dog. Nor was Ustad Mangu overly fond of their fair complexion. He would feel nauseated at the sight of a fair and ruddy gora soldier's face. 'Their red wrinkled faces remind me of a dead body whose skin is rotting away,' he used to say.

After an argument with a drunken gora, he would remain depressed for the entire day. He would return to his adda in the evening and curse the man to his heart's content, while smoking his Marble brand cigarette or taking long drags at his hookah.

He would deliver himself of a heavyweight curse, shake his head with its loosely tied turban and say, 'Look at them, came to the door to borrow a light and the next thing you knew they owned the whole house. I am sick and tired of these offshoots of monkeys. The way they order us around, you would think we were their fathers' servants!'

But even after such outbursts, his anger would show no sign of abating. As long as a friend was keeping him company, he would keep at it. 'Look at this one, resembles a leper! Dead and rotting. I could knock him out cold with one blow, but the way he was throwing his git-pit at me, you would have thought he was going to kill me. I swear on your head, my first urge was to smash the damn fellow's skull, but then I restrained myself. I mean it would have been below my dignity to hit this wretch.' He would wipe his nose with the sleeve of his khaki uniform jacket and keep murmuring curses. 'As God is my witness, I'm sick of suffering and humouring these Lat sahibs. Every time I look at their blighted faces, my blood begins to boil in my veins. We need a new law to get rid of these people. Only that can revive us, I swear on your life.'

One day Ustad Mangu picked up two fares from district courts. He gathered from their conversation that there was going to be a new constitution for India and he felt overwhelmed with joy at the news. The two Marwaris were in town to pursue a civil suit in the local court and, while on their way home, they were discussing the new constitution, the India Act.

'It is said that from 1 April, there's going to be a new constitution. Will that change everything?'

'Not everything, but they say a lot will change. The Indians would be free.'

'What about interest?' asked one.

'Well, this needs to be inquired. Should ask some lawyer tomorrow.'

The conversation between the two Marwaris sent Ustad Mangu to seventh heaven. Normally, he was in the habit of abusing his horse for being slow and was not averse to making liberal use of the whip, but not today. Every now and then, he would look back at his two passengers, caress his moustache and loosen the horse's reins affectionately. 'Come on son, come on, show 'em how you take to the air.'

After dropping his fares, he stopped at the Anarkali shop of his friend, Dino the sweetmeat vendor. He ordered a large glass of lassi, drank it down, belched with satisfaction, took the ends of his moustache in his mouth, sucked at them and said in a loud voice, 'The hell with 'em all!'

When he returned to the adda in the evening, contrary to routine, no one that he knew was around. A storm was roaring in his breast and he was dying to share the great news with his friends, that really great news which he simply had to get out of his system. But no one was around to hear it.

For about half an hour, he paced about restlessly under the tin roof of the Station adda, his whip under his arm. His mind was on many things, good things that lay in the future. The news that a new constitution was to be implemented had brought him at the doorstep of a new world. He had switched on all the lights in his brain to carefully study the implications of the new law that was going to become operational in India from 1 April. The worried words of the Marwari about a change in the law governing interest or usury rang in his ears. A wave of happiness was coursing through his entire body. Quite a few times, he laughed under his thick moustache and hurled a few words of abuse at the Marwaris. 'The new constitution is going to be like boiling hot water is to bugs who suck the blood of the poor,' he said to himself.

He was very happy. A delightful cool settled over his heart when he thought of how the new constitution would send these white mice (he always called them by that name) scurrying back into their holes for all times to come.

When the bald-headed Nathoo ambled into the adda some time later, his turban tucked under his arm, Ustad Mangu shook his hand vigorously and said in a loud voice, 'Give me your hand, I have great news for you that would not only bring you immense joy but might even make hair grow back on your bald skull.'

Then, thoroughly enjoying himself, he went into a detailed description of the changes the new constitution was going to bring. 'You just wait and see. Things are going to happen. You have my word, this Russian king is bound to do something big.' And as he talked, he continued to slap Ganju's bald head, and with some force as well.

Ustad Mangu had heard many stories about the socialist system the Soviets had set up. There were many things he liked about their new laws and many of the new things they were doing, which was what had made him link the king of Russia with the India Act or the new constitution. He was convinced that the changes being brought in on 1 April were a direct result of the influence of the Russian king.

For the past several years, the Red Shirt movement in Peshawar and other cities had been much in the news. To Ustad Mangu, this movement was all tied up with the 'king of Russia' and, naturally, with the new constitution. Then there were the frequent reports of bomb blasts in various Indian cities. Whenever Ustad Mangu heard that so many had been caught somewhere for possessing explosives or so many were going to be tried for treason, he interpreted it all to his great delight as preparation for the new constitution.

One day he had two barristers at the back of his tonga. They were vigorously criticizing the new constitution. He listened to them in silence. One of them was saying, 'It is Section II of the Act that I still can't make sense of. It relates to the federation of India. No such federation exists in the world. From a political angle too, such a federation would be utterly wrong. In fact, one can say that this is going to be no federation.'

Since most of this conversation was being carried on in English, Ustad Mangu had only been able to follow the last bit. He came to the conclusion that these two barristers were opposed to the new constitution and did not want their country to be free. 'Toady wretches,' he muttered with contempt. Whenever he called someone a 'toady wretch' under his breath, he felt greatly elated that he had applied the words correctly and that he could tell a good man from a toady.

Three days after this incident, he picked up three students from Government College who wanted to be taken to Mozang. He listened to them carefully as they talked.

'The new constitution has raised my hopes. If so and so becomes a member of the assembly, I will certainly be able to get a job in a government office.'

'Oh! There are going to be many openings and, in that confusion, we will be able to lay our hands on something.'

'Yes, yes, why not!'

'And there's bound to be a reduction in the number of all those unemployed graduates who have nowhere to go.'

This conversation was most thrilling as far as Ustad Mangu was concerned. The new constitution now appeared to him to be something bright and full of promise. The only thing he could compare the new constitution with was the splendid brass and gilt fittings he had purchased after careful examination a couple of years ago for his tonga from Choudhry Khuda Bux. When the fittings were new, the nickel-headed nails would shimmer and where brass had been worked into the fittings it shone like gold. On the basis of that analogy also, it was essential that the new constitution should shine and glow.

By 1 April, Ustad Mangu had heard a great deal about the new constitution, both for and against. However, nothing could change the concept of the new constitution that he had formed in his mind. He was confident that come 1 April, everything would become clear. He was sure that what the new constitution would usher in would soothe his heart.

At last, the thirty-one days of March drew to a close. There were still a few silent night hours left before the dawn of 1 April and the weather was unusually cool, the breeze quite fresh. Ustad Mangu rose early, went to the stable, set up his tonga and took to the road.

He was extraordinarily happy today because he was going to witness the coming in of the new constitution.

In the cold morning fog, he went round the broad and narrow streets of the city but everything looked old, like the sky. His eyes wanted to see things taking on a new colour but, except for the new plume made of colourful feathers that rested on his horse's head, everything looked old. He had bought this new plume from Chaudhry Khuda Bux for fourteen annas and a half to celebrate the new constitution.

The road lay black under his horse's hooves. The lamp posts that stood on the sides at regular intervals looked the same. The shop signs had not changed. The way people moved about, the sound made by the tiny bells tied around his horse's neck were not new either. Nothing was new, but Ustad Mangu was not disappointed.

Perhaps it was too early in the morning. All the shops were still closed. This he found consoling. It also occurred to him that the courts did not start work until nine, so how could the new constitution be at work just yet.

He was in front of Government College when the tower clock imperiously struck nine. The students walking out through the main entrance were smartly dressed, but somehow their clothes looked shabby to Ustad Mangu. He wanted to see something startling and dramatic.

He turned his tonga left towards Anarkali. Half the shops were already open. There were crowds of people at sweetmeat stalls, and general traders were busy with their customers, their wares displayed invitingly in their windows. Overhead, on the power lines perched several pigeons, quarrelling with each other. But none of this held any interest whatever for Ustad Mangu. He wanted to see the new constitution as clearly as he could see his horse.

Ustad Mangu was one of those people who cannot stand the suspense of waiting. When his first child was to be born he had spent the last four or five months in a state of great agitation. While he was sure that the child would come to be born one day, he found it hard to keep waiting. He wanted to take a look at his child, just once. It could then take its time getting born. It was because of this desire that he could not overcome that he had pressed his sick wife's belly and put his ear to it in an attempt to find out something about the baby, but he had had no luck.

One day he had screamed at his wife in exasperation, 'What's the matter with you! All day long you lie in bed as if you were dead. Why don't you get up and walk about to gain some strength? If you keep lying there like a flat piece of wood, do you think you will be able to give birth?'

Ustad Mangu was temperamentally impatient. He wanted to see every cause have an effect, and he was always curious about it. Once his wife, Gangawati, watching his impatient antics, had said to him, 'You haven't even begun digging the well and already you're dying to have a drink.'

This morning he was not as impatient as he normally should have been. He had come out early to take a look at the new constitution with his own eyes, in the same way he used to wait for hours to catch a glimpse of Gandhiji and Pandit Jawaharlal Nehru being taken out in a procession.

Great leaders, in Ustad Mangu's view, were those who were profusely garlanded when taken out in public. Anyone bedecked in garlands of marigolds was a great man in Ustad Mangu's book. And if because of the milling crowds a couple of near-clashes took place, the leader's stature grew in Ustad Mangu's eyes. He wanted to measure the new constitution by the same yardstick.

From Anarkali he turned towards the Mall, driving his tonga slowly on its shiny surface. In front of an auto showroom, he found a fare bound for the cantonment. They settled the price and were soon on their way. Ustad Mangu whipped his horse into action and said to himself, 'This is just as well. One might find out something about the new constitution in the cantonment.'

He dropped his passenger at his destination, lit a cigarette, which he placed between the last two fingers of his left hand, and eased himself into a cushion in the rear of the tonga. When Ustad Mangu was not looking for a new fare, or when he wanted to think about some past incident, he would move into the rear seat of the tonga, with the reins of his horse wound around his left hand. On such occasions, his horse after neighing a little would begin to move forward at a gentle pace, glad to be spared the daily grind of cantering ahead.

Ustad Mangu was trying to work out if the present system of allotting tonga number plates would change with the new law, when he felt someone calling out to him. When he turned to look, he found a gora standing under a lamp post at the far end of the road, beckoning to him.

As already noted, Ustad Mangu had intense hatred for the British. When he saw that his new customer was a gora, feelings of hatred rose in his heart. His first instinct was to pay no attention to him and just leave him where he was. But then he felt that it would be foolish to give the man's money a miss. The fourteen annas and a half he had spent on the plume should be recovered from these people, he decided.

He neatly turned around his tonga on the empty road, flicked his whip and was at the lamp post in no time. Without moving from his comfortable perch, he asked in a leisurely manner, 'Sahib Bahadur, where do you want to be taken?'

He had spoken these words with undisguised irony. When he had called him 'Sahib Bahadur', his upper lip, covered by his moustache, had moved lower, while a thin line that ran from his nostril to his lower chin had trembled and deepened, as if someone had run a sharp knife across a brown slab of shisham wood. His entire face was laughing, but inside his chest roared a fire ready to consume the gora.

The gora, who was trying to draw on a cigarette by standing close to the lamp post to protect himself from the breeze, turned and moved towards the tonga. He was about to place his foot on the foothold when his eyes met Ustad Mangu's and it seemed as if two loaded guns had fired at each other and their discharge had met in mid-air and risen towards the sky in a ball of fire.

Ustad Mangu freed his left hand of the reins that he had wrapped around it and glared at the gora standing in front of him, as if he would eat every bit of him alive. The gora, meanwhile, was busy dusting his blue trousers of something that couldn't be seen, or perhaps he was trying to protect this part of his body from Ustad Mangu's assault.

'Do you want to go or are you again going to make trouble?' the gora asked.

'It is the same man,' Ustad Mangu said to himself. He was quite sure it was the same fellow with whom he had clashed the year before. That uncalled for argument had happened because the gora was sozzled. Ustad Mangu had borne the insults hurled at him in silence. He could have smashed the man into little bits, but he had remained passive because he knew that in such quarrels it was tongawalas mostly who suffered the wrath of the law.

'Where do you want to go?' Ustad Mangu asked, thinking about the previous year's argument and the new constitution of 1 April. His tone was sharp like the stroke of a whip.

'Hira Mandi,' the gora answered.

'The fare would be five rupees,' Ustad Mangu's moustache trembled.

'Five rupees! Five rupees! Are you . . .?' the gora screamed in disbelief.

'Yes, yes, five rupees,' Ustad Mangu said, clenching his big right fist tightly. 'Are you interested or will you keep making idle talk?'

The gora, remembering their last encounter, had decided not to be awed by the barrel-chested Ustad Mangu. He felt that the man's skull was again itching for punishment. This encouraging thought made him advance towards the tonga. With his swagger stick, he motioned Ustad Mangu to get down. The polished cane touched Ustad Mangu's thigh two or three times. Ustad Mangu, standing up, looked down at the short-statured gora as if the sheer weight of a single glance would grind him down. Then his fist rose like an arrow leaving a bow and landed heavily on the gora's chin. He pushed the man aside, got down from his tonga and began to hit him all over his body.

The astonished gora made several efforts to save himself from the heavy blows raining down on him, but when he noticed that his assailant was in a rage bordering on madness and flames were shooting forth from his eyes, he began to scream. His screams only made Ustad Mangu work his arms faster. He was thrashing the gora to his heart's content while shouting, 'The same cockiness even on 1 April! Well, sonny boy, it is our Raj now.'

A crowd gathered. Two policemen appeared from somewhere and with great difficulty managed to rescue the Englishman. There stood Ustad Mangu, one policeman to his left and one to his right, his broad chest heaving because he was breathless. Foaming at the mouth, with his smiling eyes he was looking at the astonished crowd and saying in a breathless voice, 'Those days are gone, friends, when they ruled the roost. There is a new constitution now, fellows, a new constitution.'

The poor gora with his disfigured face was looking foolishly, sometimes at Ustad Mangu, other times at the crowd.

Ustad Mangu was taken by police constables to the station. All along the way, and even inside the station, he kept screaming, 'New constitution, new constitution!' but nobody paid any attention to him.

'New constitution, new constitution! What rubbish are you talking? It's the same old constitution.'

And he was locked up.

A TALE OF 1947

Mumtaz was speaking with great passion, 'Don't tell me a hundred thousand Hindus and the same number of Muslims have been massacred. The great tragedy is not that two hundred thousand people have been killed, but that this enormous loss of life has been futile. The Muslims who killed a hundred thousand Hindus must have believed that they had exterminated the Hindu religion. But the Hindu religion is alive and well and will remain alive and well. And after putting away a hundred thousand Muslims, the Hindus must have celebrated the liquidation of Islam; but the fact is that Islam has not been affected in the least. Only the naive can believe that religion can be eliminated with a gun. Why can't they understand that faith, belief, devotion, call it what you will, is a thing of the spirit; it is not physical. Guns and knives are powerless to destroy it.'

Mumtaz was very emotional that day. The three of us had come to see him off. He was sailing for Pakistan, a country we knew nothing about. All three of us were Hindus. We had relatives in West Punjab, now Pakistan; some of them had lost their lives in anti-Hindu riots. Was this why Mumtaz was leaving us?

One day Jugal had received a letter, which said that his uncle who lived in Lahore had been killed. He just couldn't believe it. He had said to Mumtaz, 'If Hindu–Muslim killings start here, I don't know what I'll do.'

'What'll you do?' Mumtaz had asked.

'I don't know. Maybe I'll kill you,' he had replied darkly.

Mumtaz had kept quiet and for the next eight days he hadn't spoken to anyone; on the ninth day he had said he was sailing for Karachi that afternoon.

We had said nothing to him nor spoken about it. Jugal was intensely conscious of the fact that Mumtaz was leaving because of what he had said: 'Maybe I'll kill you.' He wasn't even sure if the heat of religious frenzy could actually bring him to kill Mumtaz, his best friend. That afternoon Jugal was very quiet; it was only Mumtaz who didn't seem to want to stop talking, especially as the hour of departure drew close.

Mumtaz had started drinking almost from the moment he climbed out of bed. He was packing his things as if it was a picnic he was going on, telling jokes, then laughing at them himself. Had a stranger seen him that morning, he would have concluded that his departure from Bombay was the best thing that had ever happened to him. However, none of us was fooled by his boisterousness; we knew he was trying to hide his feelings, even deceive himself.

I tried a couple of times to talk about his sudden decision to leave Bombay but he didn't give me an opportunity.

Jugal fell into an even deeper silence after three or four drinks and in fact left us to lie down in the next room. Brij Mohan and I stayed with Mumtaz. There was much to do. Mumtaz wanted to pay his doctor's bill; his clothes were still at the laundry, etc. He went through all these chores with the utmost aplomb. However, when we went to buy cigarettes from our regular shop in the corner, he put his hand on Brij Mohan's shoulder and said, 'Do you remember, Brij . . . ten years ago when we were all starving, this shopkeeper, Gobind, lent us money?' His eyes were moist.

He didn't speak again till we got home—and then it was another marathon, an unending monologue on everything under the sun. Not much of what he was saying made a great deal of sense, but he was talking with such utter sincerity that both Brij Mohan and I had no option but to let him go on, getting in a word edgeways when we could. When it was time to leave, Jugal came in, but as we got into the taxi to go to the port everyone became very quiet.

Mumtaz was looking out of the window, silently saying goodbye to Bombay, its wide avenues, its magnificent buildings. The port was crowded with refugees, mostly poor, trying to leave for Pakistan. But as far as I was concerned, only one man was leaving today, going to a country where no matter how long he lived he would always be a stranger.

After his baggage was checked in, Mumtaz asked us to come to the deck. Taking Jugal's hand, he said, 'Can you see where the sea and the sky meet? It is only an illusion because they can't really meet but isn't it beautiful, this union which isn't really there?'

Jugal kept quiet. Perhaps he was thinking, 'If it came to that, I may really kill you.'

Mumtaz ordered cognac from the bar because that was what he had been drinking since morning. We stood there, all four of us, glasses in our hands. The refugees had started to board. Jugal suddenly drank his glass down and said to Mumtaz, 'Forgive me. I think I hurt you very deeply that day.'

After a long pause, Mumtaz asked, 'That day when you said, "It is possible I may kill you," did you really mean that? I want to know.'

Jugal nodded. 'Yes, I am sorry.'

'If you had killed me, you would have been even sorrier,' Mumtaz said philosophically. 'You would have realized that it wasn't Mumtaz, a Muslim, a friend of yours, but a human being you had killed. I mean, if he was a bastard, by killing him you wouldn't have killed the bastard in him; similarly, assuming that he was a Muslim, you wouldn't have killed his Muslimness, but him. If his dead body had fallen into the hands of Muslims, another grave would have sprung up in the graveyard, but the world would have been diminished by one human being.'

He paused for breath, then continued, 'It is possible that after you had killed me, my fellow Muslims may have called me a martyr. But had that happened, I swear to God, I would have leapt out of my grave and begun to scream, "I do not want this degree you are conferring on me because I never even took the examination." In Lahore, a Muslim murdered your uncle. You heard the news in Bombay and killed me. Tell me, what medals would that have entitled you to? And what about your uncle and his killer in Lahore? What honour would be conferred on them? I would say that those who died were killed like dogs and those who killed killed in vain.'

'You are right,' I said.

'No, not at all,' he said in a tense voice. 'I am probably right but what I really wanted to say, I have not expressed very well. When I say religion or faith I do not mean this infection, which afflicts ninety-nine per cent of us. To me, faith is what makes a human being special, distinguishes him from the herd, proves his humanity.'

Then a strange light came into his eyes. 'Let me tell you about this man. He was a diehard Hindu of the most disreputable profession, but he had a resplendent soul.'

'Who are you talking about?' I asked.

'A pimp,' Mumtaz said.

We were startled. 'Did you say a pimp?' I asked.

He nodded. 'Yes, but what a man, though to the world he was a pimp, a procurer of women!' Then Mumtaz began his story.

'I don't remember his full name. It was something Sehai. He came from Madras and was a man of extremely fastidious habits. Although his flat was very small, everything was in its right place, neatly arranged. There were no beds, but lots of floor cushions, all spotlessly clean. A servant was around but Sehai did most things himself, especially cleaning and dusting. He was very straight, never cheated and never told you anything which was not entirely true. For instance, if it was very late and the liquor had run out, he would say, "Sahib, don't waste your money because in this neighbourhood they will only sell you rubbish at this hour." If he had any doubts about a particular girl, he would tell you about her. He told me once that he had already saved up twenty thousand rupees. It had taken him three years, operating at twenty-five per cent. "I need to make only another ten thousand and then I'll return to Benaras and start my own retail cloth business." Why he wanted to earn no more than that I didn't know nor did I have any idea what he found so attractive about the retail cloth trade.'

'A strange man,' I said.

Mumtaz continued, 'First I thought he cannot really be what he appears to be. Maybe he is nothing but a big fraud. After all, it was hard to believe that he considered and treated all the girls that he supplied to his customers as his own daughters. I also found it strange that he had opened a postal savings account for each of them and insisted that they should put their earnings there. There were some whose personal expenses he subsidized. All this was unreal to me because in the real world these things do not happen. One day when I went to see him, he said to me, "Both Ameena and Sakeena have their weekly day off. You see, being Muslims, they like to eat meat once in a while but none is cooked in this house because the rest of us are all strictly vegetarian." One day he told me that the Hindu girl from Ahmedabad, whose marriage he had arranged with a Muslim client of his, had written from Lahore, "I went to the shrine of the great saint Data Sahib and made a wish which has come true. I am going again to make another wish, which is that you should quickly make thirty thousand so that you can go to Benaras and start that retail cloth business of yours." I had laughed, thinking that he was only telling me this story about the popular Muslim saint because I was a Muslim.'

'Were you wrong?' I asked Mumtaz.

'Yes—he really was what he appeared to be. I am sure he had his faults but he was a wonderful man.'

'How did you find out that he wasn't a fraud?' Jugal, who hadn't spoken until now, asked.

'Through his death,' Mumtaz replied. 'The Hindu–Muslim killings had started. Early one morning, I was hurriedly walking through Bhindi Bazaar, which was still deserted because of the night curfew. There were no trams running and taxis were out of the question. In front of the JJ Hospital I saw a man lying in a heap on the footpath. I first thought it was a patiwala, who was still sleeping, but then I saw blood and stopped. I detected a slight movement and bent down to look at the man's face. It was Sehai, I realized with a shock. I sat down on the bare footpath. The starched and spotless twill shirt that he habitually wore was drenched by blood. He was moaning. I shook him gently by the shoulder and called his name a couple of times. At first, there was no response but then he opened his eyes; they were expressionless. Suddenly his whole body shook and I knew he had recognized me, "It's you," he whispered.

'I showered him with questions. What had brought him to this preponderantly Muslim locality at a time when people preferred to stay in their own neighbourhoods? Who had stabbed him? How long had he been lying here? But all he said was, "My day is done; this was Bhagwan's will."

'I do not know what Bhagwan's will was but I knew mine. I was a Muslim. This was a Muslim neighbourhood. I simply could not bear the thought that I, a Muslim, should stand here and watch a man, whom I knew to be a Hindu, lie there dying at the hands of an assassin who must have been a Muslim. I, who was watching Sehai die, was a Muslim like his killer. The thought did cross my mind that if the police arrived on the scene I'd be picked up, if not on a murder charge, certainly for questioning. And what if I took him to the hospital? Would he, by way of revenge against Muslims, name me as his killer? He was dying anyway. I had an irresistible urge to run, to save my own skin, and I might have done that except that he called me by my name. With an almost superhuman effort, he unbuttoned his shirt, slipped his hand in but did not have the strength to pull it out. Then he said in a voice so faint I could hardly hear it, "There's a packet in there . . . it contains Sultana's ornaments and her twelve hundred rupees . . . they were with a friend for safe custody . . . I picked them up today and was going to return them to her . . . these are bad times you know . . . I wanted her to have her money and the ornaments . . . Would you please give them to her . . . tell her she should leave for a safe place . . . but . . . please . . . look after yourself first!"'

Mumtaz fell silent but I had the strange feeling that his voice had become one with the dying voice of Sehai, lying on the footpath in front of the JJ Hospital, and together the two voices had travelled to that distant blue point where sea and sky met.

Mumtaz said, 'I took the money and ornaments to Sultana, who was one of Sehai's girls, and she started crying.'

We stepped down the gangplank. Mumtaz was waving.

'Don't you have the feeling he is waving to Sehai?' I asked Jugal.

'I wish I were Sehai,' he said.

THE GREAT DIVIDE

The 1947 upheavals came and went, much like the few bad days you get in an otherwise sunny Punjabi winter. Karim Dad lived through them, refusing to be cowed down. The will of God it might have been, as they said, but he was not one to surrender. He had fought many brave encounters during the last few months, not because he wanted to inflict defeat on anyone, but because it seemed to him that if you gave in you were less than a man.

At least, that is how he appeared to others; he had never thought consciously about these things. Had someone actually asked him in so many words if surrender to the enemy was a negation of one's manhood, he would have been confused, as if he had been told to solve an intricate mathematical equation.

Karim Dad was not interested in adding, subtracting or multiplying things. The 1947 upheavals were over. He took no interest in the balance sheets everyone was busy drawing up now. How many dead? How much in property losses? All he knew was that he had lost his father, Rahim Dad. He had carried his father's dead body over his shoulder and buried him near a well in a grave he had dug with his own hands in the soft earth.

A great deal had happened in their village. Hundreds of young and old people had been killed. Scores of girls had gone missing; others had been brutally raped. Those whom the upheavals had affected directly would not be able to forget their misfortune or the cruelty of the enemy for a long time.

As for Karim Dad, he had shed no tears. In fact, he was proud of the bravery of his father who had fought nearly thirty armed men single-handed, till he fell. All Karim Dad had said when he had been told about his father's death was, 'He should have listened to me. Didn't I tell him one must keep at least one weapon on one's person these days?'

Then he had gone out, picked up his father's body from the fields where it lay and buried it next to a well. His last words to him were, 'Only God knows about good and bad deeds, but may you end up in paradise.'

Rahim Dad, who was not only Karim's father but his best friend as well, had been killed mercilessly. The villagers even now became angry and abusive when they mentioned his killers, but Karim Dad had never said a word. His standing crop had been burnt to the ground, two of his houses had been gutted, but he had never once tried to recount his losses. The nearest he had come to doing that was, 'Whatever happened was because of our own mistakes.' He had never gone into details.

The village was still busy mourning those terrible days when Karim Dad married Jeena, a girl he had had his eye on for some time. She had lost her only brother in the riots. He was a giant of a man and the only one she had in the world after her parents died. Though Jeena loved Karim Dad as much as a woman can love a man, this love now lay buried under her grief for her dead brother. She would cry often.

Karim Dad hated people crying or feeling sorry for themselves. He hated to see Jeena in mourning, though he never told her that. She was a woman and he was afraid he might hurt her. However, one day when they were working in the fields, he couldn't contain himself. 'It is one year since we buried the dead. Even they by now must be tired of your mourning. Try to get over it. Save your tears; God knows how many more we are fated to mourn while we are alive.'

At first, Jeena had felt offended, but because she loved him, she finally convinced herself that Karim Dad was right. When word had first leaked out in the village that Karim Dad was planning to marry Jeena, the elders had opposed it. However, it was a feeble kind of opposition, because the fact was that the people were so sick of mourning the dead that they just didn't have the will to take a stand on the issue. So the wedding had gone ahead and it had been a lot of fun. It was after a long time that the village had seen a bride.

This was the first happy thing to have happened since the upheavals of Partition and the celebrations were spontaneous. To some it almost felt like a ghost wedding, so unused had they become to lights and laughter. When one of Karim Dad's friends mentioned this to him, he thought it was the funniest thing he had ever heard. He even told Jeena, but she did not think it was funny. In fact, a shudder ran through her body.

On their first night together, Karim Dad took hold of Jeena's bangled wrist and said, 'This ghost is going to haunt you for the rest of your life. Even Rahim Sain, the village witch doctor, will discover that his mumbo-jumbo does not work on the ghost called Karim Dad.'

Jeena put her hennaed finger between her teeth and blushed. 'Keemay, is there nothing you are afraid of?' Touching his moustache with the tip of his tongue, he said, 'Is fear anything to be afraid of, silly?' They laughed.

Jeena had almost forgotten the tragedies of the past. Her mind was now on her baby because she was pregnant. Karim Dad would look at her and say, 'I swear by God, you never looked more beautiful; but if you have put on this special look for that one you are carrying, then I'm telling you, he has a rival . . . me.'

Jeena would blush, try to cover her protruding belly with her dupatta and Karim Dad would laugh. 'Don't hide this thief. Don't I know all the things you are doing behind my back for this little swine!'

Jeena's face would darken. 'Don't abuse him.'

'He is a little swine because I am a big swine myself,' Karim Dad would say, bellowing with laughter.

The festival of Chotti Id came, followed by the Burri Id, both of which Karim Dad celebrated with great gusto. It was twelve days before the last Burri Id when the village had been attacked and his father, Rahim Dad, and her brother, Fazal Elahi, were killed. Jeena had wept bitterly remembering their deaths but Karim Dad was not one to let past sorrows darken his present.

Jeena found it hard to believe sometimes that she was beginning to forget such a great tragedy in her life. She didn't remember the deaths of her mother and father, but her brother, Fazal Elahi, who was six years older than her had become both father and mother to her. She also knew that it was because of her that he had not married and it was known to the entire village that he had laid down his life to save her honour. His death was the greatest tragedy in Jeena's life. It was like doomsday that had come to pass exactly twelve days before Burri Id. And now when she thought of it, she felt surprised at how quickly that great trauma had begun to be forgotten.

When the month of Muharram arrived, for the first time Jeena asked Karim Dad to fulfil her one ardent desire. She wanted to watch the Muharram procession go past with its riderless horse and commemorative floats. She had heard a lot about this from her friends. So she said to Karim Dad, 'Will you take me to watch the Muharram procession go by if I am well?'[1]

'I'll take you even if you are not well . . . and that little swine too,' he replied with a wink.

For some time now there had been rumours that a war would break out between India and Pakistan. Actually, the moment Pakistan was born, it somehow seemed to have been decreed that there would be a war. When it would take place, no one in the village could say. If someone asked Karim Dad, he always had this cryptic answer: 'It will be when it will be, why waste time worrying about it now?'

Jeena had also heard the rumours and she was terrified. She hated violence; she had seen enough of it in her young life; she did not wish to see any more.

Meanwhile, Karim Dad had bought a gun and trained himself to become an expert marksman. He was strong and he was brave. When he was with her, she never felt any fear, but when she was with other women, she felt very scared.

Bakhto, the village midwife, who came regularly to look at Jeena, one day brought the news that the Indians were going to dam the rivers which brought water to their villages in the Punjab. Jeena did not understand what this meant, so when Karim Dad came home that evening, she said to him, 'They are saying that the Indians are going to take away our water. Why would they do that?'

'So that our lands turn to waste,' he replied matter-of-factly.

'But that is cruel,' she said, quite convinced now that the rumours were correct.

'Was Bakhto here today?' he asked.

'Yes.'

'And?'

'She said the baby would come in ten days.'

'Zindabad,' Karim Dad shouted gleefully.

---

[1]The month of Muharram commemorates the martyrdom of Hussain, the Holy Prophet's favourite grandson, and his companions, who chose death instead of allegiance to Yazid, whom they considered an unjust and illegitimate ruler.

'You are rejoicing. God knows what is going to happen to us,' Jeena answered.

Karim Dad went out, spending the rest of the evening gossiping with the other men in the village common. Chaudhry Nathoo, the headman, was there trying his best to answer all the anxious questions being put to him. There were some who were abusing Pandit Nehru; others were cursing India. Though not one man was prepared to believe that the rivers could actually be dammed and diverted.

'Which rivers are they going to dam?' Jeena had earlier asked Bakhto.

'The ones that irrigate our lands,' the midwife had replied.

'You can't be serious, auntie,' Jeena had said. 'No one can dam rivers; they are not drains, they are rivers.'

Bakhto, who was massaging her belly, had replied, 'I don't know girl, but I have told you what I heard. They say it is in the newspapers.'

'What is in the newspapers?'

'That they are going to dam our rivers.' Then she had run her hand expertly over Jeena's belly and said, 'He should be here in ten days.'

Karim Dad had merely said, 'Well, that's what they say,' when she asked him again about the rumours.

Some people in the village were of the view that this was a punishment from God and the only way of averting this catastrophe was to gather in the mosque and pray.

Nobody was abusing the Indians more than Chaudhry Nathoo. It made Karim Dad squirm in his seat to hear the old man go on and on. 'It is mean and unfair; it is a bastardly act, a great sin, the greatest ever. It is what Yazid did when he dammed the river that brought water to Karbala where Hussain and his brave companions were fighting for survival. Many of them died of thirst, and that is what the Indians are doing.'

Karim Dad coughed two or three times, which meant that he wanted to say something. Chaudhry Nathoo had once again begun his tirade against the Indians, using the most filthy words he could think of. Suddenly, Karim Dad cut him short, 'Don't abuse them, Chaudhry.'

Chaudhry Nathoo, who was about to regale his audience with tales about the doubtful origin of the Indians and the morals of their mothers, couldn't believe his ears. 'What did you say?'

In a low but determined voice, Karim Dad replied, 'I said don't abuse them.'

Chaudhry Nathoo rasped back, 'What are they to you?' then addressed himself to the others, 'Did you hear that? He says I shouldn't abuse the Indians. Why don't you ask him what is his exact relationship to them? We would all like to know, I am sure.'

In a calm voice, Karim Dad replied, 'I'll tell you: they are my enemies.'

The headman laughed. 'Did you hear that! They are his enemies, he says, which means one should love one's enemies.'

'I didn't say one should love them. All I said was you shouldn't abuse them,' Karim Dad replied quietly.

'And why?' Miran Bux, one of Karim Dad's childhood friends, asked.

'What will you gain by that? They want to lay waste your lands and you think you will get even by abusing them. Is that wise? You only abuse when you have run out of other options,' Karim Dad said to Miran Bux.

'Do you have an option?'

'How can I answer this? It's not I alone who am involved, but hundreds upon thousands of others. How can I answer on their behalf? One has to think about these things coolly. They can't dam and divert our rivers in a couple of days; it will take them years, but you people will have vented all your anger in one day by abusing them.'

'He is talking nonsense,' Chaudhry Nathoo said.

'I am not talking nonsense. When it is war, everything is permissible. Haven't you seen two feuding wrestlers in a ring, fighting to the finish? There are no holds barred in such contests,' Karim Dad replied.

'You have a point there,' his friend said, scratching his head.

Karim Dad smiled. 'It follows then that they have every right to dam our rivers. It may appear to us as an act of cruelty, but it is no such thing to them. I think it is fair.'

'Fair, you said!' Chaudhry Nathoo screamed. 'When your tongue is hanging out because you have no water to drink, I will ask you if it is fair. When your children long for a mouthful of food, I will ask you if it is fair.'

'I will still say the same thing, Chaudhry,' Karim Dad replied.

'Why do you forget that it is not they alone who are our enemies; we are their enemies too. Had it been in our power, we would have seen to it that they received neither water to drink nor food to eat. I just don't think it is right to call the Indians mean, bastardly and cruel.'

'Hear that!' Chaudhry Nathoo shouted.

Karim Dad ignored him, turning to Miran Bux. 'It's foolish to expect your enemy to be kind to you. It is like complaining during battle that the other side is using heavier guns or bigger bombs compared to yours. What sort of a complaint is that?'

'But they are going to dam our waters and starve us, that is the issue. They want us to perish,' Chaudhry Nathoo said almost imploringly.

'Look Chaudhry Nathoo,' Karim Dad said, 'once you declare someone your enemy, then why complain that he is trying to starve you to death, that he is trying to turn your green fields into barren land? What do you expect him to do? Lay out a banquet for you?'

'You are talking nonsense,' was all that the headman could counter Karim Dad with.

But Karim Dad had not finished. 'It just so happens that the Indians are now in a position to take our water away from us. So, let's do something about it, instead of sitting here and abusing them. Don't expect the enemy to dig canals for you and fill them with milk and honey; expect him to poison your water so that you drink it and die. You will call it barbarism. I don't. If it is war, then it is a war, not a wedding contract with preconditions and the rest of it. You can't say, all right we will go to war, provided you don't starve us or take away our food. Or that if you must fire at us, use only a certain brand of cartridge. Be reasonable.'

'And how do I do that?' Chaudhry Nathoo asked.

Karim Dad did not answer, but rose and left.

He almost bumped into Bakhto as he walked through the front door. She was smiling. 'A boy like the new moon. Have you thought of a name?'

'Yes, I have,' he answered. 'Yazid, that's what he is going to be called.'

Bakhto's face went white because no Muslim child is ever called Yazid, as no Christian child can be called Judas. It is an evil name because it was Yazid at whose orders Hussain, the Prophet's grandson, and his companions were deprived of water and finally massacred.

Karim Dad ran into the house. Jeena was lying in bed, looking very pale. Next to her lay a tiny pink baby boy, his thumb in his mouth. Karim Dad touched him on the cheek. 'My little Yazid,' he said proudly.

'Yazid!' Jeena almost screamed.

'Yes, Yazid . . . that is his name,' Karim Dad said looking at the baby.

'What are you saying?' she asked in a shocked voice.

Karim Dad smiled. 'Yes, that's right, it is only a name after all.'

'But do you know whose name that is?' she asked.

'It is not necessary that this little one here should be the same Yazid. That Yazid dammed the waters; this one will make them flow again.'

FREE FOR ALL

In every city, town and village of the newly independent state, word went forth that anyone found begging on the street would be sent to gaol. Arrests began immediately, causing a lot of public joy because the curse of beggary had at last been abolished.

Only the wandering minstrel Kabir was grief-stricken.

'What is the matter with you, weaver?'—because that is what he was by caste—asked the citizens.

'I am sad because cloth is woven with two threads. One runs horizontally, the other vertically. The arrests are horizontal, but feeding the hungry is vertical. How are you going to weave this fabric?'

A refugee from India, a lawyer by profession, was given ownership of two hundred abandoned handlooms. Kabir passed that way and began to weep.

'Are you crying because I've been given what by right should have been yours?' asked the lawyer.

'No, what made me cry was the knowledge that these looms will never weave cloth again, because you'll sell the thread for a profit. You have no patience with the clickety clack of a loom, but that noise is a weaver's only reason to live.'

On the street a man was turning the printed leaves of a book into paper bags.

Kabir picked one up and as he began to read the print, tears welled up in his eyes.

'What troubles you?' the astonished bag-maker asked.

'Inscribed on the paper out of which you have fashioned these bags is the mystic poetry of the blind Hindu saint, Bhagat Sur Das,' answered Kabir.

The bag-maker didn't know any Hindi, but he did know that in his

native Punjabi Sur Das did not mean blind devotee—it meant pig.
'How can a pig be a saint?' he asked.

One of the most magnificent buildings in the city was adorned with a statue of the Hindu goddess of good fortune, Lakshmi. However, the new occupants, refugees from across the border, had covered it with an ugly length of cloth made from jute fibre. Kabir saw it and began to cry.

'Our religion forbids idolatry,' they told him.

'Does it not forbid the degradation of beauty?' Kabir asked.

A general was addressing his troops: 'We are short of food because our crops have been destroyed, but there's no cause for anxiety. My soldiers will fight the enemy on empty stomachs.'

Slogans of the impending victory were raised.

'My valiant general, who will fight hunger?' Kabir asked.

'Dear brothers in faith, grow beards, shave off your sinful whiskers and wear your trousers as ordained—an inch above the ankle. Dear sisters in faith, don't paint your faces, and cover yourselves with a veil. That is the divine command.'

Tears came to Kabir's eyes.

'You have neither brother nor sister and your beard is not black, but dyed. Don't you like to show your white hair?' Kabir said.

A heated intellectual argument was in progress.

'Art for art's sake.'

'Nonsense, art for life.'

'To hell with you!'

'To hell with your Stalin!'

'Shut up. Today art is another form of propaganda.'

'To hell with the reactionaries of the world and their Flauberts and Baudelaires!'

Kabir began to weep.

'He is undergoing a bourgeois trauma,' said one of the intellectuals.

'No, I weep because I want you to understand what art is for,' Kabir said.

'He is a proletariat joker.'

'No, he is a bourgeois clown.'

A new law was proclaimed requiring the city's prostitutes to get married within thirty days. When Kabir looked at their ravaged and anxiety-ridden faces, he wept.

A religious leader asked him, 'Why do you weep, my good man?'

'Who will find them husbands?' Kabir asked.

The religious leader began to laugh. It was the funniest thing he had ever heard.

A politician was addressing a crowd: 'My dear brothers, our greatest problem is the recovery of our women abducted by our enemies across the border. If we do nothing, I fear they will all end up in the prostitutes' quarter. We must save them from this fate. I call on you to take them into your homes. When you next think of a match for a member of your family, you should bear these unfortunate creatures in mind.'

When Kabir heard these words, he wept inconsolably.

'Look at this good man,' the leader told the crowd. 'How deeply my appeal has moved him.'

'No, your call did not move me,' Kabir said. 'I wept because I know that you have remained unmarried because you haven't yet found a rich bride.'

'Throw this lunatic out,' the crowd hissed.

Muhammad Ali Jinnah, the father of the nation, died. The country was plunged into mourning. Everyone went round with black armbands.

Kabir watched them in silence with tears rolling down his cheeks.

'So much cloth for so many armbands. It could have covered the hungry and the naked,' he said to the mourners.

'You are a communist,' they said.

'You are a fifth columnist.'

'You are a traitor to Pakistan.'

And for the first time, Kabir laughed that day. 'But my friends, I am wearing no armband, black, green or red.'

THE GIRL FROM DELHI

The religious killings had shown no sign of abating. India had been partitioned, but the bloodletting continued: Hindus killing Muslims, Muslims killing Hindus.

So one day, Nasim Akhtar, the young and much-sought-after nautch girl from Delhi's 'red light' quarter, said to her old mother, 'Let's get out of here.'

The old woman carefully placed a betel leaf in her toothless mouth and asked, 'But where will we go, sweetheart?'

'Pakistan,' Nasim Akhtar replied, and looked at her music teacher, old Ustad Achhan Khan. 'Khan sahib, what do you think? Is it any longer safe for us Muslims to live in Delhi?'

Achhan Khan had perhaps been thinking along the same lines, because he immediately said, 'You are quite right, but we must have your mother's—our burri baiji's—permission.'

But that was the difficult bit. Despite Nasim Akhtar's fervent pleading, the old woman would not go along. One day, the young woman told her mother, 'It is going to be Hindu raj; they don't want any Muslims around.'

'So what,' her mother replied. 'We are in business because of our Hindu patrons and clients. All your admirers and regulars are Hindus, don't you forget that. There's nothing the Muslims can do for us or that we want from them, I am telling you.'

'Don't say that mother,' Nasim Akhtar reacted sharply. 'The Quaid-e-Azam, Jinnah sahib, has worked so hard and got us our own country, Pakistan, and that's where we should go and live.'

In his opium-saturated voice, Mando the musician, chipped in, 'Chotti bai, may God protect you, what a wonderful thing you have said! I am prepared to go to Pakistan this very minute. If I die there and my bones are placed in its earth, my soul will rest in eternal peace.'

The other musicians were also equally enthusiastic about moving to Pakistan, but since the burri bai was against the idea, no more was said about it.

The burri bai, herself the toast of Delhi in her youth, sent a message to Seth Gobind Prakash, one of Nasim Akhtar's ardent and rich admirers and a frequent visitor to the kotha. The message conveyed that her daughter was terrified of all this Hindu–Muslim business and would he kindly come and set her mind at rest?

He came the next morning and Nasim Akhtar's mother said to him, 'Please talk to her. This girl wants us all to move to Pakistan, but I have been trying to reason with her. With such kind and generous friends as yourself, why should we leave Delhi? In fact, I have no doubt that in Pakistan we will be reduced to sweeping the streets. Sethji, I need a favour from you.'

The seth who was only half-listening to the burri bai, as his mind was elsewhere, asked, 'Ah, yes, what is that?'

'Could you have two or three armed guards posted outside our kotha for a few days so that this girl can feel safe?'

'No trouble at all. I can speak to the chief of police right away, so don't you worry. He will post a special police guard for your place, by this very evening, I promise,' the seth said expansively.

'May God bless you!' said the burri bai, much moved.

'Perhaps I will drop in myself this evening. Wouldn't it be nice to see our Nasim Akhtar's mujra?'

The old courtesan rose. 'Yes, indeed, this is your own place and this girl is always here at your service. Also, you must dine here tonight, seth sahib.'

'Unfortunately, I am on a diet these days,' he said, running his hands over his big belly.

After the seth's departure, the house was given a thorough cleaning. The big floor cushions, on which the clients reclined as they sat and watched Nasim Akhtar perform, had their covers changed, new lights were installed and a special tin of scarce cigarettes was ordered for Seth Gobind Prakash.

While the final touches were still being given to these elaborate preparations, the servant burst into the room, his face white with fear. He even had difficulty speaking, but finally managed to tell them that he had seen five Sikhs pounce on a Muslim street vendor just around the corner and stab him to death in the most gruesome manner.

Nasim Akhtar nearly fainted when she heard what had happened. Ustad Achhan Khan made gallant efforts to reassure her but she was just too shaken by what she had heard. Finally her mother said, 'This is not the first time a man has been killed in the street; these things are always going on. Now, child, don't you think it is time you got ready for the evening? Seth sahib could be here any minute.'

Although that was the last thing she felt like doing, Nasim Akhtar put on her silks and brocades, her peshwaz, painted her face, did her hair and took her customary place in the room where all the entertaining was done. But she couldn't get over that poor Muslim street vendor lying dead in a pool of blood. She wanted to throw off her ornaments, get out of her shimmering clothes, put on something plain and beg her mother to listen to her because she was sure something terrible was going to happen to them.

Finally she told her mother what had been going through her mind, but the old woman merely replied, 'Why should anything happen to us? We haven't offended anybody.'

'And who had that poor vendor offended? They killed him nevertheless, didn't they?' Nasim Akhtar said gravely. 'They cut him into pieces. It is the bad ones who escape and the innocent who get killed.'

'You don't know what you are saying,' her mother retorted irately.

'Who *does* these days? All I know is that blood is flowing in the streets of Delhi,' the young woman said. Then she rose, walked to the balcony and surveyed the street below. She saw four men with guns. She waved to Ustad Achhan Khan to come and take a look. 'Are they the armed policemen seth sahib had promised to arrange?' she asked him.

'They don't look like police to me; they are not wearing uniforms. They look like goondas to me,' the old man whispered.

'Goondas!' Nasim Akhtar nearly screamed.

'God only knows. They are coming towards the kotha. Nasim, I think you should take the stairs and go to the rooftop and I'll follow you in a few minutes. There is definitely something very wrong here.'

Nasim Akhtar slunk out of the room. The old woman had not noticed. Ustad Achhan Khan came soon after. Nasim Akhtar's heart was sinking. 'What is going on?' she asked the old man.

'Just what I had feared. The four men came up as soon as you had left the room. They said they had been sent by Seth Gobind Prakash to fetch you to his residence since he couldn't make it himself. Your mother was pleased and said it was very kind of him. She thought you were in the bathroom. She told the men she would have to come along too, but one of them said, "We don't want you, you old hag. We have come for the young one." 'When I heard that, I slipped out and rushed here to warn you,' the old man said breathlessly.

'What should we do?' Nasim Akhtar asked desperately.

Ustad Achhan Khan scratched his head. 'Let me think of something. Perhaps we should get out of here as fast as we can.'

'And my mother?' she asked.

'God will protect her, but we should escape while there is time,' he replied after a pause.

The adjoining roof, a few feet lower, was that of the local laundry. Without much difficulty, they jumped on to it. Luckily, there were stairs leading from the roof to the street and in a few minutes they were safely out. They walked a block or two and found a tonga owned by a Muslim who agreed to take them to the railway station.

On their way, they saw an army truck with Muslim soldiers who were evacuating people from Hindu areas and taking them to the station where special refugee trains for Pakistan were being run. They got a ride and were in time to board a train going to Lahore in Pakistan, where they arrived the next morning.

They were taken to a refugee camp in a place outside the city called Walton. They lived there for a few weeks and then Ustad Achhan Khan sold some of Nasim Akhtar's jewellery and they moved to a small, inexpensive hotel. After a few days, the old man rented a kotha in Hira Mandi, Lahore's famous 'red light' courtesan district.

One day Ustad Achhan Khan said to her, 'I think we need to invest in some purchases, I mean musical instruments, floor cushions, that sort of thing and, with God's blessings, we can take up where we left off in Delhi.'

But to his surprise, Nasim Akhtar replied, 'No, Khan sahib, my heart is not in that sort of thing any more. I don't even want to live in this neighbourhood. Please find me a small place in some nice, normal locality. Delhi is behind me. That life for me is finished. I just want to live like a normal woman.'

'What are you talking about, girl?' Achhan Khan asked.

'That was all a long time ago. I don't even want to think about those days. Please pray for me; may God give me the strength to make a break from my past.' Nasim Akhtar's eyes were full of tears.

Over the next few days, Ustad Achhan Khan tried his best to talk her out of her strange resolve but her mind really seemed to be made up. One day she said to him, 'I would like to get married, that is, if someone would have me; otherwise I will remain a spinster.'

Achhan Khan could not understand what had happened to her.

Was it the partition of the country that had unhinged her? Women in this profession were not like this. But he soon gave up on her. She really had changed. He found her a small house in a quiet locality, far away from Hira Mandi; but he moved back to the area himself, where he felt at home, and was hired by a rich and popular courtesan as her music teacher.

Nasim Akhtar was happy. It was a hard life, but that was what she wanted. A young boy-servant did her shopping and helped her around the house. The money from the sale of the rest of her ornaments was enough to keep her going for some time yet. She had become very religious, praying five times a day, and abstaining from food and drink during Ramadan.

Over the last couple of months, an old woman called Jannatey had begun to visit her off and on. Nasim Akhtar was grateful for her company; what she did not know was that this woman was a procuress who enticed young girls and sold them into prostitution. If they had a talent for song and dance, they became rich courtesans; otherwise they became part of Hira Mandi's infamous flesh trade.

One day, while Jannatey was out in the courtyard, she heard Nasim Akhtar singing most beautifully as she washed her hair. She had not sung for a long time and even now was not conscious of the fact that she was singing. By instinct and experience the old woman knew the moment she heard the singing that this strange girl from Delhi who never talked and lived alone could find a place in Hira Mandi, where she could become one of Lahore's leading singing girls. The question was how to go about it.

She tried a number of ruses, made some indirect, some direct references to the possibility, but none of them worked. Finally, one day, she threw her arms around Nasim Akhtar and kissed her on the forehead affectionately. 'Daughter, I beg of you, don't misunderstand me. I was only testing you, but you are a young woman of great piety and virtue, and not for you those things. I am sorry.'

Nasim Akhtar was taken in; she even told the old woman that she wanted to get married to a nice and simple man as it was not safe or advisable for a young woman to be living all alone without anyone to look after her.

This was just the opening Jannatey had been looking for. 'You leave that to me; I will find you the perfect husband, a man who will worship you.'

In the next few days, the old procuress brought Nasim Akhtar a number of fake proposals, making none of them sound too good, until one day she burst into the house announcing that she had found the man she was looking for. He was not too old, had a lot of property, was of a fine, upright moral character, and if Nasim Akhtar would trust her, she would go right ahead with the arrangements.

Nasim Akhtar was mentally prepared for any proposal that sounded good, more so because she had complete faith in the old woman. So she said Jannatey could proceed with the arranged marriage. She did not need to see or meet the man.

A date was set and a simple ceremony took place and Nasim Akhtar was married. She was happy that she had found a good husband who would look after her. However, her happiness was not to last beyond twenty-four hours, because the very next day she overheard her husband talking to two old courtesans from Hira Mandi. They were haggling over her price. She was being sold off. Jannatey was the mediator.

Nasim Akhtar rushed into her bedroom, tears running down her cheeks. She cried for a long time, then she dried her eyes and unpacked the clothes she had brought with her from Delhi, the ones she had been wearing that last evening, and quietly walked out of the house, making straight for the kotha where Ustad Achhan Khan was employed.

BITTER HARVEST

When Qasim walked through the door, all he was conscious of was a burning pain in his thigh because of the embedded bullet. But when he saw the blood-soaked body of his wife lying in the courtyard, he forgot his pain. He wanted to grab his axe and rush out of the house, killing everyone who came in his path, smashing everything that caught his eye. Then he thought of his daughter, Sharifan.

'Sharifan! Sharifan!' he shouted.

The doors of the two rooms in the house were shut. Was she hiding behind one of them, he wondered. 'Sharifan! Sharifan!' he screamed. 'This is me, your father.' There was no answer. He pushed open the first door with both hands. What he saw was so horrifying that he almost fainted.

On the floor was the nearly naked body of a young girl, her small, upturned breasts pointing at the ceiling as she lay on her back. He wanted to scream but he couldn't. He turned his face away and said in a soft, grief-stricken voice, 'Sharifan.' Then he picked up some clothes from the floor and threw them over her. He did not notice that they had missed their target by several feet.

As he ran out of the house, axe in hand, he was no longer conscious of the bullet in his thigh or the blood-soaked body of his wife, but only of Sharifan, the naked Sharifan lying dead in a heap on the floor of her room.

Axe in hand, he began to move like molten lava through the deserted streets of the city. He saw a Sikh in the main square, a big hulk of a man, but so ferocious and sudden was Qasim's attack that the man fell to the ground like an uprooted tree, blood gushing out of his severed head.

Qasim could feel his own blood surging through his body, like boiling oil over which cold water is being sprinkled. He saw a group of five or six men at the far end of the road and moved towards them like an arrow. 'Har Har Mahadev,' they shouted, obviously taking him for a fellow Hindu. 'Motherfuckers,' he screamed and rushed at them, swinging his axe wildly.

In a few seconds, three of them had fallen to the ground in a blood-smeared pile; the others had run away. Like a man demented, he kept hitting them, till he fell on top of one of the dead bodies himself. He wasn't sure if he had fallen or been overpowered. He lay there waiting for the blow to come, but nothing happened. After a few minutes, he slowly opened his eyes. There was no one on the road, just three dead men among whom he lay.

He almost felt disappointed that he had not been killed, but then he remembered Sharifan's naked body, an image that seared his eyes like molten lead. He picked up his axe and was soon running in the streets, shouting obscenities.

The city was deserted. He turned randomly into a small side street, but was soon out of there when he realized that it was a Muslim neighbourhood. So far he had been hurling abuse at the mothers and sisters of his enemies; now he began to abuse their daughters.

He came to a stop in front of a small house. On the wooden door was a sign in Hindi. Qasim began to swing his axe at it and in a few minutes he had smashed the wood into a pulp. 'Come out, you bastards, come out!' he screamed as he went in.

One of the doors in the house creaked on its hinges and opened slowly to reveal a young girl. 'Who are you?' he asked. 'I am a Hindu,' she replied, running her tongue over her dry lips. She could not have been more than fourteen or fifteen.

Qasim threw away the axe and pounced on her like a wild beast, throwing her to the ground. Then he began to tear at her clothes and for half an hour he ravaged her like an animal gone berserk. There was no resistance; she had fainted.

When he finished, he realized that he was clutching her throat with both hands, his nails embedded into her soft skin. He released her with a violent jerk.

He closed his eyes and saw an image of his daughter, lying dead on the floor, her small breasts pointing upwards. He broke into an icy sweat.

Through the smashed street door, a man ran into the house, a sword in his hand. He found Qasim squatting on the floor, trying to spread a blanket over someone lying there.

'Who are you?' the stranger roared.

Qasim turned his face towards him.

'Qasim!' the man screamed in disbelief.

Qasim blinked his eyes; his face wore a blank expression. He couldn't even see properly.

'What are you doing in my house?' the man shouted.

With a trembling finger, Qasim pointed to the blanket-covered heap on the floor. 'Sharifan,' he said in a hollow voice.

The other man pulled off the blanket. The sword fell from his hand; then he staggered out of the house wailing, 'Bimla, my daughter, Bimla.'

A STRANGE TALE

In the large garden attached to the big house, a cat gave birth to several kittens behind the bushes, all of which were eaten by a tomcat. Then came along a bitch who gave birth to pups in the same spot. They grew into big dogs and ran in and out of the house at all hours, barking and making a nuisance of themselves. They were poisoned one by one, as was their mother. Had the father been alive, he would have been poisoned too.

It is hard to say how much time had passed after these incidents took place. Anyway, the bushes in the garden had been trimmed thousands of times since. In between, many cats and dogs had given birth to their litters in the same spot. None had survived. This spot had also become the favourite hideout for hens who came here to lay their eggs.

And every morning, she would take away the eggs.

In the same garden, a young man had murdered her maid in cold blood. He had strangled her with a red silken cord with pompons, the cord that she had purchased from a street vendor a week ago for eight annas and which was used to hold her trousers in place. The murderer had strangled her so savagely that her eyes had nearly popped out of their sockets.

She had seen the dead woman and it had made her ill. So high was her fever that she had fallen unconscious. Perhaps she was still unconscious. But that couldn't be, because after the murder it was not hens that had come to lay eggs but cats that had used the place to give birth to kittens. There had also been a wedding. The bride was a bitch with a pretty red dupatta with sequins draped around her. Her eyes had not popped out; they had become even more deeply embedded in their sockets.

A band had played in the garden. Soldiers in red tunics with bagpipes had produced strange sounds from their instruments. Their uniforms were adorned with pompons. Some of them had fallen and the onlookers had picked them up from the ground and tied them to the cords that kept their trousers in place. Next morning, no soldier could be seen. They had all been poisoned.

The bride had decided to give birth not behind the bushes but in her bed. It was a lovely baby, like a red pompon, but the bride's mother had died, as had her father. The baby had killed both of them. Had his own father been around, he would have killed him too.

The soldiers in red uniforms and big pompons had not returned. The garden had become the hunting ground of wild tomcats that glared at one another and mistook her for a basket of animal entrails but all it contained was oranges.

One day, she took out two of her oranges and placed them in front of a mirror. She went behind the mirror but could not see the oranges, perhaps because they were small. Then the oranges grew big and she wrapped them in silk and placed them on the mantel.

The dogs had begun to bark and the oranges began to roll around the house, through every room, before bouncing into the garden where they were seen playing with the dogs.

Two of the dogs had taken poison and died; the rest were eaten by her fat, middle-aged maid who had replaced the young maid who had been strangled with her own trouser cord with dangling pompons.

Her mother was five or six years older than her new maid but not strong like her. Every morning, she would go for a drive. Like a stray hen, she had the bad habit of laying her eggs behind those bushes, which she would pick up and bring home. The driver was not allowed to do that. She would prepare an omelette with the eggs and invariably soil her clothes while cooking. Then she would throw the soiled clothes behind the bushes for kites to take away.

A friend had visited her one day. She had come by Pakistan Mail, car no. PL 9612. It was very hot. Daddy was in the hills and mummy had gone for a walk. She was perspiring. As soon as she was in her room, she had thrown off her blouse and stood under the ceiling fan. The milk in her breasts was boiling but it had cooled down before boiling again. Then the cold milk and the boiling milk had got mixed and turned into buttermilk.

Her friend was serenaded but the uniformed soldiers with pompons had not come this time. In their place had arrived big brass instruments that alternately produced shrill and thunderous sounds.

When she had met her friend next, she had found her changed. Now she had two bellies, one old, one new. And her milk had gone sour.

The next to be serenaded was her brother. The old maid had wept because it had reminded her of her own wedding, but her brother had calmed her down.

All night, her brother and his bride had kept fighting and while she had cried, he had laughed. In the morning, the fat, middle-aged maid had taken her brother away to console him. The bride had been bathed and her trousers tied with a cord, which had a red pompon. It was not clear why the cord was not around her neck.

She had big eyes, and had she been properly strangled, her eyes would have popped out like the eyes of a slaughtered ram. Then she would have developed a high fever, but her earlier fever had not yet gone down. Or maybe it had and it was the new fever that had knocked her unconscious.

Her mother was learning to drive. Her father lived in a hotel and only came home occasionally to meet his son, who also brought his wife home off and on, but the fat, middle-aged maid would start crying over some memory from the past. He would calm her down and she would caress him affectionately and the bride would leave.

At times, she and her brother's wife would go for a walk, joined by her friend. They would take Pakistan Mail and drive by car no. PL 9612 to Ajanta where one was taught how to paint. All three of them would turn into paintings with lots of reds, yellows, greens and blues, all very loud. The man who had created the paints would tame the colours. He wore long hair and a topcoat summer and winter. He was handsome and walked about in wooden sandals, at home and on the street. After taming the colours, he would shriek. The three women would calm him down and then shriek themselves.

The three of them had produced hundreds of abstract paintings in Ajanta but their breasts had gone dry because it was hot. They had been perspiring when they had entered the cool room and stood under the fan after throwing off their blouses. The fan had neither cooled nor warmed their milk.

Her mother was in the other room and the driver was wiping engine oil off her body. Her father was in the hotel where his secretary was rubbing eau de cologne on his forehead.

One day, she was serenaded too. The abandoned garden, decorated by the proprietor of Ajanta Studio, had come to life again.

Deep coloured lipstick evaporated in the air while the darkest shade became her pupil.

Her bridal dress had been designed by the Ajanta man. It looked different from every angle. If viewed from the front, it resembled a heap of trouser cords. Looked at from the side, it could be mistaken for a fruit basket or a curtain fluttering in a window. If seen from behind, it could be compared with watermelons. From a certain angle, it was a jar of tomato ketchup; from the top, a work of abstract art; and viewed from a low angle, the obscure poetry of Meeraji.

Those who appreciated art were pleased with the sight. The bridegroom was so impressed that he had decided the next morning to become an abstract painter. He and his wife had travelled to Ajanta where they were told that the teacher was getting married in a few days and had already moved in with his wife-to-be.

His wife-to-be was a dark lipstick, much darker than the other lipsticks. In the beginning, it was more interested in abstract art than her husband; but after the closure of Ajanta Studio, he had gone into the salt business, which had turned out to be highly profitable.

In the course of his business, he had met a girl whose breasts had not dried up and he had liked them. There was no band in attendance but they had got married nevertheless. The first one had picked up her paintbrushes and begun to live alone.

In the early days, there was bitterness between them but it had soon turned into sweetness. Her friend who had gone on a tour of Europe after dumping her husband was now ill, but she had turned the sweetness she had found into cubism. Her painting had lots of cubes, one on top of the other, surrounded by cacti. On the top you could see honeybees buzzing about trying to extract nectar.

Her other friend had poisoned herself, and when she had heard the news, she had fallen unconscious. It was not clear if her unconsciousness was old or new.

Her father was in Eau de Cologne where his hotel was rubbing the temples of his secretary. Her mother had handed over the keys of her house to the fat, middle-aged maid. She could drive a car now but she had fallen very ill. Anyway, she had not neglected the driverless puppy, which was being fed on her engine oil.

Her brother and his wife lived happily and showed much affection for one another. One night when the maid and her brother were working out the day's expenses, her sister-in-law had appeared suddenly. She was no abstract painting and carried no paintbrush, but she had wiped off both of them.

In the morning, two bloodied pompons were found in the room which her brother's wife had put around her neck.

She had regained consciousness. After her bitter quarrel with her husband, her life had acquired a certain sweetness, so to inject it with a shot of bitterness, she had started to drink but it had not worked because she only drank small quantities. Then she had begun to drink heavily and people were sure she would drown in liquor but she had invariably managed to bob up to the surface, wiping the liquor off her mouth and laughing hysterically.

When she had woken up in the morning, she had felt that all night her body had been gushing out tears. All the children she could have borne, all the graves that could have been dug for them, all the milk that could have been theirs to drink had simply not come to pass. The children were crying inconsolably but where was her milk? The tomcats had come and drunk it.

She would have liked to drink more so that she could drown in a bottomless sea but it had never happened. She was intelligent, educated and she could talk about sex without inhibition. She did not see anything wrong in going to bed with men. On nights when she was alone, she wanted to be like one of her hens, go behind the bushes and lay an egg.

She was hollow, no more than a bag of bones. People avoided her, but she was not bothered. She lived alone, smoked cigarette after cigarette, drank, and always kept thinking. She needed very little sleep and at night she kept walking around the house.

In the servant quarters, the driver's motherless son cried constantly, asking for engine oil but her mother had no more of it. The driver had met with an accident. The car was in the garage and her mother in the hospital where one of her legs had been amputated. The other was going next.

Sometimes she would peep into the servant's room where the driver's son was. She would feel the milk that was still in her breasts bubble but it was never enough to even moisten the lips of the child.

Her brother was gone. One day he had written to her from Switzerland, saying he was under treatment but his nurse was nice. He was going to marry her as soon as he got out of the hospital.

The fat, middle-aged maid had disappeared after stealing her mother's ornaments, cash and clothes. Her mother had died following an operation.

Her father had come for the funeral but that was the last time she had seen him.

She was all alone now, having sacked the servants including the driver. All she was left with was a nurse for the child. Nothing bothered her any longer, except her thoughts. If someone came to the house, she would scream, 'Go away, whoever you are. I wish to see no one.'

In a locked safe, she had come upon her mother's ornaments. She had also found some of her own but she had no real interest in them now, though every night she would sit in front of the mirror naked. She would bedeck herself with the ornaments, drink and sing ribald songs in an offbeat voice. She had no neighbouring house and was free to do what she liked.

She had bared her body but it was her soul she wanted to see naked. Was it possible? Through drink perhaps, she thought, as she drank some more.

She was tired of painting and her paintbrushes and colours had remained boxed since long. One day, she had opened the box, mixed the paints in separate bowls, washed and cleaned the brushes and gone and stood naked in front of her mirror. Then she had painted her body because she sought absolute nudity.

It had taken her all day to paint the front of her body. Without food or drink, she had stood facing the mirror, confidently painting her body with strange lines and loops. At midnight, she had examined herself and found the result satisfactory. Then she had put on all her ornaments and looked in the mirror one more time.

Startled by a noise, she had turned and found a masked man with a knife standing behind her. He had screamed, dropped the knife and run out in panic.

She had run after him, screaming, 'Stop, stop, you have nothing to worry about, stop.'

But the thief had jumped over a wall and disappeared. Returning home, she had seen the knife lying near the door which she had picked up and taken inside. Returning to the mirror, she had examined herself, noticing the sheath she had painted where her heart was. She had placed the knife against the painted spot but found it to be too large, so she had chucked it aside. Then she had picked up the bottle, taken four or five large swigs and walked around restlessly for a few minutes before emptying every other bottle in the house. She had not eaten.

She had stood in front of the mirror wearing a necklace with pompons, but it was not a real necklace; she had painted it on.

Suddenly, she had felt the necklace tightening itself like a noose around her throat, cutting into the flesh. She had stood there watching her eyes bulge out and the veins in her face become visible. She had screamed and fallen to the floor on her face.

A QUESTION OF HONOUR

If you happen to be on Faras Road, Bombay, and turn into the street called Sufaid Gulli, you run into a cluster of cafes and restaurants. Nothing special about that, Bombay being a city of cafes and restaurants. However, there is something special about Sufaid Gulli. It is the city's 'red light' district where prostitutes of every race and description can be found.

If you went past Sufaid Gulli, you came to Playhouse, a noisy all-day cinema.

There were actually four cinemas in the area, each with its bell-ringing barker. 'Walk in, walk in. First-class show for only two annas.' Sometimes, unwilling passers-by were physically pushed inside by these enterprising salesmen.

Street masseurs were always around. Getting your head massaged was a popular pastime in Bombay. I would watch men contentedly getting their skulls reconditioned. It never failed to amuse me.

If you felt like massage at three in the morning, a malashia could easily be sent for, no matter in what part of the city you lived. These fellows were omnipresent, yelling 'pi, pi, pi'—short for champi or massage.

The name Faras Road was used to describe the entire prostitutes' quarter. The small side streets had their own names, but collectively they were referred to as Faras Road or Sufaid Gulli.

The women sat in small rooms behind bamboo screens. The price varied from eight annas to eight rupees, and from eight rupees to eight hundred rupees. You could find your choice in this versatile buyers' market.

There was also a small Chinatown. It was not clear what occupations its residents were engaged in, though some certainly ran restaurants, their names scrawled in funny insect-like letters outside.

Another street in the area was called Arab Gulli, with twenty to twenty-five Arabs living there, all apparently in the pearl trade. Others were Punjabis or Rampuris.

It was in Arab Gulli that I had a rented room, which was so dark that the light had to be kept on at all times. The monthly rent was exactly nine rupees, eight annas.

If you have never lived in Bombay, you would find it hard to believe that its people simply do not interfere in each other's business. If you are dying in your room—kholi in Bombaiya—nobody is going to give a damn. If a murder takes place in the neighbourhood, nobody is going to bring you the news.

However, there was one man in Arab Gulli who was informed about every single resident of the area. His name was Mammad Bhai. He came from Rampur and had the reputation of being the master of every known martial art. I was told many stories about him when I first moved in, but it was a long time before I got an opportunity to meet him.

I used to leave my kholi early in the morning and return late at night. However, this character Mammad Bhai had begun to fascinate me. It was said, for instance, that, single-handed, he could fight off twenty-five men armed with lathis. One by one, he could fell them to the ground. It was also said that a knifer of his dexterity was hard to find in Bombay. He could slash an adversary with demonic speed. His victims were said to walk away without noticing anything amiss and then suddenly crumble to the ground . . . stone dead. 'Nobody has Mammad Bhai's touch,' it was whispered.

My curiosity to meet Mammad Bhai grew every day. You were always conscious of his presence in the area. He was the dada, the burra badmash, but everyone swore that he was a puritan as far as women were concerned, or, as the local expression went, he was 'wedded to the sanctity of his loincloth'. He was also a sort of local Robin Hood.

Not only in Arab Gulli, but also in the surrounding streets, every poor woman without means knew Mammad Bhai. He used to help them regularly. It was always one of his apprentices—shagirds, as they were called—who was sent over. He never went himself.

I did not know what means of income Mammad Bhai had. He was said to dress well, eat well and drive himself around in a dandy pony tonga, invariably accompanied by two or three shagirds. They would make a round of the bazaar, stop at a local shrine briefly, then trot back into Arab Gulli and get into one of its Iranian cafes for a long session, with Mammad Bhai holding forth on the intricacies of martial arts.

Next to my kholi was the kholi of a male dancer from Marwar who had told me hundreds of stories about Mammad Bhai. He once said, 'Mammad Bhai is simply peerless. Once I came down with cholera. Somebody informed Mammad Bhai and he got every Faras Road doctor into my kholi, warning them that if something went wrong with Ashiq Hussain, he would bump them off personally.'

Then Ashiq Hussain added in an emotional voice, 'Manto sahib, Mammad Bhai is an angel. When he threatened the doctors, you could see them trembling. Then they really got down to the treatment and I was bouncing about like a ball in two days flat.'

There were other stories I had heard about Mammad Bhai in the filthy and third-class cafes of Arab Gulli. One man, probably a shagird, told me that Mammad Bhai always carried a razor-sharp steel dagger tucked against his thigh, so sharp that he could shave himself with it. It was kept unsheathed and was so lethal that had Mammad Bhai not been a careful man he could have seriously injured himself with it.

So, with each passing day, my keenness to meet this man increased. I would try to imagine him. A tall, muscular, formidable figure, the kind of man they used as a model to advertise the Hercules bicycle.

Tired after my long day, I would generally hit my bed and fall asleep immediately. There was never time to meet Mammad Bhai. I often thought of skipping work one day to catch a glimpse of him. Unfortunately, I was never able to do that. I had a ridiculous job.

One day, I suddenly came down with high fever. I am hardy by nature and have never required care, but God knows what kind of a fever it was. It felt as if someone was slowly crushing my spine. For the first time in my life, I felt in need of help, but I had nobody around.

For two days I lay in agony all alone. There were no visitors, not that I had expected any. I hardly knew anyone. The few friends I had lived in far-flung areas. If I had died, for instance, they would never even have come to know and, in any case, who cared in Bombay whether you lived or died.

I was in terrible shape. Ashiq Hussain the dancer had gone back home because his wife was ill, according to the tea boy—chhokra—from the Iranian cafe.

One day, I decided to try the impossible—get up from my bed

and go to one of the bazaar doctors. Suddenly, there was a knock at the door. I thought it was the chhokra. In a barely audible voice, I said, 'Come in.'

The door opened to reveal a man of slight build. The first thing I noticed about him was his moustache. It was his entire personality, and without it, one would hardly have noticed him.

He walked in, giving his Emperor Kaiser Wilhelm moustache a twirl. He was followed by three or four other men I did not know.

The man with the Kaiser Wilhelm moustache said to me in a very soft voice, 'Vimto sahib, this is no good. Why didn't you send me word you were ill?'

That I had been called Vimto instead of Manto was nothing new, nor was I in the mood to correct him. All I could say in my weak, feverish voice to the moustache was, 'Who are you?'

'Mammad Bhai,' came the cryptic answer.

I almost rose from my bed. 'Mammad Bhai . . . Mammad Bhai, the famous dada?'

It was a bit tactless, but he ignored it. With his little finger he gave his moustache a slight lift and smiled. 'That's right, Vimto bhai, I am Mammad, the famous dada. It was the chhokra who told me how sick you were. This is no sala good. You should have sent me word. When something like this happens, Mammad Bhai sala loses his cool.'

I was about to say something, when he ordered one of his companions. 'Hey, what's your name, go run to what's his name that sala doctor. Tell him Mammad Bhai wants him here double quick. Tell him to run. Drop whatever he is doing. And let the sala not forget to bring his stuff with him.'

The man whom Mammad Bhai had commissioned for the errand disappeared. I looked at him and remembered the stories I had heard about him, but all I could see was his moustache. It was a terrifying sight—and an impressive one. His features were soft and it seemed he had grown a moustache to give himself a macho touch.

Since there was no chair, I invited Mammad Bhai to sit on my bed, an offer he refused, saying drily, 'Never mind.'

He began to pace around, although the room was hardly capable of offering such luxury. Presently, he produced his famous dagger from somewhere. It was a dazzling sight. At first I thought it was made of silver. He ran it gently over his wrist and any hair that came in its path was instantly shaved away. This seemed to please him and he began to trim his nails with it.

His mere arrival had brought my fever down several degrees, or so it seemed. 'Mammad Bhai,' I said, 'this dagger that you carry is awfully sharp. Aren't you afraid you'll hurt yourself?'

Neatly slicing off another nail, he said, 'Vimto bhai, this dagger is meant for my enemies. How can it hurt me?'

He sounded like a father speaking fondly of his child. 'How can my own child hurt me?'

Finally the doctor came. His name was Pinto—and I was Vimto. He greeted Mammad Bhai respectfully and asked what the matter was. 'I'll tell you what the matter is,' he replied sternly. 'If you don't get Vimto bhai well, sala you're going to pay for it.'

Obediently, Dr Pinto began to examine me. He took my pulse, put his stethoscope on my chest, tapped my back, checked my blood pressure and asked me how and when I had fallen ill. Then he said to Mammad Bhai—not me—'Nothing to worry. It is only malaria. I'll give him a shot.'

Mammad Bhai shaved some more hair off his wrist and said, 'I know nothing about these things. If you want to give him a shot, then give him a sala shot, but if anything happens to him, remember . . .'

'No, Mammad Bhai, everything is going to be fine. Now let me give him a shot.' He opened his bag and took out a syringe.

'Wait, wait,' Mammad Bhai screamed. Pinto put the syringe back into the bag and looked at Mammad Bhai nervously.

'I just cannot watch anybody getting the needle,' he said and walked out, followed by his entourage.

Dr Pinto gave me a quinine injection neatly, although normally it is a very painful affair. When he was done, I asked him what I owed him. 'Ten rupees,' he said. I reached for my wallet, which lay under my pillow, and had just paid him when Mammad Bhai entered the room.

'What's going on?' he screamed. 'I was only paying the doctor his fee,' I said. 'Sala, what do you think you are doing?' he screamed at Pinto. 'Mammad Bhai, I swear I didn't ask for it,' Pinto replied meekly.

'Sala, if you want your fee, you get it from me. Give Vimto sahib back his money.' It was immediately returned.

Mammad Bhai twirled his moustache and smiled. 'Vimto sahib, how can a doctor from my area take money from you? Had he done that, I swear I would have had my moustache shaved off. Everyone here is your slave.'

I asked Mammad Bhai how he knew me.

'How do I know you? Is there anyone here whom Mammad Bhai doesn't know? My friend, Mammad Bhai is the king and looks after his people. My detectives keep me informed about everything. Arrivals, departures, who is doing what.'

Then he added, 'I know everything about you.'

'Is that so?' I asked.

'Sala—don't I know? You come from Amritsar. You are a Kashmiri. You work here for newspapers. You owe ten rupees to the Bismillah Hotel in the bazaar, which is why you no longer pass that way. In Bhindi Bazaar there is a paanwala who curses you day and night. You owe him twenty rupees ten annas for the cigarettes he sold you on credit.'

It was humiliating.

Mammad Bhai patted his moustache and smiled.

'Vimto bhai, you are not to worry. All your debts have been paid. You can start with a clean slate. I have warned these salas never to bother you. You have Mammad Bhai's word.'

That was nice of him, but since I was not feeling too good after my shot, all I could manage to murmur was, 'Mammad Bhai, may God bless you.'

Mammad Bhai gave his moustache another twirl and left.

Dr Pinto came twice a day, but when asked what he was owed, he would say, 'No, Mr Manto, it is between Mammad Bhai and me. I wouldn't dream of charging you.'

It was comical. The doctor was paying for my treatment.

Mammad Bhai himself came daily, sometimes in the morning, sometimes later, but never without five or six of his shagirds. 'You are going to get better. It is only sala malaria,' he would console me.

In about two weeks, I was back on my feet. By now, I had come to know Mammad Bhai quite well. He was between twenty-five and thirty and a fast mover. Arab Gulli residents swore that when he threw his dagger at an enemy, it went straight through the unfortunate man's heart.

One day, I ran into him outside one of the Chinese restaurants in Arab Gulli.

I said to him, 'Mammad Bhai, this is the age of guns and revolvers. Why do you go around with this dagger?'

Mammad Bhai touched his moustache and replied, 'Vimto bhai, guns are boring. Even a child can fire them. What is the point? All you do is press the trigger and bang they go. But daggers and knives . . . by God, it is fun using them. What was that you once said? Yes, art. It is an art.

'What is a revolver? Nothing but a toy. But look at this dagger and how sharp it is.' He wet his thumb and ran it lovingly over the edge. 'It makes no sound. Just push it into the belly and the sala doesn't even so much as squirm. Guns are rubbish.'

Whenever I tried to thank him for what he had done for me, he would say, 'What favour are you talking about?'

In the eyes of the law he was a dada, a goonda but what I could not understand then—and do not understand now—was why he was considered dangerous. There was nothing dangerous about him, except his moustache.

Somebody once told me that Mammad Bhai always massaged his moustache after each meal with butter, because it was guaranteed to provide nourishment to the hair. So, who was the real Mammad Bhai: the moustache or the dagger?

The prostitutes of the area treated him like a pir, and as he was the acknowledged dada, it was only natural for him to have a mistress or two among them, but my inquiries had failed to reveal any such liaison.

One morning, while I was on my way to work, I heard in the Chinese restaurant that Mammad Bhai had been arrested. This was surprising because he had influence with the local police.

I asked around and was told that an Arab Gulli woman, Shirin bai, who had a young daughter, had gone to Mammad Bhai the day before in a distraught state. Her daughter had been raped. 'You are the dada and my daughter has been raped. What are you going to do about it? Sit at home?' she had screamed.

Mammad Bhai had first abused the old woman, then asked, 'What do you want me to do? Go rip open that bastard's stomach?'

Finally, he had pulled out his dagger, run his finger along the sharp, glittering edge and said, 'Go home. The necessary will be done.'

The necessary was done within half an hour. The man who had raped the old woman's daughter was stabbed to death.

Mammad Bhai was arrested, but he had done the job so quickly and with such care that no witnesses could be found. And in any case, even if there had been witnesses, none would have testified against Mammad Bhai in court. He was bailed out.

He had spent two days in the lockup, but had been kept in comfort. The police constables and the inspectors knew him well. However, when he came out, one noticed that his brush with the law had been a big shock to him. Even his moustache looked somewhat droopy.

I met him in the Chinese restaurant. His clothes, normally so neat, looked shabby.

I did not mention the murder to him, but he himself said, 'Vimto sahib, I am sorry the sala took such a long time dying. It was all my fault. I did not stab him cleanly. I botched it.'

You can imagine my reaction. He was not sorry the man had died, but that he had not been able to dispatch him neatly and forthwith.

The court case was to come up soon and Mammad Bhai was worried. He had never seen the inside of a court in his life. I don't know if he had committed any murders before, but what I do know is that he simply had no idea what sorts of birds magistrates, lawyers and witnesses were. They had never entered his life before.

One could see that he was worried. When the date for the first hearing was announced, Mammad Bhai said to me, 'Vimto sahib, I would sooner die than appear in court. I don't know what kind of a place it is.'

His Arab Gulli friends assured him that there was nothing to it. There were no witnesses and the only thing that might go against him would be his moustache. It might prejudice the magistrate.

As I have said, had it not been for his moustache, Mammad Bhai could never have been mistaken for a dada.

As the date approached, Mammad Bhai began to show unmistakable signs of anxiety. When I met him in the Iranian cafe, his agitation was obvious. His friends had told him, 'Mammad Bhai, if you have to go to court, then for God's sake do something about that moustache. One look and the magistrate will jail you.'

One day, while we were sitting in the Iranian cafe, he pulled out his dagger and threw it into the street. 'Mammad Bhai,' I exclaimed, 'what have you done?'

'Vimto bhai, everything is going downhill. I have to appear in court. Everybody tells me that one look at my moustache and the sala magistrate will convict me. What do I do?'

I could not help feeling what a criminal that moustache made him look. Finally I said, 'Mammad Bhai, your moustache is most likely to affect your chances in court. The decision will be not so much against you as against your moustache.'

'Should I then get rid of it?' he asked, running his hand lovingly over the offending feature.

'If you want to,' I replied.

'It is not what I want, it is what everybody seems to think I should do to make a good impression on the sala magistrate. What do you think, Vimto bhai?'

'Well, get it over and done with then,' I replied.

The next day Mammad Bhai had his moustache shaved off, since that had been the universal advice.

His case was heard in the court of Mr F.H. Tail. Mammad Bhai appeared without his moustache. There were no prosecution witnesses, but the magistrate nevertheless declared him a dangerous goonda and ordered him out of the province of Bombay. He was given just one day to settle his affairs.

When we got out of the court, we said nothing to each other. Involuntarily, his fingers rose to his face, but there was no longer anything there to caress.

In the evening, we met in the Iranian cafe. About twenty of his shagirds sat around him drinking tea. He did not greet me when I entered. He looked very harmless. And he was depressed.

'What's on your mind?' I asked.

He swore loudly, then added thoughtfully, 'The Mammad Bhai you knew is dead.'

'What does it matter, Mammad Bhai—one has to live. If not in Bombay, then elsewhere,' I said.

He began to abuse everything under the sun. 'Sala, I am not bothered where I live. What bothers me is why I got my moustache shaved off.'

Then he began to abuse everyone who had persuaded him to get rid of his moustache. 'If I had to be exiled from the province anyway, I should have gone with, not without, my moustache.'

I couldn't help laughing. 'Sala, what sort of a man are you, Vimto? God is my witness, I wouldn't have cared if they'd hanged me. But look at me now. Sala. I got terrified of my own moustache.'

Then he beat his breast with both hands and cried, 'A curse on you, sala Mammad Bhai. Scared of your own moustache. Go sleep with your mother.'

Tears welled up in his eyes, an odd sight on an egg-smooth face.

DOING GOD'S WORK

I come from Gujarat Kathiawar in the west of India, and am a bania by caste, trader by tradition. Last year, when the world went topsy-turvy following the Partition of the country, I was temporarily out of work, except for the odd buck I made through my cocaine deals.

Thousands of refugees had begun moving from here to there, or there to here, so one day I also decided to migrate to Pakistan. There would always be something to do, I said to myself. If not in cocaine, then something else. So I set out. It took me some time to get there, but in the end I managed, even making a little cash as I went along.

Since I had moved to Pakistan to start a business, I began to study the situation carefully. The going thing seemed to be allotment of property left behind by the Hindus. Since I have the gift of the gab and can get around people, I was able to make friends easily in the right quarters and soon a house was allotted in my name. I sold it promptly, making a nice packet in the process. This looked promising and I began to move from city to city, getting property allotted and disposing of it as soon as I had the documents.

All work takes effort. Nothing in life is easy. Well, I could not hope to be an exception. It was a constant struggle. Sometimes flattery would get the necessary done; other times a bribe or a dinner invitation, even a 'good time' in the evening. What I do know is that I was constantly on my feet. I would arrive in a city, survey the residential areas, pick out a nice house and then try to get hold of it.

Hard work always gets rewarded and so it happened that in a year's time I had managed to pile up a tidy fortune. I now had everything a man needs to live well: a nice house, plenty of cash in the bank, servants, a big car, not to mention commercial property.

But I felt restless. When I was in cocaine, I sometimes used to get this strange depression, but it was nothing compared to what I was going through now. I felt under a kind of weight. What it was I could not define.

I am an intelligent man. If something is bothering me, I always manage to find out what it is. I was determined to get to the bottom of this one as well. What was wrong with me?

Women? Well, I was unencumbered. I had lost my wife in Gujarat. However, there were other women. My gardener's wife, for instance. There is no accounting for taste. I believe that the only thing that matters in a woman is youth. It is not essential that she should have an education or be able to dance or what have you. I can only speak for myself. I like them young. That's all.

As I said, I am an intelligent man and I knew that something was missing in my life. My business was OK, my bank account was growing by the day and I had people working for me. In fact, I had reached a stage where money was coming in without much effort on my part. After much reflection, I found the answer. I was restless because I hadn't done a single good deed since coming to Pakistan.

Back in Kathiawar, I had quite a few good deeds to my credit. For example, when my friend Pandorang died, I brought his wife to live in my house and thus was able to prevent her from getting into the oldest profession in the world for at least two years. Another friend, Vinayak, broke his wooden leg and I promptly bought him another. Cost me forty rupees. And so on and so forth. However, I hadn't done anything by way of a virtuous deed since moving to Pakistan, which was perhaps why my heart was restless.

I tried to think how best to go about doing good deeds. Alms? Well, I walked around the city one day and found that it was full of naked and hungry wretches. Could I feed and clothe all of them single-handed? What about setting up a community kitchen? Did not seem practical. It would mean buying huge quantities of foodgrains which could only be had on the black market. What would be the point in doing something morally reprehensible for the sake of a good deed?

I spent hours every day listening to tales of woe and misfortune. Everybody had a sad story to tell: those who slept on the street and those who lived in vast and expensive houses. The pedestrian was unhappy because he did not have a new and comfortable pair of shoes. The man who had the money to be chauffeured around was depressed because he could not afford to buy the latest model of car. In fact, all complaints were genuine and reasonable.

I remembered a ghazal I had once heard Amina Bai Chitalkar of Sholapur (may God rest her soul in peace) sing. One of the lines ran: no man can fulfil another's need. So there I was, willing to help, but actually unable to. There were just too many who needed aid. After much reflection, I came to the conclusion that charity was not the answer. I visited many refugee camps and found that because of charity most of the inmates had become idle. They no longer wanted to work. I found them lolling around in their camps all day, playing cards or just gossiping, waiting all the while to be fed free of charge. How could these wretches do anything for Pakistan? I came to the conclusion that alms-giving was in no way akin to a good deed. So what was I going to do?

Hundreds of inmates were dying in these refugee camps. Epidemics were frequent and the city hospitals were full. I decided to construct a free hospital. I prepared the complete scheme. I would call for tenders, collect a tidy sum in tender fees, set up my own company and give it the contract for, say, a hundred thousand rupees (the building would never cost more than seventy thousand, leaving me a neat thirty thousand) and thus achieve my aim. However, I gave up the idea because what if I managed to save all those lives? Damn it, there would be a population explosion. How would the nation handle that?

Come to think of it, the whole trouble was that there were too many people. While the size of the population kept increasing, the land that grew food remained the same size. The rainfall did not necessarily keep pace with the proliferating numbers. I therefore came to the considered conclusion that it was pointless to build a hospital.

Then I thought of building a mosque. May God keep old Amina Bai Chitalkar of Sholapur in His heavenly peace, for she used to sing something about doing a good deed to keep your name alive after you were gone. And what were the good deeds she used to sing of? Digging wells and building bridges and constructing mosques. But this kind of thing was no good, because there were far too many mosques in the city. More mosques meant more fights among the believers, more sectarian divisions. I did not wish to add to them.

I decided to go on a pilgrimage to Mecca instead. But before I could embark on my journey, God Himself provided me with an answer. There was a public rally in the city and it broke up in complete pandemonium. Thirty people were killed, trampled underfoot. When the story appeared in the papers the next morning, it was said that they had not been killed but 'martyred'.

This set me thinking. I called on various leading religious scholars in the city and was assured that those who died in accidents were blessed because, since it had not been their fault, martyrdom had been conferred on them. And that was the highest state a man could aspire to. I said to myself: if instead of dying plainly people could be martyred, wouldn't that be wonderful? What was the point of dying an ordinary death? A complete waste. It was martyrdom alone that could give meaning to a drab life.

I did some more thinking on this very delicate issue. I looked around and what did I see? Hordes of miserable creatures with sunken eyes, their faces yellow with malnutrition, crushed by the weight of poverty, walking about like ghosts in tattered clothes. They looked like junk thrown on the rubbish heap, living in ramshackle huts, crawling about the city bazaars like unclaimed animals. Why were these people alive, I asked myself. What were they living for and how? Nobody knew. There they were, dying by the thousands, dying of hunger and thirst, dying of cold, dying of heat and, what was more, dying unmourned, unremembered.

And when they died, what happened to them? Nothing at all. So I hit upon my great idea. Why should these people not die as martyrs, instead of living in perpetual hunger, sickness and pain? Why should they not win for themselves a place of honour in this world, become the subject of veneration among those who did not even want to look at their ravaged faces today?

The question was: would these people be willing to be martyred? I was confident they would be, because they were good Muslims and all good Muslims longed for the exalted state of martyrdom. Even Hindus and Sikhs were now aspiring to martyrdom. I was therefore extremely disappointed when I was told by an emaciated wretch (I had asked him if he wanted to become a martyr) that he had no such ambition.

I just could not understand what this miserable creature was going to get out of being alive. I tried to argue with him. I said, 'Look my friend, you are an old man and you are not likely to live more than a month or a month and a half. As it is, you are so weak you can't even walk. When you go into one of your coughing fits, it is a wonder that you come out of it at all. You haven't a penny to your name. You have never had a day of comfort in your life. There is no question of a future in your case. Why do you want to live? For what? You are too old to join the army; otherwise, you might have had a chance to die fighting for your country. Why not make arrangements to get martyred?'

'How can that be arranged?' he asked. So I explained to him how. 'Lying in front of you on the ground is a banana skin. Supposing you were to slip on it, it is obvious you wouldn't survive the shock and would die and become a martyr.' However, he did not buy my argument. Instead, he said, 'You think I am so out of my mind that I should let myself slip on that banana skin with my eyes open. Don't I love life?' My God! That's what that miserable bag of bones said. He thought he was living life.

His attitude really depressed me. I was even more depressed when I heard a couple of days later that he, who could so easily have attained martyrdom, had died coughing on a bare steel bed in a charity hospital.

Then there was this woman, with no teeth in her mouth and no intestines in her belly. She looked as if she would breathe her last any minute. I felt very sorry for her. All her life had been spent in grief and poverty. I lifted her up in my arms and placed her on the railway track, but as soon as she heard the train approach, she bounced up like a wound-up toy on a spring and ran away.

It broke my heart, but I did not give up. I had seen the straight and narrow path of virtue and I was not going to be deflected so easily.

There was an empty building in the city, dating back to the time of the Mughal kings. There were exactly 151 tiny rooms in it. With my experienced eyes, I estimated at one glance that the first big rain would bring its leaking roof down. I bought the place up for a few thousand rupees and let it out to about one thousand homeless people, charging them no more than a rupee a month. For two months I received rent and, as I had estimated, at the beginning of the third, the first rains came to the city and the roof caved in, martyring seven hundred men, women and children.

My heart felt light. There were now seven hundred less to feed and clothe in the world and, what was more, they had all attained martyrdom and gone to heaven.

My good work has continued. No day passes when two or three people do not drink the sweet cup of martyrdom through my efforts.

All work needs labour, and as old Amina Bai Chitalkar of Sholapur used to sing . . . but let that pass. I can't recall the words. Suffice it to say that I have had to try very hard to attain my noble objective. There was one miserable creature whom I was unable to dispatch to heaven after having thrown banana skins in his path about ten times. However, like death, martyrdom is preordained and one day he slipped in his bathroom and joined the exalted company of martyrs.

These days I am engaged in constructing a huge residential building. The contract—worth two hundred thousand rupees—is being executed by my own company. I am sure to make a profit of at least seventy-five thousand rupees. I have also had the building insured. I estimate that when the third storey is raised, the whole thing will come tumbling down, for such are the substandard materials I have used. And of the three hundred men who are engaged in the construction work, given luck, not one would survive, but immediately attain eternal martyrdom.

And if there are survivors, it would mean that they are sinners, and God, who is merciful and compassionate, is not willing to admit them to the exalted state of martyrdom.

KHUSHIA

Khushia was thinking.

He had just got himself a paan laced with black tobacco from the shop across the road. He was sitting in his usual place, the cemented plinth by the roadside that served as a showroom for tyres and motor spares during the day. Evenings, it was his. He was masticating his black-tobacco-laced paan slowly and he was thinking of what had happened just half an hour earlier.

He had gone to the fifth street in Khetwari because around the corner lived his new girl, Kanta, who had come from Mangalore. Someone had told him that she was planning to move and he had gone to check it out. He had knocked at her door and she had asked who it was. 'It is I, Khushia,' he had answered. She had opened the door and what he had seen had nearly thrown him. She was naked, or nearly naked because all she had covering her was a skimpy towel which was simply not adequate because whatever women keep covered normally was there in full view.

'Khushia, what brings you here . . . I was about to take a bath . . . sit down . . . you should have ordered some tea from the shop across the road before you came in . . . that blasted boy Rama who used to work for me has run off.'

Khushia, who had never seen a woman naked or even half-naked, was confused. He did not know how to react or what to say. His eyes wanted to be elsewhere rather than on Kanta's body.

But all he could manage to mutter was, 'Why don't you go and take your bath?' And then, 'If you were not quite dressed, why did you answer the door? You could just have said you were not ready and I would have come another time . . . But go and take your bath.'

Kanta smiled, 'When you said it was Khushia, I asked myself what harm there was in letting you in. After all, I thought, it is Khushia, our own Khushia . . .'

He sat there thinking of the smile on her face as she had spoken to him. The sensation was almost physical, electrifying his mind and body. He could see her standing in front of him naked like a wax figurine. Her body was beautiful. For the first time, Khushia had realized that women who rent out their bodies could be beautiful also. This was like a revelation. But what had thrown him was her standing in front of him without the least sense of shame or self-consciousness. Why?

But then had she not answered that question herself when she said that she had let him in because, after all, he was 'Khushia, our own Khushia'.

Both Kanta and Khushia were in the same line of work, she being the goods that he hawked. In that sense, he was her 'own' but did that justify her standing in front of him without her clothes? Khushia could not figure it out.

He could still see her as she had stood there. Her skin was taut like skin over a drum and her body did not seem to be aware of itself. He had gazed at her brown nakedness exploratively but there had been no reaction from her. She had just stood there like an emotionless statuette. She should have reacted to his gaze. After all, there was a man staring at her, and men's eyes could penetrate through a woman's clothes, but she had shown not the least nervousness. He also remembered that her eyes had a washed and laundered look. Whatever it was, he said to himself again, she should have felt some sense of self-consciousness, given some sign that her modesty had been outraged. Her face should have turned red with embarrassment. It is true she was a prostitute but did prostitutes stand undressed in front of men as she had done?

He had been in this business for ten years and he knew all the secrets of this profession and the women who worked it. He knew, for instance, that at the end of the street the girl who lived with a man she said was her brother, and who used to play a song from the movie *Achoot Kanya* on her broken harmonium, was in love with the actor Ashok Kumar. Many boys had taken her to bed on the promise that they would introduce her to Ashok. He also knew that the Punjabi girl who lived in Dadar wore a jacket and trousers because a customer had once told her about Marlene Dietrich, the star of the movie *Morocco*, who was said to wear trousers because her legs were so beautiful that they needed to be protected. They were said to be insured for a lot of money. She had seen that movie many times. The trousers sat tightly over her buttocks but it didn't matter. Then there was the girl from the Deccan who lived in Mizgaon and who ensnared handsome college students because she wanted to have a good-looking baby, though she knew it was unlikely to happen as she was infertile. There was also the dark one from Madras with diamond earrings who wasted most of what she earned on lotions, creams and medicaments that promised to turn dark skin into fair, though in her heart of hearts she knew it would never happen and she was wasting her money.

All these women for whom he worked he knew inside out but what he did not know was that one day one of them, Kanta Kumari, a name he found difficult to remember, would stand in front of him naked, an experience he had never had before. Beads of perspiration appeared on his brow. His pride had been hurt. When he thought of Kanta's bare body, he felt a deep sense of insult. He was speaking to himself. 'It is an insult, is it not! Here is a girl who is practically naked and she stands bang in front of me and says, "Come in, after all, you are Khushia, our own Khushia." As if I was not a man but that stupid cat which is always sprawled on her bed.'

As he sat there thinking, he became convinced that he had been insulted. He was a man and he expected women, whether housewives or the other kind, to treat him like a man, a male. He expected them to maintain the distance laid down by nature between man and woman. He had gone to Kanta's house to find out if she was really moving and, if so, where. It was a business call. When he knocked at her door, he had had no idea what she might be doing. He had thought maybe she was lying in bed with a bandage around her head to fight a headache or delicing her cat or removing the hair from her armpits with that foul-smelling powder he could not stand. She could even be playing a game of cards with herself.

She lived alone. It could not have even remotely occurred to him that Kanta, the girl whom he had always seen properly dressed, would open the door and stand there in front of him in her birthday suit. She was naked because that skimpy towel could hardly cover anything. But what had she really felt when she had let him in? As for himself, it was as if he had been holding a banana in his hand and suddenly the eatable part had slipped out and fallen on the ground and all he held now was its skin. Her words kept ringing in his ears. 'When you said it was Khushia, I said to myself that there was no harm in letting you in. After all, I said to myself, it is Khushia, our own Khushia.'

'The bitch was smiling,' he kept murmuring. It was a smile as naked as she was. He could not help thinking of her body, which was like smoothly polished wood. He suddenly remembered this woman from his childhood who used to say to him, 'Khushia, my son, go get me a bucket of water.' And when he returned with it, she would say from behind a makeshift curtain, 'Come, place it next to me. I cannot see because I have soaped my face.' He would lift the curtain from a corner and place the bucket next to her. He would see a naked woman with her entire body soaped, but it would mean nothing. He was only a child then and women did not hide themselves from children when they were naked.

But now he was a man, a twenty-eight-year-old man. How could a woman, even an old woman, bare herself in front of him? What did Kanta think he was? Was he not equipped with everything that a young man is supposed to be equipped with? While it was true that her bare body had startled him, he had looked at her stealthily. He could not help noticing that, despite the daily use to which her body was subjected, everything was where it should be, and in good shape too. She charged ten rupees for a throw and that was not much considering what she had on offer. The other day, the bank clerk who had gone back because she would not bring down the price by two rupees was surely an ass. He recalled experiencing a strange tautening of the body. He wanted to stretch out his arms and release the tension until his bones began to rattle. Why had this wheat-coloured girl from Mangalore not seen him as a male? Instead, she had let him gaze at her nakedness because to her he was Khushia, just Khushia.

He got up, spat on the road and jumped into the tram that he always took to get home.

Once there, he took a bath, put on fresh clothes, stepped into the neighbourhood barber shop, looked at himself in the mirror, combed his hair and, on second thought, sat down for a shave, his second that day. The barber said to him, 'Brother Khushia, have you forgotten? I shaved you only this morning.' Khushia ran his hand over his face and replied, 'Your razor was not sharp enough.'

After the shave, he rubbed his face with a bit of talcum powder and crossed the road to a taxi stand. 'Chi chi,' he said—the standard

Bombay call for hailing a taxi. The driver opened the door for him, 'Where sahib?' he asked. Khushia was pleased at being called sahib. 'I will let you know. Go towards Pasera House first via Lemington Road, understand,' he replied in a friendly voice. The driver switched on his meter and took off. At the end of Lemington Road, Khushia asked him to turn left.

The taxi turned left and before the driver could change gears, Khushia had told him to stop. He then stepped out, walked across to a paan shop, exchanged a few words with a man who was standing there and after helping himself to a paan came back with the fellow he had talked to. They both got into the taxi. 'Go straight,' Khushia told the driver. The taxi drove for quite a while with Khushia doing the navigation. They went through brightly lit bazaars and, in the end, turned into an ill-lit street where some people had already settled in for the night on makeshift beds. Some were getting their heads massaged and looked contented. Khushia paid no attention to them. 'Stop here,' he told the driver as they went past a wooden hut. In a low voice, Khushia told the man he had picked up from the paan shop that he would wait for him in the car. The man got out without a word and went into the hut.

Khushia reclined into the seat and put one leg on top of the other. Then he pulled out a bidi from his pocket and lit it, but he took only a couple of drags before chucking it out of the window. He was restless. His heart was beating fast and for a moment he thought the driver had not killed the engine in order to increase the fare. 'How much extra do you think you will make by idling that engine?' he asked sharply.

The driver turned. 'Seth, the engine is not idling. It is switched off.'

As he realized his mistake, Khushia felt even more restless. He now began to bite his lips. Then he put on the black boat-like cap that lay tucked under his arm. He shook the driver by his shoulder. 'Look, a girl will soon come and get into the car. The moment she does so, drive off. And don't think anything odd is happening; everything is perfectly all right.'

The door of the hut opened and two people walked out, the man Khushia had picked up and Kanta, who was wearing a bright coloured sari.

Khushia sank further into his seat. It was quite dark in the car. The man opened the car door and gently pushed Kanta in. Then he banged the door shut. 'Khushia! You!' Kanta screamed. 'Yes, I, but you have already been paid, haven't you!' Then he told the driver to get moving.

The engine coughed and came to life. The car lurched forward and if Kanta said something it could not be heard. The man who had brought Kanta could be seen standing on the road, looking somewhat bewildered. The taxi soon disappeared into the night.

No one ever saw Khushia at his customary hangout again.

A WOMAN FOR ALL SEASONS

She was not much to look at. There was nothing about her that could be called attractive, but her first appearance on the screen made her an instant hit. Those who watched her prancing around like a butterfly in love scenes thought her most beautiful. They found her face, the way she moved, the way she acted, utterly fascinating. Her admirers were like a swarm of flies buzzing around her celluloid image.

If someone were asked what it was that was so special about her compared to other movie stars, or what distinguished her from her rivals, he would have answered without hesitation: her innocence. And it was a fact that she looked utterly without wile, an absolute angel, on the screen. She exuded simple, pure, unspoiled innocence. The movies in which she appeared were artless romances, such as the teenage daughter of a rustic weaver might be expected to conceive. She was always cast in simple roles, such as the daughter of a poor, illiterate man living a lonely life in a wooden shack away from the distractions of the world. Sometimes she was a farmer's daughter, sometimes a labourer's or a railway signalman's. She took to these roles with a natural, inborn ease.

The very mention of her name, Lateeka Rani, brought to mind a slight girl, her ghagra worn high, leaving her ankles bare, her hair done in a ponytail, tending a flock of sheep or playing in the sand, bareheaded, barefooted, her small breasts rising modestly from under a tight choli, her eyes very still, her nose sitting harmlessly on her face: in short, a woman you felt easy about.

Her first movie made her famous and she remained famous thereafter, though it is now many years since she stopped making movies. She not only earned fame during her long career but a lot of money too. In her methodical way, she kept account of every single coin that fell into her pocket. She treated fame in the same unsentimental, practical manner. She took each step up that ladder with confidence.

Lateeka Rani was a great actress but a strange woman. At the age of twenty-one, as a student in France, instead of learning French she began to learn Hindi, which was not her native tongue. A young man from Madras, a fellow student, fell in love with her and she decided to marry him, but in between she met a middle-aged Bengali on a visit to London who was studying to become a barrister, and changed her mind in his favour. It was a well-considered decision because she had seen something in the older man, which she knew would help her fulfil her dreams. The Madras man whom she had agreed to marry was studying pulmonary diseases in Germany. What could he give her except guarantee good care of her lungs! She decided that she did not need that. Prafula Roy, on the other hand, was a dreamer around whom she could weave her magic charms and make him her captive.

Prafula Roy, who came from a middle-class family, was an extremely hard-working man, and had he set his mind to it, he could have obtained the highest law degree in the world and excelled all rival candidates, but he hated law. It was to make his parents happy that he was in London, attending the Lincoln Inn dinners half-heartedly and managing to turn up for the necessary classes. His heart was not in it. But what he wanted to do, he did not quite know. He always wore a lost look and he hated crowds. He had no interest in partying. Most of the time he was by himself. Sometimes he would sit in a teahouse or chat with his old landlady, building castles in the air but certain in his heart that, one day, he would score a major achievement.

After a couple of meetings with him, Lateeka came to the conclusion that Prafula Roy was no ordinary man. She was not short of admirers because she was young and in her own way attractive. However, she was not fooled by the flattering remarks young men made to her, treating them as a boring formality. The Madrasi doctor who was in love with her did really perhaps consider her beautiful but it always seemed to her that it was her lungs, more than her, that he was taken by. One day he had told her that her lungs were spotless. She knew she was no beauty and her charms were limited. She had always felt incomplete and she also knew that without help nothing would change for her.

After meeting Prafula Roy, Lateeka felt that this apparently absent-minded man who was always smoking was looking at her in a way she had not been looked at before. She felt as if he were quietly taking her apart, every facet of her personality, her smile, her features, the way she moved, and reassembling it all according to his own particular scheme. He saw her not only with his own eyes but as others saw her. In his mind, he was reconstructing her and, happy with the result, smiling to himself quietly. He wanted to redesign her according to his own measurements. She was intelligent and she knew that Prafula Roy was not the kind of architect who would show her what he had designed, nor would he tell her what she would need to do to make the structure stand straight; and yet he knew what she wanted herself to be. Prafula Roy had a feeling that she knew what thoughts passed through his mind and that she had changed in many subtle ways just as he had wanted her to. In a sense, they were like master and apprentice though they had never spoken about it in these words.

They were happy because they could feel the chemistry between them taking shape. Without each other they were going to remain incomplete. He had become the touchstone on which she constantly tested herself. Without his saying a word, she knew what he wanted her to do. She also knew that the passion that she found in his eyes, she would not experience in his bed. But she was happy. What she had seen in his eyes was what she needed to make her dreams come true.

She always calculated her moves carefully and she was good at forecasts. In the two months that she had known Prafula Roy, she had seen the possibility of her dreams coming true. As to how it would happen and under what circumstances, she was going to leave it to him. It was for him to work it out. Lateeka was confident that his ingenious brain would manage to find the right formula, the right combination, the right moment. They had by now decided to return to India, but before setting out for India, they made a trip to Berlin. A friend took them to a famous movie studio and Lateeka knew that this was where her future lay. When Prafula was engrossed in a conversation with a famous German actress, Lateeka knew that he was looking at her as a painter might look at a piece of canvas on which he plans to draw a different face, in this case, Lateeka's.

Some time after they arrived in Bombay, Prafula ran into an Englishman at the Taj Hotel. He was a knight but at the time down at heel. However, he knew a lot of people. Aged around sixty, he stammered a little and had the most perfect manners. While Prafula was not quite sure what to make of him, the farsighted Lateeka saw in him someone who could be of great use. She decided to cultivate him, paying him the sort of attention a nurse pays to her patient. In a few days, over dinner, things worked out exactly in accordance with Lateeka's plans. A film company, it was decided, would be formed, to be headed by Prafula Roy, with two of Sir Howard Pascal's friends as directors. The difficulties normally encountered in launching new ventures were bypassed through the association of these men of influence.

Lateeka had never had any doubt about Sir Howard's usefulness, and she had been proved right. Sometimes Lateeka's attentions to the Englishman made Prafula jealous but she paid no attention to it. She knew that Sir Howard probably derived some vicarious satisfaction by having her around, but to her this was of little consequence. The two directors Sir Howard had found for the company were also motivated in part by Lateeka's looks and her come-hither manner. She found that perfectly in order as well. To her, these men were important only as long as their money was in their and not the company's account. She knew that one day Bombay's Marwari moneylenders would be willing to stake millions for the sake of catching just one glimpse of her face. However, she was in no hurry because she could see things moving exactly in the direction she wanted.

The company was established and all its shares sold. Because of Sir Howard's contacts, a plot of land, located in the most ideal spot, was found for building a studio. Next, the directors requested Prafula Roy to proceed to England and order purchase of machinery and equipment. A day before he left, like a traditional western gentleman, Prafula asked Lateeka if she would marry him. She said she would and the ceremony took place later the same day. They spent their honeymoon in England but there was nothing they needed to discover about one another, physically. These discoveries they had made much earlier. All they were interested in was to purchase the equipment and rush back to Bombay. It had never worried Lateeka that Prafula knew nothing about running a studio and making movies. What she knew was that he was a sharp and intelligent man and she had no doubt he would successfully accomplish whatever needed to be done. She also knew that when she appeared in the studio's first presentation as the leading lady, she would take the whole of India by storm.

Prafula Roy's only brush with movie-making was the few days he had spent in the German film studio trying to learn something about this industry, but when he returned to Bombay, a director and cameraman in tow, and launched the first production of India Talkies Ltd, he impressed everyone with his sure-footed handling of detail. He was a man of few words. He would arrive at the studio early and spend the rest of the day working on the screenplay and the day's schedule. Everything was well organized and happened according to the laid-down schedule. Every department was headed by a professional who reported to Prafula. He had no tolerance for impropriety of any kind, with the result that the working atmosphere was clean and well disciplined.

The first movie produced by Prafula Roy was released exactly as he had conceived it. At the time, movies were loud and extravagant. The heroine had to be of high birth and opulently costumed. The romantic side that was exaggerated had nothing to do with reality. The dialogue was theatrical. Prafula Roy had produced a movie in which everything was the exact opposite of these clichés and it was a runaway success across India. Suddenly, Lateeka Rani was the toast of the country.

Prafula Roy read the flattering write-ups in the press about the innocent beauty of Lateeka Rani and her artless acting with great joy and pride. What especially made him happy was that it was he who was the creator of this charismatic product called Lateeka Rani. As for Lateeka, success had had no appreciable effect on her. She had foreseen it, and what the days to come held in store for her, she could read as if it was an open book. She had calculated everything to the last detail well in advance. She knew what clothes she would wear on the opening night, what sort of conversation she would make with her husband in front of others, how she would divest herself of the garlands which would be placed around her neck and on whom she would bestow them and, finally, what smile she would flash on whom and when. She had worked it all out at least a month in advance.

The way she conducted herself in the studio was also carefully planned. She lived close by and Sir Howard Pascal had been given an apartment on the top floor of the studio. Lateeka would arrive early, and spend a little time with Sir Howard, who was a keen gardener. She had made it a point to talk flowers to him for half an hour every morning. Then she would return home and pay what attention had to be paid to other things, including her husband. She would then get ready for the day's work, carefully making up her face, every inch of which could have carried the inscription: invented and fashioned by Prafula Roy.

The second movie was released, then the third, fourth and fifth. All of them were hits. In fact, India Talkies Ltd had blazoned a path which other film-makers had no choice but to follow. With each new release, Lateeka's fame and popularity grew, as did that of India Talkies Ltd. However, very few knew her better half, Prafula Roy, but that never bothered him as he sat alone, his eyes seeking through the haze of cigarette smoke new and more attractive roles for Lateeka. In his movies, the hero did not really have much to do. He was like a robot who sat, stood or walked at Prafula's directions. Even in the studio, he did not have much star value. Everyone knew what the pecking order was: Prafula Roy, Mrs Roy and then the rest, none of them very important. Before long, there was a reaction to this hierarchical system and it was noticed that her leading man who had appeared with her in every movie had begun to assert himself. They were popular as a pair and taken for granted, so it was only natural that he should like to claim the recognition being denied to him by the studio.

He hated Lateeka because she did not give a damn about his rights as an actor. He had begun to talk about it openly in the studio. As was to be expected, he was dropped from her next movie by Prafula Roy. There was some protest but it soon died down. A new leading man was hired and there was much whispering about that, but only for a few days. Lateeka had absolutely no feelings for the leading man with whom she had appeared in one hit after another, and made no attempt to have his axing revoked. The new movie flopped and the second one met the same fate. Lateeka's popularity began to ebb. Then came the shocking news that she had eloped with her new leading man. The story created a sensation in the press and a woman who had until now been sold as a symbol of feminine purity now found herself mired in scandal.

Prafula was in quite a state and those who were close to him swore that he had fainted several times after he was told that Lateeka had run away with his new hero. This was the greatest shock of his life. To him she was the piece of canvas on which he painted his dreams. And now everything lay in pieces at his feet. It even occurred to him to set the studio on fire and jump into the conflagration but it needed courage, which he did not have in the required measure. Finally it was the discarded leading man who stepped forward to help. He told Prafula things about Lateeka, which he had never even guessed at. He told him, 'She is a woman utterly devoid of the capacity to love. She has not eloped with her new leading man because she loves him but because it is a move to revive her sagging career. She has gone on her own and taken him along as one takes along a domestic. Had she asked me to play this role, she would have been disappointed because I would have refused to play her game. She is now ready to return because, according to her calculations, her return is several days overdue. Maybe, I am even sharing this with you at her instructions.' Like all creative people, Prafula Roy was a simple person and when Lateeka returned he began to complain to her as a jilted lover might, accusing her of infidelity.

Lateeka said nothing. She did not even comment on what her leading man had told her husband. In fact, she asked that his monthly salary—all actors worked on monthly salaries—should be doubled. Outwardly, she was most friendly to him but there was no love lost between them. They had no mutual chemistry. They made a new movie, which hit it big at the box office as did the next one and the one following. As time passed, several new movie companies sprang up with as many new faces, some of them far more attractive than Lateeka Rani's ever was. Her first leading man was quite sure that Lateeka would leave Prafula any day to find a new man who could discover new vistas for her, but no such dramatic event took place.

There was a lot of idle talk about Lateeka and much speculation about the state of her marriage. There were some who swore that for pure sex she had chosen Ram Bharosa, the man who tended her ponies. Her relationship with her husband was ceremonial at best. This story had been circulated by her old leading man who would say, 'A woman like Lateeka can only go to bed with someone who is her inferior, such as a servant, a man who should do her whimsical bidding, who should always feel obligated to her. Had she been capable of love, she would have gone with the man she eloped with. The fact is that her day is done. This she knows and fully understands. She also knows that Prafula Roy is a spent man. Whatever vitality and talent he had, he has long since squandered on her. He is now like a squeezed mango that can offer no more sweet pulp. Mark my words, one of these days, she will walk out on him to warm the bed of another film-maker.'

Lateeka did no such thing. Her short-lived escapade appeared to have brought about little change in her. She was still making her morning call on Sir Howard Pascal and her interest in gardening had not abated. She knew the gossip about her in the studio but she had chosen to remain silent—silent and dignified. She made two more movies, both of which flopped badly. The once-scintillating name of India Talkies Ltd had by now lost much of its gloss. Lateeka was impervious to these developments but everyone knew that Prafula Roy had taken them to heart. Her old leading man, who respected the man who had given him his first break, would advise him off and on to let one of his juniors take over the day-to-day responsibilities and himself take to a stress-free life. This advice had had no effect on Prafula Roy. Some thought that he was planning a fresh start with a refurbished Lateeka as the focal point. Household servants told everyone that Prafula had become extremely ill-tempered and always looked angry. Sometimes he would abuse Lateeka in the most vile language but she never reacted. He could not sleep well at night and often Lateeka could be seen massaging his head or pressing his feet until he had gone to sleep.

In the past, Prafula had never insisted that Lateeka share his bed with him but now if he couldn't find her next to him he would look for her in the middle of the night all over the house and beg her to lie in his bed. Her old leading man would find these reports distressing. He would say, 'Prafula Roy is a great man, so it is a pity that he has placed himself at the mercy of a woman who does not deserve the privilege. She is not a woman but a witch. If I had anything to do with it, I would put a bullet through her. The tragedy is that Prafula Roy is more in love with her now than he was in the early days.'

Others were of the view that, since there was nothing more that Prafula could do for Lateeka to bring back her fame and youth, he was determined to spoil it for her. He had once seen her as an object of sanctity that must be protected against evil influences, but now, being disillusioned, he wanted her to be mired in scandal and corruption so that when someone told him next about her latest misdeed he should feel neither sorrow nor surprise. He used to live in a world of dreams, they said, but all that was long gone and he now inhabited the harsh world of reality where the logical thing seemed to be to smash Lateeka Rani's head with a rock before smashing his own.

Life still went on and the company began work on its twenty-second production. This was going to be a new experiment and so closely guarded a secret was the new project that even those working in the studio could only hazard a guess. Prafula sat in his office late into the night. Often, instead of going home, he slept there. His table was piled high with paper and his ashtray was always found chock-full of cigarette ends. A screenplay was being written, but what it was nobody knew.

The studio's costume department that had been idle for many months one day found that it had a most unexpected visitor: Lateeka Rani. She asked that a long-sleeve blouse, which she was going to wear with a black silk sari, be stitched for her. She left detailed instructions about the design. She also had a lengthy discussion with the hairdresser, Miss de Mello, about a new hairstyle. When the story spread, people linked it with the mysterious new movie. Lateeka's original leading man was of the view that it would be a tragedy, based on Prafula Roy's own life. The shooting got under way and seemed to proceed smoothly till the day Prafula Roy appeared on the set unexpectedly, watched the scene being shot for a couple of minutes and began to scream at the cameraman. He slapped him on his ear, which knocked the man out. Nobody said anything at the beginning but when Prafula Roy's rage showed no sign of abating and, in fact, gave every indication of getting worse, he was led off the set and taken home.

Several doctors were sent for but it appeared that Prafula Roy had lost his mind. He would send for Lateeka every now and then, and when she appeared, he would begin to scream at her. He wanted to tear her apart and he used such filthy language about her that no one who heard it could believe his or her ears. It was most bizarre. For four days, his condition remained unchanged. On the fifth, when Lateeka was having her morning gardening session with Sir Howard Pascal, and telling him about her husband's insanity, news arrived that Prafula Roy was fast sinking. Efforts to revive him were unsuccessful and he died.

When the pallbearers arrived to take away the coffin, Lateeka Rani appeared. Her eyes were swollen and her hair dishevelled. She was dressed in a splendid black sari and a finely cut blouse. Her old leading man took one look at her, turned his face in disgust and said, 'The bitch knew when this scene was going to be shot.'

BABU GOPI NATH

I think it was in 1940 that I first met Babu Gopi Nath. I was the editor of a weekly magazine in Bombay. One day, while I was busy writing something, Abdul Rahim Sando burst into my office, followed by a short, nondescript man. Greeting me in his typical style, Sando introduced his friend. 'Manto sahib, meet Babu Gopi Nath.'

I rose and shook hands with him. Sando was in his element. 'Babu Gopi Nath, you are shaking hands with India's number one writer.' He had a talent for coining words which, though not to be found in any dictionary, somehow always managed to express his meaning. 'When he writes,' Sando continued, 'it is dharan takhta. Nobody can get people's "continuity" together like him. Manto sahib, what did you write about Miss Khurshid last week? "Miss Khurshid has bought a car. Verily, God is the great carmaker." Well, Babu Gopi Nath, if that's not the "anti" of pantipo, then what is, I put it to you!'

Abdul Rahim Sando was an original. Most of the words he used in ordinary conversation were strictly of his own authorship. After this introduction, he looked at Babu Gopi Nath, who appeared to be impressed. 'This is Babu Gopi Nath, from Lahore, but now of Bombay, accompanied by a "pigeonette" from Kashmir.'

Babu Gopi Nath smiled.

Abdul Rahim Sando continued, 'If you are looking for the world's number one innocent, this is your man. Everyone cheats him out of his money by saying nice things to him. Look at me. All I do is talk and he rewards me with two packets of Polson's smuggled butter every day. Manto sahib, he is a genuine "antifloojustice" fellow, if ever there was one. We are expecting you at Babu Gopi Nath's flat this evening.'

Babu Gopi Nath, whose mind seemed to be elsewhere, now joined the conversation. 'Manto sahib, I insist that you come.' Then he looked at Sando. 'Sando, is Manto sahib . . . well, fond of . . . you know what?'

Abdul Rahim Sando laughed. 'Of course, he is fond of that and of many other things as well. Is it all settled then? May I add that I have also started drinking because it can now be done free of cost.'

Sando wrote out the address and at six o'clock I presented myself at the flat. It was nice and clean. Three rooms, good furniture, all in order. Besides Sando and Babu Gopi Nath, there were four others—two men and two women—to whom I was presently introduced by Sando.

There was Ghaffar Sain, a typical Punjabi villager in a loose tehmad, wearing a huge necklace of beads and coloured stones. 'He is Babu Gopi Nath's legal adviser, you know what I mean?' Sando said. 'In Punjab, every lunatic is a man of God. Our friend here is either already a man of God or about to be admitted to that divine order. He has accompanied Babu Gopi Nath from Lahore, because he had run out of suckers in that city. Here, he drinks Scotch whisky, smokes Craven A cigarettes and prays for the good of Babu Gopi Nath's soul.'

Ghaffar Sain heard this colourful description in silence, a smile playing on his lips.

The other man was called Ghulam Ali, tall and athletic with a pockmarked face. About him Sando provided the following information: 'He is my shagird, my true apprentice. A famous singing girl of Lahore fell in love with him. She brought all manner of "continuities" in play to ensnare him, but the only response she received from Ghulam Ali was: "Women are not my cup of tea." Ran into Babu Gopi Nath at a Lahore shrine and has never left his side since. He receives a tin of Craven A cigarettes daily and all the food he can eat.'

Ghulam Ali smiled good-naturedly.

I looked at the women. One of them was young, fair and round-faced, the Kashmiri 'pigeonette' Sando had mentioned. She had short hair, which first appeared to be cropped, but was not. Her eyes were large and bright and her expression suggested that she was raw and inexperienced. Sando introduced her.

'Zeenat Begum, called Zeno, a love-name given by Babu sahib. This apple, plucked from Kashmir, was brought to Lahore by one of the city's most formidable madams. Babu Gopi Nath's private intelligence sources relayed the news of this arrival to him and, overnight, he decamped with her. There was litigation and for about two months the city police had a ball, thanks to Babu Gopi Nath's generosity. Naturally, Babu Gopi Nath won the suit. And so here she is. Dharan takhta.'

The other woman, who was quietly smoking, was dark and red-eyed. Babu Gopi Nath looked at her. 'Sando, and this one?' Sando slapped her thigh and declaimed, 'Ladies and gentlemen, this is mutton tippoti, fulful booti, Mrs Abdul Rahim Sando, alias Sardar Begum. Fell in love with me in 1936 and, inside of two years, I was done for—dharan takhta. I had to run away from Lahore. However, Babu Gopi Nath sent for her the other day to keep me out of harm's way. Her daily rations consist of one tin of Craven A cigarettes and two rupees eight annas every evening for her morphine shot. She may be dark, but, by God, she is a tit-for-tat lady.'

'What rubbish you talk,' Sardar said. She sounded like the hardened professional woman she was.

Having finished with the introductions, Sando began a lecture highlighting my greatness. 'Cut it out, Sando,' I said. 'Let's talk of something else.'

Sando shouted, 'Boy, whisky and soda. Babu Gopi Nath, out with the cash.'

Babu Gopi Nath reached in his pocket, pulled out a thick bundle of money, peeled off a bill and gave it to Sando. Sando stared at it reverently, raised his eyes to heaven and said, 'Dear God of the universe, bring unto me the day when I put my hand in my pocket and fish out a thick wad of money like this. Meanwhile, I am asking Ghulam Ali to run to the store and return post-haste with two bottles of Johnny Walker Still-Going-Strong.'

The whisky arrived and we began to drink, with Sando continuing to monopolize the conversation. He downed his glass in one go. 'Dharan takhta,' he shouted, 'Manto sahib, this is what I call honest-to-goodness whisky, inscribing "Long Live Revolution" as it blazes its way through the gullet into the stomach. Long live Babu Gopi Nath.'

Babu Gopi Nath did not say much, occasionally nodding to express agreement with Sando's opinions. I had a feeling that the man had no views of his own. His superstitious nature was evident from the presence of Ghaffar Sain, his legal adviser, in Sando's words. What it really meant was that Babu Gopi Nath was a born devotee of real and fake holy men. I learnt during the conversation that most of his time in Lahore was spent in the company of fakirs, mendicants, sadhus and the like.

'What are you thinking?' I asked him.

'Nothing, nothing at all.' Then he smiled, glanced at Zeenat amorously. 'Just thinking about these beautiful creatures. What else do people like us think about?'

Sando explained, 'Manto sahib, Babu Gopi Nath is a great man. There is hardly a singing girl or a courtesan worth the name in Lahore he has not had a "continuity" with.'

'Manto sahib, one no longer has the fire of youth in one's loins,' Babu Gopi Nath said modestly.

Then followed a long discussion about the leading families of courtesans and singing girls of Lahore. Family trees were traced, genealogy analysed, not to speak of how much Babu Gopi Nath had paid for the ritual deflowering of which woman in what year. These exchanges remained confined to Sando, Sardar, Ghulam Ali and Ghaffar Sain. The jargon of Lahore's kothas was freely employed, not all of it comprehensible to me, though the general drift of the conversation was clear.

Zeenat never said a word. Off and on, she smiled. It was quite clear that she was not interested in these things. She drank a rather diluted glass of whisky, and I noticed that she smoked without appearing to enjoy it. Strangely enough, she smoked the most. I could find no visible indication that she was in love with Babu Gopi Nath, but it was obvious that he was with her. However, one could sense a tension between the two, despite their physical closeness.

At about eight o'clock, Sardar left to get her morphine shot. Ghaffar Sain, three drinks ahead, lay on the floor, rosary in hand. Ghulam Ali was sent out to get some food. Sando had got tired of talking. Babu Gopi Nath, now quite tipsy, looked at Zeenat longingly and said, 'Manto sahib, what do you think of my Zeenat?'

I did not know how to answer that, so I said, 'She is nice.' Babu Gopi Nath was pleased. 'Manto sahib, she is a lovely girl and so simple. She has no interest in ornaments and things like that. Many times I have offered to buy her a house of her own and you know what her answer has been? "What will I do with a house? Who do I have in the world?"'

He asked suddenly, 'What does a motor car cost, Manto sahib?'

'I've no idea.'

'I don't believe it, Manto sahib, I'm sure you know. You must help me buy Zeno a car. I've come to the conclusion that one must have a car in Bombay.'

Zeenat's face was devoid of expression.

Babu Gopi Nath was quite drunk now and getting more sentimental by the minute. 'Manto sahib, you are a man of learning. I am nothing but an ass. Please let me know if I can be of some service to you. It was only by accident that Sando brought up your name yesterday. I immediately sent for a taxi and asked him to take me to meet you. If I have shown you any discourtesy, you must forgive me. I am nothing but a sinner, a man full of faults. Should I get you some more whisky?'

'No, we've all had much too much to drink,' I said.

He became even more sentimental. 'You must drink some more, Manto sahib!' He produced his bundle of money, but before he could peel some off, I thrust it back into his pocket. 'You gave a hundred rupees to Ghulam Ali earlier, didn't you?' I asked.

The fact was that I had begun to feel sorry for Babu Gopi Nath. He was surrounded by so many leeches and he was such a simpleton. Babu Gopi Nath smiled. 'Manto sahib, whatever is left of those hundred rupees will slip through Ghulam Ali's pocket.'

The words were hardly out of his mouth, when Ghulam Ali entered the room with the doleful announcement that some scoundrel had picked his pocket on the street. Babu Gopi Nath looked at me, smiled, and gave another hundred rupees to Ghulam Ali. 'Get some food quickly.'

After five or six meetings, I got to know a great deal more about Babu Gopi Nath's personality. First of all, my initial view that he was a fool and a sucker had turned out to be wrong. He was perfectly aware of the fact that Sando, Ghulam Ali and Sardar, his inseparable companions, were all selfish opportunists, but you could never guess his inner thoughts from his behaviour.

Once he said to me, 'Manto sahib, in my entire life, I have never rejected advice. Whenever someone offers it to me, I accept it with gratitude. Perhaps they consider me a fool, but I value their wisdom. Look at it like this. They have the wisdom to see that I am the sort of man who can be made a fool of. The fact is that I have spent most of my life in the company of fakirs, holy men, courtesans and singing girls. I love them. I just couldn't do without them. I have decided that when my money runs out, I would like to settle down at a shrine. There are only two places where my heart finds peace: prostitutes' kothas and saints' shrines. It's only a matter of time before I shall be unable to afford the former, because my money is running out, but there are thousands of saints' shrines in India. I will go to one.'

'Why do you like kothas and shrines?' I asked.

'Because both establishments are an illusion. What better refuge can there be for someone who wants to deceive himself?'

'You are fond of singing girls. Do you understand music?' I asked.

'Not at all. It doesn't matter in the least. I can spend an entire evening listening to the most flat-voiced woman in the world and still feel happy. It is the little things which go with these evenings that I love. She sings, I flash a hundred-rupee bill in front of her. She moves languorously towards me and, instead of letting her take it from my hand, I stick it in my sock. She bends and gently pulls it out. It's the sort of nonsense that people like us enjoy. Everybody knows, of course, that in a kotha parents prostitute their daughters and in shrines men prostitute their God.'

I learnt that Babu Gopi Nath was the son of a miserly moneylender and had inherited ten lakh rupees, which he had been frittering away ever since. He had come to Bombay with fifty thousand rupees, and though those were inexpensive times his daily outgoings were heavy.

As promised, he bought a car for Zeno—a Fiat—for three thousand rupees. A chauffeur was also employed—an unreliable ruffian—but they were the sort of people Babu Gopi Nath felt happy with.

Our meetings had become more frequent. Babu Gopi Nath interested me. In turn, he treated me with great respect and devotion.

One evening, I found among Babu Gopi Nath's regulars a man I had known for a long time—Mohammad Shafiq Toosi. Widely regarded as a singer and a wit, Shafiq had another unusual side to his character. He was the known lover of the most famous singing girls of the time. It was not so commonly known, however, that he had had affairs, one after the other with three sisters, belonging to one of the most famous singing families of Patiala.

Even less known was the fact that their mother, when she was young, had been his mistress. His first wife, who died a few years after their marriage, he did not care for, because she was too housewifely and did not act like a woman of pleasure. He had no use for housewives. He was about forty and, though he had gone through scores of famous courtesans and singing girls, he was not known to have spent a penny of his own on them. He was one of nature's gigolos.

Courtesans had always found him irresistible. When I walked into the flat, I found him engrossed in conversation with Zeenat. I couldn't understand who had introduced him to Babu Gopi Nath. I knew that Sando was a friend of his, but they had not been on speaking terms for some time. In the end, it turned out that the two had made up and it was actually Sando who had brought him here today.

Babu Gopi Nath sat in a corner, smoking his hookah. He never smoked cigarettes. Shafiq was telling stories, most of them ribald and all of them about courtesans and singing girls. Zeenat looked uninterested, but Sardar was all ears. 'Welcome, welcome,' Shafiq said to me, 'I did not know you too were a wayfarer of this valley.'

Sando shouted, 'Welcome to the angel of death. Dharan takhta.'

One could not fail to notice that Mohammad Shafiq Toosi and Zeenat were exchanging what could only be described as amorous glances. This troubled me. I had become quite fond of Zeenat, who had begun to call me Manto bhai.

I didn't like the way Shafiq was ogling Zeenat. After some time, he left with Sando. I am afraid I was a bit harsh with Zeenat, because I expressed strong disapproval of the goings-on between Shafiq and her. She burst into tears and ran into the next room, followed by Babu Gopi Nath. A few minutes later, he came out and said, 'Manto sahib, come with me.'

Zeenat was sitting on her bed. When she saw us, she covered her face with both hands and lay down. Babu Gopi Nath was very sombre. 'Manto sahib, I love this woman. She has been with me for two years, and I swear by the saint Hazrat Ghaus Azam Jilani that she has never given me cause for complaint. Her other sisters, I mean women of her calling, have robbed me without compunction over the years, but she is a girl without greed or love of money. Sometimes, I go away for weeks, maybe to be with another woman, without leaving her any money. You know what she does? She pawns her ornaments to manage until I return.

'Manto sahib, as I told you once, I don't have long to go. My money has almost run out. I don't want her life to go to waste after I am gone. So often have I said to her, "Zeno, look at the other women and learn something from them. Today, I have money, tomorrow, I'll be a beggar. Women can't do with just one rich lover in their lives; they need several. If you don't find a rich patron after I leave, your life will be ruined. You act like a housewife, confined at home all day. That won't do."

'But Manto sahib, this woman is hopeless. I consulted Ghaffar Sain in Lahore and he advised me to take her to Bombay. He knows two famous actresses here who used to be singing girls in Lahore. I sent for Sardar from Lahore to teach Zeno a few tricks of the trade. Ghaffar Sain is also very capable in these matters.

'Nobody knows me in Bombay. She was afraid she would bring me dishonour, but I said to her, "Don't be silly. Bombay is a big city, full of millionaires. I have bought you a car. Why don't you find yourself a rich man who could look after you?"

'Manto sahib, I swear on God that it is my sincere wish that Zeno should stand on her own feet. I am prepared to put ten thousand rupees in a bank for her, but I know that within ten days that woman Sardar will rob her of the last penny. Manto sahib, you should try to persuade her to become worldly-wise. Since she has had the car, Sardar takes her out for a drive every evening to the Apollo Bandar beach, which is frequented by fashionable people. But there has been no success so far. Sando brought Mohammad Shafiq Toosi this evening, as you saw. What is your opinion about him?'

I decided to offer no opinion, but Babu Gopi Nath said, 'He appears to be rich, and he is good-looking. Zeno, did you like him?'

Zeno said nothing.

I simply could not believe what he was telling me: that he had brought Zeenat to Bombay so that she could become the mistress of a rich man, or, at least, learn to live off rich men. But that's the way it was. Had he wanted to get rid of her, it would have been the easiest thing in the world, but his intentions were exactly what he said they were. He had tried to get her into films, Bombay being India's movie capital. For her sake, he had entertained men who claimed to be film directors, but were no such thing. He even had had a phone installed in the flat. None of these things had produced the man he was looking for.

Mohammad Shafiq Toosi, a regular visitor for a month or so, suddenly disappeared one day. True to style, he had used the opportunity to seduce Zeenat. Babu Gopi Nath said to me, 'Manto sahib, it is so sad. Shafiq sahib was all show and no substance. Not only did he do nothing to help Zeno, but he cheated her out of many valuables and two hundred rupees. Now I am told he is having an affair with a girl called Almas.'

This was true. Almas was the youngest daughter of the famous courtesan Nazir Jan of Patiala. She was the fourth sister he had seduced in a row. Zeno's money had been spent on her, but like all his liaisons this too had turned out to be short-lived. It was later rumoured that Almas had tried to poison herself after being abandoned.

However, Zeenat had not given up on Mohammad Shafiq Toosi. She often phoned me, asking me to find Toosi and bring him to her. One day I accidentally ran into him at the radio station. When I gave him Zeenat's message, he said, 'This is not the first one. I have had several. The truth is that while Zeenat is a nice woman, she is too nice for my taste. Women who behave like wives are of no interest to me.'

Disappointed in Toosi, Zeenat resumed her visits to the beach in the company of Sardar. After two weeks of effort, Sardar was able to get hold of two men who appeared to be just the kind of gentlemen of leisure being sought. One of them, who owned a silk mill, even gave four hundred rupees to Zeenat and promised to marry her, but that was the last she heard from him.

One day, while on an errand on Hornsby Road, I saw Zeenat's parked car, with Mohammad Yasin, owner of the Nagina Hotel, occupying the back seat. 'Where did you get this car?' I asked.

'Do you know who it belongs to?'

'I do.'

'Then you can put two and two together.' He winked meaningfully.

A couple of days later, Babu Gopi Nath told me the story. Sardar had met someone at the beach and they had decided to go to Nagina Hotel to spend the evening. There was a quarrel and the man had walked out, which is how Yasin, the hotel's owner, had come into the picture.

Zeenat's affair with Yasin appeared to be progressing well. He had bought her some expensive gifts, and Babu Gopi Nath was mentally prepared to return to Lahore, because he was certain Yasin was the man Zeno could be entrusted to. Unfortunately, things did not work out that way.

A mother and daughter had recently moved into Nagina Hotel and Yasin was quick to see that Muriel, the daughter, was looking for someone to while away the time. So, while Zeenat sat in the hotel all day long, waiting for him, the two of them could be seen driving around Bombay in Zeenat's car. Babu Gopi Nath was hurt.

'What sort of men are these, Manto sahib?' he asked me. 'I mean if one has had one's fill of a woman, one just says so honestly. I no longer understand Zeenat. She knows what is going on, but she wouldn't even tell him that if he must carry on with that Christian chhokri then at least he should have the decency not to use her car. What am I to do, Manto sahib? She is such a wonderful girl, but she is so naive. She has to learn how to survive in this world.'

The affair with Yasin finally ended, but it seemed to have left no outward effect on Zeenat. One day I phoned the flat and learnt that Babu Gopi Nath had returned to Lahore, along with Ghulam Ali and Ghaffar Sain. His money had run out, but he still had some property left, which he was planning to sell before returning to Bombay.

Sardar needed her morphine and Sando his Polson's butter. They had therefore decided to turn the flat into a whorehouse. Two or three men were roped in every day to receive Zeenat's sexual favours. She had been told to cooperate until Babu Gopi Nath's return. The daily takings were around a hundred rupees or so, half of them Zeenat's.

'You do realize what you are doing to yourself?' I said to her one day.

'I don't know, Manto bhai,' she answered innocently. 'I merely do what these people tell me.'

I wanted to say that she was a fool and the two of them would not even hesitate to auction her off, if it came to that. However, I said nothing. She was a woman without ambition and unbelievably naive. She simply had no idea of her own value or what life was all about. If she was being made to sell her body, she could at least have done so with some intelligence and style, but she was simply not interested in anything, drinking, smoking, eating, or even the sofa on which she was to be found lying most of the time, and the telephone which she was so fond of using.

A month later, Babu Gopi Nath returned from Lahore. He went to the flat, but found some other people living there. It turned out that, on the advice of Sando and Sardar, Zeenat had rented the top portion of a bungalow in the Bandra area. When Babu Gopi Nath came to see me, I told him of the new arrangement, but I said nothing about the establishment Sando and Sardar were running, thanks to Zeenat.

Babu Gopi Nath had come back with ten thousand rupees this time. Ghaffar Sain and Ghulam Ali had been left in Lahore. When we met, he insisted that I should come with him to Zeenat's place. He had left a taxi waiting on the street.

It took us an hour to get to Bandra. As we were driving up Pali Hill, we saw Sando. 'Sando, Sando,' Babu Gopi Nath shouted. 'Dharan takhta,' Sando exclaimed when he saw who it was.

Babu Gopi Nath wanted him to get into the taxi, but Sando wouldn't. 'There is something I have to tell you,' he said.

I stayed in the taxi. The two of them talked for some time, then Babu Gopi Nath came back and told the driver to return to town.

He looked happy. As we were approaching Dawar, he said, 'Manto sahib, Zeno is about to be married.'

'To whom?' I asked, somewhat surprised.

'A rich landlord from Hyderabad, Sindh. May God keep both of them happy. The timing is perfect. The money I have can be used to buy Zeno her dowry.'

I was a bit sceptical about the story. I was sure it was another of Sando and Sardar's tricks to cheat Babu Gopi Nath. However, it all turned out to be true. The man was a rich Sindhi landlord who had been introduced to Zeno through the good offices of a Sindhi music teacher who had failed to teach her how to sing.

One day he had brought Ghulam Hussain—for that was the landlord's name—to Zeenat's place and she had received him with her usual hospitality. She had even sung for him at his insistence Ghalib's ghazal *'Nukta cheen hai gham-e-dil usko sunai na bana'*. Ghulam Hussain was smitten. The music teacher mentioned this to Zeenat, and Sardar and Sando joined hands to firm things up and a date for marriage was set.

One thing had led to another and now they were going to get married.

Babu Gopi Nath was ecstatic. He had managed to meet Ghulam Hussain, having had himself introduced as Sando's friend. He told me later, 'Manto sahib, he is handsome and he is intelligent. Before leaving Lahore, I went and prayed at the shrine of Data Ganj Baksh for Zeno and my prayer has been answered. May Bhagwan keep both of them happy.'

Babu Gopi Nath made all the wedding arrangements. Four thousand rupees was spent on ornaments and clothes and five thousand was to be given in cash to Zeenat.

The wedding guests from Zeenat's side were myself, Mohammad Shafiq Toosi, and Mohammad Yasin, proprietor of the Nagina

Hotel. After the ceremony, Sando whispered, 'Dharan takhta.'

Ghulam Hussain was a handsome man. He was dressed in a blue suit and was graciously acknowledging the congratulations being offered to him. Babu Gopi Nath looked like a little bird in his presence.

There was a wedding dinner, with Babu Gopi Nath very much the host. At one point, he said to me, 'Manto sahib, you must see how lovely Zeno looks in her bridal dress.'

I went into the next room. There sat Zeenat, dressed in expensive, silver-embroidered red silk. She was lightly made up, but was wearing too much lipstick. She greeted me by bowing her head slightly. She did look lovely, I thought. However, when I looked in the other corner, I found a bed profusely bedecked with flowers. I just could not contain my laughter. 'What is this farce?' I asked her.

'You are making fun of me, Manto bhai,' Zeno said, tears welling up in her eyes.

I was still wondering how to react, when Babu Gopi Nath came in. Lovingly, he dried Zeno's tears with his handkerchief and said to me in a heartbroken voice, 'Manto sahib, I had always considered you a wise and sensitive man. Before making such fun of Zeno, you should at least have weighed your words.'

I suddenly had the feeling that the devotion he had always shown me had suffered a setback, but before I could apologize to him, he placed his hand affectionately over Zeenat's head and said, 'May God keep you happy.'

When he left the room, his eyes were wet and there was a look of disillusionment on his face.

MUMMY

Her name was Stella Jackson, but everyone called her mummy. A short, active woman in her middle years, whose husband had been killed in the last great war. His pension still came every month.

I had no idea how long she had lived in Poona. The fact was that she was such a fascinating character that after meeting her once, such questions somehow became irrelevant. She herself was all that mattered. To say that she was an integral part of Poona may sound like an exaggeration, but as far as I am concerned all my memories of that city are inextricably linked with her.

I am a very lazy person by nature, which is not to say that I do not dream about great travels. If you hear me talking, you would think I was about to set out to conquer the Kanchenjunga peak in the Himalayas. It is another matter that once I get there I might decide not to move at all.

I can't really remember how many years I had been in Bombay when I decided one day to take my wife to Poona. Let me work it out. Our first child had been dead four years and it was another four years since I had moved to Bombay. So, actually, I had been living there for eight years, but not once had I taken the trouble to visit the famous Victoria Gardens or the museum. It was therefore quite unusual for me to get up one morning and take off for Poona. I had recently had a tiff at the film studio where I was employed as a writer. I wanted to get away—a change of scene, if you like. For one thing, Poona was not far and there were a number of my old movie friends living there.

We took a train, arrived, scampered out of the station and realized that the Parbhat Nagar suburb where we planned to stay with friends was quite far. We got into a tonga which turned out to be the slowest thing I had ever been in. I hate slowness, be it in men or animals. However, there was no alternative.

We were in no particular hurry to get to Parbhat Nagar, but I was getting impatient with the absurd conveyance we were in. I had never seen anything more ridiculous since Aligarh, which is notorious for its horse-drawn ikkas. The horse moves forward and the passengers slip backwards. Once or twice, I suggested to my wife that perhaps we should walk the rest of the way, or get hold of a better specimen of tonga, but she quite logically observed that there was nothing to choose from between one tonga and the next and, besides, the sun would be unbearable. Wives.

Another equally ridiculous-looking tonga was coming from the opposite direction. Suddenly, I heard someone shout, 'Hey Manto, you big horsie.' It was Chadda, my old friend, huddled in the back with a worn-out woman. My first reaction was regret. What had gone wrong with his aesthetic sense that he was now running around with a woman old enough to be his mother? I couldn't guess her age, but I noticed that despite her heavy make-up, the wrinkles on her face were visible. It was so grossly painted that it hurt the eye.

I had not seen Chadda for ages. He was one of my best friends and, had he not been with the sort of woman he was with, I would have greeted him with something equally mindless. In any case, both of us got down.

He said to the woman, 'Mummy, just a minute.' He pumped my hand vigorously, then tried to do the same to my extremely formal wife. 'Bhabi, you have performed the impossible, I mean, getting this bundle of lazy bones all the way from Bombay to Poona.'

'Where are you headed for?' I asked.

'On important business. Now, listen, don't waste time. You are going straight to my place.' He began to issue instructions to the tongawala, adding, 'Don't charge the fare. It'll be settled.'

Then he turned to me. 'There is a servant around. See you later.' Without waiting for an answer, he jumped into his tonga, where the woman whom he had called Mummy sat waiting for him. The embarrassment I had felt earlier was gone.

His house was not far from where we had met. It looked like an old dak bungalow. 'This is it,' the tongawala said. 'I mean Chadda sahib's house.' I could see from my wife's expression that she was not overly enthusiastic about the prospects. As a matter of fact, she had not been overly enthusiastic about coming to Poona. She was afraid that once there I would team up with my drinking friends and, since I was supposed to be having a change of scene, most of my time would be spent in what was to her highly objectionable company. I got down and asked my wife to follow me, which she did after some hesitation, as it was clear to her that my mind was made up.

It was the kind of house the army likes to requisition for a few weeks and then abandon. The walls were badly in need of paint and the rooms could only have belonged to a careless bachelor, an actor most likely, paid every two or three months—and that, too, in instalments.

I was conscious that this was no place for wives, but there was nothing to do but wait for Chadda, and then move to Parbhat Nagar, where this old friend of mine lived with his wife in more reasonable surroundings.

The servant in a way suited the place. When we arrived we found all the doors open and nobody in sight. When he finally materialized he took no notice of us, as if we had lived there for years. He came into the room and sailed past us without saying a word. I thought he was an out-of-work actor sharing the house with Chadda. However, when he came again and I asked him where the servant was to be found, he informed me gravely that he himself was the holder of that office.

We were both thirsty. When I asked him to get us a drink of water, he began looking for a glass. Finally, he produced a chipped glass mug from the bottom drawer of a cupboard and murmured, 'Only last night, sahib sent for half a dozen glasses. Now what on earth could have happened to them!'

My wife said she did not want a drink after all. He put the mug back exactly where he had unearthed it—in the bottom drawer of the cupboard—as if without this elaborate ritual the entire household would come tumbling down. Then he left the room.

While my wife took one of the armchairs, I made myself comfortable on the bed, which was probably Chadda's. We did not say anything to each other. After some time, Chadda arrived. He was alone. He seemed quite indifferent to the fact that we were his guests.

'What's what old boy,' he said. 'Let's run up to the studio for a few minutes. With you in tow, I'm sure I can pick up an advance, because this evening . . .' Then he looked at my wife. 'Bhabi, I hope you haven't made a mullah out of him.' He laughed. 'To hell with all the mullahs of the world. Come on, Manto, get moving. I am sure bhabi won't mind.'

My wife said nothing, although it wasn't difficult to guess what she was thinking. The studio was not far. After a noisy meeting with Mr Mehta the accountant, Chadda succeeded in making him cough up an advance of two hundred rupees. When we returned to the house, we found my wife sleeping in the armchair. We did not disturb her and moved into the next room, where I noticed everything was either broken or in an advanced state of disrepair. At least it gave the place a uniformity of sorts.

There was dust on everything, an essential touch to the bohemian character of Chadda's lodgings. From somewhere, he found the elusive servant, handed him a hundred rupees and said, 'Prince of Cathay, get us two bottles of third-class rum, I mean, 3-X rum and six new glasses.'

I later discovered that the servant was not only the Prince of Cathay, but the prince of practically very major country and civilization in the world. It all depended on Chadda's mood of the moment.

The Prince of Cathay left, fondling the money he had been given. Lowering himself on the bed, which had a broken spring mattress, Chadda ran his tongue over his lips in anticipation of the rum he had ordered and said, 'What's what. So you did hit Poona after all.' Then he added in a worried voice, 'But what about bhabi? I'm sure she's bloody upset.'

Chadda did not have a wife, but he was always worried about the wives of his friends. He used to say that he had remained single because he felt insecure when dealing with wives. 'When it's suggested to me that I should get married, my first reaction is always positive. Then I start thinking and in a few minutes come to the conclusion that I don't really deserve a wife. And that's how the project gets thrown into cold storage every time,' was one of his favourite explanations.

The rum arrived, and with it, the glasses. Chadda had sent for six, but the Prince of Cathay had dropped three on the way. Chadda was unconcerned. 'Praise be to the Lord that at least the bottles are unharmed,' he observed philosophically.

Then he opened the bottle hurriedly, poured the rum into virgin glasses and toasted me: 'To your arrival in Poona.' We downed our drinks in long swigs. Chadda poured more, then tiptoed into the other room to see if my wife was still asleep. She was. 'This is no good,' he announced 'Let me make some noise so that she wakes up . . . but before that let me organize some tea for her. Prince of Jamaica,' he shouted.

The Prince of Jamaica materialized at once. 'Go to Mummy's place and ask her to kindly prepare some first-class tea and have it sent over. Immediately.'

Chadda drank up, then poured himself a more civilized measure and said, 'For the time being, I am watching my drinking. The first four drinks make me very sentimental and we still have to go to Parbhat Nagar to dump bhabi.'

The tea came, set on a nice tray. Chadda lifted the lid of the teapot, smelled the brew and declared, 'Mummy is a jewel.' Then he sent for the Prince of Ethiopia and began screaming at him. When he was sure that the racket had awakened my wife, he picked up the tray daintily and told me to follow him. He put it down with an exaggerated flourish on a table and announced, 'Tea is served, madam.'

My wife did not appear too amused by Chadda's antics, but she drank two cups and said, not so ill-humouredly, 'I suppose the two of you have already had yours.'

'I must plead guilty to that charge, but we did it in the secure knowledge that we'd find forgiveness,' Chadda said.

My wife smiled, encouraging Chadda to continue. 'Actually, both of us are pigs of the purest breed who are permitted to eat every forbidden fruit on earth. It is therefore time that we took steps to move you to a holier place than this.'

My wife was not amused. She did not care for Chadda. The fact is that she did not care much for any of my friends, especially him because she thought he was always transgressing the limits of what she considered correct behaviour. I don't think it had ever occurred to Chadda how people reacted to him. He considered it a waste of time, like playing indoor games. He beamed at my wife and shouted, 'Prince of Kababistan, get us a Rolls-Royce tonga.'

The Rolls-Royce tonga came and we left for Parbhat Nagar. My friend Harish Kumar was not at home, but his wife was, which we found helpful. Chadda said, 'As melons influence melons, in the same way, wives influence wives. We are off to the studio now, but we will soon return to verify the results.'

Chadda's strategy was always simple. Create so much confusion that enemy forces get no opportunity to plan theirs. He pushed me towards the door, giving my wife no time to object. 'Operation successfully accomplished. What now? Yes, Mummy great Mummy,' Chadda declared.

I wanted to ask him who this Mummy of his was, daughter of what Tutankhamun, but he began to speak about totally unconnected matters, leaving my question to wither on the vine.

The tonga took us back to the house which was called Saeeda Cottage. Chadda had christened it Kabida Cottage, the abode of the melancholy, as it was his theory that all its residents were in a state of advanced melancholia. Like many of his other theories, this one too was not quite consistent with the facts.

Chadda was not the only resident of Saeeda Cottage. There were others, all actors, and all working for the same film company which paid salaries every third month—in the form of advance. Almost all the inmates of the establishment were assistant directors. There were chief assistant directors, their deputies and assistants who, in turn, had their own assistants. It seemed to me that everyone was everyone's assistant and on the lookout for a financier to help him set up his own film company.

Because of the war, food rationing was in effect, but none of the Saeeda Cottage residents had a ration card. When they had money, they used to buy from the black market at exorbitant prices. They always went to the movies and, during the season, to the races. Some even tried their luck at the stock exchange, but no one had so far made a killing.

Since space was limited, even the garage was used for residential purposes. It was occupied by a family. The husband was not an assistant director, but the film company chauffeur, who kept odd hours. His wife, a good-looking young woman, was named Shireen. She had a little boy who had been collectively adopted by the residents of Saeeda Cottage.

The more liveable rooms in the cottage were occupied by Chadda and two of his friends, both actors, who had yet to make the big time. One was called Saeed, but his professional name was Ranjeet Kumar, a quiet, nice-looking man. Chadda often referred to him as the tortoise because he did everything very, very slowly.

I do not now remember the real name of the other actor, but everybody called him Gharib Nawaz. He came from a well-to-do family of the princely state of Hyderabad. He had come to Poona to get into the movies. He was paid two hundred and fifty rupees a month, but since being hired a year earlier had been paid only once—an advance against salary. The money had gone to rescue Chadda from the clutches of a very angry Pathan moneylender. There was hardly anyone in Saeeda Cottage who did not owe money to Gharib Nawaz.

Despite Chadda's theory, none of them was particularly melancholy. In fact they lived fairly happily, and even when they talked of their straitened circumstances it was in an offhand, cheerful manner.

When Chadda and I returned, we ran into Gharib Nawaz outside the front gate. Chadda pulled out some money from his pocket and gave it to him—without counting—and said, 'Four bottles of Scotch. If I've given you less, then I know you'll make up for it. If I've given you more, I know I'll get it back. Thank you.'

Gharib Nawaz smiled. 'This is Mr—one two,' he said to him, meaning me. 'Detailed discussions are not possible at this stage because he has had a few rums. But wait until the evening when the Scotch begins to flow.'

We went inside. Chadda yawned, picked up the half-empty bottle of rum, took stock of its contents and shouted for the Prince of the Cossacks. There was no answer. 'I think he is drunk,' he observed, pouring himself another drink.

Chadda's room was like an old junk shop. However, it had a window or two, through one of which I now saw Venkutrey the music director, another old friend of mine, peeping in. It was difficult to tell by looking at him what race he belonged to—whether he was Mongol, Negroid, Aryan or something completely unknown to anthropology.

While one particular feature might, for a moment, suggest certain origins, it was immediately cancelled out by another feature, pointing at entirely different possibilities. However, he was from Maharashtra. His nose, unlike that of his famous forebear, the warrior Shivaji, was flat, which he always assured people was a great help in reproducing certain notes.

'Manto seth,' he screamed when he saw me.

'The hell with seths,' Chadda said. 'Don't stand there. Come in.' Venkutrey appeared, put a bottle of rum on the table and said he was at Mummy's when he was told that one of Chadda's friends was in town. 'I was wondering who that could be. Didn't know it was sala Manto the old sinner.'

Chadda slapped his head. 'Shut your trap. You've produced a bottle of rum, that's enough.' Venkutrey picked up my empty glass and poured himself a large measure. 'Manto, this sala Chadda was telling me this morning, "Venkutrey, I want to get drunk tonight. Get some booze." Now I was broke and I was wondering where I was going to get the money . . .'

'You are an imbecile,' Chadda said.

'Is that so, then where do you think I managed to get this big bucket of rum from? It wasn't a gift from your father, I can tell you that.' He finished his glass. 'What did Mummy say?' Chadda asked. 'Was Polly there, and Thelma . . . and that platinum blonde?'

Chadda didn't wait for his answer. 'Manto, what a bundle of goods that one is! I had always heard of platinum blondes, but by God I had never set eyes on one, that is, until yesterday. She's lovely. Her hair is like threads of fine silver. She is great, Manto. I tell you she's great. Mummy zindabad. Mummy zindabad.' Then he said to Venkutrey, 'You bloody man, say Mummy zindabad.'

Chadda grabbed my arm. 'Manto, I think I am getting very sentimental. You know in tradition the beloved is supposed to have black hair like a rain cloud, but what we have here is an entirely different bill of fare. Her hair is like finely spun silver . . . or maybe not . . . now I don't know what platinum looks like. I have never seen the bloody thing in my life. How can I describe the colour! Just try to imagine blue steel and silver mixed together.'

'And a shot of 3-X rum,' Venkutrey suggested, knocking back his.

'Shut up,' Chadda told him. 'Manto, I am really going bananas over this girl. Oh, the colour of her hair. What are those things fish have on their bellies, or is it all over? The pomfret fish. What are those things called? Damn fish, I think snakes have them too, those tiny, shimmering things. Scales, that's right, they're called scales. In Urdu they're called "khaprey", which is a ridiculous name for something so beautiful. We have a word for them in Punjabi. I know it. Yes . . . "chanay". What a lovely word. It sounds right. It sounds just right. That's what her hair is like . . . small, brilliant, slithering snakes.'

He got up. 'To hell with small, brilliant, slithering snakes. I'm going out of my mind. I'm getting sentimental.'

'What was that?' Venkutrey asked absent-mindedly.

'Beyond your feeble powers of comprehension, my friend,' Chadda replied.

Venkutrey mixed himself another drink. 'Manto, this sala Chadda thinks I don't understand English. You know I'm a matriculate. My father loved me. He sent me to . . .'

'Your father was mad. He made you the greatest musician in the world. He twisted your nose and made it flat so that you could sing flat notes. Manto, whenever he has had a couple of drinks, he starts talking about his father. Yes, he's a matriculate, but should I then tear up my BA degree?'

I drank. 'Manto,' Chadda said, 'if I fail to conquer this platinum blonde, I promise you Mr Chadda will renounce the world, go to the highest peak in the Himalayas and contemplate his navel.'

He said he was throwing a big party that night. 'Had you not hit town, that rascal Mehta would never have given me the advance. Well, tonight is the night.' He began to sing in his highly unmusical voice. Before Venkutrey could protest at this most foul murder of music, the door opened to reveal Gharib Nawaz and Ranjeet Kumar, each holding two bottles of Scotch. We poured them some rum.

It turned out that the name of this jewel was Phyllis. She worked in a hairdressing salon and was generally to be seen with a young fellow, who, everybody assured me, looked like a sissy. The entire male population of Saeeda Cottage was infatuated with her.

Gharib Nawaz had declared that morning that he might rush back to Hyderabad, sell some property, return with the proceeds and sweep her off her feet. Chadda's only plus was his good looks. Venkutrey was of the view that she would fall into his lap the moment she heard him sing. Ranjeet Kumar was in favour of a more direct approach. However, in the end, it was clear that success would depend on whom Mummy favoured.

Chadda looked at his watch. 'Let the bloody platinum blonde go to blazes. We have to be in Parbhat Nagar, because I am sure by now Mrs Manto is angry. Now, if I get a sentimental fit in her presence, you'll have to look after me.' He finished his drink and called for the Prince of Egypt, the land of mummies.

The prince appeared, rubbing his eyes as if he had just been disinterred from the earth after hundreds of years. Chadda sprinkled his face with some rum and told him to conjure up two royal Egyptian chariots.

The chariots came and soon we were on our way to Parbhat Nagar. My friend Harish Kumar was home and my wife seemed to be in a good mood. Chadda winked at him as we entered to indicate that something was on the cards for the evening.

Harish asked my wife if she'd like to come to the studio to watch him shoot a couple of scenes. She wanted to know if a musical sequence was being filmed. When told that it would be the next day, she seemed to lose interest. 'Why not tomorrow then?' Harish's wife suggested. The poor woman was sick of taking guests to the studios. She told my wife, 'You look tired. I think you should take some rest.'

Harish said it was a good idea. 'Manto, you'd better come with me to see the studio chief. He has expressed an interest in your writing a film for him.' My wife was pleased. Chadda provided the final touch to the drama. He said he was leaving as he had something important to do. We said our goodbyes. When we met later on the road, Chadda shouted lustily, 'Raja Harish Chander zindabad.'

Harish did not come with us. He had to meet his girlfriend.

From the outside, Mummy's house looked like Saeeda Cottage, but there the resemblance ended. I had expected to find myself in a sort of brothel, but it was a perfectly normal, middle-class Christian household. It looked a bit younger than Mummy, perhaps because it was simple and wore no make-up. When she walked in, I felt that while everything around her had remained the same age as the day it was bought, she had moved on and grown old. She was wearing the same bright make-up.

Chadda introduced her briefly: 'This is Mummy the great.' She smiled, then admonished him gently. 'You sent for tea in such an unholy hurry that I am sure Mrs Manto could not have found it drinkable. It was all your friend Chadda's fault,' she told me.

I said the tea was great. Then she said to Chadda, 'I fixed dinner, otherwise you always get impatient at the last moment.' Chadda threw his arms around her. 'You are a jewel, Mummy. Of course we are going to eat that dinner.'

Mummy wanted to know where my wife was. When we told her that she was with friends in Parbhat Nagar, she said, 'That's awful, why didn't you bring her?'

'Because of the party tonight,' Chadda replied.

'What party? I decided to call it off the moment I saw Mrs Manto.'

'What have you done, Mummy?' Chadda exclaimed. 'And to think that we planned this entire charade just for that!'

Then on an impulse he jumped up. 'But you only thought of calling the party off. You didn't actually call it off. As such, hereby I call off your decision to call off the party. Cross your heart.' He drew a cross across Mummy's heart and shouted, 'Hip hip hurray!'

The fact was that Mummy had called off the party. I could also see that she didn't want to disappoint Chadda. She touched him on the cheek affectionately and said, 'Let me see what I can do.'

She left. Chadda's spirits rose. 'General Venkutrey, report to headquarters and arrange immediate transportation of all heavy guns to the battlefront.'

Venkutrey saluted smartly and left for Saeeda Cottage. He was back in ten minutes with the heavy guns—the four bottles of Scotch—with the servant bringing up the rear. 'Come in, come in, my Caucasian prince. The girl with hair the colour of snake scales is coming tonight. You too can try your luck.'

I was thinking about Mummy. Chadda, Gharib Nawaz and Ranjeet Kumar were like little children waiting for their mother who had gone out to buy them toys. Chadda was more confident because he was the favourite child and he knew that he would get the best toy. The others were not altogether without hope. Every situation has its own music. The one in Mummy's home had no harsh notes. Drinking did not feel like something which should not be done. It was like imbibing milk.

Her make-up still bothered me, however. Why did she have to paint her face like that? It was an insult to the love she showered with such generosity on Chadda, Gharib Nawaz and Venkutrey . . . and who knew how many more.

I asked Chadda, 'Why does your Mummy look so flashy?'

'Because the world likes flashy things. There are not many idiots around like you and me who wish colours to be sober and understated, music to be soft, who don't want to see youth clad in the garments of childhood and age in the mantle of youth. We who call ourselves artists are actually second-class asses, because there is nothing first class on this earth. It is either third or second class, except . . . except Phyllis. She alone is first class.'

Venkutrey poured his drink over Chadda's head. 'Snakes scales . . . you have gone mad.'

Chadda lapped it up. 'This has cooled me down.'

Venkutrey began his long, rambling story about how much his father loved him, but Chadda was having none of that.

'To hell with your entire family,' he said. 'I want to talk about Phyllis.' He looked at Gharib Nawaz and Ranjeet Kumar, who were huddled together in a corner whispering in each other's ears. 'You leaders of the great gunpowder plot, your conspiracies will never succeed. Victory in battle will kiss Chadda's feet. Isn't that so, my

Prince of Wales?'

The Prince of Wales seemed more worried about the bottle of rum, which was getting emptier by the minute. Chadda laughed and poured him a hefty measure.

The lights had been switched on, and outside, the evening had fallen. Then we heard Mummy on the veranda. Chadda shouted a slogan and ran out. Ranjeet Kumar and Gharib Nawaz exchanged glances, waiting for the door to open.

Mummy came in, followed by four or five Anglo-Indian girls—Polly, Dolly, Kitty, Elma, Thelma—and a young man who answered to the description that had been provided to me of Phyllis's friend.

Phyllis was the last to appear. Chadda had his arm around her. He had already declared victory. Gharib Nawaz and Ranjeet Kumar looked positively unhappy at this unsporting behaviour.

All hell broke loose. Suddenly everyone was jabbering away in English, trying to impress the girls. Venkutrey failed his matriculation several times in a row. Soon he went into a corner with Thelma, offering free instruction in Indian classical dance.

Chadda was surrounded by a bevy of giggling girls. He was reciting dirty limericks which he knew by the hundred. Mummy was busy with her arrangements. Ranjeet Kumar sat alone, smoking cigarette after cigarette. Gharib Nawaz was asking Mummy if she needed any money.

The Scotch was brought in ceremoniously. Phyllis was offered a drink, but she shook her head. She said she did not like whisky. Even Chadda was refused. Finally, Mummy prepared a light drink, put the glass to her lips and said, 'Now be a brave girl and gulp it down.'

Chadda was so thrilled that he recited another twenty limericks. I was thinking. Man must have got bored with nakedness when he decided to don clothes, which is why sometimes he gets bored with them and reverts to his original state. The reaction to good manners is certainly bad manners.

I watched Mummy. She was surrounded by the girls and was giggling with the rest of them at Chadda's antics. She was wearing the same vulgar, tasteless make-up under which her wrinkles could be seen in high relief. She looked happy. I wondered why people thought escape to be a bad thing. Here was an act of escape. The exterior was unattractive, but the soul was beautiful. Did she need all those unguents, lotions and colouring liquids?

Polly was telling Ranjeet Kumar about her new dress, which she had picked up as a bargain and had done something to at home. And now it was perfectly lovely. Ranjeet Kumar was offering to buy her two new ones, although he was unlikely to get an advance in the near future. Dolly was trying to talk Gharib Nawaz into lending her some more money. He knew perfectly well that he would never see it again, but was still trying to convince himself to the contrary.

Thelma was being tutored in the intricacies of Indian classical dance by Venkutrey, who knew that she would never make a dancer. She knew that too, but she was still listening to him with great concentration. Elma and Kitty were drinking steadily.

In this tableau it was difficult to be sure about the rights and wrongs. Was Mummy's flashiness right or a part of the situation? Who could say? In her heart there was love for everyone. Perhaps she had coloured her face, I said to myself, so that the world should not see what she was really like. Maybe she did not have the emotional strength to play mother to the whole world. She had just chosen a few.

Mummy did not know that during her absence in the kitchen, Chadda had persuaded Phyllis to take a massive drink, not on the sly, but in front of the others. Phyllis was slightly high, but only slightly. Her hair was like polished steel, waving gently from side to side like her young sinuous body.

It was midnight. Venkutrey was no longer trying to make a classical dancer out of Thelma. Now he was telling her about his father, who loved him to the point of distraction. Gharib Nawaz had forgotten that he had already lent some more money to Dolly. Ranjeet Kumar had disappeared with Polly. Elma and Kitty were sleepy.

Around the table sat Phyllis, her friend and Mummy. Chadda was no longer sentimental. He sat next to Phyllis and it was evident he was determined to take her tonight.

At some point, Phyllis's friend got up, laid himself down on the sofa and went to sleep. Gharib Nawaz and Dolly left the room. Elma and Kitty said their goodnights and went home. Venkutrey, after praising his wife's beauty one more time, cast a longing look at Phyllis, put his arm around Thelma and took her out into the garden.

Suddenly a loud argument developed between Mummy and

Chadda. He was drunk, angry and foul-mouthed. He had never spoken to her like that. Phyllis had given up her feeble efforts to make peace between the two. Chadda wanted to take her to Saeeda Cottage and Mummy had told him that she would not permit that. He was screaming at her now. 'You old pimp, you have gone mad. Phyllis is mine. Ask her.'

'Chadda, my son, why don't you understand? She is young, she is very young,' Mummy said to him, but Chadda was beyond reason. For the first time it occurred to me how young Phyllis was, hardly fifteen. Her face was like a raindrop surrounded by silver clouds.

Chadda pulled Phyllis towards him, squeezed her against his chest in a passionate B-grade movie embrace. 'Chadda, leave her alone. For God's sake let her go,' Mummy screamed, but he paid no attention to her.

Then it happened. She slapped him across the face. 'Get out, get out!' she shouted.

Chadda pushed Phyllis aside, gave Mummy a furious look and walked out. I followed him.

When I arrived at Saeeda Cottage, he was lying on his bed, face down, fully clothed. We did not speak. I went to my room and slept.

I got up late next morning. Chadda was not in his room. I washed and as I was coming out of the bathroom I heard his voice outside. 'She is unique. By God, she is great. You should pray that when you reach her age you should become like her.'

I did not want to hang around much longer. I waited for him to come back to the house, but after about half an hour I left for Parbhat Nagar.

Harish hadn't returned home. I told his wife that we had had a late night, so he had decided to sleep at Saeeda Cottage. We took our leave and on the way I told my wife about the night's incident. Her theory was that Phyllis was either related to Mummy or the old woman wanted to save her for some better client. I kept quiet.

After several weeks I had a letter from Chadda. All it said was, 'I behaved like a beast that evening. Damn me.'

I went to Poona a few months later on business. When I called at Saeeda Cottage, Chadda was out. Gharib Nawaz was playing with Shireen's son. We shook hands. I learnt from him that Chadda hadn't spoken to Mummy after that night, nor had she visited Saeeda Cottage.

She had sent Phyllis back to her parents. It turned out that she had run away from home with that young fellow. Ranjeet Kumar—who had just walked in—was confident that had Phyllis stayed on, he would have scored. Gharib Nawaz had no such illusions, but he was sorry she was gone.

They said Chadda had not been well for some time, but refused to see a doctor. As we were talking, Venkutrey rushed in. He looked very nervous. He had met Chadda on the street, found him feeling groggy and put him in a tonga to get him home, but Chadda had fainted on the way. We ran out. Chadda lay in the tonga looking very ill. We brought him in. He was unconscious.

I told Gharib Nawaz to get a doctor. He consulted Venkutrey and left. They returned a little later with Mummy. 'What has happened to my son?' she asked. 'What kind of friends are you? Why didn't you send me word?' she said.

She immediately took charge. 'Get hold of some ice and rub his forehead. Massage his feet. Fan his face.' Then she went out to get a doctor. Everyone looked relieved, as if the entire responsibility of bringing Chadda back to health was now Mummy's.

Chadda had begun to regain consciousness when Mummy returned with the doctor. The doctor examined him, then took Mummy aside. She told us there was no cause for worry. Chadda was still a bit disoriented. He saw Mummy. He took her hand in his and said, 'Mummy, you are great.'

She ran her hand gently over Chadda's burning face. 'My son, my poor son,' she said.

Tears came to Chadda's eyes. 'Don't say that. Your son is a scoundrel of the first order. Go get your husband's old service revolver and shoot him.'

'Don't talk rubbish,' she said. She rose. 'Boys, Chadda is very ill. I'm going to take him to the hospital.'

Gharib Nawaz sent for a taxi. Chadda could not understand why he was being taken to hospital, but Mummy told him that he would be more comfortable there than at home. 'It's nothing,' she said.

He was laid up for many days, with Mummy spending most of her time with him. However, he did not seem to be getting better. His skin had become sallow and he was losing strength. The doctors were of the view that he should be taken to Bombay, but Mummy said, 'No, I'm going to take him home and he's going to get well.'

I had to leave Poona, but I phoned from Bombay every other day. I had started to lose hope, but slowly, very slowly, Chadda began to come round. I had to go to Lahore for a few weeks. When I returned to Bombay there was a letter from Chadda. 'The great Mummy has reclaimed her unworthy son from the dead,' he had written. There was so much love in that line. When I told my wife, she observed icily, 'Such women are generally good at these things.'

I wrote to Chadda a few times, but he didn't answer. Later, somebody told me that Mummy had sent him to the hills to stay with friends. He was soon better—and bored—and returned to Poona. I was there that day.

He looked weak, but nothing else had changed. He talked about his illness as if he had had a minor bicycle accident. Saeeda Cottage had seen a few changes in his absence. A Bengali music director called Sen had moved in. He shared his room with Ram Singh, a young boy from Lahore who had come to Bombay, like so many others, to get into films.

Ranjeet Kumar had been picked up to play the lead in a movie. He had been promised the direction of the next one, provided the one under production did well. Chadda had finally managed to raise an advance of one thousand five hundred rupees from the studio. Gharib Nawaz had just come back from Hyderabad and the general finances of Saeeda Cottage were in good shape as a result of that. Shireen's boy had new clothes and new toys.

My friend Harish was currently trying to seduce his new leading lady, who was from Punjab. He was, however, afraid of her husband, who had a formidable moustache and looked like a wrestler. Chadda's advice to Harish had been sound: 'Don't worry about him at all. He may be a wrestler, but in the field of love he is bound to fall flat on his face. All you need to learn are a few heavyweight Punjabi swear words from me. I'll settle for one hundred rupees per lesson. You'll need them in awkward situations.'

Harish had struck a deal and, at the rate of a bottle of rum per choice Punjabi swear word, had learnt half a dozen of them. However, there had been no occasion to test his new powers. His affair was doing well without them.

Mummy's parties had been reconvened and the old crowd—Polly, Dolly, Elma, Thelma etc.—was back. Venkutrey had still not given up his efforts to induct Thelma into the mysteries of Indian classical dance. Gharib Nawaz was still lending money and Ranjeet Kumar, who was about to hit the big screen, was using his new position to ingratiate himself with the girls. Chadda's dirty limericks were still flowing.

There was only one thing missing—the girl with the platinum blonde hair, the colour of snake scales and blue steel and silver. Chadda never mentioned her. Occasionally, one would see him looking at Mummy, then lowering his eyes, recalling the events of that night. Off and on, after his fourth drink, he would say, 'Chadda, you are a damned brute.'

Mummy was still the Mummy—Polly's Mummy, Dolly's Mummy, Chadda's Mummy, Ranjeet Kumar's Mummy—still the wonderful manageress of her unique establishment. Her make-up was still flashy, and her clothes even flashier. Her wrinkles still showed, but for me they had come to assume a sacred dimension.

It was Mummy who had come to the rescue of Venkutrey's wife when she had had a miscarriage. She had taken charge of Thelma when she had caught a dangerous infection from a dance director who had promised to put her in the movies. Recently, Kitty had won five hundred rupees in a crossword puzzle competition and Mummy had persuaded her to give some of it to Gharib Nawaz, who was a bit short. 'Give it to him now and you can keep taking it back,' she had advised her.

There was only one man she didn't like: the music director Sen. She had told Chadda repeatedly, 'Don't bring him to my house. There is something about him that makes me uneasy. He doesn't fit.'

I returned to Bombay carrying with me the warmth of Mummy's parties. Her world was simple and beautiful and reassuring. Yes, there was drinking and sex and a general lack of seriousness, but one felt no emotional unease. It was like the protruding belly of a pregnant woman: a bit odd, but perfectly innocent and immediately comprehensible.

One day I read in the papers that the music director Sen had been found murdered in Saeeda Cottage. The suspect was said to be a young man named Ram Singh.

Chadda wrote me an account of the incident later.

'I was sound asleep that night. Suddenly, I felt someone slump into my bed. It was Sen. He was covered in blood. Then Ram Singh rushed into the room holding a knife. By this time, everyone was up. Ranjeet Kumar and Gharib Nawaz ran in and disarmed Ram

Singh. Sen's breathing grew uneven and then stopped. "Is he dead?" Ram Singh asked. I nodded my head. "Please let go of me. I won't run away," he said calmly.

'We didn't know what to do, so we immediately sent for Mummy. She took stock of the situation in her unruffled manner and escorted Ram Singh to the police, where he made a statement confessing to the killing. The next few weeks were awful. Police, courts, lawyers, the works. There was a trial and the court acquitted Ram Singh.

'He had made the same statement under oath that he had made to the police. Mummy had said to him, "Son, speak the truth. Tell them what happened." Ram Singh had spoken the truth. He had told the court that Sen had promised to get him to sing for films, provided he would sleep with him. He had let himself be persuaded, but was always troubled by what he was doing. One day he had told Sen that if he tried to force him to perform the unnatural act again, he would kill him. And that was exactly what had happened that night. Sen had tried to force him and Ram Singh had stabbed him repeatedly with a kitchen knife.'

Chadda had written, 'In this age of untruth, the triumph of truth is astonishing.'

A party had been organized to celebrate Ram Singh's acquittal and when it was over Mummy had suggested that he should return to his parents in Lahore. Gharib Nawaz had bought him a ticket and Shireen had prepared food for him to take on the long journey. Everyone had gone to the station to see him off.

A week or so after this, I was asked by the studio to come to Poona to complete an assignment. Nothing had changed at Saeeda Cottage. It was still the way it always was. When I arrived, a minor party was in progress to celebrate the birth of another son to Shireen. Venkutrey had got hold of two tins of Glaxo baby food from somewhere, not an easy thing at the time. Suggestions were also being invited on a name for the child.

Everybody was trying to look cheerful, but I couldn't help feeling that there was something the matter with Chadda, Gharib Nawaz and Ranjeet Kumar. A vague sadness hung in the air. Was it the weather which was beginning to turn chilly or was it Sen's murder? I could not decide.

For one week I was shut up in Harish's house because I was in a hurry to complete my assignment. I was a bit surprised that Chadda hadn't come to see me all this time, nor Gharib Nawaz for that matter.

Then one afternoon Chadda burst into the house. 'This rubbish you've been writing, have you been paid something for it yet?' he asked. I told him I had received two thousand rupees only the other day and the money was in my jacket. He took out four hundred rupees and rushed out, pausing just long enough to tell me that there was a party at Mummy's house that evening and I was expected.

When I arrived, it was already in full swing. Ranjeet and Venkutrey were dancing with Polly and Thelma. Kitty was dancing with Elma, and Chadda was jumping around like a rabbit with Mummy in his arms. Everyone was quite drunk. My entrance was greeted with guffaws and slogans. Mummy, who had always maintained a certain formality with me, took hold of my hand and said, 'Kiss me, dear.'

'That's enough dancing,' Chadda announced above the din. 'I want to do some serious drinking now. Open a new bottle, my Prince of Scotland.' The prince, who was very drunk, appeared with a bottle and dropped it on the floor. 'It is only a bottle, Mummy. What about broken hearts?' Chadda said before she could scold the servant.

A chill fell over the party. A new bottle was duly produced. Chadda poured everyone a huge drink. Then he began to make a speech: 'Ladies and gentlemen, we have among us this evening this man called Manto. He thinks he's great story writer, but I think that's rubbish. He claims that he can fathom the depths of the human soul. That too is a lot of rubbish. This world is full of rubbish. I met someone yesterday after ten years and he assured me that we had met only the other week. That too is rubbish. That man was from Hyderabad. I pronounce a million curses on the Nizam of Hyderabad who has tons of gold but no Mummy.'

Someone shouted, 'Manto zindabad,' but Chadda continued with his speech. 'This is a conspiracy hatched by Manto, otherwise my instructions were clear. We should have greeted him with catcalls. I have been betrayed. But let me talk of that evening when I behaved like a beast with Mummy because of that girl with hair the colour of snake scales. Who did I think I was? Don Juan?

'Be that as it may, but it could have been done. With one kiss, I could have sucked in all her virginity with these big fat lips of mine. She was very young, very weak . . . what's the word, Manto? . . . yes, very unformed. After a night of love, she would either have carried the guilt with her the rest of her life, or she would have completely forgotten about it the next morning.

'I am glad Mummy threw me out that night. Ladies and gentlemen, now I end my speech. I've already talked lot of rubbish. Actually, I was planning a longer speech, but I can't speak any longer. I'm going to get myself a drink.'

Nobody spoke. It occurred to me that he had been heard in complete silence. Mummy also looked a bit lost. Chadda sat there nursing his drink. He was quiet. His speech seemed to have drained him out. 'What's with you?' I asked.

'I don't know—tonight the whisky is not battering in the buttocks of my brain as it always does,' he answered philosophically.

The clock struck two. Chadda, who in the meanwhile had begun a dance with Kitty, pushed her aside and said to Venkutrey, 'Sing us something, but I warn you, none of your classical mumbo-jumbo.'

Venkutrey sang a couple of songs, set to the melancholy evening raga Malkauns. The atmosphere grew even sadder. Gharib Nawaz was so moved that his eyes became wet. 'These Hyderabadis have weak eye-bladders. You never know when they might start dripping,' Chadda observed.

Gharib Nawaz wiped his eyes and took Elma on to the floor. Venkutrey put a record on. Chadda picked up Mummy and began to bounce around.

At four o'clock, Chadda suddenly said, 'That's it.' He picked up a bottle from the table, put it to his mouth and drank what was left of it. 'Let's go, Manto.'

When I tried to say goodbye to Mummy, he pulled me away. 'There are going to be no goodbyes tonight.'

When we were outside, I thought I heard Venkutrey crying. I wanted to go back, but Chadda stopped me. 'He too has a faulty eye-bladder.'

Saeeda Cottage was only a few minutes' walk. We did not speak. Before going to bed, I tried to ask Chadda about the strange party, but he said he was sleepy.

When I got up the next morning, I found Gharib Nawaz standing outside the garage wiping his eyes.

'What's the matter?' I asked him.

'Mummy's gone.'

'Where?'

'I don't know.'

Chadda was still in bed, but it seemed he hadn't slept at all. He smiled when I asked him if it was true. 'Yes, she's gone. Had to leave Poona by the morning train.'

'But why?' I asked.

'Because the authorities did not approve of her ways. Her parties were considered objectionable, outside the limits of the law. The police tried to blackmail her. They offered to leave her alone if she would do their dirty work for them. They wanted to use her as a procuress, an agent. She refused. Then they dug up an old case they had registered against her. They had her charged with moral turpitude and running a house of ill repute and they obtained court orders expelling her from Poona.

'If she was a procuress, a madam, and her presence was bad for society's health, then she should have been done away with altogether. Why, if she was a heap of filth, was she removed from Poona and ordered to be dumped elsewhere?'

He laughed bitterly. 'Manto, with her a purity has vanished from our lives. Do you remember that awful night? She cleansed me of my lust and meanness. I am sorry she's gone, but I shouldn't be sorry. She has only left Poona. She will go elsewhere and meet more young men like me and she will cleanse their souls and make them whole. I hereby bestow my Mummy on them.

'Now, let's go and look for Gharib Nawaz. He must have cried himself hoarse. As I told you, these Hyderabadis have weak eye-bladders. You never know when they might start dripping.'

I looked at Chadda. Tears were floating in his eyes like corpses in a river.

THE PATCH

When a suppurated boil appeared on Gopal's thigh, he was terrified.

It was summer and mangoes were in season and plentiful: in bazaars, streets, shops and even with street vendors. Wherever you looked, you saw mangoes. They came in all colours: red, yellow, green, multi-hued. Heaps upon heaps of them—and in all varieties—were on sale in the fruit and vegetable market at throwaway prices. The shortage experienced a year earlier had been more than made up for.

Outside the school, Gopal had had his fill of them at fruitseller Chootu Ram's stand. All the money he had saved during the month he had spent on those mangoes, saturated as they were with juice and honey. After school closed that day, Gopal, the taste of mangoes still in his mouth, had decided to stop by at Ganda Ram, the sweetmeat seller's, for a glass of buttermilk. He had asked him to prepare the drink but the man had refused, saying, 'Babu Gopal, settle the old account first and you can have fresh credit, not otherwise.'

Had Gopal not gorged himself on mangoes or had he had any money on him, he would have settled Ganda Ram's account there and then. He would then have paid for his glass of buttermilk which had in fact been prepared by Ganda Ram, and a piece of ice could be seen floating about in it. This sweetmeat seller had made a face and put the glass behind his back on a round iron dish. There was little Gopal could do and then, on the fourth day precisely, this big boil had appeared on his thigh. It had kept growing for the next three to four days. This had made Gopal very nervous, not quite knowing what to do. The boil itself did not bother him as much as the pain it was beginning to cause. What made things worse was that with each passing day the boil was getting redder and redder and some of the skin that covered it had begun to come off. At times Gopal felt as if under all that red there was a pot on the boil and whatever was in it wanted to burst out all in one go. So big had it become that once he felt as if one of his glass marbles had jumped out of his pocket and ledged itself in his thigh.

Gopal said nothing about the boil to anyone at home. He knew that if his father found out, all the anger that he felt over his fly-infested police station would be taken out on him. It was also possible that he might thrash him with the stick that the lawyer Girdhari Lal's assistant had brought for him from Wazirabad the other day. His mother was no less hot-tempered. Had she chosen not to punish him for eating all those mangoes, she would have boxed his ears red for having wolfed down all those mangoes all by himself. The principle his mother had laid down was, 'Gopal, even if it is poison that you want to take, you should do so at home.' Gopal knew what was behind this: her wish to sample the same delights that Gopal was enjoying.

Be that as it may, the fact was that this boil was destined to appear on Gopal's thigh and it had done so. As far as Gopal could work it out, it was the mangoes he had eaten that had caused this boil to appear. He had made no mention of it to anyone at home, because he still remembered the dressing-down he had got from his father, Lala Prashotam Das, police inspector, as he sat under the big municipal tap wearing only a loincloth, with the water gushing over his bald head and his big belly jutting forth. He was sucking mango after mango through the filter of his moustache. A dozen mangoes lay in front of him in a pail that he had taken from a street fruitseller in return for tearing up the ticket he had earlier given him. Gopal was rubbing his father's back, peeling away layers of dirt from it. When he had dipped a clean hand into the pail to quietly pull out a mango, Lalaji had prised the tiny fruit from his hand and put it in his mouth, along with his moustache, and said, 'How shameless! When will you learn to be respectful of your elders?'

And when with a weepy face Gopal had replied, 'Father, I too want to eat mangoes,' the Inspector sahib, chucking away the stone in an open drain that ran in the street, said, 'Gopu mangoes are just too hot for you, but if you want boils and carbuncles, then you are most welcome to them. Let it rain three or four times and then you can eat them to your heart's content. I will ask your mother to make you some buttermilk. Now get back to rubbing my back.' Gopal, having run into this roadblock, quietly resumed his assigned chore. The very thought of the mango's sour taste had made his mouth water and he kept swallowing it for a long time.

The very next day he gorged himself on those mangoes and four days later a boil appeared on his thigh. What his father had said had come true. Now, had Gopal mentioned his boil to anyone at home, he would have received a good beating, which was why he had kept quiet, while all the time thinking of some way of stopping the boil from growing any further.

One day on returning home from the police station, his father called out Gopal's mother and announced, as he handed her a packet, 'This Bombay balm is something of great value, one remedy that equals a hundred remedies. This is the time of year when boils and carbuncles are common, so all you need to be rid of them is just one single application. That's all. This is something special from Bombay, so tuck it away somewhere safe.'

Gopal was playing cricket in the courtyard with his sister, Nirmala. It just happened that, when the Inspector sahib was busy explaining to his wife something about the balm he had given her, Nirmala lobbed the ball towards him and since Gopal was trying to listen to his father the ball hit him precisely on the spot where his boil was. The pain was excruciating but he said not a word as he was used to bearing pain in silence. He had become used to being caned at school by his teacher, Hari Ram. Pain was nothing new to him. Just as the ball landed on his boil, he heard his father say, 'Just apply a little balm on the boil and all will be well in a jiffy. Like this!' As he snapped his fingers, something clicked in Gopal's mind. Now he knew how to be rid of his pain.

His mother placed the balm in her sewing basket, where Gopal knew she kept all things she considered valuable. The most carefully guarded thing in that basket was a pair of tweezers, which she used every ten or fifteen days to pull out hair over her forehead to make it appear broader than it was. The white ash she used to apply afterwards at the spots from where she had pulled out the hair was also kept in this basket. However, to be absolutely certain, Gopal lobbed the ball under the bed and while retrieving it made sure that the balm had been duly placed in the sewing basket.

In the afternoon, with Nirmala in tow, he went to the rooftop, where sacks of coal used to be stored under a rain shelter, duly armed with the small pair of scissors with which his father used to clip his nails, the balm and a bit of cotton cloth that his mother had saved to finish the sewing of his father's loose pyjamas. They sat down on the floor next to the sacks of coal. Nirmala produced the piece of cotton and spread it out on her thigh, over the sleek, silken surface of her shalwar. When Gopal looked at her with his dancing eyes, it seemed as if this eleven-year-old girl, who was lissome as a reed growing on a river bank, was readying herself for a great task. Her little heart, which used to beat in fear of her parents' admonitions and her dolls getting soiled, was now all aflutter with the thought that she was about to view the boil on her brother's thigh. Her ear lobes had gone red and they felt warm.

Gopal, who had not whispered a word about his boil to anyone, had told her his secret and how he had eaten all those mangoes without letting anyone know, how he had not been able to drink any buttermilk after and how this boil as big as a coin had appeared on his thigh. After he had told her his story, he said to her in a confidential voice, 'Look, Nirmala, no one at home is to know this.' A serious look appeared on Nirmala's face. 'I am not mad that I should.' Gopal, being sure that Nirmala would keep the confidence, rolled up his trouser over one leg and showed her the boil, which she touched lightly with her finger, keeping herself at as much distance as she could. She trembled involuntarily, made a whistling noise, looked at the quite red boil and said, 'How red it is!' 'It is going to get even redder,' Gopal bragged with manly courage. 'Really?' Nirmala exclaimed with astonishment. 'This is nothing, the boil I saw on Charanji was much bigger and redder than this,' Gopal replied, while running two of his fingers across the boil. 'So, is it going to grow in size?' Nirmala asked, slipping closer. 'Who knows, it's still growing,' Gopal answered, pulling out the balm from his pocket. Nirmala was scared. 'Will this balm make it right?' Gopal uncovered the balm by peeling away the paper that covered it and shook his head affirmatively. 'One application and it will burst open.' 'Burst open!' Nirmala felt as if a balloon had just popped next to her ear. Her heart was beating fast. 'And whatever is in there will gush out,' Gopal said, dabbing his finger with balm.

Nirmala's pink complexion by now was pale like the Bombay balm. With her heart in her mouth, she asked, 'But why do these boils spring up, brother?' 'By eating things with hot properties,' Gopal replied like an expert physician. Nirmala remembered the two eggs she had eaten two months ago. She began to think. They talked some more and then they got down to the business at hand. With great delicacy, Nirmala cut a round patch of cloth, which was faultless. It was round like the round roti her mother baked every day. Gopal applied some balm on the round patch, spread it out and examined his boil with great care. Nirmala, bent over Gopal, was watching everything he was doing with great interest. When Gopal placed the patch on his boil, she trembled as if someone had put a piece of ice on her body. 'Will it get all right now?' Nirmala asked, but half-questioningly. Gopal had not yet answered her when they heard steps, which were their mother's who was coming up to pick up some coal. Gopal and Nirmala looked at each other at the same time and, without saying a word, hid everything under the box in which their cat Sundri used to give birth to her kittens. Then without a word, they slunk away.

When Gopal ran down the stairs, his father sent him out on a buying errand. When he returned, he ran into Nirmala on the street. He handed over the cold, sweet drink he had brought for his father to her and went over to Charanji's house. In the process, he forgot to put back the things he and Nirmala had hidden under that box when they had heard their mother walking up. He was at Charanji's quite long, playing cards. After they had had their fill, the two left the room, hand in hand. Something that made Charanji laugh highlighted an old mark on his left cheek, which reminded Gopal of his boil and the things he had hidden under the box. Wresting himself free, he ran towards home.

He studied the situation. His mother was sitting in the courtyard, while his father read out the day's news from the newspaper *Milap*. They were both laughing over something. Gopal went past them and, though they looked at him, they did not say anything. This reassured Gopal that his mother had not taken a look at her sewing basket yet. Quietly, he walked upstairs to the rooftop. He was about to step out on it when something he saw made him stop.

Nirmala was sitting next to the box. Gopal stepped back so that he could see without being seen what was up. With great concentration, Nirmala, her long, thin fingers delicately working the scissors they held, was cutting a piece of cloth into a round patch. After she was done, she applied a little balm on it, then bending her neck, she unbuttoned her shirt to uncover a protrusion on the right side of her chest, which resembled a half bubble in a faucet.

Nirmala blew on the patch and placed it on that slight protrusion.

THE SUPPLICATION

As the bottle was lowered into Hamid's glass, a feeling of unease came over him. Malik, who was on his third drink, immediately realized that Hamid was undergoing some sort of spiritual struggle. He had known Hamid for the last seven years and he had often witnessed such fits, which had always puzzled him. He did, however, understand that there was some sort of weight on his slightly built friend's conscience, which always came to the fore when he was drinking. It was like a person being nudged in the ribs when he is inattentive.

Hamid was the happy-go-lucky type, used to fun and games, quick witted and gifted with a literary temperament. Ever since his friend Malik had come to know him more closely, he had found that Hamid's greatest quality was his sincerity. He was so sincere that sometimes Malik felt he was dealing with a romantic tale from earlier times. The most unusual thing that Malik had noted in Hamid was that his eyes had never known tears. Although he himself was somewhat miserly when it came to crying, he did know that if the occasion warranted it tears would come to his eyes. He was always affected by tragic things, but he only let them stay on his mind for about as long as an agile horse tolerates a fly. However, Hamid, who stayed away from worries and was always full of good cheer, would sometimes lapse into silence, the silence of a graveyard. Who could say what event in his past life was responsible for this! At such moments, his face would take on the colour of liquor to which three-day-old dead soda water has been added.

In the last seven years, Hamid had experienced several similar fits but Malik had never asked him what caused them. It wasn't that he wasn't curious to find the cause, but Malik was laid-back and lazy and the very thought of having to listen to a long, rambling explanation had kept him from probing the matter any further. He did not want the pleasure that his third drink was giving him to be wasted. He considered it the height of tastelessness to narrate long life stories after a few drinks. Nor was he much experienced when it came to listening to stories. Since he was quite happy with not ever wanting to listen to Hamid's story, he had never asked him about his fits.

Kirpa Ram poured a third drink in Hamid's glass and placed the bottle on the table. Then he said to Malik, 'Malik what is with him?' Malik kept quiet, but Hamid became restless and his already taut nerves shook violently. He tried to look at Kirpa Ram and smile but he did not succeed, which made things worse for him. Hamid's great weakness was his inability to keep any secret and when he tried to do so he became like a woman who is trying to cover herself with a single article of clothing in a violent storm.

Malik downed his third drink and, to revive the pleasant atmosphere that had existed but a moment earlier, laughed his inappropriate laugh and said to Kirpa Ram, 'Kirpa, you have got to admit that he has fallen in love, the kind of love that we associate with Ashok Kumar's movies. This Ashok Kumar is a strange bird. When he is playing a love scene on the screen, it is as if he was drunk on castor oil.' Kirpa Ram knew Ashok Kumar about as much as he knew Emperor Ashoka and his iron pillar. The thing was that he had no interest in either movies or history, though he knew of their benefits. He used to say, 'When I don't get sleep, I either start watching a movie or reading the history book written by Chakravarty.' He would always get a kick out of calling the mathematician Chakravarty a historian. Kirpa Ram had now downed four drinks and intoxication had reached the farthest recesses of his brain. Squeezing his eyes as if he was focusing a camera, he said to Hamid, 'Your glass is still untouched.' Hamid made a face as if he had a headache and replied, 'I won't be able to take any more.'

'You are an idiot, no not an idiot, but something else. You will have to drink, understand! He who says no to a drink is not a man but an animal, not even an animal, because if animals were turned into men, they would never decline this lovely thing. Are you listening, Hamid? If I do not pour this entire drink down your throat, then my name is not Kirpa Ram but Ghaseeta Ram artist.' Ghaseeta Ram artist was one man Kirpa Ram hated because despite being an artist he carried the name Ghaseeta Ram. Malik's mouth was full of whisky, which he expelled like a fountain as he broke into laughter hearing Kirpa Ram's remark. 'Kirpa Ram, you should please never mention Ghaseeta Ram's name because it creates a storm in my intestines. And look here, my trousers are all spoiled. Hamid, my brother, you will have to drink now. Kirpa Ram may not turn into Ghaseeta Ram but I will certainly become Kirpa Ram, if you don't down your glass. Come now, drink up, drink up. Why are you looking at me like that? Why do you look crestfallen? Kirpa Ram, get up, there are some who only respond to force. I am afraid that's what we'll have to use.'

Kirpa Ram and Malik rose together and tried to force the drink down Hamid's throat. Mentally troubled as Hamid was, when Kirpa Ram and Malik began to wrestle with him, he felt physically assaulted. Hamid's discomfort pleased Kirpa Ram and Malik greatly. They were now treating the whole thing as a game. Their tactics became even more tiresome. Kirpa Ram picked up the glass and poured some of the drink over Hamid's head, then he rubbed it into his hair like barbers do. Hamid was so affected by this horseplay that big tears welled up in his eyes and his voice thickened. His whole body began to tremble. Lowering his shoulders, he said in a dead, weepy voice, 'I am sick, for God's sake, don't tease me.' Kirpa Ram, who thought this was an excuse, was about to think of another device, when Malik with a wave of his hand asked him to move aside. 'Kirpa, he is really not feeling well . . . look he is crying.' Kirpa Ram bent from his fat waist, taking an intent look at Hamid. 'You really are crying,' he said. Tears were rolling down Hamid's eyes, which triggered a torrent of questions from his friends. 'What is the matter with you . . . is everything all right?' 'Why are you crying?' 'We were only joking.' 'You should at least let us know what is bothering you.'

Malik sat down next to Hamid. 'Please forgive me, if I offended you.' Hamid pulled out a handkerchief from his pocket, wiped his tears, tried to say something but was overcome by emotion and could not say anything. Before the third drink, he had worn a cheerful look and his conversation had been fresh and bubbly like soda, but now it all resembled a stale drink. He sat there like a pair of wet trousers. The way his body rested in the chair suggested that he was ashamed of himself and in order to hide his secret he had become a lifeless joke, badly told. Malik felt sorry for him. 'Hamid, for God's sake, please stop. Believe me, I feel pained by your tears. All the fun is gone and I feel saddened by your sudden burst into tears. God alone knows what is troubling you.'

'It's nothing at all. I will be all right soon. I am sometimes like this. I would like to leave now,' he said as he rose to go. Kirpa Ram was staring at the whisky in the bottle and while Malik kept telling himself that he would certainly get it out of Hamid today as to why he suffered such fits, he was already gone.

When Hamid got home, he was feeling even worse. Since he was all by himself in his room, he could not even cry because his tear-filled eyes needed more than mere furniture to make them shed. He wished there were someone with him so that he could cry after being teased. At the same time, he wanted to be alone. What he was experiencing was a strange inner struggle. He sat in his chair like a piece that has been knocked off the chessboard. On the table in front of him was one of his framed pictures, which he glanced at sadly. The seven years that lay between the time the picture was taken and now began to unfold like a length of rolled cloth. Exactly seven years earlier—it was the same rainy season as now—he had been sitting at the railway station restaurant with his friend Malik Abdul Rehman. What a world of difference there was between the Hamid of then and now! He could feel the difference intensely. The man in the picture was someone he had not met for ages. He looked at the picture carefully and was overcome with bitterness. He felt that the Hamid in the picture was far superior as a human being than the one who was now sitting in a heap in his chair. This realization caused him to feel a pang of jealousy.

Only one supplication, just one, had brought him to this sorry pass. Exactly seven years to this day, he had sat in the railway station restaurant with his friend Malik Abdul Rehman. It was then that he had decided to play a trick on his friend. He would have a full measure of odourless gin poured in a glass of lemonade and after his friend had drunk it down he would whisper in his ear, 'Maulana, a full measure of drink has now entered your piety-filled belly.' He had already arranged it with the waiter. He would order a bottle of lemonade that would contain a full measure of gin, which would be served to Malik. While Hamid sipped his whisky, Malik downed the drink served to him without realizing what it was. Hamid wanted to have three drinks and after a bit of gossip he said to his friend, 'Malik, why are you sitting there doing nothing? I take my time finishing my third drink. You should order another lemonade.' Malik agreed and another lemonade was brought to him, which was of course spiked with gin by the waiter. Their friendship was new and it was not right for Hamid to have played this trick upon his friend, but he was very lively and mischievous back in those days. When the waiter brought the second lemonade, Hamid smiled at the thought that soon there would be not one but two drinks inside Malik's belly. Malik kept sipping his spiked lemonade and Hamid kept clucking like a pigeon who finds a female pigeon perched next to him. Hamid finished his third drink and asked Malik if he would like another drink. Malik replied with uncharacteristic sombreness, 'If you want another drink, go ahead but I have to leave to attend to some important business.'

After this brief conversation, they both rose to leave. Hamid went across to pay the bill and when they left the restaurant a cool breeze greeted them. Hamid wanted to confess to Malik about the trick he had played on him but he decided to wait for a good opportunity. Malik had become very quiet, while Hamid felt overcome by a deep sense of mirth, his heart full of countless thoughts that would rise like tiny fireworks and go out as suddenly. They kept walking in silence for a long time. When they came to Company Garden, Malik sat down on a bench like a thinker in deep thought. For a few moments, nothing was said. Hamid wanted to get up and leave. He no longer felt any sense of mirth. But it was Malik who rose from the bench, saying, 'Hamid, you have hurt me spiritually. You should not have played this trick on me.' His voice was now full of pain. 'You do not know how spiritually tortured I feel. May God forgive you.' Then he left. Hamid felt intensely guilty. He wanted to apologize but Malik was already out of the garden and on the road. Hamid began to debate as to what distinguished sin from virtue. Everything he had ever been told by others about liquor being forbidden began to ring in his ears. 'Drink damages character.' 'Drink destroys families.' 'A drunken man becomes rude and shameless, which is why drinking is forbidden.' 'Drink destroys health. It peppers the lungs with holes.' All that now ran through Hamid's mind was an unending litany about drink and its evils.

He felt that the worst thing he had done was to cheat a nice, harmless man by making him drink alcohol without his knowledge. 'Maybe he is the kind of person who offers regular prayers and abstains from all evil. There is no doubt that I am the one at fault and I have earned the wages of sin. But how can I make up for the spiritual agony I made him suffer! That, as God is my witness, was not my intention. I did not want him to suffer on any account. I will beg his pardon but even then my sin will not be mitigated. First, I drank liquor and then I cheated another person by making him drink without his knowledge.' The whisky he had drunk began, as it were, to yawn in his mind, which intensified his sense of guilt. Should he stop drinking and lead a life free of sin? It was only two years since he had begun to drink and he still wasn't quite used to it. So, while walking back home, he decided that he would never touch a drink in his life. After all, it wasn't anything a person could not do without. He could live without it. It is commonly said, he thought, that once you start drinking you cannot give it up. 'Let them say what they will, but I will give it up. I will prove them wrong,' he said to himself. This made him feel like a hero. He thought of God who had pulled him away from the edge of destruction. He felt that he should thank God who had filled his heart with light; otherwise he would have kept lying in the ditch where he was.

He had by now arrived in the street where he lived. There were some clouds in the sky that looked like soapsuds. The breeze was cool and there was a silence in the atmosphere. Hamid thought of God and the fact that he had given up drinking and he felt overcome. He wanted to go down in supplication to thank God there and then but desisted, afraid that he might be seen. But then he thought that it might enhance his value in the eyes of God, so he went down, his forehead touching cold, bare stone. When he got up, he felt like a great man and when he looked around all the high walls that met his eyes appeared low in comparison with his stature. A month and a half after this incident, one day his friend Malik burst into his room, the same room where he now sat looking at his seven-year-old picture. Malik took out a half bottle of Black and White Scotch, banged the table with his fist and said, 'Hamid, let's drink and drink to our hearts' content. When we have run through this, we will get more.'

Hamid was so surprised that he could not say anything. Malik pulled out a bottle of soda from his other pocket, picked up a glass from the table, poured whisky into it, uncorked the soda with his thumb and drank down two pegs as Hamid stared at him in disbelief. Hamid stammered, 'But that day you cursed me so much!' Malik laughed loudly. 'You played a trick on me and in return I also responded in the same manner. But the fact is that the kick those two pegs gave me that day, I will never quite experience again. Now forget that story. Drink whisky. If you want to drink, whisky it is that you should drink.' Hamid felt as if the supplication he had offered in the street that day had got stuck to his forehead. It was like an evil spirit that he could not get rid of, which was why he began to drink again, but to no avail.

During the last seven years that lay between the time his picture was taken and now, that act of supplication had belittled him in his own eyes many times. That single act had robbed him of his self-respect, creativity and a life of warmth. That single act had become like a faulty brake that makes wheels come to a stop with a thud. His seven-year-old picture stood there staring at him. The entire incident ran through his mind again and he felt sick. He rose anxiously and began to rub his forehead against the wall as if he wanted to rub off the mark that his supplication had left. It was physically painful. Exhausted, he sat down in his chair and in a tired voice said, 'God, return to me what I offered that day.'

GREEN SANDALS

'I can no longer live with you—I want a divorce.'

'The devil take it all! What are you saying! That's your greatest fault; every now and then, you get these fits and you end up losing your senses.'

'But you have all your wits about you, round the clock drunk that you are.'

'Drink I do, but I do not take leave of my senses as you do without a drop. I don't talk the errant nonsense you do.'

'So I have been talking errant nonsense?'

'When did I say that, but think about it! What would you call this demand that you want a divorce?'

'Well, that's what I want. Other than a divorce what else can you demand of a husband who simply does not care about his wife!'

'Barring a divorce, there is nothing that you cannot ask of me.'

'There is nothing that you can possibly give me!'

'Now this is a new charge you have thrown at me. Can there be a woman luckier than you who while sitting right at home . . .'

'To hell with such luck!'

'Don't send your luck to hell . . . I simply cannot understand why you are so upset. Let me assure you in all sincerity that I am madly in love with you.'

'May God protect me from such love.'

'Now, let's not talk so bitterly . . . Tell me, have the girls gone to school?'

'What interest do you have in them, whether they go to school or to hell! I pray that they die.'

'One day I will have to pull out your tongue with white-hot tongs. Aren't you ashamed of mouthing such nonsense about your own offspring?'

'I am telling you, don't you use such language with me. You should be ashamed of yourself, speaking in this cheap way to a woman who is your wife and whom you are duty-bound to respect.

It is all because of the bad company you keep.'

'And what accounts for your lack of sanity?'

'You, who else!'

'It is always I whom you blame . . . I just do not understand what's the matter with you.'

'The matter with me! The same that is the matter with you. You are always breathing down my neck. I have already told you, I want a divorce.'

'You want a second marriage . . . Are you tired of me?'

'Phew! What sort of a woman do you think I am!'

'What good will a divorce do you?'

'I will go whichever way I can. I will labour and earn to feed my children.'

'How will you labour . . . rise as you do at nine in the morning and hit the bed again after breakfast. Then you sleep three hours after lunch, so don't fool yourself.'

'All right, so I am sleeping all the time and you are up and about all the time. Only yesterday, somebody from your office was here and he said you were always resting with your head on the office table.'

'Who was that offspring of an owl?'

'Mind your language.'

'I got angry and when you are in that state you lose control of your tongue.'

'I am angry with you but I haven't used one single rude word. One should never infringe the limits of politeness. But it is all due to the bad company you keep that you use such words.'

'I have a question. Will you identify the bad company I keep?'

'Well, what is that fellow's name who calls himself a cloth merchant? Have you ever noticed the clothes he wears? Always cheap and dirty. He may be a graduate but his habits, his manners are such that one can only feel disgusted.'

'He is mystically inclined.'

'What on earth is that?'

'You won't understand and I will be wasting my time for nothing.'

'Your time is very precious and will get wasted even if it is one single sentence you have to utter.'

'What is it that you really want to say?'

'There is nothing I want to say; what I had to say, I have already said. I want you to divorce me so that I am rid of it all. My life is one unending hell because of these daily quarrels.'

'Your life becomes hell even when one whispers a word of love in your ear. What can one do about it!'

'Divorce is what can be done about it.'

'Then send for some mullah, because if that is your wish, I would not say no.'

'From where am I going to get hold of a mullah!'

'Well, it is you who want a divorce. Had it been me, with a flick of my fingers, I would have produced ten mullahs by now. Do not expect me to be of any assistance to you in this matter. It is your business—you deal with it.'

'You can't even do that much for me?'

'No.'

'Up till now you have been saying that you love me madly.'

'That is correct, but as long as there is companionship, not if someone is leaving.'

'Then what should I do?'

'Whatever you wish to do . . . and look, don't bug me about this any more. Have a mullah sent for; he would write up the divorce deed and I will sign it.'

'What about the money I was promised at marriage?'

'Since it is you who want a divorce, there can be no question of such a demand.'

'What's that supposed to mean?'

'Your brother is a barrister; why don't you write to him and ask? When a woman wants a divorce, she is not entitled to anything.'

'Then do it, divorce me.'

'Why should I do such a thing! After all, I love you.'

'These little tricks are what I do not like. Were you in love with me you would not have treated me this way.'

'How have I treated you?'

'As if you do not know. Only the day before, you dusted your shoes with my new sari.'

'By God, I didn't!'

'Then who did it? Angels?'

'All I know is that it was your three daughters who were dusting their shoes with your sari. I remember screaming at them.'

'They are not so impertinent.'

'They are quite impertinent, because you have not given them the right upbringing. When they return from school, you can ask them whether they were making an improper use of your sari or not.'

'There is nothing I need ask them.'

'There is something gone wrong with you today. If only I could find out what it is, I might be able to come to a conclusion.'

'You are free to come to your conclusions, but I have come to mine. Now give me a divorce. What is the point of living with a husband who doesn't care about his wife?'

'I have always cared for you.'

'You know that tomorrow is Id.'

'I know. Why, only yesterday, I bought the girls new shoes and also lengths of cloth for their frocks. And eight days ago, I gave you sixty rupees.'

'Which was a great favour to my father and my grandfather.'

'It's not a question of favours. But what is the matter?'

'Well, if you want to know, sixty rupees was just not enough. It cost forty to buy three frock lengths for the children and the tailor charged seven rupees for stitching each frock, so tell me what great favour did you do to me and my girls?'

'So you had to pick up the tab for the rest?'

'What else? How could I otherwise have got them their frocks?'

'You can have what you paid from me right now. Is that all that was bugging you!'

'I say tomorrow is Id.'

'I know, I know, I am sending for two chickens and then there will be vermicelli. Have you made any other arrangements?'

'What arrangements can I make!'

'Why?'

'I wanted to wear a green sari tomorrow and I had ordered a pair of green sandals. How many times have I asked you to go to that Chinese shoemaker and see if the sandals are ready or not, but since you have not the least interest in me, why should you have gone?'

'Good God! So that was it then, green sandals! I picked up your sandals day before yesterday and they are lying in your closet, but since you are asleep most of the time, I do not expect you to have looked into your closet.'

THE BLOUSE

For some days past, Momin had been feeling very restless. His entire body was like a boil about to erupt. A strange pain had taken hold of him, whether he was working, talking or even thinking. Had he tried to explain what he felt, he would not have been able to do that. He would suddenly jump up and faint; silent thoughts which normally rise in the mind like bubbles and disappear as quickly would come thundering down to him only to explode noisily. On the delicate membranes of his heart and brain, he would feel thorn-footed ants crawling all the time. He had developed a strange and painful stiffness in his limbs. Sometimes the pain would become unbearable, and he would feel like asking someone to throw him in a big cauldron and beat him down with heavy blows.

In the kitchen, when spices were being pounded in a deep mortar with a metal-tipped pestle, the impact produced would bounce back from ceiling to the floor and it would feel good to Momin's bare feet. The sensation would travel to his stiff legs, and go right through his thighs to his heart, which would begin to throb like the flame of a clay lamp in the wind.

Momin was fifteen, going on sixteen, but he wasn't really sure about his age. He was a strong and healthy boy whose boyhood was racing towards youth, a race of which Momin was utterly unaware, but every drop of his blood was affected by this. Sometimes, he would try to work it all out but without success.

Several changes were taking place in his body. His neck had thickened and the muscles of his arms felt taut. His voice was breaking and there was an extra layer of fat on his chest. For some days now, his nipples had felt swollen and when he touched them they were painful. Sometimes, while at work, he would touch his nipples without wanting to, and his body would shudder. Even the thick and rough cloth of his shirt caused him pain when it touched those sensitive spots.

At times, while washing himself in the bathroom or when he was alone in the kitchen, he would unbutton his shirt and look at his marble-like nipples and rub them, producing sharp darts of pain. His body would shake like a fruit-laden tree. But he would continue with that pain-generating exercise. When pressed harder, his nipples would flatten out and exude a sticky discharge. On such occasions, his face would redden up to the lobes of his ears and he would feel that he had committed a sin.

Momin's knowledge of sin and virtue was extremely limited. Anything that a person could not do in front of others was a sin in his view. He would quickly button up his shirt and promise himself never to do such a bad thing again. However, every second or third day, when alone, he would engage in the same old game. The family he worked for was pleased with him. He was a hard-working boy who would do what was assigned to him at the appointed time. He would provide no opportunity for anyone to complain. He had worked at the deputy sahib's house for only three months but, in this brief period, he had impressed every member of the family with his natural industry. He had been hired as domestic help at six rupees a month but had earned a raise of two rupees in the second month of service, something that had made him very happy because he knew that he was being appreciated. However, for the last several days, he had been restless. He felt like walking about the bazaars all day without any purpose, or go to some lonely spot and lie down.

Although his heart was no longer in his work and he felt listless, by nature he was not lazy, which was why no one in the house was aware of his troubled mental state. There was Razia, who spent her entire day playing the harmonium, learning the latest movie tunes and reading magazines. She had never bothered Momin. Shakeela, however, would use Momin to do her odd jobs and even scold him sometimes. For the last several days, she had been busy copying different blouse designs, having borrowed a number of blouses from a friend who was fond of wearing new-fangled clothes. Shakeela had borrowed eight of her friend's blouses and was busy making notes so that she could replicate them. That was why for the last several days she had paid no attention to Momin.

The deputy sahib's wife was not a harsh woman. There were two servants in the house besides Momin, and an old woman who mostly worked in the kitchen. Momin would help her off and on. If the deputy sahib's wife had noticed some slackening in Momin's work, she had not mentioned it. In any case, she could not possibly be aware of the storm blowing across Momin's heart and mind because she did not have a son. She was therefore unable to understand the physical and mental changes which Momin was undergoing. And then Momin was only a house boy. Who cares about servants anyway! They pass from childhood to old age without those around them even noticing it.

This was also Momin's situation. In the last few days, he had taken a turn on the road of life that had put him on a course which, though not long, was extremely hazardous. Sometimes, he would take quick steps; at other times, he would slow down. He did not really know how to walk the stretch where life had brought him. Should he hurry or should he take his time while negotiating this road? Under Momin's bare feet lay the round, slippery pebbles of adolescence, which made it hard for him to keep his balance. This was why he felt so restless. Sometimes, while at work, he would grab hold of a hook in the wall with both hands and use it to lift himself from the ground. At such times, he would wish someone would pull him down by his legs and keep stretching them till his legs turned into a fine wire. All these thoughts came to life in a corner of his brain, though he did not fully understand them.

Subconsciously, he wanted something to happen, but what? The fact was that he just wanted whatever was to happen to happen. Dishes stacked on the table should start jumping up and down; the kettle should come to a boil in one go and its lid should fly away; a little pressure on the water faucet should bend it like a pin causing it to expel a fountain; or his body should stretch so much that every joint should come apart and relax. Or something should happen that had not happened before. Momin was one restless boy.

Razia was busy learning new tunes and Shakeela was busy with her blouse designs. When she was done, she picked out the one that had pleased her most and began to cut one from a length of azure satin. It also made Razia leave her harmonium and songbook to find out what her sister was up to. Shakeela did everything with great aplomb and care. When sewing, she would seat herself in a calm, comfortable position, not like her younger sister Razia, who was always rushing about. Shakeela sewed every stitch diligently to rule out mistakes. The measurements she took were precise. She would first make a paper cutout of the design and then cut the cloth accordingly. Time consuming though it all was, the end product was an exact copy.

Shakeela was a well-built girl. Her hands were well padded and at the base of each long finger was a tiny dimple. When she worked her sewing machine, these dimples would appear and disappear in quick succession. She would work the machine calmly, turning the handle with her long, shapely hand. She would bend her wrist slightly and put her neck at an angle, while a lock of her hair that seemed to have no place to go would come hanging down. So busy would Shakeela be with her work that she would make no attempt to shake it back. When she was ready to cut the azure length of satin for the blouse, she realized that she needed a measuring tape. Their old tape had been used so long that it had fallen to pieces. There was a measuring rod but it was useless for measuring her waist and chest. She had her old blouses of course, but as she had put on a little weight since, she wanted everything remeasured.

She took off her shirt and shouted for Momin. When he came into the room, she told him to run out and borrow a measuring tape from flat No. 6. 'Tell them it is Shakeela bibi who needs it.' Momin's eyes rested on Shakeela's white vest. He had seen her in a vest many times in the past but today he felt a certain hesitation in looking at her, and turned his eyes away. Then he asked nervously, 'Bibiji, what kind of tape?' 'A tape to measure cloth . . . the measuring rod is lying right here in front of you. It is made of steel; but what is needed is a soft tape. Now run and get it from No. 6. Tell them Shakeela bibi needs it.'

Flat No. 6 lay close by and Momin was back in no time with the tape, which Shakeela took from him and said, 'Just stay here so that you can return it.' Then she spoke to her sister Razia, 'If you keep anything you have borrowed from these people, that old woman can't stop bugging you for its return . . . Come here now, take this tape and measure me.' Razia began to measure Shakeela's waist and chest as the two talked, with Momin standing by the door listening to them. 'Razia, why don't you tighten it a bit . . . that's what happened last time when you measured me and the blouse turned out to be all wrong. If the fit on the top is not precise, the bits under the armpits begin to hang down.' Razia said, 'Where should I measure you and where should I not? You confuse me. I had begun to take a measurement here and you said I should move lower. The thing is if the finished product is a bit loose, that won't exactly be a calamity.' 'Why, the beauty of good clothing is that it should fit. Look at Surayya. What a tight fit her clothes are, nothing loose anywhere, even if you look for it! Now measure me.' After saying this, Shakeela took a deep breath to expand her chest and held it there. 'Get it now,' she said in a strangled voice. When Shakeela exhaled, Momin felt as if several balloons had exploded in his chest. Nervously he said, 'Give me the measuring tape bibiji and I will return it.' 'Just wait,' Shakeela said sternly.

As she spoke, the tape measure got wrapped around her arm and, when she tried to get rid of it, Momin saw a bunch of black hair under her fair armpit. Similar hair had begun to sprout in Momin's own armpits, but he liked the bunch he had glimpsed. His body felt electrified. He wanted that the bunch of hair he had seen should turn into a moustache and grow on him. As a child, he used to pretend that he had a blond or black moustache with hair you find on a corn cob. When he placed that hair over his upper lip, he would tremble slightly, which was what was happening now to his upper lip and nose. Shakeela had lowered her arm now and her armpit could no longer be seen, but he could not banish from his mind's eye the image of that bunch of black hair he had seen in her armpit.

After a few minutes, Shakeela handed over the tape measure to Momin, saying, 'Go, return it and say thank you very much.' After returning the tape, Momin came back and sat down in the courtyard. Vague thoughts had begun to rise in his head and for a long time he tried to understand them, but he failed. He then opened his small trunk in which he kept the new clothes he was going to wear for Id. When he lifted the lid, and the smell of his unworn cotton clothes hit his nose, he felt an urge to wash himself thoroughly, put on those new clothes and go straight to Shakeela bibi to say, 'Salam bibiji.' His new cotton shalwar would produce a rustling noise and his Rumi cap would . . .

As he thought of his cap, its black tassle at the top turned into the bunch of black hair that he had seen in Shakeela bibi's armpit. He pulled out his Rumi cap and began to run his hand over its soft, black silken tassle. Then he heard Shakeela bibi call, 'Momin!' He returned the cap to the trunk, closed the lid and went into the room where Shakeela had already cut several pieces of soft, slippery azure satin, which lay in a corner. 'I called you several times, had you gone to sleep?' she asked. Momin stuttered, 'No, bibiji.' 'So what were you doing?' 'What . . . nothing at all.' 'You must have been doing something,' Shakeela was firing all these questions at him but what was really on her mind was the blouse in which she had put temporary stitches. 'I was looking at my new clothes in my trunk,' Momin said, laughing bashfully. Shakeela burst out laughing too, as did Razia.

Shakeela's laughter gave Momin a strange sense of satisfaction and he felt an urge to do something silly which should make Shakeela laugh even more. Lisping like a girl, he said shyly, 'And I will take some money from the elder bibiji and buy myself a silk handkerchief.' 'And what will you do with that handkerchief?' Shakeela asked, still laughing. Momin replied awkwardly, 'I will tie it around my neck, bibiji . . . it will feel good.' Both Shakeela and Razia began to laugh at his reply. 'If you tie it around your neck, I will hang you with it,' Shakeela said, trying to control her laughter. 'The wretch has made me forget why I had called him Razia,' Shakeela said.

Razia did not answer and began to hum a new popular song that she had learnt two days earlier. Meanwhile, Shakeela remembered why she had called Momin. 'Look Momin, I will take off my vest, which I want you to take to that new store next to the pharmacy and ask them what six such vests would cost. You remember you went there with me that day. Ask them for a discounted price. Understand!'

'Yes,' Momin answered.

'Go, be on your way now.'

Momin came out of the room and stood behind the half-open door. In a few moments the vest landed at his feet, followed by Shakeela's voice, 'Tell them this is exactly what we need. There should be no dissimilarity.'

Momin picked up the vest, which was slightly damp because of perspiration, as if somebody had placed it over a steaming pot and then removed it quickly. The lingering body odour in the garment and its sweet warmth felt good to Momin. Rubbing the undershirt, which was soft like a kitten, between his hands, he went to the bazaar, found out the price and by the time he came back Shakeela had begun stitching the azure satin blouse, which was brighter and softer than the tassle on Momin's cap.

This blouse was probably being readied for Id, which was coming up. Momin was now being summoned several times a day, to get thread, to fetch the iron, to pick up a new needle because the one in use had snapped. In the evening, when Shakeela was done for the day, she asked Momin to pick up the loose bits of thread and satin trimmings which could be put to no further use. Momin swept the place up nicely and threw out the waste, but the shiny satin trimmings he put in his pocket, without quite knowing what he would do with them.

The next day, he pulled out the trimmings from his pocket, found a bit of privacy and began to dethread them. He spent a lot of time doing that and finally he had a tiny ball of thread in his hand, which he kept rubbing and pressing, while thinking of Shakeela's armpit and the bunch of black hair he had caught a glimpse of. The other trimmings he put back in his pocket. That day too, Shakeela called out to him a number of times. He watched the azure blouse through its various stages of production, from being cut to being stitched. These images kept popping up before his eyes, from the point where temporary white stitches were threaded through it to its being ironed to smooth out the wrinkles and make it appear even shinier to Shakeela putting it on and showing it to Razia, then standing in front of the dressing table and examining herself from every angle. When she was fully satisfied, she took it off and made what adjustments were necessary, so that it would fit perfectly. She tried it one more time before she began to apply the final stitches.

While the blouse was being readied, the stitches in Momin's brain were coming undone. When summoned to the room, his eyes wouldn't leave the shiny garment, wanting all the time to touch it, and not merely that, but to keep caressing its silken smooth texture with his rough hand. He knew from the satin trimmings in his pocket how smooth the blouse was. The tiny ball of thread he had made was even smoother with its rubber-like elasticity. Whenever he walked into the room and looked at the blouse, his mind would race back to the sight of the black hair he had seen in Shakeela's armpit. Momin wondered if it was as smooth as satin.

The blouse was ready at last. Momin was cleaning the floor with a wet rag, when Shakeela came into the room and took off her shirt, throwing it on the bed. She was wearing the white vest that Momin had been sent out to find the price of. She stood in front of the mirror and put on her new blouse. While continuing to clean the floor, Momin looked up at the mirror. The blouse had come to life and at one or two places it was stretched so tight as to have lost colour. Shakeela's back was turned towards Momin and he could see the deep cleft of her spine. He could not help himself and said, 'Bibiji, you have excelled even master tailors.' Shakeela was pleased by the praise, but she was restless because she wanted to know what Razia thought of her handiwork, so all she said to him was, 'Good, isn't it!' and ran out of the room. Momin kept staring at the mirror where he could still see an image of the shimmering blouse.

At night, when he went to the stitching room to place a pitcher of water there, he saw the blouse hanging there by a hook. There was no one in the room, so he stepped forward, looked at it carefully and then, apprehensively, ran his hand over it, which made him feel as if someone was caressing his entire body with an exceedingly light and airy touch. When he went to bed that night, he had many meaningless dreams. There was the deputy sahib who, standing in front of a heap of coal, was asking him to break the larger pieces into smaller ones. When Momin picked up a piece, put it on the ground and hit it with a hammer, it turned first into a ball of fine black hair and then into a ball of spun black sugar, which rose to the sky to break up into several balloons. High up, very high up, the balloons burst. At that point, a violent wind rose. Momin dreamt that he had lost the black tassle on top of his Rumi cap, so he began to look for it, going from place to place, some known, some utterly strange to him. He could smell something that he identified as fresh white cotton cloth. Next he found himself clutching a black satin blouse in his hand. He could also feel a throbbing object that lay under his hand. He woke up with a start and for a few minutes he could not understand what had happened. A spasm of fear, surprise and sweet pain shook his body. It was a most strange feeling. First he felt a painful warmth come over him, which was replaced after a few moments by a cool wave that crawled all over his body.

ON THE BALCONY

She comes to the balcony, wearing a white, sequinned sari that seems to set off silver-hued fireworks. The sequins embedded in the undulating silken fabric of the garment shimmer and my entire body feels titillated. For quite some time now, she has been my titillation.

I have seen her nearly two hundred times and each one of those images is engraved in my mind. Once I saw her chasing a butterfly in her courtyard. She flashed past my eyes only once. Whenever I think of that incident, it feels as if a bird is fluttering in my heart, which might fly away suddenly out of fear. One day, I saw her standing on the balcony in the sun, shaking her wet hair dry. When I try to summon that image, I see it sometimes in dark outline; other times it appears brightly lit.

I have seen her so many times that I can summon her whenever I wish, even without appearing before her. At first, I found this exercise difficult but that is no longer true. Only last evening, while I was sitting at a friend's place, I felt a sudden desire to see her. Without even closing my eyes, I had her standing in front of me. She looked exactly as she normally does. Neither my friend nor his sister, who was sitting in a chair in front of me, could guess anything. For a moment, I pulled her out of the tiny box in my mind where I keep her and then put her back immediately so that no one should know what I had done. I kept talking to them while I looked at her, and not for a minute did my mind wander. And what was I saying? 'Yes, dried fish smells. God knows how people eat it! My nose can't . . .' And for a long time afterwards, we talked about noses and how different they all are.

I like her nose. I have a light pink tea service which I like because the handles of its cups resemble her nose. You will laugh but one morning when I saw her from close, a strange desire rose in me to hold her by the nose and drink the nectar of her lips. I find her lips lovely, maybe because they always look moist, like a peeled orange. If I feel a desire to kiss them, it is not because that is what I have read in books or that is what I have heard from others about kissing women's lips, no, that's not it. Had I known none of those things, I would still have wanted to kiss them. That's the way her lips are—they form an incomplete kiss.

She is the only daughter of my neighbour who is a doctor. All day long, she sits in her father's dispensary. Sometimes when passing by, I have seen her standing next to the medicine cabinet, looking like a long-necked bottle with something colourful and bubbly inside. One day I walked into the dispensary to ask the doctor for a cold remedy. Doctor sahib said to her, 'Child, sprinkle a few drops of eucalyptus on his handkerchief.' She took my handkerchief from me, pulled out a small bottle from the cabinet and put a few drops on it. At that moment, I wanted to get up, hold her by the hand and say, 'Please cork this bottle; instead give me a single teardrop from your eyes and I will be healed of all ailments.' But I sat there silently, looking at the colourless drops which were being sprinkled on my handkerchief.

Since I began to notice her, it has been my heartfelt desire that she should cry and I should watch tears floating in her eyes. In my imagination, I have seen her eyes getting melancholy many times, which is the real reason I want to see her cry. Tears flickering over her thick eyelashes will look lovely. It will be like raindrops dancing down a shuttered window. It is possible that you may not think tears to be necessary in women's eyes, but I cannot even imagine a woman's eyes without tears. Tears are the perspiration of the eyes. A worker's brow is only a worker's brow when it is shining with perspiration. A woman's eyes can only be a woman's eyes when they are drowned in tears.

She came in a white, sequinned sari on the balcony, setting off silver-hued fireworks. The sequins embedded in the undulating fabric of the garment shimmered and my entire body felt titillated. She suddenly turned towards me, as if she had become aware of a presence other than her own in the silence of the night. Two pearls rolled down her eyes . . . she was crying . . . she . . . she was crying. And as I looked and before I could do anything, the tears from her eyes, the first perspiration of her youth, fell to the floor. Perhaps they could not bear my intrusive eyes. They may have wished to lie, like newborn babies, in the soft and tender swings of her eyes. It was my eyes that made them come down. She was crying, but I was happy. Her moist eyes looked like fog-covered lakes, very mysterious, very thought-provoking. Under the shallows of her tears, the black and white of her eyes shimmered like those tiny fish that are afraid to come to the surface.

I stopped looking at her, only concentrating on her eyes, which looked like two clay lamps flickering on a cold, wet December night. Her eyes looked at me from far, very far, as I began to move towards her . . . then two tears formed, came up, dangled over her thick eyelashes for a while and slowly rolled down her pale cheeks. In her right eye, another tear rose, rolled down, stayed for a fleeting moment on her cheek and like a traveller who, approaching the end of his journey, takes a breather, it slid past the corner of her lips whose moisture made it thin out. With her washed eyes, she looked at me intently and asked, 'Who are you?' She knew who I was, and in asking who I was she was asking herself who she was. I answered, 'You are Sheela.'

Her clenched lips trembled and she said between sobs, 'Sheela . . . Sheela . . . She . . .' She sat down on the balcony. She looked tired, but then suddenly she thought of something, as if in a dream. She shook it off and stood up. In an anxious voice she said, 'I . . . I . . . what was I saying? . . . Nothing is the matter with me . . . I am all right . . . And how did I come to be here?' I consoled her, 'Do not be worried, Sheela . . . you have said nothing to me . . . such things are neither said nor heard.' Sheela looked at me as if I had caught her doing something she shouldn't have been doing. 'What things . . . what things . . . there is nothing.'

I said to her, 'Day before yesterday in the dispensary when you were playing with that parrot, sticking out your red tongue at him, your crystal fingers were creating music when they touched the bars of his cage. At that moment, you were an incomplete woman. But today, when tears are rolling down your eyes, you are complete as a woman. Don't you feel the difference? You must. What you were yesterday, you are not today. And what is today will not be there tomorrow. But the mark the hot iron of happiness has left on your heart will always remain there, just as it is . . . isn't it a good thing to have happened? That will remain something in your life that will always be entirely yours. Something over whose ownership there would be no doubts. I wish my heart could become your heart . . . a woman's heart . . . which struck once remains content thereafter . . . in the immensity of a woman's heart, many wildernesses can find space . . . these numberless wildernesses are by themselves a refuge and a settlement . . . you are fortunate . . . the day for which you would have had to wait has come so early in your life . . . you are fortunate.'

There was a look of astonishment on her face; she was like a hen which has laid an egg for the first time. She began to speak in a monologue. 'Fortunate . . . I am fortunate . . . how is that? How do you know?' I answered, 'When a kite is cut away and the boys are screaming from their rooftops in an attempt to grab the string, does anything have to be said? Where is the kite that you had flown into the immensity of the sky? Till yesterday, you held the string in your hand, but where is it now?' Tears began to roll down her eyes. 'I am fortunate,' she said in tear-drenched words. 'Please tell those boys who get on their rooftops and start screaming because they want the kite that has been cut away . . . that they are so noisy.' Her tears became more abundant and she looked at me through their rain and asked, 'Whose parched throat do you want to moisten with these tears? I know why you are subjecting me to these pinpricks.'

Then she turned her face away in disgust. Her rational mind at that moment resembled an oversharpened knife. I spoke to her calmly, 'All that has happened is in my knowledge, but if I had asked you then to forget it all, offered you false sympathy and like a juggler made your pain, your grief disappear with a magic spell, you would have thought of me as a friend, but I can't do that . . . your heart is yours and what it has experienced is also yours. Why should I rob your heart of its wealth? Why should I ask you to forget the pain which is the treasure of your life? This pain, this sad event that has come to pass, these are what you will have to lay the foundations of your future life on . . . I do not want to lie, Sheela, but if you want, I can do even that for your satisfaction. Tell me what you want to hear.' Her reply was sharp, 'I do not need anyone's sympathy.' I said, 'I know . . . in such situations, no sympathy is needed . . . if the game consists of jumping into the fire, no instructions are required. The cortege of love needs to be borne on no one's shoulders. This dead body we will have to carry on our backs for the rest of our lives.'

She cut me short. 'I will carry it . . . what is that to you . . . why are you trying to frighten me by saying such terrifying things? I have only loved him . . . And do I not love him still . . . He betrayed me . . . he was false to me . . . but this betrayal has come at the hands of the one I love . . . I know that he has destroyed my life. I have nowhere to go, but what does it matter . . . It was a game that I played and lost . . . You want to frighten me, taunt me, but I . . . I do not now care about death . . . I have spoken of death . . . and this has made you tremble. You fear women, but look at me, I am not afraid of death.'

I looked at her. There was a forced smile playing on her lips and from her eyes, under the tears, a strange light shone forth. She was trembling, ever so slightly. I looked at her intently once again and said, 'I am afraid of death because I want to live. You are not afraid of death because you do not know how to live. A person who does not know the art of living, for him to be alive is like being dead . . . If you want to die, then go ahead.'

She looked at me with surprise. I continued, 'You want to die because you think that you will not be able to free yourself of this mountain of grief that has fallen on you so suddenly . . . That is not true . . . If you have the strength to love, you also have the strength to survive heartbreak . . . The joy, the ecstasy that you drew from being in love, is the essence of your life. Take good care of it and spend the rest of your life by drinking deep of those magic moments . . . The one who loved you is not so important, or even necessary, as the love you bore him . . . forget him but remember your love and live on that remembrance . . . the remembrance of those moments for whose sake you destroyed the most precious thing in your life. Can you ever forget those moments which you bought with a pearl whose value was beyond imagining? No, never! Man can forget such moments, and does forget them, because he pays no price for them . . . but a woman cannot forget because in return for those fleeting moments she has sacrificed her entire life. Do you want to die? Do you want to abandon the refuge for which you paid such a high price? Live, make use of this life! We all have to die, which is why it is necessary to live.'

My words had left her exhausted and she sat down. 'I am tired,' she said.

'Go to sleep . . . rest and gather your courage to fight other calamities.' I was about to walk off after saying this when it suddenly occurred to me—and the thought made my heart miss a beat—that she might kill herself. If that happened, I would lose something. I turned, came close to her and said in the voice of a supplicant, 'Sheela, I've a request.'

Sheela lifted her head and looked at me. 'Look, Sheela, I beg of you to banish the thought of suicide . . . you should live, you must live.'

She asked, 'Why?'

'Why? Why do you ask me, Sheela? You know very well in your heart why I am making this request. But let's not talk about such things . . . I hold nothing against you, nor anything against myself . . . what we started, I want it to reach a conclusion. Am I selfish? Every man is selfish . . . I am begging you not to die . . . this is selfishness . . . Live, if you live, my love will always remain young . . . I want my love to be inseparable from every phase of your life . . . but only with your permission.'

She kept thinking for a long time; she had grown quite sombre. 'I will have to live,' she said in a soft voice.

Her voice was an indication of her determination. Leaving her tired youth in sleepy moonlight, I walked down from the rooftop to my flat and went to sleep.

HARNAM KAUR

Nihal Singh was worried. For the last two hours and a half, he had been nervously sucking the ends of his black-grey moustache and thinking of his son Bahadur, now a young man.

Nihal Singh's sharp eyes were surveying the large village common where he had played all kinds of games as a child. There was a time when he was considered the bravest and most dashing young man in the village. He had seduced any number of self-willed village girls by simply grabbing them by the wrist in the middle of a sugarcane or corn field and making them yield to him. He would expel his spit with such force that it would land fifteen yards away. He was handsome and he was fun-loving. When he would set out for the village fair, a lance in hand and a jaunty, striped turban over his head, old men would exclaim, 'If you want to know what Sundar Jat must be like, just take a look at Sardar Nihal Singh.'

Sundar Jat was a famous dacoit, a folk hero, whose exploits had been made immortal in songs which people knew by heart. But Nihal Singh was not a dacoit. His youth had the sharp edge of a kirpan, which was why women swooned over him. His torrid love affair with Harnam Kaur who had once smitten his heart was remembered to this day.

When Sardar Nihal Singh thought of Harnam Kaur and reminisced about his youth, for a moment an electric current ran through his middle-aged body. What a flashy beauty she was, always sucking her dainty red lips! One day when the trees were laden with berries, Nihal Singh came upon her. She was picking up the berries that had fallen to the ground and sucking her dainty red lips. At the sight, Nihal Singh began to sing a snatch from a folk song, 'Who was the lover who brought you that bowl of hot milk which burnt your red lips?'

Harnam Kaur picked up a stone, took aim and threw it at Nihal Singh. Unmindful of the hurt it had caused, he stepped forward and grabbed her by the wrist, but in a flash, as mercurial as a fish, she freed herself and ran off. Nihal Singh felt as if someone had thrown him on his back in a wrestling bout. This feeling of having been defeated grew even more intense when the story of his slight spread in the village.

Nihal Singh made no comment, quietly listening to both friend and foe. Three days later, he saw her outside the gurdwara under the banyan tree. Harnam Kaur was sitting on the ground with a brick in hand, trying to knock back a nail that had come loose from her sandal. When she noticed Nihal Singh, who had come close by now, she tried to run away, but it was too late. And this time he got what he wanted.

In the evening, when people heard Nihal Singh singing loudly 'O Harnam Kauray, O Harnam naray', they knew what castle he had conquered. However, the next day he was arrested and charged with rape. After a brief trial, he was sentenced to six years in prison, which became seven and a half because of the two fights he had got himself into. After his release, he walked back to the village along the railway track, past the gurdwara, where he saw Harnam Kaur standing under the same banyan tree, sucking her lips. Before he could say anything or even think, she leapt forward and threw her arms around him, clinging to his broad chest.

Nihal Singh picked her up and began to walk away from the village. 'Where are you going?' Harnam Kaur asked. *'Jo bolay so nihal, Sat Siri Kaal,'* Nihal Singh shouted. Both of them burst out laughing. Nihal Singh married Harman Kaur and they made their home in a village about forty miles from the one where they used to live. Their first child, Bahadur, was born after six years, and much praying it had taken. He was born on the day of Baisakhi, the harvest festival. He was only two and a half months old when Harnam Kaur's mother died. Harnam Kaur died soon after. Nihal Singh asked his widowed sister to take Bahadur and raise him with her four daughters. When Bahadur turned eight, he brought him home.

Four more years passed. Bahadur, now under his father's care, bore a close physical resemblance to his mother, being slim and delicate like her. Sometimes when Nihal Singh would catch him sucking his thin red lips, he would shut his eyes. Nihal Singh loved Bahadur deeply. He would bathe him himself and wash his hair with yogurt to make it soft. He would feed him well and take him out for walks, telling him stories and making him exercise, but Bahadur had no interest in such things. He always looked a bit sad, which Nihal Singh attributed to his missing his aunt with whom he had lived for so many years. When Nihal Singh joined the army and was shipped out to fight in the war, he left Bahadur with his sister again.

Another four years passed. At long last, the war came to an end and Nihal Singh returned. He was now fifty years old but looked as if he were in his sixties because he had undergone tremendous suffering in a Japanese prisoners' camp. Bahadur, by Nihal Singh's reckoning, was now sixteen, but he was unchanged from what he had been four years earlier, slim, delicate and very good-looking. It was Nihal Singh's view that his sister had not raised him properly, her attention being entirely directed at her four daughters, who were always jumping around the courtyard like pesky calves. He exchanged words with his sister, after which he brought Bahadur back to his village.

During his absence, his land had turned into a waste, so the first thing Nihal Singh got down to was its rehabilitation, which did not take him long. He next turned his attention to Bahadur, for whom he bought a brown buffalo, but it remained a matter of regret to him that Bahadur felt no fondness for milk, yogurt or butter. He preferred other things, which angered Nihal Singh though he never made that apparent because he loved his son to distraction. Although Bahadur had been raised by his aunt, everyone said, when they noticed his odd habits, that he had been spoiled by an overly indulgent father. Bahadur, unlike boys of his age, was not interested in physical activity; neither did Nihal Singh want his son to work in the field like a labourer and plough the land from morning till evening because God had given him enough. He had a sizeable income, and then there was his army pension. But he did want Bahadur to do things. What things, he wasn't quite sure himself. Often he would ask himself what he wanted Bahadur to do, but never found a satisfactory answer. He would then get nostalgic about his days of youth and forget Bahadur, reliving his long-lost past.

It was now two years since Nihal Singh had returned from the war. Bahadur had turned eighteen; in other words, he was in the full flush of youth. This realization troubled Nihal Singh and he would take it out on Bahadur. 'I named you Bahadur, which means brave, so show me some bravery some time,' he would say. In reply, Bahadur would suck his lower lip and smile. Nihal Singh then thought of finding Bahadur a bride and began to look around for a suitable match. He also mentioned it to his friends, but then he thought of his own youth and decided that, like him, Bahadur should find his bride himself. As to when, he did not know, because he had so far not seen in his son the flash that could indicate his precise state of mind. Bahadur was good-looking, but he was no Sundar Jat. He had large, black eyes, dainty red lips, an aquiline nose, a slim waist and very fine jet-black hair. Village girls would look at him from a distance, whisper to one another but beyond that pay no attention to him. After much thought, Nihal Singh came to the conclusion that perhaps Bahadur liked none of those girls. With that thought, the image of Harnam Kaur flashed before his eyes, which stayed with him for a long time. He then tried to picture every village girl, one by one, but none of them could match Harnam Kaur in beauty. Nihal Singh's eyes lit up. 'Bahadur is my son, and he would not even care to look at these run-of-the-mill types,' he consoled himself.

But time kept passing. The seasons when berries ripen on the trees came and went, came and went. The corn grew tall, as tall as Nihal Singh, year after year, and one rainy season followed another but Bahadur still did not find a girl he liked. Nihal Singh's nervousness increased, but before he could come to a final decision about Bahadur's marriage, disturbances broke out all over the place. Strange news began to filter into the village. Someone said that the British were going to leave, while another brought information that the Russians would impose their raj now. Someone would announce that Congress had won, while another would report that he had heard it on the radio that the country was going to be divided. There were as many stories as there were people. By now, Nihal Singh was utterly at his wit's end. He was not interested in any of these stories. The truth was that he was not even interested in the war in which he had fought for four years. What he wanted above all was that Bahadur should get married and he should have a daughter-in-law in the house.

It all happened suddenly. The country was divided and word went out that from now on Hindus and Muslims were going to be living separately. There was utter pandemonium and large-scale to-and-fro movement of people. There were reports that thousands had been killed and hundreds of girls had been abducted. There was widespread looting. Not long after, caravans of people could be seen moving on the metalled road that bypassed the village, for whose residents it turned into a carnival of sorts. They had begun to form marauding bands of a hundred or two hundred to waylay the caravans and bring home the loot, which included cows, buffaloes, horses, personal baggage—and young women. By now—and this had been going on for days—every village youth had an 'accomplishment' to his credit, even the pygmy hunchback Varyam Singh, son of Mukhia. He was severely disabled and hobbled around on bandy legs but just four days earlier he was in a raiding party and had come back with a young woman, whom Nihal Singh saw. She was beautiful, very beautiful, but not as beautiful as Harnam Kaur, he decided.

The village had acquired a new life. Young men sauntered around drunk, singing bawdy songs. If a girl ran out of a house, she was chased noisily. At times, there were disputes over looted goods, leading to violence. There no longer was a quiet moment to be enjoyed. The one person who had not ventured out was Bahadur, who sat at home all day without saying a word. In the beginning, Nihal Singh did not notice it, but when the upheaval intensified, his fellow villagers began to crack jokes about it. When someone would say, 'Sardar Nihal Siyaan, we hear your Bahadur has performed many deeds of courage,' Nihal Singh's face would turn red with shame. One evening in the village common, the jaundice-eyed sweetmeat seller, Basheshar, said to Nihal Singh, 'Two of them my son Ganda Singh has brought in and my own score is one—but she is like an unopened bottle.' Then he produced a smacking noise as if a bottle of aerated water was being uncorked. 'Only the fortunate get to uncork these unopened bottles, Sardar Nihal Siyaan,' he said with a smirk.

These words burnt Nihal Singh to a cinder. He thought with contempt of Basheshar and Ganda Singh, one suffering from jaundice, the other from tuberculosis. A little later, when he was in a cooler frame of mind, he felt sorry because what Basheshar had said was true. Regardless of what the father and son were like, the fact was that there were three young women in their house. Since Nihal Singh was a neighbour, for several days now, he had been hearing women's cries from Basheshar's house. One day near the gurdwara, he heard two young men talking and laughing. One said, 'There are many stories we have heard about Nihal Siyaan.' The other quipped, 'Leave that aside, let's talk about Bahadur—he is hiding at home like a woman.' This was much too much for Nihal

Singh, so when he returned home, he tried to appeal to Bahadur's manliness. 'Have you heard what people are saying? That you are hiding at home like a woman in bangles. I swear by the Guru that by the time I was your age, countless young girls had lain between my legs . . .'

Nihal Singh said no more because he noticed Bahadur getting red in the face with embarrassment. He left the house in a troubled state of mind and walked to the village well and sat there, across from the village common where he had performed such memorable athletic feats. In the end, he came to the conclusion that Bahadur was just shy, and he was shy because of his flawed upbringing. He cursed his sister silently and decided to get Bahadur out of his reverie. A stratagem came to his mind. There were reports that a caravan was due to pass over the unpaved road that ran by the village. It was a dark night and when a band of men left the village to raid the caravan Nihal Singh joined it. They attacked the caravan, which was unarmed, and in no time its members were running pell-mell, trying to save themselves. While others looted what goods or valuables those people carried, Nihal Singh took no part in that. He was looking for something else.

Because of the dark night, the village men were carrying hand-held torches to identify objects of interest. Some torches had gone off, but in that murky atmosphere Nihal Singh saw several fleeing shadows, who were possibly women. He wasn't sure which one he should try to grab and so a good deal of time passed. The frenzy of the looters had also subsided. In his restless state, as Nihal Singh began to run sometimes in one direction, at times in another, he noticed someone with a bundle under the arm run past him. He chased this figure and when he got close he found that it was a young woman. Nihal Singh threw a sheet over her like a net, as if she were a fish. Then he picked her up, placed her like a bundle on his shoulder and walked back home, taking a rarely used path.

When he got home, he found it dark. Bahadur was asleep in his room. Nihal Singh did not want to wake him up, so he opened his door, pushed the girl in and bolted it from the outside. He also beat upon the door to wake up Bahadur. He laid out his cot outside the room and began to imagine excitedly what must be happening between the young woman and Bahadur. He could see a flickering light inside Bahadur's room where there had been none before. Nihal Singh shuddered, feeling transported to the days of his youth when he would grab any young woman he fancied and take her to a lonely sugarcane field. He was up all night, with strange thoughts passing through his head. When the cocks began to crow at the break of dawn, he got up to walk into his room, but stopped at the entrance. 'They must have gone to sleep, totally exhausted and maybe . . .' he said to himself, as his body began to tremble. To calm his nerves, he sat down on his cot, sucked at his moustache and smiled.

After the sun rose, he unbolted Bahadur's door. There were rustling noises from the room. When he opened the door, he found the girl sitting in a heap on the bed, wrapped in a saffron-coloured dupatta. Her back was towards him and he could see her long, snake-like black ponytail. He stepped into the room, which made her wrap the dupatta even more securely around her body. A clay lamp was still flickering in the alcove. Nihal Singh blew it out and suddenly he thought of Bahadur. Where was he? He looked around the room but there was nobody there. 'Where is Bahadur?' he asked the girl.

She did not answer. There was a rustling noise under the bed and out came another girl. Nihal Singh was flabbergasted as his astonished eyes saw that the girl who had rushed out of the room by now had a beard, but one that had been shaved.

Nihal Singh advanced towards the bed on which sat the girl, who squeezed her body into a ball, but Nihal Singh pulled away her dupatta and turned her face towards him. Stepping back, he screamed, 'Harnam Kaur.'

It was Bahadur wearing women's clothes, his hair parted in the middle, a ponytail over his back. He was also sucking his lips.

THE MAN WHO LIKED TO LOSE

People only like to win, but he derived great enjoyment from losing.

He had never found it hard to win, but he often had to work hard to lose. In the beginning, when he was working at a bank, he wanted to make heaps of money, but when his family and friends only made fun of it, he left the bank to move to Bombay where he was soon able to earn enough to help his family and friends with their needs off and on.

There were many things he could have done in Bombay but he chose the movies because therein lay money and fame. That was where he could make millions and then spend it all away. That being so, to this day he has remained in that business. He has earned not millions, but hundreds of millions and spent it all. He took less time in spending what he earned than the time spent earning it. In the beginning, he wrote lyrics for a movie, which earned him a hundred thousand rupees. That sum he showered on singing girls, go-betweens, races and gambling dens, though it took him some time to blow it all away.

He also made a movie, which earned him a million. The question was how to spend it. He went about the task by acquiring three cars, one new, two used ones, though he very well knew that the latter were quite useless. He parked them outside his house where he expected them to stand and rot. The new one he locked in the garage on the excuse that petrol was hard to come by. He continued to go about in taxis. He would hire one in the morning, make it stop at a gambling house, go in, only to reappear hours later after having lost a couple of thousand rupees, to get back into the cab and return home. He would not pay the driver and, when in the evening he would come out, he would find the cab waiting. 'You silly man, are you still here?' he would ask. 'All right then, take me to the office so that I can pay you what you are owed.' He would go into his office and let the waiting cab wait on.

One after the other, three of his movies had turned out to be smash hits, breaking all previous records. He now had more money than he knew what to do with. His fame had touched the skies. Exasperated, he made three films in quick succession, which bombed at the box office. He not only lost heavily himself, but took down several others with him. He did not let this get him down but made another movie that turned out to be a gold mine. His dealings with women were also along the same lines. He would pick up a woman, from a party or the bazaar, see to it that she became famous and, after getting his fill, create opportunities for her to find another lover. While on the hunt, he had crossed swords with many millionaires and several dashing young men, but he would always manage to reach into those thorny bushes to pluck the flower of his choice. He would put that flower in his lapel the next day so that some rival should snatch it from him.

These days he had taken to visiting a gambling house in Faras Road. This had gone on for the last ten days because he was in the mood to lose, although he had recently lost a most beautiful actress and a million rupees in a movie that was a disaster. But these mishaps had only whetted his appetite, having occurred rather suddenly, contrary to his estimates. This was why he had been visiting the Faras Road gambling house, having measured out the sum of money he planned to lose there.

Every evening, he would put two hundred rupees in his pocket, get into a cab and drive towards Pawan Bridge on his way to Faras Road. The cab would crawl along the tiny cubicles in which sat the city's prostitutes behind an iron grill, waiting for customers. The taxi would come to a stop near a lamp post and he would step out, adjust his thick spectacles over his nose, straighten his loincloth and glance to his left where a most plain-looking woman was always to be found applying make-up to her face with the help of a broken hand-held mirror. He would ignore her and walk up a flight of stairs to the gambling den. In the last ten days that he had been coming here, he had been dutifully losing two hundred rupees every day. Sometimes he would lose the entire sum in two or three hands and sometimes it would be early morning before he was rid of the money.

On the eleventh day, when his taxi came to a stop at the lamp post, he stepped out, adjusted his thick spectacles over his nose, straightened his loincloth, looked to his left and realized that he had seen this ugly woman every day for the last ten days applying make-up with the help of a broken mirror. He stopped in front of the iron grill behind which she sat and examined her carefully. She was middle-aged, dark with oily skin, and there were tattooed blue circles on her cheeks and chin. Her teeth were crooked and her gums had rotted because of the tobacco-filled betel leaves she was obviously addicted to. He wondered about the men who came to her. He came a step closer to the grill and she smiled, putting the mirror to one side. Then she asked crudely, 'Well, seth, you going to stay?' He took another look at the woman and felt surprised that, even at her age, she was still hopeful of attracting customers. 'Bai, how old are you?' he asked her. This question clearly hurt her feelings, because she made a face and mumbled something in Marathi, probably a word of abuse. Realizing his mistake, he asked her with great sincerity, 'Bai, please forgive me, my question did not imply anything, but I find it surprising that you sit here every day, ready and made-up. Do you get visitors?'

She did not answer him. Realizing his mistake again, he asked, without showing much curiosity, 'What is your name?' The woman, who was about to go behind a curtain, stopped in her tracks and replied, 'Gangoo Bai.' 'Gangoo Bai, how much do you make every day?' There was sympathy in his voice. Gangoo Bai came close to the grill and said, 'Six or seven rupees; on some days, nothing.' As Gangoo Bai spoke, he thought of the two hundred rupees that lay in his pocket, only waiting to be lost. Suddenly, a thought came to him, 'Look, Gangoo Bai, you earn six or seven rupees a day, but I can give you ten rupees every day.' 'To stay?' she asked. 'No, but just assume that I want to stay.' He put his hand in his pocket and pulled out a ten-rupee bill which he slipped to her through the grill. Gangoo Bai took the money but there was a question mark on her face. 'Look, Gangoo Bai, I will give you ten rupees every day, but on one condition.' 'Condition?' 'The condition is that after taking the money, you will eat, then go inside to sleep.' A strange smile appeared on Gangoo Bai's lips. 'Don't laugh, I am a man who keeps his promises,' he said. Then he took the stairs to the gambling den. While on his way up, he thought, 'I come here to lose anyway, so instead of losing two hundred, let me lose ten rupees less.'

Several days passed. Every evening, his taxi would come to a stop near the lamp post and he would step out, adjust his thick spectacles over his nose, straighten his loincloth and walk past Gangoo Bai, who would be sitting in her cubicle behind the iron grill. He would approach her, slip her a ten-rupee bill through the grill, which she would clutch, then raise her hand and touch her forehead by way of a greeting. He would lose the hundred and ninety rupees he was left with, and come down, generally late at night, to find Gangoo Bai's door closed.

One evening, after slipping her the usual tenner, he lost all his money rather earlier than usual. He came down to get into his waiting cab and found Gangoo Bai's door open. She was sitting there and it looked as if she was waiting for a customer. Her face clouded when she saw him walking towards her. 'Gangoo Bai, what is this?' he asked. Gangoo Bai kept quiet. 'I am sorry, but you did not keep your word. Did I not tell you that I did not want that light in your room to be lit at night, but here you are sitting and waiting, just as you used to.' He sounded hurt. 'You are bad,' he said, and turned to go. 'Wait, seth,' Gangoo Bai said. He stopped. Each word that she now spoke was uttered with deliberation. 'I am bad, but who is good here? Seth, by doling out ten rupees, you can manage to put out one light, but just look at all those lights down the street.'

Through his thick glasses, he looked at the naked bulb that hung over Gangoo Bai's head, then at her dark face. He lowered his head, but all he could say was, 'No, Gangoo Bai, no.'

When he got into his cab, his heart was as empty as his pocket.

NIGHT WHISPERS

'Please don't tease me . . . for God's sake, don't tease me.'

'You have become very hard-hearted lately.'

'Yes, that is right; I've become hard-hearted.'

'That is no answer.'

'That is my answer and I have given this to you over and over.'

'I am going to listen to no such answer today.'

'Please, don't tease me, I swear by God, I am telling you the truth; if you tease me, I will start screaming.'

'Don't raise your voice; you'll wake up the little girls.'

'You want little girls in droves.'

'That's how you always taunt me.'

'You should give it some thought then . . . I've just about had it.'

'True . . . but . . .'

'No ifs and buts.'

'Actually, you don't really care about me . . . The fact is that you no longer love me . . . It is not the way it was eight years ago . . . You have no interest in me as a person any more.'

'Yes, sir.'

'Those were the days, when we first got married. You took such good care of me. We were like milk and sugar . . . but now! Sometimes you use the excuse that you are sleepy, other times you are tired and there are times when you just plug both your ears and simply stop listening.'

'I am prepared to listen to nothing.'

'You are not capable of showing any mercy.'

'Please let me sleep.'

'Go to sleep then . . . but I will keep turning in my bed all night . . . but what do you care!'

'Please do not raise your voice . . . Think of the neighbours.'

'I don't care.'

'You really are impossible . . . What will they say if they hear us!'

'They will say what a headstrong wife I have.'

'Oh!'

'Please speak in a low voice. Look one girl has woken up.'

'O God, O God! O please God . . . go to sleep child, God, O God! By God, you are really impossible!'

'Dear God, dear God! You don't even know how to put a child to bed.'

'But you do . . . which is what you do all day at home.'

'How can I stay home all day . . . but whenever I can, I come home to help you out.'

'I don't need to be helped out. Please stay away from home to have a good time with your friends.'

'Good time?'

'I don't want to say much.'

'All right, just answer one question.'

'For God's sake, don't tease me any more.'

'Where should I go?'

'Wherever you wish.'

'Really?'

'Won't you please keep quiet?'

'No, I am going to keep talking tonight; I will neither sleep myself, nor will I let you do so.'

'I am telling you the truth. You are sending me over the bend . . . what kind of a man is this, dear God! He just refuses to understand, instead all the time, all the time . . .'

'You are most certainly going to wake up the girls.'

'Then you should not have caused them to be born.'

'Who am I to cause them to be born . . . They are God's gift . . . So go to sleep, go to sleep.'

'Now, who woke the girl up?'

'I am sorry.'

'So all you can come up with is, "I am sorry" . . . You have been shouting at the top of your voice, utterly unmindful of neighbours. You don't even care what they might say. By God, you are sending me up the tree.'

'May your enemies go up the tree!'

'You are my enemy.'

'Then may God send me up the tree.'

'You are already there.'

'Yes, that is true. I am crazy, but I am crazy about you.'

'Don't try to flatter me.'

'I can't seem to bring you around, this way or that.'

'I want to sleep.'

'Go to sleep then. I will keep talking my nonsense.'

'Is this nonsense that important?'

'Well, it is . . . Just turn towards me.'

'I say, please don't tease me or I'll start crying.'

'Why do you hate me so much? You are my life, my entire life. I just don't understand what has come over you. If I have done something wrong, please tell me what it is.'

'Three of your wrongs are stretched right across that bed.'

'When will these reprimands stop?'

'And when will your demands stop?'

'All right, you won't hear a word from me this moment on. Go to sleep. I will move downstairs.'

'Where?'

'To hell.'

'What madness is this! There are too many mosquitoes downstairs . . . and there's no fan there either . . . I am serious . . . You are crazy . . . I won't let you go.'

'What will I do here . . . downstairs, there are mosquitoes and there is no fan . . . but it doesn't matter, I've lived through hard times and I do not care for creature comforts . . . I will go to sleep on the sofa.'

'You will remain awake all night.'

'What do you care!'

'I won't let you go . . . You always make a mountain out of a mole hill.'

'It won't kill me . . . Let me go.'

'O the words you utter! I am asking you not to go.'

'I won't be able to sleep here.'

'Doesn't matter.'

'What strange logic . . . I am not leaving after a fight.'

'Is there anything left to fight over! By God, you sometimes behave like a child . . . Why else would you want to sleep in mosquito-infested heat . . . Anyone in my place would have gone bonkers by now.'

'What do you care!'

'All right, all right! What do you want?'

'Now you are talking.'

'Don't flatter yourself. I am doing no such thing.'

'Come on now.'

'God forbid!'

'Is your sari back with its embroidered border?'

'No!'

'What a rascal that tailor is . . . he said he would bring it today.'

'He did, but I sent it back.'

'Why?'

'It needed some more work.'

'O . . . well, I say, let's go see the movie *Barsaat* tomorrow. I have complimentary tickets.'

'How many?'

'Just two. Why?'

'The big sis wanted to come too.'

'Forget the big sis, she can see it another day. It is not easy to get complimentary tickets in the opening week . . . your body is shimmering in this moonlit night.'

'I hate moonlight. It gets into my eyes; it won't let me sleep.'

'All you want to do is sleep.'

'You will know why if you had to take care of three girls. You will then know what I am talking about. While you are changing one, the other has already soiled her clothes. One is put to bed and the other gets up, while the third is busy wolfing down food from the pantry.'

'There are two servants in this house.'

'Servants do nothing.'

'Then throw them out.'

'Lower your voice, please, the youngest just stirred.'

'Sorry, just pat her on the back.'

'The middle one is also restless.'

'Did you have her go to the toilet before you put her to bed?'

'Yes.'

'Then why?'

'It is far too warm today . . . please get away from me.'

'No, no.'

'In the end, I am the one who always have to admit defeat.'

'Your defeat is no defeat, it is a victory . . . only God knows how much I love you.'

'Your love only comes to the surface on these occasions.'

'So, should I show my love when we are in the street? Look here, look at me.'

'You will have your way, won't you?'
'Because you are my sweetheart.'
'I said, get away from me.'
'Why?'
'Don't you see, the eldest is awake.'
'Oh!'
'Didn't you hear?'
'What?'
'She wants milk. "Daddy milka," she just said.'
'Yes, I heard. Give her milk.'
'I left it downstairs.'
'Downstairs?'
'Yes, in the pantry . . . Go get it.'
'Bring it from downstairs?'
'Hurry, or she will start crying.'
'Yes, I am going.'
'I say, listen, warm the milk before you bring it.'
'All right, all right . . . I heard you.'

SONARAL

When Bushra took three Sonaral sleeping pills for the third time in an attempt to commit suicide, I became suspicious. I mean if she wanted to kill herself, there were far more effective means available, such as opium or one of the more effective poisons, and they were not so hard to come by. So why did she always take Sonaral pills?

While there is no doubt that if taken in a large quantity these pills will result in death, it was curious that all the three times Bushra had tried to kill herself she had taken Sonaral. My first thought was that since her first two attempts had led to no fatal results, she had settled on these particular pills, because whatever effect she planned to create by her brush with death could be safely created by taking Sonaral. But the fact was that I wasn't really sure because taking sleeping pills is a touch-and-go thing. In any case, it was hardly a safe method of achieving her ends.

The next time she took thirty-two Sonaral pills. Her husband, a sub-overseer in the Public Works Department, came to know of it at 6.30 in the morning, when he found her lying senseless on the bed like a paralysed buffalo. She had taken the tablets three or four hours earlier. He rushed to my place, looking utterly shaken, which surprised me greatly, because after marrying Bushra he had completely ignored me, whereas earlier he used to spend a good deal of time with me every day, drinking beer. In those days, he used to live in straitened circumstances, using a bicycle to go to work. However, after he met Bushra and married her, everything changed, including his living conditions.

He began to be seen in well-cut suits. A car soon appeared on the scene and new furniture arrived at the house. He took to going to the races and instead of local rum he now drank only Scotch whisky. Bushra too liked a drink and the two appeared to be living happily. Qamar, the sub-overseer, was around fifty and Bushra was about five years younger. She must have been fairly good-looking at one time, but she had not aged well. Her face was lined, which she would paint with excessive quantities of make-up. She had also started colouring her hair, but her body had become loose-jointed like the string of a kite that has been cut away. Her breasts she uplifted with the help of her crane-like brassiere and her eyes were thickly lined with antimony. To me she looked like a crude parody of femininity.

All that had attracted Qamar was solely Bushra. Her father was a big landlord from the Punjab and she had inherited a good deal of land from him, which brought her a regular monthly income of five to seven hundred rupees. Apart from that, she had ten to fifteen thousand rupees sitting in a bank. Qamar was just an ordinary sub-overseer. He was already married and had six children, two of whom were at college. Poverty reigned supreme in his household, but it had not prevented him from having a roving eye and writing poetry. A drink in the evening was also a must. Given those habits, there was hardly anything left for the children.

Qamar told everyone that he had married Bushra, but I was never sure of it. I suspected that being the wily kind, he was trying to fool people. After all, in his fifty years, he had sampled life in more ways than one. He had gone through good times and bad, and seen many ups and downs. How could such a man live with the additional inconvenience of another marriage, I asked myself. However, the Bushra liaison had done him good. His three daughters, who used to waste their time playing all day, were now in a missionary-run school. His first wife's appearance and clothes had improved and the family was eating better. Speaking for myself, I was pleased that the second marriage had not just been good for him but also good for Bushra, who had found a husband. Qamar had found a woman who might not be beautiful but who had money. But the arrangement did not last long. We heard one day that after a big argument, both of them had swallowed Sonaral pills. When they were found, Qamar was unconscious on the floor and Bushra lay lifeless on the bed.

They were both taken to the hospital from where they were discharged in good health the next day. However, fifteen days later, there was another episode involving the two of them, and once again, Sonaral. I am not sure if they were rushed to the hospital or whether they were taken care of at home, but they survived. For the next one year, there was no untoward incident, till one day I was told that Bushra had swallowed thirty-two tablets of Sonaral.

Qamar was beside himself with worry and appeared utterly incapable of knowing what to do. I phoned the hospital, had an ambulance sent for, got Bushra there, pulled out the house surgeon from his quarters and told him the story. My urgent tone had no effect on him and in a somewhat pitiless voice he said, 'Manto sahib, let them die, why are you worried?' He knew that Bushra had been brought to the hospital two or three times in the past in a similar condition. I went no further with him and came home.

It is not that I did not know Bushra's background and her previous life. I had met her many times and she always called me brother Saadat. I also had drunk with her several times. One of her daughters was named Pervez, whose picture I saw for the first time when Bushra moved to Qamar's home as his new wife. Her things were laid out in a set of rooms on the lower floor. I noticed the framed picture of a young and pretty woman on the mantelpiece. When we were drinking beer, I asked Bushra who she was. She told me it was her only daughter Pervez, who had committed suicide. When I asked why, this is what she told me. If I were writing a story, that is also exactly how I would write it.

Pervez was Bushra's firstborn. Her first husband, a rich landlord named Allah Bux, had died a few years after their marriage. He had begun to hate Bushra because she was flirting with another man. She too had had enough of his contempt and hatred, and left him. He died without leaving her anything, but he did leave something for his daughter Pervez. Educated and liberal as she was, Bushra took another husband, a successful barrister from Peshawar. They had two boys, but the marriage did not last long, and Bushra asked for a divorce because she wanted to live an independent life. That barrister is still alive and both the boys are now grown men who live with their father. They don't meet their mother because they do not like her character.

This is a thumbnail sketch of Bushra's life, but the story of her daughter Pervez is longer. She grew up in the country. She was a delicate child who would be out playing in the open fields all day, often by herself. Her parents did not encourage her to mix with the children of those who tilled the land. When she became older, she was sent to a boarding school in Lahore, where most students came from rich families. She was intelligent and talented. After completing school, she went to college, having by now grown into a beautiful young woman. Her restless mind was always on the lookout for her ideal man. She had a sweet voice and when she sang she captivated her listeners. She had also learnt to dance and was a marvellous dancer, given her graceful and supple body. So good was she that even with the least perceptible movement of her limbs, she could hold her audience spellbound.

Pervez was simple and artless, as most village people are. At her English-medium school and college, she had made friends with several intelligent and street-smart girls. But she herself was different, always floating above the din of everyday life. She did not care for money but dreamt of meeting a young man whom she could worship. That is the way she wanted to spend her life, perpetually in love with the man with whom she would fall in love. Her mother once took her to Abbottabad, where in a mixed party she persuaded her daughter to dance. Pervez surveyed the audience and her eyes rested for a moment on a well-dressed young Pathan. He noticed her and they exchanged glances, which were akin to messages. Pervez, who was not planning to dance, changed her mind and soon had everyone sitting up. She used her soft and supple body to express every desire that had remained hidden in her heart up till now. She held nothing back and he got the message.

The young man's name was Yusuf Ghilzai and he came from a rich tribal family. He had finished his education and was now actively involved in national politics. No stranger to women, he took little time in falling under Pervez's spell. Their marriage took place with great pomp and ceremony, and they settled in Abbottabad. Pervez was happy, so happy that she felt like dancing all the time and making music. She had come to worship Yusuf and she had given him everything a woman could give a man. She was so happy that she did not even notice how quickly the first three years of their marriage passed. She had given birth to a daughter, but so much in love with Yusuf was she that she sometimes neglected the child. When her daughter was born, her love for Yusuf grew more intense because after all it was he who had made that possible. That was how much she loved Yusuf.

However, the man she worshipped did not stay faithful because by nature he was a pleasure seeker. He was like a honeybee, always wanting to suck the nectar of every flower that caught his fancy. Before long, he broke away the chains that Pervez's love had thrown around him and reverted to his old ways. He had money, youth and a captivating personality. Because of his politics, he had begun to gain countrywide fame. He had also come to view Pervez's love for him as nothing more than ignorance. He had actually become tired of her. He would feel irritated when she touched or kissed him. He had no patience with such overt expressions of affection. He did not want Pervez to capture him in the gossamer web of her love because he was convinced that if he let that happen he would never be able to free himself. He would be like an insect that gets caught and dies because it could not untangle itself. He did not want to end up like that insect.

When Pervez realized that Yusuf was not entirely hers, she went into a state of shock and for days afterwards she moved around as if in a swoon. What she had seen as her ideal now lay smashed in bits. She said nothing to Yusuf, nor did she ever bring up the matter of his neglect of her and his infidelities. She withdrew into herself and although nothing could be easier than to rid herself of Yusuf she simply was not prepared for a life without him. She it was who had made him into a god. How could she now turn away from him! In the end, she decided that she would never leave Yusuf because she it was after all who had chosen him for worship as others worship their god. She was prepared to pay any price for that. In fact, she began to make it convenient for Yusuf to pick up women, whom he promptly dropped after deriving a few moments of pleasure from their bodies. Some might have seen it as shameless on her part, but in order to hold on to what little of him she still had, she was willing to suffer this humiliation.

Pervez would behave very nicely with Yusuf's women. She would show them hospitality, put up with their shameless ways and provide her husband with the opportunity to have a good time with them. She would prepare all kinds of food for these women. And when to please them, her husband would ask Pervez to dance and sing, she would do so, while struggling to hold back her tears. She would sing songs of joy when her heart felt wounded. She would put a smile on her angry and trembling lips and dance with all the intensity she could muster. When she was alone, she would break down and cry so much that she would feel life ebbing out of her body. At the same time, these emotional storms would give her new strength and she would resume what really amounted to pimping for Yusuf. She had convinced herself that she was doing nothing of which she should be ashamed.

During this period, her mother had come to visit her several times, but Pervez never complained to her about her husband, nor shared her troubles with anyone else. She saw it as a very personal situation. She had even come to reconcile herself to the emotional devastation she had suffered as she had convinced herself that she was doing the right thing because those women pleased the man she loved to distraction. Bushra currently was without a man in her life but was enjoying herself. She would come to Abbottabad to spend a couple of weeks, and Yusuf would take her around. During her stay with them, his contact with other women remained suspended. Bushra and Yusuf would spend hours playing cards, while Pervez would keep them entertained and looked after. She wanted her mother to stay longer than she usually did so that the other women, who were worse than bazaar prostitutes, would stay away from her home. However, Bushra was never the kind to stay at one place for too long. She would leave and it would only take a couple of days for Yusuf's women to return, with Pervez showing them the usual hospitality in order to please her husband.

She had become so used to this pattern that it did not cause her much pain now. She had convinced herself that this was the role the drama called life had assigned to her. The bitterness and unhappiness she used to feel earlier, she was no longer troubled by. She was, in fact, happy and had begun to pay more attention to her daughter than she used to. Once she went to Lahore for a couple of days where something had come up. When she returned, she found the door to Yusuf's room bolted from inside. She could hear sounds of laughter. When she glued her eyes to the crack in the door to see what was going on, she began to tremble, her pink face drained of all colour. I learnt this from a reliable source. What Bushra told me was different from what my source had told me. According to Bushra, one night, utterly sozzled, with his arm around one of his mistresses, Yusuf asked Pervez to take off all her clothes and dance. She did as she was told, but while her naked body undulated rhythmically, tears flowed down her cheeks. At the end of the dance, she put on her clothes, stepped out of the room, drank poison and died.

My source had a different story. After Pervez took a peek into Yusuf's room through that crack in the door, she decided to end her life. She got into her car, drove to a chemist's and asked for a bottle of Sonaral. She realized when she was about to pay that she had left her handbag at home. However, when she told the storekeeper that she was Mrs Yusuf Ghilzai and she had forgotten her handbag at home, he let her have the pills, confident that the bill would be settled by her husband. She came home, asked her maid to grind the contents of the bottle into a soft powder and put the powder in a warm glass of milk. When it was brought to her, she drank it down. After a while, a servant came in to say that her mother had arrived and her husband wanted to see her. Pervez's eyes were dry but sleepy because the pills had begun to take effect. She washed her face, arranged her hair, went into the room, embraced her mother and sat down on the carpeted floor with Yusuf. While talking to her mother, she felt giddy and fell unconscious. Her face began to turn blue. Yusuf, who was drunk, said there was nothing wrong with Pervez; she was merely pretending. Then he shook Pervez by her shoulder and said in a commanding voice, 'Get up! I don't like this acting.' Bushra also tried to make her daughter get up but she did not. Finally, a doctor was sent for, but when he arrived, Pervez was already dead. There were other stories about Pervez's suicide but what I had learnt, I kept to myself, awaiting confirmation.

But to return to the most recent incident, when Qamar came back from the hospital, I went to see him. He no longer had a car. When I asked him about it, he replied with poetic indifference, 'It was taken by the one who owned it.' 'Meaning?' I asked. 'Meaning that it was never mine, but hers and it is no longer in my use. I go to work on my bicycle. When she needs to go some place, I act as her chauffeur.' I asked if there had been a falling out. 'Well, you can say that; I have actually divorced Bushra.' When I probed further, he confessed that they were never married but he had to pronounce a formal divorce because he did not want people to know that they had never been married and had lived in sin for two years. The break-up came, said Qamar, when Bushra began to have an affair with a middle-aged aristocrat, a refugee, from Hyderabad. In other words, she no longer found Qamar of any interest, nor did she feel attracted to him in a physical way. I was sorry to hear that. I also learnt later that Qamar's three daughters had been pulled out of that nice school. As for Qamar, he had given up smoking expensive cigarettes, settling for the cheap Stork brand. He was like a camel on the loose.

He told me a good deal about Bushra but what I could not understand was that if Bushra had an affair with the Hyderabad man and he, Qamar, had decided to end his relationship with her, why had he taken thirty-two Sonaral tablets to kill himself. On the face of it, her affair with the man from Hyderabad was what had unhinged Qamar, but the more I thought about it, the less convinced I felt about his story. One day, I finally asked him, 'This Sonaral tradition that Pervez established, why did you and Bushra have to follow it? Also, do please tell me what caused Pervez to kill herself? You have told me several times that Pervez was reconciled to the dissipated lifestyle of her husband, Yusuf Ghilzai, and, in fact, was a party to it, so why should she have killed herself? When a woman reaches that point of degradation, it simply doesn't seem logical for her to kill herself. If you ask me, I think she killed herself because she found out that her mother was sleeping with her husband.' Qamar confirmed what I had surmised. 'That's the truth. One day when she was drunk, Bushra confessed to me, while crying, that that's exactly what had happened.'

The same evening, I learnt that the aristocrat from Hyderabad had taken twenty-four tablets of Sonaral, while Bushra had swallowed her usual thirty-two. They were both in hospital, lying unconscious. The man died the next day, but Bushra survived. These days she is mourning her lover, while the man to whom she had recently sold her car is said to be with her all times of day and night, offering comfort.

DRAMA

IN THIS VORTEX

A Melodrama

CHARACTERS

Begum (mother, an invalid)
Amjad and Majid (Begum's sons)
Saeeda (Amjad's new bride)
Asghari (maid)
Karim and Ghulam Muhammad (house helpers)

SCENE I

A room in Nigar Villa. Its beautiful glass windows open on undulating hills, as far as the eye can see, till they disappear in the dusty blue of the sky. The silk curtains in the windows wave gently in the light morning breeze. To the right of the windows is a bed with a mosquito net strung across mahogany posts. A glass table lies next to it with a crystal goblet, a glass and a timepiece on it. Behind it lies a pink taffeta-covered set of sofas on which the two house helpers are now placing cushions. Not far from them is the young, plain-looking maid who is trying to rearrange the already well-placed objects, which are not many in number, on the mantelpiece. There is a virgin-like quality to the atmosphere, which can be robbed by the slightest movement. The sound of gentle tapping on the tiled floor can now be heard getting closer to the room. The three servants look startled for a second but continue with what they are busy doing. A handsome woman in her middle years enters through the door on crutches, looks around and expresses satisfaction with what she sees.

BEGUM (*ambling around the room with the aid of her crutches and finding everything where she thinks it should be*): Good! (*removes one crutch from under her armpit in order to sit on the sofa, then changes her mind, and places one hand on the silk-covered arm of the sofa, where it ruffles up the fabric. With a corner of her stole she flattens it out, readjusts her crutch in her armpit and speaks to the young maid*) Asghari!

ASGHARI (*suddenly attentive*): Yes please!

BEGUM (*realizing that she can't quite remember what she wanted of her*): What was I going to say?

ASGHARI (*smiling*): You were going to say that you were not quite satisfied. That's what I also think. The bride is very beautiful and when she enters this room, all the embellishments that have been done to its décor will pale in comparison (*she looks at a picture of the bride that hangs over the fireplace, suspended by a silk cord*).

BEGUM (*smiling, moves towards the fireplace and looks at her daughter-in-law's picture carefully. She seems happy, but suddenly her face clouds*): Asghari!

ASGHARI: Yes!

BEGUM: Since morning, I have had this feeling of unease.

ASGHARI: Because Amjad is arriving with his bride.

BEGUM (*lost in thought*): Yes, he should be here any minute now. Kamal has taken the car to the railway station to pick him up.

ASGHARI: Get Majid married off next year and this house will be full of fun and good cheer.

BEGUM: God willing . . . by His grace, that wedding too will take place with great fanfare (*whispers*), God willing!

ASGHARI (*looking at the bride's picture and obviously impressed by her looks*): May God protect her from the evil eye.

BEGUM (*nearly screaming though without wanting to*): Asghari!

ASGHARI (*scared*): Yes!

BEGUM: Nothing . . . when does the train arrive from Karachi?

ASGHARI: I don't know.

BEGUM (*to one of the helpers*): Look Karim, make a phone call to inquire, but the train arrived at Rawalpindi yesterday. There was a telegram from Majid.

KARIM: Yes.

BEGUM (*in a worried voice*): And I have sent Kamal to the station. God knows what is wrong with my memory. Amjad was to spend the night in Rawalpindi with his friend Saeed. But I think they must have left by now. (*To the other servant*) Ghulam Muhammad.

GHULAM MUHAMMAD: Yes?

BEGUM: Go look for Kamal . . . where did he take the car?

GHULAM MUHAMMAD: I will do that (*leaves*).

BEGUM (*leaning over Asghari's shoulder*): I haven't been feeling well since morning . . . Had I not been handicapped and had that confounded Dr Hidayatullah not forbidden it, I would have gone myself to bring the bride home. (*The phone rings in the distance.*) I think it's Amjad's friend informing us that they have left. Go Asghari, run (*Asghari runs out*). (*To Karim as if to reassure herself*) They should be here any minute now.

KARIM: May God bring them home safely!

BEGUM (*nearly screaming*): What do you mean?

KARIM (*terrified*): Just this, I mean . . .

ASGHARI (*almost shouting*): Begum, Begum sahib!

BEGUM (*bewildered*): Why, what happened? (*Asghari enters the room in a highly agitated state*)

ASGHARI: Begum, Begum sahib!

BEGUM (*her hands firmly on her crutches*): What?

ASGHARI: Majid has phoned—there has been a train accident.

BEGUM (*her grip on her crutches now even firmer*): And?

ASGHARI: Amjad and the bride were injured and are lying in hospital.

BEGUM (*her grip on her crutches loosens and they fall to the ground. She stands for a moment like a stone figure, then she moves towards the door*): Get hold of Kamal . . . We are driving to Rawalpindi. (*Begum is walking towards the door as Ghulam Muhammad and Asghari watch her in disbelief. Asghari screams and Begum turns to look at her*) What's it?

ASGHARI: You . . . you are walking . . . you can walk!

BEGUM: Me? (*realizing that she no longer has her crutches*) How can I walk? (*she reels and falls to the floor, unconscious*)

ASGHARI (*rushing forward*): Ghulam Muhammad, go phone the doctor. (*Ghulam Muhammad leaves, as Asghari tries to bring Begum around.*)

SCENE II

(*The same room, but it wears a lived-in look, as if all that is in it has been in use for long. It is morning and the silk curtains in the windows can be seen waving in the light breeze. On the mahogany bed with the mosquito net lies the bride, Saeeda, under a blanket. The tiny timepiece on the glass table begins to vibrate and sounds a faint alarm. There is movement under the blanket, Saeeda turns on *her side, opens her eyes, bends to look at the timepiece, and smiles. As she smiles, her thick eyelashes on her quite beautiful face flutter. She props herself up on the pillows and looks happy as a child at the enticing sight of the hills that stretch into the far distance. She throws the blanket aside with a swing of her legs and jumps down from the bed. She moves the curtains aside and looks out. She hears a bird singing and looks lost in thought. She is young and she is wearing loose silk nightclothes, which do not quite hide her lovely contours. She is not only beautiful but also fully aware of her beauty. Asghari's harsh voice is heard, a sharp contrast to the sweet birdsong. Saeeda is startled. Silently, she uses her eyes to ask what is up.*)

ASGHARI: Majid sahib has just returned from the hospital and he wanted me to see if you were awake.

SAEEDA: What news has he brought?

ASGHARI: I will go get him. (*Leaves the room. Saeeda moves away from the window to the dressing table, looks at herself in the mirror for a moment, arranges her hair casually with both hands and approaches the bed where she picks up her white georgette stole that is hanging by one of the bedposts and throws it over her shoulders unconcernedly. We hear approaching footsteps. She reacts slightly, then looks towards the door, through which enters Majid, a well-built young man of average height and light brown complexion. He looks older than he is.*)

MAJID: Salam, bhabijan.

SAEEDA: Salam.

MAJID (*comes and stands next to the sofa*): How do you feel?

SAEEDA (*disinterestedly*): All right (*sits down*), what news have you brought from Rawalpindi?

MAJID (*standing in front of her*): Nothing much (*half sighs*), but we will bring him home now.

SAEEDA: Why?

MAJID: He is tired of it all (*pulls up a settee and sits down*). Had I been him, it is quite possible I would have committed suicide.

SAEEDA (*gets up, walks to the window*): Who knew this was what fate had in store for me? So many died; I could have died with them.

MAJID: That was not God's will.

SAEEDA (*looking at the hills*): Yes, that was not God's will . . . What God willed was that I should get a slight scratch on my leg, but the rest of my life should lie shattered (*starts to cry, then wipes her tears with her white stole*). God willed that my husband should break his back and I should waste away like a kite that has been cut away (*sobs*).

MAJID (stands up): Bhabijan, one should be strong . . . who knows he may get better.

SAEEDA (*as if reprimanding him*): Majid, at least do not try to fool me. For the last six months he has been glued to that hospital bed. I know quite well what the doctors have decided . . . he is never going to get well . . . both his legs are now useless . . . but, but I would say that he has a lot of courage . . . Whenever I have gone to see him, he has always said to me, as he made me sit next to him, that I, Saeeda, should never worry, he is going to get well very soon. And then he is going to take me to walk among those hills about which he used to tell me in Karachi. He is in love with those hills, he tells me. He loves them so much that I could well be jealous of them. Then he tries to keep my courage up by saying that this world is but another name for accidents. He says he is grateful to God that I did not lose my life, otherwise . . . but I am terrified of repeating what he says next.

MAJID: What?

SAEEDA (*her eyes wet with tears*): That after he is gone, I will become someone else's (*trembles*). Why does he think of such things, Majid?

MAJID: I don't know.

SAEEDA: You should know (*taking small steps, she moves towards the sofa and sits down. Her stole slips away and her breasts can be seen heaving under her silk nightdress*). You are a man . . . his brother . . . what if you had been in this accident?

MAJID: I would never have thought of such things as brother Amjad does.

SAEEDA: Why?

MAJID: We are both men . . . brothers . . . but we have different hearts and minds.

SAEEDA (*murmurs*): Hearts and minds.

ASGHARI: Majid sahib, Begum sahib wants to see you.

MAJID: All right, I will only be a minute.

ASGHARI: She wants you to come right away.

MAJID: All right (*looks at Saeeda*), I will be back (*leaves*).

(*Asghari sits on the floor on the rug, at Saeeda's feet, and begins to press them.*)

SAEEDA (*pulling them back*): Let go, Asghari.

ASGHARI (*practically embracing her feet*): No, Dulhan Begum (*presses her toes*). What news did Majid sahib bring?

SAEEDA: Says he wants to come here.

ASGHARI: That is very good news.

SAEEDA (*sadly*): Yes!

ASGHARI: But Begum sahib was quite annoyed that Majid sahib had taken so long . . .

SAEEDA: So long where?

ASGHARI: Here, with you.

SAEEDA: With me? What did Begum sahib say?

ASGHARI: Nothing . . . She is very curt with everyone these days, nothing seems to please her . . . She is less sorry about Amjad sahib than about you. She is always thinking about you . . . So, has Amjad sahib recovered?

SAEEDA (*annoyed, pulls away her feet*): Yes, he has (*Begum sahib enters. Asghari stands up*): Salam, auntie.

BEGUM: Salam, my child, may you live long (*puts her hand on Saeeda's head affectionately*)! So Majid has told you . . .

SAEEDA: Yes . . .

BEGUM: The poor man is tired of the hospital (*looks at Asghari*). Asghari, you get going (*Asghari leaves*). It is . . . it is his wish that he should come here and be with you. He has told me that if he has to die, he wants to have his Saeeda before his eyes.

(*Tears begin to form in Saeeda's eyes; she embraces the older woman, who is crying too.*)

BEGUM: He . . . he is madly in love with you, but he wanted that you be asked if you have any objection to his coming back to live here.

SAEEDA: Objection!

BEGUM: Child, because that may add to your grief.

SAEEDA: Why does he think like that, auntie, why does he think like that?

BEGUM: Child, that's the sort of person he is, always thinking of others.

SAEEDA: He should come, why shouldn't he come (*her voice almost a wail*), but he should not talk like that.

BEGUM: The doctors have said that if he remains happy mentally, he should be able to walk with the help of crutches in a couple of months (*begins to cry bitterly*), crutches, which his train accident freed me from. Had I known that crutches were going to become part of his life, I would have held on to them tightly. But child, in this vortex that they call life, you can sink in even the sturdiest boat and a mere straw can get you across to the shore. (*After a pause*) Saeeda, my child, Amjad also wanted me to ask something else of you.

SAEEDA: What, auntie?

BEGUM: Do you love him?

SAEEDA (*flabbergasted*): Love!

BEGUM (*runs her hand over Saeeda's head*): I don't want to burden you too much (*leaves*).

SAEEDA (*drying her tears with her stole, murmurs*): Love . . . love? (*walks to the fireplace where her picture hangs on the wall, suspended by a silk cord*) Tell me, will you love him? (*There is sound of china rattling on a tray. Asghari enters with the breakfast tray, places it on a wheeled trolley.*)

ASGHARI: Dulhan Begum, if you do not love Amjad sahib, who will?

SAEEDA (*startled*): What did you say?

ASGHARI: Nothing at all . . . I was only talking to myself . . . Here's breakfast.

SAEEDA: Please go.

ASGHARI: Yes. (*Casts a glance at her and then her picture and leaves. Saeeda, thinking, slowly moves towards the bed and lies down on it, staring at the ceiling*) Dulhan Begum, if you do not love Amjad sahib, who will (*in a louder voice*), who will . . . who can?

SCENE III

(*The Nigar Villa garden. In the middle, surrounded by trimmed hedges, a fountain is playing; the sun is out in a clear sky. There is something virginal about the atmosphere, but utterly without self-consciousness. Every object, every atom appears to be waiting to be accepted. The breeze seems to have paused so that the buds in the garden should be able to preen themselves, the flowers redden the glow in their cheeks and the black moths kiss the blossoms of their choice at leisure. On the green lawn, several chairs have been placed, on one of which sits Saeeda, dressed in pink, which is a reflection of her looks. The warmth of the sun is irradiating the atmosphere with Saeeda's beauty. In another chair sits Majid, puffing at a cigarette and blowing blue smoke rings. He looks at peace with himself. Across him sits Amjad in a wheelchair. He looks helpless like his chair, which cannot move without help. His face is pale but his eyes are bright, as if echoing Saeeda's beauty.*)

AMJAD (*looking around*): What lovely weather!

SAEEDA (*suddenly attentive*): Yes.

AMJAD: Majid, you should take Saeeda out in those hills (*tries to turn his head*), I am sorry, I am unable to turn. Majid, get up and turn my chair . . . I want to see those hills. (*Majid gets up, but Saeeda has already turned Amjad's wheelchair. All three are now facing the hills, Amjad, as if drinking in the sight*) Saeeda, there lie the hills that I love, love so much that I am unable to express it. (*to Majid*) Go Majid, take Saeeda with you and let her see those hills. (*to Saeeda*) Saeeda, when you get breathless climbing and you are breathing hard, you will realize that there is no greater pleasure in this world than that feeling. I used to take Majid against his will there but he would give up after one steep climb. He would say, 'Brother, this is one hobby of yours I do not like . . . what is the point of getting breathless climbing' (*laughs*)! He will never understand the beauty of climbing, the urge to conquer those hills. Saeeda?

SAEEDA (*smiling*): Yes.

AMJAD (*to Majid*): Go, my friend, take Saeeda. Do some work for a change.

MAJID (*to Saeeda*): Come bhabijan . . . but I bet that after today, she will never go in that direction again.

SAEEDA: No, no . . . how can you say that?

AMJAD: Because he is of a different heart and mind.

SAEEDA: Heart and mind? What on earth are those?

MAJID: You will find out after climbing just one hill.

AMJAD (*laughing*): Rubbish, Majid. Saeeda's life ahead is like climbing a mountain . . . If she gets tired after climbing just one hill, then . . .

SAEEDA: Let's go, Majid.

MAJID: Right. (*They leave, Amjad smiles*)

(*Asghari enters, carrying a plate with sliced apples. She looks at Majid and Saeeda with meaningful eyes, then addresses Amjad.*)

ASGHARI: Have a slice of apple.

AMJAD (*watching Saeeda and Majid going down the hill*): I will.

ASGHARI (*also looking at the two receding figures*): How lovely Dulhan Begum looks today!

AMJAD (*turning away*): Looks?

ASGHARI (*smiling slightly, but looking perplexed*): Yes . . . yes.

AMJAD (*looks again at Saeeda and Majid*): She is beautiful. She does not look beautiful, she is beautiful. There is a world of difference between something being something and something looking like something.

ASGHARI: That's true.

AMJAD: Give me the apples.

ASGHARI (*offering him the plate*): Here they are, already sliced.

AMJAD: Meaning?

ASGHARI: What is sliced can mislead (*laughing*) . . . they have lost their red cheeks to the knife.

AMJAD (*laughs*): Asghari, you have become very naughty, you little devil . . .

ASGHARI (*serious*): Naughty? Amjad sahib, you once told me that the Devil was God's principal angel but he refused to bow before Adam who was formed from ordinary clay.

AMJAD: Yes, and . . .

ASGHARI: And this headmaster of the angels was punished.

AMJAD: That's correct.

ASGHARI: Then this is correct too.

AMJAD: What?

ASGHARI: Nothing really . . . after all, what is correct? It is what you think is correct or try to think is correct. Or it is like a mistake that you once make, hoping that it will correct itself or that correct act that you are trying to turn into a mistake, hoping that you will turn it around again. But all this is rubbish . . . I am a stupid woman.

AMJAD: What sort of talk is this today?

ASGHARI: I am a stupid woman, but I am a woman, Amjad sahib.

AMJAD: I still do not understand.

ASGHARI (*picks up a slice of apple and brings it to Amjad's mouth*): Eat some apple.

AMJAD (*taking the slice between his teeth*): You never talked like this before.

ASGHARI: The weather is so beautiful today.

AMJAD: What's that?

ASGHARI (*picking up another apple slice*): Have another slice (*puts it in Amjad's mouth*).

AMJAD (*munches the apple, then after a while, speaks*): Asghari!

ASGHARI (*absorbed in looking at the hills*): Yes?

AMJAD: Shall we get you married?

ASGHARI: Marriage?

AMJAD: Yes, it is time you were married.

ASGHARI: Why?

AMJAD: Marriage is a good thing . . . Everything under the sun should be married . . . There is no greater joy in life . . . I am going to ask mother to get you married, quickly.

ASGHARI: No, Amjad sahib, no.

AMJAD: Why?

ASGHARI: I am afraid.

AMJAD: Of whom?

ASGHARI (*sits down on the lawn, and says in a worried tone*): Of marriage.

AMJAD (*laughs*): Crazy girl!

ASGHARI: That is true, Amjad sahib . . . I am really afraid . . . To begin with, what significance can a maid's marriage have! It may happen, it may not happen, it doesn't really matter . . . but if it does take place and if the train gets derailed and . . .

AMJAD (*touched*): Asghari!

ASGHARI (*still talking*): If the train gets derailed and Asghari escapes with her life, but loses a leg, an arm and an eye, then half of Asghari would have disappeared and only one half would have survived . . . no, no, Amjad sahib, please do not even mention marriage. Marriage is something whole and solid, not something that is a half or a quarter.

AMJAD (*thinking*): Asghari!

ASGHARI (*in a stifled voice*): Yes!

AMJAD: You are right (*his voice acquiring great pathos*), but please do not make me sad. I want to remain happy, even on these two broken legs of mine . . . Do not tease me . . . it makes my heart ache.

ASGHARI (*at Amjad's feet*): Please forgive me, Amjad sahib (*tears welling up in her eyes*), God knows what nonsense I talked. I want you to be happy. May God keep you happy!

AMJAD (*bravely*): Don't mention God . . . Had He wanted to keep me happy, why would He have had me in this accident . . . and yes He did that, but then why didn't He put me in His hunter's bag of slain game . . . Don't mention Him . . . We are no longer friends . . . If I have to remain happy, I want to be happy on my own, with what is left of my body. On these broken branches I have to build a small nest of happiness.

ASGHARI: Just for your happiness?

AMJAD (*deeply grief-stricken*): Asghari, for God's sake . . . Why are you so cruel . . . If you have been given a tongue, it is to be used to increase my happiness . . . I beg of you to help me, help an invalid live the few days of a broken life that are left to him.

ASGHARI: You do not have to beg . . . It shatters me . . . You are the master, you can command me. I lie on the line for you (*her tears fall on Amjad's slippers . . . she gets up and moves to one side*).

(*Amjad looks down at his tear-stained slippers, raises his head to see Asghari leave. Begum appears from a side of the house, wrapped in a shawl, carrying a couple of boxes of jewellery.*)

BEGUM: Amjad, my son.

AMJAD (*hurriedly hiding his feet*): Yes!

BEGUM: The jewellery that you chose for Saeeda has arrived (*places the boxes in his lap*).

AMJAD (*with child-like enthusiasm, he opens the boxes one by one, looks at the jewellery, bubbling with pleasure*): Very nice . . . very fine . . . very beautiful. . . but not as beautiful as Saeeda . . . Asghari . . . Asghari, come here (*Asghari, standing next to a cypress, comes up and is shown the jewellery*). What do you think?

ASGHARI: You yourself said it is beautiful, but not as beautiful as Dulhan Begum.

AMJAD (*to his mother*): Mother, when will the dresses be delivered?

ASGHARI: By tomorrow.

AMJAD: And that film projector . . . why is it not here yet?

BEGUM: Son, Majid has already ordered it, just give it a couple of days.

AMJAD (*hesitatingly*): Mother!

BEGUM: Yes, son.

AMJAD: We should order a few more things for Saeeda . . . I do not want to see her unhappy even for a minute . . . There should be something new for her every day.

BEGUM: It is all up to you, do what you wish.

AMJAD: Up to me? (*hesitates*) So . . . Mother . . .

BEGUM: Yes?

AMJAD: Send Kamal to the sports store and get every game that they have. Saeeda and Majid will play and I will watch, and please tell him to get a couple that I can play with Saeeda.

BEGUM (*deeply moved, takes Amjad's head in her hands*): My child! (*Amjad starts crying inconsolably. Asghari lowers her eyes and runs into a corner. Begum cries silently.*)

SCENE IV

(*The same room. It is night and very quiet. Stretched out on the bed is Saeeda, her head with its semi-golden hair resting on a heap of pillows. She is reading a book, but her eyes seem resting not so much on her book as her heart. Where the blanket covers her breasts, there are ripples that betray what it covers. To the right is another bed, the kind one finds in hospitals. Amjad sits in his wheelchair, also holding a book as if it were something made of glass. His eyes surveying everything restlessly. From the printed page, they sometimes rest on Saeeda's hands, or on her golden-haired head buried in the pillows. Finally, he puts the book aside and addresses Saeeda in a very low voice.*)

AMJAD: Saeeda.

SAEEDA (*startled*): Yes?

AMJAD: I think you should go to sleep now.

SAEEDA (*turning towards Amjad*): If you want to go to sleep, I will send for Ghulam Mohammad and Karim and they will help put you to bed.

AMJAD (*in an empty voice*): Put me to bed . . . no Saeeda . . . I am tired of lying down . . . I will sleep in my chair today . . . If it is no trouble, could you please put out the bright light and switch on the green one?

SAEEDA (*rises*): Why do you mention my convenience time and again?

AMJAD: Because of the inconvenient state in which I find myself.

SAEEDA (*irritated*): I realize that, Amjad sahib . . . but tell me what can I do for you . . . I am prepared to do whatever I can . . . but the trouble is you are always thinking of my convenience . . . I am in no way inconvenienced.

AMJAD: Saeeda, you're so good.

(*Saeeda switches off the light and for a moment everything goes dark, only to be immediately bathed in faint green light.*)

SAEEDA: I wish I were good . . . could be good (*gets up and sits down in the sofa, her agitated state apparent from her heaving breast*).

AMJAD: You couldn't be better, Saeeda.

SAEEDA (*sharply*): No, you do not know.

AMJAD (*very softly*): If I have annoyed you in any way, please forgive me.

SAEEDA (*looks at Amjad, gets up, smiles and combs his hair with her long, shapely fingers*): The truth, Amjad sahib, is that I am not worthy of you.

AMJAD (*grabs Saeeda's hand*): That is the goodness of your heart if you think so, but the reality is its exact opposite.

SAEEDA (*running her fingers through his hair*): Go to sleep . . . you have been up for so many nights, in fact ever since you came you haven't slept a wink.

AMJAD: I can't sleep, Saeeda.

SAEEDA: Why?

AMJAD: I don't know . . . it just seems that I will never be able to sleep again. I have even forgotten what sleeping at night was like.

SAEEDA: I wish I could gift my sleep to you.

AMJAD: No, Saeeda . . . I can never snatch such a precious thing from you. I want it to always remain resting in your eyes, which look even more beautiful when you are asleep . . . Go to bed now.

SAEEDA: That blasted sleep will come anyway.

AMJAD: Don't say such things . . . May God always keep a benevolent eye on you . . . Go to sleep now.

SAEEDA (*in an irritated voice*): Why are you always so thoughtful and kind to me . . . Amjad Sahib, it really bothers me . . . By God, your soft manner, your self-denial, your humility will one day make me lose my sanity. (*Gets up looking upset, then throws herself on the bed*)

AMJAD: It seems to me that the words I speak are also in a broken state.

(*Saeeda says nothing and turns away from Amjad, who picks up the book from his lap and starts to turn its pages. It is very quiet and because of the faint green glow in the room, it feels even quieter. Nothing breaks that silence for a long while. It is an enervating silence. The green light on Amjad's face resembles the green cloth people place on graves. His eyes leave his book repeatedly to look at Saeeda, only to return to the book in an ecstatic state. Some more time passes. Amjad is very restless now.*)

AMJAD: Saeeda!

SAEEDA: Yes!

AMJAD: I . . . have a request to make.

SAEEDA (*without turning*): What?

AMJAD: Can . . . can this be our first night?

(*Saeeda trembles in her bed*)

AMJAD: That night which has so far not come.

(*Saeeda remains silent*)

AMJAD: Saeeda!

SAEEDA: Yes.

AMJAD: Can you accept my request?

SAEEDA (*turns to look at Amjad, a stricken desire to give herself floating in her eyes*): How, Amjad sahib?

AMJAD: Just pretend . . . only to make me feel good. You should pretend that I am lying next to you . . . and I will pretend that you are lying next to me . . . I will begin to say things to you that I was to say to you on our first night . . . and you answer me as you would have . . . Just for my sake . . . can you play this little game for me, Saeeda?

SAEEDA (*her eyes no longer longing to give herself, but full of tears out of pity*): I am at your service, Amjad sahib.

AMJAD: Thank you.

(*Long pause*)

AMJAD: Tonight is our first night, Saeeda . . . the night when youth takes its first step towards earthly paradise . . . the night into whose mysteries two souls plunge themselves and become one . . . Do not be shy . . . This is the night when all that had remained hidden wishes to be unveiled . . . a faint whisper, a low sigh, a slight touch, a whiff of breath can lift the veil from what had stayed hidden . . . and it all happens so gently, so imperceptibly that it does not even make a sound and one is suddenly permitted, in a flash, to view the full splendour of the vision . . . This is the night when eyes meet eyes and stars cascade from the sky and come to rest on the foreheads of two who have come together . . . this is the night when Adam's body was slashed and his rib given to Eve . . . this is the night that poets wish would never end . . . this is the night the young pray for . . . this is the night when nature itself unravels all the knots that modesty had kept hidden . . . this is the night when the entire workshop of nature is busy in chiselling only one implement . . . the implement that gives life to the entire universe . . . this is the night when all other sounds recede into their receptacles so that the one sound that was heard at the beginning of creation can be heard . . .

this is the night all of whose curtains are made of light . . . this is the night at whose feet lie in supplication all the nights that are yet to come . . . this is the night when every pore in the body speaks and gets to hear all unrevealed secrets, all unsung melodies (*screams*) . . . Cover it . . . cover it . . . Saeeda, cover your body . . . it is like a snake that bites me . . . Each line of this body is like the sharp edge of a sword slashing at my desires . . . cover it . . . for God's sake, cover your body . . . for God's sake, cover your body.

SAEEDA (*lying like a dead body made of soft green blades of grass under the green glow, trembles, each pore in her body trembles*): Yes.

AMJAD (*starts crying inconsolably*): Cover your body. (*Saeeda covers herself with a blanket as Amjad, his hand covering his eyes, continues to sob . . .*)

SCENE V

(*Nigar Villa garden, evening, the fountain playing. The shadows have lengthened and in the background the darkening hills have receded. The sky is ashen and a silence has descended on the grassy lawn. There is an emptiness to the atmosphere, like a frame that awaits the mounting of a picture. Majid and Saeeda are heard laughing. They enter, still laughing, but looking tired. Saeeda drops herself into a chair, while Majid stands next to her.*)

SAEEDA (*drumming her thighs with her fists*): Oh! Oh!

MAJID (*laughs*): You are exhausted. Shall I press your legs?

SAEEDA (*anxiously*): No, no, please send Asghari, I can't even walk two steps.

MAJID (*smiling*): Good . . . (*moves forward to put aside a lock of golden hair from Saeeda's face*)

SAEEDA (*with great anxiety*): I'll go in (*tries to get up*).

MAJID (*turns his head*): There, Asghari has come of her own . . . come Asghari, press bhabijan's feet.

ASGHARI (*the corners of her lips are trembling as if she is desperate to say something*): Dulhan Begum, you look exhausted today.

SAEEDA (*beating her thighs with her fists*): Yes!

ASGHARI (*sits down on the ground and starts pressing one of Saeeda's calves, but her words are addressed to Majid*): It is all Majid sahib's fault. Such a long outing and in such a rush (*her tone suddenly sharp*) . . . Everything should happen at a slow, even pace (*to Saeeda*) . . . right, Dulhan Begum? Do you feel somewhat better now?

SAEEDA (*nervously shaking her free leg, her agitated state of mind quite evident*): Yes, all right, it's all right.

ASGHARI (*to Majid*): Majid sahib, go and wash yourself, your face looks like a dusty, muddy potato.

MAJID (*sharply*): You have become very impertinent . . . it's all . . .

ASGHARI (*interrupting him*): Dulhan Begum's fault, who indulges me (*looks at Saeeda*) and how lovely she is. (*Majid leaves, looking furious*)

ASGHARI (*laughing*): Majid sahib is so good-looking normally but when he is angry, his face gets distorted . . . what do you think?

SAEEDA: Don't say such things to me (*wants to get up but Asghari tightens her grip*), let me go.

ASGHARI (*pressing her legs*): I don't want to be denied this privilege of serving you (*removes Saeeda's sandals*). Majid sahib was saying that I have become impertinent . . . is that so Dulhan Begum?

SAEEDA: Absolutely correct.

ASGHARI (*pressing her feet in utter absorption*): This is very bad . . . a maid must not be impertinent . . . You should box my ears.

SAEEDA: Keep quiet!

ASGHARI: This is not fair . . . It is very unfair to silence someone, Dulhan Begum . . . What have I said to displease you?

SAEEDA (*agitated*): Everything that you say I find unbearable.

ASGHARI: What can poor Asghari do (*after a pause*). . . but I used to think that having been in the service of an educated mistress like you for a year now, I had come to learn all I needed to learn, but it seems I was mistaken. I have learnt nothing from you . . . but whose fault is it? The teacher's or the pupil's?

SAEEDA (*pulling away her legs with an air of finality*): What is it that you want to say?

ASGHARI (*faking surprise*): I?

SAEEDA: Yes, you . . . what do you want to say?

ASGHARI (*thinking*): There is much that I want to say.

SAEEDA (*walking on grass in her bare feet*): Then say it today . . . I do not like the way you taunt me lightly every day . . . Whatever you have to say, I am ready to listen to.

ASGHARI: You have great courage, Dulhan Begum.

SAEEDA: Whether I have courage or whether I am a coward . . . it is not important . . . Spit out whatever you want to say.

ASGHARI: If I spit it out, it would be painful for both you and me.

SAEEDA: Don't you worry about me . . . I can bear it.

ASGHARI (*thinking*): I had thought that you would be afraid after eyeing the sharp dagger that I am holding between my teeth, but it seems you have reached a point where you are not afraid of being wounded . . . I am beginning to be afraid of you.

SAEEDA (*restlessly walking about*): Asghari!

ASGHARI (*startled*): Yes?

SAEEDA: Tell me, if Amjad had died in the train accident, what would I have done?

ASGHARI: You? I don't know what you would have done.

SAEEDA: I am young and beautiful . . . I have a thousand desires in my heart that I have nurtured for seventeen years with the honey of my dreams. I cannot strangle them. I have tried, Asghari . . . my God is my witness, I have tried hard but I have not been able to persuade myself to murder my desires . . . You may call me weak . . . cowardly . . . characterless . . . You are a maid . . . and I am confessing before you that I cannot lay waste the garden of my youth and its leaves and flowers . . . The blood of my virgin youth courses through my veins . . . I cannot permit anyone to close my eyes, place locks on my senses and throw me into the well of old age and widowhood . . . I cannot let myself be pushed down the turbulent rocks of desire. I am standing at the summit fighting off the stormy winds that are trying to blow me off . . . You have my permission to do the same.

ASGHARI (*defeated*): Dulhan Begum, no more.

SAEEDA: I am at a crossroads where the earth ripples under my feet; whichever way I turn, the path moves away from me. Whatever resolution I make, escapes from me. I chase after it blindly, but when I catch up with it, I realize that it is made of sand. The moment I touch it, it falls in a heap at my feet . . . Asghari, you do not know how long I have lain restlessly on this bed of live coal, on which I sprinkle water but it only produces clouds of hissing steam that push me up into high air, shake and toss my body around and then make me fall to the ground . . . each bone in my body is now crushed . . . Asghari, it would have been better if, instead of Amjad, I had become a cripple. (*Long pause. Asghari says nothing. Saeeda keeps walking about restlessly*) What should I do?

ASGHARI (*as if waking up from a trance*): What should you do?

You should wait for Amjad sahib to die.

SAEEDA (*thinking*): You'll call me stone-hearted, but Asghari, I want to know when he is going to die.

ASGHARI: When God so wills (*murmurs*), but Amjad sahib is no longer friends with Him.

SAEEDA: What did you say?

ASGHARI: Nothing at all (*walks away, taking unsteady steps, while Saeeda keeps walking up and down the lawn restlessly*).

SCENE VI

(*Nigar Villa's living room, large and furnished with heavy old-fashioned furniture, the kind that lasts. There are oil paintings of various family members on the wall, including one of Begum as a young woman, under which she sits on a sofa, presenting a contrast between what was and what is. In the painting, she wears a carefree look compared with the worried expression on her face as she sits there knitting. Her thoughts are like spun wool which she unravels only to see them get tangled up again. Enter Asghari.*)

BEGUM: Did you find Majid?

ASGHARI: Yes.

BEGUM: Where was he?

ASGHARI: In the garden.

BEGUM: What was he doing?

ASGHARI: Doing? . . . He was sitting by himself.

BEGUM (*looks at Asghari, then lowers her eyes*): Is he coming?

ASGHARI: Yes.

BEGUM: You may leave now.

ASGHARI: I will. (*She leaves, enter Majid looking at her receding figure*)

MAJID: What is it, Mother?

BEGUM: Nothing . . . sit down.

MAJID (*sits next to her in a chair*): It is cold here.

BEGUM: Yes . . . it is cold here. (*pause*)

MAJID (*feeling ill at ease*): I think you have sent for me to tell something to me.

BEGUM: Yes.

MAJID: Please say it.

BEGUM: I want to send you away from here.

MAJID: Me (*gets up*)? Where?

BEGUM: Sit down.

MAJID (*sits down*): All right.

BEGUM: I have not spoken to Amjad yet.

MAJID (*gets up again*): About what?

BEGUM: My sending you away from here.

MAJID: But why do you want me to leave . . . is it on a special assignment or . . .?

BEGUM: Sit down.

MAJID (*sits down*): Is it something special?

BEGUM: No.

MAJID: Then why is it necessary to send me away?

BEGUM: Because I think that is for the best.

MAJID: Best? Best for whom?

BEGUM: All of us . . . this family.

MAJID (*gets up*): You're talking in riddles, Mother.

BEGUM: Majid, you are my son. I am your mother . . . Nothing should pass between us that can smear, even in the slightest, our sacred relationship. I want you to leave for Karachi today and stay there for as long as I want you to.

MAJID: But, Mother . . .

BEGUM (*cuts him short*): You have many friends there and I am sure that with their help you will be able to get across this vortex called life.

MAJID (*wants to say something but is unable to; he sits down*): Very well . . . I will go.

BEGUM: Your decision . . . (*she stops as Amjad comes into the room, his wheelchair being pushed by Karim*)

AMJAD (*to Majid*): Hey pal! You are a strange character. There I was in my room waiting for you so that we could together think of a present for Saeeda's birthday but I find you sitting here. (*To his mother*) Mother, what have you decided . . . what kind of a present should it be? I just can't think of anything, I simply can't.

BEGUM: Why don't you ask Saeeda?

AMJAD: Listen to that (*laughs*). Mother, come on, if I were to ask her, the element of surprise would be gone, which is the real thing. (*To Majid*) Right, Majid? (*Majid remains silent*)

AMJAD: Say something, pal.

MAJID (*gets up*): Ask mother, I am leaving.

AMJAD (*surprised*): Where are you going?

MAJID: Karachi!

AMJAD: You are out of your mind . . . What are you going to Karachi for?

MAJID: What am I going for (*a faint smile appears on his lips*)? To pull out my boat from the vortex.

AMJAD (*to his mother*): What is the matter with him? (*to Majid*) Sit down, pal, day after is her birthday . . . Let's come to a decision right now.

MAJID: The decision has been made.

AMJAD: What?

MAJID: That I am going to Karachi and I am never going to return.

AMJAD: What rubbish are you talking? (*to his mother*) Mother, what is going on?

BEGUM: Nothing . . . mother and son have had an argument.

AMJAD: About what?

BEGUM: You are not to ask.

AMJAD: I may be defying you but Majid is my brother and if there is anything that has come between you and him, it is my duty to remove it . . . I know Majid better than you do . . . He is incapable of doing anything that can hurt others. (*to Majid*) Come here, Majid.

MAJID: I have to pack.

AMJAD: What the heck! What is all this! (*to his mother*) Mother, for God's sake, stop him, if not for me, then for Saeeda. He is the only one in this house who has kept her from getting depressed. There is so much he puts up with for my sake. If you let him go, mother, I don't know how I would deal with that. He takes Saeeda for walks and I imagine that it is not he who is with her but I. When he plays a game with her, the chasm that nature has so cruelly created in my life somehow feels filled. I sometimes think that if Majid weren't there, the debris that is my life would not be worth dumping even at the lowliest place. Mother, please stop him. He is my arm, why are you separating him from me? Mother, don't play God (*starts to cry*).

MAJID: Mother, I am leaving.

BEGUM: Wait (*Majid stops*)!

BEGUM (*gets up, pats Amjad on the head affectionately*): Son, do not cry . . . Majid won't go . . . everything will remain where it is . . . because that is the way it is fated. (*to Majid*) Majid, sit with your brother and think about Saeeda's birthday (*leaves*).

MAJID (*thinks for a while, then moves towards Amjad's*

wheelchair): Brother, please let me go.

AMJAD (*raises his head*): Where should I let you go? Don't be crazy.

MAJID: You don't understand, brother.

AMJAD: I understand all . . . Take out your handkerchief and wipe my tears. (*Majid pauses, then pulls out his handkerchief and wipes off Amjad's tears, but very quickly*) What are you doing? You don't even know how to wipe off tears (*smiles*), such a simple thing to do.

MAJID: It's not so simple, brother.

AMJAD (*smiling*): All right, it is very, very difficult . . . Come sit by me, let's think of a birthday present for Saeeda. Sit down.

MAJID (*takes a chair next to Amjad*): Think.

AMJAD (*sighs*): I will, brother, that is all one does now, think (*both of them look lost in thought*).

SCENE VII

(*Nigar Villa garden, evening, the fountain is no longer playing, as if it had got tired. In the background, the hills appear to be trying to hide their petrified bodies in the dark. The grass looks trampled upon. To the right of the fountain, behind thick bushes, sits Amjad in his wheelchair, which Asghari begins to push.*)

AMJAD: No, Asghari, wait. . .

ASGHARI (*stops*): But, Amjad sahib . . .

AMJAD: I want to suffer the last injury of my life today.

ASGHARI: If you must suffer that injury, suffer it in your imagination . . . but you have already suffered your injury . . . Why do you want to reopen that wound?

AMJAD (*trying to smile*): Someone in my condition is foolish beyond imagination . . . he wants to undo the stitches of his wounds . . . considers himself a great martyr (*laughs*). Asghari, you have never had something of yours broken, so you do not know what people go through, how lying in the pit of misery, completely humbled and broken, they try to raise sky-high structures in their imagination.

ASGHARI (*smiles*): I have gone beyond those limits, Amjad sahib. The high structures I once raised, I have since brought down with my own hands. I have reached a point where my heart is nothing but a hollow pit.

AMJAD (*trembles*): Asghari . . . you are terrifying.

ASGHARI (*laughs*): Every wilderness is terrifying . . . but what terror can I hold for anyone, I, whose time is taken up with bewailing my own fate. How can I terrify others when I myself live in a state of fear and foreboding!

AMJAD: Did your life suffer an accident?

ASGHARI: No . . . what accident need I meet, being an accident myself?

AMJAD: I smell burnt flesh from your words.

ASGHARI: It is only that your sense of smell is aroused.

AMJAD: Was it asleep before?

ASGHARI: Yes, in deep sleep.

AMJAD: Who woke it up?

ASGHARI: The train that got derailed.

AMJAD (*murmurs*): The train . . . that got derailed (*in a louder voice*) . . . Will it again get derailed?

ASGHARI: What God wills will happen.

AMJAD: Don't name Him . . . My friendship with Him has ended.

ASGHARI: No, Amjad sahib, people like us never end our friendship with Him. It snaps only to get whole again and again.

AMJAD: That's all rubbish. (*They are startled as they hear footsteps. Majid and Saeeda appear, both quite breathless. Saeeda, who looks very tired, sits down on one side of the fountain.*)

SAEEDA: I am exhausted today.

MAJID: Although we didn't venture out too far.

SAEEDA: Yes.

MAJID: It would have been good had I gone to Karachi.

SAEEDA: It would have been good.

MAJID: I am in a dilemma. Say I had gone to Karachi, the question is: would I have been able to pull my boat out of this vortex? No . . . I would have certainly failed.

SAEEDA: I know.

MAJID: You know . . . I know . . . except my brother, everyone knows, which is the most tragic aspect of this story.

SAEEDA: I have thought many times of telling him (*gets up*) but I am afraid he would not be able to bear the shock.

MAJID: That is what I am also afraid of . . . The doctors have said that he is not going to live beyond a year . . . it would be cruel to snatch away from him what life he is left with.

(*Amjad clenches his teeth as Asghari tightens his grip on his shoulder.*)

SAEEDA: It should always be the effort to keep him happy as long as he is alive. His sentiments must not be hurt, even in the slightest way.

MAJID: And if in the meanwhile, our bubble were to burst?

SAEEDA (*almost screaming*): That would be a disaster.

MAJID: Which is why I think I should go . . . for as long as my brother . . .

SAEEDA (*interrupting him*): Don't say that, Majid . . . don't be so cruel.

(*Amjad trembles in his wheelchair. Asghari places her hand on his other shoulder too.*)

MAJID: Love is cruel and selfish, Saeeda . . . not even ashamed of rejoicing over the death of others.

SAEEDA: We must not think such thoughts.

MAJID: That's right, but if they come to one's mind, what can one do!

(*Saeeda starts walking towards the house, Majid follows her, taking slow steps . . . behind the bushes, Amjad sits in his wheelchair, head down, with Asghari standing behind him like a statue.*)

ASGHARI: Should we go?

AMJAD (*head still bent*): No . . . not yet . . . I am thinking.

ASGHARI: What?

AMJAD: I don't know . . . perhaps I am thinking what I should think.

ASGHARI: Such thoughts are useless.

AMJAD (*raising his head*): Useless, yes, but then what can I do. (*after a pause*) They are not as cruel as you . . . You even forbid me to think . . . you are very cruel, Asghari.

ASGHARI (*smiles*): Love is cruel and selfish, Amjad sahib . . . It even rejoices over its own death.

AMJAD: Come in front of me.

(*Asghari comes in front of him; Amjad looks into her eyes, thinks, then murmurs something.*)

AMJAD: Where had this book been lying all this while?

ASGHARI: In the trash bin . . . where it belongs.

AMJAD: Let's go, take me away.

(*Asghari pulls his chair towards the house.*)

SCENE VIII

(*The same room as seen in Scenes II and IV, night; the room is bathed in a green light, everything appears to have changed, the atmosphere akin to that of a psychotic patients' ward; the bed is empty, as if nobody has ever slept in it. Asghari enters, rolling Amjad's wheelchair.*)

ASGHARI: Why has Dulhan Begum gone into Begum sahib's room?

AMJAD: She was afraid.

ASGHARI: Of you?

AMJAD (*smiling*): Who will be afraid of me? She was afraid of herself.

ASGHARI: She is not that weak, Amjad sahib.

AMJAD: Time can wear down a mountain . . . she is only a young woman.

ASGHARI (*after a pause*): Would you like to sleep?

AMJAD: Sleep? (*laughs*) Don't make fun of me Asghari . . . Don't laugh at my burning wounds.

ASGHARI (*hesitates*): Are you in love with Saeeda?

AMJAD: No.

ASGHARI: Then what are these burning wounds?

AMJAD: Let me think . . . will you permit me to think?

ASGHARI: You may think (*Amjad is lost in thought for a long time*).

AMJAD: I am not in love with Saeeda . . . as one picks out a good thing from the market, I chose her out of hundreds of girls as my wife . . . I was proud of my choice, still am, because Saeeda is beautiful beyond words . . . My only claim on her is that I chose her and made her my companion for life, a life that now lies crippled in this chair which cannot move without someone's help . . . The doctors have given me at best a year to live . . . I don't understand why I want to keep her in chains, each component of which is as undependable as my life . . . I am not sure what I should do (*thinks*). It can be only her youth and beauty that make me want to keep her; (*in a startled voice*) that is the only reason, none other (*feels the pain of what he is saying*). Oh! Oh! the sight of her, how can I ever forget that . . . that sight, she lying in this bed in the full splendour of her beauty, so beautiful that no finery in the world could be worthy of her . . . That is the sight that keeps me glued to her . . . or I to it (*after a pause*), Asghari?

ASGHARI (*startled*): Yes!

AMJAD: Can there be some way of banishing this vision from my consciousness?

ASGHARI: The key to every difficulty lies in the difficulty itself.

AMJAD: Then it should be looked for . . . but . . . but why do I feel shy?

ASGHARI: Don't know why . . . this difficulty lies nowhere but with you, so if you want to remove it, the hand with which you banish it, will be your hand, no one else's.

AMJAD: I know . . . I am fully conscious of my rebellious heart that beats in rhythm with an emotion which is false . . . but today is the day when a decision will be made.

ASGHARI: What decision?

AMJAD: Come in front of me (*she does so*). Now go and lie in that bed.

ASGHARI (*hesitant*): Amjad sahib, I do not have that beauty or that youth that can render the world's most precious finery unworthy of me . . . My youth is worthy of nothing better than a rough jute mat.

AMJAD: Go lie in that bed.

ASGHARI (*tears welling up in her eyes*): No, Amjad sahib, it will be unfair to that bed . . . it is used to the soft and delicate body of Dulhan Begum.

AMJAD: I order you.

ASGHARI (*lowers her head*): You are the master (*goes and lies down in the bed, her eyes glued to the ceiling*).

AMJAD: Do you know what night this is? This is the night when a shattered and disfigured youth will become whole. This is an awesome night, a night of artistry, when the soul will find immortality by melting into this night's dark and eternal crucibles. This is the night that will be followed by no more nights. Its blind eyes will be lit with dark and everlasting antimony. This is the night when grand edifices will rise from the womb of shattered dreams, such proud and magnificent edifices that they will touch the highest reaches of the sky. This is the night when the waters of the sacred spring of Zam Zam will crawl away into the recesses of the earth and where there was water, dust will rise, dust that the purest of souls will perform their ablutions with. This is the night when He who writes in the book of fate will overturn the inkpot in which He dips his pen to write and find some corner of the sky where He can hide and weep. This is the night on which Amjad pronounces three divorces on all the beauties of the world and weds an ugliness (*screams*), Asghari . . . Asghari . . . (*Asghari has in the meanwhile left her bed, walked up to the window and thrown them open. She stands on the sill, staring down at the depths.*)

AMJAD (*screams*): What are you doing, Asghari?

ASGHARI (*looks at Amjad from where she is standing on the window sill*): My master, there must be an exchange of vows (*leaps out*).

Amjad (*covering both his eyes with his hands*): Asghari! (*uncovers his eyes and stares at the dark towards the open window which is like a black gaping wound*) Exchange of vows (*murmurs*), yes, there must be an exchange of vows (*with great difficulty drags his wheelchair forward and finally manages to reach the window*). I did not know this was how the difficulty would be resolved . . . I needed someone to hold my hand (*grabs hold of the window sill with both hands firmly and with a great effort lifts his paralysed body up and swings it over*). My hills, my lovely hills, my lovely Asghari (*he slides across and then his entire body is swallowed up by the dark*).

(*Curtain*)

SKETCHES

A SWEET MOMENT

XXX . . . XXX . . . Reports are coming in of sweets having been distributed in the Indian cities of Amritsar, Gwalior and Bombay to celebrate the death of Mahatma Gandhi . . . x x x . . . x x x

WAGES

There was looting and rioting everywhere and to them had now been added widespread arson.

Quite unmindful of it all, a man was waltzing down the street, a harmonium strung around his neck, and a popular song on his lips:

She went away to a far land
Breaking my heart
Never again will I love another,
Never again . . .

A young boy went running by, cradling dozens of packets of papads in his arms. He tripped slightly and dropped one packet. As he stooped to try and pick it up, an older man with an obviously stolen sewing machine on his head said, 'Why bother to do that son? The road is so hot that your papads will soon turn to a crisp.'

A gunnybag landed on the street with a thud. A man stepped forward and slashed it open with his big hunting knife, expecting perhaps to find a bleeding fugitive inside, but what came cascading out was sugar: white, fine-grained sugar. Soon a crowd gathered and people began to help themselves to the unexpected prize. One man in the crowd was only wearing a length of cloth loosely wrapped around his middle. As if it was the most normal thing to do, he freed himself of it and, standing stark naked, began to throw fistfuls of sugar into what was now a makeshift carrier-bag.

'Make way, make way, look out, look out.' It was a tonga, loaded with gleaming furniture made of fine wood.

From the top-floor window of a house overlooking the street, someone threw down a rolled length of muslin, but on its way down it was licked by flames leaping out of a lower-storey window, and by the time it hit the ground it was nothing but a handful of ash.

They finally managed to haul the big steel safe out of the house and although there were many of them, all armed with sticks, they just could not get it to open.

One man stepped out of a shop carrying several tins of Cow & Gate dry milk. No one paid any attention to him as he disappeared down the street, taking slow, careful steps.

'Come on, boys, treat yourself to cool lemonade. It is summer time,' came the loud invitation. One man with a car tyre around his neck picked up two bottles and walked off without even saying thank you.

Someone screamed, 'Send for the fire brigade; otherwise all these precious goods will be lost to the flames.' However, no attention whatsoever was paid to this eminently sensible suggestion.

And so it went on all day with the heat from the sun and the many fires blazing in all directions becoming almost unbearable. Suddenly, there was a sound of gunfire. By the time the police appeared, the street was quite deserted . . . except for a receding human figure at the other end moving very fast. The policemen, furiously blowing their whistles, ran towards what looked like an apparition appearing and disappearing through the haze and the smoke. And then he was in the clear, a Kashmiri seasonal labourer, one of thousands who came to the plains in search of daily work. There was a big gunnybag on his back. The policemen began to blow their whistles even more furiously but he did not stop. He was running as if what he was carrying on his back was no heavier than a feather.

The policemen began to tire. Even their whistles seemed to have gone hoarse. In exasperation, one of them pulled out his revolver and fired, hitting the Kashmiri labourer in the leg. The gunnybag fell off his back. He stopped, saw blood gushing out of the wound, but paid no attention to it. Picking up the gunnybag with one mighty heave, he broke into a sprint.

'Let him go to hell,' the policemen said, but just then he staggered and fell to the ground in a heap, with the gunnybag resting on top of him.

The policemen took both the man and the gunnybag to the station. On the way, several times, he tried to soften the hearts of his captors but to no avail. 'Exalted sirs, why you catch this poor fellow? All he take is one little bag of rice. Brave ones, why you shoot down this poor man when all he done . . .'

At the station, he made many efforts to present his case. 'Exalted sirs, other people steal big things. All poor me take is one bag of rice. Me very poor man, just eat rice . . .'

Ultimately, he gave up. Wiping his brow with his dirty skullcap, he looked at the bag of rice longingly and, spreading both his hands in supplication before the police inspector, said, 'All right, exalted sir, you keep the rice, all poor me ask is my wages for carrying this bag . . . just four annas.'

COOPERATION

A crowd, forty or fifty strong, armed with sticks, advanced determinedly towards the big residential house. Its intention was quite obvious: looting.

Suddenly, a slim, middle-aged man emerged from the midst of the throng, pushed everyone aside, waved his arms high over his head as politicians do and began to speak. 'Brothers,' he said, very much in the style of a populist leader, 'there is great wealth in this house, much that is precious. Let's take it all and then divide it equally among ourselves.'

Sticks waved in the air, clenched fists bobbed up and down and loud slogans greeted the suggestion.

The crowd led by the slim, middle-aged man began to close in on the house, which was said to contain immense wealth.

As they came to the front door, the slim man spoke again. 'Brothers, whatever is in there belongs to you; that being so, there is no need to be impatient, no need to get into fights over who should take what. Let's go!'

'But there is a lock on that door,' someone shouted.

'Pull down the door, yes pull it down,' several of the men screamed.

Sticks waved in the air, clenched fists bobbed up and down and loud slogans greeted the suggestion.

The slim man, a faint smile playing on his lips, gestured to the rioters to stay calm. 'Brothers, I am going to unlock this door with the help of a key.'

Then, from his pocket, he produced a bunch of keys, carefully selected one and slipped it into the lock, which gave way. As the heavy wooden door swung back on its hinges, the crowd went mad with excitement.

The slim man wiped his brow with his sleeve and said, 'Brothers, go easy. As everything in there belongs to you, is there any point in getting agitated?'

This had an immediate calming effect on the rioters, who could be seen entering through the main door in an orderly fashion, almost queuing. However, once they were all inside, they turned unruly, ruthless and greedy.

In a voice full of pain, the slim man spoke again. 'Brothers, we should be gentle. There is absolutely no need to fight one another or snatch what the next one is holding. Let's work in a spirit of cooperation. If you see one of you with an object of value, don't envy him. This is a large house, and surely all of you can find something equally valuable. But let's not act like savages; otherwise you will only end up breaking what belongs to you. It will be your loss.'

Discipline returned to the crowd once again. The house began to be emptied of its contents slowly and methodically.

Occasionally, the slim man would offer advice.

'Look, my friend, lift that radio gently or you might damage it. Yes, don't leave the antenna behind.'

'This is a walnut table with ivory inlay work. It folds nicely . . . like this.'

'No, no, don't drink here; it may go to your head. Take the bottle with you.'

'Watch out, let me switch the mains off or you could get a bad shock.'

There was a scuffle in one room, with four of the looters quarrelling over a rolled length of silk. This time there was almost admonition in the slim man's voice. 'You will only end up tearing it to shreds. I am sure there is a tape measure in this house somewhere and a pair of scissors. Let's look for them, measure the cloth and then cut it into four equal parts.'

Suddenly, there was the sound of a dog barking and then like a flash of lightning a big Alsatian leapt into the room. He pounced on three or four of the intruders, pinning them to the floor.

'Tiger, Tiger!' the slim man screamed.

Tiger, who was about to go for the windpipe of one of the terrified men, immediately let go of him and, tail between his legs, eyes to the floor, went to the slim man.

Everyone had run away, except the man whom Tiger had been about to savage.

The solitary intruder looked at the slim man. 'Who are you?'

'I own this house.' He smiled. 'But watch out or you will drop that crystal vase. It seems to be slipping out of your fingers.'

DIVISION

He chose the largest of the wooden chests for himself, but no matter how hard he tried, he couldn't move it.

Another man, who had been unable to find anything worthwhile to take, came up to him. 'Do you need help?'

He said yes and the volunteer picked up the deadweight with his strong hands and with one mighty heave placed it on his broad back.

However, the weight was so crippling that the volunteer felt, as they took to the street, that his back would break or his legs would give way. What kept him going was the expectation of reward.

The man who had spotted the chest was not in a very good physical shape; however, in order to assert his ownership, he kept one hand firmly on the prize as they slowly moved towards a safe spot.

Once they were there and the chest had been safely placed on the ground, the man who had done all the hard work said, 'I want to know what my share is.'

'One-fourth,' came the reply.

'That's not enough!'

'No? But remember it was I who found it.'

'Yes, but it was I who brought it all the way here on my back.'

'What about fifty-fifty?'

'That's a deal. Let's see what is inside.'

What came out was a man with a sword, with which he immediately subdivided the two shareholders into four.

PROPER USE

After firing ten rounds and killing three men, the Pathan felt that he too had joined the band of the brave.

There was utter pandemonium. People were running helter-skelter. Some were engaged in looting, some in killing. The Pathan, his gun held proudly in one hand, joined the fray and after wrestling about for an hour or so, managed to win a prize—a thermos flask.

When the police arrived, everyone ran, including the Pathan.

He narrowly escaped being shot through the head, but he did not let go of the red flask.

With much pride, he showed his friends the great prize, at which one among them smiled. 'Khan sahib, what have you got there?'

With loving eyes, the Pathan looked at the shimmering lid of the flask. 'Why?' he asked.

'Don't you know what this is? A special bottle which keeps cold things cold and warm things warm.'

Tucking the flask in his big pocket, the Pathan said, 'Good, it will do nicely. Keep my snuff cold in winter, warm in summer.'

THE BENEFITS OF IGNORANCE

The trigger was pressed and the bullet spun out ill-tempered.

The man leaning through the window doubled over without making a sound.

The trigger was pressed a second time. The bullet swished through the air, puncturing the water-carrier's goatskin. He fell on his face and his blood, mixing with the water, began to flow across the road.

The trigger was pressed a third time. The bullet missed, embedding itself into a mud wall.

The fourth felled an old woman. She did not even scream.

The fifth and sixth were wasted. Nobody got killed and nobody got wounded.

The marksman looked frustrated, when suddenly a running child appeared on the road. He raised his gun and took aim.

'What are you doing?' his companion asked.

'Why?'

'You are out of bullets.'

'You keep quiet. How does a little child know?'

FOR NECESSARY ACTION

When the attack came, some members of the minority community in the neighbourhood were killed, while the survivors ran off. One man and his wife, however, hid themselves in the basement of their house.

For two nights they were cooped up there, expecting to be discovered any moment.

Two more nights went by and the fear of death began to recede, replaced by pangs of hunger.

Four more nights passed, but by now they had reached a point where they did not really care whether they lived or died. They came out of their hideout.

In a voice which could be barely heard, the man said to the new occupants of his house, 'We give ourselves up. Please kill us.'

'Our religion forbids us to kill,' they answered.

They were Jains, but after mutual consultations, the fugitive couple was handed over to residents of a neighbouring locality 'for necessary action'.

MIRACLE MAN

Homes were being raided by the police to recover looted goods.

Out of fear, people started to chuck their 'hot cargo' out of their windows after nightfall. There were some whose keenness to stay out of the law's mischief was so great that they even got rid of legitimately acquired goods.

One man, however, had a problem. He had two large sacks of sugar in his house, which he had helped himself to when the local grocery story was ransacked. One night, he managed to drag them to the neighbourhood well. One he pushed down the shaft quite easily, but fell in himself with the second.

His screams woke up everyone. Ropes were lowered but to no avail. Finally, two youths went down and pulled him out, but he died a few hours later.

The next morning when people drew out their drinking water from the well, it was found to be sweet.

That night, there were prayer lamps illuminating the miracle man's grave.

JELLY

At six in the morning, the man who used to sell ice from a pushcart next to the service station was stabbed to death. His body lay on the road, while water kept falling on it in steady driblets from the melting ice.

At a quarter past seven, the police took him away. The ice and blood stayed on the road.

A mother and child rode past the spot in a tonga. The child noticed the coagulated blood on the road, tugged at his mother's sleeve and said, 'Look, mummy, jelly.'

INVITATION TO ACTION

When the neighbourhood was set on fire, everything burnt down with the exception of one shop and its sign.

It said, 'All building and construction materials sold here.'

PATHANISTAN

'Hey, you there, speak at once, who're you?'

'I . . . I . . . !'

'You offshoot of the devil, at once . . . are you Indoo or Musalmeen?'

'Musalmeen.'

'Who is your Prophet?'

'Mohammad Khan.'

'OK, let him go.'

WARNING

After a great deal of struggle, the owner of the house was dragged out and kicked to the ground.

But he got up immediately, dusted off his clothes with great dignity and wagging a finger at the rioters said, 'You can kill me, but I am warning you, don't you dare touch my money!'

PERMANENT VACATION

'Catch him, catch him, don't let him get away!'

After a brief chase, the quarry was overtaken and was about to be lanced to death when he said in a tremulous voice, 'Please don't kill me, don't kill me please . . . you see I am going home on vacation.'

THE GARLAND

The rampaging mob suddenly changed direction, its wrath now directed at the statue of Sir Ganga Ram. Sticks were swung through the air; bricks and stones were put to liberal use. One man smeared the statue's face with coal tar. Another strung together a garland of shoes and was about to place it around the statue's neck when the police arrived, guns blazing.

The man with the garland of shoes was shot, then taken to be bandaged at Sir Ganga Ram Hospital.

OUT OF CONSIDERATION

'Don't kill my daughter in front of my eyes.'

'All right, all right. Peel off her clothes and shoo her aside!'

DUE SUPERVISION

Introducing his friend as one belonging to the same religion, A was able to get B a ride with a convoy, which was being moved to safety under military escort.

During the trip, B, whose religion had been changed for the sake of safety, asked the soldiers, 'Have any incidents taken place in this area of late?'

'Nothing much,' the soldiers answered, 'except that a mongrel was gunned down in a nearby neighbourhood the other day.'

Terrified, B asked, 'Anything else?'

'No, only three dead bitches were found floating in the canal.'

'Doesn't the military do anything about it?' A asked the soldiers, hoping to reassure B.

'But of course, everything is done under its due supervision.'

DETERMINATION

'Under no circumstances am I prepared to be converted to a Sikh. I want my razor back.'

MODESTY

The rioters brought the train to a stop. Those who belonged to the other religion were methodically picked out and slaughtered. After it was all over, those who remained were treated to a feast of milk, custard pies and fresh fruit.

Before the train moved off, the leader of the hosts addressed the passengers: 'Brothers and sisters, since we were informed late of your train's arrival time, we were not able to offer you the kind of hospitality we would have wished.'

THE FOOL

Commenting on his suicide, a friend of his said, 'What a fool! I kept arguing with him that if his beard had been shaved off and his long hair scissored, it did not mean he had lost his religion. Daily use of yogurt and the benediction of the Guru will return him to the shape he was in.'

BESTIALITY

With great difficulty, the husband and wife managed to get away with a few household valuables. The teenage daughter was nowhere to be found. The baby girl, however, the mother kept close to her breast. The brown buffalo they had was taken away by the rioters. The cow was still with them, but her calf had gone missing.

All four—the husband, the wife, the baby girl and the cow—were now in safe hiding. It was very dark. When the little girl began to cry because she was afraid, it was like bongo drums in the night's stillness. The terrified mother covered the baby's mouth with her hand, and for additional protection, the father threw a thick sheet over her.

A few minutes passed. Suddenly, a calf mooed in the near distance. The cow heard him, jumped up, answered the call loudly and began to run around in circles as if she were demented. They tried hard to calm her down but in vain.

The noise alerted their pursuers. In the distance, they could see the glow of hand-held torches.

'Why did you drag this beast along?' the woman asked her husband angrily.

LOSING PROPOSITION

The two friends finally picked out a girl from the dozen or so they had been shown. She cost forty-two rupees and they brought her to their place.

After spending the night with her, one of them asked her, 'What is your name?'

When she told him, he was taken aback. 'But we were told you were the other religion.'

'They lied,' she replied.

'The bastards cheated us!' he screamed as he ran to his friend, 'selling us a girl from our own faith. Let's go and return her!'

RITUALISTIC DIFFERENCE

'I placed my knife across his windpipe and, slowly, very slowly, I slaughtered him.'

'And why did you do that?'

'What do you mean why?'

'Why did you kill him the halal way?'

'Because I enjoy doing it that way.'

'You idiot, you should have chopped his neck off with one single blow. Like this.'

And the halal killer was dispatched in accordance with the correct ritual.

MISHTAKE

Ripping the belly cleanly, the knife moved in a straight line down the midriff, in the process slashing the cord, which held the man's pyjamas in place.

The one with the knife took one look and exclaimed regretfully, 'Tut tut tut! . . . Mishtake.'

TIDINESS

The train was stationary.

Three gunmen appeared on the platform. 'Any turkey in there?' they asked the passengers.

'None,' they replied. One passenger was about to say something but then changed his mind.

A few minutes passed. Suddenly four men holding lances stuck their heads through the windows of the carriage. 'Any turkey in there?' they asked.

The man who had decided to keep quiet the last time spoke now. 'I don't know. Perhaps you could check out the lavatory.'

The men stepped in, broke down the lavatory door and came out with a 'turkey'.

'Slash his throat,' suggested one of the men holding the lances.

'No, no, not here!' said his friend. 'It'll mess up the carriage. Take him out.'

GOD IS GREAT

The evening finally came to an end and the singing girl's clients left one by one.

The old man in charge of the arrangements, said, 'We came here after having lost everything on the other side, but Allah has showered us with all these riches in a few days.'

SOCIALISM

He loaded all his belongings on to a truck and was driving to another town when he was waylaid by a mob. Eyeing the goods greedily, one man said to the other, 'Just look at all that booty he is decamping with.'

The owner smiled proudly. 'What you see there is my personal property.'

Two or three men laughed. 'We know it all.'

One man yelled, 'Don't let this rich man get away. He is a robber with a truck.'

DOUBLE CROSS

'Look, this is hardly fair. You sold me impure petrol at black-market prices and not even one shop could be put to the torch.'

RESTING TIME

'He is not dead. There is still some life left in him.'

'O leave it, my friend, I am exhausted.'

LUCK

'That is rotten luck, my friend. After so much hard work, all I was able to get was this box . . . and all it contained was pork.'

UNGRATEFUL LOT

'What sort of people are we! After all the trouble I took to slaughter fifty pigs in this mosque, what happens! Not a single customer! And there on the other side, people queuing up to buy beef? Here no one wants to buy swine flesh.'

PRECAUTIONARY ARRANGEMENT

The first incident took place in front of the hotel in the corner. A sentry was immediately put on duty there.

The second incident happened the next evening, not too far from the general store. The sentry was moved to the site of the new occurrence.

The third incident took place at midnight in front of the laundry.

The sentry was ordered to stand guard at the new spot. 'Please post me where the next incident is going to take place,' he suggested.

MISTAKE REMOVED

'Who are you?'

'And who are you?'

'Har Har Mahadev, Har Har Mahadev!'

'Har Har Mahadev!'

'What is the evidence that you are who you say you are?'

'Evidence? My name is Dharam Chand.'

'That is no evidence.'

'All right, I know all the four Vedas by heart, test me out.'

'We know nothing about the Vedas. We want evidence.'

'What?'

'Lower your trousers.'

When his trousers were lowered, there was pandemonium. 'Kill him, kill him.'

'Wait, please wait . . . I am your brother . . . I swear by Bhagwan, I am your brother.'

'Then what is this?'

'The area through which I had to pass was controlled by our enemies; therefore, I had to take this precaution . . . just to save my life . . . this is the only mistake, the rest is in order.'

'Remove the mistake.'

The mistake was removed . . . and with it Dharam Chand.

PORTRAITS

JINNAH SAHIB

'The year was 1937. The Muslim League was young—and so was I. I was at an age when you want to do something . . . anything. I was well built and strong, always ready to take on whatever came my way. I was rearing to go. I would have even wanted to fashion a creature with my own hands and then go for him in a no-holds-barred physical fight. Such is youth. You are perpetually restless because you want to do things, hoping they will be big things. You simply cannot sit still.'

This was Mohammad Hanif Azad the film actor, a name familiar to most people. Before the partition of the country, he used to be in the movies in Bombay. He has since lived in Lahore, where, like the rest of his fellow actors, he has been struggling to survive, such being the state of the industry in Pakistan. Someone once told me that he had been Quaid-e-Azam Muhammad Ali Jinnah's chauffeur for many years. I was keen to know if it was true and had sought him out one day. I was to hold many more meetings with him to help him relive the old days. But let Azad speak himself.

'Like Ghalib had once been young, so was I. I do not know if the great poet ever found himself sucked into a political movement, but I can tell you that I was a committed worker of the All India Muslim League. I was a sincere member of the Ghaziabad Corps, as were many other young people like me. I say sincere because sincerity was all I had.

'I recall clearly when Muhammad Ali Jinnah came to Delhi and was taken out in a procession the like of which had not been seen before. We, the youth of Ghaziabad, had played no small part in making the event a great success. Our corps was led by Anwar Qureshi, a strapping young man, who was later known as the poet of Pakistan. He had written a special poem for the occasion, which we were all singing in chorus as we marched. I do not know if we were offbeat, but singing we were and very lustily too. We couldn't care less if the notes that left our throats were right or wrong. Remember what Ghalib said: "It does not matter how you say it nor if what you say is in or out of rhythm. The important thing is to say it." Our historic procession set out from Delhi's historic Jamia Mosque with sky-renting slogans and wound its way to the Muslim League office through Chandni Chowk, Lal Kunwan, Hauz Qazi and Chowri Bazaar.

'It was during this procession, I think, that Muhammad Ali Jinnah was spontaneously given the title of Quaid-e-Azam—the Great Leader. He was in a phaeton drawn by six horses, and every leading Muslim League leader marched that day with us. There were men on cycles, motorbikes and even camel carts. It was all very disciplined, which seemed to please our leader greatly, since he was a strict believer in discipline.

'My response to that procession was deeply emotional. I was completely overwhelmed. I do not even remember now what exactly I felt when I first set eyes on Jinnah sahib. When I look back and analyse my reaction, I realize that I was so taken with him, even before I had seen him, that if someone had pointed at a man, any man, and said to me, "There goes your Quaid-e-Azam," I would have believed him immediately and felt deliriously happy. That's the way faith is. Pure and without the slightest trace of doubt. As our procession wound its way through the streets of old Delhi, I got a chance to look at Jinnah sahib from many angles. Then suddenly a thought came to my mind. How could my Quaid, my Great Leader, be so gaunt, so weak, so frail!

'Ghalib had once marvelled at his beloved actually coming to visit him. In wonder, the poet had gazed at her and then at the home, which she had graced. I felt more or less the same way. I would look at the Quaid's fragile figure and then at my strong and well-built body and wish that I would either shrink or become like him or have him become like me. I also had prayed that he be safe from those who wished him ill, and it was said there were many such.

'Life moved on, and it so happened that this deep and hidden urge I have always had to do something artistic now began to add to my restlessness. One day, therefore, I decided to travel to Bombay and try my luck in that city. I was always inclined towards drama and acting. So here I was, no longer smitten with the desire to serve the nation so much as to become an actor. What a bundle of contradictions a human being is! When I arrived in Bombay, the Imperial Film Company ruled the roost, but it was next to impossible to get into it. But I persisted and finally managed to get a foot in as an extra on a daily wage of eight annas. That did not stop me from dreaming about becoming a great star of the silver screen. I am gregarious by nature. I may not have a sweet tongue but I am not that bad a talker either. Urdu, my mother tongue—something with which all the great stars of the company were unfamiliar—came to my rescue, ironically in Bombay where it was not spoken and not in Delhi where it was. Since the language of the movies was Urdu or Hindustani, I was always in demand to read and write the lines the actors were required to speak. I would also read their fan mail for them and write the replies. However, this reading and writing did not help me in my ambition. Extra I was and extra I remained.

'It was during those days that I became friends with the personal chauffeur—a man named Buddhan—of the owner of the Imperial Film Company, Seth Ardeshir Irani. The first thing he did for me was to teach me how to drive. This he would do during his spare hours, which were not many. He was always afraid that if the seth found out what he was doing he might be laid off. Because of this constraint, and despite my intelligence and enthusiasm, I did not quite master the art of motor driving. All I could manage was drive Seth Ardeshir Irani's Buick on the arrow-straight roads of Bombay whenever I had the opportunity. As to what made a car move or what its body parts were, I knew absolutely nothing.

'I was obsessed with acting, but that was in my head. My heart was still filled with the love of the Muslim League and its moving spirit, Quaid-e-Azam Muhammad Ali Jinnah. One talked endlessly of the treatment meted out to the Muslims by the Congress, whether while whiling away time at the Imperial Film Company or loafing around Kennedy Bridge, Bhindi Bazaar, Muhammad Ali Road or the Playhouse. Everyone knew at Imperial that I was an ardent Muslim League supporter and a follower of Quaid-e-Azam Muhammad Ali Jinnah. In those days a Hindu did not become your enemy just because you liked the Quaid-e-Azam. The formal demand for Pakistan had yet to be made. Not everyone at the Imperial Company perhaps knew about the Quaid. Some might have thought when I praised him that I was referring to a movie actor whose fan I was. One day, the most celebrated hero of those days, D. Billimoria, passed on a copy of the *Times of India* to me and said, "Look, here is your Jinnah sahib." I thought it was a picture of his which had appeared that day, but when I found nothing on any of the pages, I asked, "But where is his picture then?" Billimoria, who sported a John Gilbert moustache, smiled and said, "There is no photo-voto but an ad." "What kind of an ad?" I asked. Billimoria took the paper away from me and pointed at a column. "Mr Jinnah wants a motor mechanic who should take charge of his garage and all the cars in it." I looked at the spot which Billimoria had touched with his forefinger and said, "Oh!" as if I had read every word instantaneously, though the fact was that I knew about as much English as Billimoria did Urdu.

'As I have already said, my driving prowess consisted of the ability to get the car moving, provided the road was straight like an arrow. I was quite ignorant about how cars worked. All I knew was that when you pressed the self-starter the engine caught. Sometimes it failed to do so, but if someone had asked me why, I would have replied that it was all part of the immutable laws of motor driving, which the human mind could not fathom. I asked Billimoria what address the ad carried and memorized it. Next morning, I decided to go to the Quaid-e-Azam's house, not to get the job but to get a chance to see him again. The only diploma I had under my arm was my devotion to the Quaid. I arrived at his residence on Mount Pleasant Road, Malabar Hill. There was a Pathan security guard outside the magnificent bungalow, wearing a spotless, generously cut white shalwar and a huge silk turban, tied just right. I was delighted. Here was another well-built man. Mentally, I tried to compare myself with him and was satisfied that the difference, if any, was marginal.

'There were quite a few hopefuls there already, and each of them had certificates and diplomas testifying to his suitability for the position. I joined them quietly. I might add that I did not even possess a driving licence. All I was waiting for was to take one more look at the Quaid-e-Azam. I was hoping he would appear any moment now. Then suddenly there he was on the porch. Everyone came to attention, while I slunk to one side. Next to him stood his tall and graceful sister, Fatima, whose pictures I had often seen in newspapers and magazines. Standing a few steps away at a respectful distance from the Quaid was his secretary Matloob sahib [Matloob Hussain Syed].

'The Quaid adjusted his monocle and scrutinized each candidate carefully. His monocled eye came to rest on me. I shrank even more. Then I heard his penetrating voice: "You . . ." That much English I understood, but who was "you"? I was sure it was the man standing next to me, so I nudged him. "He has called for you." My companion stammered, "Sahib, I?" The Quaid-e-Azam's voice rose again: "No . . . you." His thin but steel-like finger was pointed at me. I began to tremble. "Sir, I?" "Yes," he replied. This one word went through me like a bullet out of a Royal Enfield .303 rifle. My throat, from which I had raised so many slogans for the Quaid, was now utterly dry. I could not speak. He took off his monocle and said, "All right." It seemed to me that he had somehow come to know how I felt and in order to end my agony had said, "All right." He turned, looked at his young and handsome secretary, said something to him and then went back into the house with his sister. I was about to run off when Matloob spoke: "Sahib has asked that you report here tomorrow at ten." I could not even ask him why I had been called, nor could I tell him that I had no qualifications for the job the Quaid-e-Azam had advertised for. I could not. Then Matloob sahib walked back into the house and I returned home.

'Next morning, I duly reported at the house and was informed by the Quaid's secretary that the sahib had liked me and I was to immediately take charge of the garage. My first thought was that I should confess that I knew nothing and that the Quaid-e-Azam had been misled. I had walked in just like that and was in no position to take the responsibility being given to me, but I don't know why I just kept quiet. I was given the keys to the garage and put in charge of the Quaid's four cars. The only car I had off and on driven was Seth Ardeshir Irani's Buick and that too on a straight road. The Malabar Hill was full of hair-raising bends and turns and I, poor Azad, was now required to drive a man on whose life depended the survival of millions of Muslims, all along this hazardous route and God alone knew where else.

'I had a wild urge to drop the keys on the ground and run all the way home, pick up my things and get on a train bound for Delhi, but thought better of it. It would be best to tell Jinnah sahib the truth, ask his forgiveness and go back to where I belonged, I said to myself. However, believe me, such an opportunity did not come my way for six months.'

'How?' I asked Mohammad Hanif Azad.

'This is how it was,' he explained. 'I was informed six months after I had joined that I was to drive the car into the porch and wait. I almost fainted but consoled myself with the thought that as soon as the Quaid appeared I would salute him, hand over the keys of the garage to him and then fall at his feet. That did not happen. The moment he walked into the porch, I was so dumbfounded that I could not utter a single word. Fatima sahiba, his sister, was also with him, and Manto sahib how can you fall at someone's feet in a woman's presence? It wouldn't have been right somehow. So Manto sahib I had to start the car, a new Packard it was. I silently prayed to God and managed to drive it out on the road through the front gate without a hitch. I negotiated all the turns of the Malabar Hill quite well, but when I came to the red light on the main road, I ran into trouble. My master Buddhan had taught me to use the brake gently, but I was so nervous that when I yanked it down, the car came to a stop so suddenly and with such a jolt that the cigar the Quaid was smoking fell out of his hand and Fatima sahiba was practically thrown out of her seat. She began to curse me and I thought I would die. My hands began to tremble and I felt my head reeling. The Quaid-e-Azam picked up his cigar from the floor and said something in English, which I thought meant I should return to the residence. Once we got back, he asked for another car and another driver and drove off. My next opportunity to serve him did not come until six months later.'

'And you served him the same way?' I asked, smiling.

Azad smiled too. 'Well, the thing was that sahib did not try me all this time. There were other drivers who were used. They all wore sahib's livery and very smart it was. Matloob sahib would inform us a night before who the driver for the next day was going to be and which car was to be taken out. Off and on, I would ask about myself but he would say nothing. The fact was that nobody could say with certainty what the sahib had in mind, nor could anyone dare ask him. He was very matter-of-fact and would only speak when it was necessary to speak, and listened only to that which was necessary to listen to. That was why despite being physically close to the Quaid, I could never find out why he had chucked me aside in his garage as a useless spare.'

I ventured a guess: 'Maybe he had forgotten all about you.' Azad laughed loudly. 'No, sir, no way the sahib had forgotten or would forget anything. He well knew that Azad had been feasting around for the last six months without doing the least bit of work. And Manto sahib when Azad feasts away, it takes a lot to keep him happy. Just look at me and my big body.'

I looked at him. He was indeed a big and strong man. I could imagine what he must have been in the year 1937 or 1938. Since I had learnt that he had once been the Quaid's chauffeur, I had been looking for an opportunity to talk to him. I was to meet him several times and ask him about his days with the Quaid. As I began to write this account, it occurred to me that the Quaid-e-Azam liked strength, as Allama Mohammad Iqbal, the poet, liked tall people. The Quaid's choice of those who worked for him was governed by this basic consideration: strength. During Azad's time, everyone who worked for the Quaid was physically strong and good-looking. Matloob, his secretary, was well built and handsome, as were the drivers and the security guards. Mr Jinnah may have been physically weak but he had nerves of steel. It makes psychological sense that he did not wish to be associated with weaklings. One always takes good care of what one likes. The Quaid was no different. He was very particular about the smart turnout of his staff. The Pathan watchman was under orders to always wear his traditional dress. Azad, though not a Punjabi, was often asked to wear a turban because it made men look tall and impressive. If his turban was well and properly tied, he would sometimes earn himself a special tip.

Come to think of it, the secret of Quaid-e-Azam's strong character lay in his physical infirmity. He was always conscious of his fragility and it was this awareness that was his greatest strength. It manifested itself in everything, from the way he carried himself to how he spoke. Azad told me that the Quaid-e-Azam ate very little. 'He was such a small eater that I would often wonder what it was that kept him alive. Had I been put on that diet, I would have begun to vanish in a matter of days. Every day, four to five chickens were prepared in the kitchen and all Jinnah sahib ate would be a small bowl of soup. Fresh fruit would come to the house in large quantities every day but he would hardly eat any; it all went into the servants' bellies. Every day before going to sleep, he would indicate from a list what he wished to be prepared the next day. I would be handed a hundred-rupee note to cover the shopping.'

'A hundred rupees every day?' I asked Azad.

'Yes sir, one hundred rupees. The Quaid-e-Azam never asked us to account for it. What was not spent would be divided among the staff. On some days, it would be thirty rupees, on others forty and sometimes even sixty or seventy. He certainly knew about it but he never once asked for accounts. Miss Jinnah, however, was different and would often say that we were all thieves and were charging more for our shopping than what we had paid. We would listen to her quietly because we knew that the sahib did not really care about such things. On such occasions, he would tell his sister, "It's all right, it's all right."

'However, there was one occasion when it did not turn out to be "all right" and Miss Jinnah was so angry with the cooks that she laid off both of them. One was exclusively assigned to cook European meals, while the other was in charge of Indian cuisine. The latter would often be idle, sometimes for months on end. When his turn came, he would spring into action, but the Quaid-e-Azam was not really overly fond of Indian food. He kept quiet when both cooks were sacked because he would never interfere in his sister's affairs. For several days, both of them would go to the Taj to eat their meals. This was great as far as we were concerned. We would take the cars out in search of new cooks and gallivant around the city royally, only to come back and report that we had failed to find anyone suitable. In the end, Miss Jinnah asked the two old cooks to come back.

'Small eaters are either jealous of those who eat more than they do or are happy to see them eat well. The Quaid fell in the latter category of small eaters. That was why he never asked us what we had done with the money we had obviously not spent on meat and groceries. Let me tell you a story. The year was 1939. I was gently driving the Quaid in his white Packard along the Marine Drive, the waves beating languidly against the shore. There was a touch of cold in the air. I could see that Jinnah sahib was in a pleasant mood. I thought it was a good opportunity to mention the Id festival, which was around the corner. I could see him in my rear-view mirror. There was a faint smile on his lips. He knew what I meant. I wanted some money. His faithful cigar was between his lips. Finally, he spoke, "Well, well, you have suddenly become a Muslim . . . try being a bit of a Hindu for a while." Only four days earlier, the Quaid had tipped me two hundred rupees and thus made a good Muslim out of me, which was why he was now advising me to embrace a bit of Hinduism since I wanted more money.'

The Quaid-e-Azam's domestic life has always been a mystery and will remain so. It has been generally said that his domestic life was non-existent because all his time was taken up by politics. He had lost his wife years earlier and his daughter had married a Parsi against his express wishes.

Azad told me, 'This was a great shock for the sahib because he wanted her to marry a Muslim, no matter what caste or colour he was, but his daughter would argue with him. She would say that if he himself had exercised his freedom to choose a wife why was he not willing to accord the same freedom to her?'

The Quaid-e-Azam had married the daughter of a prominent Bombay Parsi, something that had been deeply resented by the Parsi community, which wanted the slight avenged. Some people said that the marriage of the Quaid's daughter to a Parsi was the result of a well-thought-out plan. When I mentioned this to Azad, his reaction was, 'God knows best, but all I know is that after his wife's death, this had come as the greatest shock to the Quaid-e-Azam. When he learnt of the marriage, you could see the grief on his face. He was very transparent that way. You could know how he felt by merely looking at him. He was a sensitive man and even a minor incident could upset him. His brow would furrow and you would know that he was angry or upset. Only he could measure the extent of his grief, but those who saw him during those days knew how restless he was. For two weeks, he would not receive visitors. He would just keep smoking his cigars and pacing up and down in his room. He must have walked hundreds of miles in those two weeks.

'He would always pace about the room when he was thinking, often late at night, all alone, up and down the spotless floor of his room, taking measured steps. His brown-and-white or black-and-white brogues would produce a rhythmic pattern of sound as the night wore on. It was like a clock ticking. The Quaid-e-Azam loved his shoes. Was it because they were always at his feet and would do exactly what he willed?

'After two weeks he resurfaced. There was no sign of grief on his face, nor any tension. His head was again held high, although for two weeks he had tended to keep it bent. But this did not mean he had forgotten what had happened or really recovered from it.'

I asked Azad how he knew that. 'Nothing is hidden from servants,' he replied. 'He would sometimes ask for a certain metallic chest to be brought to his room and unlocked. It was full of clothes that belonged to his dead wife and his headstrong daughter when she was a little girl. The clothes would be taken out and sahib would gaze at them without saying a word. His gaunt, transparent face would become clouded. "It's all right, it's all right," he would say, then remove his monocle, wipe it and walk away.

'The Quaid had three sisters, Fatima, Rehmat and a third one whose name I do not remember. They used to live in Dongri. Rehmat Jinnah lived at Chowpati Corner near Chinoy Motor Works. Her husband was employed somewhere and did not earn much. Sahib would give me a sealed envelope every month with money in it, and sometimes a packet, which probably contained clothes. These I had to deliver to Rehmat Jinnah. Off and on, sahib and Miss Jinnah would go and visit her. The other sister who lived in Dongri was married too and, as far as I knew, was well off and in no need of financial assistance. The Quaid had a brother whom he used to help regularly, but he was not allowed to come to the house. I once saw him in Bombay. It was at the Savoy bar. He looked like the Quaid and he had just ordered a small rum. He had the same nose, the same general features, the same combed hair with a grey streak in the middle. When I asked someone who that person was, I was told it was Mr Muhammad Ali Jinnah's brother, Ahmad Ali. I watched him for a long time. He sipped his rum slowly and paid the bill—which was less than a rupee—with a flourish as if it was a vast sum of money. The way he sat there, you would have thought he was not in a third-class Bombay watering hole but the Taj Mahal Hotel itself. Before the historic Gandhi–Jinnah meeting, there was an equally historic meeting of Bombay Muslims, which a friend of mine attended. He told me that as the Quaid-e-Azam spoke in his characteristic style, in a back corner stood his brother, Ahmad Ali, muttering, a monocle fitted to his eye.

'The only indoor sport the Quaid-e-Azam liked was billiards. Whenever the urge to play came upon him, he would order the billiards room to be opened and although it used to be cleaned and dusted every day, the servants would still take one extra look at everything on such days to be sure that all was spick and span. I was permitted to go to the billiards room because I too had a bit of a liking for the game. Twelve balls would be placed in front of the sahib and he would carefully choose three and then begin playing. Miss Jinnah would often be there too. Sahib would place his cigar between his lips and study the position of the ball that he planned to hit. This would take several minutes, as he would examine it from every angle. He would weigh the cue in his hand, run it over his long and slim fingers as if it was a bow he was going to play a stringed instrument with, take aim and then stop short of executing the stroke because he had thought of a better angle. He only played his shot when he was fully satisfied that it was the right one. If the shot went through as planned, he would smile triumphantly at his sister.

'In politics, the Quaid-e-Azam was equally meticulous. He never made a hasty decision. As at billiards, he would examine the situation from every angle and only move when he was sure he would get it right the first time. He would take the measure of his quarry and choose the right weapon to bring it down. He was not one of those who would hurriedly pick up a gun and shoot without looking, confident that they would not miss. The Quaid was mindful of every pitfall before going into attack.'

According to Azad, the Quaid-e-Azam avoided casual visitors because he hated idle talk. 'He only had ears for relevant and brief conversation. In the special room where he received visitors, there was only one sofa with a small side table. He would flick the ash from his cigar in an ashtray that lay on that table. There were two glass-front cabinets resting against the opposite wall where he kept copies of the Holy Quran presented to him by his admirers. His personal papers were also kept here. Most of his time was spent in that room. If one of us was sent for, we were expected to stand at the door and listen to his instructions. Then we would leave. The papers he was looking at would lie scattered on the sofa. If he wanted to have a letter written, he would send for Matloob or his stenographer and dictate it in a harsh, decisive voice. Although my knowledge of English was limited, I always felt that he emphasized words which did not need emphasis.'

The harshness Azad refers to was perhaps an unconscious defensive reaction to his physical frailty. His life was like a bubble on moving waters but he gave the world the appearance of a giant whirlpool. It was his lack of physical strength that kept him alive so long. Azad said the Quaid's best friend, with whom he had the most informal relations, was the late Nawab Bahadur Yar Jang. 'He would often come to stay and the two would talk for hours on national and political issues. The Quaid was a different person when he was with the Nawab. He was the only man with whom he talked as one talks to a close, personal friend. They were like two childhood buddies. When they were together in a room, you would often hear them laughing loudly. There were others who came to visit, including Raja Sahib of Mahmoodabad, I.I. Chundrigar, Maulana Zahid Hussain, Nawabzada Liaquat Ali Khan, Nawab Sir Mohammad Ismail and Ali Imam. However, the sahib dealt with them in an official kind of way. Gone was that easy informality which one associated with Bahadur Yar Jang's visits.'

I asked Azad if Liaquat was a frequent visitor.

'Yes, he was,' Azad answered. 'The Quaid treated him as his most talented pupil. Liaquat would show the utmost deference to him and carry out his orders to the last detail. Sometimes when he had been sent for, he would ask me before being shown in what kind of a mood the sahib was in. I would always tell him because when the Quaid was in a bad mood everyone knew, even the walls of the Malabar Hill home. The Quaid-e-Azam was particular about the appearance and conduct of his servants and staff. He hated everything that lacked cleanliness, including human character. He liked Matloob very much but when he learnt that he was carrying on with a Muslim League woman volunteer, he was annoyed because he was not one to tolerate such deviant behaviour. Matloob was called in, questioned and sent home. However, whenever the Quaid met him later, he always treated him like an old friend.

'Once I came home very late. You see I had gone out to town and spent quite a few hours at a bar. I thought the sahib would not know how late I had been, but I was wrong. He sent for me the next day and told me in English that I was spoiling my character, then added in broken Urdu, "Well, *ab hum tumhara shadi banai ga*"—We will have to get you married off now. Four months later when he came to Delhi from Bombay to attend a meeting of Muslim League, as desired by him, I was duly married. It was because of my association with him that I found a wife who came from a Syed family. I was a Sheikh by caste but had been accepted as a son-in-law by the Syeds because I was in the service of the Quaid-e-Azam.'

I asked Azad if he had ever heard the Quaid-e-Azam say 'I am sorry.' Azad shook his head. 'No, I am sure if the words had ever escaped his lips, he would have excised them from the dictionary for good.' This one observation contains the key to Quaid-e-Azam Mohammad Ali Jinnah's character, I think.

Mohammad Hanif Azad is alive in the Pakistan that his Quaid-e-Azam gifted to him, a country which is trying to survive in a harsh world under the leadership of his talented pupil, Liaquat Ali

Khan. On this piece of free land, he sits on a broken cot outside the office of Punjab Art Pictures, close to a betel-leaf seller, and waits for his sahib and prays for the day when he would be paid his salary on time. He is even prepared to become a bit of a Hindu, just as the Quaid-e-Azam had advised, provided there is an opportunity.

Last time I spoke to him about the Quaid, he was depressed. I realized that he did not have enough on him to buy himself even a betel leaf. I talked to him of this and that and managed to get his mind off his troubles.

He sighed. 'My sahib is dead. How I wish I was with him on his last journey, driving his white Packard with the roof down. How I wish I could have driven him gently to his destination. His delicate temperament was not suited for a rough, jolting ride. I have heard—and I do not know if it is true or untrue—that when his plane brought him to Karachi, on what was to be his last trip, the ambulance which was to take him to the Governor General's house broke down. The engine stalled after it had gone a short distance. I know how much that must have upset my sahib.'

There were tears in Azad's eyes.

BARI ALIG: THE ARMCHAIR REVOLUTIONARY

Autocratic and oppressive rulers meet their well-deserved fate
Streets of Russia echo with cries of revenge
The last nail in the coffin of the Romanoff dynasty

Large, life-size posters with these screaming headlines had gone up on various walls of the city of Amritsar. Most people never read beyond the headlines as they exchanged whispered remarks. I do not remember the year but it was the season of arrests, something not uncommon in Amritsar. There was also the occasional bomb blast and incendiary materials being pushed into the city's red letter boxes. There was much tension in the air, which explained the interest passers-by took in the sensational wall posters. However, they never stopped for long, afraid of being caught reading such seditious material.

The headlines on the posters were a direct borrowing from one of Oscar Wilde's inferior plays named *Vera* that my childhood friend Hasan Abbas and I had published in Urdu translation. The poet Akhtar Shirani had corrected the manuscript. Bari sahib, who was our guru, had helped us with the translation. We had managed to get the book printed at the Sanai Electric Press and Bari sahib had personally carried the plates home for safekeeping because he was afraid the police would raid the press and remove everything. Both Hasan Abbas and I were greatly thrilled by these developments. Our boyish minds were incapable of realizing what awaited those who were sent to jail or the treatment meted out to those interrogated at police stations. We did not even want to think about such things, being entirely taken with the idea that if you went to jail you were making a sacrifice for the nation. We were sure that on release we would be garlanded by the people and ceremonially taken out in a procession.

Vera concerned the revolutionaries and terrorists of Russia who were fully armed, compared to us. If anyone in the Amritsar of the time had dared ask for so much as an air gun, he would have been placed at the business end of a cannon and blown off till kingdom come. Moscow may have been a long way away from Amritsar but Hasan Abbas and I were not new to the ranks of revolution. Back in tenth grade at school, we had charted out on a map a land route all the way to Russia. Those were early days and Ferozuddin Mansour had yet to become Comrade F.D. Mansour and Sajjad Zaheer was still probably called Bannay Mian. Our Moscow was Amritsar and it was in the streets of that city that we wanted to see autocratic and oppressive rulers get their just deserts. We wanted the last nail in the coffin of the Russian imperial house to be hammered in at Chowk Farid, Katra Jamil Singh or Karmoon Deori. It had never occurred to us that the last nail may not be quite straight or the hammer may flatten our fingers instead of the nail. Bari sahib was our guru and it was for him, not for us, to think. However, it had occurred to me more than once that the man we had chosen as our leader was weak of heart. Even a rustle in the trees was enough to startle him; it was only our sincere enthusiasm that had kept him going.

Now that one looks back, all those things appear to be like little toys, but at the time we saw these very toys as giant, impregnable enterprises. Had our khalifa Bari sahib not been timid, all four of us (Abu Saeed Qureshi had by now joined our triumvirate) would have been hanged, thus joining the ranks of those martyrs of Amritsar who, if later asked what they thought they were up to, would have replied that they did not know where their boyish enthusiasm was taking them.

I have called Bari sahib timid but it is not an attack on his personality. The fact is that timidity was a prominent and integral part of his personality, and had he not been timid, he would not have been the man he was. He would have been somebody quite different: a world-famous hockey player in the lifelong service of some princely state or a primary school teacher who became a university reader or even another Bhagat Singh the bomb-thrower (he personally knew Bhagat Singh, who came from his area, Lyallpur). It was only his timidity that prevented him from making anything of himself. He remained suspended in mid-air as it were. It is my belief that the many bright ideas that came to him from time to time also remained suspended from a hook called timidity.

Bari sahib would come up with the most original schemes and forget them just as soon. Sometimes he would discover an island and draw up plans as to how that island should be reached and conquered. He would conjure up for his listeners in graphic detail the hidden riches that awaited those lucky enough to get there, and before he had finished there was more than one volunteer ready to set out for that dream island. However, it would be noticed almost immediately that there was no Bari sahib to be seen anywhere. And when he reappeared and someone asked him about the island, he would start describing an even more fascinating island that he had since discovered.

That was exactly what had happened after those posters went up. Abbas and I were so apprehensive of being picked up that we hardly slept that night. The next day, like new bridegrooms, we went around looking for our experienced mentor Bari to ask him what our next move was. He was missing. We went to his usual haunts but he wasn't at any of them. He appeared after fifteen days, full of his latest scheme, namely the publication of a weekly. He told us in his characteristic style, 'I was not idling my time away like you fellows; I was busy making arrangements that are now complete. All we need is permission from the government. I am going to start writing articles as of today.'

The posters promising the last nail in the coffin of the Russian imperial house were mostly gone, the few that were left were half covered by others advertising male potency drugs. Our enthusiasm for revolution was now concentrated on the new weekly. All copies of *Vera* I had locked up at home because of its atrocious printing and get-up. It was *Khalq* the weekly that had our full and complete attention now. The first issue was printed at the Sanai Electric Press and Bari sahib and I carried the copies home. We were quite pleased with the way it looked. Among Bari sahib's patrons was a leather merchant whose name I have now forgotten. This black-bearded gentleman had played a big role in financing *Khalq* and was willing to invest even more, except that Bari sahib once again ran away.

The first issue carried his article 'From Karl Marx to Hegel', on page one; it was a history of the evolution of socialism, something quite beyond Hasan Abbas and me. We knew of neither Hegel nor Karl Marx though the latter's name we had heard several times from Bari sahib. All we knew was that he was a great friend of the working class, but as to what his philosophy was and where and how it linked up with that of Dr Hegel we hadn't the faintest idea. I would like to add as an aside that my first story, 'Tamasha', was printed in the same issue, but it did not carry my name because I was afraid of being laughed at. However, Bari sahib, despite knowing how limited my knowledge was, always encouraged me, to the extent that he never pointed out my mistakes. All he would say was, 'It is just fine.'

The first few days after the appearance of *Khalq* were heady. Abbas and I felt as if we had made some great achievement and we would walk in Katra Jamil Singh and the Hall Bazaar with our noses up in the air. However, after a few days we realized that nothing had changed and to the city of Amritsar we were the same time wasters we used to be. The cigarette vendors continued to pester us to pay what we owed them and the older members of the family remained convinced that we were up to no good. That was not too far from the truth because some plainclothesmen, it turned out, had been making inquiries about us. When this news reached Koocha Wakeelan, where we lived, my brother-in-law, Khwaja Abdul Hamid, who had recently retired as instructor at the Police Training School, Philor, buttonholed the policemen who had come looking for us. 'Go do something else because this Hegel and Marx is beyond your ken. Even poor Bari doesn't quite know what it is all about.'

Having been at the police school, he knew practically everyone. He also knew Bari sahib and was familiar with his interest in history. He was particularly fond of Bari sahib's oratorical style, which was why he told the plainclothesmen to buzz off, assuring them that there was nothing in what Bari had written that could cause the overthrow of the British government in India. However, when Bari sahib found out that something was up, he produced only one more issue of *Khalq*—that he left with me—and disappeared. He was away for a long time and even sent me a postcard from Multan that said, 'From the observatories of Multan, I am studying my stars.' This was his favourite sentence, and whenever he wrote to me from wherever he was, this line always made an appearance. I believe that wherever he happened to be, he never forgot to study his stars. Even in the dark observatories of the grave, he is no doubt studying his stars, though it is a pity he can't mail me a postcard from there.

He liked postcards because they cost less than envelopes but he was lazy when it came to answering letters. I remember once writing several letters to him from Amritsar but never having even one answered. Finally, I enclosed two five-paisa stamps in my next letter and urged him to write. In a few days, a card arrived that said, 'I sold the stamps you sent and have purchased this postcard. All your letters have duly arrived.' This angered me and I travelled to Lahore where he was, determined to give him a piece of my mind, but as we sat in Arab Hotel and before I could tell him how mean he was, he was busy studying my stars from the observatories of Lahore. His finding was: 'Sort things out with the family, move to Lahore and get a job with a newspaper.'

It was not the first time this sort of thing had happened. On several occasions in the past, when I had been quite determined to tell him what I thought of him and on that note end our friendship, he had always managed to disarm me. He had a round, dark brown face, an outsize head, and his lips and gums were dark. He was not very tall. When he smiled, his dark face lit up. It was at moments such as these when I think even the stars, bored with his constant ogling, may have smiled at him.

Bari sahib was a coward, by God, he was a big coward. If he ate too much, he would be gripped by the fear that he was developing a paunch; although even when he was starving, this part of his anatomy continued to grow. He would never run, being afraid it would affect the heart, although it was this very organ that let him down in the end. He would prepare large blue maps of massive red uprisings but the sound of a cracker going off would terrify him. He was in love with a young woman but his parents had found another match for him. As soon as they discovered that Bari had his eye on someone else, they fixed a date for the wedding. Bari sahib and I were sharing lodgings at the time. A few days before the wedding, he disappeared but not for long because the bride-to-be sent him a message that if he did not marry her she would stab him in the belly. Bari sahib was terrified and quietly got married.

When he arrived at the observatories of Burma to study his stars, his star got entangled with that of a Burmese girl so he sent for his wife, but when the stars continued to remain in a confusing configuration, he ran away, using the outbreak of war as an excuse. He was always running away from women. At one time, he was much taken with Iqbal and his philosophy of the self. Iqbal had written that so deep should a man go into his self that the Almighty should Himself ask him, 'Speak, what is thy will?' Bari sahib worked very hard on his self but the Almighty never asked him what his will was. In the end, Bari sahib himself went over to the other world to ask Iqbal about the confusion he had created.

Late at night, after putting the newspaper to bed, Bari sahib would go to Iqbal's grave and spend hours conversing with him over the philosophy of the self. He was always hard up and salaries in the office were not paid with any regularity. Even when salaries were paid, they were paid by instalment because the proprietors of the newspaper were convinced that those who worked for them were some kind of load-carrying oxen who should be grateful for whatever was thrown their way. Bari sahib was a sensitive man. If he took a loan, he would groan under its burden. He had taken the philosophy of the self so high that it wasn't possible to take it any higher. In exasperation, he had gone to Iqbal's tomb and asked him some pretty defiant questions which I am sure, had the poet been alive, he would have found difficult to answer.

In the end, the rebel in him simmered down. Had he not been timid, he would have come up with some new interpretations of Iqbal's philosophy, but because of his intrinsic timidity, ideas that could have blossomed from his hyperactive brain withered on the vine. I am not sure if his other friends would agree, but had he been more steadfast and had he had the ability to fight back, he would have written a tome akin to *The French Revolution* called 'The Indian Revolution', and it is also possible that he may have become a firebrand revolutionary of the kind seen during the 1857 Mutiny. Like Iqbal he kept telling God: there is much to do here on earth, so You wait for me now. But when God sent for him, he did not have the courage to tell Him that there was much he still had to do on earth and He should wait. He just left, as Iqbal had earlier. Iqbal had written about the humble sparrow that, if motivated, can take on the eagle. Bari sahib was always ready to match his sparrow against the imperial eagle, but when the time for a showdown arrived, he threw the cage on the ground and ran, giving the little bird no opportunity to test its beak against the eagle's.

Bari sahib was a great day-dreamer and he could dream up the most fantastic schemes. I recall the time he closed down *Khalq* after only two issues and, having failed to earn any money from the couple of newspaper jobs he had taken, decided to bring out another weekly, which was to be called *Mochna*, or tweezers. He worked out to the last detail the headlines the paper would run and the articles it would carry. He described its early issues to us so graphically that we could actually see them lying in front of us or falling upon our heads like rain from the sky. Another time, he got so disgusted with the profession of journalism that he decided to instal a fresh animal-fodder-cutting machine. He described it to me in his characteristic way and so deep an impression did he make on me that when I joined the All India Radio, I wrote a play called *Journalist*, whose central character was called Bari. Its broadcast created an uproar and every Urdu newspaper wrote editorial notes denouncing it because the play was seen as insulting to newspaper proprietors. The irony was that the very journalists whose plight my play had described had been used to denounce me.

It may be interesting to quote some excerpts from the play. The journalist Bari sets up a fresh animal-fodder-cutting machine and is very happy with his new life. Here he is talking to himself.

BARI: I earn up to two rupees a day. My evenings are spent at a drinking joint across the road that I find most relaxing. When I am done, I walk back to my place. There is no news to translate, no copy to paste, no phone calls, no calligraphers, no Reuters service. Boy, am I grateful to that friend of mine who first suggested that I do this! When winter comes, I will lay my bed next to my bales of fodder and sleep peacefully. Isn't this a great life! My advice to all those editors who are killing themselves working in newspapers is to follow my lead and set up a fresh animal-fodder-cutting machine. I am sure they will bless me for the rest of their days.

(Life is good to the journalist but then the Second World War breaks out and the dormant journalist in Bari comes to life. He is in the drinking joint when he learns that the world is at war. The drunks around him are discussing quail fighting. Bari cannot bear it.)

BARI: Silence. What rubbish are you talking! You are a bunch of ignoramuses. There is a war on in Europe that could wipe out many countries from the map of the world forever. Millions will be killed. And here you are discussing quail fighting.

FIRST DRUNK: What rubbish is he talking?

SECOND DRUNK: *(laughs)* I don't know what he's saying. *(To Bari)* Bari, what's come over you today?

FIRST DRUNK: He has had too much to drink.

SECOND DRUNK: Drink is an awful thing.

BARI: What nonsense are you talking! I am fully in my senses; it is you who are drunk. What I am thinking at this moment, even my country is incapable of conceiving.

FIRST DRUNK: Bravo, bravo my mullah!

BARI: You make fun of what I am saying (*laughs*), but it is not your fault, it is mine. So far I have kept my identity a secret but let me tell you who I am. You have no idea how important I am in the world of politics.

FIRST DRUNK: OK, so you are the champion wrestler of this age. All right? Let's talk about something else.

BARI: You will continue to make fun of me till you know who I really am. Do you know who I am? My name is Maulana Abdul Bari, editor, *Khalq*.

The irony in the last line needs no embellishment because in the end Bari did leave journalism and set up a fresh animal-fodder-cutting machine. However, this machine was not his property but that of the British government (in his last years, he had taken a job with the British Information Service in Lahore). People used to make fun of him because all his life he had abused the British and in the end had agreed to take up employment under them. I am sure in his own mind he kept saying, 'You will continue to make fun of me till you come to know who I really am. I have kept my real identity hidden from you so far.'

It is my considered view that Bari sahib always looked for escape routes and even when he had escaped he continued to exercise the utmost caution, which was why the real Bari remained unknown to others. He had nobody to blame but himself. Initially, he would step out to take on the most formidable challenge but suddenly change direction and go elsewhere. In my play, the character Bari says:

BARI: If we study the events between the two world wars, we would find to our regret that the civilized world has allowed itself to be caught in a net of degradation. While science has marched on, mankind has continued to stand where it was. Racism and religious enmities have flourished and the result is there for all to see. War-like peace has made way for peace-like war. I ask only this: where is this civilized world of ours headed? Are we returning to the dark ages? Will the blood of man once again be sold cheaper than water?

Will our flesh and bones be traded as if they were mere commodities? What is going to happen? Will someone tell me what lies in store for us? Abandonment of principles has created thousands of divisions. Man is pitched against man, nation against nation, country against country. This is the story of the twentieth century.

These ideas are actually those of Bertrand Russell but I have put them in Bari sahib's characteristic oratorical style. His intellect was no less formidable than Russell's, but he was born in a country where he found himself at the mercy of newspaper owners to whom he could have said, 'You say you serve the nation, so do I, but for this service I am never paid in time and, often, I am not paid at all. In the last four months, I have been paid only sixteen rupees. I am a human being not a stone. I get hungry, sometimes I may want to eat a delicacy but how can I? You appointed me editor of a newspaper, not a sadhu or a saint who has turned his back on the material world.'

I may have exaggerated his total takings for four months of work, but it is a fact that when he was working for the daily *Ehsan* he used to have to steal old newspapers from the office so that he could sell them and get something to eat. Raja Mehdi Ali Khan was also working in the same newspaper at the time, but while Bari sahib was a cautious, careful man, Raja was reckless by nature. When Bari sahib confided to Raja what he was doing to make an extra buck, he was excited. On the first day, he stole two bundles but the next day he declared that he was not interested in small-time theft. 'We should move into big time,' he added. That evening, he brought two huge sacks, which he and Bari sahib stacked with old newspapers. Bari sahib was scared, because while Raja was busy filling the sacks, he was standing guard. Two labourers were summoned to carry the sacks. That evening, according to Raja, both of them went to the movies.

Raja Mehdi Ali Khan tells another story. Once, he swears, the two of them had to beg in the street. It was a Bari scheme. He had worked out exactly how they should ask for alms. They were to wear expressions of helplessness and misery on their faces and explain their plight in emotionally charged language. However, when the time came, Bari sahib lost his nerve and was able to get no more than a few annas while Raja took in nearly three rupees. Another Raja story also deserves to be recalled. Raja was begging in the

Anarkali area when he saw a milkman with a huge pitcher on his head walking towards him. Raja, who had heard various lectures from Bari sahib on human psychology, felt that the man was monied and if he told him of his condition he would easily manage to get a good sum of money out of him, at the very least a rupee. He stepped forward and told his tale of woe to the milkman. 'Help me get this pitcher down,' he told Raja. This was a tough job but Raja managed it somehow. The milkman then put his hand in a secret pocket, pulled out a thick wad of money and placed just one paisa on Raja's outstretched palm. Then he said, 'Now, young man, help me get this pitcher back on my head.'

I also know that during really hard times Bari sahib and Hasan Abbas used to steal fruit from the shop directly under the single room that they had rented in Lahore's Old Anarkali. The room had no light, but Bari sahib had instructed Hasan Abbas as to how they could establish their own power house, a project involving the theft of electricity direct from the overhead wiring in the street.

I recall another incident connected with this room. I had come from Bombay after seven years and I knew where to find Bari sahib and Hasan Abbas. Off and on, I used to exchange letters with them. In those days, there was no prohibition and at railway stations you could buy liquor from a cart that the salesmen of the Spenser company plied to and fro. I was meeting Abbas after a long time and so we decided to begin celebrating early in the day. There was much that we needed to catch up on. For our heart to heart get-together, we relied on that old cheer leader, Johnny Walker. I was hoping to meet Bari sahib at the railway station but he had failed to turn up, or to quote Hasan Abbas, one more time, he had acted 'ignominiously'. We got into a tonga and set out on a search for him. Finally, we found him. It turned out that he was hiding because he was afraid that with my arrival some serious drinking would be on the agenda. He wanted to be no part of it, but when we reminded him of our old friendship, while cursing him in between, he relented.

We also ran into our old Amritsar buddy Abu Saeed Qureshi, who had either already stormed the citadel called Bachelor of Arts or was getting ready for the assault. He was still as romantic as he used to be, dreaming of whiling away the moonlit evening by the water with a femme fatale while reciting Omar Khayyam. Bari sahib declared that for that sin he deserved to be fined one bottle of Johnny Walker. The sentence was acceptable to the convict. We gathered in the Old Anarkali room: Bari sahib, Abu Saeed Qureshi and Abdulla Malik (who is more handsome now than he was then). Rajindra Singh Bedi also dropped in for a while.

Bari sahib was a neatness freak, to the extent possible. He used to spend a lot of time arranging and rearranging his table, almost like a child. The nail cutter had to be placed next to his pen-holder, which in turn had his cut-throat razor as its companion. If he found a round stone somewhere he would press it into service as a paperweight. His books wore hand-designed dust covers and if you looked, on top of them, you would find thread and needle. Bari sahib loved to use scissors. Why, I do not know. He used to make the page himself, carefully clipping news stories and pasting them on the page that was later transferred on litho and sent for printing. While I know that this is one of the duties of news editors, what I cannot understand is why he was so fond of using scissors long before he became a news editor. I can see him sitting in his chair in the office of the Amritsar newspaper *Musawat* with a pair of scissors in his hand. He looked like a man who was about to embark on a most fascinating task.

His table always rested against a wall so that when he sat down to write he should see nothing but a wall when he looked up. He had to have something blocking his view when he was writing. Once when he came to my house and wanted to write something, I moved the table so that it did not face a wall. He sat down but looked uneasy. When I asked why, he replied, 'Unless I have something blocking my view, I cannot write.' Then he picked up a big world atlas and placed it in front. But I am digressing. I should have stayed in the Old Anarkali room. Actually, if a memory crops up while I am writing, I put it down immediately as I am afraid I might otherwise lose it. He was also in the habit of grinding his teeth while he wrote. He formed his letters so round and so small that sometimes it was difficult to tell them apart.

In that Old Anarkali room, there also hung on the wall a historic group photograph taken in Amritsar that showed Abbas, Bari sahib, Abu Saeed Qureshi and me. Under the picture, Bari sahib had scrawled 'Amritsar School of Thought'. He was very fond of this picture and had taken it along to Burma when he had walked out of the office of the newspaper *Milap* or *Pratap* for a 'short while' and had next surfaced in Burma. By the way, he had left his jacket behind, hanging at the back of his chair. As I entered the room which was now the sole living accommodation shared by Bari sahib and Hasan Abbas, the first thing that Bari sahib pointed out to me was that picture. 'Look at this Khwaja sahib,' he said with cheery, childish enthusiasm. He could not say more. He was smiling and his face had lit up.

He loved me and he was also proud of me but he had said no such thing to me ever. I do not know if he had ever told anyone that Manto was his creation, though that would have been the truth. He it was who set me on the path of writing. Had I not run into him in Amritsar, I would have died unknown or I might have been serving a long sentence for armed robbery. Abbas and I were quite high by now. Abu Saeed Qureshi's bottle was uncorked and a drink poured out for everybody. Bari sahib became more and more interesting as alcohol entered his bloodstream. Gone was his reserve and the sobriety with which he usually carried himself. All one wanted at such moments was that he should go on talking and we should go on listening. It is another matter that when in his cups, nobody else could get a word in edgeways.

Rajindra Singh Bedi was talking about Mikhail Sholokhov's *And Quiet Flows the Don,* which none of us had read. However, the way Bedi was going on, I had to pretend that I too had read the book. When I said that, it seemed to rattle Bedi. Bari sahib, who was watching the exchange, intervened at this point and began a lecture on Sholokhov as a novelist. After some time, Bedi had to confess that he hadn't read the book. I followed with an identical confession. This sent Bari sahib into convulsions. When he calmed down, he said that the first time he had heard the name Sholokhov was that very evening from Bedi's lips. What he had said about his novel writing was pure invention. Bedi, who had to go far, left early.

It was December and hence very cold. Since I had lived away from the Punjab winter for many years, I was feeling particularly cold. Bari sahib rose, went out, came back with some firewood that he placed methodically in a makeshift steel basket with a solid bottom, sprinkled some Johnny Walker on his arrangement, lit a matchstick and soon had a fire going. Almost immediately, he went down on the floor in supplication crying, 'Zoroaster, Zoroaster.'

I was reminded of our days in Amritsar when Bari sahib used to offer not five, as ordained, but eight and sometimes ten prayers a day. Whenever he came to visit me at home, we would go to my room that he had named 'The Red Retreat'. If he felt like praying, he would call my mother (we called her Bibijan) and ask for a jug of water for his ablutions and a prayer mat. Sometimes when he felt guilty about something he had done, he would go down on the floor touching it repeatedly with his forehead and asking God to let bygones be bygones. Bari sahib did not like me to drink during our early days in Amritsar, but I was sure he was putting on an act. One evening, he and I took a walk, dropping in at the railway station refreshment room where I ordered a whisky and a ginger ale for Bari sahib with a shot of gin but without his knowing it. Bari sahib always had one or another stomach ailment. 'I don't want to drink anything because I have a bad stomach,' he said.

He was not an obstinate man and after a little while I convinced him—as you could convince him of anything after a short lecture—that ginger was the most effective defence against all maladies of the stomach. He agreed and the waiter brought us our drinks. After a couple of swigs, it was clear that he had begun to enjoy the 'ginger' drink. When I ordered another whisky, he expressed a desire to have another ginger ale. A spiked one was duly brought by the waiter whom I had earlier instructed. The two drinks put Bari sahib in a very good mood. 'I had read about the wondrous qualities of ginger in a book on eastern medicine and there is no doubt that ginger is an amazing thing in nature. The depression that I had been feeling since morning is now entirely lifted,' he said.

I laughed and had to tell him that the wondrous thing in his drink was not ginger but gin. This upset him greatly and, though he forgave me this childish prank, I felt that I had caused him an injury. So, on an impulse, I promised him that I would never touch the stuff again. This incident had a great effect on me. When I returned home that night, before going in, I supplicated myself on the threshold and prayed to God for forgiveness while beseeching Him to give me the strength to keep my promise. While I felt lighter in a way, at the same time, I could not dismiss the thought that I wouldn't be able to drink any more. As days passed, my listlessness increased, but what kept me going was a certain sense of satisfaction that I had kept my word to God and was also rid of the demon called drink.

One evening, Bari sahib came to see me and found me sitting by the window. He asked me how I was. 'Don't ask. I suppose I'm all right,' I replied, smiling wanly. 'I'll be back in a minute,' he said and disappeared. When he returned, he had half a bottle of whisky hidden under his shirt. I was taken aback and wanted to say something but he refused to listen, sat down and uncorked the bottle. Just at that moment, Abbas walked in. All doors were closed as per Bari sahib's instructions. We sent for some food from the kitchen but none of us ate anything. We kept the curry and the glasses, while returning the other dishes. Abbas went out to get water from the street well. We kept drinking and though I was uneasy I said nothing. To tease Bari sahib, Hasan Abbas said, 'Everyone respects you in this house. Bibijan knows you as an observing Muslim who prays regularly, which is why she has such enormous regard for you. Now what if she were to walk into the room and see you?'

Bari sahib replied, 'I would open the window, jump out and never show her my face again.'

All his life, Bari sahib had a window he could open and jump out from, leaving it ajar though it was never to see his face again. I do not say this to denigrate him. I am thinking of the system established by the British that Bari sahib had been born into, through which he had lived and worked and which he had seen departing. Then he found himself under another system where he tried to refashion his life in the evening gloom, a system unsheathed by the very swords of which the poet Iqbal had spoken and which were now the daily refrain of Radio Pakistan. There were many windows in the new country that opened by themselves the moment someone even so much as thought of jumping out.

But I am digressing again. I was in that room in Old Anarkali where in the freezing cold of winter we were drinking. Every now and then, Bari sahib would step out and bring in more logs. Since we had met after years, we were not conscious of how long we had been sitting. Bari sahib kept the fire going for a long time in the name of Zoroaster. Next morning, when I went out, I noticed that a wooden fence I had seen the day before was no longer around. However, its ashes were intact inside the room. Abbas told Bari sahib that if the landlord found out what we had done to his fence, he would turn into a red-hot cinder and throw us out. Bari sahib, timid that he was, tried to laugh it off but I could see that he looked worried. 'Before he finds out, we'd have fled,' he said to Abbas. The trouble was that before he could fly anywhere, it became public knowledge. When he left his jacket hanging behind his chair in the office of the newspaper *Milap* or *Pratap* and disappeared to Burma, he was sure nobody would ever find out, but everyone did.

Bari sahib studied his stars from various observatories in various cities, and in the end it was the observatory of Lahore where he came to rest. For some time, it was the Arab Hotel that was his observatory, followed by Nagina Bakery, where many accomplished star-gazers gathered every day to scout the heavens. Some of them went beyond the stars during his lifetime and others whose stars had no luminosity were forced to seek favours from those who lived in higher elevations.

Whenever I watched Bari sahib holding forth, I thought of a hot cup of coffee from which tiny clouds of swirling steam rise, dance around in the air for a while and go to sleep in its moist lap. In those warm, charged and uncaring gatherings, so many ideas rose like aromatic steam from Bari Sahib's pot-like head, danced around delicately for a few moments in the heavy atmosphere and vanished. Bari sahib was the king of conversation. In Amritsar, he would come to 'The Red Retreat', rest himself against the pillow that he called 'Wali Allah' and will soon get going like a river in full flow. Muhammad Sarwar, later the editor of *Afaq*, Lahore, would drop in off and on and show an interest in me and what I was doing. Like Bari sahib, he too would give me encouragement, assuring me that before long I would have several books under my belt.

Another Amritsar story. When Bari sahib, Hasan Abbas, Abu Saeed Qureshi and I were together, we did not want to be disturbed by any outsider. We all knew Comrade Ferozuddin Mansour, and now and then he would pay a visit to 'The Red Retreat'. We never quite liked it. Bari sahib used to say that the comrade was into manufacturing potassium permanganate bombs, while Abbas used to call him Fraud-ud-Din Mansour. We put up with him for some time till Bari sahib found a way out. One day as he entered the room, Bari sahib winked crudely at Abbas and said, 'Khwaja sahib, let's move; otherwise we might be late.' He got up and bolted all the windows, giving Mansour no time to sit down. Out in the bazaar, Bari sahib excused himself and a few minutes later was back at 'The Red Retreat'. He was very happy and could not stop laughing. Little things could please him. In this he was like a child. He had a paunch and when he laughed it seemed to laugh with him, but this extra weight always worried him.

Bari sahib was utterly sincere, so sincere that he could never have picked up an argument with death when it overtook him. He always avoided arguments because he was a man with a sweet and peaceable temperament. He had had a heart ailment for long but he never treated it aggressively, treating it most peaceably. I remember that two days before his death, I ran into him on Lahore's Mayo Road. He was in a tonga. He saw me first and got down. I was annoyed with him, highly annoyed, because after taking up a job in the British High Commission he had withdrawn into himself and when he ran into an old friend he looked embarrassed.

We shook hands and he asked how I was. I did not like this formality and I did not mince my words. 'Bari sahib,' I said, 'how much lower can you sink—you have stopped meeting me altogether! Your entire character has gone down the drain since you started working for the British.' He did not respond but a faint, sickly smile came to his lips. His face was pale and his voice was weak. 'How are you?' I asked. My question made him go into a long, serious explanation of the countless treatments he had tried for his heart condition and how none of them had worked. Then he told me that he was on his way to see a homoeopath on Mayo Road. I joked, 'So this was the only untried observatory from which you are now going to study your stars. Drop it Bari sahib, there is nothing the matter with you whatever. You are a hypochondriac and even Hippocrates could not cure that. You eat more than you should and that is why you always have an upset stomach. That affects your heart. That is all there is to it. The rest is your imagination.'

He immediately agreed (he always agreed immediately) and said, 'I think you are right. This stomach problem I do have . . . and some doctors have confirmed that.' We talked for a long time. He told me that he was writing an extended history of the world in several volumes (he never completed it). He was also looking for similarities between the Turkish and Punjabi languages. He had always loved Punjabi. There was a time when he wanted Punjabi to be the official language of the Punjab. In those days, he was editing *Ajit*, a Punjabi newspaper owned by the Sikhs. Wherever he would go in those days, he would talk about the various schemes he had drawn up to popularize the Punjabi language. He would tell everyone, 'Instead of Urdu, you should write in Punjabi.' It was his view that only that language is robust which has robust and formidable swear words. It was his faith that no language of the world could compare with Punjabi when it came to swear words. The interesting thing is that not once in his life did he write a single sentence in Punjabi.

Before the partition of the country, there used to be a Kailash Hotel in Anarkali, which had a bar. Whenever I would come to Lahore to deal with this or that legal suit, a couple of evenings were invariably spent at this bar with my publisher Chaudhri Nazir. We would always drag Bari sahib along and walk up to the top storey, where a Sikh waiter served us. After a couple of shots, Bari sahib would start speaking to him in the purest Punjabi. He would tell him about the need to establish the supremacy of Punjabi. After four drinks, he would turn to Urdu and hold forth on its universal character. He would say that Punjabi was the language of hoodlums and gangsters. It was an uncivilized tongue that was harsh on the ears. After five or six drinks, his love for Urdu would shrink as he would begin to sing praises of the sweetness of Persian. Then he would try to speak Persian in a pure Iranian accent, but the seventh and eighth drink would set him off on the stony trail of Pushtu. Another drink later, all these languages would turn into a cocktail in his head.

Bari sahib was very fond of listening to his own voice but did not have the courage to speak in a public meeting. He used to make do with his friends. Once he walked out of Delhi Muslim Hotel in Anarkali with a spoon he had filched. When we were in the middle of Anarkali, he produced the spoon, placed it on his shoulder like the shovel that volunteers of the semi-militant Khaksar movement carried as they marched on the street saying 'chup raast', or left right, and began to make a rousing Khaksar-like speech. Soon a small crowd gathered to listen to him as Bari sahib's eloquence increased. We raised slogans of 'Allama Mashriqi zindabad', bought white motia flower garlands and threw them around our necks. Bari sahib wrapped one around his wrist and said, 'Khwaja sahib, let's go to Hira Mandi . . . that is the direction in which the aroma of these flowers is leading us.'

We arrived in Hira Mandi, the famous courtesan quarter of Lahore. Bari sahib was happy and drunk. We walked around its dark streets for some time with Bari sahib holding conversations in Pushtu with a number of Pathan women standing in doorways. It was during one of those conversations that one of his acquaintances happened to pass by. Bari sahib stepped forward, shook hands with him and when the man asked what Bari sahib was doing there he replied, 'I was discussing the current international situation with this young lady.'

In the morning, Hasan Abbas narrated the evening's incidents, duly garnished, to Bari sahib in such a way that he should feel bad about them. Bari sahib turned to me for confirmation and with feigned seriousness I said, 'Bari sahib, it is a fact that you did some disgraceful things last night. Such conduct is not expected of you.' He was immediately repentant and to even scores performed his ablutions and began to pray.

Bari sahib was fond of becoming a reformer. It was his heartfelt desire that he should become a great leader with his statue in every city square. He should do a deed great enough to be remembered by succeeding generations. However, in order to go down in history, you need courage and initiative. The courage and initiative that Bari sahib displayed in the streets of Hira Mandi while discussing the current international situation with Pathan courtesans would next morning lead him to the prayer rug. That was where he did his moral dry-cleaning. All his life, with a pair of scissors, he kept clipping his ideas and pasting them in the book of his life, but he never got around to transferring the impression on litho because he was afraid that the stone may get crushed under the weight of his thoughts. He was always afraid of something getting crushed under something else, though what he ended up doing was crush his ideas into a powder and use it like snuff.

He was a great enemy of the British but what an irony it was that when the British left India it was under them that he took a job. He wrote a rebellious book like *Company ki Hakoomat* but he spent the last precious years of his life under the former masters of that East India Company. I was talking about my last meeting with Bari sahib when he was on his way to see a homoeopath for his heart ailment. But his heart was so well-mannered that it went along with Bari sahib's timidity and stopped beating. When we met for the last time, I had recently published a piece on Agha Hashr Kaashmiri, the renowned playwright, in which I had described Jija's hotel in Amritsar where we used to hang out.

Bari sahib had written me a letter after reading the article and reminded me of those days when Abu Saeed, Hasan Abbas, Ashiq photographer, he and I used to roam around the streets like distracted men. We had no purpose in view and we did not really want anything. We had also set up something we called 'Free Thinkers'. The rules and regulations of this madcap society laid down that any member could do anything he wanted without the need to explain to other members why he had done what he had done. Often, when all four of us would be walking together, Bari sahib would turn into a side street without a word and disappear. We would be in the middle of a heated discussion when Abbas would suddenly fall silent and leave.

That day we talked about the letter he had written me. I said to Bari sahib that he always bragged about his retentive memory but he had forgotten much about our Amritsar days. He apologized in a weak voice and said that he had written that letter with the utmost sincerity and there was so much he wanted to say but his heart was not at peace. When he mentioned his heart again, I remonstrated with him. Why, I asked, was he after his heart with which there was nothing wrong?

But two days later, as I lit my first cigarette after my morning cup of tea and picked up the day's issue of the newspaper *Imroze*, I saw a headline on page one that said, 'Famous socialist writer Bari Alig is dead'. For a moment, I was lost, then I looked at the news story again, which had run under a three-column headline. It seemed to me that Bari sahib had himself cut the copy neatly with his scissors and pasted it perfectly on the page.

Socialist writer Bari, my friend, my mentor, my guide who kept pasting major and minor headlines in the book of life, but never got down to writing under those headlines the stories that came to birth in his head and disappeared like steam in the charged atmosphere of Lahore's restaurants and bakeries.

Bari sahib is in his grave. Is there a window in there through which he could jump out?

ASHOK KUMAR: THE EVERGREEN HERO

When Najmul Hasan ran off with Devika Rani, all of Bombay Talkies was in turmoil. The film they were making had gone on the floor and some scenes had already been shot. However, Najmul Hasan had decided to pull the leading lady out of the celluloid world into the real one. The worst affected and the most worried man at Bombay Talkies was Himanshu Rai, Devika Rani's husband and the heart and soul of the company.

S. Mukherjee, Ashok Kumar's brother-in-law, who was to make several hit movies in the years to come, was at that time sound engineer Savak Vacha's assistant. As a fellow Bengali, he felt sorry for Himanshu Rai and wanted to do something to make Devika Rani return. Without saying anything to Rai, he somehow managed to persuade her to come back, which meant that he talked her into abandoning the warm bed of her lover Najmul Hasan in Calcutta and return to Bombay Talkies where her talents had a greater chance of flourishing.

After Devika Rani came back, Mukherjee convinced the still-shaken Himanshu Rai to accept his runaway wife. As for Najmul Hasan, he was left to join the ranks of those who are fated to be deserted by their beloved for less emotional, but weightier political, religious or simply material considerations. As for the scenes he had already done, they were trashed. The question now was: Who was going to be his replacement?

Himanshu Rai was a very hard-working man, a film-maker totally absorbed in his craft, and basically a loner. He had set up Bombay Talkies on the lines of a teaching institution, choosing the village of Malad outside Bombay as the site. He wanted nosy outsiders to be kept out—outsiders like Najmul Hasan. A replacement was needed. Once again, Mukherjee came to the rescue of his emotionally disturbed boss. His wife's brother Ashok Kumar, after taking a bachelor's degree in science and reading law in Calcutta, had joined Bombay Talkies as an unpaid laboratory apprentice. He was quite good-looking and could sing a little. Mukherjee suggested him as

Najmul Hasan's replacement. Himanshu Rai, who had spent his entire life experimenting, agreed to look at the young fellow. His German cameraman Wirsching gave Ashok a screen test and showed it to Himanshu Rai, who was satisfied. His German film director, however, had a different opinion, but there was no one who could overrule Himanshu Rai. And so it came to pass that Ashok Kumar Ganguly, who was then no more than twenty-two years old, was chosen to play Devika Rani's leading man.

They made one film, then another, then another, becoming filmdom's inseparable team. Most of their movies were hits. The doll-like Devika Rani and the young and innocent Ashok Kumar looked just right together on the screen. Her artless gestures and girlish ways won the hearts of film-goers who had until then been fed on love's 'heavier', more aggressive screen version. These two delicate, almost fragile-looking young lovers became the toast of India. So popular were they that college girls would pine for Ashok Kumar, while boys would go about wearing long and loose Bengali shirts, sleeves unbuttoned, one of which Ashok Kumar had worn in that famous duet with Devika Rani: *Mein banki chidiya banke bolun re* (I shall become a forest bird and sing from grove to grove).

I had seen some of Ashok's films and as far as acting was concerned, Devika Rani was streets ahead of him. In the beginning, he used to look like someone made of chocolate but as time passed he matured and his style became more assertive.

When he moved from the laboratory to acting, his monthly salary was fixed at seventy-five rupees, a sum he accepted happily. In those days, for a single person living in a far-flung village, which Malad was, it was a lot of money. When his salary was doubled, he was even happier. Not long after, when it was raised to two hundred and fifty rupees, he was very nervous. Recalling that occasion, he said to me, 'My God . . . it was a strange feeling. When I took the money from the studio cashier, my hand was trembling. I did not know where I was going to keep it. I had a place, a tiny house with one bed, two or three chairs and the jungle outside. What would I do if thieves paid me a visit at night? What if they came to know that I had two hundred and fifty rupees? I felt lost . . . I have always been terrified of thefts and robberies, so I finally hid the money under my mattress. That night I had horrible dreams, so next morning I took the money to the post office and deposited it there.'

While Ashok was telling me this story, outside, a film-maker from

Calcutta was waiting to see him. The contract was ready but Ashok did not sign it because while he was offering eighty thousand rupees, Ashok was insisting on one lakh. And to think that only some years earlier he had been at a loss to know what to do with two hundred and fifty rupees!

With Ashok doing so well, Mukherjee, an intelligent and highly observant man, also flourished, soon rising to become a big-time producer who made several silver and golden jubilee hits for Bombay Talkies. He established a new style of scripting movies. I, for one, always considered him my teacher.

Ashok's popularity grew each passing day. He seldom ventured out, but wherever he was spotted, he was mobbed. Traffic would come to a stop and often the police would have to use lathis to disperse his fans. He was not too generous with his admirers. In fact, he would get irritated because they wanted to get close to him. He would sometimes react as if someone had abused him. I would often say to him, 'Dadamoni, your reaction is most ridiculous. Instead of being flattered by the attention you receive, you get upset. Can't you understand that these people love you?' However, his brain appeared to me to be devoid of those cells which help you understand unquestioning admiration.

Till the time I left Bombay in 1948, he was totally unfamiliar with love. I am unaware of what changes occurred in him in later years. Hundreds of beautiful women came into his life but he treated them all with the greatest indifference. Temperamentally, he was a rustic. His living style and his food habits also had a touch of rusticity.

Devika Rani tried to have an affair with him but he rebuffed her rather curtly. Another actress once picked up her courage and invited him to her home. Once he was there she told him tenderly how much she loved him. Ashok reacted so brusquely that to save face she had to assure him she was just testing him and had only sisterly feelings towards him. The amusing thing was that Ashok liked her and would have loved to get her into bed. She always wore a washed and scrubbed look, which Ashok found irresistible. When she told him that he was like a brother to her, he felt rather let down.

Ashok was not a professional lover but he liked to watch women, as most men do. He was not even averse to staring at them, especially at those areas of their anatomy that men find attractive. Off and on, he would even discuss these things with his friends. Sometimes he would experience a strong urge to make love to a woman but he would never step forward. Instead he would say something like, 'Yaar Manto . . . I just do not have the courage.' Courage he certainly lacked, which was a good thing for his marriage. I am sure his wife, Shobha, was happy about her husband's timidity, praying that he would never lose it.

I always found it odd that Ashok should be scared of women when hundreds of them were willing to jump if he told them to jump. His mailbag would be full of love letters from thousands of girls, but I do not think he ever read more than a hundred of them in his life. It was his tubercular-looking secretary, de Souza, who would read each letter like a voyeur, only to look even more insubstantial. A few months before Partition, Ashok was in Calcutta for a Chander Shekher film. Huseyn Shaheed Suhrawardy was the chief minister of Bengal at the time. Ashok had been to his home, where they had watched 16-mm home movies. While driving back, two pretty Anglo-Indian girls flagged his car down, wanting a lift. Ashok stopped and they jumped in. However, he had to pay dearly for this vicarious pleasure because one of them not only smoked his cigarettes but also took away his cigarette case. Ashok knew where they lived and often thought of starting something with them, but could never muster up the courage.

Once Ashok was shooting a film in Kolhapur. It was the kind of rubbish where swords, shields and maces are the actors' mainstay. Ashok's scenes had almost all been done but since he did not like the movie he was not too enthusiastic about shooting the rest of his scenes. He returned to Bombay, where he received message after message begging him to come to Kolhapur. Since a contract was a contract, he did in the end go, but dragged me along, though I was busy writing *Eight Days* for Filmistan. Since Ashok was to produce and direct the movie, I couldn't say no, especially when he said, 'Come, yaar, we can work there in peace.'

But how could there be peace? Word soon went around that Ashok Kumar was in town. Our hotel was now almost constantly surrounded by fans. The manager was a clever man and he would somehow manage to make the crowd go away on one pretext or the other. The diehards, however, were not to be fooled or discouraged and would hang around for hours to see their idol. Ashok's attitude was what it had always been: unfriendly, something that I found irritating.

One evening, we went out for a walk with Ashok suitably

'camouflaged' in dark glasses. He had a walking stick in one hand and the other was on my shoulder so that he could manoeuvre me back and forth in case of emergency. We went into a store, as Ashok wanted some anti-allergy tablets to counter the dirt and dust of Kolhapur. The shopkeeper paid no attention to us and turned around to get the medicine from his cabinet. Then something occurred to him. It was like a delayed bomb.

'Who . . . who are you?' he asked.

'Who am I? I am who I am,' Ashok replied. The store owner looked at him carefully. 'You are Ashok Kumar,' he said.

'Ashok Kumar must be somebody else. Let's go, Manto,' Ashok said.

Then he placed his hand on my shoulder and walked out of the store without buying the medicine. As we were turning towards our hotel, three Maharashtrian girls appeared. They were pretty and their hair was parted in the middle with the parting sprinkled with kumkum. They were also wearing flowers in their hair. One of them had a couple of oranges in her hand and she was the one who noticed Ashok. She began to quiver and said to her friends in a stifled voice, 'Ashok.' As she said it, the oranges fell from her hands. Ashok let go of my shoulder and ran towards the hotel. He was always like that with women.

I first met Ashok at Filmistan, which S. Mukherjee had founded after walking out of Bombay Talkies with his entire team. I had caught glimpses of Ashok Kumar here and there but I only got to know him when I joined the new company. Every actor has two personalities, one that you see on the screen and one as he or she really is. When I saw Ashok for the first time at close quarters, he was quite different from what I had seen of him in the movies. He was quite dark with rough and chubby hands, strong of body and semi-rustic in manner. He was also quite formal but in a tense, uneasy kind of way.

Ashok spoke excellent Urdu. He did try to learn to read and write it, but could never go beyond the first primer. However, he learnt enough to write a line or two in the language. When we were introduced, I said, 'I am very pleased to meet you.' Ashok's reply was self-conscious but well rehearsed. Once a visitor to Filmistan said to Ashok in the most formal Urdu, 'I have a feeling that this most humble servant of yours has in the past had the honour of meeting you.' Ashok's reply, delivered in accented Urdu, contained a huge malapropism, of which he soon became conscious, and he slunk away without saying another word. After I left Bombay to come to Pakistan, he wrote me a letter in broken Urdu asking me to come back but for some reason I did not write back.

My wife, like most women, was among Ashok's admirers. One day I brought him home and as we entered I shouted, 'Safia, come out. Ashok Kumar is here.' Safia was cooking. She finally came out since I kept bugging her. I introduced them. 'This is my wife, Dadamoni, shake hands with her.' They both became self-conscious. I took hold of Ashok's hand. 'Dadamoni'—which in Bengali means older brother—'why are you shying away from shaking hands with my wife?' I said. So he had to shake hands. That day my wife had prepared keema parathas. Ashok liked it so much that he ate three parathas. It was strange that whenever my wife prepared keema parathas, somehow Ashok would always appear. None of us could explain why. I suppose it is fated who will eat what, when and where.

I began to call Ashok 'Dadamoni' because he insisted that I should. 'But what makes you think you are older? I can prove to you that I am older,' I argued. When we worked it out, he turned out to be two months older, so from that day on, I began to call him 'Dadamoni' instead of 'Mr Ganguli'. In any case, I liked the sound of the word 'Dadamoni' because it had the gentle sweetness of Bengali culture. In the beginning, he used to call me 'Mr Manto' but when I began to call him 'Dadamoni' he switched to just 'Manto', a form of address for which I did not really care.

Ashok looked soft on the screen but in real life he was a tough person who exercised regularly. He could hit a door hard enough to crack the wood. He used to box at home and was crazy about shikar. He was capable of doing the most arduous job cheerfully. However, he had no interest in keeping an elegant home. Had he wanted, he could have had the best-furnished home in the city but he never bothered about such things and when he tried, the results were disastrous. He would pick up a brush and paint a perfectly nice chair all blue or turn a fine sofa into a divan by removing its back.

Ashok lived in a seafront house but it wasn't very nice. The salt had eaten through the grill that guarded the windows and it was now badly rusted. The place did not smell very nice. However, none of these things had the least effect on Ashok. His refrigerator was parked on the veranda and his big Alsatian slept against it. His children would be creating a rumpus in the living room and Ashok, quite unmindful of them, would be in the loo, working out which horse would win the next big race. He would also rehearse his lines while sitting in the WC.

Ashok was well versed in astrology, which he had learnt from his father. He had read many books on the subject and when he had time he used to tell the fortunes of his friends. One day he asked me my birth date and after working out something on a paper asked if I was married. 'You know that I am,' I replied. He was quiet for a while, then said, 'I know, but Manto, tell me something. You have no children so far, have you?' 'Why do you ask?' I wanted to know. He hesitated before saying, 'Well, the first child of those with your combination of stars is a male, but he does not survive.' Ashok did not know that I had lost my son when he was a year old.

Ashok later told me that his first child, a son, was stillborn. He explained that his and my stars were in more or less the same configuration and it was not possible for such people to have their firstborn male child not die. Ashok was a complete believer in astrology as long as the calculations were accurate. 'As you can never get the correct balance if even one paisa is wrongly added, similarly, if you do not work out the stars with absolute accuracy, you will get the most misleading results, which is why you should not rely on these things totally because it is possible that your basic data is wrong,' he once told me.

Ashok would place his racing bets on the basis of astrological calculations. He would spend hours working out the winning horses. However, he would never place more than a hundred rupees on any one horse. He would sometimes win ten rupees or come out even, but he never lost. He backed horses not so much to win as to divert himself. He would always be accompanied to the race course by his lovely wife, Shobha, mother of his three children. A few minutes before the start of the race he would give her money and ask her to place it. She would also be the one who would later queue up at the window to pick up the winnings. Shobha was a housewife with a modest education. Ashok would joke about her being illiterate but they had a happy marriage. Despite their money, Shobha would do most of the housework herself, clad like a true Bengali in a cotton sari with the house keys tied in a big bunch around her waist and hanging by the side. Over drinks in the evening, she would prepare delicacies for us to nibble on. Since I drank more than others, she would tell Ashok, 'Look, do not give Mr Manto too much to drink; otherwise his wife will protest to me.'

Our wives were good friends. Often Shobha would take Safia along when she went shopping. Every shopkeeper knew who she was: wife of the famous actor Ashok Kumar. They would, therefore, produce the most sought-after things for her from under the counter. Bombay men, I should point out, generally speaking, were a soft touch, compared to the women. If you had to get your money from a bank or mail a registered letter or buy a cinema or a train ticket and you were a male, you would have to stand in line for hours. However, if you were a woman, you could do the necessary in a matter of minutes. While Ashok never took advantage of his fame and popularity, some others were not that scrupulous. Raja Mehdi Ali Khan was one such.

He worked for Filmistan, which I had left in between, and at the time of the incident was busy writing a story for director Wali sahib. One day, Ashok's secretary phoned to say that Raja was ill. When I went to look him up, he was in bad shape with a throat so sore that he could hardly talk. He was so weak that he could not get up without help. He had been gargling with salt water and rubbing some balm on his chest but it was not working. I was afraid that he might have diphtheria, so I put him in a car and phoned Ashok, who told me to take him to a doctor friend of his, who confirmed that it was indeed diphtheria. On the advice of the doctor we put him in the infectious diseases hospital, where he was given a number of injections. I phoned Ashok and told him about Raja's illness but he showed little concern. I got angry at his attitude and told him so. 'It is strange that here is this man infected with a most serious disease and there you are, behaving in a totally unconcerned manner. You know he has no one to look after him.'

All Ashok said in reply was, 'We will go look him up this evening.' I got off the phone and went to the hospital. Raja was somewhat better. The doctor had suggested certain injections and I had brought the vials with me. I stayed for some time and came away telling Raja not to worry and to hang in there. In the evening, Ashok picked me up from Wali sahib's office. I was still a bit upset with him but he talked me out of my annoyance. He apologized to Raja, explaining that he would have come earlier except that he had been busy. After some time he left. The next day when I went to the hospital, I found everything transformed. Raja really looked like a raja. His sheets were bright and clean and the pillows had fresh covers. He had a packet of cigarettes and there were flowers in a vase on the windowsill. He was wearing crisp hospital clothes and reading a newspaper. 'What is all this, Raja?' I asked.

Raja smiled through his thick moustache. 'This is nothing. You wait and watch.'

'What?' I asked.

'I have everything that a man needs. If I stay here for a few more days, I will have a harem going in the next room. God bless my Ashok Kumar . . . but where is he?' He then told me that his changed circumstances were entirely due to Ashok Kumar. The hospital management had found out that Ashok had come to see how he was and since then he had half the nursing staff waiting on him, wanting to know if Ashok really had come, and how close their friendship was, and if he would be coming again, and when.

Raja told everyone that Ashok was his dearest friend and was prepared to lay down his life for his sake. That Ashok even wanted to move into the hospital with him but the doctors would not agree to the arrangement. That he would have come twice a day but he was busy working. However, the good news was that he was due to drop in that evening. It had paid off. In that free hospital, every facility was now Raja's. I was about to leave as the visitors' hour had come to an end when a bunch of girl students from the medical college came in. Raja smiled. 'Khwaja, I don't think this adjoining room will be large enough for the harem,' he said to me with a wink.

Ashok, always a fine actor, could only work at his best if he was teamed up with people he knew well. Films where that had not been the case showed him performing indifferently. With his own team around him, he would come alive. He would advise the technicians and accept advice from them. He would ask people their opinion about his acting, and would play a scene in many different ways before deciding upon the final version. He would listen to others, but once he was involved in work, he hated to be interrupted. Being educated and having spent so many years with an institution like Bombay Talkies, Ashok had come to acquire a basic working knowledge about every department of film-making. He understood the finer points of photography and was well informed about all technical aspects of the business. He had practical knowledge of editing and had studied direction seriously. So when Rai Bahadur Chunilal, one of the leading lights of the industry, asked him to produce a movie for Filmistan, he agreed right away.

Filmistan had just completed its war propaganda movie *Shikari*, and all the members of the company were enjoying a well-earned holiday with their families. One day, Savak Vacha dropped in to see me. 'Saadat,' he said after some small talk, 'write a story for Ganguli.' I could not understand what he meant. I was a Filmistan employee and it was my job to write stories. I did not need a recommendation from Savak to write for Ganguli. Any responsible Filmistan official could have asked me to write a story and I would have started doing so there and then. I later learnt that since Ashok himself was going to produce the movie, he wanted me to make a special effort to write a story that would be unique. We gathered at Savak's nice, well-laid-out flat some days later. It was not clear what kind of a story Ashok wanted. 'Manto, I don't know . . . but it should be something sensational. Remember, it is my first film as a producer,' he said.

We sat there for hours, searching for an idea but couldn't come up with any. At the time, a huge stage was being built at the Brabourne Stadium, very close to where Savak lived, in connection with the diamond jubilee celebrations of the Aga Khan's birthday. I thought that might inspire me to think of something, but nothing came. A fine piece of sculpture in Savak's flat also failed to get my creative juices flowing. I tried to get an idea from one of my earlier stories but still nothing clicked. In the evening, after a long and barren day, we placed our chairs on the terrace and began to drink brandy. Savak was a great aesthete when it came to drinks and he had produced an excellent brandy. One sip and you were in seventh heaven. We could see Churchgate station down below and the street was full of people. The sea lay beyond. Expensive cars, shimmering under the street lights, moved about noiselessly. Suddenly from nowhere, one of those huge, ugly roadrollers appeared. It was an odd sight but it gave me an idea. I thought, if a young and beautiful girl standing in her balcony were to drop a piece of paper from above and vow to marry the man who picked it up, she could well find herself married to the driver of the roadroller rather than the owner of one of those sleek, expensive cars. Anything could happen.

When I told Ashok and Vacha, they seemed greatly amused. We poured ourselves some more brandy and began to speculate and throw up ideas and fictional situations in the air. When we parted, it was with the understanding that a story should be worked out on the idea I had come up with. I wrote a story but, of course, it was different. There was no girl in the balcony and no roadroller. I favoured a tragedy but Ashok wanted the story to have a happy ending with fast action. We all zeroed in on 'the story' now. Finally, it was done. Ashok liked it and we began to shoot. Every single frame was prepared under Ashok's supervision. Few people knew that the entire direction of *Eight Days*, the movie we produced, was the work of Ashok Kumar though D.N. Pai's name appeared as director in the credits. He had not directed even an inch of the movie. At Bombay Talkies the film director was not a prima donna as elsewhere. It was all team effort and when the film was ready for release one member of the team would be credited with its direction. We had adopted the same system at Filmistan. D.N. Pai was a film editor and a good one, so it was decided that he should be mentioned as the director of the film.

It was during the making of *Eight Days* that I realized that Ashok was as good a director as he was an actor. He would take great pains over even the smallest scene. A day before the scene was to be shot, he would go over the screenplay—which I had already gone through one final time—and spend hours in the loo ruminating over it. Oddly, Ashok could only concentrate when he was in the loo.

There were four new faces in the movie: Raja Mehdi Ali Khan, Upinder Nath Ashk, Mohsin Abdullah (husband of the actress Neena who was publicized as the 'Mystery Woman') and I. It had been decided to give a small role to Mukherjee as well but he copped out at the last moment because I had copped out of his film *Chal Chal Re Naujawan* as I was terrified of the camera. But that was only an excuse. The fact was that he was equally terrified of the camera.

Mukherjee was to have played a shell-shocked soldier. Everything was ready including the uniform, and when he said no Ashok was very upset. The shooting had to remain suspended for several days. Rai Bahadur Chunilal began to get worked up about it. One day Ashok burst into my room, where I was busy rewriting a number of scenes. He picked up my papers, put them aside and said, 'Come, Manto.' I got up because I thought he wanted me to hear one of the new songs in the movie. However, when we ended up on the set, I asked him what was up. 'You are playing the crazy,' he announced. I knew that Mukherjee had said no and Ashok had been unable to find a replacement, but I had never imagined he would pick me out, so I said to him, 'You are out of your mind.' Ashok became serious. 'No, Manto, you have got to do it.' Raja Mehdi Ali Khan and Upendranath Ashk felt the same way. Raja said to me, 'Look, I have been asked to play the husband of Ashok's sister, and I find it very embarrassing to be "married" to my good friend's sister, even if it is only in a movie. So what is odd about your playing a man who has lost his marbles?' In the end, I did play Flight Lieutenant Kirpa Ram, the shell-shocked officer, but only God and I know how terror-stricken I felt in front of the camera.

The film was released and it was a success. The public felt that it was a great comedy, which pleased Ashok and me greatly. We wanted to make another new type of film but fate had other things in mind. Savak Vacha had gone to London soon after we began to shoot *Eight Days* for the treatment of his mother. When he returned, the movie industry was in a crisis. Many companies had gone bankrupt and Bombay Talkies was in bad shape. A few years after the death of her husband, Himanshu Rai, Devika Rani had married a Russian émigré by the name of Svetoslav Roerich. She had also turned her back on movies. Many efforts had been made to put Bombay Talkies back on track but nothing had succeeded. Savak Vacha with the help of Ashok, now made a last-ditch effort to save the company.

Ashok left Filmistan. In the meanwhile, I had been cabled an offer from Lahore by Moti B. Gidwani to work for him at a salary of one thousand rupees a month. I would have gone but I wanted to wait for Savak. When he returned and took Ashok with him to Bombay Talkies, I went with them. This happened on the eve of Partition. The British were now putting the final touches to the map of the subcontinent so that when the whole thing went up in smoke, they would be able to watch it from a distance. Hindu–Muslim riots had begun, and as wickets fall in cricket matches, so were people dying. There were big fires everywhere.

Savak ran into a number of problems right away when he tried to reorganize Bombay Talkies. A lot of people, almost all of them Hindus, were given the sack as they were found to be redundant. This caused an uproar since their places were mostly filled by Muslims. Apart from me, there was Shahid Latif and his wife, Ismat Chughtai. Then there were Kamal Amrohi, the movie director, Hasrat Lukhnavi, Nazim Panipati and the music director Ghulam Haider. This created great resentment against Savak Vacha and Ashok Kumar among the company's Hindu employees. When I mentioned it to Ashok, he laughed. 'I will tell Vacha to sort those johnnies out,' he said.

This was done but it had the opposite effect. Vacha began to receive hate mail. He was told that if he did not get rid of the Muslims, the studio would be set on fire. He would get very angry when he read the letters. 'These salas say I am in the wrong. Well, if I am in the wrong, then the hell with them! If they set fire to the studio, I will push them all into it.' Ashok was utterly devoid of any communal feelings. They were foreign to his nature. He could not even understand why those people were threatening to set fire to the studio. 'Manto, this is madness . . . it will go away; it is only a matter of time.' However, it never went away, this madness. Instead, as time passed, it became more and more virulent. I felt somehow responsible for all that had happened. Ashok and Vacha were my friends and they would seek my advice because they trusted me and they knew I was sincere. However, my sincerity had begun to atrophy. I used to ask myself how I would face Vacha and Ashok if something bad were to happen to Bombay Talkies.

The religious killings were now at their height. One day Ashok and I were returning from Bombay Talkies. We stopped at his place, where I stayed for several hours, and then he offered to drop me home in the evening. He took a short cut through a Muslim neighbourhood. A wedding procession led by a band was approaching us from the other side of the street. I was horrified. 'Dadamoni, why have you come here?' 'Don't you worry,' he said. He knew what I was thinking. But it failed to calm my nerves. We were in an area that no Hindu would dare enter. And the whole world knew Ashok was a Hindu, a very prominent Hindu at that, whose murder would create shock waves. I could remember neither prayers in Arabic nor an appropriate verse from the Quran. But I was cursing myself and praying in broken words, 'O God, don't let me be dishonoured . . . let no Muslim kill Ashok because if that happens, I will carry that guilt to my grave. I am not the entire Muslim nation. I am only an individual but I do not want the Hindu nation to curse me for ever and ever if something happens to Ashok.'

When the procession reached the car, some people spotted Ashok and began to scream, 'Ashok Kumar . . . Ashok Kumar.' I went cold. Ashok had his hands on the steering wheel and he was very quiet. I was about to scream to the crowd that I was a Muslim and Ashok was taking me home when two young men stepped forward and said, 'Ashok bhai, this street will lead you nowhere. It is best to turn into this side lane.'

Ashok bhai? If Ashok was their brother, then who was I? I looked at my clothes which were homespun cotton . . . had they thought I was another Hindu? Or had they not even noticed me because of Ashok? When we got out of the area, I relaxed and thanked God.

Ashok laughed. 'You were nervous for nothing. These people never harm artists.'

A few days later, at a meeting held to discuss a story written by Nazir Ajmeri—which was later filmed as *Majboor*—I made some critical remarks, suggesting changes. Nazir turned to Ashok and Vacha and said, 'You should not let Manto sit in on such meetings. Since he is a story writer himself, he is prejudiced.'

It upset me and I felt that it was time I took a decision. I thought about it for several days but couldn't make up my mind. Then I said to myself, 'Manto bhai, this street will lead you nowhere. It is best to turn into this side lane.'

So I took the side lane that brought me to Pakistan, where I was soon tried for obscenity for writing a story called 'Thanda Gosht'.

V.H. DESAI: GOD'S CLOWN

'Lights on . . . fan off . . . camera ready . . . start, Mr Jagtap!'

'Started.'

'Scene thirty-four . . . take one.'

'Neela Devi, you don't have a thing to worry about. I have also drunk the urine of Peshawar . . .'

'Cut, cut!'

The lights came on. V.H. Desai placed the rifle against a prop and with the utmost calm asked Ashok Kumar, 'OK, Mr Ganguli?'

Ashok, who was about to turn from a red-hot cinder into pure ash, looked at Desai with murderous eyes, controlled his anger with a superhuman effort, brought a forced smile to his face and said, 'Wonderful.' Then he looked at me and said, 'Well, Manto?'

I embraced Desai. 'Wonderful!'

All around us on the set, people were having a hard time trying to control their laughter. Desai looked extremely pleased. It was after a long time that he had heard such fulsome praise from me. Earlier, Ashok had instructed me never to show my irritation because this would throw Desai off balance and the entire day would be lost.

After a few minutes, Desai asked Dixit, the dialogue prompter, 'Next dialogue, Dixit sahib?'

Ashok, the director of *Eight Days*, the movie we were shooting, now addressed me: 'Manto, I think we should do another take of the last scene.'

I looked at Desai. 'Desai sahib, what do you say? Let it be an even more wonderful shot.'

Desai shook his head in a typical Gujarati gesture and replied, 'Go right ahead . . . I am hot.'

Dattaram shouted, 'Lights on.'

The lights came on. Desai picked up the rifle.

Dixit leapt towards Desai, the script in his hand. 'Desai sahib, what about going over the lines once again?'

Desai asked, 'Which lines?'

Dixit answered, 'The same lines that you delivered so wonderfully just now. Let's go over them one more time.'

Desai rested the rifle soldier-like on his shoulder and said with absolute confidence, 'I remember them.'

Dixit looked at me. 'Manto sahib, why don't you hear them?'

I placed my hand on Desai's other shoulder and said in a friendly tone, 'So what are those lines, Desai sahib? . . . Neela Devi, you don't have a thing to worry about. I have also drunk the water of Peshawar.'

Desai adjusted the Peshawari-style turban on his head at a rakish angle and said to Veera, who was playing Neela Devi, 'Neela Devi, you do not have a thing to Peshawar about. I have also drunk your water.'

Veera burst out laughing hysterically. Desai looked worried. 'What happened, Miss Veera?'

Veera, with the loose end of her sari between her teeth to control her laughter, ran off the set. Desai, who now looked positively anxious, asked Dixit, 'What was the matter?'

Dixit turned his face away because he too was having a hard time trying not to laugh. To set Desai's mind at rest, I intervened, 'Nothing serious. It was her cough.'

'Oh!' Desai said, relieved. 'Neela Devi, you do not have a thing to cough about, I have also had Devi's . . .'

Ashok, with clenched fists, was hitting himself in the head. This really had Desai worried. 'What is the matter, Mr Ganguli?'

Ashok hit himself one more time. 'Nothing, I have a headache. So let's do this scene.'

Desai shook his pumpkin-like head. 'Done.'

In a dead voice, Ashok called, 'Camera ready . . . ready, Mr Jagtap?'

'Ready,' came Jagtap's thin voice through his hand-held hailer.

'Start.'

The camera began rolling. The clapper boy did his bit.

'Scene thirty-four . . . take two.'

Desai waved the rifle and addressed Veera, 'Neela Devi, you do not have to Devi a thing. I have also had Peshawar's . . .'

'Cut, cut!' Ashok screamed like a banshee.

Desai placed the gun carefully on the floor and asked Ashok in a worried voice, 'Any mistake, Mr Ganguli?'

Ashok looked at Desai with murder in his eyes, then immediately assumed a lamb-like expression. 'None . . . it was very good . . . very, very good.' Then he said to me, 'Manto, come out for a minute.'

Ashok almost burst into tears as soon as we were off the set. 'Manto, what are we going to do? We have been at it since morning. He just doesn't seem to be able to say "the water of Peshawar" . . . Why don't we break for lunch?'

It was just as well because to expect Desai to get his lines right once his mind was derailed was one of nature's impossibilities. The trouble was that his retentive memory was absolutely zero. He just could not commit anything to memory, not even one line. If he was ever able to get his lines right, even one line, the first time, it was considered a pure accident. The funny thing was, no matter how many times he fumbled his lines, he remained totally unaware of his boo-boos. He had no idea which line he had turned into what. After rendering yet another rib-tickling version of the lines given to him, he would look at those present on the set, waiting to be complimented. One or two gaffes were always cause for general amusement, but when it went on and on, it was no exaggeration to say that everyone present on the set would have been more than happy to chop him up into a hundred pieces and be done with it.

I spent three years at Filmistan and during this period Desai made four films there. I do not remember a single occasion when he got his lines right the first time. He must have wasted hundreds of thousands of feet of film in his life. Ashok once told me that Desai's retake record stood at seventy-five. That was at Bombay Talkies. When he got it wrong for the seventy-fourth time, the German director Franz Osten wailed, 'Mr Desai, the problem is that the audience likes you. The moment you appear on the screen, it starts laughing. Had that not been the case, I would have lifted you myself and chucked you out today.'

During those seventy-four retakes, practically every studio employee had to be pressed into service to assure Desai that he was doing just fine. The trouble was that once he was in one of those grooves of his, nothing, including prayer, worked. The practice, therefore, was to go on shooting the same scene over and over again, hoping all the time that at some miraculous moment the will of God and Desai's memory would come together and the scene would get done as scripted.

During lunch break, as was the custom, nobody said a word to Desai about the botched lines for fear that it might remind him of the gibberish he had been speaking since morning. Ashok pretended to chat happily, while Desai kept up a steady humorous banter, which was not at all funny. However, everybody laughed at his jokes. When shooting was about to be resumed, Ashok asked, 'Desai sahib, do you remember your lines?'

'Yes, sir!' Desai answered confidently.

The lights came on. Scene thirty-four, take three began to roll. Desai waved his rifle in the air. 'Neela Devi . . . you . . . you.' He suddenly stopped. 'I am sorry.'

Ashok's heart sank, but to keep Desai in a good mood, he said, 'That's all right, but hurry up.'

Scene thirty-four, take four got under way. However, Desai was unable to separate urine from Peshawar. The trouble was that in Urdu the word for urine was 'peeshap', which was perilously close to Peshawar. When a few more efforts also failed to produce results, I took Ashok aside and said, 'Dadamoni, when Desai speaks his lines, let him say them with his back to the camera. Let him not drink the urine of Peshawar while facing the camera.'

Ashok immediately understood that this was the only way of getting out of this conundrum because we could then dub the lines in his voice by joining different sound clips. But, if he was facing the camera, his lip movements would not be in sync with the soundtrack.

When this was explained to Desai, he was shattered. He assured us that this time he would get it right but the water was by now over our heads, and what was more, it was the water of Peshawar. We all begged him to go along and say whatever came to his lips. He was greatly disheartened. 'That is all right, Manto, I will turn my face away from the camera, but mark my words, I will get the lines letter perfect.'

'Scene thirty-four . . . take fourteen,' the words rang out. Desai waved his rifle in the air with a determined flourish and said to Veera, 'Neela Devi, you do not have a thing to worry about. I have also drunk the peeshap of Peshawar.'

'Cut!' Desai rested the rifle on his shoulder in triumph and asked Ashok, 'Yes, Mr Ganguly?' Ashok, whose heart by now had turned into stone, replied dryly, 'Fine, fine.' Then he said to Hardeep the cameraman, 'Let's do the next shoot tomorrow.'

We packed up the shift and I remembered that I had to go to Churchgate with a friend who was in a hurry to get to the railway station. As I stepped into the carriage, I found Desai sitting there bragging to his fellow passengers. I joined him. 'What should be done to those who forget their lines on the set?' I asked at one point.

Desai's answer was immediate. 'I don't know, I have never forgotten my lines, even once.'

He was innocence itself, being completely unaware of the disease called 'forgetting your lines'. I am quite sure he was convinced that he was incapable of making any mistakes. This was understandable because one can only be aware of mistakes if one knows what is right. Since that part of the human brain that makes such distinctions was altogether missing in Desai's case, he lived in a perpetual state of bliss. Those who thought him to be a great comedian were wrong. He was not even an actor. If people burst out laughing at what he did on the screen, the credit was due to nature's pulling mankind's leg. God had fashioned him out of funny bones.

Once at the racecourse, I pointed out Desai to my wife. She took one look at him from a distance and began to laugh. 'Why are you laughing when you can't even see him clearly?' I asked her.

She had no answer; all she could come up with was, 'I don't know.'

Desai was crazy about racing and would always bring his wife and daughter with him to the races, but he never bet more than ten rupees. He used to say that he knew many jockeys who gave him the inside dope which he passed on to his friends with instructions not to share the 'info' with anyone. Funnily enough, he never used those tips himself but relied on what someone else had told him. When I introduced him to my wife at the race-course, he immediately gave her a 'sure' tip. When it failed to produce a winner, he told her in a surprised voice, 'How odd! This tip was supposed to be one hundred per cent accurate.' He himself had backed another horse, of course, which had placed.

Information about Desai's early life is sketchy. All I knew was that he came from a middle-class family of Gujarat. After his graduation, he took a law degree and for six or seven years knocked around Bombay's lower courts, making just enough to manage. Then he sort of flipped and remained half-crazy for some time. This was a very difficult time for him financially. His treatment had worked up to a point, but the doctors had warned him not to do any work involving intellectual activity or he might flip again. That was a tough one for Desai. Law was out because it required the brain to go full blast. He could have gone into business but he had no interest in it.

It was at this point that he asked Chiman Lal Desai of Sagar Movietone to get him some work at the studio. What he meant was a chance at acting. Since Chiman Lal was both a Gujarati and a Desai, he hired V.H. and because of him some directors gave him bit parts. However, all of them came to the conclusion that once was more than enough. For some time, V.H. remained at Sagar Movietone drawing a salary and doing nothing.

Meanwhile, Himanshu Rai had set up Bombay Talkies and had made a number of hit movies. This company was quite justifiably known for having a soft spot for educated people, so it was only a matter of time before Desai knocked at its doors. After two or three visits and a couple of letters of recommendation that he managed to obtain, he met Himanshu Rai. Because of his looks and despite his lunacy, Rai took him on, as he wanted to introduce an actor to the Indian cinema who was completely ignorant of the art of acting.

However, in his very first film, Desai became the centre of attention. What torture the staff and the technicians of Bombay Talkies suffered during the making of that movie, it is not possible to describe. Many times, they almost gave up on him but persisted because they saw it as a challenge. After his first film, Desai became a Bombay Talkies icon. No film coming out of that studio was considered complete or sufficiently amusing unless it starred Desai. He, of course, was delighted but not at all surprised because he was convinced that the secret of his success lay in his intelligence, application and tireless efforts; but as God is my witness, none of these things had anything to do with his fame and fortune. It was one of nature's jokes that Desai became Indian cinema's leading comedian.

During my time at Filmistan, he acted in three of its productions, *Chal Chal Re Naujawan*, *Shikari* and *Eight Days*. On numerous occasions, I nearly gave up on him, but since Ashok Kumar and Mukherjee had warned me what to expect, I persisted. It was a most trying experience. I have a restless temperament, so it is a wonder that I did not give up the ghost during the making of the first movie, *Chal Chal Re Naujawan*. There were days when I wanted to pick up the camera and throw it at him or push the sound boom down his throat and place all the studio lights on his immobile body. But one look at him and I could not help laughing.

I do not know how the angel of death was able to claim Desai's life. Didn't he roll over with laughter while approaching him? Even if angels do not have human characteristics, there can be no question that even for the angel of death it must have been a most amusing experience. I am reminded of the final scene in *Shikari* in which we had to kill Desai. It was the cruel Japanese who had to do the deed. However, he had a line to speak before dying. He was to tell his apprentice Badal, played by Ashok Kumar, and his beloved Veera that they should not grieve over his death but continue the good work. The nightmare of his lines was there, of course, as always; the problem was to have him die in a way that would not make the audience laugh. I had already announced my view that even if Desai was to be actually killed the audience would still laugh because they just would not believe that he had died or even that he could die.

Had it been left to me, I would have deleted this scene from the movie altogether, but the difficulty was that the direction the story had taken was such that Desai's character absolutely had to die. For days we toyed with various ideas but came to the conclusion that there could be no two ways about it: Desai simply had to die.

The lines did not really matter. We began to rehearse the scene. One thing that we all immediately noticed was that the way Desai died after having spoken for the last time to Ashok and Veera was extremely funny. This was supposed to be a poignant moment. The way he flailed his arms about made him look like a wound-up toy that was unwinding. This was bound to cause laughter. We told him to fall and not wave his arms about, but it seemed that, like his brain, his body too was not under his control. Finally, Ashok came up with a suggestion. He proposed that he and Veera, the heroine, should each grab Desai's hands so that he would not be able to wave his arms in that very funny way. Everyone was relieved that a solution had been found, but on the opening night, when this scene came, the entire auditorium burst out laughing. For the next showing, we partly edited the scene, but there was not much change in audience reaction. Finally, we decided to let it run as it had been shot.

Desai was a great miser and had never been known to spend a paisa on his friends. He had once bought Ashok's old car from him—on monthly instalments, of course—and since he could not drive himself, he employed a driver. However, we noticed that every ten days or so, he had a different one. When I asked him why, he gave me a roundabout answer. But soon the cat was out of the bag. Jagtap, the sound recordist, told me that every driver was hired without pay on a ten-day trial basis and was sacked on some excuse on the eleventh. This went on for several months, which gave Desai enough time to learn to drive himself.

Desai had long been an asthma patient and, on someone's advice, he had got into the habit of trying a little dried marijuana every day as an antidote. In winter, he would also help himself to a couple of glasses of brandy and then chirp merrily like a canary.

In *Eight Days* one of the scenes required him to sit in a bathtub. The weather was pleasant the day this scene was to be shot, but Desai kept complaining that it was cold. We had the water in the tub heated to keep him comfortable, while instructing the production manager to keep some brandy at hand. Those who have seen the movie will remember how Tekam Lala, which was his character's name in the film, gets into the bathtub in Sir Narindra's flat with an ice pack on his head and a fan blowing cool air in his face. He is supposed to have had a few drinks because he keeps saying, 'On all four sides is the sea and that big mountain made of ice . . .'

After the scene was shot and Desai had dried and changed, we gave him a large peg of brandy, which he downed happily. One peg was all it took to get him tipsy. He and I were alone in the room and he began to regale me with stories of his great exploits as a lawyer and how he used to score dramatic court victories for his clients. He was a great admirer of the legal acumen of Quaid-e-Azam Muhammad Ali Jinnah and Bhulabhai Desai. He had met the Quaid-e-Azam many times and heard him plead some of his celebrated cases.

While we were shooting *Eight Days*, I received a notice from Lahore, which said that the government of Punjab had issued warrants against me under Section 292 as my story 'The Odour' had been found to be pornographic. When I mentioned this to Desai, he began to brag about his encyclopaedic legal knowledge and this made me think of a prank. I decided that I would have Desai defend me. His mere entry into the courtroom would have people in stitches. When I mentioned this to Mukherjee, he agreed that it was a great idea. My list of defence witnesses also included the other great comedian of Indian cinema, Noor Mohammad Charlie. The mere thought of both these characters in one courtroom defending Saadat Hasan Manto was hilarious; Desai had begun 'preparing' my defence, which was totally unnecessary since all I wanted was entertainment. Noor Mohammad Charlie was also readying his testimony. Unfortunately, because of unremitting work at the studio, I found it impossible to get out of Bombay even for a day.

Desai was sorry that he had not found an opportunity to prove his legal genius. He did not, of course, realize that I had no interest in his knowledge of law. I had wanted him to do in court what he did in movies—to keep forgetting what he was supposed to say. I wanted him to make the court do one retake after another by turning Peshawar into peeshap and peeshap into Peshawar. Pity it never came to pass.

Desai has since died. The only time in his entire life when he did not need a retake or even a rehearsal was when he dutifully carried out the instructions of the angel of death and did exactly what he was asked to do, namely, slide into the valley of death without making any more people laugh.

RAFIQ GHAZNAVI: THE LADIES' MAN

I am not sure why, whenever I think of Rafiq Ghaznavi, I am reminded of Mahmud of Ghazni who invaded India seventeen times. If there was one thing common to the two of them, it was that they were both iconoclasts. While Mahmud ransacked the great temple at Somnath with its golden idol, depriving it of its treasures, Rafiq's conquests were made up of a dozen or so courtesans.

Rafiq's name would suggest that his ancestors came from Ghazni. I am not sure if he ever saw Ghazni; all I know is that he used to live in Peshawar and could speak both Pushto and Afghan Persian. Normally, he would speak Punjabi. He wrote well in English, and had he chosen to write in Urdu, he would have made a name for himself. He was much given to Urdu literature and his collection of books was large. When I first met him in Bombay at his Gulshan Mahal place and saw books scattered all over the floor, I was surprised. I had thought he was just a musician who had no use for literature, but when we began to talk he named authors of whom I had never heard. He told me about one Abdul Fazal Siddiqui who wrote stories only about animals and birds. When I read him later, I found him good.

I am not sure where I should start as I sit down to write on Rafiq Ghaznavi, but I have already begun writing and, if all goes well, I shall somehow reach the end. Let me try to remember when I first met him. I knew of him before we actually met. How I knew of him and for how long, I do not recall now. However, it must have been about twenty-five years ago when a betel-leaf seller in Bijli Chowk, Amritsar, called after me as I went past his shop. 'Babu sahib, it has been a long time. I think you should settle my account.'[1] I was taken aback because I had never taken any credit from him. 'What are you talking about? I have never bought anything here,' I said. He smiled. 'That's what they all say when they do not wish to pay what they owe.' I asked him for details and it was only then that I learnt that he had mistaken me for Rafiq Ghaznavi. I assured him that I was Saadat Hasan. 'But you bear a remarkable resemblance to him,' the shopkeeper remarked. I had heard of Rafiq Ghaznavi and until then I had had no desire to meet him, but when I heard that I looked like him I became curious.

Those days, I was wholly idle, restless and bored all the time. I wanted to sample everything I came upon, no matter how bitter the taste. I would go to shrines, walk in graveyards or spend hours sitting under a tree in Jallianwala Bagh, dreaming of the revolution that would destroy the British Raj in one instant. On seeing a bunch of schoolgirls on the street, I would pick one out and imagine that I was having an affair with her. I would try to invent bomb-making methods or would listen to noted classical singers and try to fathom the mysteries of their music. I once even tried my hand at poetry. I would write long love letters to sweethearts who did not exist, read them over and tear them up because they were such rubbish. I tried marijuana, cocaine and drinking but nothing cured me of my restlessness.

It was during that time that I developed an intense desire to meet Rafiq Ghaznavi. I looked for him at shrines, cheap drinking haunts and even asked about him in the bazaar where the dancing girls lived and performed, but no one could tell me where he was. Off and on, I would hear that he was in Amritsar and every time I heard that, I would go looking for him but never found him. One day, I learnt that he was in Amritsar and staying at the house of a friend, a tailor whose name I no longer remember. He had a shop in a small street of the Karmoon Deori area, not far from where I lived. When I went there, I was told that Rafiq was to be found at the tailor's home, which was outside the city in a thinly populated area. It was my friend Bala who had obtained the information for me. He was, in fact, on his way to this place and agreed to take me along. This is as good a place as any to introduce Bala. It pains me to write that he used to be known as Bala Kanjar—or Bala of the prostitutes' clan. I have never understood why human beings are associated with the professions of their families.

Bala was a young man of taste who was educated, handsome, witty and poetical. He had talent and much promise. He knew what people called him, but he did not care. He used to live in that area of the city where women make their living by selling their bodies. After Independence, he moved to Karachi and began to sell his paintings. I once read in a newspaper that he had held an exhibition of his works which had been greatly appreciated. Bala also liked to sing, though he had a bad voice. Along with him, Captain Waheed, Anwar the painter, Ashiq Ali the photographer, the poet Faqir Hussain Salees, and Giani Aror Singh the dentist formed our group of bohemians.

Most of our time was spent either at Anwar's or at the dental clinic of Giani Aror Singh. We could also be found at Jeeja's Hotel Shiraz or the shop of the tailor whose name I have forgotten.

While together, we would do marijuana. It would either be cooked with meat or ground into a mixture with milk and sugar. There would be much singing of the light classical variety—thumri, dadra and tappa. Ashiq Ali had a thin but sweet voice and he would often sing in Rafiq Ghaznavi's popular style. Captain Waheed played the tabla and Anwar just nodded his head and enjoyed the music. Giani Aror Singh would forget all about teeth and sing the raagni Pahari after the manner of Khan Sahib Ashiq Ali Khan of Patiala, son of Taan Kaptaan Khan Fateh Ali Khan. Ashiq Ali Khan's voice was awesome, deep and powerful in all three octaves. Bala used to tell jokes and, off and on, recite his latest poems. I still remember a verse, something about a teardrop dangling on an eyelash. It was good, as such poetry goes.

Giani Aror Singh was doing quite well as a dentist, but once the art bug bites you, you rarely survive, which was what happened. He closed down his business and disappeared. The same fate was in store for Anwar. I have no idea what happened to Jeeja, though I heard once that he was in Lahore practising herbal medicine. As for Faqir Hussain Salees, he went into soap-making. Giani Aror Singh eventually became a successful actor, but some time later I heard that he had renounced the world and become a hermit. Captain Waheed married a woman who already had five children. He became a contractor.

As for Rafiq Ghaznavi, he did not change. After moving to Pakistan, he raced horses in Karachi and composed music for the movies, which was exactly what he used to do in Bombay. I have begun to reminisce about things that happened a long time ago and I find myself getting carried away. I had begun writing about Rafiq and I went into unrelated things, though the truth is that it is these unrelated things which I like. Isn't life itself the sum total of unrelated happenings and people?

So here I was with Bala on my way to see Rafiq Ghaznavi. It was a cool evening in April and our tonga travelled for a long time before it came to a stop in front of a single-storey house in semi-darkness.

Although this happened nearly twenty-five years ago, I distinctly remember that it was surrounded by trees and bushes. In the light of a lantern, that tailor whose name I cannot remember, and another character by the name of Meeda Mota, plus some others, were playing cards and drinking. I disliked Meeda Mota, first because he was fat, big and strong and, second, because he would always induce me to play cards, cheat and put me under a debt of eight or ten rupees. Some days later, he would waylay me, pull out a knife and ask me to pay, else . . . When Bala asked the tailor about Rafiq, he replied that he had been missing for two days, but he could not state with certainty where he was. Then he added, 'Bala, you know when Rafiq steps into a kotha he does not come out for weeks.' Bala smiled, which suggested that he knew that. As for me, another attempt to meet Rafiq had failed.

A year later, I saw a photograph of Rafiq Ghaznavi floating in a flat, open pan in Ashiq Ali's darkroom. Ashiq Ali was an innovative photographer, the first in Amritsar to use unorthodox techniques. Normally, photographers pander to the vanity of their subject by retouching all the lines in his face, lines that express his real character. They turn his face into a peeled potato without a mark or a line. Ashiq Ali used to say, 'It is the duty of the photographer to show people as they are. The camera must record what it sees accurately.' He loved using light and shadow, and the picture I saw that day was one of his masterpieces. Rafiq was dressed like an Arab. He had a long face and though some of it was in shadow I could see that his features, though not too sharp, were attractive. He was handsome. His nose was long and generously proportioned. His lips were thin and compressed, creating tiny triangles at either end, while his hair was long and swept back carefully, with long sideburns. I saw no resemblance between our two faces. God alone knows what that betel-leaf seller had seen in me that he thought I shared with Rafiq. Ashiq Ali told me that Rafiq had been at his studio a day earlier but had gone back to Lahore in the evening. So I went to Lahore after him, but was told that he had gone to Rawalpindi and since I had no intention of following him there I returned to Amritsar. A week later, I learnt that Rafiq had all along been cooped up in the kotha of a dancing girl. To hell with it, I thought. After this, years passed, but I still had not found an opportunity to meet Rafiq. In fact, I had nearly given up, though I kept up with the gossip, which had him sleeping with practically every leading courtesan of Amritsar.

Rafiq had popularized a certain style of ghazal singing and every girl in the bazaar dutifully followed it. The stories that went around about Rafiq had to be heard to be believed. 'And what is it that you are singing?' 'Oh, that is one of Rafiq's things.' 'And what style would that be?' 'Rafiq Ghaznavi's, of course.' 'You know, this smashed watch that you see is Rafiq's. Yesterday, as he began to develop a note, he waved his arm in the air and his hand hit the wall, smashing his watch into a thousand pieces.' 'Yesterday, Rafiq Ghaznavi was getting ready to sing at one of the kothas and had just finished tuning the instruments when he noticed something. "Tune your tabla," he said to the tabla player. "Done that already," the tabla player replied. "Do it one more time . . . there was a fly sitting on the right one a minute ago. It might have disturbed the tonal balance."'

Rafiq also used to write poetry and one of his ghazals was very popular those days; I now confuse its words with one of Iqbal's, such being my memory. One day, I heard that Rafiq had gone to Lahore to play the lead in the first talkie being made in Punjab, based on the love legend of Heer Ranjha. Rafiq, being the hero, was Ranjha and the heroine was a courtesan from Amritsar by the name of Anwari (who later married Ahmed Salman of All India Radio—later of Radio Pakistan—whose Hindu name at birth was Jugul Kishore Mehra). The role of Qaido, the villainous uncle of Heer, had been given to M. Ismail. The film was made and released but I could not go to Lahore—why, I do not remember Rumours were rampant at the time that Rafiq had quarrelled with the movie's producer and director, A.R. Kardar, and also that Rafiq was having a torrid affair with Anwari, and that Anwari's mother was most upset and one of these days knives would be out and somebody would get hurt. Then came the news that Rafiq had run off with Anwari in a most dramatic manner.

The story was true. Rafiq really had decamped with Anwari, her distraught mother notwithstanding. Some really rough characters had been sent after Rafiq but they had failed to make him let Anwari go. Only when he was satiated did he send her back to her mother with the message, 'Here is your precious daughter—all yours.' This was a catastrophe for Anwari's family because a courtesan who is no longer a virgin fetches no price. The family had waited for the big day when the virgin Anwari would be 'married'—for a few nights—to the highest bidder, but now that she was 'soiled goods', it was not going to happen. The family, therefore, asked Rafiq to keep her. This was

Rafiq's first recorded assault in this realm. Anwari eventually gave birth to a daughter, who was named Zarina—she played Roohi in A.R. Kardar's famous film *Shahjahan* (1946) and was later given in marriage by her 'father' Ahmed Salman, deputy director general of Radio Pakistan, to a rich businessman from Karachi.

In the meantime I left Amritsar and landed in Bombay where I worked for various publications. There I learnt that Rafiq had left Anwari and was now in Calcutta writing film music scores. I too had moved to films, having wasted enough time in journalism. The first couple of years were spent chasing shadows but eventually I landed at Hindustan Cinetone owned by Seth Nanoobhai Desai, who had set up and bankrupted many film companies in his time. His new enterprise did not look too promising either. I had written the story for a movie called *Keechar*, which he had liked because it was based on socialist ideas. I never could understand why the seth, every inch a dirty capitalist, had taken a shine to it. One day, I was busy writing the dialogue for *Keechar* when someone said Rafiq Ghaznavi had just arrived and wanted to meet me. The first question that came to my mind was: How does he know me? I was still wondering when a tall, strapping fellow in a finely tailored suit walked into my room. It was Rafiq Ghaznavi. A fully articulated Punjabi curse rolled off his tongue, followed by, 'So you are hiding in here?' I suddenly had a feeling that I had always known him.

There was something carefree about Rafiq. The picture I had seen floating in Ashiq Ali darkroom in Amritsar was different from the real man in only one respect. It did not talk. His style of conversation did not go with his general personality. When he talked, his mouth opened in a cavernous way and I could not fail to notice that he did not have good teeth and gums. I would not have minded his bad teeth and gums if his conversation had not reeked of the bazaar. I did not like the way he moved his hands like a dancer when he talked. He spoke to me as he spoke to his social inferiors, which was something I disliked right away. However, since this was our first meeting and one I had sought for so long, I did not let these minor details affect my overall judgement of the man.

He invited me to come to his hotel in the evening. The first thing I saw when I entered his room was a vichitra veena, a stringed sitar-like instrument, which lay in a corner on the floor, sheathed in silk. In the other corner lay Rafiq's shoes in a neat row. Then I noticed a woman who appeared to have come straight from the bazaar—and, in fact, had. Her name was Zohra. She later married a struggling film director by the name of Mirza and came to be known as Zohra Mirza. She had two children, a boy and a girl. The girl, who was older, was called Parveen and came to the movies under the name Shaheena. She made at least one film called *Beli* in the early days of Pakistan, based on one of my stories. It was a disaster at the box office. When I met Rafiq in Bombay, Parveen must have been around five. She had blue eyes, but Zohra, Parveen's mother, did not have light eyes. The girl had inherited her eyes from her grandmother who had lovely big blue eyes.

I forgot to record that when I was hired as a 'munshi' or resident writer at the Imperial Film Company, Zohra's two younger sisters had joined the outfit at the same time. One of them was rather plump, while the other was slim and pretty. Their names were Sheedan and Heeran. Sheedan was blithe, flirtatious and restless, and found it hard to sit still even for a minute. She spoke so rapidly that her words overrode each other. It was quite unnerving to talk to her. It was she who told me that Rafiq or Pheeko bhaijan, as she called him, had left Anwari and was now married to her (Sheedan's) elder sister Zohra. Heeran, compared to Sheedan, was awkward, which was why she could not make it in the movies, unlike her sister who had a part in Imperial's *Hind Mata*, which did quite well.

One day I went to Imperial Film Company to meet with Seth Ardeshir Irani, the owner. As I walked into his room through the swing door, I found him pumping one of Sheedan's breasts as if it was one of those old-fashioned car horns. I turned right around without saying a word.

To return to my visit, one look at Rafiq's room was enough to tell me that he was down on his luck those days. There was one thing about him. Whenever he was going through a bad patch—or what in Bombay is known as 'karki'—he would dress with the greatest care and in the most expensive clothes. Once he was over the hump, he would revert to ordinary clothes. He was one of those people who not only know how to dress but also look good in whatever they wear. We sat in his room for some time and then walked out into the hotel's small garden. I had brought a bottle of whisky with me, which we shared.

While there, we were joined by a woman. She smiled at Rafiq and took a chair next to him without any formality. Rafiq introduced her to me. She was a Sikh and had plenty of money of her own, but the film bug had bitten her and she had a crush on Ashok Kumar, which was why she came to Bombay every now and then, just to catch a glimpse of her idol. She was a big woman and Rafiq said to me in her presence, 'I have told this sali several times that she should cure herself of this Ashok Kumar obsession. Just think about it. Were Ashok to lie on top of her, he would look like a parrot trying to fire a cannon.' Rafiq kept laughing at his own joke for a long time. She did not react. That was another thing about him. He would laugh so much at his own stories that in the end those present had to join in. The Sikh woman had average looks and was slightly masculine in appearance. Although Rafiq kept conversing with her, it was clear that he had no interest in her. But that notwithstanding, he continued to drop broad hints about wanting to take her to bed. She, of course, had eyes only for Ashok Kumar. Finally, she told him in a characteristic rustic Punjabi way, 'Now listen, Rafiq, I would rather couple with a dog than . . .' But Rafiq did not let her finish. 'Say no more . . . you have no idea what a pedigreed dog I am!' Pedigree I do not know about, but what I would say is that Rafiq was indeed a dog though only courtesans and prostitutes could make him wag his tail. Housewives and straight women meant nothing to him.

This was our first real meeting and it led to many more. Rafiq was mean, selfish and low. He cared only about himself. He believed in accepting hospitality, but never offered any. However, if he had an axe to grind, he would throw a big party for you. But he would then scout the table and eat the best pieces of meat himself! He hardly ever offered anyone a cigarette. During the war it was difficult to buy good cigarettes except in the black market. One day, Rafiq walked into a studio where I was working, holding a tin of Craven A cigarettes, my favourite brand. When I tried to take one, he moved his hand so that the tin was beyond my reach. 'Let me have one,' I said. Rafiq stepped back, shoved the tin into his pocket and said, 'No, Manto . . . to begin with, I never offer anyone a cigarette; secondly, I do not want to spoil you. Go on smoking your Gold Flakes.' There were a couple of people around and I felt deeply humiliated.

Rafiq was utterly without a sense of honour although, as a Pathan, it was one quality he should have had. It was said that, before his affair with Zohra, he had had an affair with her mother. He had next seduced Mushtri, Zohra's elder sister, followed by Zohra and, finally, Sheedan, the youngest sister. Rafiq used to live on Bombay's Mahim Road. In fact, he lived in the same building as my sister. I was already married and living in Adelphi Chambers, Clare Road, where Rafiq used to visit me. We would also run into each other at All India Radio's Bombay station. One day I asked him, 'So what keeps you busy these days?' 'Love-making, but it is beginning to affect my health.' A few days later, I heard that Sheedan had tried to commit suicide by taking a large dose of opium. She must have pinched it from Zohra who, like her mother, had a taste for the drug. It turned out that there had been a fight between the two sisters over Rafiq. Zohra had told Sheedan that she was stealing her husband from her. Sheedan was too young and too infatuated with her Pheeko bhaijan to know what was good for her. Anyway, she survived and was spared the dubious honour of becoming a martyr to love. As a result of this incident, Rafiq left Zohra and set himself up with Sheedan.

When Rafiq's love life was at its most active, it so happened that a Hindu gentleman from Lahore came to Bombay with a young woman companion by the name of Zebunissa. He rented a flat in Gulshan Mahal on Lady Jamshedji Road in Mahim. He was a strange character. Obviously rich, he did not really care what his Zeb did as long as he did not know. He was quite happy with the way things were. Rafiq had somehow got to know him and had been over to his flat a couple of times, which was enough to have got Zeb interested in him. She was so taken with Rafiq that she would spend all her money on him and even bring him anything of value she found in her flat. The affair did not last as Rafiq got tired of her. When I asked why, he replied, 'She is too straight . . . not the sort of woman I enjoy.' He had no interest in women who were nice and homely, because the ones he had known all his life were from the bazaar, women who swore and drank and told dirty stories. He felt no sexual excitement if a woman showed 'wifely' qualities. He was husband to every prostitute and dancing girl who entered his semi-Byronic life. He was a very special client of these women, a client who gave nothing, but took what he could. He considered life itself to be some kind of a prostitute, a bazaar woman. He would sleep with it every night, get up in the morning and start exchanging dirty stories with it. Then he would ask it to perform, and return the favour by performing himself. He believed that was how life should be lived.

I never found Rafiq depressed. He was always shamelessly happy, which was perhaps the secret of his good health. His advancing years had done nothing to him; in fact, the older he grew, the more attractive he became to women. I used to say that when Rafiq reached the age of hundred, he would be transformed into a baby sucking its thumb.

When Sheedan give birth to a stillborn child, my wife and I went to his Shivaji Park place to condole. We saw a strange scene. Rafiq was sitting on the floor wearing a Turkish cap as if he were about to offer his prayers, while Zohra was dressed in black. She had not done her hair and her eyes were swollen. Mirza, the man she had married, was around and appeared to be rather overcome by the occasion. We heard Sheedan sobbing in the next room. Zohra leapt through the door and began to console her sister. It was all very odd.

Let me work it out. Rafiq was married to Zohra at one time and had two children by her, Parveen and Mahmood. He was now married to her sister Sheedan, and Zohra was married to Mirza. Sheedan was Zohra's sister as well as her sister-in-law. Rafiq's children by Zohra were Sheedan's nephew and niece and also her stepson and stepdaughter. Sheedan's stillborn child was Zohra's nephew as well as her stepson. Parveen and Mahmood were thus the stillborn baby's half-sister and half-brother, as well as his cousins. Rafiq and Mirza were brothers-in-law and so on and so forth. It was a mystifying rigmarole.

'Let's get out of here,' Rafiq said to me as we walked out on the veranda. He threw his cap on a chair and lit a cigarette. 'The hell with it . . . my face has become long because of the mournful expression I have had to wear since morning.' Then he burst out laughing.

Another time I had to travel to Lahore from Bombay to attend a court hearing. I met Rafiq there at an auction house run by one Syed Salamatullah Shah, a most colourful character. I was told that Rafiq was very happy as he had just returned from Amritsar where he had gone to meet his daughter by Anwari, Zarina alias Nasreen. Rafiq had only seen her as a little girl because Anwari had never encouraged him to visit her, having told her daughter that her father was an ugly rake. His friends arranged a meeting between Rafiq and the daughter he had only seen as a child. Rafiq told me that day in Lahore, 'Manto, she is tall and extremely beautiful, full of youth. When I took her in my arms and embraced her, it was like being in heaven.' I do not wish to comment on this statement. Rafiq also told me that when he was about to leave, Anwari came in and tried to pick a fight with him, but he silenced her with just one line. 'Shut up, Anwari . . . you should be grateful to me that I have made you the owner of a gold mine.' I have no idea how many such gold mines

Rafiq gifted to how many women in his lifetime. I suppose we will only find out on the day of judgment. Rafiq once said to me, 'Frankly, I have no idea how many sons and daughters I have fathered. God alone knows because He is the greatest counter of them all.'

Rafiq also had a 'proper' wife, the one his family had found for him. She died three or four years after their marriage. They had a daughter by the name of Zahira, who was the film director Zia Sarhadi's first wife. The marriage ended in a divorce and the last I heard she was living in Karachi, where she had moved in 1947 with Rafiq Ghaznavi. That girl had a sad life but I hold Rafiq responsible for her ill fortune because he always advised her to live her life as he had lived his. When she was in Bombay, she got briefly involved with the film journalist Nazir Ludhianwi while she was also seeing Zia Sarhadi. Rafiq's advice to her was, 'Look child, if you cannot marry Nazir Ludhianwi, you should marry Zia Sarhadi, and if you can't make up your mind, you should marry both. If they betray you, don't take it to heart. Remember I am your biggest husband, being your father.' Nazir was betrayed by Zahira and Zahira by Zia. Subsequently, she came to live with the biggest husband of them all, Rafiq Ghaznavi. She used to smoke bidis, looking for her lost youth in their ashes, a youth which was destined to come to nothing. I do not wish to write another word about Zahira because I find it agonizing.

Rafiq was always very boyish. He would laugh at the slightest joke, and if he felt happy, he would actually jump up and down. At that time we were making *Chal Chal Re Naujawan* for Filmistan, starring Naseem and Ashok Kumar. Rafiq too was playing a role in it. He told me that he used to know Naseem's mother, the famous Delhi courtesan Shamshad alias Chammiya. One evening, with some of the city's richest patrons in attendance, she was singing and sipping a drink out of a crystal glass, when she noticed Rafiq, smiled and waved to him to come sit next to her. He said he sat there all night, taking one drink after another from her dainty hand. 'I was there for the next fifteen days and nights,' he told me. I introduced him to Naseem. The last time Rafiq had seen her, she was a little girl running around the room with a chunnariya over her head. Naseem knew Rafiq. Their conversation was rather stilted and formal because Naseem was always extremely polite. She did not allow Rafiq an opportunity to say anything 'loose', but he was thrilled to be in her company. When he came to my room, he began to dance and praise Naseem's beauty. He jumped on a table, dropped to the floor with a thud, swerved and swivelled for some time, then crept under a table, hit his head against it, re-emerged, stood up and started singing. I think Rafiq was quite keen to have something going with Naseem but he had no luck, not that he ever gave up trying.

Nur Jehan he would have seduced but she was so smitten by Shaukat Hussain Rizvi that she had no time for anyone else. Sitara, however, without quite wanting to and without being asked, ended up in Rafiq's bed, he having taken advantage of her simultaneous affairs with Arora and Nazir. When Sohrab Modi was filming *Sikander*, Meena, a young girl from Bombay's courtesans' quarter, Pawan Pull, was also around, having been spirited away by a man called Zahoor Ahmed, who had married her. She had found a job in Minerva Movietone. Rafiq, who was scoring the music for the movie, had written a chorus—*Zindagi hai pyar se, pyar se bitai ja; Husn ke hazoor mein, apna sar jhookai ja* (Life is love, spend it in the pursuit of love; when you see beauty, bow down before it). Rafiq had duly bowed in front of Meena but just three or four times. Then he rolled up his prayer mat and disappeared.

Then there were those two singing girls from Agra, both sisters, who had recently moved to Pawan Pull from Hyderabad, where they had served the pleasure of Prince Moazzam Jah. The elder one was called Akhtar, while the younger one, who was only fourteen or fifteen, was named Anwar. They used to perform at their kotha and were very popular. Haldia, a friend of mine from Delhi, had a crush on Akhtar. On one of his visits to Bombay, we spent an evening listening to the two sisters. I don't know how but Rafiq Ghaznavi's name came up during our conversation. 'He is a bastard,' I said. The younger one smiled at me flirtatiously and said, 'You bear a close resemblance to him.' I was left speechless.

I mentioned this exchange to Rafiq but he did not know the girls. However, after some time he began to visit them. His interest lasted just a year. His prediction that Anwar would become a great thumri singer came true. I saw her several years later at All India Radio's Delhi station where I was then working. She was a bag of bones. The change was shocking. Gone were her youth and vivaciousness. Who had reduced her to this state, I wondered. She sat in front of the microphone, a couple of pillows cradling her back, her head resting against the tanpura to spare her fragile neck the burden of supporting that weight. But when she sang, the listeners felt as if her voice was penetrating their souls.

As for Rafiq, it was always my opinion that he was more of a trick performer than a singer. He would have you swaying before even a single note had left his lips. He would place his finger on one of the keys of his harmonium and his face would assume an other-worldly look. Then he would emit a long 'hai'—as if he was in pain or his soul was leaving his body—electrifying his listeners. This would be followed by another sound of unbearable pain (or was it pleasure?) and just when it felt that he was about to swoon, he would burst out laughing. The actual performance would come next, like water being sprinkled gently on parched earth. He would make strange faces when singing, as if his stomach was bothering him, especially when he was singing a classical composition. He appeared to be in such agony that you would pray to God to release him from his ordeal.

When Ezra Mir set up a film company in association with some other well-to-do Jews of Bombay and announced its first production, *Sitara*, Rafiq was chosen as music director. Mir was a handsome man and so were his associates, but even standing among them, Rafiq's personality was undiminished. He was the kind of man who stood out in a crowd. His style of work was unique. There he would be, standing in the middle of a hundred musicians and giving them their final instructions; with the Punjabis, he would crack jokes, while the Christian musicians would be addressed in English; to the Urdu-speaking ones, he would talk in chaste Urdu. One day Rafiq, Ezra Mir and I were together in Mir's room discussing a composition, while the musicians were in one of the studios rehearsing. Suddenly, Rafiq trained an ear in the direction of the music, which we could only hear faintly, pulled a face and said in an agonized voice, 'Dash it, one of the violins is not properly tuned.' Then he left us to attend to the offending instrument.

I have no taste for music and though I have listened to most of the great singers of our time, somehow I have never become privy to the mysteries of music. However, I do know that Rafiq did not have a good voice. I do not know enough about the subject to give an opinion about his knowledge of music. I have heard it said that when he sang, he was often off-key. I once told this to Nur Jehan. Her reaction was spontaneous. She put her tongue between her teeth and touched both her ears with her thumb and index fingers. 'Oh no, oh no . . . this is calumny . . . He was a master . . . one of a kind.' Age, she agreed, always affected one's voice but there could be no question about Rafiq's knowledge of music. It was his special gift.

But the special gift that Rafiq possessed in my view was his utter lack of a sense of honour and shame. I would not call him characterless because he was not an ordinary person but an artist. He may not have believed in any religious edicts but he always observed the basic ground rules. He may have been nobody's friend but neither was he anyone's enemy. He was never the traditional husband but, in all fairness, it must be pointed out that he never expected any woman to play the traditional wife to him.

There was this woman from one of Delhi's respected Hindu families who fell in love with Rafiq. She would write him long, rambling letters. I discovered this because I ran into Rafiq one day and noticed that something appeared to be bothering him, which was quite untypical. When I asked him what it was, he told me the story. 'Manto, this girl has taken leave of her senses. I am not a one-woman man. I do not believe in platonic love. She says she is going to leave home and come to me . . . She can if she wants to but how long will I be able to stay glued to her pure love? I wish to God all good women would remain in their homes, get married, give birth to children and go to hell. I am all right without their pure, platonic love, thank you. All my life I have dealt in counterfeit coins; it is too late for me to fool around with real ones.' Then he wrote a coldly worded letter to the girl from Delhi and never heard from her again.

This piece on Rafiq leaves me with a feeling of incompletion because I cannot do justice to his multifaceted personality in a handful of pages; but if I live longer, I promise to do a whole book on him. Let me close with a story. When we were making *Chal Chal Re Naujawan,* Rafiq invited all of us to dinner at his flat in Shivaji Park: the producer S. Mukherjee, the director Gyan Mukherjee, Ashok Kumar, Santoshi, Shahid Latif and myself. Rafiq was sitting on the floor, humming, with a harmonium in front of him. Next to him sat Sheedan and her brother. He welcomed the others formally but greeted me with the usual jocular Punjabi abuse. We had a few drinks, but while the others were served Scotch, I was given Indian Solan whisky, which I drank quietly. In between, Rafiq would roll a swear word in my direction, but I was determined not to show any reaction. Finally, food was served and, as was to be expected, Rafiq served the best pieces of meat to himself. After eating, everyone left except me. Sheedan also retired but her brother kept me company. Rafiq, who was not much of a drinker, was dozing because of all the good food he had eaten.

My turn had now come. I rose, tiptoed into the next room, found the bottle of Scotch, which was still half full, brought it out and began to drink. Off and on, I would pour one for Sheedan's brother. Then I would try to wake up Rafiq but he would go back to sleep after swearing at me. It was my turn this time. So I began to curse Rafiq. I cursed him so much that he woke up, looking bewildered and overwhelmed. My vocabulary of swear words was limited, so I kept repeating the ones I knew, sometimes using them in new combinations. When this became too repetitive, I decided to say whatever came to my lips, nonsense words, swear words, all kinds of words.

Rafiq was drunk, sleepy and he felt helpless. In the end, he surrendered and begged me in a half-dead voice, 'Manto, please . . . I am exhausted, I have no strength left to return your abuse.' That was the moment I had waited for all evening. I felt that I was finally even with him. I am sure he will curse me when he reads this but since I am in Lahore and he is in Karachi, I am safe for the time being. When he comes to Lahore, I am sure I will get a mouthful from him. Then I will throw a party, pour spirit in a glass of Gymkhana whisky and drink it down.

SHYAM: KRISHNA'S FLUTE

It was 23 or 24 April. I do not really remember. I was in the mental hospital at Lahore, recuperating after having earlier gone on the wagon, when I read in a newspaper that Shyam was dead. I was in a strange state at the time, suspended between consciousness and a complete lack of it. It was not possible to determine where one ended and the other began. The two states had become intertwined in a way that was hard to work out. I felt as if I was in no-man's-land.

When my eye caught the news item about Shyam's death, I thought it had something to do with my having stopped drinking. In the past weeks, various members of my family had died in my semi-conscious condition; I learnt later that they were all well and alive and praying for my recovery.

I distinctly remember that when I read about Shyam, I said to the inmate in the room next to mine, 'Do you know that a very dear friend of mine has died?'

'Who?' he asked.

'Shyam,' I replied in a tearful voice.

'Here? In the lunatic asylum?'

I did not answer his question. Suddenly, one after another, several images sprang to life in my fevered brain: Shyam smiling, Shyam laughing, Shyam screaming, Shyam full of life, utterly unaware of death and its terrors. So I said to myself that whatever I had read in the newspaper was untrue . . . even the newspaper that I held in my hands was only a figment of my imagination.

But as time passed and the mist of alcohol began to lift from my mind, I reasserted my hold on reality. The entire process was so slow and drawn out that when I finally realized that Shyam was dead I did not experience any shock. I felt as if he had died long ago and I had mourned his passing at some remote point in the past. Only the symptoms of that grief now lingered, a debris through which I was digging in the hope that in this broken mass of brick and stone I may somewhere find the buried smile that once belonged to Shyam, or the sprightly peal of his laughter.

Outside the mental hospital in the world of the sane, it was believed that Manto had gone mad after being told of Shyam's death. Had that actually happened, I would have been extremely sorry because Shyam's death should have made me wiser, heightened my awareness of the impermanence of the world. It should have made me acquire the vengeful determination to live to the hilt what was left of life. To have gone mad after learning of Shyam's death would have been madness itself.

Ghalib wrote that the legendary lover Farhad, when told of his beloved Shireen's death, killed himself with one blow of the instrument he was using to break stones. Ghalib did not consider this an act worthy of a great lover. Why had he terminated his life through a traditional, mechanical method? He should have just ceased to be. How could I, therefore, insult Shyam, who hated every conventional thing, by going mad?

Shyam is alive. He is alive in his two children, who are a result of his effulgent love for Taji whom he used to call 'my weakness'. He is alive in the person of all those women whose stoles of silk and muslin once brought shade and shelter to his loving heart. And he is alive in my heart which grieves because, when he was dying, I could not stand over him and shout, 'Shyam zindabad'.

I am sure he would have kissed death with the utmost sincerity and said in his characteristic style, 'Manto, by God, those lips are something else.'

When I think of Shyam, I am reminded of a character from a Russian novel. Shyam was a lover, but to him the act of love was not to be performed for its own sake. He was prepared to die for anything that was beautiful—and I think death must have been beautiful; otherwise he would not have died.

He loved intensity. People say the hands of death are cold, but I do not believe it. Had it been true, Shyam would have flung them aside and said, 'Go away woman, you have no warmth.'

He writes in a letter:

> Pal, the long and short of it is that everyone here is 'hiptullha' but the real 'hiptullha' has gone far, far away. As for me, there appears to be no reason for complaining . . . Life is steaming ahead, good times and drinking, drinking and good times. Taji has returned after six months. She continues to be my one great weakness. And you know there is no greater pleasure in life

than to experience the warmth of a woman's love . . . After all, I am a human being, a normal human being.

I run into Nigar [the actress Nigar Sultana] off and on, but the first right is that of 'T'. In the evenings, one misses your wise rubbish.

Shyam has used the word 'hiptullha'—and that needs an explanation.

I was working for Bombay Talkies. At the time, Kamal Amrohi's story *Haveli*, which was later filmed as *Mahal*, was being given the final touches. Ashok Kumar, Vacha, Hasrat Ludhianwi and I used to have discussion sessions every day where not only the story but all kinds of things, from gossip to scandal, came up. Shyam, who was shooting *Majboor* in those days, often joined us after knocking off work.

Kamal Amrohi was given to using heavyweight literary words and expressions even in normal conversation, which caused me problems because when I said something in simple words I could see that he was not impressed. And if I chose to say it in his heavy style, it would fly over the heads of Ashok and Vacha. Consequently, I had begun to employ a strange melange of words to make myself understood.

One morning while on the train from my home to Bombay Talkies, I opened the newspaper at the sports page to read the scorecard of a cricket match that had been played at the Brabourne Stadium, when I came across a strange name: 'Hiptullha'. I had never heard such a name before. I assumed, therefore, that it was a corrupt form of 'Haibatullah'.

When I got to the studio, the script conference was already in session. In his typical and ornate style, Kamal was describing one of the episodes. After he was done, Ashok looked at me. 'Well, Manto?'

I don't know why, but I heard myself saying, 'It is all right—but it lacks "hiptullha".'

Somehow 'hiptullha' managed to convey my meaning. What I wanted to say was that the sequence lacked force.

Later in the meeting, Hasrat presented the same sequence with variations. When I was asked my opinion, I said, this time consciously, 'Hasrat, dear friend, it doesn't do the trick. Come up with something which is hiptullha—I mean hiptullha.'

When I said 'hiptullha' for the second time, I looked around at the others for their reaction and was delighted to discover that the word had gained acceptance. In fact, it was used freely by everyone through the rest of the session, and with variations, such as: 'This thing has no "hiptullhity"' or 'It needs to be "hiptullhized".' At one point, Ashok collared me. 'What is the actual meaning of "hiptullha" and which language does it come from?'

Shyam had joined us by then. He began to laugh and his eyes narrowed. When I saw that odd name in the paper, he was with me on the train. Almost rolling over, he informed the meeting that it was Manto's latest Mantoism; when all else failed, he dragged 'hiptullha' into the film world. Soon the word gained popular currency in Bombay's film circles.

In a letter dated 29 July 1948, Shyam writes:

Dear Manto,

Once again you have gone silent and I am annoyed, really, although I am conscious of your mental lethargy. Anyway, I go berserk—and I cannot help it—when you suddenly slip into one of your silences. While it is true that I am no great letter monger myself, I get a special thrill out of receiving and writing letters, which are of a 'different kind', in other words, 'hiptullha'.

But 'hiptullha' has become a rare bird here. If you try to write it down on a piece of paper, it becomes 'hiptullhi' and if one can't even grab 'hiptullhi', you can imagine how annoying it can be. Excuse me if I have started 'hiptullhizing', but what can I do? When what is real gets lost, one begins to 'hiptullhate', but I don't give a damn as to what you think or what you don't. All I know is—and you can't be unaware of it—that I am the only person who has had the honour of humbling on the battlefield a big 'hiptullha' like you.

Manto, someone has said that when a lover runs out of words, he begins to kiss; and when a speaker runs out of words, he starts to cough. I want to make an addition to this saying: When a man runs out of manhood, he begins to look back on his past. But don't you worry, I am some distance yet from that final point. Life is full and it is rushing along. I find little time for that special madness, although I need it badly.

The film with Naseem [*Chandni Raat*] is nearly half-complete and I have signed a contract for one more with Amarnath. Guess who my heroine is. Nigar, and it was I who proposed her name, just to find out if it was possible to revive on the screen the feelings which we once felt for each other in real life. It was a joy once, but now it is work. But what do you think? Would this not be a lot of fun and frolic?

Taji is still in my life and Nigar is very good to me. She treats me with such gentleness. For some time now, Ramola has also been in Bombay and when I met her I discovered that she had not quite been able to overcome the weakness she once felt for me. So we have had some fun and games.

Old boy, these days I am receiving advanced training in the art of flirtation, but pal, this entire business is very complicated, and as you know, I love complications.

The wanderer, adventurer and seeker in me are still very powerful. I am not of a given place and do not wish to be of a given place. I love people and I hate people, so that is how life is passing. Come to think of it, life is my one and only sweetheart. As for people, they can go to hell.

I have forgotten the name of the author and all I remember is this line—which may not even be correct—but what it says is, 'He loved people so much that he never felt lonely; and when he hated them he felt quite alone.' I cannot add to that.

In both letters, there is mention of Taji, which was what Mumtaz was called. And who was Mumtaz? In Shyam's own words, his 'great weakness'. The truth was that Nigar, Ramola and all of them were his weaknesses. Women were his greatest weakness, and also his greatest strength.

Mumtaz was the younger sister of Zeb Qureshi. She arrived in Bombay with Zeb and fell in love 'heavily', it should be said, with the thickset actor Zahoor Raja. However, she rid herself of him quickly and returned to Lahore where she met Shyam and thus their great romance began. When Shyam started to do well in Bombay, he married her for the sake of the children he wanted to have with her.

Shyam loved children, especially cute children, even if they were impertinent. In the eyes of the fussy and the snooty, Shyam himself was the most impertinent. Some women disliked him intensely because of his straight, no-nonsense style, but he didn't give a damn about that. He had never tried to 'improve' himself to win their approval. Shyam's exterior was a reflection of his inner self. 'Manto,' he would say, 'these salis who look down at me are fake—they live in an artificial world of cosmetics and make-up.'

There were some women, though, who loved him because he was rough and straight. They found his conversation utterly free of the lewd stench of the adulterous bed. Shyam would talk to them in an unselfconscious and open way and they would say things to him that would not be considered fit for utterance in polite society. Shyam would be there laughing his head off, jumping up and down, tears running down his face, and I would feel as if in a corner of the room, on a bed of sharp nails, lay the goddess called inhibition praying for forgiveness of his sins.

When and where I first met Shyam, I no longer remember clearly. It now seems as if I had known him even before we were introduced. Our first meetings, I am reasonably sure, took place on Lady Jamshedji Road where my sister had a place. On the top floor of a building called 'High Nest', lived a woman named Diamond. Shyam and I met on the stairs leading up to her flat a couple of times; these encounters were quite casual and informal. During one such encounter, Shyam told me that Diamond, who was officially known in the building as Mrs Shyam, was not his wife at all, though they were like husband and wife in all other ways. Shyam wasn't a believer in the fig leaf called marriage, though once when he had to get Diamond admitted to a hospital in order to deal with a certain 'problem', he had registered her in the records as his wife.

Long after the affair was over, Diamond's husband filed a suit against Shyam and the matter dragged on for quite some time. It was finally sorted out, because Diamond had by now entered the world of movies and seen the money-lined pockets of the men who inhabited it. Shyam was no longer a part of her life, though he would often talk about her.

Once I remember the two of us were walking in a park in Poona and Shyam said to me, 'Manto, Diamond was a great woman. By God, a woman who can bear the trauma of an abortion can face up to the greatest challenge in life.' Then he had paused. 'But Manto, why is a woman afraid to face the outcome of a relationship? Is it because she sees it as the fruit of her sin? But what is this rubbish about sin and virtue? A banknote can be genuine or fake; a child cannot be legitimate or illegitimate. It is not like putting an animal under the knife in the name of the God of the Muslims or decapitating it in the manner approved by the Sikhs. A child is the outcome of that divine and magnificent madness which first gripped Adam and Eve. Oh! That madness!' And then he had kept reminiscing about his innumerable bouts with that madness.

Shyam had a high-pitched personality. His conversations, his movements, his manners were all expressed in the higher notes. He was not a believer in the middle way. To him nothing could be more comical than to sit in company with a grave expression on your face. If, while drinking, someone fell silent or tried to philosophize, Shyam would blow his top. There were times when he would even smash the bottle and glasses on the table and storm out.

I remember an incident that happened in Poona. Shyam and the writer and poet Masood Pervez were both living in a house called 'Zubaida Cottage'. I was in town to sell a film story. Masood by nature was a quiet man and after a few drinks would go into a sepulchral silence. One day we began a rum drinking session quite early in the day. Many came, downed a few, got drunk and left. Only Masood, Shyam and I stayed the course. Shyam was in a great mood because he had been making much noise with the drunken ones practically all day. By evening he felt that Masood had isolated himself from us, perhaps having had too much of Shyam's raucousness. Shyam narrowed his intoxicated eyes, looked at Masood and said sarcastically, 'Hazrat Pervez, have you completed your elegy?'

Masood smiled in his characteristic manner and said nothing. Just at that point, in walked Krishan Chander, the short-story writer, and Shyam forgot about Masood Pervez and his frozen smile. After a couple of rounds, Shyam told Krishan about the 'unbearable iciness' of Masood. Krishan needed only two drinks to unlock his tongue, which happened quickly. 'What kind of a poet are you?' he said to Masood. 'You have been drinking since morning and you have yet to say something even slightly offensive. By God, a poet who cannot talk rubbish is incapable of writing poetry. I am astonished you actually write poetry. I am quite sure your poetry is rubbish. Look at yourself now. You've turned into a bottle of castor oil after all that good liquor.'

Shyam was so amused by this simile that he fell on the floor laughing, tears running down his cheeks.

We kept teasing Masood, but he did not react. Then suddenly he got up, emptied all our glasses in gulp after gulp and declared, 'Let's go.'

We stepped out of the house and, at Masood's suggestion, we took off our shoes, tucked them under our arms and began to run. It was around midnight and the streets of Poona were deserted. The four of us and another person, whose name I cannot recall, were running like madmen and screaming our heads off, not knowing where we were headed and not particularly interested either.

At one point, we found ourselves in front of Krishan Chander's house and noticed that he had run ahead of us and gone in. We forced him to open the door and spent some time teasing him. His friend Samina Khatoon, who was asleep in the next room, woke up and came in to investigate. Krishan begged us to leave him alone, which we finally did. Then we hit the road again.

Poona is a city of temples and you have to walk barely a couple of hundred yards to come upon one. Masood's next act was to go into the first temple we passed, pull the cord and ring the bell. When we heard the sound, Shyam and I prostrated ourselves, our foreheads touching the bare road, piously intoning, 'Shiv Shambhu, Shiv Shambhu.' From then on, the bell of each temple we came across was dutifully sounded and after we had risen from our supplications, we would break into laughter. Once or twice we even woke up a priest, but before the astonished and bleary-eyed man could say anything, we were off.

At three in the morning, Masood Pervez stopped in the middle of the road and let out such a torrent of abuse that we could not believe our ears. In my entire life, I had never heard him utter one impolite word. I must also add that all the while that he was unburdening the choicest abuse I had ever heard, I felt that those words did not sit right on his tongue.

We returned to Zubaida Cottage at four in the morning and hit the sack, though Masood remained up, composing poetry.

Shyam was not particularly given to moderation when it came to drinking, but he remained in control. Like an experienced player, he would carefully survey the field around him and then try his best to stay within its confines. He used to say to me, 'I prefer fours—sixers I hit by pure chance.'

Here is a sixer.

A few months before Partition, Shyam moved over to my place from Shahid Latif's house. In Bombaiya, those were karki times. We were all extremely hard up, but there had been no let-up in our drinking which continued unabated. One evening, we all had had more than a few. Raja Mehdi Ali Khan, the poet and lyricist, was also around. A curfew used to go into effect every night. He was getting ready to go home when I told him, 'Are you out of your mind? You will be hauled up.'

'Why don't you sleep here? Taji is not around these days,' Shyam said jokingly.

Raja smiled. 'But I can never sleep on a spring bed, absolutely can't.'

Shyam fixed a huge measure of brandy in keeping with Raja's ample proportions and said, 'Drink this and you will sleep like a log.'

Raja downed the glass in one go. We kept talking about Taji for a long time. She had had a fight with Shyam and had gone to stay with her sister. They used to argue over trivial things every eight or ten days, but I had learnt not to interfere because Shyam did not like it. There was an unstated understanding between us that we would not interfere in each other's private affairs.

Taji had gone with such finality this time that it seemed she would never come back. Shyam had said goodbye to her in a manner that suggested that he did not expect to see her again and wouldn't want to, anyway. However, they both pined for each other. In the evenings, Shyam would get so sentimental over Taji that I would be sure he would stay awake the rest of the night thinking of her. But he was so fond of sleeping that he would be gone minutes after hitting the bed. There were only two rooms in my flat; one was used as the bedroom, the other as a lounge. I had given the bedroom to Shyam and Taji, and I would sleep in the living room on a mattress placed on the floor. Since Taji was not around, Raja Mehdi Ali Khan was allotted one of the two beds in that room. It was very late when we turned in.

I woke up, as was my habit, at a quarter to six in the morning and noticed that somebody was lying next to me. It couldn't be my wife because she was in Lahore. When I rubbed my eyes and could see clearly, I found it was Shyam. How had he got here? Then I smelt burnt cloth. There was a sofa next to the mattress which had a hole burnt in it because of a cigarette that had not been put out properly. But that had happened many months ago. How could it be smouldering after all this time? I was now more or less awake and could feel the sting of smoke in my eyes. I could also see a faint cloud of smoke in the air. I walked into the bedroom and found that the bed on which Shyam used to sleep was smouldering, while Raja was sound asleep on the other, his big mound of a belly undulating with the rhythm of his snores.

I examined the burnt mattress carefully and found that it had a hole as big as a dinner plate, which was emitting whiffs of smoke. It appeared as if somebody had tried to put out the fire because there was a lot of water on the bed, but since the mattress was lined with coconut fibre and cotton, the fire had not been killed fully. I tried to wake up Raja but he turned on his side and began to snore even more loudly. Suddenly, a red flame leapt out of the black hole in the mattress. I ran into the bathroom, filled a bucket with water and extinguished the fire completely. Then I woke up Raja, which was not easy because he had little intention of getting up.

When I asked him what had happened, he replied in his typical style, exaggerating the events of the night and inventing all kinds of details, swearing they were all true. 'This Shyam of yours is actually Maharaj Hanuman, the monkey god. Last night, after immersing myself in a pool of brandy, I went to sleep. At about two in the morning, I heard strange sounds, which woke me up. I saw Shyam who had turned into Hanuman, with his tail on fire. He was jumping up and down on the bed, trying to set it on fire with his tail. When it caught fire, I closed my eyes and dived into the pool of brandy and hit the bottom. I was about to stay there for the rest of the night when it occurred to me that if I did that your poor bed would turn into ashes. I got up and found Shyam missing. I went to the next room to awaken you and apprise you of the situation, but found Shyam, who had once again resumed his human form, sleeping next to you. I tried to wake you up. I screamed out your name. I sounded gongs, even detonated a couple of atom bombs, but you just would not get up. Finally, I whispered in your ear, "Get up, Khwaja, a whole crate of Scotch whisky has just arrived." You immediately opened your eyes and asked, "Where?" I said, "Wake up . . . the house is on fire . . . fire, you understand? Fire." "Don't talk rubbish," was your answer to that. In the end, you decided to believe my statement, but returned to sleep after advising me to inform the fire brigade. Disappointed by you, I tried to awaken Shyam and explain to him the delicacy of our situation. When he finally managed to follow what I was saying, he said, "Why don't you put it out, pal? It is after all every citizen's duty to do so." Then, gathering all my feelings for humanity in my hands, I became a virtual fire brigade. Picking up the jug I had once given you for your birthday and filling it with water, I poured the contents down that hole in the mattress and since my job was done, leaving the rest to God, I went to sleep.'

When Shyam woke up after having slept his full quota, Raja and

I asked him how the fire had started. He did not seem to know what we were talking about. After thinking long and hard, he said with finality, 'I am unable to shed any light on the incident involving a fire.' We went to the next room, picked up Shyam's badly singed silk shirt and brought it to him. He took one look at it and declared, 'An investigation is called for.'

Our joint inquiry revealed that the vest Shyam was wearing had two or three burn marks. And two burn marks on his chest, big and round like rupee coins, provided further evidence that he had had a brush with last night's fire. It was at this point that Sherlock Holmes said to his friend Dr Watson, 'It now stands conclusively proved that there definitely was a fire and Shyam left the bed quietly to go to the other room to spare his friend Raja Mehdi Ali Khan any discomfort.'

When Shyam married Taji in a regular ceremony to satisfy social conventions, it was my view that the huge party he threw was just his way of getting even with those who had drawn up such customs. This party remained the talk of the film world in Bombay for a long time. Enormous quantities of liquor were downed that night but the ugly spots on the scanty cloth with which polite society always insists on covering itself refused to come off.

Shyam was not only a lover of women and drinking, he loved every good thing in life. He loved a good book as much as he loved a good woman. He had lost his mother as a child but he loved his stepmother just as if she were his real mother. He loved his stepbrothers and sisters more than he would have loved his own siblings. After his father's death, it was he who looked after the entire family, which was quite large.

For a long time and with the utmost devotion, he tried to get rich and famous, but lady luck would always give him the slip at the last moment. Shyam never let these setbacks get him down. He would say, 'Sweetheart, one day you are going to land in my arms.' And sure enough, the day did come when he became both rich and famous. When he died, he was earning thousands of rupees a month and he lived in a lovely house in the Bombay suburbs. There had once been days when he didn't have a place to stay, but even during those times of dire poverty, he was the same happy and perennially smiling Shyam. When the two ladies called Fame and Fortune came, he greeted them not as people greet deputy collectors; he made them sit next to him on his wrought-iron bed and planted big kisses on them.

During those days of hardship Shyam and I shared a place. Our economic condition was quite unspeakable. Like the politics of the country, it was passing through a most delicate phase. I was employed at Bombay Talkies, and Shyam had just signed a contract with the studio for a movie and had been given ten thousand rupees. This bonanza had come his way after months of unemployment. However, though contracts were signed, money was never paid on time. But we always used to manage somehow. Had we been husband and wife, there would have been arguments over money, but as far as Shyam and I were concerned, we never kept an account of who was spending what.

One day after a great deal of haggling, he managed to get five hundred rupees from the studio, quite a large sum of money at the time. I was absolutely broke. We were both on the train returning home from Malad. On the way, Shyam decided that he had to see a friend in Churchgate. My stop came first, but before I got down, he shut his eyes, took out a thick wad of banknotes from his pocket, divided it down the middle without counting and said, 'Hurry up, Manto . . . pick any.'

I took one, slipped it into my pocket and got down. As the train moved, Shyam said, 'Ta ta,' pulled out another wad of money and waved it in the air. 'What do you think? For the sake of safety, I had kept some of the loot aside . . . Hiptullha!'

In the evening, when Shyam returned, he was not in a good mood. The friend he had gone to see was KK (which was how the actress Kuldip Kaur was known among friends), who had wanted to speak to him in private. Shyam poured a large measure from the bottle of brandy tucked under his arm and told me, 'The private matter that she wanted to talk about was that once, in Lahore, I had told someone that KK had a massive crush on me. But in those days I had no time for her. Today, she said to me—and I was at her house—that what I had said in Lahore was rubbish and she had never had a crush on me. So I said to her. "Well, you can develop one tonight." She tried to play it haughty and I hit her with my fist.'

'You hit a woman?' I asked.

Shyam showed me his hand, which was injured. 'The witch moved aside and I ended up hitting the wall.'

Then he laughed for a long time. 'Sali! She is just playing hard to get.'

I have mentioned money earlier . . . Two years ago, I was in great mental agony because of the state of Lahore's film industry and the obscenity case filed against me because of my story 'Thanda Gosht'. I had been convicted by the lower court and sentenced to three months in jail with hard labour and fined three hundred rupees. I was so disillusioned that I wanted to throw everything I had ever written into the fire and start doing something else which had nothing to do with literature. Perhaps a job at an octroi post with plenty of bribe money so that I could take proper care of my family. I no longer wanted to criticize anyone or even offer an opinion on anything.

It was a strange time of frustration and listlessness. Some people were of the view that my actual profession consisted of writing stories and then having them tried in court on an obscenity charge. Some said I wrote because I sought cheap fame, while others were of the opinion that I derived satisfaction from exciting people's baser sentiments. I had been tried four times and I alone knew what those four cases had done to me.

Not that I had been doing all that well anyway, but the last thing I now wanted to do was write. I would spend most of my time away from home, hanging around with people who had nothing to do with literature. In their company, I was busy committing physical and spiritual suicide.

Then one day I received a letter from the proprietor of Tehsin Pictures, the film distributors. He wanted me to see him without delay because he had received some instructions from Bombay. Just to find out who the sender of those instructions was, I went to their office and was told that Shyam had sent telegram after telegram from Bombay, urging them to find me wherever I was and give me five hundred rupees. When I arrived at Tehsin Pictures, someone was writing a reply to yet another telegram from Shyam, saying that despite efforts they had been unable to find Manto.

I took the five hundred rupees and tears welled up in my intoxicated eyes. I tried very hard to write a note of thanks to Shyam and to ask him why he had sent me this money. Did he know how hard up I was? I wrote many letters but tore them all up because they read like a mockery of the feelings that had prompted Shyam to send me the money.

A year ago when Shyam came to Amritsar for the release of one of his films, he also came to Lahore and asked many people about me as soon as he arrived. I had already come to know that he was in Lahore, and I practically ran out of the house to be at the cinema where he was going to appear after a dinner.

With me was Rashid Attrey, the music director and Shyam's old friend from Poona. When Shyam drove up in front of the cinema and saw us, he screamed and told the driver to stop the car. However, so thick was the crowd of fans that the driver could not do so. With him was the actor Om Prakash. Both of them were wearing similar clothes and Panama hats. They entered the cinema from the back door, while we went in from the front. It was the same Shyam, laughing, smiling, full of life.

He ran forward and threw his arms around us and we made so much noise that nobody could follow a word. We were talking about a hundred things, all at the same time, and we buried ourselves under a heap of conversation. Once the public ceremony at the cinema was over, he took us with him to a film distributor's office. It was impossible to have a coherent conversation because we were constantly being interrupted and the flood of people was unremitting. In the street outside, a crowd had gathered because word had spread that Shyam was in there. The crowd was demanding that he should come to the balcony so that they could see him.

Shyam was in a strange mental state. He was intensely conscious of his presence in Lahore, the same Lahore whose streets had once been witness to his numerous romances. This Lahore was now thousands of miles from Amritsar. And how far was his beloved Rawalpindi where he had spent his boyhood? Lahore, Amritsar and Rawalpindi were all where they used to be, but those days were no longer there, nor those nights which Shyam had left behind. The undertaker of politics had buried them deep, only he knew where.

Shyam said to me, 'Stay by my side.' But his emotional agitation had reduced me also to such a state that I did not want to stay. Promising to meet him at Faletti's Hotel in the evening, I came home.

I had met Shyam after such a long time, but instead of happiness I felt an inexpressible melancholy. I was so upset that I wanted to get into a physical fight with someone, beat him up, get beaten and when exhausted, fall asleep. I tried to analyse my feelings but it was like untangling badly messed-up thread. I felt even more miserable when I went to Faletti's where I began to drink in a friend's room.

At about nine or nine thirty, there was a noise outside and I knew that Shyam had returned. His room was full of people who wanted to meet him. I sat there for some time but I could not talk to him. It seemed as if someone had put a lock on our feelings and threaded the keys in a huge ring with other keys, which the two of us were now trying to find.

I felt tired. After dinner, Shyam made a very emotional speech but I did not listen to a single word. My mind was broadcasting on a different and louder frequency. When Shyam finished his rubbish, the crowd roared its approval and broke into applause. I left and went to his room where film director Fazal Karim Fazli was already waiting. We had an argument over something very trivial. When Shyam arrived, he said, 'All these people are going to Hira Mandi, come with us.'

I almost began to cry. 'I don't want to go, you go and let your people go.'

'Then wait for me . . . I won't be long.'

Shyam left with the group that was going to Hira Mandi. I sat there, abused Shyam and the entire film industry, and said to Fazli, 'I think you will wait here, but if it is possible, please drop me home in your car.'

I had strange disjointed dreams all night. I fought with Shyam several times. In the morning when the milkman came, I was saying in hollow anger, 'You scoundrel, you are mean, you are disgraceful . . . you are a Hindu.'

I woke up and felt as if the greatest word of abuse in the world had just left my lips. But when I looked inside my heart, I knew that it was not my mouth but the blower of politics which had disgorged that vile word. While I took milk from the vendor which was one-fourth water, I thought of Shyam. I felt great solace at the realization that though Shyam was a Hindu, he was not a mixed-with-water Hindu.

Once, during the time of Partition when a bloody fratricidal civil war was being fought between Hindus and Muslims with thousands being massacred every day, Shyam and I were listening to a family of Sikh refugees from Rawalpindi. They were telling us horrifying stories of how their people had been killed. I could sense that Shyam was deeply moved and I could understand the emotional upheaval he was undergoing. When we left, I said to him, 'I am a Muslim, don't you feel like murdering me?'

'Not now,' he answered gravely, 'but when I was listening to the atrocities the Muslims had committed . . . I could have murdered you.'

I was deeply shocked by Shyam's words. Perhaps I could have also murdered him at the time. But later when I thought about it—and between then and now there is a world of difference—I suddenly understood the basis of those riots in which thousands of innocent Hindus and Muslims were killed every day.

'Not now . . . but at that time, yes.' If you ponder these words, you will find an answer to the painful reality of Partition, an answer that lies in human nature itself.

In Bombay, the communal atmosphere was becoming more vicious by the day. When Ashok and Vacha took control of the administration of Bombay Talkies, all senior posts somehow went to Muslims, which created a great deal of resentment among the Hindu staff. Vacha began to receive anonymous letters that threatened him with everything from murder to the destruction of the studio. Neither Ashok nor Vacha could care less about this sort of thing. It was only I, partly because of my sensitive nature and partly because I was a Muslim, who expressed a sense of unease to both of them on several occasions. I advised them to do away with my services because the Hindus thought that it was I who was responsible for so many Muslims getting into Bombay Talkies. They told me that I was out of my mind.

Out of mind I certainly was. My wife and children were in Pakistan. When that land was a part of India, I could recognize it. I was also aware of the occasional Hindu–Muslim riot, but now it was different. That piece of land had a new name and I did not know what that new name had done to it. Though I tried, I could not even begin to get a feel for the government which was now said to be ours.

The day of Independence, 14 August, was celebrated in Bombay with tremendous fanfare. Pakistan and India had been declared two separate countries. There was great public rejoicing, but murder and arson continued unabated. Along with cries of 'India zindabad', one also heard 'Pakistan zindabad'. The green Islamic flag fluttered next to the tricolour of the Indian National Congress. The streets and bazaars reverberated with slogans as people shouted the names of Pandit Jawaharlal Nehru and Quaid-e-Azam Muhammad Ali Jinnah.

I found it impossible to decide which of the two countries was now my homeland—India or Pakistan. Who was responsible for the blood that was being shed mercilessly every day? Where were they going to inter the bones that had been stripped of the flesh of religion by vultures and birds of prey? Now that we were free, had subjection ceased to exist? Who would be our slaves? When we were colonial subjects, we could dream of freedom, but now that we were free, what would our dreams be? Were we even free? Thousands of Hindus and Muslims were dying all around us. Why were they dying?

All these questions had different answers: the Indian answer, the Pakistani answer, the British answer. Every question had an answer, but when you tried to look for the truth, none of those answers was of any help. Some said if you were looking for the truth, you would have to go back to the ruins of the 1857 Mutiny. Others said no, it all lay in the history of the East India Company. Some went back even further and advised you to analyse the Mughal empire. Everybody wanted to drag you back into the past, while murderers and terrorists marched on unchallenged, writing in the process a story of blood and fire, which was without parallel in history.

I stopped going to Bombay Talkies. Whenever Ashok and Vacha dropped in, I would pretend I wasn't feeling well. Shyam would look at me and smile. He knew what I was going through. I began to drink heavily, but got bored and gave it up. All day long, I would lie on my sofa in a sort of daze. One day, Shyam came to the flat straight from the studio. I was lying listlessly on the sofa. 'Chewing the cud, Khwaja, are we?' he asked.

I was upset. Why did he not think like me? Why did he look so calm? Why did he not feel the terrible upheaval that was raging through my heart and soul? How could he keep laughing and cracking jokes? Or had he perhaps come to the conclusion that the world around us had gone so completely insane that it was futile even to try to make sense of it?

It happened suddenly. One day I said to myself, 'The hell with it all. I am leaving.' Shyam was shooting that night. I stayed up and packed. He came quite early in the morning, looked around and asked, 'Going?' 'Yes,' I replied.

We never mentioned the subject again. He helped me move odds and ends around while keeping up a steady patter of amusing stories about the night's shooting. He laughed a lot. When it was time for me to leave, he produced a bottle of brandy, poured out two large measures, handed me a glass and said, 'Hiptullha!'

'Hiptullha!' I answered.

Then he threw his arms around me and said, 'Swine!'

I tried to control my tears. 'Pakistani swine,' I said.

'Zindabad Pakistan,' he shouted sincerely.

'Zindabad Bharat,' I replied.

Then we walked down the stairs to a truck waiting to take me to my ship that was bound for Karachi.

Shyam came to the port. There was still time to board the ship. He kept telling funny stories. When the gong was sounded, he shouted, 'Hiptullha!' one last time and walked down the gangway, taking long, resolute strides. Never even once did he look back.

From Lahore, I wrote him a letter, to which he answered on 19 January 1948.

> Everyone misses you and feels the absence of your upbeat humour, which you used to squander on these characters with such generosity. Vacha says you left without telling him; he finds your leaving paradoxical, since you were the one man who used to oppose the entry of Muslims in Bombay Talkies and it was you who became the first to run off to Pakistan, thus becoming a martyr to your own credo . . . However, that is Vacha's view and I hope you have written to him, and if you haven't, decency demands that you do.
>
> Yours,
>
> Shyam

It is 14 August today, the day when India and Pakistan became free. There are celebrations on both sides, and at the same time, full preparations for attack and defence are in hand . . . I say to Shyam's spirit, 'Dear Shyam, I left Bombay Talkies. Can't Pandit Nehru leave Kashmir? Now isn't that hiptullha?'

KULDIP KAUR: TOO HOT TO HANDLE

KK they called her, short for Kuldip Kaur. She appeared in countless films. Whenever I saw her name flashed across a billboard, I would always think of her nose because she had the pertest nose I have ever seen on anyone.

When Punjab was engulfed in communal rioting at the time of Partition, Kuldip Kaur was in Lahore making movies. She left for Bombay with the actor Pran, who was like her male mistress. He had already made a name for himself through his roles in films produced by Pancholi Studio. He was a handsome man and a popular figure in Lahore because of his impeccable clothes and the most elegant tonga in the city, which the rich of those days used for joyrides in the evening. I am not sure when the affair between Pran and Kuldip began because I was not living in Lahore at the time, but such liaisons between people in the movie world are not uncommon. During the making of a film, an actress could be carrying on with more than one man associated with the production. While the affair between Pran and Kuldip was on full blast, Shyam returned to Lahore, a city he loved to distraction, after having tried his luck in Bombay. A ladies' man by nature, it was only a matter of time before he turned his attention towards Kuldip. They would certainly have had a fling had another woman, Mumtaz, later popularly known as Taji, not entered Shyam's life just at that point.

Kuldip was offended by Shyam's sudden change of course and never forgave him. She was not the kind of woman who changes her mind once it is made up. One day in Bombay, the three of us—Shyam, Kuldip and I—were going home by train and it so happened that we were the only occupants of our first-class carriage. Shyam was boisterous by nature and, when he realized that he was practically alone with Kuldip, he began to flirt with her, hoping, of course, to pick up the thread from where he had let it drop in Lahore. He had just had a fight with Taji. Of his other friends, the actress Ramola was in Calcutta, and Nigar Sultana was currently the mistress of the lyricist Dina Nath Madhuk. So, in his own words, he was 'empty-handed'. He was teasing Kuldip. 'Sweetheart, why are you always trying to slip away from me? Why don't you sit next to me?' Kuldip's nose looked even more pert as she replied sharply, 'Shyam sahib, don't try these tricks on me.' I recall the rest of the conversation, but on second thought, I would rather leave it out because it was quite risqué. Shyam was incapable of speaking in a serious manner so, in his characteristic style, he said to Kuldip, 'Darling, dump that owl's offspring you call Pran and come to me. He is a friend of mine; I will explain it to him.'

Kuldip, with her pert nose and big eyes which she used to full effect, replied even more sharply, 'Keep your paws off me.' This kind of rebuff from women never had an effect on Shyam. He laughed. 'Sweetheart, you used to be mad about me in Lahore, or have you forgotten?' Kuldip now laughed sardonically. 'You fool yourself.' 'That is not true. You were mad about me,' Shyam insisted. I looked at Kuldip and I could feel that she still had a crush on Shyam but her obstinate temperament was in the way, so she batted her eyes a few more times and replied, 'I was, but no longer.' Shyam's response was typical of him. 'Look, if not today, then tomorrow, you are fated to come to me.' Kuldip was angry. 'Look here Shyam, let me tell you for the last time that there can never be anything between us. You just stop preening yourself the way you do. It is possible that I might have fancied you once in Lahore, but since you showed indifference then, I am determined to have nothing to do with you now. You'd better forget that Lahore business here and now.' There the matter ended, but only for the time being as Shyam did not have the patience for long discussions.

Kuldip came from a rich Sikh family of Attari in Punjab, one of whose members had a long relationship with a Muslim woman from Lahore. It was said to have continued after Partition. He was also believed to have spent millions on her. After 1947, he continued to come to Lahore, stay at Faletti's Hotel, spend a few days with his friend and return home.

During the division of the country, Pran and Kuldip had left Lahore in such a hurry that Pran's car—which Kuldip had probably paid for—had to be abandoned. Kuldip, not one to be afraid of anything, including men, whom she could wrap around her little finger, came to Lahore while the communal rioting was in full fury and drove the car all the way back to Bombay. I only came to know the story when

I once asked Pran about his car. Kuldip had driven back without incident, he told me, except for a 'minor problem' in Delhi, but he did not say what it was. She told me once about the atrocities the Muslims had committed against Sikhs. The way she narrated those stories almost convinced me that she was about to pick up a butter knife from the table and plunge it in my belly. But she was just being emotional. She was not the kind of person who would have borne the Muslims any grudge for being Muslims. She was not religious in that sense but a woman who believed in pure animal instincts.

Kuldip's nose made her face look highly expressive. She had finely chiselled features and she talked with great intensity. When I left Filmistan and joined my friends Ashok Kumar and Savak Vacha at Bombay Talkies, it was clear to everyone that we were living in unsettled times and there was not much work to be had. One day Kuldip and Pran came to Bombay Talkies to see if there was something going. I had met Pran earlier through Shyam and we had become friends immediately, as he was a man without malice towards anyone. My relationship with Kuldip was on the formal side. But it so happened that three films were about to go into production at Bombay Talkies and Vacha, after taking one look at Kuldip, asked our German cameraman Josef Wirsching to do a screen test on her. Wirsching had come to Bombay from Germany with Himanshu Rai and had been placed under detention at Devlali during the war. He was released only after the war and he returned to Bombay Talkies. He was a good friend of Vacha's, head of the sound recording laboratory at the studio.

The lights came on while Kuldip Kaur went to the make-up room. Wirsching stood waiting behind a new camera, his cigar in his mouth. Kuldip appeared after some time and stood facing the camera without any self-consciousness. She was ready for action but I noticed that the German felt somewhat overawed by her presence. When he saw her through the lens, he was bewildered because from whichever angle he framed her, all he could see was her pert nose. He began to sweat, then turned to me. 'Let's have a cup of tea in the canteen.' I could guess what his problem was. As we sat down with our cups, he wiped his brow and said, 'Mr Manto, what can I do with her nose? It practically plunges into the lens. Her face merely follows.' Then he brought his lips close to my ear and whispered, 'And she is not quite right there, but how can I tell her?' He was referring to the fact that she was less than well endowed. Nose, he said, he could somehow manage but 'the other thing', well, some way would have to be found to deal with it. I assured him that I would get 'the other thing' worked out, and I did. When Kuldip was leaving the studio, I told her in plain words what Wirsching had said. I also told her that for thirty-five rupees, she could purchase at the Whiteway Laidlaw store something that would do the trick. The test in the meanwhile had been put off for a day.

Kuldip was not in the least bashful. She said it was no big deal and she would do the necessary, which she did right away. The next day when she came to the studio, she was a different woman. I silently saluted the inventors of these most ingenious devices. Wirsching took one look at her and was satisfied. He was still bothered about her nose, but 'the other thing' being the way he wanted it, he took her screen test and when we saw it in the projection room later everyone agreed that she was fine, especially in roles depicting 'the other woman'.

Off and on, Kuldip would come with Pran to one of our evenings. She lived in a hotel not far from the beach. Pran lived close by with his wife and child but most of his time was spent with Kuldip. One day, Shyam, Taji and I were on our way to a hotel for a glass of beer when we were waylaid by D.N. Madhok, the famous lyricist, who insisted that we go with him to the bar of Eros Cinema. Madhok was Bombay's king of taxis. For instance, the big jalopy waiting for him in the parking lot he had had in tow for the last three days. After we came out of the bar, Madhok said he was going to visit his current girlfriend, Nigar Sultana, who once used to be Shyam's girlfriend. She lived not far from Kuldip's place. Shyam suggested that we should go and look up Pran, so we all filed into Madhok's taxi, and while he got dropped off at Nigar Sultana's, the driver took us to Kuldip's hotel. Pran was there. He had had a couple because he looked sleepy. Shyam proposed that we should play cards, which might wake up Pran. Kuldip agreed right away but said it would have to be flush and with stakes. Kuldip sat behind Pran, her pointed chin on his shoulder. Every time he won a hand, she would pick up the money. I had often played before, but I had never been in a game like this. Of the money I had, seventy-five rupees was gone in fifteen minutes flat. 'The cards are stacked against me today,' I consoled myself. Shyam said to me, 'That's enough.' Pran smiled and asked Kuldip to return my money.

I said there was no question of that because he had won the money. Pran replied that I should know that he was the best card sharper in town and since I was a friend he could not cheat me. My first thought was that he wanted to return the money to me out of sympathy but when he picked up the pack and dealt it four times in a row, with him holding the highest cards each time, I was convinced that he was right. Pran asked Kuldip to return my money but she refused. Shyam was furious; Pran was not too happy either and he walked out in a huff. He also had to take his wife somewhere. Shyam and I sat for some more time. 'Let's go out,' I suggested. Kuldip was game. We sent for a taxi and took it towards Byculla. I lived by myself on Clare Road but had Shyam staying with me. I took them home. As soon as we entered, Shyam began to flirt with Kuldip. She kept warding him off, but with good humour, because she was not the kind of woman who was easily offended by such things. She knew what she wanted and she had a lot of self-confidence.

I forgot to mention that before we arrived at my place, Kuldip asked the driver to stop at a store as she wanted to buy a perfume. Shyam was angry because she was going to buy the perfume with my money out of which I had been cheated. I told him to forget the whole thing as it was of no consequence. I went into the store with Kuldip. She picked up a bottle for twenty-two rupees eight annas, slipped it into her handbag and told me to pay. I did not want to, but the store owner knew me and the way she had asked me to pay ensured that I would do so out of male vanity. I paid. When Shyam learnt what had happened, he was even angrier. He abused both Kuldip and me but cooled down after some time. He still had hopes of Kuldip. I put in a word for him as well and she appeared to soften. I offered to leave them alone so that they could work out the details of their new 'agreement', but Shyam said it would have to be finalized at her hotel. The taxi was still down there, waiting, so they took it. I was pleased that at least something had worked out.

Shyam was back within thirty minutes and he looked angry. I poured him a brandy and noticed that he had an injured hand. 'What happened?' I asked. It turned out that Kuldip had taken him to the hotel where she lived, but contrary to what he thought she wanted, she had asked him to leave. In frustration, he had tried to hit her, but she had moved and he had hit the wall instead. She had burst out laughing and left the room, leaving Shyam with injured male pride and a bleeding hand.

Some years after Independence, there was a story in the papers that Kuldip had been charged with spying for Pakistan. I have no idea if there was any truth in that report but I felt that a woman like Kuldip Kaur who was utterly straightforward could never be a Mata Hari.

NARGIS: NARCISSUS OF THE UNDYING BLOOM

It was a long time ago. The Nawab of Chattari's daughter Tasnim—later Mrs Tasnim Saleem Chattari—had written me a letter: 'So what do you think of your brother-in-law, my husband? Since his return from Bombay, he has been talking ceaselessly about you, much to my delight. He was apprehensive of meeting you, my unseen, unmet brother. In fact, he used to tease me about you. Now for the last two days he has been insisting that I should come to Bombay and meet you. He says you are a fascinating person. The way he talks about you, it would seem that you are his brother rather than mine . . . in any case, he is very happy that I choose people carefully. My own brother got here before Saleem did and lost no time in telling me of his meeting with you. Nargis he never mentioned, but when Saleem arrived and spilled the beans, including your fracas with Nakhshab, only then did everything fall into place. Saleem is apologetic about the second visit to Jaddan Bai's house and holds his brother Shamshad, whom you have met, responsible for it . . . You do know, of course, that if Saleem was ever infatuated, it was with Leela Chitnis, which, at least, shows good taste.'

When Saleem dropped in to see me in Bombay, it was our first meeting, and he already was, as Tasnim put it, my brother-in-law, being her husband. I showed him what hospitality I could. Movie people have one 'present' they can always give: take their visitors to see a film being shot. So, dutifully, I took him around to Shri Studio where K. Asif was shooting *Phool.*

Saleem and his friends should have been happy with that but it appeared to me that they had other plans, which they obviously had made before arriving in Bombay. So at one point, quite casually, Saleem asked me, 'And where is Nargis these days?'

'With her mother,' I replied lightly. My joke fell flat because one of the nawabs asked with the utmost simplicity, 'With Jaddan Bai?'

'Yes.'

Saleem spoke next, 'Can one meet her . . . I mean my friends here are quite keen on doing that. Do you know her?'

'I do . . . but only just,' I answered.

'Why?' one of them asked.

'Because she and I have never worked on a movie together,' I said.

'Then we should really not bother you with this,' Saleem remarked.

However, I did want to visit Nargis. I had decided to do so several times but I had not been able to bring myself to go there. These young men whom I would be taking to see her were the kind who just stare at women with their eyes practically jumping out of their sockets. But they were an innocent lot. All they wanted was to catch a glimpse of Nargis so that when they went back to their lands and estates they would be able to brag to their friends that they had met Nargis, the famous film star. So I told them that we could go and meet her.

Why did I want to meet Nargis? After all, Bombay was full of actresses to whose homes I could go any time I wished. Before I answer that question, let me narrate an interesting story.

I was at Filmistan and my working day was long, starting early and ending at eight in the evening. One day, I returned earlier than usual, in fact, in the afternoon, and as I entered my place, I felt there was something different about it, as if someone had strummed a stringed instrument and then disappeared from view. Two of my wife's younger sisters were doing their hair but they seemed to be preoccupied. Their lips were moving but I couldn't hear a word. It was obvious they were trying to hide something. I eased myself into a sofa and the two sisters, after whispering in each other's ears, said in chorus, 'Bhai, salaam.' I answered the greeting, then looked at them intently and asked, 'What is the matter?' I thought they were planning to go to the movies but it was not so. They consulted one another, again in whispers, burst out laughing and ran into the next room. I was convinced they had invited a friend of theirs and since I had come in unexpectedly I had upset their plans.

The three sisters were together for some time and I could hear them talking. There was much laughter. After a few minutes, my wife, pretending that she was talking to her sisters but actually wishing me to pay attention, said, 'Why are you asking me? Why don't you talk to him? Saadat, you are unusually early today.' I told her there was no work at the studio. 'What do these girls want?' I asked. 'They want to say that they are expecting Nargis,' she answered. 'So what? Hasn't she been here before?' I replied, quite sure they were talking about a Parsi girl who lived in the neighbourhood and often visited them. Her mother was married to a Muslim. 'This Nargis has never been here before. I am talking of Nargis the actress,' my wife replied. 'What is she going to do here?' I asked.

My wife then told me the entire story. There was a telephone in the house and the three sisters loved to be on it whenever they had a minute. When they got tired of talking to their friends, they would dial an actress's number and carry on a generally nonsensical conversation with her, such as, 'Oh! We are great fans of yours. We have arrived from Delhi only today and with great difficulty we have been able to get your phone number . . . We are dying to meet you . . . We would have come but we are in purdah and cannot leave the house . . . You are so lovely, absolutely ravishing and what a wonderfully sweet voice you are gifted with—' although they knew that the voice which was heard on the screen was that of either Amir Bai Karnatiki or Shamshad Begum.

Actresses had unlisted numbers; otherwise their phones would never have stopped ringing. But these three had managed to get almost everyone's number with the help of my friend the screenwriter Agha Khalish Kashmiri. During one of their phone sessions, they had called Nargis and they liked the way she talked to them. They were the same age and so they became friends and would talk on the phone often, but they were yet to meet. Initially, the sisters did not let on who they were. One would say she was from Africa while the other was from Lucknow who was here to meet her aunt. Or she was from Rawalpindi and had travelled to Bombay just to catch a glimpse of Nargis. My wife would at times pretend to be a woman from Gujarat, at others, a Parsi. Quite a few times, Nargis would ask them in exasperation to tell her who they really were and why they were hiding their real names.

It was obvious that Nargis liked them, although there could have been no shortage of fans phoning her home. These three girls were different and she was dying to know who they really were because she did very much want to meet them. Whenever these three mysterious ones called, she would drop everything and talk to them for hours. One day, Nargis insisted that they should meet. My wife told her where we lived, adding that if there was any difficulty in locating the place she should phone from a hotel in Byculla and they would come and get her. When I came home that day, Nargis had just phoned to say that she was in the area but could not find the house, so they were all getting ready in desperation to fetch her. I had entered at a very awkward time.

The two younger sisters were afraid I would be annoyed, while my wife was just nervous. I wanted to pretend I was annoyed but it did not seem right. It was just an innocent prank. Was my wife behind this madcap scheme or was it her sisters'? It is said in Urdu that one's sister-in-law owns half the household and here I was, not with one but two. I offered to go out and fetch Nargis. As I walked out of the door, I heard loud clapping from the other room.

In the main Byculla square, I saw Jaddan Bai's huge limousine—and her. We greeted each other. 'Manto, how are you?' Jaddan Bai asked in a rather loud voice. 'I am well, but what are you doing here?' I asked. She looked at her daughter who was in the back seat and said, 'Nothing, except that Baby has to meet some friends but we can't find the house.' I smiled. 'Let me guide you.' When Nargis heard this, she drew her face close to the window. 'Do you know where they live?' 'But of course!' I replied. 'Who can forget his own house!' Jaddan Bai shifted the paan she was chewing from one side of her mouth to the other and said, 'What kind of storytelling is this?' I opened the door and got in next to her. 'Bibi, this is no story, but if it is one, then its authors happen to be my wife and her sisters.' Then I told them everything that had happened since I returned home. Nargis listened with great concentration, but her mother was not so amused. 'A curse be on the devils . . . if they had said at the start that they were calling from your home, I would have sent Baby over right away. My, my, for days we were all so curious . . . By God, you have no idea how excited and worked up Baby has been over these phone calls. Whenever the phone rang, she would run. Every time I would ask her who it was at the other end with whom she had been carrying on such a sweet conversation for hours, and she would reply that she did not know who they were but they sounded very nice. Once or twice, I also picked up the phone and was impressed by their good manners. They seemed to be from a nice family. But the imps would not tell me their names. Today Baby was beside herself with joy because they had invited her to their place and told her where they lived. I said to her, "Are you mad? You don't know who they are." But she just would not listen and kept after me, so I had to come myself. Had I known by God that these goblins lived in your house—'

'Then you would not have come personally.' I did not let her complete her sentence.

A smile appeared on her face. 'Of course, don't I know you?'

Jaddan Bai was well read and always read my writings. Only recently, one of my pieces, 'The Graveyard of the Progressives', had appeared in *Saqi*, the Urdu literary magazine edited by Shahid Ahmad Dehlvi. God knows why, but she now turned to that. 'By God, Manto, what a writer you are! You can really put the knife in, as you did in that one. Baby, do you remember how I kept raving about that article for the rest of the day?'

But Nargis was thinking of her unseen friends. 'Let's go, bibi,' she implored her mother impatiently.

'Let's go then,' Jaddan Bai said to me.

We were home in minutes. The three sisters saw us from the upstairs balcony. The younger two just could not contain their excitement and were continually whispering in each other's ears. We walked up the stairs, and while Nargis and the two girls moved into the next room, Jaddan Bai, my wife and I sat in the front room. We amused ourselves by going over the charade the girls had been playing all these months. My wife, now feeling calmer, got down to playing the hostess while Jaddan Bai and I talked about the movie industry and the state it was in. She always carried her paandaan with her because she could not be without her paan, which gave me an opportunity to help myself to a couple as well.

I had not seen Nargis since she was ten or eleven years old. I remembered her holding her mother's hand on movie opening nights. She was a thin-legged girl with an unattractive long face and two unlit eyes. She seemed to have just woken up or about to go to sleep. But now she was a young woman and her body had filled out in all the right places, though her eyes were the same—small, dreamy, even a bit sickly. I thought she had been given an appropriate name, Nargis, the narcissus. In Urdu poetry, the narcissus is always said to be ailing and sightless.

She was simple and playful like a child and was always blowing her nose as if she had a perennial cold; this was used in the movie *Barsaat* as an endearing habit. Her wan face indicated that she had acting talent. She was in the habit of talking with her lips slightly joined. Her smile was self-conscious and carefully cultivated. One could see that she would use these mannerisms as raw material to forge her acting style. Acting, come to think of it, is made up of just such things.

Another thing that I noticed about her was her conviction that one day she would become a star, though she appeared to be in no hurry to bring that day closer. She did not want to bid farewell quite yet to the small joys of girlhood and move into the larger, chaotic world of adults with its working life.

But back to that afternoon. The three girls were now busy exchanging their experiences of convent schools and home. They had no interest right now in what happened in movie studios or how love affairs took place. Nargis had forgotten that she was a film star who captivated many hearts when she appeared on the screen. The two girls were equally unconcerned with the fact that Nargis was an actress who was sometimes shown doing rather daring things in the movies.

My wife, who was older than Nargis, had already taken her under her wing as if she were another of her younger sisters. Initially, she was interested in Nargis because she was a film actress who fell in love with different men in her movies, who laughed and cried or danced as required by the script, but not now. She seemed to be more concerned about her eating sour things, drinking ice-cold water or working in too many films as it could affect her health. It was perfectly all right with her that Nargis was an actress.

While the three of us were busy chatting, in walked a relation of mine whom we all called Apa Saadat. Not only was she my namesake, but also a most flamboyant personality, a person who was totally informal, so much so that I did not even feel the need to introduce her to Jaddan Bai. She lowered herself, all two hundred plus pounds of her, on to the sofa and said, 'Saffo jaan, I pleaded with your brother not to buy this excuse for a car but he just wouldn't listen. We had only driven a few yards when the dashed thing came to a stop and there he is now trying to get it going. I told him that I was not going to stand there but was taking myself to your place to wait.'

Jaddan Bai had been talking of some dissolute nawab, a topic Apa Saadat immediately pounced on. She knew all the nawabs and other rulers of the states that dotted the Kathiawar region because her husband belonged to the ruling family of the Mangrol state. Jaddan Bai knew all those princes because of her profession. The conversation at one point turned to a well known courtesan who had the reputation of having bankrupted several princely states.

Apa Saadat was in her element. 'God protect us from these women. Whosoever falls into their clutches is lost both to this world and the next. You can say goodbye to your money, your health and your good name if you get ensnared by one of these creatures. The biggest curse in the world, if you ask me, is these courtesans and prostitutes . . .'

My wife and I were severely embarrassed and did not know how to stop Apa Saadat. Jaddan Bai, on the other hand, was agreeing with all her observations with the utmost sincerity. Once or twice, I tried to interrupt Apa Saadat but she got even more carried away. For a few minutes she heaped every choice abuse on 'these women'. Then suddenly she paused, her fair and broad face underwent a tremor or two and the tiny diamond ornament in her nose sparkled even more than it normally did. She slapped herself on the thigh and stammered, looking at Jaddan Bai, 'You, you are Jaddan. You are Jaddan Bai, aren't you?'

'Yes,' Jaddan Bai replied soberly.

Apa Saadat did not stop. 'Oh you, I mean, you are a very high-class courtesan, isn't that so Saffo jaan?' My wife froze. I looked at Jaddan Bai and gave her a smile, which must have been a sheepish one. Jaddan Bai did not flinch, but calmly and in great detail continued her story of this most notorious courtesan. However, the situation could not be recovered. Apa Saadat had finally realized her faux pas and we were too embarrassed to say anything. Then the girls walked in and the tension evaporated. When Nargis was asked to sing, Jaddan Bai told us, 'I did not teach her to sing because Mohan Babu was not in favour of it, and the truth is I too was against it. She can sing a bit though.' Then she said to her daughter, 'Baby, sing something.'

Like a child, Nargis began to sing. She had no voice at all. It was not sweet nor was the timbre good. Compared to her, my youngest sister-in-law was a thousand times better. However, since Nargis had been asked and asked repeatedly, we had to suffer her for two or three minutes. When she finished, everyone praised her, except Apa Saadat and I. After a few minutes Jaddan Bai said it was time to go. The girls embraced one another and promised to meet again. There was much whispering. Then mother and daughter were gone.

This was my first meeting with Nargis.

I met her several times after this. The telephone was kept busy; the girls would phone her and she would get into her car without her mother and come over. The feeling that she was an actress had almost disappeared. The girls met as if they were related or had known one another for years. Many times, after she had left, the three sisters would say, 'There is nothing actress-like about her.'

A new movie starring Nargis was released around this time with quite a few love scenes which showed her whispering coyly to the hero, looking at him longingly, nuzzling up to him, holding his hand and so on. My wife said, 'Look at her, the way she is sighing, one would think she really was in love with this fellow.' Her two sisters would say to each other, 'Only yesterday she was asking us how to make toffee with raw sugar and here she is . . .'

My own view of Nargis's acting abilities was that she was incapable of portraying emotion. Her inexperienced fingers could not possibly feel the racing pulse of love. Nor could she be aware of the excitement of love, which was different from the excitement of running a race in school. Any perceptive viewer could see from her early movies that her acting was untouched by artifice or deception. The most effective artifice must appear to be natural, but since Nargis was callow and inexperienced, her performances were totally artless. It was only her sincerity and her love for the profession that carried her through her early movies. She was naive about the ways of the world and some of that genuine innocence came through in her performance. Since then, given age and experience, she has become a mature actress. She knows well the difference between love and the games she played at school. She can portray all the nuances of love. She has come of age.

It is good that her journey to acting fame was a slow one. Had she arrived there in one leap, it would have hurt the artistic feelings of perceptive filmgoers. If her off-screen life in her early years had been anything like the roles she was given to play, I for one would have died of shock.

Nargis could have become only an actress, given the fact of her birth. Jaddan Bai was getting on and, though she had two sons, her entire concentration was on Baby Nargis, a plain-looking girl who could not sing. However, Jaddan Bai knew that a sweet voice could be borrowed, and if one had the talent even the disadvantage of ordinary looks could be surmounted. That was why she had devoted herself entirely to Nargis's development and ensured that whatever talent her daughter had was fully brought out and made central to her personality. Nargis was destined to become an actress and she did become one. The secret of her success, in my opinion, was her sincerity, a quality she always retained. In Jaddan Bai's family there was Mohan Babu, Baby Nargis and her two brothers. All of them were the responsibility of Jaddan Bai. Mohan Babu came from a rich family and had been so fascinated with the musical web Jaddan Bai's mellifluous voice had woven around him that he had allowed her to become his entire life. He was handsome and he had money. He was also an educated man and enjoyed good health. All these assets he had laid at her feet like offerings in a temple. Jaddan Bai enjoyed great fame at the time. Rajas and nawabs would shower her with gold and silver when she sang. However, after this rain of gold and silver was over, she would put her arms around Mohan because he was all she really cared about. He stayed by her side until the end and she loved him deeply. He was also the father of her children. She had no illusions about rajas and nawabs; she knew that their money smelt of the blood of the poor. She also knew that when it came to women, they were capricious.

Nargis was always conscious that my sisters-in-law, whom she came to meet, and spent hours with, were different from her. She was always reluctant to invite them to her home, afraid that they might say it was not possible for them to accept her invitation. One day when I was not around, she told her friends, 'Now you must come to my home some time.' The sisters looked at one another, not sure what to say. Since my wife was aware of my views, she accepted Nargis's invitation, but she did not tell me. All three went.

Nargis had sent them her car and when it arrived at Marine Drive, Bombay's most luxurious residential area, they realized that Nargis had made special arrangements for them. Mohan Babu and his two grown-up sons had been asked not to stay around because Nargis was expecting her friends. The male servants were not allowed into the room where the women were. Jaddan Bai came in for a few minutes, exchanged greetings and left. She did not want to inhibit them in any way. All three sisters kept saying later how excited Nargis was by their presence in her home. Elaborate arrangements had been made and special milk shakes had been ordered from the nearby Parisian Dairy. Nargis had gone herself to get the drinks because she did not trust a servant to get the right thing. In her excitement and enthusiasm, she broke a glass, which was part of a new set. When her guests expressed regret, she said, 'It's nothing. Bibi will be annoyed but daddy will quieten her down and the matter will be forgotten.'

After the milk shakes, Nargis showed them her albums of photographs, which had stills from many of her movies. There was a world of difference between the Nargis who was showing them the pictures and the Nargis who was the subject of those pictures. Off and on, the three sisters would look at her to compare her with the movie photographs. 'Nargis, how do you become Nargis?' one of them asked. Nargis merely smiled. My wife told me that at home Nargis was simple, homely and childlike, not the bouncing, flirtatious girl whom people saw on the screen. I always felt a sadness floating in her eyes like an unclaimed body in the still waters of a pond whose surface is occasionally disturbed by the breeze.

It was clear to me that Nargis would not have to wait long for the fame which was her destiny. Fate had already taken a decision and handed her the papers, signed and sealed. Why then did she look sad? Did she perhaps feel in an unconscious way that this make-believe game of love she played on the screen would one day lead her to a desert where she would see nothing but mirage followed by mirage, where her throat would be parched with thirst and the clouds would have no rain to release? The sky would offer no solace, and the earth would suck in all moisture deep into its recesses because it would not believe she was thirsty. In the end, she herself would come to believe that her thirst was an illusion.

Many years have passed and when I see her on the screen, I find that her sadness has turned into melancholy. In the beginning, one felt that she was searching for something but now even that urge has been overtaken by despondency and exhaustion. Why? This is a question only Nargis could answer.

But back to the three sisters at Nargis's house. Since they had gone there on their own, they did not stay long. The two younger ones were afraid I would find out and be annoyed, so they took Nargis's leave and came home. I noticed that whenever they talked about Nargis, it would come to the question of marriage. The younger ones were dying to know when or whom she would marry, while my wife, who had been married for five years, would speculate about what kind of mother Nargis would make.

My wife did not tell me at first about their visit, but when she did I pretended to be displeased. She was immediately on the defensive and agreed that it was a mistake. She wanted me to keep it to myself because, according to the moral and social milieu in which the three had been brought up, visiting the home of an actress was improper. As far as I know, they had not told even their mother that they had gone to see Nargis, although the old lady was by no means narrow-minded. To this day, I do not understand why they thought they had done something wrong. What was wrong with going to see Nargis at her home? Why was acting considered a bad profession? Did we not have people in our own family who had spent their entire lives telling lies and practising hypocrisy? Nargis was a professional actress. What she did, she did in the open. It was not she but others who practised deception.

Since I began this account with Tasnim Saleem Chattari's letter, let me return to it because that is what set the whole thing off. Since I was keen to meet Nargis at her own place, I went along with Saleem and his friends despite being busy. The correct thing would have been to phone Jaddan Bai to see if Nargis was free or not, but since in my daily life I was no great believer in such formalities, I just appeared at her door. Jaddan Bai was sitting on her veranda, slicing betel nut. As soon as she saw me, she said in a loud voice, 'Oh! Manto, come in, come in.' Then she shouted for Nargis, 'Baby, your sahelis are here,' thinking that I had brought my two sisters-in-law. When I told her that I was accompanied not by sahelis but sahelas, and also who they were, her tone changed. 'Call them in,' she said. When Nargis came running out, she said to her, 'Baby, you go in, Manto sahib has his friends with him.' She received Saleem and his companions as if they were buyers who had come to inspect the house. The informality with which she always spoke to me had disappeared. Instead of 'Sit down', it was 'Do please make yourselves comfortable', and 'Want a drink?' had become 'And what would you prefer for a drink?' I felt like a fool.

When I told her the purpose of our visit, her rather studied and stylized reply took me aback. 'Oh! They want to meet Baby? The poor thing has been down with a bad cold for days. Her heavy work schedule has taken the last ounce of energy out of her. I tell her every day, "Daughter, just rest for a day." But she does not listen, so devoted is she to her work. Even director Mehboob has told her the same thing, offering to suspend the shooting for a day, but it has no effect on her. Today, I put my foot down because her cold was bad. Poor thing!'

Naturally, my young friends were gravely disappointed when they heard that. They had caught a glimpse of her from the taxi when she had briefly run on to the veranda, but they were dying to see her from close quarters and were disappointed that she was ill. Jaddan Bai, meanwhile, had begun to talk of other things and I could see that my young friends were bored. Since I knew there was nothing the matter with Nargis, I said to Jaddan Bai, 'I know it is going to be hard on Baby but they have come from so far; maybe she could come in for a minute.'

After being summoned three or four times, Nargis finally appeared. All of them stood up and greeted her in a very courtly manner. I did not rise. Nargis had made the entry of an actress. Her conversation too was that of an actress, as if she were delivering her given lines. It was quite silly. 'It is such a great pleasure to meet you'. 'Yes, we only arrived in Bombay today'. 'Yes, we will be returning the day after'. 'You are now the top star of India'. 'We have always seen the opening show of every one of your movies'. 'The picture you have given us will go into our album'. Mohan Babu also joined us at one point but he did not say a word, just kept looking at us with his big eyes before going into some reverie of his own.

Jaddan Bai spoke most of the time, making it clear to her visitors that she was personally acquainted with every Indian raja and nawab. Nargis's entire conversation was pure artifice. The way she sat, the way she moved, the way she raised her eyes, was like an offering on a platter. Obviously, she expected them to respond in the same self-conscious, artificial manner. It was a boring and somewhat tense meeting. The young men felt inhibited in my company, as I did in theirs. It was interesting to see a different Nargis from the one to whom I was accustomed. Saleem and his friends went to see her again the next day, but without telling me. Perhaps this meeting was different. As for my argument with the poet Nakhshab to which Tasnim Saleem had referred in her letter, I do not have the least recollection of it. It is possible he was there when we arrived because Jaddan Bai was fond of poetry and liked to entertain poets and have them recite. It is possible I may have had a tiff with Nakhshab.

I saw another aspect of Nargis's personality once when I was with Ashok. Jaddan Bai was planning to launch a production of her own and wanted Ashok to play the lead, but since Ashok, as usual, did not want to go by himself, he had asked me to come along. During our conversation, we discussed many things but discreetly, things such as business, money, flattery and friendship. At times, Jaddan Bai would talk as a senior, at others as the movie producer and at times as Nargis's mother who wanted the right price paid for her daughter's work. Mohan Babu would nod his agreement now and then.

They were talking big money, money which was going to be spent, money which had been spent. However, each paisa was carefully discussed and accounted for. Nargis was pretty businesslike. She seemed to suggest, 'Look Ashok, I agree that you are a polished actor and famous but I am not to be undermined. You will have to concede that I can be your equal in acting.' This was the point she wanted to hammer home. Off and on, the woman in her would come to life, as if she were telling Ashok, 'I know there are thousands of girls who are in love with you, but I too have thousands of admirers and if you don't believe that, ask anyone . . . maybe you too will become my admirer one of these days.'

Periodically, Jaddan Bai would play the conciliator. 'Ashok, the world is crazy about you and Baby, so I want the two of you to appear together. It will be a sensation and we will all be happy.' Sometimes, she would address me. 'Manto, Ashok has become such a great star and he is such a nice man, so quiet, so shy. God grant him a long life! For this movie, I have had a role specially written for him. When I tell you all about it, you will be thrilled.'

I did not know what role or character she had got specially written for Ashok, but anyway I was happy for her. It did occur to me though that Jaddan Bai herself was playing a most fascinating role, and the one she had chosen for Nargis was even more fascinating. Had this been a scene being shot with Ashok, she could not have spoken her lines with more conviction. At one point, Suraiya's name came up and she pulled a long face and started saying nasty things about her family and pulling her down as if she were doing it out of a sense of duty. She said Suraiya's voice was bad, she could not hold a note, she had had no musical training, her teeth were bad and so on. I am sure had someone gone to Suraiya's home, he would have witnessed the same kind of surgery being performed on Nargis and Jaddan Bai. The woman whom Suraiya called her grandmother, but who was actually her mother, would have taken a drag at her hookah and told even nastier stories about Jaddan Bai and Nargis. I know that whenever Nargis's name came up, Suraiya's mother would look disgusted and compare her face to a rotting papaya.

Mohan Babu's big, handsome eyes have been eternally closed for many years and Jaddan Bai has been lying under tons of earth for a long time, her heart full of unrequited desires. As for her Baby Nargis, she stands at the top of that make-believe ladder we know as the movies, though it is hard to say if she is looking up, or if she is looking down at the first rung on which she put her tiny child's foot many years ago. Is she seeking a patch of dark under those brilliant arc lights that illuminate her life now, or is she searching for a tiny ray of light in that darkness? This interplay of light and dark constitutes life, although in the world of movies there are times when the dividing line between the two ceases to exist.

SITARA: THE DANCING TIGRESS FROM NEPAL

As a writer, I have had to go through and overcome many difficulties, but I have never felt more hesitant than I do now as I sit down to record my memories of the famous dancer and film star Sitara. To most, she was known as an actress who was a superb dancer, but I happened to have the opportunity to study her character, hence this piece. Sitara was a living case history, and only a psychologist could write about her as she deserved to be written about. Over the years, I have known and analysed many women but the more I learnt about her, the closer I came to the view that she was not a woman but a typhoon which did not blow in and out as typhoons do, but which retained its force and fury without showing any signs of weakening. She may have been a woman of average build but she was stronger than most people I have known. Had another woman suffered as many illnesses as she did, she could not have survived. Sitara was made of a different clay and was both brave and strong-minded. She never missed her morning dance exercises and spent at least an hour dancing as if there was no tomorrow.

Every morning, she would dance with bone-breaking vigour for an hour, but I never found her looking tired. She had amazing stamina and there was never a sign of fatigue on her face. She loved her art in the same total way as she loved her men. Even for an ordinary performance, she would rehearse for hours and give it everything she had. She always wanted to do new things. Her movements were swift and she was one of those restless people who cannot sit still even for a minute. She was always up and about.

She had two sisters, Tara and Alaknanda, which made them a female trinity. These three sisters were probably born in a Nepalese village and came to Bombay one by one to seek their fortune. Her sisters faded out long ago and there would be few who would even recall their names, but in their time they had lived interesting lives. Tara had many affairs, including one with Shaukat Hashmi who was married to Purnima who later divorced him. Alaknanda passed through many hands and in the end settled down with the famous Prabhat Studio actor Balwant Singh. How long she lived with him, I do not know. Of the three sisters, only Sitara was able to make a mark. I hesitate to write about her because she was not one but several women, and so many were the men with whom she had affairs that it would be impossible to deal with them all in one short piece.

Were the sisters to have a biographer, the book would run into thousands of pages. I have often been denounced as a writer of pornography. Those who do so never give me credit for refusing to write about smutty people, and God knows there are enough of them in this world. People, in my view, do smutty things either out of instinct or because of the surroundings in which they live. What comes instinctively to a human being can perhaps be kept under control if he tries, but if he is indifferent, then whom can he blame except himself?

Whenever I think of Sitara, I am reminded of a typical five-storey Bombay high-rise with many flats and rooms, all inhabited. It is a fact that she had the ability to be involved with many men at the same time. When she came to Bombay, she was with a gaunt-looking Gujarati film director whose name I do not recall but it was some Desai. They were probably married too. He was very good at his work but obstinate by nature, which earned him many rejections. I met him at a time when Saroj Film Company was still in business but dying slowly. We became friends right away because he understood film-making and had a taste for literature. Sitara had just left him but he had few regrets because he told me that he did not have the ability to cope with a woman like her. She then lived with someone else but, off and on, she would come to see Desai. He would welcome her but never encourage her to stay long. There was no divorce under Hindu law. Desai and Sitara had had a Hindu marriage and, despite her affairs with a succession of men, technically she remained Mrs Desai.

I am taking you back to the time when Mehboob's star was rising. He cast her in one of his movies and soon there was a roaring affair going on between the two of them. I won't write about it because only Ishrat Jahan—known to movie-goers as Bibbo—can do justice to this story. Mehboob was shooting outdoors in Hyderabad and, despite his affair with Sitara, his routine was unchanged. He would offer his prayers with the greatest devotion and make love to her with the same single-minded enthusiasm. Mehboob was completing a movie at Film City Studio where P.N. Arora (later to make his mark as a producer) was the sound recordist. Fazalbhai who was all-in-all at Film City, had earlier sent Arora to England for training. The recording laboratory was under the overall charge of Seth Shiraz Ali. Mehboob was still carrying on with Sitara. But according to Diwan Singh Maftoon, editor of the famous journal *Riasat*, she was also having it on the side with Arora. After the Mehboob movie was done, she moved in with Arora. Then there appeared on the scene the handsome Al-Nasir who had just arrived from Dehra Dun to become an actor. Because of his looks, he was given a role in a movie which also starred Sitara. It was only to be expected that he would get added to her list. In effect, besides Al-Nasir, she was maintaining relations with three other men all more or less simultaneously: her husband Desai, Arora and Mehboob.

Her fifth man was Nazir whose mistress, a Jewish actress by the name of Yasmin, had recently left him. I don't know exactly how Nazir and Sitara met, but they instantaneously fell for each other. Nazir was a very forthcoming and open-hearted person. When we met, for instance, instead of shaking hands, he would shower me with the choicest abuse, his way of showing affection. He had a heart of gold and he was straight as an arrow. His affair with Sitara lasted for several years. Because of his strong personality, she temporarily gave up the other men but it was not going to last because Sitara was not a one-man woman. Before long, she had fallen into her old ways with time for everybody: Arora, Al-Nasir, Mehboob and her husband. This was too much for a self-respecting man like Nazir who believed in maintaining a relationship faithfully, once it had been formed. Sitara was made of different clay and even a man like Nazir could not keep her from hopping into bed with other men. His former mistress Yasmin was both very feminine and quite beautiful, but when she told Nazir that she would like to settle down with a husband and home, he, whom many considered a hard man, had said to her in all sincerity that, since they were not going to get married, she was free to marry whom she pleased. How that kind of a person could carry on with a woman like Sitara for so long always baffled me.

I first met Nazir at Hindustan Cinetone. It was a bad time for the movie industry. Many financiers had become bankrupt because of playing the stock market to make quick money. The original name of Cinetone used to be Saroj Film Company, and God knows what else before that. I had written a story called *Keechar*, which Seth

Nanoobhai Desai had liked immensely. It was the sort of story that no producer would have been willing to film because of its theme, which was sure to provoke the government's ire. Nanoobhai was a brave man and he had bought my story, but the project had remained incomplete because of other difficulties he had run into. I had specially written a character—that of a labourer—for Nazir, which he had liked. On learning that Nanoobhai was unable to make that 'heretical' film, he had offered to buy the story and promised to film it no matter what it took. Since Nanoobhai really liked the story, he had declined the offer. He had also in the meantime arranged the money, and the film, which was in the Gujarati language, was directed by Dad Gunjal, completed and released. Nazir had been playing with the idea of forming a film company of his own for some time and, being at a loose end since the end of his affair with Yasmin, he had concentrated on this project and managed to set it up. As far as I can remember, his first production was *Sandesa*, followed by *Society*, which starred Sitara. And that was when she had really got him under her spell though, true to form, she had not stopped meeting her other lovers, especially P.N. Arora.

Here is an interesting story. After I left Bombay for a year to work for All India Radio in Delhi, it was only natural that I would remain largely unaware of the gossip in Bombay. One day I ran into Arora on the street. He was walking with the help of a stick and his back was bent. He had always been thin but he looked in extremely poor shape that day. I felt that he had difficulty even walking, as if there were no life left in him. I was in a tonga and I asked the driver to stop. Expressing surprise at his appearance, I asked him what was wrong. Almost out of breath with fatigue, he managed a faint smile and replied. 'Sitara . . . Manto, Sitara.'

Al-Nasir, who lost his slim, upright and handsome figure after a few years, and became fat and flabby, was a sensation when he first came, with his fair, almost pink complexion, nurtured by the cool hill air of his native Dehra Dun. He was so good-looking that one could almost compare him to a beautiful woman. When I returned to Bombay from Delhi after accepting an offer from Shaukat Hussain Rizvi, I met him at Minerva Movietone. I just could not believe my eyes. His pink complexion had become ashen and his clothes hung loose on him. He seemed to have shrunk, and all energy and strength appeared to have been squeezed out of him. 'My dear, what have you done to yourself?' I asked because I was worried about his health.

He whispered the answer in my ear, 'Sitara . . . my dear, Sitara.'

Sitara was everywhere. I wondered if Sitara's only purpose in life was to infect men with pallor, from the England-trained Arora to the Dehra-Dun-born Al-Nasir. So I took Al-Nasir aside and asked him to give me the lowdown on her. He said it was Sitara who had drained him out, and he had come to a point where he knew that if he did not fight free of her and run it would be the end of him. So one day, he had just hopped on a train bound for Dehra Dun where he had spent three months in a sanatorium and recovered some of his strength. He said she had been writing him long letters in Hindi, which he was unable to read, but added that he dreaded their arrival. He again whispered in my ear, 'Manto sahib, that woman . . . I tell you!'

Women like Sitara are rare, perhaps one in a million. She survived illnesses so dangerous that few other women could have scraped through them. She had determination, and so formidable was her constitution that not once, but several times, she successfully cheated death. Many thought that after such grave bouts with a host of ailments, she would lose her will and ability to dance, but they were wrong. She danced as she had always danced, in her later years as in her early youth, giving it everything she had. She would never miss her daily practice and she would have herself massaged every day. She always had two house servants, a man and a woman. The man always performed the massage. As for the woman, she invariably chose one who looked like an old-fashioned procuress.

Sitara was mostly to be seen in a fine muslin sari, which left nothing to the imagination. It wasn't too pretty a sight. She never talked much but she had sharp eyes that noticed everything. When she was fifty-five, she had the agility of an eagle-eyed young woman. For a time she lived alone in Dadar's Khodadad Circle. Khodadad in Urdu means God-given and the truth is that her talent and her qualities were God-given. Nazir, who later got tied up with the actress Swaran Lata (whom he married), despite his tolerance and generosity, could only take so much of Sitara and no more. In the end, he gave up on her because she could never be satisfied with one man. I am told that he had once stood in front of her with his hands joined together in supplication and begged her, 'Sitara, please let me go. I made a mistake and I am sorry for it and I want you to forgive me.'

Nazir used to rough up Sitara occasionally but she did not seem to mind. Perhaps she was one of those women who derive sexual pleasure from this sort of thing. There is an interesting sub-plot to the Sitara–Nazir affair. His nephew K. Asif (later to become a film-maker of note) was staying with his uncle when Sitara was living in the house. Asif was a big, strong man, still tender in years, who, as far as I know, had never known a woman in his life. He was keen on movies and curious to learn everything about them because he had ambition, and he had come to know many film personalities, including actresses, since he had moved in with his uncle. He must also have witnessed what went on between Sitara and Nazir. A restless young man, he was raring to go, and though Sitara may have appeared to him like a stone wall, she was the kind of wall which men like Asif would be challenged to scale.

Nazir's flat was off a courtyard in front of Ranjit Studio. It had three rooms, one of which served as the office of his company, Hind Pictures. The place did not offer much by way of privacy, so it is to be assumed that young Asif must have witnessed, and certainly heard, what a man and a woman do when they are alone. This must have been a new experience for someone whose knowledge of such things consisted of stories he had heard his married friends tell. His opportunity came one day when he actually saw 'action play' between his uncle and his mistress. It reminded him of a fight between two wild dogs who were trying to bite and tear each other apart as, frothing at the mouth, they carried on with their savage encounter. A shiver ran down his spine. Man, he said to himself, was an animal, and love was a deadly encounter, and he wanted to be in just one such encounter himself. His body was young, sinewy and powerful, his blood warm; all he wanted was an opportunity to prove his manhood.

The talented but luckless Pakistani film director Nayyar was also living in Bombay in those days and staying with Nazir. He and Asif were the same age, both bachelors with wild and youthful fantasies. They would talk about women who were to be theirs in the future that stretched ahead. Whenever Sitara's name came up, they would tremble and feel transported to a world inhabited by demonic spirits. They did not know what a nymphomaniac was, nor could they have known that if, on the one hand, there were women like Sitara, the flip side of the coin was that there were others who were frigid like slabs of ice. They did not know then that Sitara was not faithful though she was Nazir's mistress. They did not know that she still made love to Arora, her husband Desai and Al-Nasir. But they did know why every other day there were scratch marks on Nazir's rhinoceros skin.

Sitara would be up at the crack of dawn and begin the day by dancing like a savage for an hour. Her drummer would get exhausted but not she. The earth would tremble under her feet as she completed her exercises. This was followed by an extended session with her masseur. Then she would bathe, put on fresh clothes and go to Nazir who would still be asleep. She would wake him up and make him drink a cup of milk or something else. That over, another dance would begin. Asif and Nayyar were aware of all this. They were still at an age when you look into empty rooms and peek through windows, when the slightest sound makes you come to a standstill, when you try to read a meaning into everything. Nayyar was slightly built compared to Asif and his sexual urges were also less headstrong than his friend's. Asif's body was full of the static of youth and raw passion, which made him long to knock down a woman like a thunderbolt which falls on the earth's stony surface on a dark night.

Sitara would spend hours chatting to Asif. He felt less shy with her than when he had first come from Lahore, but he still could not muster the courage to touch her. He was terrified of his uncle's temper. However, there was one thing he was in no doubt about: Sitara was attracted to him. If he were to grab her wrist, she would come with him, no matter where he took her, even on a bed of stones on a black, stormy night. Asif was restless. He did not want to wait. The two of them were like two trains which are programmed to collide headlong one day. This bothered him because he wanted the collision to take place today. He felt close to her but they were running on parallel tracks, near yet far. There was no physical contact. The two would talk as passengers riding on trains going in opposite directions, only to move apart. Asif was waiting for that dark and stormy night when he would take the leap. Nazir, in the meanwhile, had become suspicious, and he was horrified. One day he screamed at Sitara and ordered her to pack up and leave. He also beat her up.

Sitara was, after all, a woman, and after the violence and unpleasantness with Nazir, she did not have the strength to just walk out of the door. She wanted help, but how could she ask for it? Nazir was frothing at the mouth with anger because he knew what she was up to. That night he went into his office and slept there. Asif knew that his chance had arrived and he slipped into Sitara's room and rubbed her body where it hurt, then he helped her pack and took her to her Khodadad Circle flat in Dadar. Sitara thanked him for his kindness and, encouraged by that, he took her hand and said, 'You don't have to thank me.' She did not try to free it and one thing led to another. And so it came to pass that young Asif joined the long line of men on whom she had cast her siren spell.

Sitara gave him the time of his life. Had it happened during the day, he would have surely seen stars in the sky, but it had taken place at night in the privacy of her flat at Khodadad Circle. Asif was smitten. 'Look,' he said to her, 'we should have a strong relationship; it is time you stopped going with other men. You should belong to just one man.' Sitara promised that she would not look at another man from that day on. Asif was happy and left as he was afraid his uncle might ask him where he had been. He promised to be back the next day. After he left, Sitara went to her dressing table, brushed her hair, put on a fresh sari, walked down to the street, hailed a taxi and gave the driver P.N. Arora's address.

Sitara hated the sight of me. I was editing the film weekly *Mussawar* in which I wrote a couple of satirical but amusing pieces about her. My columns 'Nit Nai' (The Latest) and 'Baal ki Khal' (Splitting Hairs) were popular and always in good taste, but Sitara did not like what I had written; not that I cared because, frankly, there was nothing I wanted from her. It was also my effort, as far as possible, to keep well away from film personalities. When I wrote a rather naughtily embellished account of her quarrel with Nazir, she was beside herself with rage and was said to have abused me all day. When my spies gave me details of her affair with Asif and I made indirect references to it in my columns, she asked him to beat me up, adding that if he didn't she would hire someone to do it. She also asked him to have some other journalist attack me in his paper. Asif did nothing because he could take a joke; he just let Sitara curse me to her heart's content.

Things between Asif and his uncle, meanwhile, had reached a rather delicate stage. Nazir was getting very, very suspicious about his nephew's movements. Asif was out of the house until the small hours and when he was asked where he had been he would come up with one excuse or another. But excuses, no matter how good, run out in the end. Nazir had banished Sitara from his life and once his mind was made up he never changed it. Sitara he did not give a damn about, but he was worried about his nephew whom he had brought all the way from Lahore so that he could make something of himself. He did not want him to fall into Sitara's clutches. He knew her well and he also knew that she fed on young men like Asif. She had a way with men. Most of the time, she did not even have to try; they just fell into her lap willingly and, once there, found all escape routes blocked.

Once a man caught Sitara's fancy, he had to be on call all hours of the day and night. Asif, therefore, had begun to be absent from home much of the time. Once or twice, Nazir asked him if it was Sitara who was the cause of his disappearances. 'Uncle, I wouldn't even think of it,' Asif would say. Not that Nazir believed him. He was too old in tooth and claw not to know that this boy, his own nephew, was Sitara's latest acquisition. As for Asif, had it been a woman other than his uncle's former mistress, he would not have lied; but this was different. How could he tell his uncle that he was having an affair with his ex-mistress? Not only did Asif have no desire whatsoever to turn away from Sitara, he would not even have been able to, had he tried.

Nazir's anger was mounting, but slowly. He did not wish to act until he had caught the two in a compromising position himself. And one day, that opportunity came his way. I do not now remember how Nazir caught Asif, but catch his nephew he did. Asif still swore that there was nothing between Sitara and him, but it was no use. Nazir's first impulse was to break every bone in their bodies, but thanks to the actor Majid (who came to Lahore after 1947), who was in his good books, he cooled down. Majid, on his own, had tried several times to warn Asif about Sitara and the dangerous game he was playing, but Asif was beyond advice. He was also foolish enough to believe that his affair with Sitara would remain a secret. Nazir may have had a temper but he was also a tender-hearted man. He had had a long physical relationship with Sitara. He did not want his nephew to fall into her hands because he knew it would do him no good. Even if Asif had not been his nephew, he would still have given the young man the same advice. Nazir, a man of great sincerity—although he gave the impression of being hard—was not happy with what he had done, rather, not done. And he was nobody's fool; he was perceptive and, what was more, he knew Sitara as few men knew her.

Asif began to get home earlier so as not to provoke his uncle's ire. Once he left, Sitara would make her up face, change and hop into a taxi to spend the rest of the night with Arora on whom the potions of Delhi's herbal medicine miracle-workers had had a salutary effect. He had regained some of his old vigour and he no longer had that hollow-cheeked look. She had not given up on her other old flames either. They—Al-Nasir, Mehboob and God alone knows how many others—remained on her 'active list'. Asif had reduced his visits because of his uncle, but he had not eliminated them. And how could he, even if he had tried. Sitara was like a sorceress of old who turns her lovers into flies and sticks them on the wall. In fairy tales, it always required a prince bearing a special amulet to break the spell and release the sorceress's prisoners. Was a prince going to come to Asif's rescue, because he was bewitched by one on whom even the most potent black magic could not have much effect? She was a fort that could not be stormed; so Asif continued to see Sitara and his relationship with his uncle kept worsening. By the way, after Nazir threw out Sitara, the famous musician Rafiq Ghaznavi had tried to make peace between them but without success. Once he invited Sitara, Arora and Nazir to his flat for drinks but despite his best efforts—he was a most persuasive conversationalist—he could not manage to change Nazir's mind. In the end, everybody left and Sitara spent the night with Rafiq, who kept assuring her that her time with Nazir was a thing of the past and she should accept it. That was the beginning and the end of his peace mission. It was also the first and last night she spent with Rafiq. One wonders why. Was it that he had found her to be less than a perfect dancer and she had discovered that he was not the musician he fancied himself to be?

Sitara was perhaps the first woman in Asif's life and she had taken a shine to him. Nazir, unfortunately, caught them in flagrante delicto one more time, but I do not know who got Asif off the hook this time. Some days later, I heard that Asif had disappeared from Bombay. Then I was told that Sitara was not to be seen anywhere either. When people asked, they were told that she had gone to a Hindu shrine. Had it been the annual Haj pilgrimage season, some wags would have quipped that Asif had gone to the holy land, but it wasn't. Then came the news that both of them were in Delhi, were married, and Sitara had become a Muslim and taken the name Allah Rakhi. One can imagine the effect it must have had on Nazir. Under Hindu personal law there was no divorce. Once a woman was married, she remained married for life. She can have a hundred men but she will remain the wife of the man to whom she first got married. Even if a Hindu woman changes her religion, she remains married to her first husband. From that point of view, Sitara may have become Begum K. Asif; but to all intents and purposes, she was still Mrs Desai.

Once the story was confirmed, I had a field day with it in my *Mussawar* columns. Every week, I would write about the newlyweds in a cutting manner. When the two returned to Bombay after their honeymoon, Nazir was so embarrassed and angry that it is not possible to describe it in words. One day at the races I saw Asif in a sharkskin suit with his arm around Sitara's waist. When he saw me, he smiled, then began to laugh. He shook my hand and said, 'Brilliant, the columns you are writing are most amusing, by God I say.' Sitara made a face and stood aside, but Asif paid no attention to her and kept talking to me for quite some time. He may have had little education but he had the ability to take a joke. In Bombay, the word along the bazaar grapevine was that someone called Asif had married Sitara. In Bhindi Bazaar and Mohammed Ali Road, traditionally Bombay's Muslim-dominated localities, men would sit in Iranian cafes sipping tea and expressing satisfaction over the fact that a Muslim had married a Hindu and converted her to Islam. Most of these devout Muslims often happened to be ardent supporters of the All India Muslim League. Some would say that Asif should not allow this sali to appear in movies; others would say there was nothing wrong with it, as long as she observed purdah when she left home. Some cynics would declare, 'It is all a stunt.' Once I asked Asif if he had really married Sitara in a Muslim ceremony. 'What ceremony, what marriage!' he answered. Only God knows what the truth was.

Asif had no place of his own, so he was living in Sitara's flat and driving her around in her car. In Delhi, Asif had met a financier, Lala Jagat Narayan, and talked him into investing in a movie he wanted to make. He must also have taken an advance because he did not appear to be hard-pressed for funds. Asif had a lot of self-confidence and could get the better even of famous directors and writers. He had great native intelligence, and plenty of horse sense. When he became a director, he did not confine himself to the advice of a small coterie, as so often happens, but invited a cross section of people to advise him, never hesitating to accept a good suggestion or idea.

I am reminded of a story that involves me. When Asif was going to make *Phool* and I was living in a flat on Clare Road, one day I heard persistent honking in the street. I came out on the balcony and found a huge car parked in front of my building. I had a first-floor flat and I bent over to see who the occupant was. It was Asif, who stuck his head out of the car window and smiled. 'Come in,' I said.

He opened the car door, said something to Sitara who was in the back seat and replied, 'In a minute.' The car drove off and Asif walked in. He shook hands warmly and said, 'I want to read you my story.' 'I charge a fee as you know,' I said jokingly. Without another word, Asif walked out. I called after him and even ran out to the street but he would not return. All he said was he would come back when he had my fee. I felt ashamed of my bad joke, though I had been quite sure that he would take it in the spirit in which I had made it. When I told my wife what had happened, she said it was silly of me to have said what I had. Asif, after all, was not a close friend and it was understandable that he had reacted the way he had.

Of course, I had not had the least intention of injuring his feelings, nor had I expected him to give me money. On the other hand, I really wanted him to narrate to me the story of his yet-to-be-made film. There were many 'third-class' directors in Bombay who had asked me to listen to their stories not once but twice and even thrice because they wanted my opinion. I had never asked them for money. I regretted having upset Asif. One day, there was a knock at the door. I opened it and found a man with an envelope, which he gave to me, and left. I had not even opened it when I heard a car honk in the road. It was Sitara's car. The envelope contained five hundred rupees and a one-line note, 'Here's the fee. I will come tomorrow.' I was floored. Next day, Asif appeared at nine. 'Well, doctor, have you received your fee?' he asked. I was speechless but I apologized and tried to return the money, but he would not take it. He sank into the sofa and said, 'Manto sahib, what are you thinking? This money is not mine, nor my father's, but the producer's. It was my mistake that I arrived without a fee because I wasn't thinking. I do not believe in getting things done free. You are going to spend your time, so it is only right that you should be paid for it. By God, that is what I believe. But let's forget about this nonsense and let me tell you the story.'

Without giving me an opportunity to answer, he sat down on a sofa and I took a chair facing him. I had never heard him tell a story and it was quite an experience. He rolled up the sleeves of his silk shirt, loosened his belt, pulled up his legs and assumed the classic posture of a yogi. 'Now listen to the story. It is called *Phool*. What do you think of the name?' 'It is good,' I replied. 'Thank you, I will narrate it scene by scene,' he said. Then he began to speak in his typical manner. I do not know who the author was but Asif was playing all the characters, raising his voice, moving around all the time. Now he would be on the sofa, the next minute his back would be against the wall, then he would push his legs against it and his upper torso would be on the floor. At times, he would jump from the sofa on to the floor, only to climb on to a chair the next minute. Then he would stand up straight, looking like a leader asking for votes in an election. It was a long story, like the intestine of the devil, as the expression goes. After he finished his narration, we were silent for a few moments. 'What do you think about it?' Asif asked. 'It is trash,' I replied. Asif bit his lips, sat upright on the sofa and asked furiously, 'What did you say?' Had it been somebody else, that person might have flinched, but I am not made that way. 'It is trash,' I repeated.

Asif tried many of his conjurer's tricks to impress me but they had no effect on me. Also, I simply have no patience with loudness, which was one of Asif's characteristics. Finally, I decided to give it to him. 'Look here, Asif, I suggest you get hold of a big, heavy stone, place it on top of my head and hit that stone with a hammer, once, twice, thrice, and as long as you like. And by God, I swear I would still say that your story is trash.' Asif stood up, took my hand in both of his and said, 'By God, it is trash. I had come only to hear you say that.' I first thought he was joking but he was serious, so we sat down and began to think of improvements.

Asif and Sitara stayed 'married' for quite some time, which reminds me of another story, which predates my friendship with Asif and his relationship with Sitara. Asif had pimples on his face, which are associated with adolescence. I used to think that if youth were so ugly and painful, then may it please God not to bless anyone with youth. (I am thankful to the Almighty that he did confer such youth on me.) I used to dabble in herbal medicine and I wanted to do something for Asif's appearance. I also consulted a couple of doctor friends and one day I brought a handful of medicines for him, but they did him no good. When Sitara came into his life, every pimple on his face disappeared.

Kamal Amrohi and I used to be colleagues at Bombay Talkies. I recall the time when we were trying to put his story, later filmed as *Mahal*, into final shape. One day I noticed a pimple on his face and thought nothing of it, but in a few days it became so painful that we felt something had to be done to rid him of it. 'I have a treatment that can't miss,' I told Kamal. 'What?' he asked. 'Do you know where Sitara lives?' I asked. 'I do,' he replied. 'All you have to do is go there, walk up the stairs right up to her door but under no circumstances are you to enter. There is your cure,' I said. Kamal was an intelligent man and burst out laughing. He knew what I meant.

Meanwhile, Sitara and Asif were living together in Mahim where I visited them several times. Their third-floor flat was at the other end of a street facing the church on Lady Jamshedji Road. Asif had finished *Phool* and was thinking of making *Anarkali*, which Kamal Amrohi had scripted for him, but he was not too happy with it and had asked various people including me to give it a new twist. I used to get to his place by eight in the morning and the door would be answered by an old woman wearing a thin muslin sari, which always made me uneasy. She looked like an old Arabian Nights witch to me. I would go in and sit on the sofa. From the next room, which was the bedroom, I would hear strange noises, which sent a shiver down my spine. After some time, Asif would appear, smacking his lips. He used to be a sight, with his nightshirt torn in various places and blue marks on his chest and arms, his hair dishevelled, and his breathing uneven. He would greet me casually and then fall in a heap on the floor. After some time, Sitara would send him a cup of custard, which he would eat with undisguised reluctance. Then we would begin our work, which was more gossip than anything. The two of them seemed to be doing well, though rumours were spreading that Asif was marrying a girl from his family, that a date had been set, and soon he would be travelling to Lahore with his friends for the ceremony.

I was busy when all this happened; otherwise I would have met him and asked what it was all about. I never got an opportunity until many days later. 'Well, I have decided to put an end to it and I will,' was all he said. He was in a car and I was walking. He had stopped and was in a hurry so we could not have a proper conversation. A few days later, I learnt that Asif had gone to Lahore with a large party of friends and a big wedding had taken place there with drinks flowing and dancing girls performing. Then I heard that Asif had returned to Bombay with his new bride and had rented a portion of a house on Pali Hill, Bandra. I later found out that it was actually Nazir's house and he had vacated one half of it for his nephew. I am not sure what Sitara thought of it, but I do know that her visits to Arora continued. Asif had now begun to make preparations to make *Mughal-e-Azam* (completed several years after Independence).

Then a most interesting development took place. Asif began disappearing from home and it came to light that he was again spending his nights with Sitara. Consequently, the new marriage failed. Nazir's grown-up son was also around at the time and one is not sure what exactly happened, but this much was known that Asif had stopped going home at night. There was much unpleasantness and then we heard that a divorce was in the offing. All through this crisis, Asif kept meeting Sitara. It seemed they were together again. There were many stories in the market about Asif's new wife but I have no wish to go into them because I am not sure if they were true. All I know is that Asif had married in Lahore with great fanfare and brought his bride to Bombay, settled down on Pali Hill and, in less than three months, the marriage was on the rocks. Who but Sitara could have been responsible for it? She was a woman of experience and knew how to make herself attractive to a man, rendering him useless for other women. That was how she had weaned Asif away from his new bride and that was why he had come back to her. That woman Sitara had something other women lacked. Asif left his wife because she probably did not have the qualities that he had found in Sitara. Was it that she had left Asif with no taste for inexperienced virgins?

I have written this account and I know that it will not annoy Asif because he is a big-hearted man. Sitara, of course, would be angry, but after some time, she will forgive me because, in her own way, she too is a big-hearted woman. In my book, she walks tall. I do not know what she thinks of me but I have always thought of her as a woman who is born once in a hundred years.

NAWAB KAASHMIRI: AN ACTOR'S ACTOR

Though he was merely an actor—I say 'merely' because actors, like writers, are given little respect in this society—I had more respect for him than I have for anyone else who may fall in the 'merely' category. He was a master of his art. This is something about which a cabinet minister may not have been able to tell you anything. But if you had put the same question to a working man in rags who had spent his hard-earned money to see Nawab Kaashmiri in a movie, he would have told you about Nawab's great achievements as an artist. When an English king dies, they announce: 'The King is dead; long live the King.' Nawab Kaashmiri is dead, but there is no one who can take his place and for whose long life I can pray because, compared to him, all actors look like ordinary pawns.

I first met Nawab Kaashmiri in a Bombay studio. We sat together for a long time and talked. I narrated one of my film stories to him but it had no effect on him. He told me without any ceremony, 'It's all right, but I don't like it.' I was impressed by his frank criticism. The next day, I narrated another story of mine to him. At many points in the narrative, I saw tears well up in his eyes. When I was finished, he pulled out a handkerchief, dried his eyes and said, 'Whom are you selling this story to? I would very much like the role of the pimp.' I told him that no producer was prepared to buy the story. 'Let them go to hell,' Nawab said.

I saw him for the first time in *Yahudi ki Ladki.* Rattan Bai was the female lead and Nawab played the Jew traitor. I had never met a Jew in my life, but when I went to Bombay and saw them, I felt that Nawab's rendition had been close to life. He told me that in order to do justice to the part and get it right, he had spent a good deal of time with Bombay's Jews. Only when he was confident that he understood them had he said yes to B.N. Sarkar, owner of New Theatre. He was unforgettable in that movie. He had had all his teeth extracted to lend credibility to his role as an old man. He was indeed a great actor and would never accept a role unless he sincerely felt that he could do justice to it. Before signing a contract, he would listen to the entire story and think about it for several days. He would stand in front of a mirror to get right the various facial expressions the character would need. When he was fully satisfied that he was on top of the character he had been asked to play he would sign the papers.

He loved the plays of Agha Hashra Kashmiri, but it is strange that a man who was one of the most admired actors of the old Imperial Theatrical Company which staged Hashra's major works would so completely change his style after coming to motion pictures. There was no theatricality in his acting style on the screen. He would speak his lines as people talk in daily life. Nawab's performances in Imperial Theatrical Company plays such as *Khoobsoorat Balaa*, *Noor-i-Watan* and *Baagh-i-Iran* made him famous all over the country. He was the only son of the Mufti-i-Azam of the biggest imambara in Lucknow. It is ironical that the son of the Shi'as' biggest religious personality in Lucknow should have gone to the stage and then the cinema, but he had been inclined that way from childhood. The story is that a roving theatrical company once came to Lucknow and the young Nawab used to go and watch its presentations regularly and avidly. He felt that if there was one reason he had come into this world, it was to be an actor. He would come home from the theatre and for hours he would rehearse and repeat the lines of dialogue he had heard earlier that evening.

One day, he appeared at the roving theatrical company and asked that he be tested. When the director saw him act and deliver his lines, he was swept off his feet. Nawab was hired immediately—at what salary, I do not know. He went with the company to Calcutta and established himself there in a very short time. When Cowasji Khataoji of Alfred Theatre Company watched Nawab perform, he made him an offer which he accepted. Before long, he had established his reputation as a character actor. The owner of another famous company, Seth Sukh Lal Karnani, was a colourful character. When he heard that an actor by the name of Nawab was drawing in the audience, he said in his typical style, 'So get hold of that bull.' That bull was got hold of, given a higher salary and for two years he played in every major company production. I am not sure if it was around the time when Bombay's Imperial Film Company was making its first talkie, *Alam Ara*.

The talkies were now here to stay. One of the first men to seize the opportunity was B.N. Sarkar, an educated man of vision, who set up New Theatre and persuaded Nawab to move from the stage to the cinema. He was an admirer of the actor and treated him not as an employee but as one of his heroes. He was a man of literary and artistic taste. Nawab's first film was the celebrated *Yahudi ki Ladki.* The heroine was Rattan Bai, whose hair was so long that it touched her ankles. The movie was directed by the Bengali director Atorthy. The music was scored by Bali. The third member of the team was a man called Hafizji. It was quite a trinity. Atorthy was an educated man. He once said to me, 'An actor like Nawab the world will not see again. He takes to his role as a glove takes to the wearer's hand. He is a master of his art.' Hafizji too used to say that he had never seen an actor like Nawab.

Nawab was offered the role of a pickpocket in a movie by the name of *Maya.* When he heard the story, he refused to take it, saying he could not play it since he was not a pickpocket and did not know how to pick someone's pocket. However, he began spending his time in a third-class Calcutta hangout where he got to know a number of pickpockets and other street characters. He would sit with them and drink, although he was not a drinking man. After a week of this, he was satisfied that he could play the role. He had learnt their ways and become familiar with their tricks. He was a success in the part. In real life, he was a good and pious man. One of his relatives, M.A. Ammad, told me once that he was an observing Shi'a and would never undertake anything major unless he had first prayed and asked for divine guidance. Personally, I do not know the difference between the Sunni and the Shi'a sects. But I do know that when they fight each other, they prove conclusively that they are off their rockers.

Who can forget that scene in the film *Mukti* when Nawab offers his wife, who has been unfaithful to him, a plate of roasted corn. He was able to express more emotion by the mere movement of the hand that held the plate than other actors could with their faces. In *Devdas*, when K.L. Saigal slaps him, he rubs his cheek for a long time, then says, 'You hit Deeno Bhai.' That one line used to run like a strong electric current through the audience. In the movie *Ziddi*, when his nephew's wife, played by Kuldip Kaur, rushes past him—he is in his invalid's chair—with her lover, played by Pran, he looks at her and says philosophically, '*Phur* . . . she is gone.'

As for his personal life, his first wife was from his hometown, but when they had got married, I do not know. There were no children. When he lost hope of her bearing a child, he began to look around and obtained the hand of the daughter of Prince Mehr Qadar, the eldest son of the Nawab of Oudh. When his wife learnt that he had married another woman, she had a breakdown, but Nawab paid no attention. In the end, she committed suicide. She sprinkled kerosene on her quilt, rubbed her body and her clothes with it liberally, calmly lay down on her bed, lit a match and set everything on fire. Nawab was with his new wife in another house, ignorant of how his first wife had greeted the news of his second marriage. When he did learn, he arranged for her burial. She had left a will that said that her life insurance, which was worth ten thousand rupees, should be given to her husband. She had also left him a huge quantity of gold. Nawab was surprised by her last testament. For a long time, he must have smelt kerosene after he was told of it.

When I think of Nawab Kaashmiri, I sometimes feel like a kerosene can, which is about to ignite. I am also a Kashmiri but I am not so cruel as to drive my wife to kill herself just because she could not beget a child. I love Kashmiris but I hate those who ill-treat their wives. I admired Nawab Kaashmiri and I considered him a great artist but whenever I see him on the screen, I smell kerosene.

May God keep him in hell where he would be happier.

NEENA: THE INSCRUTABLE HOUSEWIFE

Shahida was a happy housewife, married to Mohsin Abdullah. They had fallen in love in Aligarh and married and remained in love. She was the kind of young woman who did not even look at another man, but Mohsin was different. He relished variety, not that Shahida knew anything about it. She did know, though, that her husband's sisters were liberal women and mixed with men without any self-consciousness and even discussed such things as sex with them. Shahida was never comfortable with that. One of Mohsin's sisters, Dr Rashid Jahan, was particularly 'advanced'. She later married Sahibzada Mahmood-ul-Zafar who was teaching at MAO College, Amritsar, where I was a student. He was a handsome man and he had socialist ideas. Faiz Ahmed Faiz, the poet, with whom I had the friendliest of relations, also used to teach at our college and he always reminded me of a lotus-eater. He would often ask me to shop for him, something I would do happily. He used to go to Dehra Dun to meet Dr Rashid Jahan with whom he was in love, I think. I have no idea to what extent he was successful, but I do know that he wrote some wonderful love poems at the time, despite his laziness. I mention these interconnected facts because they form the background to the story I am about to tell.

Mohsin Abdullah moved to Bombay when he landed a job at Bombay Talkies, which was the most prestigious institution of its time, headed by the formidable Himanshu Rai who believed in hiring educated young people. Mohsin worked in the laboratory and lived in the Malad area where the studio was located. It was company policy that middle-level and junior employees live as close to work as possible, and accordingly Mohsin and Shahida had rented an old, dilapidated house in the area. He was a good worker and had made a fine impression on Himanshu Rai. He made about the same money as Ashok Kumar who was fast becoming successful. Azuri, the dancer, and Mumtaz were also at Bombay Talkies, as was S. Mukherjee who was assistant to the sound recordist Savak Vacha. It was a happy crowd.

When *Puner Milan* was being shot—it starred Snehprabha Pradhan, who was an educated girl—Khwaja Ahmad Abbas, the writer (later to become a famous producer), also happened to be employed in the company's publicity department. Mohsin and Abbas both fell in love with Snehprabha who belonged to Sind and had come to Bombay to do a nursing course, which she had successfully completed. They both wanted her to 'nurse' them but she was a smart woman who played both of them along without letting them get anywhere near her. Mohsin had also developed a passion for gambling and would lose his entire salary on his new pastime, much to the misery of Shahida who had to borrow money from her parents every month. They also had a child who was always sick. One day Shahida said to her husband as gently as she could, 'Mohsin, even if you don't take care of me, at least take care of your child.' This had no effect on him because he was obsessed with Snehprabha Pradhan and gambling.

At the time I was working at Nanoobhai Desai's Hindustan Cinetone. V. Shantaram, who had made one hit after another for Prabhat Film Company, had earlier invited me to come to Poona on a get-acquainted visit and meet a group of writers and journalists who were also to be there. One of those invited was W.Z. Ahmed, who was working with Sadhana Bose, translating dialogue from Bengali into Urdu. We spent two days in Poona, but I did not really get to know him. W.Z. Ahmed always wore a kind of mask that was hard to penetrate. Everything about him, including his smile, struck me as a pose. I did notice though that, like the well-known Jewish director Ernst Lubitsch, he always had a long cigar tucked in his mouth. I next met W.Z. at the actor Ramshakal's place where he was drinking rum. We exchanged cold, formal greetings and I could see that he was by nature reserved, like a tortoise which draws in its head so as not to be seen. 'Why don't you say something?' I asked him. He laughed. 'You have been talking to Ramshakal, is that not enough conversation?' he replied. I did not like his answer, which was more suited to a politician, a breed that I hate. I met him several times in the same house but he hardly ever opened his mouth. He would just sit in a corner, quietly drinking rum with the two of us jabbering away.

Two years later, I heard that W.Z. was setting up a film company. I was surprised that a man who was making his living translating dialogue from Bengali to Urdu could do that. He had decided to call it Shalimar Studio and it was to be based in Poona. The first production was already being aggressively advertised. I noticed that every advertisement was centred on a new actress described as 'the inscrutable Neena'. I could not understand what mystery could be attached to an actress. Once she appeared on the screen, all her mystery would be lost. For nearly two years, he kept selling Neena as 'the mystery lady'. I asked many people who this Neena was but no one knew. Once, when I was working for Baburao Patel, editor of *Filmindia*, I asked him who this Neena was. 'Sala, don't you know? What kind of an editor are you . . . You know that Mohsin Abdullah?' Baburao asked. 'Yes, I have heard of him . . . I even know a little bit about him,' I replied. 'Neena is his wife, understand?' Patel said. 'But I don't understand. His wife's name is Shahida,' I replied. Patel then informed me that Shahida was the sister-in-law—bhabhi—of the actress Renuka Devi whom I had seen in *Bhabhi*, a film that had impressed me. So now we had two bhabhis: Renuka and Shahida alias Neena.

I met W.Z. Ahmed a few more times and came to the conclusion that he was both a careful planner and an adventurer. Like Soviet dictators, he would plan for years before embarking on anything. Then he would sit back and wait for results. I am a man in a hurry, so we were temperamentally incompatible. I talked too much; he was a man of few words. He was very formal whereas I hated formality. When he spoke, he sounded like a recording. I must admit though that whatever he said often had a lot of weight. He spoke many languages: Marathi, Gujarati, English and Punjabi. A Punjabi, he was the brother of Maulana Salahuddin Ahmed, editor of the literary magazine *Adabi Duniya*. Another brother, Riazuddin Ahmed, was a government officer. Most people would not have known that Salahuddin and W.Z. were brothers, though they certainly had one thing in common: they loved flattery. By the way, the 'W' in the name stood for Waheed. He was married to the daughter of Sir Ghulam Hussain Hidayatullah, who was Governor of Sindh after the establishment of Pakistan. How this match had come to be arranged, I haven't the least idea.

I ran into W.Z. Ahmed the other day at my barber's shop on Hall Road, Lahore, and dragged him home where I told him that I wanted to write a piece on Neena and asked him if I had his permission. His answer was typical, 'I will get back to you in a day or two.'

Several days passed but I did not hear from him. A few days later when I ran into him again, I asked, 'How much time do you need?' He was smoking a pipe. He smiled vaguely and his half-bald head shone even more. 'I am busy these days. I need a week,' he said. This conversation took place in the office of the film magazine *Director* owned by Chaudhri Fazle Haq and edited by Shabab Keranwi (who later became a film director). 'That's fine, a week goes by quickly,' I replied.

Two more weeks passed and there was no word from him, so I said to myself that actors and actresses were public property and one did not need permission to write about them. Hence the piece that you are now reading.

When Shalimar was established, Mohsin Abdullah was put in charge of the laboratory. Shahida was the domestic type and had no ambition to become a film star; she only wanted a calm home life. W.Z. Ahmed, being the Soviet-style planner that he was, drew up a five-year plan and began to implement it stage by stage. He aroused no suspicion, using his tortoise technique. Mohsin, meanwhile, was busy trying to entice Snehprabha Pradhan. He was also very hard up, had given his gambling losses, so one day he said to Shahida, 'You are so conservative. Look at my sisters; how modern and enlightened they are.' She replied that she was quite happy the way she was. There were many arguments between the two because Mohsin wanted her to become an actress, a line of work in which she had no interest.

Ismat Chughtai, the writer and wife of director-writer Shahid Latif who was associated with such famous films as *Ziddi*, *Arzoo* and *Buzdil*, told my wife, Safia, that Shahida and she had been at school in Aligarh and she knew what a simple girl she was. 'How do you know?' my wife asked. 'I know, she is my friend,' Ismat replied. 'What do you think of me?' my wife asked. 'You are just a woman,' Ismat answered. 'Is there something wrong with that?' my wife asked. 'No, but you are different from Shahida,' replied Ismat. 'How?' 'She is artless, you are not. You know how to keep an eye on your husband; she does not.' 'Tell me more.' 'I know her well. I know her whole family. She was really a very simple girl. We used to make fun of her in college.' Ismat told my wife that Shahida knew nothing about men or falling in love and she for one could not understand how she had fallen in love with Mohsin and married him. He must have chased her hard and she must have relented because she had a soft personality. Naive by nature, she could never work out the consequences of the actions that she took.

In the end, Mohsin succeeded in persuading his wife to join the movies though it was against her instincts. Shalimar Studio, therefore, was built on her fragile shoulders. Ahmed became a producer and turned the simple Shahida into 'Neena, the mystery girl'. He ran a huge publicity campaign to introduce his star. You only had to pick up a movie magazine in those days to read about her. This propaganda barrage created much public curiosity because people were keen to know who this mysterious star was. The film that launched her career was *Ek Raat*, based on Hardy's *Tess*. Shahida had been given the role of the peasant girl who is raped and then married off. She is so simple that she tells the story to her husband who throws her out.

Ahmed's five-year plan was on course. He would meet Shahida as Molotov would meet an ambassador. Mohsin was doing his own thing, though he was not having much luck with Snehprabha. Ahmed had become a close friend of Shahida's and would call her 'Begum' and treat her with great deference. He would rise when she entered the room, bowing from the waist to greet her. This was all well thought out. He wanted her to notice the difference between him and the unconcerned Mohsin. He was prepared to wait, one, two, even five years. He knew that ultimately he would capture her. In moviedom, most men succeed through women. Ahmed knew that and so he kept Mohsin happy while keeping an eye on his wife. He had hired Mohsin on a good salary so that he would get even more involved in his favourite pastimes. Shahida would complain to Mohsin off and on about his conduct, but it had no effect on him. From the confining atmosphere of Bombay Talkies, he had been catapulted into the open spaces of Shalimar and he was taking full advantage of this freedom. Shahida may have become an actress but she still wanted to return to private life. She did not much like being called 'the mystery girl'.

But as time passed and she began to excite people's curiosity, she began to change. She became sensitive to the differences between Ahmed and Mohsin. While one was the very picture of good manners and thoughtfulness, the other was rude and careless. Shahida's biggest embarrassment was the unabashed manner in which Mohsin chased women. Ahmed had put Mohsin in charge of the laboratory but he knew that he would not be able to manage it. It was all part of his plan. He had never asked Mohsin why he gambled or went to the races or ran after studio girls. He wanted him to get even more involved in these diversions. It was all very obvious but not to the simple Shahida. She did not even realize that she herself was changing. She would sit in front of the mirror while make-up was being applied, look at herself and blush. She sometimes felt like Tess who was going to be raped. When shooting began, she became less self-conscious. There was now a widening gulf between Mohsin and her, something she did not want, but Ahmed kept assuring her that there was no cause for worry because the relationship would heal by itself. Ahmed moved slowly and with care, finally convincing Shahida with the greatest subtlety that her husband was dissolute and a wastrel. He also made her realize that he had given him a job because of his concern for him but he had to confess that Mohsin had betrayed his trust.

This was indeed true. Mohsin's work at the laboratory was not satisfactory, and though Ahmed had an abundance of patience, one day he sent for Mohsin Abdullah and said to him in his soft voice, 'Perhaps you do not do what needs to be done because you think this sort of work is beneath you. I am prepared to continue paying you your salary, but I am going to place the laboratory under someone else's charge.' Mohsin's first reaction was anger, but Ahmed cooled him down and put him on the promised pension which, for all practical purposes, it was. Mohsin, who could be either highly sensitive or utterly otherwise, must have been feeling 'otherwise' when he accepted Ahmed's offer. He also seemed to be oblivious of the fact that his long-neglected wife, whom he always wanted to see emulating his 'enlightened' sisters, was slowly being drawn to another man. The fact was that he was not really much interested in his wife, preferring his horse races in Poona and Bombay and his card-playing to her.

Meanwhile, the film was progressing and Ahmed, being the director, was using every opportunity his position gave him to wean Shahida away from her husband, who had failed to realize that his virtual dissociation from the studio could affect his relationship with his wife. He was foolishly confident that since theirs had been a love marriage she would always remain faithful to him. Ahmed was a man who kept his word and he was paying Mohsin his salary in time even when there was not enough money to pay others. Not by nature mean or small-minded, he exhibited all the qualities generally associated with people who come from good families and solid backgrounds. He was in the movie business, although by temperament he was more suited to politics. He had brought no capital with him but had enough tact and imagination to raise millions. He never wasted his money on frivolities, but he had one weakness. He would hold court like a Mughal prince and lap up the flattery heaped on him by his hangers-on.

Ahmed had a whole stable of writers and poets working for him, among them Sagar Nizami, Josh Malihabadi, Jan Nisar Akhtar, Krishan Chander and Bharat Vyas, apart from Dr Abdullah Chughtai and my nephew Masood Pervez. They would sit in Ahmed's room and hold heated discussions on the film being shot, sometimes for the whole night, but without arriving at any useful conclusions, which was not surprising as the atmosphere was that of a court full of sycophants. Josh would be kept happy with a pint of rum every evening. He would come up with a verse that was appropriate to the subject under discussion and receive effusive praise. Masood Pervez, who was very quick-minded in those days, would add a few verses on the spot, which would inspire Sagar Nizami, who would recite an entire poem in his sweet voice. Krishan Chander, being a story writer, would just sit there like an owl, unable to join in the spontaneous versification. Very little work would get done during such meetings. Bharat Vyas would feel out of it because of his poor knowledge of Urdu. To make up, he would try to impress the company with his Sanskritized Hindi. And every time Ahmed said something witty, Josh would shower him with praise, 'Ahmed sahib, you are a poet.' When the meeting came to an end, Ahmed would shut himself in his room and try to write a ghazal, but as far as I know, he had not been able to compose one even once. All these people were Ahmed's groupies.

In the beginning, everyone used to be paid regularly but it did not last. The permanent staff had to subsist on advances. The atmosphere at Shalimar was strange. There was one director with about a dozen assistants, who, I suspect, had their own assistants. How these people managed to survive, I never could understand. It was a tribute to Ahmed that he had somehow kept Shalimar going because he was a clever man who remained cool no matter how hard the times were. He would just sit there unperturbed, pick out a betel leaf from a silver paandaan, add his favourite condiments, including a pinch of tobacco, roll the leaf, place it in his mouth, and smile.

He had every quality that a successful politician needs, and that was how he had been able to set up Shalimar Studio. That was also how he had stolen Shahida from her husband. I could never understand what was so attractive about her that he had built an entire studio practically on her body. Could it be that she was the only woman he could get? The fact was that she was not the acting type at all, so what was it about her that he had found so irresistible? Was he so impressed with her housewifely qualities that he had fallen in love with her? It is also possible that he was not in love with her at all, but had simply used her for his own purposes. And although he had worked long and hard to wrest her away from Mohsin, I do not think he ever succeeded fully because even when Mohsin and she were going through a divorce Shahida did not want to leave him. But in the end, she really did leave him; she lived alone for a while and ultimately moved in with Ahmed.

Which year it was I no longer remember, but I was working at Filmistan with S. Mukherjee as the company's production controller. One day he asked me why I did not write a story for him. I sat down and turned out four stories in five days, but when he asked me to read them to him, I refused and sent all four to my nephew Masood Pervez who worked for Ahmed at Shalimar, as I have stated earlier. The first story was called 'Controlistan'. Four days later, I travelled to Poona. The first thing that I did on arrival at Shalimar was to go to the loo because it is my view that if you wanted to know quickly what was going on all you had to do was read the graffiti. 'Nobody gets paid here; the rest is OK,' was the first news that greeted me. That was enough to nearly make me take the next train back to Bombay but Masood insisted that I meet Ahmed now that I was here. We met in his office. He was in his chair, a long cigar between his lips. On one side sat Shahida, on the other Josh Malihabadi, with whom I exchanged greetings. He was holding a pint of rum, courtesy, no doubt, W.Z. Ahmed. I spoke to Ahmed in Punjabi but immediately realized that Shahida and Josh did not understand the language, so I slipped into Urdu. When I had first seen Ahmed at Prabhat he was a fine, handsome young man but he now looked somewhat burnt out. He greeted me with his usual courtesy and introduced me to Shahida alias Neena the mystery girl. She was plain and there was no mystery to her whatever. She looked like a watercolour that has been under a dripping tap and as a result taken on an even more washed-out look. There was nothing actress-like about her. She just sat there in her chair quietly. She knew who I was and she also must have known that Mohsin was a friend of mine. I mostly talked to Josh, who was holding on tightly to his daily ration of rum, while Ahmed was mimicking one of Bombay's German film directors. We never talked about the story which I had come to sell. I had a couple of drinks, and when I have had a couple, I do not stand on ceremony. So I turned towards Neena and told her, 'I do not know where your mystery lies, but I do know that you cheated your husband.' Ahmed looked at me, apologized that he would have to step out for a minute because he had to see someone and, before leaving, he took Josh with him. He had stolen Shahida under a long-term scheme as one steals a pigeon from a pigeon coop. So now that he had her, he wanted her to lay any eggs that she might wish to lay in his coop. It was not Neena who was mysterious but Ahmed. She had laid an egg at Mohsin's, which had not produced a very healthy chick, but Ahmed was taking as good care of it as if he were the mother.

After Ahmed and Josh left, I had a conversation with Neena, telling her that Mohsin often pined for her. An ironic smile appeared on her wilted lips and she said, 'Manto sahib, you do not know that man. Every tear that he sheds is a crocodile tear. It is not he who sheds tears but tears which shed him.' I did not know what that meant but the grimness with which she spoke suggested that she was convinced that whatever she had said was true.

Ahmed in the meanwhile had begun making preparations to film *Meerabai*. He had chosen Bharat Bhushan to play Krishna, but since he was very thin, he used to be fed lumps of butter and other nourishing food every day so that he would put on weight and look the part. It was yet another five-year Ahmed plan.

Let me also tell the story of Ahmed's first and real wife, Safia, daughter of Sir Ghulam Hussain Hidayatullah. When a man neglects his wife, she is bound to go with another, which was what happened in this case. It is said that Safia began an affair with the famous communist leader Syed Sibt-e-Hassan. Years later, I asked Sibt-e-Hassan in Lahore about it and wanted to know if it was true that he had followed Safia to America where she had gone to some conference and, further, that the two of them had got married. Had

Sibt-e-Hassan not been arrested by the government soon after our conversation, I would have solved the mystery. He was released after three years and when I met him soon afterwards there were too many people around for me to bring it up. 'When will you go to jail again?' I asked instead. He drew at his pipe and replied, 'In a few days.' Just as he had said, fifteen days later, he was in jail again.

But let me get back to our story. It was I who helped Mohsin Abdullah get a job at Filmistan because he was in a bad way. I told S. Mukherjee, 'Are you not ashamed that Mohsin and you were once colleagues at Bombay Talkies and while you are the big boss at Filmistan, the production controller of the company, your old friend is almost starving?' Mukherjee sent for him the next day and hired him at Rs 400 a month, regardless of the fact that Mohsin never did much work, expecting others to do it for him. We were very busy with *Eight Days*, a film I had written, and Mohsin would keep advising me about the script, something I would ignore because it was always technically absurd. He would also tell me that he still missed Shahida, though I knew he was trying to start an affair with Veera, a young woman we had picked up for a starring role in *Eight Days*. Mohsin normally used to travel second class on the train that brought us every morning to Filmistan, a trip of about twenty miles from Bombay, but after Veera was hired by Rai Bahadur Chunilal, Mohsin would travel only first class, just to impress her.

One day I was in a taxi going down Lamington Road when I spied Mohsin. I told the driver to stop. 'Mohsin, what's up?' I asked. A smile appeared on his broad face. 'These days I measure the roads with my feet,' he replied. 'How long and broad is Lamington Road then?' I asked. 'As long as you and as broad as me,' he answered. 'Get into the taxi and I will drop you wherever you have to go,' I offered, but he did not accept my invitation. He looked restless and I could understand why. He had lost his wife to Ahmed (the two were living together in Poona) and Snehprabha Pradhan was paying no attention to him. He had lost whatever money he had in gambling, and to top it all he had no work. 'And how is Miss Pradhan?' I asked. He smiled bitterly. 'She is all right. Khwaja Ahmad Abbas is trying his luck with her these days. I predict he will lose all his hair in two to three months.' 'Why?' I asked. 'You do not know her. She is not a woman, she is a safety razor and what she shaves off never grows again.' I have always had a lot of body hair and I wished for a moment I could get hold of this miracle safety razor called Miss Pradhan so as to be rid of all that ungainly hair. Luckily, I did not try or I would have met the same fate as Khwaja Ahmad Abbas and Mohsin Abdullah. Both of them eventually went bald.

BABURAO PATEL: THE SOFT-HEARTED ICONOCLAST

I think it was in 1938 that I first met Baburao Patel. I was at the time editing the weekly *Mussawar* on a monthly salary of forty rupees. Nazir Ludhianwi, who owned the magazine, was keen that I make some extra money, which was why he had introduced me to Baburao Patel, the editor of *Filmindia*.

Before I write about that meeting, let me first say a few words about how *Filmindia* came to be born. There was a time when the Poona-based Prabhat Film Company was at the height of its success, having already produced such runaway all-India hits as *Amrit Manthan* and *Amar Jyoti*. It was no longer just another company but a nationally acclaimed institution. Everyone who worked for it exuded the confidence and self-assurance that had become the company's hallmark. On its rolls were men like V. Shantaram, Saeed Fatelal and K. Dhailbar, who tried to excel their rivals in the art and technique of film-making. As a result, the company had grown in strength and reputation, and had already given birth to three siblings: Famous Pictures, the sole distribution agency for Prabhat movies, headed by Baburao Pai; B.B. Samant and Company, in charge of the printing and production of the entire range of Prabhat publicity materials; and the New Jack Printing Press, which, though unknown in the trade, was entrusted with the actual job of printing all posters, handbills and books relating to Prabhat movies. It was headed by a man named Parker.

Filmindia was a child of the New Jack Printing Press as Parker and Baburao Patel were good friends. Parker did not have much of an education but the plan to launch a magazine was as much his as his friend's. They had the press and paper, was easily available because it was cheap in those days. B.B. Samant and Company could be depended upon to provide the advertising, not only for Prabhat-made movies but possibly others as well. All essential ingredients were in place. Baburao was a hard-working and thorough man who did not believe in dreaming, and as the English idiom has it, he liked to hit the nail on the head. It is a fact that with its very first issue *Filmindia* started a new trend in Indian film journalism.

Baburao wrote with eloquence and power. He had a sharp and inimitable sense of humour, often hurtful. There was a tough-guy assertiveness about his writing. He could also be venomous in a way that no other writer of English in India has ever been able to match. What established his name and reputation was his subtle sense of satire, mixed with aggressiveness, which had been until then unknown in Indian journalistic writing. Soon he had his readers hooked on his stuff.

He was a man of great dignity. You realized it the moment you set foot in the large office he had set up in Mubarak Building on Bombay's Apollo Street. That was where I first met him. By then, about seven or eight issues of *Filmindia* had appeared, which one simply could not fail to admire. I had imagined that the author of such elegant and finely honed humour would be slim and good-looking, but when I saw a peasant sitting in a revolving chair behind a huge table, I was disappointed. There was nothing in his features to even remotely connect him with his writing. He had small eyes embedded in a big face and his nose was large and bulbous. His teeth were not very good and he had a big forehead. When he rose to shake hands with me, I realized that he was much taller than I was and quite a strong man. His handshake, however, was limp. For me the caving in of the roof, so to speak, came when he began to talk in Urdu. He was a peasant and, like all true Bombaywalas, every sentence that came out of his mouth was liberally studded with the word 'sala'. He also had a wide vocabulary of swear words.

I first thought that he spoke like that because his grip on Urdu was weak, but when he got on the phone I became convinced that this man could never be the Baburao Patel who wrote those delightful *Filmindia* editorials or the 'Bombay Calling' column, or who came up with those amusing answers to questions sent to the magazine. His accent was atrocious; he sounded as if he was speaking English in Marathi and Marathi in street Bombayese. And, of course, before every full stop, there was the ubiquitous 'sala'. So I said to myself, 'If this sala is Baburao Patel then this sala, that is me, is not Saadat Hasan Manto.' Nazir Ludhianwi, who had introduced me to Patel, praised me effusively. 'I know,' said Patel, 'that sala Abid Gulrez often comes here and reads *Mussawar* to me every week.' Then he turned to me. 'And what does this sala name Manto mean?' I calmly explained to him what it meant. He then asked me if I would translate a Prabhat film booklet—'chopri' in Gujarati—into Urdu. I took the booklet that Baburao Patel had written, translated it and asked Nazir Ludhianwi to pass it on to Baburao. I was told that he liked it very much.

We did not meet for a while as most of my time was spent at the *Mussawar* office, and because even in those days I considered it undignified to run after film companies in search of work. I learnt, though, that Baburao had talked V. Shantaram into bringing out a magazine called *Prabhat*, which would publicize, but in an original way, the production of this thriving film company. Shantaram may have been a man of limited education but he had the temperament of an artist who always wished to break new ground. He readily agreed and Baburao brought out the magazine, which delivered exactly what he had promised. It was well produced and it was original. It certainly did a great public relations job for Prabhat Film Company. Nazir Ludhianwi was the kind of person who never let a good opportunity pass, so one day he suggested to Baburao that some sections of his new magazine should be reproduced in *Mussawar* in Urdu translation. Baburao agreed because he had once known poverty and he always had a soft corner for those who needed work. He knew all about Nazir's precarious financial situation, and when he learnt that I would be doing the translations he felt reassured and gave him the go-ahead.

To tell the truth, my knowledge of English was limited. What Baburao wrote, though not beyond my ken, was not easy to translate with precision either. He had a certain style and his use of language was different from that of others. He was familiar with both English and American usage and he had a natural talent for playing with words. I decided that the best way to translate him was to read what he had written and put it in my own words, taking care to retain the spirit of the original. When Nazir took the first issue to Baburao, I was with him. He looked at me and said, 'Sala, are you trying to be Baburao?' His cigarette was nestling, villager style, between the third and the little fingers of his right hand and he drew on it vigorously. 'Yesterday, I sala had this stuff read to me by Abid Gulrez. I enjoyed it . . . then I said to him (here he swore) "Hey you! Weren't you saying that this sala is a big-time Urdu writer?"' I accepted the compliment because it was one. It was decided that the arrangement would continue. Unfortunately, the magazine folded after two issues because Prabhat felt it could not afford the expense.

I will not go into details about the magazine because they will draw me into areas I do not wish to be drawn into. What I really want is to write about Baburao Patel and my impressions of him. Because of certain things, my relation with Nazir . . . no, no, no, that comes later . . . Well, it happened that I decided to get married. I left the magazine and got a job with Imperial Film Company at eighty rupees a month, but it only lasted a year, with Imperial owing me four months' salary. My next job was with Saroj Film Company. I had just joined when rumours began to circulate that the company was going to sink. Was I jinxed? The company did go bust but thanks to some quick footwork, our boss, Seth Nanoobhai Desai, managed to set up another company on the debris of the defunct Saroj and I was hired at a hundred rupees a month. Three-fourths of a story that I had written had already been filmed. In the meantime, my nikah had also taken place and all that remained was for me to bring my bride home. But I needed money to rent a flat where we could live. So what was I to do but go see Seth Nanoobhai and ask him for some cash which he flatly refused to part with. I told him of my situation but it had no effect on him. We got into an argument and he fired me. That was a shattering blow. I felt so insulted that I decided to stage a hunger strike bang in front of the company. Someone must have told Baburao because he picked up the phone and abused Seth Nanoobhai and when that had no effect he arrived in person and, after a long discussion, persuaded him to settle my dues in part, if not in full. Though I was owed twelve hundred rupees, I was paid eight hundred rupees, which I pocketed on the basis of the old maxim that something is better than nothing. It did enable me though to bring my wife home.

I forgot to mention that during my time at Imperial, one of the actresses with the company, the quiet and modest Padma Devi, who played the lead in my first film *Kisan Kanya*, which was in colour, had a thing going with Baburao Patel. He used to keep a stern eye on her. He already had two wives, one of whom, a doctor, I had once seen.

Meanwhile, Nazir Ludhianwi had behaved badly with me and terminated my services. My sincere and selfless friendship and all the hard work I had done for him had been disregarded. Besides a salary, he used to pay me a monthly house rent allowance of twenty-five rupees, which I now lost, but I was not sorry. I was doing some radio writing but more money was needed because I had a family now. My old mother was also living with me. To celebrate my wedding, I had thrown a party for my friends from the film industry, but it was clear that my mother would not be able to manage the party chores on her own. I was in a bit of a fix when something unexpected happened. Somehow, Baburao came to find out and the next thing I knew Padma Devi had arrived at my flat and was helping my mother with the cooking. She had also brought some sort of an ornament for my wife as a wedding gift.

I went to see Baburao after some days. I knew that just to help his friend Abid Gulrez he had brought out the Urdu weekly *Karwan*, but Abid, a poet, was the carefree kind, and had left to try his luck in the movies, writing dialogue, film scripts and lyrics. I showed Baburao the dismissal letter Nazir had sent me. He was taken aback, but he recovered, abused everyone and asked, 'So?' I knew he was about to offer me a job, so I nodded my head to indicate that I would say yes. Baburao spoke again, 'Sala, why don't you come here? There is this sala magazine *Karwan* with nobody to look after it.'

'I am ready,' I answered.

Baburao shouted, 'Rita!'

The door opened and a strong-legged, bosomy, dark-complexioned Christian girl walked into the room. Baburao winked at her. 'Come here.' She walked up to his chair. 'Turn around,' Baburao told her. When she did, he slapped her bottom resoundingly. 'Get some paper and a pencil.' The girl who was called Rita Carlyle was Baburao's secretary, stenographer and mistress, all in one. When she returned with a shorthand notebook and a pencil, Baburao started dictating my appointment letter to her. When he came to my salary, he stopped. 'Well Manto, what will it be?'

Then without waiting for a reply, he said, 'A hundred and fifty will do.'

'No,' I said.

Baburao became serious. 'Look Manto . . . This sala magazine *Karwan* cannot afford more.'

'You got me wrong,' I told him. 'I will work for sixty rupees a month, neither more nor less.'

Baburao thought I was joking, but when I assured him that I was serious, he said in his characteristically peasant way, 'Sala mad mullah!'

I replied, 'Mad mullah I may be, but I have asked for sixty rupees because I will come and go when I want. *Karwan*, I can assure you, will continue to appear on time.'

We agreed that we had a deal.

I worked with Baburao for six or seven months and, during this time, I came to know a lot about his strange personality. He was in love with Rita Carlyle and it was his opinion that no woman in the world could excel her in beauty and charm. Rita Carlyle was not a one-man woman but because of Baburao she had become more upmarket. I am sure if only she could speak Urdu, he would have made her a top film star in a short time. He believed that if he were to pick up a piece of wood and declare it to be the world's greatest dancer, after some time it would indeed become one and the world would acknowledge it too. Padma Devi was not well known when he took charge of her, but he transformed her into the film industry's 'Colour Queen'. He used to print dozens of her pictures in *Filmindia* with witty captions, which he used to write himself.

He was a self-made man. Whatever he was then and whatever he became later was entirely due to his own efforts. He owed nothing to anybody. In his early youth, he had fallen out with his father and cut off all relations with him. Whenever I asked him about Patel the elder, he would invariably say, 'That sala is a pucca bastard.' While it is difficult for me to say which of the two was a pucca bastard, I can say that if the elder Patel was one, then Baburao was a much bigger one.

An analysis of his pungent style would take us back to his childhood. Baburao was always bringing people down from their high pedestals and demolishing shibboleths. Was it because when he was young his father had tried to tame him so that he would become like him? He had also forced him to marry against his will. The second marriage was Baburao's own doing, but this time it was he who had made a mistake. In his pantheon, there were scores of half-shattered statues of the great and the famous—all lying on their faces—scores of old, senile bastards, and hundreds of courtesans and prostitutes. He had demolished them all, deriving the same pleasure in this act as Mahmud of Ghazni must have experienced when despoiling the great temple at Somnath.

Baburao simply could not stand anyone who put on airs. On the other hand, he was always willing to walk a mile to pick up someone who had fallen by the wayside and make him stand upright again.

But, once he had him standing, he did everything in his power to bring him down. He was a bundle of contradictions. There was a time when he considered V. Shantaram the world's greatest film director, but when he turned against him he tried to demolish not only his movies but also the man himself. He used to hate the director-producer A.R. Kardar but when he became his friend Kardar could do no wrong. Then came 1947 and he denounced Kardar and tried his best to have his studio and his property confiscated by the government on the ground that the owner had gone to Pakistan and abandoned his assets. Kardar was lucky and survived the assault.

Once Baburao had announced that it was only the 'Mian Bhais'—a nickname for Muslims—who knew how to make movies because no Hindu was capable of equalling the style, methodology, technique and artistry, which were natural to Muslim directors. I remember the days when he considered Prithviraj of no more significance than a crawling insect. He also used to feel the same way towards Kishore Sahu. These extreme likes and dislikes were like fits that would periodically affect him. Psychologically, he was unbalanced; some blind and powerful force always kept ramming his insides. It was my view that he was an artist who was so supremely confident of his own talent that he had lost his way. When I was working for *Karwan*, you could not make him stop praising me but when I left he would say to people if my name came up, 'Manto . . . who is that monster?' But Baburao being Baburao, when my film *Eight Days* was released, he wrote that Manto was India's most brilliant, most extraordinary storyteller.

During Baburao's association with Prabhat Film Company, Shanta Apte was considered India's most glamorous film actress, but the moment she left the outfit she became the ugliest woman in India. Baburao wrote such venomous pieces about her in *Filmindia* that, being the true Maharashtrian that she was, she burst into Baburao's office one day, dressed in her riding gear, and whipped him six or seven times with her riding crop. Years earlier, the grand old man of Bombay's English journalism, B.G. Horniman, had taken a few swipes at Baburao in *Bombay Sentinel*. This had angered Baburao so much that he had filed a defamation suit against him, much to the amusement of the eighty-year-old editor who sent a message to him through a common friend that if he did not want his nose bloodied, he should quietly slip him two thousand rupees and the entire episode would be forgotten. Baburao's first reaction had been anger; but on reflection he had sent Horniman a thousand rupees and called it quits.

Baburao may have been foolish and at times frivolous but he was very human with a soft corner for the poor. At that time, postmen were not allowed to use lifts when delivering mail to high-rise buildings but were required to take the stairs. Baburao wrote so much on this inhuman practice that it was finally discontinued. His services to Indian cinema are too numerous to list. Western film-makers who used to make fun of Indian movies and India itself had met their match in Baburao, who gave them a run for their money. He toured Europe, met many of Indian cinema's detractors and gave them his frank views about the quality of the stuff they inflicted on the world.

Baburao must have fathered many children; if not dozens, certainly a dozen. One day when I went to his house, he told all his brood to appear so that I could see them. He was a most affectionate father, but . . . this 'but' marks the point where I bring out the 'other' Baburao. I noticed it when he was beginning to evolve into his other persona. I felt that the resentment he always bore against authority was beginning to get out of hand. I was afraid it were going to assume horrifying proportions if it were not checked, which was what happened. Irked by the popularity of Jawaharlal Nehru, he denounced him as Gandhi's protégé and a nuisance for the entire nation. After Pakistan's establishment, he turned against the new country because he could see it making a place for itself in the world, which ran counter to his petulant temperament.

Filmindia, as the name suggested, should have had only material related to films but slowly it began to get politicized. Things reached a point where politics, filmdom and sex became so inextricably intertwined in its pages that one could only explain them as being a reflection of Baburao Patel's own perverted personality. You could read in one place, all together, about Pakistan, Morarji Desai, women's menstrual problems and about actress Veera's 'papaya-like face'. He even turned against Gandhiji. Did he think politics was a Rita, a Sushila or a Padma whom he could put like a puppet on a string, have it perform tricks according to his instructions? He was too intelligent a man not to know that he had failed as a film-maker and that his chances of succeeding in politics were even slimmer; or was it that he could not help finding fault with everything, that being his nature!

My own theory is that Baburao was not interested in India or

Pakistan; he only hated eminence, including the eminence of age and genius. Otherwise he was quite happy in his expensive Oomer Park bungalow, as he was with his secretary Sushila Rani whom he praised to the sky for two years in *Filmindia*. He even had her star in a film and to save her from the lascivious advances of other men he directed the film himself, with disastrous results. Not that he cared because he had his Rani, his race horses, his luxurious office and his suspected cancer, which he was confident he could deal with any time he chose to fly to America.

There was one and only one thing, however, which constantly gnawed at Baburao's heart. He could neither forget it nor come to terms with it. He could not understand why Muslims were undependable. It was not that some of them had betrayed him; so had many Hindus. He was bitter because he liked them. He felt comfortable with them, the way they lived, even the way they looked. Most of all, he loved their food. He was an enlightened man with an open and secular mind, but when one of his daughters fell in love with a Muslim worker in his press, he was upset. The man was illiterate and the girl, being Baburao's daughter, was well bred and educated, but love is impervious to such things, and the two of them, sensing opposition from the family, ran away. Baburao, who managed to find and bring them back, cursed his daughter and ordered her to end the affair but she refused. 'What do you want?' he finally asked her. 'I want to marry him,' she replied. 'All right then,' he said and set about making arrangements for the marriage. I met him some time later and when he began to talk about it there were tears in his eyes. 'What kind of people are you . . . you sala Mussalman? You snatch away our chhokri and then you ask us for food.'

Baburao's later anti-Muslim writings should perhaps be analysed in the light of this episode. Can there be anything more foolish than to avenge the wrongs of a few by damning an entire community or a religion? Baburao was a student of history. Did he not know that religion and nationalism are realities and not a mirage in the desert? People can continue to say bad things about Islam and the man who brought its message to the world, but it makes not the least difference. So much hatred was spread against the idea of Pakistan, but it came into being. What is particularly tragic is to see an artist succumbing to hatred and bigotry. It should not be in the nature of an artist to hurt others. Baburao Patel was an artist but he degenerated into an ordinary mortal.

Some of *Filmindia*'s later issues made me sick because I just could not believe Baburao had sunk so low. It seemed that the artist who had once inhabited his soul had either turned into a cancer in his belly or now lay buried in the cut and blow-dried hair of Rita Carlyle or the beds of Padma Devi and Sushila, cursed by his two wives.

PARO DEVI: THE GIRL FROM MEERUT

Chal Chal Re Naujawan had bombed at the box office, a shock that we at Filmistan were slowly trying to absorb. Meanwhile, Gyan Mukherjee was busy writing a war propaganda story for us. We had signed up the actress Nalini Jaywant, and a Rs 25,000 contract, duly approved by her husband, Virendra Desai, had been finalized. It was valid for a year. However, the story had yet to be passed by the censors, this being wartime. S. Mukherjee took a full ten months before he was satisfied with the story idea and the treatment. He always took time making up his mind. Gyan was sent to Delhi to clear the story with the censors, which he managed without difficulty. However, just as shooting was due to begin, Virendra Desai insisted that another contract be signed with Nalini Jaywant since the earlier one was about to run out. Rai Bahadur Chunilal, our owner, was a tough man in these matters and decided to go to court rather than sign a fresh contract. He lost the case, which placed the studio under a further financial obligation of Rs 25,000.

Rai Bahadur Chunilal was keen that the film should be over and done with quickly because enough time had already gone by, so he sent for the director Wali Sahib and his wife, the dancer and actress Mumtaz Shanti, and signed them up. He slipped them an advance of Rs 14,000 under the table without asking for a receipt so that the studio wouldn't have to show it in its books. On the second day of shooting, everyone agreed that the rushes of a brief exchange between Ashok Kumar, the lead, and Mumtaz Shanti, the heroine, were awful. Mumtaz used to come to the studio wearing a burqa and Wali had made it clear that she was not to be so much as touched, so everything was a bit stilted. This inhibiting deal was unacceptable because there were scenes where she would have to be shown semi-nude. It was inevitable that Mumtaz Shanti would be fired and so she was, and thus another Rs 14,000 went down the drain with her. Because of the failure of *Chal Chal Re Naujawan*, the financial health of the company was poor and it was already in the red to the tune of Rs 39,000 without an inch of film to show for it.

One day, Savak Vacha, Dattaram Pai, Ashok and I were chatting about our troubles when Ashok told us that the Rs 14,000 which Rai Bahadur Chunilal had given to Mumtaz was borrowed from him. He was scratching his knee when he said it and it sounded rather comical. We burst out laughing but stopped as we noticed a rather attractive woman going towards the make-up room. Pai looked lecherously at her and nudged Ashok. 'Who is she?'

Vacha smacked him gently over his head. 'Sala, why do you want to know?' As Pai got up, Vacha pulled at his wrist. 'Sit down, don't bother going after her. One look at you and she will run away in horror.' Pai quietened down but Ashok, who had been silent so far, spoke, 'She is not bad-looking, is she?' 'Not displeasing to the eye,' I suggested. 'What?' Ashok asked, not having understood my Urdu. 'I mean the woman who just went past us is pleasant looking, a bit short though but she will do, won't she, Vacha?' Pai asked. 'Dadamoni, you do know who she is, don't you?' Vacha asked. 'No,' Ashok answered. 'All that Mukherjee told me earlier this morning was that there was to be a screen test today.'

When we saw the rushes and heard the sound of her voice, there were different opinions. Ashok, Vacha and I did not like her because her movements were wooden and she moved her body in an unnatural way. When she spoke she raised her eyebrows like a professional dancing girl. Her smile wasn't very nice either. However, Pai seemed to have developed a crush on her and told Mukherjee, 'She has a wonderful screen face.' In the end, she was chosen for the forthcoming war propaganda film, despite our reservations, but on a low monthly salary. Her name was Paro and she would report to the studio every day. She came from the courtesans' quarter, had a happy disposition and was extremely friendly. She came from Meerut where she was a big hit with all the rich men of the city. She had money of her own and quite a bit of it; all she wanted was to become an actress. When I got to know her a little more, it turned out that among those who frequented her kotha were the poets Josh Malihabadi and Sagar Nizami.

Her pronunciation was excellent and she had a lovely skin. In her half-sleeved tight blouse, her arms looked as if they were made of ivory. Her skin was translucent like freshly shaved wood. She would come early, looking washed, scrubbed and very clean, wearing a white or a light-coloured sari. When she left for home in the evening, she would look just as fresh as she did in the morning. Pai was smitten. We had not yet begun shooting and there was plenty of leisure time. Pai would never miss an opportunity to engage Paro in conversation. How she found him attractive, we could not understand. But then she was a courtesan and courtesans have a lot of patience with every male type.

I was given an outline of the movie story to study and suggest additions and deletions. I found the whole thing so disjointed that I was at a loss and did not know what to propose because it had neither head nor tail. But since I felt as if I were on trial, I knocked it into some sort of shape. I was also keen to do my best because it was to be directed by Savak Vacha, who was a very good friend of mine.

When the new outline was presented before the full bench of Filmistan, I felt as if I were in the dock. S. Mukherjee's verdict was short and quick, 'Good, but there is much room for improvement.' When Gyan Mukherjee was asked, he first kept his mouth shut, then finally emitted just one sentence, 'It's almost all right.' He was the man whose name used to appear as director on all movies directed by S. Mukherjee when he had not directed even a single foot of the film. But that was how we worked at Filmistan. Pai, who had no idea what a film story was, would frequently advise me on how to write one. Only someone who has ever written a propaganda movie can understand how trying the task can be. My difficulty was that I had to write a role for Paro, keeping in mind her looks and the way she talked and carried herself. At last the script was finalized and the work started.

We decided that Paro's scenes would be shot last as, by that time, she would be used to the atmosphere of the studio and may also have lost her fear of the camera. However, scene or no scene, she was always on the set. Pai had become quite friendly with her to the extent that they would play tricks on one another. I found Pai's constant attentions to Paro somewhat annoying and when Paro was not around I would make fun of him. His reaction was always the same. 'Sala, why are you jealous?' Paro was a cheerful girl and she became popular with everyone in the studio. The junior staff began to call her Paro Devi out of respect and the name caught on and was even used in the movie credits. Pai, meanwhile, decided to take things one step further and arrived at her house one day where he was offered much hospitality. Soon, these visits became weekly affairs.

Paro did not live alone; there was a middle-aged man who lived in the house. He was twice her size and looked more of a minder than a husband, though he probably was the latter. Pai used to boast about his visits to Paro's; and Vacha and I used to laugh at his foolishness, but it had no effect on him whatsoever. A number of times, I joked about his crush on Paro in her presence, but she was not offended and kept smiling. It was the same smile that had made half the men in Meerut lose their heads over her.

Paro was not like other women of the bazaar. She had none of the brashness or vulgarity one normally associated with her professional sisters. Paro was now perfectly at home in the studio and had the confidence to hold her own in sophisticated company and make cultured conversation. One reason for her impeccable manners was the high-grade clientele she entertained in Meerut. It often happens in the film world that newcomers, if they are women, are immediately taken under the wing of one or the other of the old hands, but it did not happen to Paro because Filmistan had a more 'moral' atmosphere than most other studios. Paro, on her part, was in no hurry to get involved with anyone. Among the people there, Mohsin Abdullah, tired of his monotonous, dry bachelor life, was trying to start something with the Parsi girl Veera, who was also a new arrival. Mohsin no longer travelled with us by second class but invariably bought a first-class ticket to share the ride with Veera. She had a dog and Mohsin would often find himself walking her dog in and out of the train. Vacha was not interested in women. He had just got rid of his ill-reputed French wife with some difficulty. S. Mukherjee was trying to interest Naseem Bano, the star who was said to have the face of a fairy, so he did not have eyes for anyone, including Paro. Gyan Mukherjee was not into this sort of thing at all. As for me, what I liked about Paro was her lovely skin. When I mentioned this to my fellow-writer and friend Shahid Latif, he said, 'You like her skin, but do you know what lies under it?' Only Pai was completely out of control. One day, Paro invited him over and poured two large pegs of Johnny Walker for him with her own dainty hands. The whisky travelled to his head right away and Paro gently made him lie on the sofa and doze off, which convinced him that Paro was in love with him, and that we who had failed were jealous. What Paro thought of this fantasy, we did not know.

The shooting of *Shikari* was proceeding well. Veera was the heroine, while Paro had the side role, playing a Burmese tribal girl from the heart of the jungle who is feline and coquettish. I was a bit apprehensive about her acting abilities and began to get nervous as the time to shoot her scenes came closer. I was not sure she could do it. I recall clearly the day her first scene was to be shot. She was all made-up and costumed in a tight bra with a part of her midriff showing and her skirt hanging several inches above her ankles. She did not look in the least scared by the bright lights and the camera. She knew her lines and we were all hoping she would not fumble with them. However, when the time came for the 'take' she suddenly froze, becoming wooden. When she delivered her lines, she did so flatly. We put her through several rehearsals but she remained wooden and lifeless. She would raise her eyebrows like professional dancing girls as if she were quoting a price for her services, but she just could not manage the scene. After four retakes, I began to lose hope. Vacha was the kind to get worried rather quickly and said to me that there was nothing right about her and that S. Mukherjee would have to find some way to deal with the situation.

Mukherjee also tried, but what could he do? That was the way she was. Finally, one take, which was somewhat better, was approved so that we could go on to the next scene. Meanwhile, we were all trying to make her less wooden but we were getting nowhere. It was not that she had any fear of the camera or the microphone; it was only that when the time came, she froze. We had not written her off and were still hopeful that she would get over this problem. Since I was the one who had the least hope in her, I began to rewrite her role so that she would be called upon to do very little by way of acting. She found this out through Pai and after a couple of days I noticed that she was spending much of her spare time chatting me up. She talked well, in a very cultured way. She made no attempt to flatter me but, once or twice, she invited me to her place; I would have gone but I was too busy and obsessed with the revised screenplay of the movie. I had help in the form of Raja Mehdi Ali Khan, Mohsin Abdullah and Dixit, but while Raja had no time because most of it was spent writing letters to his estranged wife, Mohsin was busy chasing Veera, which left Dixit who, poor fellow, would make honest efforts to make Paro speak her lines properly, but without success.

In the meantime, I had begun to notice that when Ashok and Paro did a scene, she gave him looks which clearly implied that if he wanted to do in real life what was being shot for the screen she was willing. Ashok was always a shy person and could never bring himself to declare love to a woman, though I knew that he found Paro attractive. He simply did not have the courage to grab her and take her to bed. So many women had come into his life and he could have become another Lord Byron, but because of his basic shyness, he had always ended up running for the door. In those days, Ashok could have tried his luck with any actress and succeeded with most. I was not surprised that Paro had developed an interest in him. She was new and if her name came to be linked with Ashok's she could become well known very quickly. In the movie, she played a wild, headstrong and aggressive tribal girl who was in love with Ashok, who, in turn, was in love with the other woman, Veera. One outdoor shot involved two boats, in one of which we were going to show Ashok and in the other, Paro. What Paro was expected to do was to jump into Ashok's boat when the two boats drew close and touched. The water was deep and during the take, as she jumped, Ashok's boat suddenly swung away and she fell. Vacha screamed and two or three people jumped after her and pulled her out. She was not scared and, as soon as her clothes were dry, she said she was ready for a retake.

When she was squeezing water out of her clothes, Ashok and I caught sight of her leg all the way up to the thigh. When we had packed up and were driving home, Ashok said to me, 'Manto, that was quite a leg. I felt like roasting it and eating it.' Ashok normally kept his feelings hidden but this time he had spoken his mind. We were in Ashok's MG, as we were every day, and we always went past the street where Paro lived. That evening as we drove by that point, Ashok stopped the car. 'What is it?' I asked. He told me that Paro had thrown a party as it was Holi, and he had been invited. 'Should I go or not?' he asked. 'Go,' I answered. 'You come too,' he suggested. 'Why should I? She has not invited me,' I responded. 'So what?' he said as he turned the car around, coming to a stop in front of her flat, and honked. We looked up and saw Vacha and Pai on her balcony. When Pai saw me, he said, 'Oh, you too are here.' 'Come Dadamoni, we were all waiting for you,' Vacha shouted to Ashok.

Paro was wearing much finery, not something she did normally. She rose as we entered and apologized to me for having forgotten to invite me. Drinks were brought out and just one was enough to send Pai reeling. Vacha asked Paro to sing something but she looked suggestively at Ashok and asked, 'Ashok sahib, would you like me to sing?' Ashok became self-conscious and replied with his usual awkwardness, 'If you sing, I will listen.' She began with a thumri, followed it up with a ghazal and then a film song. Her husband, or whoever he was, kept filling our glasses with whisky and soda. Two drinks and Pai was almost asleep. Ashok was never much of a drinking man and did not take more than a peg and a half. Vacha placed his hand over his glass after his third. Paro concluded with a Hindu devotional song, a bhajan. She must have realized that I was a Muslim and began to sing a naat, a composition in praise of the Holy Prophet. I stopped her, 'Paro Devi, this is a party . . . we are all drinking. I think it may be better that we do not refer to the black-cloaked-one.'[1] She realized her faux pas and apologized.

The food was excellent. Ashok ate quickly and wanted to wash his hands. Paro led him to the bathroom. When he returned, he looked jumpy and ill at ease. 'Let's go, Manto,' he said. We did not talk on the way and he dropped me home. The shooting meanwhile was proceeding according to schedule. One evening when Ashok and I were in his car driving past Shivaji Park where Paro lived, he slowed down and said, 'Manto, let me tell you an interesting story.' His voice trembled a little. 'Do you remember when we went to Paro's and she said she would show me to the bathroom when I wanted to wash my hands?' 'I do,' I replied. 'When she was handing me a towel, she said in a quiet voice, "Tomorrow come all by yourself at six thirty in the evening." It made me so nervous that I dropped the towel and rushed back to the living room.' At this point, he stopped the car.

'Did you go?' I asked. 'Yes . . .' He lifted his hands from the steering wheel, 'but I ran away again.' 'I want the entire story,' I said. 'You know I am a coward,' Ashok continued. 'God knows what comes over me on such occasions. She made me sit on a sofa and sat herself on the floor and snuggled up to me. She poured me two drinks and took a small one herself. Then she began to express her love for me. As I listened to her, I got more and more nervous by the minute. When she grabbed my hand and pressed it, I shook it free. I could see tears in her eyes, but they disappeared almost immediately and she began to smile. "Ashok bhaiyya, I was only testing you," she simpered. I almost fell back. "Ashok sahib, I take you as my brother," she said as I got up to leave. I did not say anything and left. When I got home, I took a small drink and felt sorry for myself. I mean where was the harm in it?' 'Yes, there was no harm in it,' I said. His tone became even more wistful. 'And . . . I even liked her.'

My mind went back to the scene we had shot the very day this incident had taken place. It was cold and we were filming outdoors. Everyone was dancing, including Ashok who had his arms around his beloved, Veera. Away from the merrymakers stood Paro, all by herself, looking very sad.

NUR JEHAN: ONE IN A MILLION

I think I first saw Nur Jehan in *Khandan*. She was certainly no 'baby' then, no sir, by no stretch of imagination. She was as well stacked as a young woman would wish to be with the assets women bring into play when required by the situation. To the moviegoers of those days, Nur Jehan was provocative, a ticking bombshell for whom they pined. Speaking for myself, I never found any such appeal in her. To me, there was just one thing about her that was phenomenal—her voice. After Saigal, she was the only singer who impressed me. Her voice was as pure as crystal. Even the suggestion of a note was discernible when she sang, perfectly in command whether the notes she employed were in the lowest range, the middle ones or the highest. I was sure, if she so wished, she could stay on the same note for hours, like those street performers who can walk the entire length of a tightly stretched rope with perfect poise and the greatest ease.

In later years, her voice lost the resonance, richness and innocence that were once its hallmark, but Nur Jehan remained Nur Jehan. aonly had to strike a note to make you sit up. Not many people know that she was as conversant with the intricacies of classical music as any acknowledged maestro, being equally adept at singing thumri, khayal and even dhrupad—the last form with an authority that was astonishing. Music was bound to be in her bones because of the family and the surroundings in which she was born, but she spent years learning it. Her talent, there can be no question, was God-given. Technically, a singer may be the most adept but if the voice lacks 'juice', technical knowledge alone cannot move the listener. Nur Jehan had both knowledge and a God-given voice. When these two things come together, the total effect is dazzling.

While one would think that a natural gift is always well looked after, often it is the other way round. Most gifted people are indifferent to their gift and, in fact, try consciously or otherwise to destroy it. Liquor is bad for the throat but the late K.L. Saigal drank heavily all his life. Sour and oily things are bad for the voice but who does not know that Nur Jehan ate large quantities of pickles in oil and, interestingly enough, when she had to record a song, she practically feasted on pickles, followed by iced water. Then and only then did she go and stand in front of the microphone. She had a theory about it. She believed that such things sharpened and enlivened the voice. How that is possible, only she could explain. I may add though that I have seen Ashok Kumar munching ice, especially when he had to record a song. Whatever the secret, as long as there is recorded music, the voice of K.L. Saigal will live, and so will that of Nur Jehan, delighting generation after generation of listeners.

I had seen Nur Jehan only on the screen, never in person. I was a fan, not of her looks, but of her talent as a singer. She was young and it always astonished me how she could sing in such a masterly way. In those days, there were two big names in Indian film music: Saigal and Nur Jehan. There was also Khurshid who had her own following, and much praise was heaped on Shamshad. But the fact is that once Nur Jehan came on the scene, all voices except hers were, so to speak, lowered. Suraiya arrived later. It will always be my great regret that while Saigal and Suraiya were brought together in one movie (*Parwana* with music by Khwaja Khurshid Anwar), it never occurred to any producer to team up Saigal and Nur Jehan. For some reason, the two never worked in a film together. Had they sung together, it would have wrought a delightful revolution in the world of music.

How, when and where I met Nur Jehan for the first time is a long story. After spending many years in Bombay, for certain personal reasons, I had moved to Delhi in a none-too-happy mental state and found a job with All India Radio, but before long I got bored. Meanwhile, Nazir Ludhianwi, editor of the weekly *Mussawar*, had been pestering me in letter after letter to return to Bombay because the man who had directed the recent hit movie *Khandan*, Syed Shaukat Hussain Rizvi, was now in Bombay and staying with him, and was keen that I should write a story for him. So I left Delhi. The political situation in India was turbulent. The Cripps Cabinet Mission had failed and gone back. I think I arrived in Bombay on 7 August 1940 and my first meeting with Shaukat took place at 17 Adelphi Chambers, Clare Road, which served as both his office and his residence.

He was a tall and dashing young man, fair with pink cheeks, a fine John-Gilbert-style moustache and curly hair, extremely well dressed in his spotless, well ironed trousers and a jacket set off with a jauntily knotted tie. He even walked stylishly. We became friends from the word go.

I found him to be a sincere person. I had brought a good stock of my favourite Craven A cigarettes from Delhi because, on account of the war, they were hard to find, especially in Bombay. When Shaukat saw my hoard of over twenty tins and nearly fifty packs, he was delighted. I moved into 17 Adelphi Chambers. We had two huge rooms, one serving as the office, the other as our living quarters, though we always ended up sleeping in the office. Mirza Musharraf, the comedian, and some others would drop in during the evening and before leaving they would make our beds. We were having a great time. There were the Craven A cigarettes and the Deer brand Nasik whisky which was quite atrocious, but which was all we could obtain. Although Shaukat had become a big director after the success of *Khandan*, his long stay in Lahore after the success of the movie had accounted for all the money he had made. Life in Lahore was full of action and, consequently, expensive. All I had was a few hundred rupees, which I had already sunk in Nasik whisky.

However, we managed somehow through those unsettled times. I remember that two days after my arrival in Bombay, on 9 August, the year being 1940, when I tried to make a phone call, the line was dead. We learnt later that, since the leaders of the Indian National Congress were being arrested, city phone lines had been made non-operational as a precautionary measure. Gandhiji, Jawaharlal Nehru, Abul Kalam Azad and other leaders had all been arrested and taken to some unknown place. The city felt like a cocked gun that could go off any moment, so there was no question of going out. For several days, we were cooped up inside, trying to kill time by drinking that dreadful Deer brand whisky. Because of political uncertainty, the film industry had suffered badly, with no one willing to invest money in a new production. The people Shaukat had been negotiating with had let things drift, waiting for more settled times. Meanwhile, we were eating the bad food sent to us by Nazir Ludhianwi and sleeping until late in the morning. Off and on, we would get excited and start talking about new film scripts.

It was during those days that someone told me about Nur Jehan's presence in Bombay. Now, who told me that? My memory appears to be failing me, but I think I knew on 8 August, which was before I met Shaukat, that she was in the city. I wanted to go to Mahim to meet some relatives and also to find out what had become of Samina, who later had an affair with Krishan Chander. She was a radio artist I had met in Delhi at All India Radio. She wanted to get into the movies and I had given her letters for Prithviraj and Brij Mohan. She was bright, good-looking and could speak her lines fluently. I was keen to know if she had been given a break or not. I was fairly confident though that she would make it.

Someone told me that she lived at Shivaji Park but it was such a sprawling neighbourhood that with just her name, Samina Khatoon, to guide me, I could never have hoped to find her. I remembered that Nizami, whose wife Geeta Nizami became a famous movie actress and who married a string of men after she left him, lived at Shivaji Park. It was the same Nizami who had trained Mumtaz Shanti, overseen her career and taught her the ways of the world. Geeta Nizami, I should add, was later involved in many court cases. In the early years of Pakistan, she organized a dance troupe, with a young and lovely woman as her lead dancer, which had performed from city to city. So far Nizami and I had only exchanged letters, and formal ones at that. Were I to really describe our first meeting, it would run into ten to fifteen pages, so I will be brief. When I appeared at his place at Shivaji Park that morning, he let me in with great warmth. He was wearing just a vest and a dhoti. He asked what had brought me to him and when I told him, he replied, 'Samina Khatoon, I will have her here in no time.' He had an emaciated Hindu manager whom he summoned. 'Get hold of Samina Khatoon and bring her to Manto sahib right away.' After he had issued this order, he assured me that there was nothing he would not do for me. Then he offered to me—in words only, of course—not only a fine, expensively furnished flat but also a car to go with it.

I thanked him for his kind thoughts in appropriate words, which he did not seem to need as he was a fan of my short stories. Nizami, who was as generous as a king when it came to empty promises, has been called all kinds of names, from procurer to pimp, but that was not my problem. I know that he was a man in search of new challenges and in that art he had no equal. I observed that day how total his hold on Mumtaz Shanti was. She was utterly under his influence, as if he were her father. Wali sahib, the director, practically danced around him, like a groom around his mounted master. In that house, Nizami was king and everybody paid him homage. His only duty was to invite producers to parties where good food was served and liquor flowed freely. He was without an equal when it came to buying petrol in the black market. He would spend time teaching Mumtaz Shanti how to become a successful actress. 'Look, if you smile in a certain way, I promise to get you a contract out of that producer,' or, 'If you shake that fat financier's hand the way I teach you, I assure you that we shall have ten thousand rupees in our pocket the same evening.'

I just sat there and wondered at the world into which I had accidentally found my way. Everything about it was artificial. At one point, Nizami asked Wali sahib to bring him his bedroom slippers, which he did and placed the pair at his feet with the utmost reverence. This, I can swear, was an unnatural gesture, something totally insincere. Mumtaz Shanti, wearing the most humdrum clothes, was in the next room hammering nails into a window with Nizami carrying on a running commentary, 'Manto sahib, this child is so simple that although she is in the world of movies, she is unaware of the ways of the world in which we all live. She does not even look at men. And it is all because of the training I have given her.' While I knew that this was all untrue, I could not help admiring Nizami. But let me get back to Nur Jehan.

After Nizami told me how he had put Mumtaz Shanti on the road to success and how exquisitely he had trained her, Nur Jehan's name came up. He said she, too, was under his tutelage and was learning the ropes like Mumtaz Shanti. I recall his words: 'Manto sahib, had this girl stayed on in Lahore, it would have been her end. I have had her come out here and I have impressed upon her that it is not enough to become a film star. There should be other means of support and security for a girl. There is no need to get into any kind of love affair in the beginning. What she should do is earn as much as she can from all possible sources and when she has enough money in the bank she can pick up a nice man and marry him so that he remains a slave to her all his life. What do you think, Manto sahib? You are a very wise man.'

What wisdom I might have had had abandoned me the moment I stepped into Nizami's flat. I had no answer to his question, so I told him that whatever he was doing appeared to be right and how could it be otherwise, since it was he who was doing it. That pleased him greatly, so he sent for Nur Jehan. We heard the phone ring in the next room, followed by Nur Jehan's voice. 'It is Kamal sahib on the line. I will be with you shortly,' Nizami smiled mysteriously. The Kamal on the line was Syed Kamal Amrohi, famous since the film *Pukar*,[1] which he had directed. Nizami spoke, 'I was telling you about my advice to her. I have drilled it into her that this marriage business is neither here nor there; she should do the best by herself first. Now Kamal can earn. If half of what he earns comes to Nur Jehan, wouldn't that be the best for her? The fact, Manto sahib, the fact is that these actresses should become adept in the art of earning money.'

'With teachers like you, they can't miss,' I said with a smile. This made him happy and he ordered one first-rate lemonade for me. So this was where Nur Jehan was being trained and educated in a scientific manner. She was being taught all the tricks of the trade under Nizami's personal supervision. Nur Jehan, having finished her call, came into the room and we met, but casually. It was my impression that this girl was growing into womanhood rapidly and the smile on her lips and her laughter were already quite commercial. She also seemed to have a tendency to become plump. But there was no doubt that she was going to prove the most talented student Nizami had ever had.

However, fate had other things in mind. It was Nizami's desire that, like Mumtaz Shanti, Nur Jehan too should remain under his thumb and accept his authority. He was like a retired madam who wanted this young woman to be a part of his establishment. Everything that Mumtaz Shanti earned, for example, remained in Nizami's custody. It was obvious that compared to Mumtaz Shanti's market value, Nur Jehan's was far greater. Nizami was too wily a man not to know that a great future lay in wait for this girl. It was only natural that he should be keen to keep this butterfly in his net.

Shaukat had had an affair with Nur Jehan in Lahore's Pancholi Studio (where *Khandan* was filmed). There was even a court case in the course of which Nur Jehan had testified that she had had no intimate relations with Shaukat who was like a brother to her. This court brother of hers was now in this vast city of Bombay, the Hollywood of India. When I told Shaukat later that I had met Nur Jehan, I did not know about their affair, nor did I know that their present relations were bad. I just told him that I had met her at Nizami's house. It was nothing more than a minor piece of interesting gossip. No sooner had the words left my lips that he banged the glass containing that dreadful Deer brand whisky on the table and exclaimed, 'Let her go to hell!' Lightly, I replied, 'I am quite happy with that but remember she played the heroine in your *Khandan*.' Shaukat understood my pun—'khandan' being family in Urdu—and said, 'Manto, you are a mischievous man, but it is like this. I just do not want to know anything about her. Of course, she is in Bombay, the sali has chased me all the way here, but I wish to have nothing to do with her.'

When I told him that she was on the phone to Kamal Amrohi and that Nizami was trying to get the two together, he pretended not to care but I knew that it had hit him hard. He at once commissioned Mirza Musharraf to go out and get another pint of Deer brand whisky and we kept drinking till late into the night. In between, after long gaps, the name of Nur Jehan would come up and it was clear to me that Shaukat was still smitten by her. The brother bit was no more than legal hair-splitting. He was still thinking of those nights when this little princess of song used to be in his arms with both of them promising each other eternal love. One day, rather abruptly, I asked Shaukat, 'Confess . . . aren't you in love with Nur Jehan?' Shaukat flicked the ash off his cigarette and replied self-consciously, 'I am . . . but the hell with her. I will get over her in time.' That, however, was not what fate intended.

Shaukat was offered a contract by Seth V.M. Vyas, owner of Sunrise Pictures, which he accepted. Vyas had earlier signed Nur Jehan for one of his movies. A word about Vyas. He started out as a tabla player, graduated to a camera coolie and became a cameraman. The next anybody knew, he was a director and with another leap, a producer in the big league. He was so thin that he would always wear a thick vest under his shirt so that no one could see his ribcage. There was no question that he was a smart fellow who worked hard at his job. He could go on from morning until night without showing the least sign of fatigue. One thing more about Vyas. He never used his own money to make a movie. After completing one film, he would announce another and sign up a star-studded cast. At that stage, there would be nothing to the movie at all, not even a story or a financier. However, sure enough, someone would swallow the dangling bait of the star cast and Vyas would ask him to put his money up front so that work could begin. Seth Vyas would then start production after having thanked the goddess Kali whose devotee he was.

As soon as Nur Jehan landed in Bombay, he signed her up because he knew that after the success of *Khandan* her name would attract many financiers. And when he realized that the movie director was also in town, he sent his men after him, held many meetings with him and, finally, signed him up to direct his forthcoming film.

No one knew what sort of movie was in the offing or what its story would be. However, when Vyas waved around the contracts he had signed with Shaukat and Nur Jehan, he was able to raise the money without the least difficulty. Destiny sometimes plays strange games. Shaukat did not know that Nur Jehan had come to Sunrise Pictures, nor was she aware that the man she had described as 'my brother' in a Lahore court was also in the same company now.

Their coming together could not have remained a secret for very long, and when it got out, it had Nizami worried because it threatened to jeopardize his plans for Nur Jehan and Kamal Amrohi. Invoking his rights as Nur Jehan's 'guardian', he informed Seth Vyas that the teaming up of the two was unacceptable to him. However, Vyas being a Gujarati—a far smarter breed than Punjabis can ever be—talked him into giving his blessing to the arrangement. In fact, then Nizami became so enthusiastic about Nur Jehan's working in Shaukat's film that he declared Vyas to be his brother and shook hands with him on the deal with great feeling, at the latter's office.

Both of them were now happy for their own reasons: Vyas because he had got what he wanted and Nizami because he had won the goodwill of a rich and resourceful man. Seth Vyas was a strict Vaishnavite, or else the same evening Nizami would have invited him over and made him feast on chicken curry and pulao prepared by Mumtaz Shanti with her own dainty hands. Had the Seth been a drinking man, Nizami would have sent out his emaciated manager and asked him to procure two bottles of Scotch from the black market. Any way, the deal was done and Nizami had placed his hand on his heart and declared to Vyas, 'Seth, now that you have called me your brother, you have my word that come hell or high water, Baby Nur Jehan will be on your set when required.'

Meanwhile, I had also signed a contract with Seth Vyas to write a story, and Shaukat and I were trying to decide what it should be. We had received our advances and if there was one thing which was not in short supply it was Nasik's Deer brand whisky. Mirza Musharraf, the comedian, Chawla and Saigal (both were to become well known film directors) would often be in attendance. Chawla would go running to Nagpada if we ran out of whisky; and if there were other errands, there was always Mirza Musharraf. After three drinks, he would invariably start crying, kiss Shaukat's hands and beg him for forgiveness for whatever he thought he had done against Shaukat in the past. 'All false, all false,' he would say. Then he would cry for his newly acquired wife and follow it with singing. It was all a masquerade but then that's what the world of films is.

Seth Vyas, meanwhile, had begun shooting his film, but none of the scenes so far had involved Nur Jehan, which meant that Shaukat and she were yet to get together. One day there was a notice on the studio bulletin board that Nur Jehan would be shooting that night. It just happened that I was at Shivaji Park where my good friend and the famous music director Rafiq Ghaznavi lived. Ghaznavi had a romance knotted into every necktie he possessed—and his collection was large. He was a friend of mine and there was no formality between us. When I arrived at his flat, I found a full house. On a sofa sat his latest wife, Khurshid alias Anuradha, and next to her was Nur Jehan. Nizami was in a chair, and Rafiq Ghaznavi was on the floor appearing to get ready to attack a latter-day Somnath in the tradition of his ancestor Mahmud of Ghazni who had invaded and ransacked the famous Hindu temple at Somnath.

I was not sure whether Rafiq was planning an 'invasion' on Nur Jehan or if Nizami or Nur Jehan suspected anything. God alone knows. Nizami told me that Mumtaz Shanti was also expected any minute. I was a bit mystified. How could this great drinking party be in full swing when there was to be a shoot at the studio? Nizami held a glass in his hand and Nur Jehan had a glass of some colourful liquid in hers, which she was sipping daintily. Khurshid alias Anuradha was taking long swigs like a seasoned drinker and as for Rafiq from Ghazni—the land which had given birth to Mahmud who had fallen in love with a boy called Ayaz—he was telling dirty stories. He had sworn at me in his fulsome way, which was his usual manner of greeting, but had changed tack immediately and said politely, 'Please, my dear, come and sit here.' He looked at Nur Jehan and asked me, 'Do you know her?' 'I know her,' I replied. Rafiq was never able to take more than four drinks. He obviously had already done that because he said to me in a slurred voice, 'No, you know nothing, Manto. This is Nur . . . Nur Jehan . . . Nur means light and she is not only the light of the world but also the spirit's elixir. By God, she has a voice sweeter than that of any houri in paradise. Were a houri to hear her sing, she would be so jealous that she would rush to earth and give her something to drink to destroy her vocal chords.'

I knew why he was building these bridges of praise. He wanted to employ them later to walk across to her bed. I noticed that Nur Jehan was not much interested in him. She was listening to him though, and off and on, she would flash an insincere smile at him. Rafiq was a great miser but that day he was overly generous. He poured a large drink from the bottle for me and insisted that I gulp it down in one go, so that he could give me another. Everyone was drinking, but Nur Jehan's drink was the lightest and she was sucking at it as honey bees suck honey from flowers. Rafiq had not stopped building his bridges of praise although his earlier structures had all collapsed. Suddenly, the phone rang.

Khurshid picked up the receiver with her delicate hand and looked upset. Then she placed her hand on the mouthpiece and whispered that it was Seth Vyas on the line wondering where Nur Jehan was. 'Dear daughter, tell him that Nur Jehan is not here,' Nizami said, which was what Khurshid told Vyas in more or less appropriate words. 'Sheedan,' Rafiq said to Khurshid as soon as she was off the phone, 'go get the harmonium . . . Seth Vyas can go to hell.' She went into another room and was soon back with a harmonium. Rafiq pushed back the top, pumped the bellows and struck a note. It was his style that, with his eyes half-shut, he would begin to swoon over the note he had just emitted from his throat. 'Hai . . . God be praised . . . Oh,' he kept saying. Every note seemed to send him into ecstasy. That was his technique. He would have his listeners applauding long before the performance had begun. But he did not sing that day because all his concentration was on Nur Jehan. At one point, he struck a note and with his half-dilated eyes said to her, 'Nur . . . sing something . . . Oh! What a divine note!'

You may have seen actors and actresses playing roles on the screen but let me take you to this live show. Nur Jehan lifted the harmonium and placed it next to her on the sofa. Khurshid came and sat beside her, holding a half-empty glass of whisky. Rafiq Ghaznavi was squatting on the floor, looking at Nur Jehan with his love-sick eyes, swaying his body and shaking his head even before she had opened her mouth. On a chair sat Nizami and next to him, this old sinner, nursing his second drink.

Nur Jehan began to sing. It was a thumri in the raag Piloo, *Toray nainaan kalar bin karey*—no antimony do your black eyes need. Then we all heard a car drive into the porch. The man who got down and walked straight in was none other than Seth Vyas. For a moment everybody was taken aback but Nizami quickly got the situation under control. He pretended that he had not seen Vyas come in and shouted at Khurshid, 'What do you think you are doing? Don't you see in what great pain she is and here you are trying to force her to sing . . . Look, she has hardly sung one line and it looks as if she is going to faint.' Then he looked at Nur Jehan and said in a worried voice, 'Lie down, Nur Jehan, lie down.' He did not wait for her to do so, but stepped forward to help her recline on the sofa. Nur Jehan began to moan loudly as if she were in great pain. Rafiq also got up, trying to look concerned. Nizami spoke to Khurshid next, 'What are you waiting for, Sheedan? Go and get her a hot-water bottle. That is a bad fit she is having.'

Sheedan went into the next room, taking quick steps. Nizami tried to calm Nur Jehan, who had now begun to wail softly, then he sat next to Seth Vyas and said, 'She has been in terrible pain since yesterday. She said to me, "Uncle, I don't think I can make it to the shooting." But I told her, "No, little one, this would be a bad omen. This is your first picture in Bombay and the first day of shooting . . . but forget that . . . What matters is that I have called Seth Vyas my brother . . . and you have to go even if you die." So we came here to get some brandy from Rafiq which might help her, and also to ask him to have his car drop us at the studio . . . you are my brother, Seth.'

Seth Vyas kept quiet, as did everyone else. Rafiq was chewing his nails and I, glass in hand, was wondering what it was all about. The story of the movie was mine, the music that of Rafiq Ghaznavi, and Seth Vyas, our boss, had caught us in the act, as it were, what with the drinks and the music. Nizami kept talking to Seth Vyas, assuring him that since they were now brothers there should be no misgivings between them. Khurshid appeared with a hot-water bottle, which she placed on Nur Jehan's stomach, and she pretended that it somewhat soothed her pain. Nizami now said to Vyas, who had begun to look more and more like the sphinx, 'You don't have to stay for this. Rafiq and I will bring Nur Jehan over to the studio.' Then he said in a loud aside. 'I think Khurshid should come along too. Women know what these women's things are.' Seth Vyas rose, put his cap on and walked out. Everyone heaved a sigh of relief. Nur Jehan put aside the hot-water bottle, which actually contained cold water, and said to Nizami, 'But uncle Nizami, hadn't you told me not to go today?' Nizami became serious. 'Little one, look, I said that for your own good. If you go on the first day without the producer coming in person to fetch you, he will start taking you for granted. Ask Mumtaz. She never goes unless the studio sends her a car, and when it comes I let the driver wait for at least an hour, although Rai Bahadur Chunilal is such a good friend of mine. I don't really care. Many times, he has had to come personally to fetch Mumtaz. Don't worry, everything is in order now. Vyas came himself to fetch you. You are very sick but you are going despite being sick. Seth Vyas will remember that.'

Nizami spent some more time explaining the delicate relationship between producer and artist. The conversation began to slowly veer towards Shaukat Hussain Rizvi. Nizami seemed keen to impress on Nur Jehan that she should have nothing more to do with Shaukat and there should be no place in her heart for him. She should follow the same path as Mumtaz Shanti had done all along under his guidance, with such successful results. I butted in at this point because Shaukat was a friend and he had told me that he was in love with Nur Jehan. It was also clear to me that the various women who were brought to him by Mirza Musharraf were needed because Shaukat was trying to bury Nur Jehan's memory in their warm embrace. He was also drinking that third-class Deer brand whisky to forget the woman with whom he was really in love.

Shaukat was like a watchmaker, a man perfect at his craft. He was always putting things right. Even if they were right, he had to put them just right. By temperament, he had no patience with anything that did not work, such as a nail which had not been pushed into a wall straight, a watch that did not keep correct time, or a pair of trousers that needed the touch of a hot iron. He was instinctively organized and disciplined, the same factors that make a watch keep good time. However, when it came to Nur Jehan, he felt helpless. How could he set right the watch that they call the heart? Had it been something he could have examined under a magnifying glass, he would have taken it to pieces and then put it back together so that it worked to perfection. This was an entirely different matter.

And there was Nur Jehan who could produce the most perfect note from her throat but who found herself unable to make Shaukat depart from her heart. She could sing the khayal with the ease of a maestro but the only thing on her mind these days was the young and willowy Shaukat, who had given her the most joyful moments of her life, who had sent a tingle through her body that the finest music had been unable to transmit. How could she forget the man who had given her such perfect physical fulfilment?

When I mentioned Shaukat to her, Nur Jehan pretended that she did not care for him. 'Look here, Nur Jehan, that's nonsense. That's not how you feel, and what that ass Shaukat tells me, I don't believe a word of it either. You are head over heels in love with each other, but you are bent upon pretending otherwise. Only yesterday we sat talking about you in the office of the magazine *Mussawar* and the day before, and the day before. Whenever Shaukat and I drink in the evening, on one excuse or another, he drags your name into the conversation. You are no different. I think I saw your eyes go wet once or twice when you mentioned his name. He is in the same state, I can tell you. I think this is no good and I am convinced that Shaukat cannot do without you. What kind of a spell have you cast on him?'

Nur Jehan listened to me as if she were in a trance. 'Look, Nur Jehan,' I added, 'don't deceive yourself. I know that Nizami sahib is a man of much worldly wisdom and the methods that he advocates may work in other departments of life; but when it comes to love, they will prove to be fake coins.' I turned towards Nizami and asked, 'Is it untrue?' He was so absorbed in what I was saying that he shook his head in an emphatic 'no'. When he realized that he had erred by agreeing with me, it was too late. I could see tears in Nur Jehan's eyes. I carried on, 'Both of you are fools. You love each other but try to hide it. From whom, may I ask? This world, Nur Jehan, cannot bear to see two people in love, but does that mean people should stop falling in love? Mumtaz Shanti's life is worth envying, I concede, and I have no doubt that under the benevolent care of her uncle Nizami she will go far.' At this point, I turned towards Nizami again. 'But you must know, Nizami sahib, that you cannot be everyone's uncle. The advice you have been giving Mumtaz may not necessarily be good for Nur Jehan. They are two different people. Am I wrong?'

I had brought Nizami to a point where he could not say no to anything I was saying. I kept talking and by the time I was done I had convinced Nur Jehan that Shaukat and she were made for each other and it was silly of them to pretend otherwise. When Nizami rose to leave, he was not a happy man. He must have been angry with me but it was not in his nature to show that. All he could do was instruct Nur Jehan that she should go to the studio with Khurshid with a hot- rather than a cold-water bottle. She was also told to complain about her 'pain' at regular intervals. He asked me about my living arrangements and assured me that he would soon have me move into a properly furnished flat, which he had already found. In fact, the key was with his manager and all I had to do was call him. If I needed petrol from the black market, it would be available too. He assured me that he sincerely wished me to accept his offer and promised to entertain me soon with roast chicken and Johnny Walker Black Label. I thanked him and declined but he was insistent that I should accept his offers. So I said yes, but I knew that the next time I went to visit him, there would be no roast chicken or Black Label whisky waiting for me. One thing was clear: I had upset Nizami's apple cart that evening.

I also learnt in the next few days that Nur Jehan had no interest in the film director Kamal Amrohi. She had been refusing to take his phone calls. When he drove up to Nizami's place in his second-hand car, she would hide in another room to avoid him. Whatever I learnt about her, I dutifully conveyed to Shaukat, though we both knew that it would not be easy to cut her loose from the old sorcerer Nizami. Finally, we held a conference, which included Nazir Ludhianwi, editor of *Mussawar*, at which it was decided to rent a flat on Cadell Road close to the beach. We were lucky to find one on the ground floor with three bedrooms, a large living area and a few other rooms. Nazir, who was sick and tired of living in his awful flat at Adelphi Chambers, said he would pay half the rent of the new place which, if I remember, was one hundred and seventy-five or two hundred rupees a month. We brought in furniture and other things and set it up nicely. Shaukat's bedroom faced the sea. Nizami's place was barely five hundred yards away. I was carrying out my 'assignment' effectively, which was to pop into Nizami's flat every now and then and give Nur Jehan the latest details of Shaukat's lovelorn days and nights. I would tell her that all she needed to do was take a walk, which would not only be good for her health but would also do wonders for her love life. Sometimes I felt like an old procuress but then what are friends for?

It is ironic to think that in those days I was dead set against marriage and even more opposed to marrying an actress. I believed that two people who liked each other should live together and go their own separate ways once they were tired of the relationship. However, Shaukat believed in putting things down in black and white so that, like inherited land, it would remain his for the rest of his life. I tried to talk him out of it and succeeded in convincing him that if Nur Jehan came to him he should live with her but not marry her. Having done what I could for my friend Shaukat, I got down to writing the screenplay of *Naukar*, a movie I had been assigned. I lived in Byculla, which was some distance from Cadell Road, which meant that our meetings became infrequent.

It was impossible in those days to get good beer. One day I came upon four magnum-size bottles of American beer and thought of sharing them with Shaukat. It was morning but breakfast with beer was not a bad idea. When I walked into his flat, it looked deserted. Nazir had already left for the day it seemed, so I tiptoed towards Shaukat's bedroom and knocked at the door. There was no answer. I knocked again, this time less gently and heard Shaukat's sleepy voice, 'Who's it?' 'Manto,' I answered. 'Wait,' he said. Three minutes later, the door opened and I saw Nur Jehan lying on the only bed in the room. Her eyes looked fresh, almost laundry-washed. Shaukat appeared to be somewhat tired. 'Has the Chittaur fort fallen?'[2] I asked. Shaukat smiled. 'Come, sit down.' I took a stool that lay in front of the dressing table. Shaukat looked triumphantly at Nur Jehan, who was trying to get under the sheets. 'Came to me tied in thin gossamer thread,' he said. Whether she had come tied in thin gossamer or a sturdier variety of thread, I do not know, but it was clear that whatever the thread, it had been knitted out of love because she had finally leapt across the five-hundred-yard gulf that had separated her from Shaukat all this time.

The long and short of it was that the one item of furniture that Shaukat's flat had lacked was now in place. As for Nizami's flat, a light had gone out of it, a light that could have lit up his entire establishment. Nizami had not given up easily. After doing his best to talk her out of her resolve to go and live with Shaukat, he had called in her brothers, who threatened her with violence if she refused to change her mind. However, nothing had worked, neither counsel nor threats. 'I think I should marry the sali,' Shaukat said to me. 'You decide. She is yours, but in my view that won't be the thing to do. Have you spoken to your family about her?' was my reaction. He did not answer and I left, hoping that he would not act in a hurry.

In those days, there was a character in Bombay by the name of Hakim Abu Mohammad Tahir Ashk Azimabadi. About seventy-five years old, he had the heart of a young man. His eyesight was perfect, his teeth were intact and he had never missed a movie opening night. He spoke five languages—Urdu, Persian, Arabic, English and Punjabi—and was one of a kind. He also dabbled in herbal medicine, wrote poetry and liked the company of friends. I had introduced him to Shaukat, who had taken to him immediately and begun calling him 'uncle'. In fact, he had found some distant family link with the old man. As I said earlier, my visits to Shaukat had become infrequent because of the distance and my work at the studio, but I liked Hakim Tahir and often sought his advice about my prose which he would happily give as he liked me, too. One day I ran into him and was told that Shaukat had married Nur Jehan. I was surprised and showed it. After some hesitation, Hakim Tahir said to me, 'Look Saadat, it was all done very quietly because it is best that people do not know. I have told you because you are like a son to me, just like Shaukat. But keep it to yourself.'

How could I argue with a seventy-five-year-old man that this secret would not remain a secret for very long? I felt a little hurt though that Shaukat had not taken me into confidence. If he wanted to marry her, why was I kept out? Why was I thrown out of the pack like the joker? I was hurt but I never mentioned it to Shaukat because it would have affected our relationship. Time passed. Nizami had given up on Nur Jehan as had Kamal Amrohi after countless unanswered calls and scores of trips to Nizami's flat in his second-hand car. Shaukat's bedroom was alive with life and laughter and the molten music of Nur Jehan's voice. Rafiq Ghaznavi was the film's music director and Nur Jehan would rehearse her songs in Shaukat's seafront love nest.

And now a story. My brother Saeed Hasan, who was a barrister in Fiji, came to Bombay after many years. He was on his way to Amritsar. I was informed that he would be arriving by air. I lived in a tiny flat so my wife and I decided that he should stay at Shaukat and Nazir's place because it had plenty of room. Nazir was a bachelor and all Shaukat seemed to use was the one bedroom in which he had his Nur Jehan. He had no interest in the other rooms. It would be perfectly convenient for them to put up my brother who would welcome a European-style room with an attached bath. When I brought him over he liked it because it was new. The landlord lived on the upper floor and there was a children's play area with a seesaw and slides just a few steps away, which was pleasant to see. The breeze from the sea blew into the rooms at all hours. Sometimes, it would be so strong that the doors and windows had to be kept tightly shut. A few days passed happily but there was trouble in store.

Shaukat was having the time of his life. He had his Nur Jehan as well as his hangers-on—Mirza Musharraf, Chawla and Saigal who were dying to be part of his team. Those who work in the movie industry are night people. During the day they are busy with their different chores but the evenings are for fun and games. Shaukat's place had a party going every evening, with his friends drinking, telling dirty stories, laughing, singing and sometimes making so much noise that the neighbours would protest. One evening Shaukat had the usual crowd over, including M.A. Mugghani—who was known all over Bombay as movie queen Naseem's drumbeater—my wife and myself. We ate and left as we had to go somewhere else. My brother was dining out so he returned late. As he stepped into the front reception area, the party was in full swing. Everyone was drunk and some people were dancing. In other words, a good time was being had by one and all. However, my brother was a serious-minded barrister who lived abroad and was a complete stranger to such goings-on. Next morning, he packed his things and moved into a place called Khilafat House. He also cursed me and my friends without mincing his words. Even today when I think of what he said I feel as if molten lead were being poured into my ears. He had spent his entire life reading his law books and fighting legal battles in Lahore, Bombay, east Africa and the Fiji Islands. How could he know what movies were all about and what kind of people were associated with them? Interestingly enough, Khilafat House was situated in a street called Love Lane.

But let me get back to Nur Jehan. Her elder sister also lived not far from Cadell Road, and she ran a whorehouse with her brother. I am not sure if the two sisters ever met in those days, but I doubt if Shaukat would ever have permitted Nur Jehan to do so. Her brother was an inveterate gambler who played cards, went to the races and had been dead set against his sister marrying Shaukat. He had tried hard with Nizami's help to talk Nur Jehan out of her obsession with Shaukat because, as far as he was concerned, she was the goose who laid the golden eggs. Shaukat was also threatened several times but it had no effect on him. In the end, everyone came to accept that Nur Jehan and Shaukat were together and intended to remain that way. Work on the movie *Naukar* was proceeding at a good pace, but I often felt that Rafiq Ghaznavi looked distinctly unhappy because Nur Jehan, whom he fancied, had been snatched away from under his very nose.

Shaukat was a hard man to please. He liked things done his way. He was never entirely satisfied with assignments carried out by others. I had given him the script and the screenplay, which he had said he liked, but I found out that he had asked various other people to come up with alternatives, including Hakim Tahir. I did not mind him because he was someone I respected as an elder, but I could not tolerate the others. One day I told Shaukat in no uncertain words what I thought of it all. He tried to calm me because he was always a very diplomatic and cool-headed person, but I am by nature obstinate and once my mind is made up nothing can make me change it. In any case, I did not like the story I had written because Shaukat had made me put in several changes of which I did not approve. Although Shaukat was a close friend and we had been drinking that awful Deer brand whisky day after day and smoking Craven A cigarettes, I knew that, though he would do whatever else I asked him to do, insofar as the movie was concerned, he would do exactly what his watchmaker's brain told him to do. I, therefore, walked out of *Naukar* quietly, normally. Shaukat knew me well and may even have welcomed my departure. Had I stayed, I could have delayed the production for several months because we would have argued endlessly.

I was cut up with Shaukat, and he may have felt the same way towards me, but our friendship remained unaffected. The movie industry was by then in trouble because of political uncertainty in the country. All you had to do to kill a handful of films under production was climb on a table and shout 'Long live the revolution'. And because of the Second World War, raw film was hard to come by. It was a very uncertain situation all around. Film directors, in particular, had been hit hard. The producers had a ready excuse to say 'No'. 'Where is the money?' they would ask when approached. There was a war on. It moved from Crete today to Finland tomorrow, and then there was the constant fear of a Japanese invasion of India. However, it was during those uncertain years that capitalists, moneylenders and film producers made their millions.

Shaukat had signed another contract, I think, with Seth Javeri who was a difficult character and, in my view, a third-class person. It was the war that had made him a seth. He had money to burn and he had set up a film company and bought two or three cars. The big actresses were outside his reach, but he had picked up a number of film extras as his women of pleasure. He signed Shaukat up and gave him an advance of Rs 3000. When he cashed the cheque, I was with him. I took him to the post office and made him send all that money to his parents. Nur Jehan must have hated me for that, but it would not have bothered me. I also persuaded Shaukat to get himself insured. He used to say 'yes' to most things I told him and he agreed to this one as well. I got him a Rs 10,000 policy. Why was I doing all those things? I do not know. I was behaving like an elder of the family, handing out advice to others while taking none myself.

Nur Jehan had blossomed after moving in with Shaukat. It is only physical contact with a man that gives the final touches to a woman's beauty, and by now Nur Jehan was a full-blown woman. The slight, girlish figure she had had in Lahore had been transformed by Bombay. Her body was now privy to all varieties of carnal pleasure and, though some people still called her Baby Nur Jehan, she was no baby, but a woman who had known love and its ecstasy. Shaukat was going to shoot one of the scenes of the movie outdoors in a garden in the suburbs of Bombay. He insisted that I go along. Since it was to appear as a night scene in the film, he was going to shoot it with a red filter on the camera. I got there in Seth Vyas's car. Nur Jehan had already arrived and was wearing a strange outfit, which was a shock to the eyes. Her shalwar was made out of a material called 'net'. Normally, it was used for window sheers but this was what either Shaukat or she had chosen to cover her lower torso. You could say that her shalwar had a thousand tiny windows through which her lower body was streaming. Her shirt was made of the same stuff. Nothing had been left to the imagination. The actress Shobhna Samarth was also present and I walked across to her because, frankly, I found Nur Jehan's dress shocking. Shobhna was an educated woman who knew how to converse. She came from a good Marathi family and there was nothing banal about her. She had superb manners. She was also doing a role in the movie. I sat next to her on the bare grass so that I could regain my composure, which had received a rude shock after one look at Nur Jehan and her vulgar outfit. I had gone there because Shaukat had insisted; otherwise I had no interest in *Naukar*, though I had written it.

I met Nur Jehan several times later at their flat and, when I studied her with more care, I noticed that she had every single characteristic associated with the background from which she came. Everything about her was a put-on. She was flirtatious but not in a cultivated way. I was surprised at how Shaukat, who came from the heart of UP could get along with this diehard peasant Punjabi girl. Shaukat would try to imitate her thick Punjabi-accented Urdu and she would try to imitate his pure UP accent. Shaukat finally completed *Naukar* and we drifted even further apart. Having tasted the joys of love, he was now concentrating on his work, as I was. Off and on, we would run into each other in a film company's office or a studio or on the roadside and exchange greetings, chat for a minute or two and go our separate ways. The movie industry had come out of the doldrums and the war psychosis was gone as far as the producers were concerned. Everyone realized that the industry had entered a boom period.

Shaukat had always had a good head for business. He took advantage of the prevailing state of the market and set up his own production company. He already had an excellent reputation as a director and editor, and his entry into production was bound to put him in the spotlight. Normally, in the film world marriages with actresses are seldom because of love alone. I am not sure if Shaukat felt the same way towards Nur Jehan. What I do know is that even if he had not married her, he would still have done well. He was a man who knew his art and who worked hard. I never understood why he left Bombay to come to Pakistan. Was it because he was always a strict Muslim and could not have countenanced even the least slight to Islam, which he might have had to experience in Bombay after Independence? I am sure if someone had said something against Islam in his presence, he would have unscrewed his skull with one of his implements, taken every piece apart and then put it back after removing the defect that made people say such things. It is also possible that it was Nur Jehan who persuaded him to leave Bombay because she had always loved Lahore: Lahore is Lahore, as all Punjabis say.

In Bombay, Shaukat was highly successful. He had made two runaway hits and he could have stayed there and minted money but he chose Pakistan as his home. Shaukat, a man whose watchmaker's mind could tolerate not the least inefficiency, came to Lahore where the movie industry was on its last legs. He bought the burnt-out Shorey Studios and turned it into a first-class production facility. Few would know that every nail in Shahnoor Studios had been put in there by Shaukat, hammered in securely with his own hands. Every plant in its gardens, and every machine in the laboratory, was put there by Shaukat himself. This is his great quality, though it has not always endeared him to people.

I have a friend in Lahore who often helps me with money. Once I went to see him and found that he had no cufflinks to go with his spotless white shirt. When I expressed surprise, he told me that he had no money to buy them. When I asked him for a cigarette, he replied that for ten days running he had been smoking others' cigarettes. This was the man in whose studio everyone used to be given cool, clean refrigerated water, where flowers bloomed, where scores of gardeners worked, where hundreds of workmen were employed, and where there was a woman called Nur Jehan who wore the most expensive clothes available and who was chauffeured around in limousines. That friend, of course, is Shaukat.

There are many stories about Nur Jehan, some of which may even be true. All I know is that she is the mother of two wonderful boys who are being educated at Chiefs College, Lahore, and whom she loves. Not long ago, there was a variety show at the college where a tableau was presented by the children, with one of Nur Jehan's boys playing the cowherd girl Radha who is in love with Lord Krishna. He had danced beautifully. Nur Jehan knows how to dance. She may even have given a few lessons to the boy Akbar, or maybe it is in his genes. One will have to see what these two boys, Akbar and Asghar, grow up to be. Will this be another family of artists like the Barrymores and the Kapoors? Only time will tell.

Nur Jehan can be arrogant. An arrogance that can't be justified by her looks, as she does not have them in any great measure, but she has a voice, a voice full of light, of which she can be justly proud. I remember once my wife asked me in Bombay if I would ask Nur Jehan to come over as some of her friends wanted to meet her. I told her it should be no problem, and asked Shaukat, who sent Nur Jehan to our place a day later. Of all the actresses I knew—and I knew scores and scores of them—Nur Jehan was the most formal in her manner, always standing on ceremony, always conscious of who she was. Everything about her was affected, her smile, her laughter, the way she greeted people, the way she asked them how they were. Could her married life also be a pretence? I think not. She came and met everyone with her usual affected warmth. I wanted to leave but a friend of my wife's insisted that I stay because she wanted me to request Nur Jehan to sing. 'Let's have a couple of songs,' I said to Nur Jehan with great informality. 'Maybe another time, Manto sahib,' she said in an affected voice. 'My throat is acting up.' I was burnt to a cinder because I know that her throat is fashioned out of steel, which nothing can damage. I knew she was putting on airs. 'This excuse won't work. You will have to sing. I have heard you a thousand times but these people really want to hear you, so whether your throat is acting up or not you should sing something for them,' I said to her.

She said 'No' a few more times, while the women insisted. My wife had had enough. 'Please let's not force her,' she said. But I am not the kind to give up. 'You will have to sing, Nur Jehan,' I said. Finally, she relented and sang Faiz's famous lines, *Aaj ki raat saaz-i-dard na chher*. It was superb. It is years since that happened but I can still feel the golden honey of her voice cascading into my ears.

There are so many men who are in love with Nur Jehan. I know cooks who prepare food for their sahibs and memsahibs while looking longingly at her picture, which they have stuck on the kitchen wall. I also know domestic servants who do not care for Nargis, Nimmi or Kamini Kaushal but who are mad about Nur Jehan. Wherever they see a picture of hers, they clip it and put it in their collection, which they hoard in a broken tin trunk so that they can soothe their eyes by looking at it in their spare hours. Were someone to say something disparaging about Nur Jehan, such men would be prepared to fight. In our own home, we have a lover of Nur Jehan who calls every young girl, every bride and every woman wearing red, 'Nur Jehan'. He knows practically all her songs. He himself is very good-looking so I am at a loss to understand what it is about Nur Jehan that he likes so much that he keeps talking about her from morning to evening.

He is closely related to me, being the son of my nephew Hamid Jalal and my sister-in-law Zakia. His name is Shahid Jalal but we all call him 'Taku'. We have tried to tell him many times that he should seriously think of falling out of love with Nur Jehan whom he cannot marry, as she is already married and has her own children, but it has no effect on him. He loves movies and if these movies do not star Nur Jehan he is very upset. He comes home and begins to sing her songs. He has told his parents that all he wants in the world is Nur Jehan. Some time ago, his grandfather Mian Jalaluddin went to meet Shaukat Hussain Rizvi and said to him, 'Look, you have a rival who is madly in love with your wife and one of these days he is going to run away with her and you will be left watching.' Shaukat asked awkwardly, 'Who is he?' Mian Jalaluddin smiled. 'My grandson.' 'Your grandson! How old is he?' 'About four.' When Nur Jehan heard the story, she declared that she would go and meet her lover and marry him. Shahid Jalal has been in seventh heaven since being given the news and is waiting impatiently for the day when Nur Jehan will come to see him and become his bride.

Recently, someone told me a story about another of Nur Jehan's lovers, who was not four, but a grown-up man, a barber by profession. He would sing her songs all day long and never tire of talking about her. Someone said to him one day, 'Do you really love Nur Jehan?' 'Without doubt,' the barber replied sincerely. 'If you really love her, can you do what the legendary Punjabi lover Mahiwal did for his beloved Sohni? He cut a piece of flesh from his thigh to prove his love,' the man said. The barber gave him his sharp cut-throat razor and said, 'You can take a piece of flesh from any part of my body.' His friend was a strange character because he slashed away a large chunk of flesh from his arm and ran away while the barber fainted after providing this proof of love. When this great lover regained consciousness in Mayo Hospital, Lahore, the first words that came to his lips were, 'Nur Jehan'.

There is a case in court against Nur Jehan these days. She is charged with beating up a young actress by the name of Nighat Sultana. Since it is sub judice, I do not wish to say much as it would amount to contempt of court, but I fail to understand why Nur Jehan beat up this girl. I had never heard of Nighat Sultana before but am told that she comes from East Bengal, from the city of Dhaka. How or when she became an actress, I absolutely have no idea.

Nur Jehan's dashing husband Syed Shaukat Hussain Rizvi is around, as are her lovely children. Then there is the Lahore barber who is prepared to cut himself with a razor to prove his love for her, not to mention her four-year-old lover, Shahid Jalal, also known as Taku, who dreams of making her his bride. And one must not forget those cooks who hang her picture on their kitchen wall and sing her songs in their tuneless voices while washing dishes. And finally, there is Saadat Hasan Manto who cannot stand the sight of her awful brassiere. What beauty she sees in her upturned front bumpers and why Syed Shaukat Hussain Rizvi permits this gross violation of good taste, I am unable to say.

NASEEM: THE FAIRY QUEEN

I had outgrown cinema-going while still in Amritsar. I had seen so many movies that, frankly, they no longer held any fascination for me. That was why, when I arrived in Bombay to edit the weekly *Mussawar*, I stayed away from movie houses altogether for months. Ours was a movie magazine and we could have complimentary tickets for any film we wished to see. The Bombay Talkies production of *Acchut Kanya* had been drawing crowds at a local cinema and I had ignored it, but when it entered its twenty-second week, I became curious. There had to be something there, otherwise why would it run so long, I said to myself.

This was to be my first film show in Bombay. It was also the first time I saw Ashok Kumar and Devika Rani together. Ashok was a bit raw but Devika Rani had given a polished performance. It was a simple story, which had been told in a simple and tasteful manner, free of the usual vulgarity. That started me off and I began to go to the movies with some frequency.

Around this time, an actress by the name of Naseem Bano was beginning to get famous. It was her great beauty which had caught the popular fancy. She was billed as '*pari chehra* Naseem', the fairy-faced one. Her picture was in every paper. She was indeed young and lovely, her most remarkable feature being her large, magnetic eyes. It is the eyes that lend beauty to a woman's face and Naseem Bano had a real good pair.

She had appeared in two movies so far, both produced by Sohrab Modi, and they had been hits but I had not seen them. Why I hadn't, I don't know. Now a new historical film called *Pukar* was being advertised widely by Minerva Movietone with Naseem playing Empress Nur Jahan. Sohrab Modi was set to play an important role as well. The film was a long time in the making, but from the stills that kept appearing in newspapers and magazines it was clear that it was going to be a big production. Naseem looked stunning as the empress.

I was invited to the release. The story was more fiction than history and the presentation was maudlin and rather theatrical. The emphasis appeared to be on dialogues and costumes. While the dialogues were unnatural and dramatized, they were impressively worded and forceful. The effect on the audience was mesmeric. It was the first such film made in India and not only did it become a source of high profits for Sohrab Modi but it brought about a revolution in the movie industry. Naseem's performance was weak, but her great beauty and lovely costumes more than made up for that. I don't recall, but I think after *Pukar*, she made two or three more films, none of which did as well.

There was no dearth of rumours and scandals about her—nothing uncommon in the movie industry. Sometimes it was said that Sohrab Modi was about to marry Naseem, while others maintained that Moazzam Jah, the Nizam of Hyderabad's son, was wooing the actress and would soon make off with her. This was half true because the prince was spending a lot of time in Bombay and had frequently been seen at her Marine Drive home. He spent millions on her and was in some sort of trouble later trying to explain where the money had gone. Money works, and the prince in the end succeeded in persuading Naseem's mother, Shamshad Begum alias Chammiya, to let him win her daughter's attentions. Both women spent some time in Hyderabad as the prince's guests.

However, before long, the worldly-wise Chammiya came to the conclusion that Hyderabad was like a prison, which would stifle her daughter. Whatever she desired by way of comfort was hers to be had but the atmosphere was constricting. And then who knew when the whimsical prince may get bored, leaving Naseem Bano high and dry. It was not easy to get out of the tightly administered Hyderabad state, but Chammiya was a wise and tactful woman and managed to get both herself and her daughter out of there and safely back to Bombay.

When she returned, there was quite a controversy. There were two groups involved in it, one speaking in favour of, and probably on the payroll of, Moazzam Jah, the other made up of Naseem Bano's sympathizers. At one point, they were sticking posters on walls maligning each other. Whatever dirt they had been able to dig up was dug up and splashed across those posters. They must have got tired because, eventually, things quietened down.

By now, I was a full-time movie person, having been engaged as a munshi or scribe by Imperial Film Company at a monthly salary of sixty rupees. I wrote nonsensical dialogues and other gibberish according to the whims of the directors. However, when Seth Nanoobhai Desai of Hindustan Cinetone offered me a hundred rupees, I moved. My first story for the company was called 'Keechar' but it was filmed as *Apni Nagariya*.

One day I read somewhere that a man by the name of Ehsan had set up a new film company called Taj Pictures, the first production of which was going to be *Ujala*, starring pari chehra Naseem. Two famous men were also associated with the company—Kamal Amrohi who had written *Pukar*, and M.A. Mugghani, who was the movie's publicity manager. There was much infighting during the making of *Ujala* between Amrohi, Mugghani and another member of the team, Amir Haider, followed by a court case, but, in the end, they managed to complete the work.

The story was pedestrian, the music weak and the direction lacked spirit, so the film fared badly and Ehsan had to suffer heavy losses, which forced him to shut shop. However, one outcome of this misadventure was that he fell in love with Naseem Bano. She was no stranger to him, because his father, Khan Bahadur Mohammad Suleman, had been her admirer too. Ehsan had therefore known Naseem before his entry into films. During the making of the movie, he got to know her better. Those who observed the two closely said that because of his shy and withdrawn nature Ehsan had been unable to make the kind of impression on Naseem that he wished. On the set, he would go to a corner and just sit there without saying a word, not even talking to her. Whatever his technique, it was successful in the end because we heard one day that the two had got married in Delhi and Naseem had declared that her movie-making days were over.

This was sad news for Naseem's admirers because the great beauty was now to provide joy and comfort to just one man: her husband. How Ehsan and Naseem graduated from courtship to love to actual marriage, I do not know. Ashok Kumar's explanation was the most interesting. One of Ashok's friends, Captain Siddiqi, was closely related to Ehsan and had invested some money in *Ujala*. Ashok used to visit him at his house almost every day but of late he had begun to notice a change in the atmosphere, though he could not put his finger on it. One day he thought he smelt perfume and asked Siddiqi what the source of the fragrance was, but received no reply.

A few days later, Ashok went to Siddiqi's place when he was not in, yet the same old fragrance, light and flirtatious, hung in the air.

Ashok went on a reconnaissance of the lower floor, sniffing the air like a hound and came to the conclusion that the source of this delightful odour was upstairs. Quietly, he tiptoed up the stairs and walked into the bedroom, the doors being wide open. What he found was Naseem sprawled on the bed with a man sitting by her side whispering in her ear. Ashok immediately recognized him because he had met him once. It was Ehsan. When Ashok told Captain Siddiqi what he had seen, he smiled. 'This thing has been on for some time,' he conceded.

Ashok's story and the light it sheds on the affair between Ehsan and Naseem needs no commentary. What happened between the two must have been what always happens between lovers. I do know though that Ehsan's mother and his sisters were dead set against the marriage and there were several quarrels in the family on this account. However, the father, Khan Bahadur Mohammad Suleman, had no objection and the marriage went ahead. Naseem left Bombay and moved to Delhi where she had grown up. The newspapers had a field day but then they forgot about it.

During this period, there were many changes in the film world. Several film companies came into being and while some survived, others perished. Many stars were born and quite a few disappeared from the scene. After the tragic death of Himanshu Rai, Bombay Talkies fell into disarray. His wife, Devika Rani, and Rai Bahadur Chunilal, his general manager, quarrelled constantly. There was a break and then Rai Bahadur left Bombay Talkies with his entire group, which included producer S. Mukherjee, director and storywriter Gyan Mukherjee and Ashok Kumar himself. They also took with them the lyricist Kavi Pradeep, sound recordist S. Vacha, comedian V.H. Desai and dialogue writers Shahid Latif and Santoshi. This group set up a new company by the name of Filmistan and S. Mukherjee was appointed production controller. He had already made his mark with a silver jubilee hit and preparations now began for the new outfit's first venture. A story was commissioned, and Mukherjee, still seething because of the old team's treatment at the hands of Devika Rani, made clear his intention of doing something that would make her sit up.

He finally hit upon a plan. He was going to talk Naseem Bano into returning to films. Based on his track record, he was confident that whatever he set his heart on, he would manage to accomplish. He devised a plan to lure Naseem back. Because of Ashok, he had developed good personal relations with Captain Siddiqi. And then wasn't Rai Bahadur Chunilal a good friend of Ehsan's father, the old Khan Bahadur? He approached Ehsan first and though, in the beginning, he was adamant, Mukherjee's persistence paid off and he said 'Yes'. Mukherjee returned to Bombay in triumph and announced to the press that the first Filmistan presentation, *Chal Chal Re Naujawan*, would star Naseem Bano. This created a sensation because it was presumed that Naseem had left the industry permanently.

I had just returned to Bombay after doing a stint lasting a year and a half at All India Radio in Delhi and was busy writing a story for Syed Shaukat Hussain Rizvi. I finished the assignment, wrote a few more stories and during this period hardly left my house. Even my wife got tired of my new domesticity, being convinced that spending so much time indoors was bad for my health. Shahid Latif, whom I had known since my Aligarh days, would drop in to see me whenever his workload at Filmistan permitted him. One day my wife said to him, 'Shahid bhai, I don't like my husband working at home. He is spoiling his health. If he had a job, at least he would be able to get out.' A few days later, Shahid Latif called from Malad saying that Mukherjee wanted to interview me because he was looking for someone for the scenario department.

I wasn't keen on a job, but I went anyway just to take a look at the Filmistan studio. It had a nice atmosphere like that of a university and I was impressed. When I met Mukherjee, I took an immediate liking to him too, and right there and then, I signed a contract. The money was meagre but I felt it might be possible to manage on three hundred rupees a month. I would have to spend an hour travelling to the studio in Goregaon from my residence but I was sure it could be done. One could also make something on the side by moonlighting.

In the beginning, I felt like a stranger in Filmistan, but in a matter of days I got to know everyone and I felt like a part of the family. With Mukherjee I was able to form a friendship, while Naseem Bano I saw only once or twice. As the script was now being written, she would only drop in briefly and then drive back home. Mukherjee was a perfectionist and it was months before he was satisfied with the story. We began to shoot the movie, starting with scenes that did not have Naseem. Then she appeared one day. I found her sitting on a folding chair outside the studio, her legs crossed, drinking tea from a thermos. Ashok introduced us. 'I have read his stories and other pieces,' she said softly.

The conversation was formal and brief. As she was still in make-up, I wasn't sure if she really was beautiful. I felt that when she spoke, she did so with an almost physical effort. There was a world of difference between the Naseem of *Pukar* and that of *Chal Chal Re Naujawan*. While she wore the splendid robes of an empress in the former, she was a uniformed volunteer of the Bharatiya Seva Dal in the latter. After I had seen her thrice without her make-up, I was convinced that she was indeed beautiful. Her mere presence in a room was enough to light up the place, such was her innate natural grace and loveliness.

She dressed with great care and I never saw a woman who had such fine taste in choosing colours. Yellow is a dangerous colour because it can make one look sickly but she wore it in a carefree, cavalier manner, which always startled me. The sari was her favourite, though off and on she would also wear a gharara or shalwar kameez. Even at home she was nicely dressed, being one of those people who take good care of their clothes, which was why even her old ones looked nearly new. I found her to be hard-working and delicate at the same time. She never showed the least sign of fatigue on the set although Mukherjee was a difficult man to please and a scene had to be rehearsed several times before he was satisfied. There she would be under powerful lights, sitting down, getting up, sitting down again, but always without complaint. I learnt later that she loved acting for its own sake. When we looked at the rushes after the day's shooting, her performance would appear lackadaisical. It lacked brilliance. She could enact scenes demanding dignified gestures and her natural good looks were always her greatest advantage, but she could not impress a critical observer who valued the pure art of acting. Her performance in *Chal Chal Re Naujawan* was the best thing she had done until then.

Mukherjee wanted her to give her portrayal an edge but Naseem was by nature a cool and laid-back woman. She could not do it. The day the film was released, there was a party at Taj Hotel. She looked splendid, almost like a Mughal princess, aloof and regal. The movie had taken two years to make, two tiring years, but contrary to expectations, it did not do very well. We were disappointed, especially Mukherjee. However, because of his contract, he was required to oversee the production of another film for Taj Mahal Pictures. He had no option but to get down to work.

Ehsan and Mukherjee had become close friends during the making of *Chal Chal Re Naujawan*. He now wanted him to take complete responsibility for the new production. Mukherjee and I had several meetings and it was decided that I should write a story called *Begum*, which would take full advantage of Naseem's beauty. I prepared a sketch and after some changes made by Mukherjee we began to shoot the movie, which we were able to complete. When I saw it on the screen, it felt like a vague reflection of what I had written on paper. During the filming of *Begum*, I had frequent opportunities to observe Naseem closely. In fact, Mukherjee and I used to take lunch at her house and often spent our evenings there going over what was to be shot the next day.

I had thought that Naseem would be living in a splendid villa, but when I entered her modest bungalow on Ghodbunder Road, I was taken aback. It was a rundown place with ordinary furniture, which was probably rented. The carpet was worn out and the floors and walls in need of paint. In the middle of this was Naseem, the woman with the face of a fairy, engaged in a discussion with the milkman on the quality of the milk he had just delivered. Her voice, which never seemed to wish to leave her throat, was fully turned on in order to extract a confession from the milkman that he had given her one full pound less than what she was paying for. One pound of undelivered milk! And that complaint from Naseem, for whose sake hundreds of Farhads would have been willing to dig any number of canals flowing with milk! I reeled as the incongruity of the situation hit me.

I found out in the course of time that the Nur Jahan of *Pukar* was a very domestic kind of woman who had every single quality that any run-of-the-mill housewife is supposed to have. When *Begum* went into production, she took charge of the costume department. It was estimated that the costumes would cost ten to twelve thousand rupees, but to save money she had a tailor permanently installed in her house, to whom she gave all her old saris, shirts and ghararas with detailed directions on how to stitch the costumes we would need.

Naseem had lots of clothes and unlike most of us she wore, rather than used, them. The fact was that whatever she wore looked good on her. In *Begum*, Mukherjee had presented her as an artless Kashmiri village damsel. He had also had her wear a Cleopatra-type costume, as well as the long-flowing Punjabi kurta and laacha, and even a modern outfit. It was our belief that *Begum* would be a hit, if for no other reason than for the lovely costumes worn by Naseem. It was a pity that, owing to poor direction and a weak score, the movie did only middling business.

We had all worked very hard, especially Mukherjee. Often we would be up until three in the morning with him putting new touches to the story, and Naseem and Ehsan doing their best to stay awake. As long as Ehsan kept swinging his leg, I knew that he was listening to us, but the moment he stopped, I knew he had gone to sleep. Naseem was always irritated by the fact that her husband could not resist sleep. What was more, he would doze off when we were discussing an important turn in the story. Mukherjee and I would tease Ehsan but Naseem would get upset and try to make him stay awake. However, the more she tried, the sleepier he would become. Finally, Naseem too would begin to show signs of sleepiness and Mukherjee would stand up and leave. I lived quite far from Ghodbunder Road and had to take a train to get home, which I could never manage before midnight. It was sheer torture and we decided after I spoke to Mukherjee that I should move in with Naseem and Ehsan for a few days.

Ehsan was a shy person and would take ages to state what was on his mind. He was keen that I should have every comfort and wanted me to know that I only had to ask for whatever I needed. However, his shyness and innate formality always prevented him from saying this in so many words. Once he asked Naseem to speak to me. 'Whatever you need, just let us know,' she said in the purest Punjabi, which she spoke perfectly. During the filming of *Chal Chal Re Naujawan*, when I told Rafiq Ghaznavi, who was playing an important role in the movie, about Naseem's Punjabi, he said in his typical manner that I was talking rubbish. I tried to convince him that I was serious but without luck.

One day during the shooting, when both Naseem and Rafiq were on the set and Ashok was trying his English tongue-twisters on her, I asked Rafiq, 'Lala, what does *uddhar vanja* mean?' 'What language is that?' he wanted to know. 'Punjabi,' I answered. 'I don't know,' Rafiq said, adding, 'you son of an *uddhar vanja*.' Naseem arched her neck slightly, smiled at Rafiq and asked in Punjabi, 'You really don't know?' When Rafiq heard Naseem speaking Punjabi, he forgot his Pushto. After the initial shock had passed, he asked her in halting Urdu, 'You know Punjabi?' Naseem kept smiling. 'Yes.' 'Then you tell me what *uddhar vanja* means,' I butted in. She thought for a few seconds, then said, '*Uddhar vanja* means the clothes you put on when you want to get comfortable at home and are not expecting any visitors.' Rafiq Ghaznavi forgot what little Pushto he still remembered.

Naseem's grandmother was a Kashmiri from Amritsar, which was how she had learnt Punjabi. Urdu she spoke with great purity because she had grown up in Delhi where her mother lived. English she knew because she had been sent to a school run by nuns. She was fond of music because of her mother, but she did not have her sweet voice, and although she sang her own songs in the movies in which she acted, her voice lacked richness. She later stopped singing altogether.

The halo around Naseem had gradually disappeared for me. What did it for me was the bath I took at their place. I expected the bathroom to be well equipped, with a variety of bath salts, exotic soaps and a whole range of toiletries that actresses and women who care about their looks use to look more beautiful. But all it had was a metal bucket, an aluminium utensil to pour water from and heavy water from a Malad well that refused to let any lather form no matter how long and hard one tried.

As for Naseem, whenever you saw her, she invariably looked fresh and lovely. Her make-up was worn light. She hated deep colours, preferring pastel shades, which were in line with her cool, laid-back personality. She loved perfumes and had a whole range of them, some both rare and expensive. She had heaps of ornaments but you would never see her weighed down with them. Perhaps a bracelet with a diamond sometimes, or a couple of gold bangles or maybe just a pearl necklace. That was all.

Her table was equally simple. Ehsan had asthma and Naseem always seemed to have a cold, so they were careful about what they ate. Naseem would remove the green chillies from my plate and Ehsan would pick out food from hers. They would have light arguments over their meals, but when you caught them looking at each other you detected love.

Once my wife invited Naseem to the house for dinner. She loved the ghee we used to cook our curries with and asked my wife, 'Where do you get this?' 'From the store. It is made by Polson. It is sold everywhere,' my wife answered. 'Could you get me two tins?' Naseem asked. I told the servant to run across the road and get two tins since I had an account at my neighbourhood grocery store. Over the next few months we purchased eight tins for her. One day she said to me, 'We should settle that ghee account.' 'There is no need,' I answered, but when she insisted, I said, 'In all there were eight tins. You can work out the cost.' Naseem was silent for a few minutes then said, 'Eight? Maybe there were seven.' 'Maybe there were seven,' I replied. 'Why maybe? If you say there were eight, then there must have been eight,' she said. 'Well you too said "maybe",' I told her. She kept going over this seven-eight business for a long time. She was sure there had been only seven. The store from where they had been purchased said there were eight, as did I. The only way this could be settled was if one of us accepted the other's figure; but since it was a question of accounts, neither side was willing to give in. Finally, Naseem asked her servant to bring out the empty tins. There were only seven of them. She looked at me triumphantly. 'You can count them . . . seven.' 'There may be seven,' I replied, 'but according to my count, there were eight.' At this point, the servant spoke, 'Yes, there were eight but the sweeper woman took one.'

I was paid five hundred rupees a month and had to account for every single paisa, but we never had any problem. Both husband and wife were happy with my work, though Ehsan was somewhat uneasy with my impatient temperament, but since he was extremely formal, he could never bring himself to say it. Outwardly, Ehsan was a weak person but he was firm with his wife. Naseem was only allowed to socialize with certain people and they did not include most actors and actresses. Naseem herself did not care for superficial types, nor had she any patience with noisy or raucous parties. Let me narrate the story of one in which she figured.

This happened at Holi. Like the 'mud-slinging party' at the Aligarh University at the start of the monsoon season, the tradition at Bombay Talkies was a Holi party. Since almost everyone at Filmistan was a former Bombay Talkies person, the tradition had been continued.

Mukherjee was the ringleader at the colour-throwers' party, while the women were under the command of his plump and good-humoured wife, who happened to be Ashok Kumar's sister. I was at Shahid Lateef's house, and his wife, Ismat Chughtai, and my wife, Safia, were busy gossiping when we heard a noise outside. 'There they are, Safia,' Ismat said. It was the Holi party indeed. Ismat was insistent that no one sprinkle any coloured water on her. I was afraid this would lead to unpleasantness since the merrymakers were in a holiday mood. Luckily, she soon relented and was drenched in colour within minutes. Shahid and I were in the same condition; in fact we all looked like multi-coloured goblins. Some more people joined us. Suddenly, Shahid shouted, 'On to pari chehra Naseem's house.'

Armed with coloured water in buckets and syringes, our raucous band ran down Ghodbunder Road towards Naseem's house and arrived there within minutes. They were both home. Naseem, perfectly made-up, was wearing a lovely, soft-coloured georgette sari. 'Go for them!' Shahid ordered, but I suggested that we give them time to change. Naseem smiled. 'I am all right the way I am.' The words were hardly out of her mouth when she was drenched in coloured water from every direction. Within seconds, she had been transformed into an evil-looking witch. The whites of her eyes and her sparkling teeth looked most odd in her multicoloured face, as if a child had upturned a bottle of ink on a painting by Behzad or Monet.

After we were done with this, a kabbadi match began. The men played first, the women followed. Whenever Mukherjee's plump wife fell to the ground, there was much laughter all around. Since my wife wore glasses, she was unable to see much and would run in the wrong direction. Naseem could not run because she wasn't used to this kind of horseplay. However, she was into the spirit of the thing and took part in everything enthusiastically.

Naseem and her husband were deeply religious, the kind who reverently kiss and touch their eyes with bits of old Urdu newspapers they pick up from the ground, fearing that the holy words printed on them may otherwise be desecrated. If they see a single star in the sky as the evening falls, they search for a group of nine and a pair for luck. You had to see Ehsan at the race course to believe how superstitious he was. If a one-eyed man were to stand next to him, he would have dropped dead. If a horse on which he had a tip but on which he had not bet, won, he would fight with Naseem. 'Why did you tell me not to back that horse?' But such arguments are a part of any marriage.

Naseem's two children were always at their grandmother's because she wanted them to stay away from film studios. She had loved her late father intensely and always kept his picture in her vanity bag. I have a strange fascination with women's bags and the bric-a-brac they contain. One day I was looking through the bag that she had left lying around when she suddenly appeared. 'I am sorry. I am indulging a bad old habit of mine,' I explained, adding, 'but tell me whose picture that is.' Naseem took the picture from my hand, gazed at it longingly and said, 'My Abbu's, who else's?' I felt that she was a little girl who was proudly showing me what her father looked like. I did not ask her what he was or where he now was. Was it not enough that he was her father . . . no, her Abbu.

One night, during the writing of the movie *Begum*, it got very late as Mukherjee and I had got involved in a long discussion on some aspects of the screenplay. It was almost two in the morning and the first local train would not leave until 3.30 a.m. My wife was with me. When we wanted to leave, Naseem said, 'No, Safia, this is no time to go. Stay here.' We said we would rather go because the weather was nice and we would walk up and down on the platform till the train arrived. But both Naseem and Ehsan were insistent that we stay on. Mukherjee left as he had a car and did not have far to go. I slept on the veranda and Ehsan lay down on a sofa in the living room. When we left after breakfast, Safia told me an interesting story.

When Naseem and she entered the bedroom, she found only one bed there. 'Why don't you take it?' my wife suggested. Naseem smiled, laid out a fresh sheet and said, 'But let us change first.' Then she gave Safia one of her new sleeping suits to wear, assuring her that it was 'absolutely new'. Safia put it on and lay down. Naseem changed languidly and then removed her make-up. Safia said she was taken aback. 'Naseem, how pale you are!' she exclaimed. A faint smile appeared on Naseem's unpainted lips. Then she rubbed her face with various ointments, washed her hands and picked up the Quran and began to recite from it. 'Naseem, I swear you are so much better than people like us,' Safia said. Then she suddenly realized that this had not been a tactful remark, and fell silent. Naseem finished her recitation and promptly went to sleep.

This was Naseem, the woman with the face of a goddess . . . the Nur Jahan of the movie *Pukar* . . . the Queen of Beauty . . . Ehsan's Roshan (his name for her) . . . Chammiya's daughter and mother of two children.

LETTERS TO UNCLE SAM

EDITOR'S NOTE

Between 1951 and 1954, Saadat Hasan Manto wrote nine letters to Uncle Sam. The first letter was written in 1951, while the rest seem to have been written in 1954. I say 'seem to have been written' because three of them bear no date. The last one is dated 26 April 1954.

These letters not only tell us a good deal about Manto and his concerns but even more about his political views. The man who speaks through these letters is well informed about international affairs and critical of American policy. We also see Manto's lighter side at play, enlivened by his caustic, at times, savage wit. We also learn a good deal about his friends and foes. He makes fun of Pakistani communists whom he always considered rather fake because they looked for a signal from their political gurus abroad before taking a position on any issue. A man with an independent temperament like Manto found such conduct pathetic and made no bones about it.

I had long wanted to translate these letters into English not so much because of their intrinsic literary and historical value but on account of their readability.

What we have here is vintage Manto.

LETTER 1

31 Laxmi Mansions,
Hall Road, Lahore
16 December 1951

Dear Uncle,
Greetings!

This letter comes to you from your Pakistani nephew whom you do not know, nor does anyone else in your land of seven freedoms.

You should know why my country, sliced away from India, came into being and gained independence, which is why I am taking the liberty of writing to you. Like my country, I too have become independent and in exactly the same way. Uncle, I will not labour the point since an all-knowing seer like you can well imagine the freedom a bird whose wings have been clipped can enjoy.

My name is Saadat Hasan Manto and I was born in a place that is now in India. My mother is buried there. My father is buried there. My firstborn is also resting in that bit of earth. However, that place is no longer my country. My country now is Pakistan, which I had only seen five or six times before as a British subject.

I used to be All India's Great Short-Story Writer. Now I am Pakistan's Great Short-Story Writer. Several collections of my stories have been published and people respect me. In undivided India, I was tried thrice, in Pakistan so far once. But then Pakistan is still young.[1]

---

[1]Manto was tried for writing 'obscene' stories three times before Independence in 1947 and three times after the establishment of Pakistan. In all six cases, he was ultimately acquitted, as the liberal intellectual establishment of the time sprang to his defence.

The government of the British considered my writings pornographic. My own government has the same opinion. The government of the British let me off but I do not expect my own government to do so. A lower court sentenced me to three months' hard labour and a three-hundred rupee fine. My appeal to the higher court won me an acquittal but my government believes that justice has not been done and so it has now filed an appeal in the high court, praying that the judgement acquitting me be quashed and I be punished. We will have to see what the high court decides.

My country is not your country, which I regret. If the high court were to punish me, there is no newspaper in my country that would print my picture or the details of all my trials.

My country is poor. It has no art paper, nor proper printing presses. I am living evidence of this poverty. You will not believe it, uncle, but despite being the author of twenty-two books, I do not have my own house to live in. And you will be astonished to know that I have no means of getting myself from one place to the other. I neither have a Packard nor a Dodge; I do not even have a used car. If I need to go somewhere, I rent a bike. If a piece of mine appears in a newspaper and I earn twenty to twenty-five rupees at the rate of seven rupees a column, I hire a tonga and go buy locally distilled whisky. Had this whisky been distilled in your country, you would have destroyed that distillery with an atom bomb because it is the sort of stuff guaranteed to send its user to kingdom come within one year.

But I am digressing. All I really wanted to do was to convey my good wishes to brother Erskine Caldwell. You will no doubt recall that you tried him for his novel *God's Little Acre* on the same charge that I have faced here: pornography.

Believe me, uncle, when I heard that this novel was tried on an obscenity charge in the land of seven freedoms, I was extremely surprised. In your country, after all, everything is divested of its outer covering so that it can be displayed in the show window, be it fresh fruit or woman, machine or animal, book or calendar. You are the king of bare things so I am at a loss to understand, uncle, why you tried brother Erskine Caldwell.

Had it not been for my quick reading of the court judgement I would have drunk myself to death by downing large quantities of our locally distilled whisky because of the shock I received when I came to know of the Caldwell case. In a way, it was unfortunate that my country missed an opportunity to rid itself of a man like me, but then had I croaked, I would not have been writing to you, uncle. I am dutiful by nature. I love my country. In a few days, by the Grace of God, I will die and if I do not kill myself, I will die anyway because where flour sells at the price at which it sells here only a shame-faced person can complete his ordained time on earth.

So, I read the Caldwell judgement and decided not to drink myself to death with large quantities of the local hooch. Uncle, out there in your country, everything has an artificial facade but the judge who acquitted brother Erskine was certainly without such a facade. If this judge—I'm sorry I don't know his name—is alive, kindly convey my respectful regards to him.

The last lines of his judgement point to the intellectual reach of his mind. He writes: 'I personally feel that if such books were suppressed, it would create an unnecessary sense of curiosity among people which could induce them to seek salaciousness, though that is not the purpose of this book. I am absolutely certain that the author has chosen to write truthfully about a certain segment of American society. It is my opinion that truth is always consistent with literature and should be so declared.'

That is what I told the court that sentenced me, but it went ahead anyway and gave me three months in prison with hard labour and a fine of three hundred rupees. My judge thought that truth and literature should be kept far apart. Everyone has his opinion.

I am ready to serve my three-month term, but this fine of three hundred rupees I am unable to pay. Uncle, you do not know that I am poor. Hard work I am used to, but money I am unused to. I am about thirty-nine and all my life I have worked hard. Just think about it. Despite being such a famous writer, I have no Packard.

I am poor because my country is poor. Two meals a day I can somehow manage, but many of my brothers are not so fortunate.

My country is poor, but why is it ignorant? I am sure, uncle, you know why because you and your brother John Bull together are a subject I do not want to touch because it will not be exactly music to your ears. Since I write to you as a respectful youngster, I should remain that way from start to finish.

You will certainly ask me out of astonishment why my country is poor when it boasts of so many Packards, Buicks and Max Factor cosmetics. That is indeed so, uncle, but I will not answer your question because if you look into your heart, you will find the answer there (unless you have had your heart taken out by one of your brilliant surgeons).

That section of my country's population, which rides in Packards and Buicks, is really not of my country. Where poor people like me and those even poorer live, that is my country.

These are bitter things, but there is a shortage of sugar here; otherwise I would have coated my words appropriately. But what of it! Recently, I read Evelyn Waugh's book *The Loved One*. He of course comes from the country of your friends. Believe me, I was so impressed by that book that I sat down to write to you.

I was always convinced of the individual genius found in your part of the world, but after reading this book, I have become a fan of his for life. What a performance, I say! Some truly vibrant people do indeed live out there.

Evelyn Waugh tells us that in your California, the dead can be beautified and there are large organizations that undertake the task. No matter how unattractive the dear departed in life, after death he can be given the look desired. There are forms you fill where you are asked to indicate your preference. The excellence of the finished product is guaranteed. The dead can be beautified to the extent desired, as long as you pay the price. There are experts who can perform this delicate task to perfection. The jaw of the loved one can be operated upon and a beatific smile implanted on the face. The eyes can be lit up and the forehead can be made to appear luminous. And all this work is done so marvellously that it can befool the two angels who are assigned to do a reckoning once a person is in the grave.

Uncle, by God you people are matchless.

One had heard of the living being operated on and beautified with the help of plastic surgery—there was much talk of it here—but one had not heard that the dead could be beautified as well.

Recently one of your citizens was here and some friends introduced me to him. By then I had read brother Evelyn Waugh's book and I read an Urdu couplet to your countryman that he did not follow. However, the fact is, uncle, that we have so distorted our faces that they have become unrecognizable, even to us. And there we have you who can even make the dead look more beautiful than they ever were in life. The truth is that only you have a right to live on this earth; the rest of us are wasting our time.

Our great Urdu poet Ghalib wrote about a hundred years ago:

If disgrace after death was to be my fate,
I should have met my end through drowning
It would have spared me a funeral and no headstone would have marked my last resting place

Ghalib was not afraid of being disgraced while he was alive because from beginning to end that remained his lot. What he feared was disgrace after death. He was a graceful man and not only was he afraid of what would happen after he died, he was certain of what would happen to him after he was gone. And that is why he expressed a wish to meet his end through drowning so that he should neither have funeral nor grave.

How I wish he had been born in your country. He would have been carried to his grave with great fanfare and over his resting place a skyscraper would have been built. Or were his own wish to be granted, his dead body would have been placed in a pool of glass and people would have gone to view it as they go to a zoo.

Brother Evelyn Waugh writes that not only are there in your country establishments that can beautify dead humans but dead animals as well. If a dog loses its tail in an accident, he can have a new one.

Whatever physical defects the dead one had in life are duly repaired after death. He is then buried ceremoniously and floral wreaths are placed on his grave. Every year on the pet's death anniversary, a card is sent to the owner with an inscription that reads something like this: 'In paradise, your Tammy (or Jeffie) is wagging his tail (or his ears) while thinking of you.'

What it adds up to is that your dogs are better off than us. Die here today, you are forgotten tomorrow. If someone in the family dies, it is a disaster for those left behind who often can be heard wailing: 'Why did this wretch die? I should've gone instead.' The truth is, uncle, that we neither know how to live nor how to die.

I heard of one of your citizens who wasn't sure what sort of a funeral he would be given, so he staged a grand 'funeral' for himself while he was very much alive. He deserved that certainly because he had lived a stylish and opulent life where nothing happened unless he wished it to. He wanted to rule out the possibility of things not being done right at his funeral; as such, he was justified in personally observing his last rites while alive. What happens after death is neither here nor there.

I have just seen the new issue of *Life* (5 November 1951, international edition) and learnt of a most instructive facet of American life. Spread across two pages is an account of the funeral of the greatest gangster of your country. I saw a picture of Willie Moretti (may his soul rest in peace) and his magnificent home, which he had recently sold for fifty-five thousand dollars. I also viewed his five-acre estate where he wanted to live in peace, away from the distractions of the world. There was also a picture of his, eyes closed, lying in his bed, quite dead. There were also pictures of his five-thousand-dollar casket and his funeral procession made up of seventy-five cars. God is my witness, it brought tears to my eyes.

May there be dust in my mouth, but in case you were to die, may you have a grander farewell than Willie Moretti. This is the ardent prayer of a poor Pakistani writer who doesn't even have a cycle to ride on. May I beg you that like the more far-sighted ones in your country, you too should make arrangements to witness your funeral while you are alive. You can't leave it to others; they can always make mistakes, being fallible. It is possible that your physical appearance may not receive the attention it deserves after you have passed away. It is also possible that you may already have witnessed your funeral by the time this letter reaches you. I say this because you are not only wiser, you are also my uncle.

Convey my good wishes to brother Erskine Caldwell and to the judge who acquitted him of the pornography charge. If I have caused you offence, I beg your forgiveness. With the utmost respect,

Your poor nephew,

Saadat Hasan Manto,
resident of Pakistan

(This letter could not be mailed because of lack of postage.)

LETTER 2

31 Laxmi Mansions,
Hall Road, Lahore

Most Respected Uncle,
Greetings!

It has been a while since I wrote to you but while there was no acknowledgment from you, some days earlier, a gentleman from your embassy, whose name I do not recall right now, dropped in to see me in the company of a young local. A brief resumé of my conversation with these gentlemen follows.

We introduced ourselves in English. I was surprised that he spoke English, not American, a language I have been unable to follow my entire life.

We spoke for nearly three-quarters of an hour. He was pleased to meet me as every American is pleased to meet a Pakistani or an Indian. I also gave him the impression that I was pleased to meet him, when the fact is that I do not derive any pleasure from meeting white Americans.

Please do not take my blunt words to heart. During the last war, when I was living in Bombay, one day I found myself at Bombay Central, the train terminus. All one could see in the city those days were Americans. Nobody any longer gave a damn about poor Tommies. All the Anglo-Indian, Jewish and Parsi girls of Bombay who slept around by way of fashion were now to be seen walking hand in hand with the Americans.

Uncle, believe me, when one of your soldiers with a Jewish, Parsi or Anglo-Indian girl on his arm would walk past these Tommies, they would burn to a cinder with envy.

You truly are different from the rest of the world. Our soldiers here don't even make enough to buy half the food they need, but you pay even your office boy so much that he can fill not one but two bellies, from bottom to top.

Uncle, forgive me for my impertinence, but is it not really something of a fraud? Where do you get all that money from? I know it is not my place to say so, but your actions have only one purpose and no other: show off. Maybe I am wrong, but it is human to make mistakes. I think you are also human, and if you are not, then there is nothing I can do about that.

I am digressing. I was talking about Bombay Central where I used to see many of your soldiers, mostly white, although one also ran into blacks. If truth be told, these black soldiers looked far tougher and in much better health than the white ones.

I can never understand why so many of your people wear glasses. The whites wore glasses and the blacks, whom you call Negroes, wore them too. Why they needed glasses, I have no idea. Maybe, it is all part of some grand strategy of yours because since you favour seven freedoms, you want those whom you can easily put to eternal sleep—and you do—should look at your world through your glasses.

At Bombay Central, I saw a Negro solider who was so muscular that at his very sight I shrank to half my size. In the end, I gathered my courage and walked up to him. He was resting his back against the wall, his kitbag was lying next to him and his eyes were half closed. I made a noise by rubbing my shoes on the floor, which made him open his eyes. I said to him in English, 'I was passing this way when I stopped, so impressed was I by your personality.' Then I offered him my hand.

The soldier who was wearing glasses took my hand in his vice-like grip and before he could crush every bone in there I begged him to let me go. A big smile appeared on his dark lips and he asked me in his pure American accent, 'Who are you?'

'I live here,' I said, massaging my hand. 'I noticed you at the station and felt like exchanging a word or two with you.'

'There are so many soldiers around, why did you pick me out?' he asked.

It was a tricky question but I answered it quite effortlessly. 'I am black, so are you. I love black people,' I told him.

He flashed a big smile at me. His dark lips looked so attractive that I wanted to kiss them. End of story.

Uncle, your women are so beautiful. I once saw one of your movies called *Bathing Beauty*. 'Where does uncle find such an assemblage of pretty legs?' I asked my friends later. I think there were about two hundred and fifty of them. Uncle, is this how women's legs look like in your country? If so, then for God's sake (that's if you believe in God) block their exhibition in Pakistan at least.

It is possible that women's legs out here may be better than legs in your country but, uncle, no one flashes them around. Just think about it. The only legs we see are those of our wives; the rest of the legs we consider a forbidden sight. We are rather orthodox, you see.

I have digressed again but I will not apologize because this is the sort of writing you like.

I wanted to tell you that the gentleman who came to see me, who belonged to your consulate here, wanted me to write a story for him. I was taken aback because I do not know how to write in English, so I said to him, 'Sir, I am an Urdu writer. I do not know how to write in English.'

'We need the story in Urdu because we have a journal that is published in the Urdu language,' he replied.

I did not want to probe, so I said, 'I am willing.'

God is my witness, I did not know that he had come to see me at your bidding. Perhaps you made him read the letter I had sent you.

But let's drop this. As long as Pakistan needs wheat, I cannot be impertinent to you. As a Pakistani (though my government does not consider me a law-abiding citizen), I pray to God that a time may come when you find yourself in need of millet and edible greens and, provided I am alive, I will send it to you.

This gentleman who asked me for the story wanted to know how much I would charge for it.

Uncle, it is possible that you lie—and you actually do, having turned it into an art—but I don't know how to.

That day, however, I did lie. 'I will charge two hundred rupees for my story.'

The truth is that the most publishers here pay me is forty or fifty rupees a story, so when I said I would charge two hundred, I felt bad and quite ashamed of myself, but it was too late.

But, uncle, I was really surprised when the gentleman you had sent replied, sounding equally surprised (real or artificial, I do not know), 'Just two hundred . . . you should charge at least five hundred for a story.'

I was really thrown because I could not imagine even in my wildest dreams that I could be offered five hundred for a story. But I was not going to go back on what I had said, so I repeated, 'Look, sir, it will be two hundred and further discussion on this matter I am not prepared for.'

He left, obviously in the belief that I was drunk. I drink and what I drink I have described in my first letter.

Uncle, I am surprised that I am still alive, although it is five years since I have been drinking the poison distilled here. If you ever come here, I will offer you this vile stuff and hope that like me you will also remain alive, along with your seven freedoms.

Anyway, next morning as I was on my veranda shaving, the same gentleman of yours appeared and said, 'Look, don't insist on two hundred, take three hundred.'

I said fine and took the three hundred he offered. After putting the money in my pocket, I said to him, 'I have charged you an extra one hundred but let me make it clear that what I write will not be to your liking, nor will I give you the right to make changes.'

He has not shown up since. If you run into him or if he has sent you a report, please do let your Pakistani nephew know about it.

Those three hundred rupees I have already spent. If you want the money back, I will pay you at the rate of a rupee a month.

I hope you are happy with your seven freedoms.

Your obedient nephew,

Saadat Hasan Manto

LETTER 3

31 Laxmi Mansion,
Hall Road, Lahore
15 March 1954

Dear Uncle,
Greetings!

I write this after a long break. The fact is that I was ill. According to our poetic tradition, the treatment for illness lies in what is called the elixir of joy served by a slender temptress straight out of the quatrains of Omar Khayyam from a long-necked crystal jug. However, I think that is all poetry. How can I speak of comely cup-bearers when one can't even find an ugly servant boy with a moustache to play the cup-bearer.

Beauty has fled this land. While women have come out from behind the veil, one look at them and you wish they had stayed behind it. Your Max Factor has made them even uglier. You send free wheat, free literature, free arms. Why not send a couple of hundred examples of pure American womanhood here so that they could at least serve a drink as it is supposed to be served?

I fell ill because of this blasted liquor—God damn it—which is poison, pure and simple. And raw. Not that I did not know, not that I did not realize, but what the poet Meer wrote applies to my condition.

What a simpleton Meer is!
The apothecary's boy who made him fall ill
Is the very one he goes to, to get his medicine

Who knows what Meer found in that apothecary's boy from whom he sought his medicine when he knew he was ill because of him. The man from whom I buy my poison is far more ill than I am. While I have survived because I am used to a hard life, I see little hope for him.

In the three months I was in a hospital's general ward, no American aid reached me. I think you knew nothing about my illness; otherwise you would have surely sent me two or three packages of Terramycin and earned credit in this world and the next.

Our foreign publicity leaves a great deal to be desired and our government, in any case, has no interest in writers, poets and painters.

Our late lamented government, I recall, appointed Firdausi-i-Islam Hafiz Jullandhri director of the song publicity department at a monthly salary of a thousand rupees. After the establishment of Pakistan, all that was allotted to him was a house and a printing press. Today you pick up the papers and what do you see? Hafiz Jullandhri bewailing his lot, having been thrown out of the committee appointed to compose a national anthem for Pakistan. He is one poet in the country who can write an anthem for this, the world's largest Islamic state, and even set it to music. He has divorced his British wife because the British are gone. He is said to be now looking for an American wife. Uncle, for God's sake, help him there so that he can be saved from a sorry end.[1]

---

[1]Hafiz Jullandhri was one of Urdu's leading poets before Independence and gained popularity for the poetic epic based on the history of Islam that he called *Shahnama-e-Islam*. He was likened to the great medieval Persian

The number of your nephews runs into millions but a nephew like yours truly you will not find even if you light an atom bomb to look for him. Do pay me some attention therefore. All I need is an announcement from you that your country (which may it please God to protect till the end of time) will only help my country (may God blight the distilleries of this land) acquire arms if Saadat Hasan Manto is sent over to you.

Overnight, my value will go up and after this announcement, I will stop doing *Shama* and *Director* crossword puzzles.[2] Important people will come to visit my home and I will ask you to airmail me a typical American grin which I will glue to my face so that I can receive them properly.

Such a grin can have a thousand meanings. For instance, 'You are an ass.' 'You are exceptionally brilliant.' 'I derived nothing but mental discomfort from this meeting.' 'You are a casual-wear shirt made in America.' 'You are a box of matches made in Pakistan.' 'You are a home-made herbal tonic.' 'You are Coca Cola,' etc., etc.

I want to live in Pakistan because I love this bit of earth, dust from which, incidentally, has lodged itself permanently in my lungs. However, I will certainly visit your country so that I can get my health back. Barring my lungs, every other organ in my body I will hand over to your experts and ask them to turn them American.

I like the American way of life. I also like the design of your casual-wear shirt. It is both a good design and a good billboard. You can print the latest propaganda item on it every day and move from Zelin's Coffee House to Pak Tea House to Cheney's Lunch Home so that everyone can read it.[3]

---

poet Firdausi, who wrote the famous epic poem *Shahnama*. Hafiz was often called Firdausi-e-Islam. After Independence, he was assigned to write the Pakistani national anthem, which he did. However, he always felt that his services had not been recognized to the extent they deserved. Manto did not think much of him, either as a poet or as a man.

[2]*Shama* and *Director*, published from Delhi and Lahore respectively, were two popular magazines of the time that ran crossword puzzle competitions that offered generous cash prizes.

[3]Zelin's Coffee House, Pak Tea House and Cheney's Lunch Home, all located on the Mall, were Lahore's most popular restaurants at the time where writers and intellectuals hung out. None of them has survived. The Pak Tea House, after teetering on the brink of bankruptcy for years, was the last to close down.

I also want a Packard so that when I go riding in it to the mall, wearing that shirt with a pipe gifted by you resting between my teeth, all the progressive and non-progressive writers of Lahore will come to realize that they have been wasting their time so far.

But look, uncle, you will have to buy petrol for the car, though I promise to write a story as soon as I have the Packard; the story would be called 'Iran's Nine Maunds of Oil and Radha'. Believe me, the moment the story is printed, all this trouble about Iranian oil will end and Maulana Zafar Ali Khan,[4] who is still alive, will have to amend that couplet he once wrote about Lloyd George and oil.

Another thing I would want from you would be a tiny, teeny-weenie atom bomb because for long I have wished to perform a certain good deed. You will naturally want to know what.

You have done many good deeds yourself and continue to do them. You decimated Hiroshima, you turned Nagasaki into smoke and dust and you caused several thousand children to be born in Japan. Each to his own. All I want you to do is to dispatch me some dry-cleaners. It is like this. Out here, many mullah types after urinating pick up a stone and, with one hand inside their untied shalwar, use the stone to absorb the after-drops of urine. This they do in full public view. All I want is that the moment such a person appears, I should be able to pull out that atom bomb you will send me and lob it at the mullah so that he turns into smoke along with the stone he was holding.

As for your military pact with us, it is remarkable and should be maintained. You should sign something similar with India. Sell all your old condemned arms to the two of us, the ones you used in the last war. This junk will thus be off your hands and your armament factories will no longer remain idle.

Pandit Jawaharlal Nehru is a Kashmiri, so you should send him a gun which should go off when it is placed in the sun. I am a Kashmiri too, but a Muslim, which is why I have asked for a tiny atom bomb for myself.

---

[4]Maulana Zafar Ali Khan, prolific poet, writer and journalist, who founded the Urdu daily *Zamindar* from Lahore. He died in the early 1950s.

One more thing. We can't seem to be able to draft a constitution. Do kindly ship us some experts because while a nation can manage without a national anthem, it cannot do without a constitution, unless such is your wish.

One more thing. As soon as you get this letter, send me a shipload of American matchsticks. The matchsticks manufactured here have to be lit with the help of Iranian-made matchsticks. And after you have used half the box, the rest are unusable unless you take help from matches made in Russia which behave more like firecrackers than matches.

The American topcoats are also excellent and without them our Landa Bazaar[5] would be quite barren. But why don't you send us trousers as well? Don't you ever take off your trousers? If you do, you probably ship them to India. There has to be a strategy to it because you send us jackets but no trousers which you send to India. When there is a war, it will be your jackets and your trousers. These two will fight each other using arms supplied by you.

And what is this I hear about Charlie Chaplin having given up his US citizenship? What did this joker think he was doing? He surely is suffering from communism; otherwise why would a man who has lived all his life in your country, made his name there, made his money there, do what he has done? Does he not remember the time when he used to beg in the streets of London and nobody took any notice of him!

Why did he not go to Russia? But then there is no shortage of jokers there. Perhaps he should go to England so that its residents learn to laugh heartily like Americans. As it is, they always look so sombre and superior. It is time some of their pretence came off.

I now close my letter with a freestyle kiss to Heddy Lamar.

Your nephew,

Saadat Hasan Manto

---

[5]Landa Bazar, Lahore's famous used and second-hand clothes market

LETTER 4

31 Laxmi Mansions,
Hall Road, Lahore
21 February 1954

Dear Uncle,

I wrote to you only a few days ago and here I am writing again. My admiration and respect for you are going up at about the same rate as your progress towards a decision to grant military aid to Pakistan. I tell you I feel like writing a letter a day to you.

Regardless of India and the fuss it is making, you must sign a military pact with Pakistan because you are seriously concerned about the stability of the world's largest Islamic state since our mullah is the best antidote to Russian communism. Once military aid starts flowing, the first people you should arm are these mullahs. They would also need American-made rosaries and prayer-mats, not to forget small stones that they use to soak up the after-drops following a call of nature. Cut-throat razors and scissors should be top of the list, as well as American hair-colour lotions. That should keep these fellows happy and in business.

I think the only purpose of military aid is to arm these mullahs. I am your Pakistani nephew and I know your moves. Everyone can now become a smart ass, thanks to your style of playing politics.

If this gang of mullahs is armed in the American style, the Soviet Union that hawks communism and socialism in our country will have to shut shop. I can visualize the mullahs, their hair trimmed with American scissors and their pajamas stitched by American machines in strict conformity with the Sharia. The stones they use for their after-drops of you-know-what will be American, untouched by human hand, and their prayer-mats would be American too. Everyone will then become your camp follower, owing allegiance to you and no one else.

It is obvious that you will do your best to uplift the lower and the lower-middle class in this country and those you need for your work will be recruited from these ranks. Even the clerks and peons employed in various offices would come from this source. The salaries paid would conform to American standards, and once they find themselves in money communism will vanish like a perished soul.

Recruitment of personnel I have no problem with but what I don't want here are your soldiers as I would not like to see our girls turning their backs on our young men for yours. I have no doubt the young men you send over would be healthy and handsome. I would also like you to know that our upper class has no qualms about anything any more, having divested itself of its inhibitions at American laundries. As for the lower classes, they continue to have certain reservations when it comes to such things.

You may like to send out American girls adept at providing first aid and teaching our young men how to dance and kiss in public so as to make them less self-conscious. It can only be to your benefit. If you can show hundreds of bare legs in the movie *Bathing Beauty*, why can't we take a leaf out of your book and replicate those legs here so that we will be able to use our only movie studio, Shahnoor, to make a movie that we can show to members of APWA[1] for their pleasure.

Yes, a strange thing called APWA has taken birth here which keeps the wives and daughters of important men suitably amused. APWA is short for All Pakistan Women's Association. I can't make it any shorter, but what is getting shorter are the blouses its members wear, short enough for people to see their bare midriffs. What is funny is that these itsy-bitsy things are sported by women over the age of forty. The years have not been too kind to their midriffs, as is to be expected. I have a confession. I cannot stand the sight of midriffs lined by age, be their owners American or Pakistani.

APWA seems game for scanty attire as long as someone can provide them with the right know-how. Women in your country can be sixty-five years of age and yet their midriffs look taut. It only makes you wonder how exactly they give birth to children. Maybe they know of a technique that can ensure the birth of the baby while sparing the skin over their middle the ravages of childbirth.

It may not be a bad idea to dispatch a couple of Hollywood experts here who know everything there is to know about skimpy outfits. Plastic surgery in your country has been turned into a fine

---

[1]APWA, acronym for the All Pakistan Women's Association, the first national women's organization that was often the butt of male jokes, which today will be considered chauvinist and anti-feminist.

art. We need at least six of your plastic surgeons who could rejuvenate some of our women so that their modish ways remain consistent with their looks.

In our traditional poetry, the beloved was supposed to have no waist. Our new poetry is otherwise, where the beloved's waist is like a solid tree trunk. Uncle, why don't you pay us a visit before you sign that military pact so that it could finally be decided whether the beloved should or should not have a waist.

One more thing. Your movie-makers are taking a great deal of interest in the Indian film industry. We cannot tolerate this. Recently, when Gregory Peck was in India, he had himself photographed with the film star Suraiya whose beauty he went on record to admire. Another American movie-maker put his arms around our star Nargis and kissed her. This is not right. Have all Pakistani actresses croaked that they should be ignored!

We have Gulshan Ara. She may be black as a pot but she has appeared as the lead in many movies. She is also said to have a big heart. As for Sabiha, while it is true that she is slightly cross-eyed, a little attention from you can take care of that.[2]

We have also heard that you are providing financial assistance to Indian movie-makers. Uncle, what is the meaning of this? It seems anyone, just anyone, who comes to call on you gets what he wants.

Let your Gregory Peck go to hell (I am sorry I am getting angry). I suggest that you send two or three of your actresses because our lone hero, Santosh Kumar, is lonely. Recently he went to Karachi, where he drank a thousand bottles of Coca-Cola and dreamt of Rita Hayworth all night.

There is something about lipstick that I need to mention to you. The kiss-proof lipstick that you sent over did not gain much popularity with our upper-class ladies. Both young girls and older women swear that by no means is it kiss-proof. My own view is that the problem lies with the way they kiss, which is all wrong. Some people kiss as if they were eating watermelon. A book

---

[2]Suraiya, famous Indian actress-singer of the late 1940s whose silky voice remained popular well into the 1960s. Gulshan Ara and Sabiha Khanum were the stars of early Pakistani cinema. While Gulshan Ara faded after a decade or so, Sabiha, married to the popular hero Santosh Kumar, remained involved in the industry, turning from a romantic heroine into a fine character actress.

published in your country called *The Art of Kissing* is quite useless here because one can learn nothing from it. You may instead like to fly an American girl over who can teach our upper classes that there is a difference between kissing and eating watermelon. There is no need to explain the difference to lower and lower-middle class people because they have no interest in such matters and will remain the way they are.

You will be pleased to know that my stomach is now quite used to American wheat. Your wheat and our eating habits seem to be compatible because we turn your wheat into chapattis. As a gesture of goodwill, you should also import some Pakistani wheat. Your soil being fertile, this new variety of Pakistani-American wheat will take root easily. It may even result in the birth of a new man whose progeny may be different from ours.

I would like to ask you in confidence if it is true (I have read this somewhere) that in Delhi young women have been seen walking about at night with tiny lights twinkling in their hair. The report said that some of them tucked these tiny lights inside their blouses. If this was your idea, you have my compliments. Why not prepare a powder that when rubbed would light up the entire body, making it leap out of the clothes?

Pandit Jawaharlal Nehru is an old-fashioned man. After all, he is the disciple of the man who told young men to cover their eyes so as not to be able to look at women. The other day, he told the women of India to take care how they dressed and to give up the use of make-up. But who is going to listen to him! Hollywood, women are always willing to listen to. So I ask you to rush this powder to India. Pandit Nehru's reaction would be most amusing.

Enclosed in this envelope is the picture of a Pakistani woman who is dressed like a fisherwoman from Bombay. Her bare midriff is visible. It is a little teaser from our Pakistani women to yours.

I hope you will accept it.

Your obedient nephew,

Saadat Hasan Manto

LETTER 5

31 Laxmi Mansions,
Hall Road, Lahore

Respected Uncle,

I have always addressed you as 'Dear Uncle' but this time I am addressing you as 'Respected Uncle' because I have a bone to pick with you. I am upset because so far you haven't sent me my gift, the atom bomb that is. Now what is the meaning of this, I ask you!

I had always heard that uncles love their nephews more than their fathers love them but it seems this is not so in the United States. And that is not the only difference between us. For instance, we have a change of ministers every other day but no such thing happens in your country. Out here there are those who claim that they are born to be prophets but you have no such birds. Here their followers can become foreign ministers, triggering countrywide disturbances that change nothing. Inquiry commissions are named to look into the disturbances but the work of the commissions is directed by an authority higher than theirs. Such interesting things do not happen in your country.[1]

Uncle, let me ask you why no prophets are born in your country? By God, all you need is just one and you will have guaranteed entertainment for life. You will find this particularly useful in your old age. It will be like a stick that will help you tend to your flock of buffaloes which I hope do exist in America.

In case you are unable to make any prophets take birth, all you have to do is let me know and I will request Mirza Bashiruddin

---

[1]This is a playful reference to Chaudhri Zafrulla Khan, Paksitan's first foreign minister, who was a member of the Ahmediyya sect that many considered controversial and not even Muslim. Muslim religious parties and mullahs, almost all of whom had opposed the creation of Pakistan, were always calling for his dismissal. In 1953, serious anti-Ahmediyya riots broke out in the Punjab, forcing the government to declare Pakistan's first martial law in certain cities to deal with the situation. In hindsight, it appears that this forced entry into the management of civilian affairs may have given the army its first encouragement to take over, which it did in October 1958.

Mahmood to send over his son to you.[2] But please hurry; otherwise a similar demand may come from your enemy Russia and you may find yourself going away empty-handed.

But to return to the atom bomb, all I wanted was a tiny one to blow up anyone wearing loose trousers with one hand inside holding a tiny stone for soaking up after-drops. It seems you did not take my request too seriously; maybe you are busy with your hydrogen bomb experiments.

Uncle, what is this hydrogen bomb anyway? In the eighth grade we were taught that hydrogen was a gas lighter than air. Can you please tell me what country's weight do you want the earth to be relieved of? Russia?

I have heard that Russia is making a nitrogen bomb. In the eighth grade we were told that nitrogen was a gas a human being could not breathe and not die. I think your answer to the nitrogen bomb would be an oxygen bomb. We were taught in the eighth grade that when nitrogen and oxygen meet, they turn into water. Won't the world have fun with all that water when the Russians lob their nitrogen bomb and you throw your oxygen bomb!

That was a joke but I hear that you have made your hydrogen bomb so that there would be lasting peace in the world. While only God knows what lies in the future, I for one have faith in you because I have eaten your wheat and, additionally, I am your nephew. Younger people must listen to their elders. For this lasting peace to be established, how many countries will need to be removed from the face of the earth? That's all I want to know. My niece who is at school wanted me to draw her a map of the world yesterday but I told her she would have to wait because I first had to talk to my uncle to find out the names of the countries that were going to survive. I promised to draw her a map after I had spoken to you.

I beg you to rid the earth of Russia to begin with, because I have a natural aversion to it. A week or so ago, a group of artists from there was visiting us as a gesture of goodwill. They are probably gone now but they included women dancers and singers who won the hearts of our simple Pakistanis by their performance. As a get-

---

[2]Mirza Bashiruddin Mahmood was the son of the founder of the Jamaat-i-Ahmediyya, Mirza Ghulam Ahmed, and at the time the khalifa or head of the Jamaat.

even measure, you must send a goodwill troupe of singing and dancing girls over to Pakistan.

I had asked you earlier to send a few million-dollar-legged girls from Hollywood but you paid no attention to your foolish nephew and remained preoccupied with your hydrogen bomb experiments.

Please ask your embassy if it is true or not that all one hears these days here are the names of Khanum and Madam Ashoora, two of the Russian performers. We have a dry and puritanical newspaper here by the name of *Zamindar*, which felt so overwhelmed by the Russians that one of its reports went like this (and I reproduce): 'When she was singing in the packed open-air theatre, the only other sound one could hear was the breathing of the audience. The star-studded sky was like an awning over her head and the green trees around the stage appeared to be lost in wonder. In this profound silence, this nightingale was singing her heart out. Her intense, deep and soul-penetrating voice was like a shaft of light stabbing the night's black bosom.'

Did you read it, uncle? I tell you this is a very serious matter and I would advise you to leave your hydrogen bombs alone for a moment and pay some attention to this situation. You are not short of women who are like firecrackers and my advice would be to rush a handful of them to us while taking care that they all have million-dollar legs. They should by no means be afraid of throwing the odd kiss to our Pakistani men. If you were to send me a plane-load of Kolynos toothpaste, I will see to it that these men get their teeth properly brushed so that they smell nice.

I promise you this will knock out the Russians, and their Khanum and Madam Ashoora would be no more than a memory. The editor of *Zamindar* will begin to see stars during daylight hours. And one more thing, uncle. If you send Elizabeth Taylor, she should be under instructions to kiss me and no one else. I happen to like her lips.

Yes, this goodwill troupe should not include Paul Robeson because he is a sala communist. I am surprised why you haven't sent him to East Africa so far where he will be shot dead as a member of the Mau Mau.

I will eagerly wait for this goodwill troupe and ask the editor of *Nawai Waqt* to launch a public relations campaign in its favour right away. He is a nice and obedient person and I am sure he would not say no to me. However, you may like to send him a signed picture of Rita Hayworth as a gift. This will be enough to please him.[3]

I also promise you that when this goodwill troupe comes to Lahore, I will take it on a tour of Hira Mandi in the company of Shorish Kaashmiri as he is the patron saint of that area (recently he has written a book on it called *In That Street*. Please order your embassy to send you a translation.). Here in Hira Mandi we have many brilliant and uncut diamonds of every colour and weight.[4]

Now to other matters. Recently Pandit Nehru criticized your decision to give military aid to Pakistan and also spoke of your policy on the Middle East and your differences with India. I am told as a result of that you have developed a strategy aimed at paying greater attention to India.

Your man in charge of South Asian and African affairs has recently spoken warmly of India and it would appear as if Washington was desperate to win Delhi's goodwill. While I know that by trying to please both Pakistan and India, you want to nurture the flickering lamp of democracy, one way of doing that would be to pour so much oil in this lamp that never again would you have to listen to another complaint about shortage of oil. Right, uncle?

You want to see Pakistan free because you love the Khyber Pass, which has been used to invade us over the centuries. The Khyber Pass is indeed a thing of beauty. I mean what else has Pakistan got!

And India you want to see free because after witnessing what Russia has done to Poland, Czechoslovakia and Korea, you are afraid that the Red Empire may pounce upon India with its hammer and sickles. If India were to lose its freedom, it would be a great tragedy and I can see that it sends shivers down your spine.

---

[3]*Nawai Waqt*, a leading Urdu newspaper founded and edited at the time by Hamid Nizami, a journalist of great courage and integrity; Manto is just being playful with him because even if this 'uncle' had sent over Miss Hayworth, Nizami would have found her of little interest.

[4]Hira Mandi, Lahore's famous courtesan district. Shorish Kaashmiri was a firebrand journalist and prolific writer who published a book in the early 1950s about Hira Mandi he called *Uss Bazar Mein*, which became quite popular, though it made the author the butt of salacious jokes, as was to be expected.

I swear by your star-studded cap that a being more sincere than you has yet to be born. May God give you a long life and may your seven freedoms continue to flourish.

We have an area here called West Punjab and its chief minister is a man called Feroz Khan Noon (his wife is British). You must have heard of him. Recently he called a meeting at his residence, which is next to Pancholi Film Studio, where he advised workers of the Muslim League (which met an ignominious defeat in East Pakistan recently) to go to their areas and intensify the struggle against the Reds.

Look uncle, please thank Feroz Khan Noon and, as a gesture of goodwill, send two or three thousand stitched dresses for his wife. But on second thought, don't, because I forgot that she now wears a sari.[5]

In any case, Noon's declaration of war against communism is a good omen because that will mean Comrade Ferozuddin Mansur again being sent to jail. I do not at all like that he is asthmatic.[6]

Now I give you a really good piece of advice. Recently, our government released Comrade Sibte Hasan from jail. Please get him abducted because he is a friend of mine and I am afraid, given his soft and charming way of talking, he may one day turn me into a communist. I am not a coward, but I can tell you that even if I were to end up as a communist, it would make not the least difference to me. However, it may cast aspersions on you. People will ask how your nephew got sucked up into that nonsense.[7]

---

[5]Feroz Khan Noon, Punjabi politician and feudal lord, who occupied several high positions before and after Independence. He was Indian high commissioner in London before 1947, where he married his secretary, an Eastern European. She took the Muslim name Viqar-un-Nissa and did a great amount of good work for the Red Cross in Pakistan, as well as for the women's movement. She outlived her husband by nearly three decades. Noon was prime minister of Pakistan in 1958 when the then army chief, General Muhammad Ayub Khan, overthrew the government with the help of Governor General Iskander Mirza, ushering in a long and recurring era of army rule in Pakistan.

[6]Ferozuddin Mansur, a lifelong communist, who like Manto came from Amritsar. Manto used to make fun of him by calling him Fraududdin Mansur.

[7]Sibte Hasan, Marxist intellectual and journalist, who was a lifelong member of the Communist Party.

A word now about making a living here. Uncle, I swear by your venerable beard that my life is hard. I am passing through such bad times that I have forgotten how to pray for good times. One can't even keep oneself properly clothed here. Cloth is so expensive that the poor cannot afford to be shrouded for burial. Those who are alive are in tatters. I have, therefore, decided to open a nudist club. The only question is what will the members eat. Each other's nakedness I suppose, though that couldn't taste very nice.

Life here is desolate, bare and harsh, but uncle no matter how tough times get, I will never forget you.

Please quickly send that goodwill delegation of sweet-voiced, pretty girls and we will manage to live through our hardships. An imprint of Miss Taylor's lips will be most welcome.

Your obedient nephew,

Saadat Hasan Manto

LETTER 6

Dear Uncle,
Greetings!

My sixth letter that I posted myself appears to have been lost. I wonder where it went.

Saadat Hasan Manto

LETTER 7

31 Laxmi Mansion,
Hall Road, Lahore
14 April 1954

Dear Uncle,
Greetings!

You will have to excuse me as I am puzzled because I have no idea if my sixth and last letter that I had posted myself arrived at all. I wonder what happened to it.

While it is true that in this country if you send a letter from Lahore to Sheikhupura, it could take two and a half to three years to get there because we Pakistanis are of a poetic temperament and things such as delayed letters are considered poetic, our postal people would never dream of playing that trick upon you; after all, they have all eaten your gifted wheat.

As far as I know, this is entirely a Russian plot and India could well be a part of it. Some time ago, there was a symposium in Lucknow on this nephew of yours with one of the speakers claiming that I was preparing the ground for America in Pakistan.

While this is entirely true, you still have to send me a couple of bulldozers, now that the whole world knows about it. By the way, someone should have asked that fool in Lucknow how exactly did he think I was going to level the ground. With my bare hands?

You do not always immediately understand what I say because you are preoccupied with your hydrogen bomb and seem to be aware of little else. Forget those bombs for a minute and consider the possibility that my letter to you may have been hijacked by the communists.

Were it left to me, I would have dealt with these mischief-makers myself, teaching them a lesson they would have remembered for the rest of their lives. The trouble is that all these communists are my friends. There is Ahmed Nadeem Qasimi and then there are Sibte Hasan, Abdulla Malik (although I hate him, he being a low kind of communist), Ferozuddin Mansoor, Ahmed Rahi, Nazish Kaashmiri, Hamid Akhtar and Professor Safdar.[1]

---

[1]All writers and members or fellow travellers of the Communist Party and/or the Progressive Writers' Movement, both of which Manto always made

Uncle, I dare not say anything to these people because they are my regular lenders. You will understand that a debtor cannot stand up to his creditor, which reminds me that you have never lent me any money. In the beginning, when I wrote you my first letter, as a gesture of goodwill, you sent me three hundred rupees. I was so touched by this gesture that I decided I was yours for life. However, you did not reciprocate this sentiment and gave me no further financial assistance.

Dear uncle, tell me what sin I have committed to deserve punishment. Not even the peon outside your Lahore establishment has anything nice to say to me. Two or three of my Pakistani brothers who work there are so full of themselves that the moment they hear my name they begin to curse me.

---

fun of for being humourless and doctrinaire, as well as without a mind of their own, always looking for direction from Moscow.

Ahmed Nadeem Qasimi, poet, story writer and critic, who, though several years younger than Manto, remained close to him. However, that did not always save him from Manto's barbed wit.

Abdulla Malik, a lifelong communist, who knew Manto in Bombay when he (Malik) was working there for the Communist Party paper in the early 1940s.

Ahmed Rahi, Punjabi poet and lyricist, was one of Manto's younger companions and admirers. Like him, Rahi came from Amritsar, an additional factor that bonded them together. Rahi's first collection of poems, *Taranjjan*, is a landmark in modern Punjabi romantic poetry. He wrote extensively for the movies but his literary output remained small, though of an extremely high order.

Nazish Kaashmiri was also from Amritsar and may have worked in Bombay as a screenwriter.

Hamid Akhtar, a communist writer and journalist, knew Manto from his Bombay days. He was a leading member of the Progressive Writers' Movement.

Professor Safdar is Safdar Mir, a Marxist intellectual, who also knew Manto in Bombay. Safdar Mir worked in the People's Theatre, Bombay, a communist-linked literary and cultural enterprise. In Pakistan he taught and wrote for leading newspapers on cultural and political matters. He was a fine poet and critic as well.

What is my fault? If I sincerely acknowledged the help you had given me, was it such a bad thing to do? You have given millions to India and so India admits. You have sent free wheat to Pakistan and so Pakistan admits. I also admit that you once sent me money. In Karachi, a camel procession was organized to thank you. Leaflets were handed out saying you had done us a great favour. It is another matter that to digest your wheat, we have had to Americanize our stomachs.

What I fail to understand is why you do not put me on a stipend when you are giving millions to India and have promised military aid to Pakistan? What will people say when they hear that after giving three hundred rupees to this great short-story writer of Pakistan, you just turned your back and walked away! I feel insulted, and so should you. So what about, say, a hundred thousand dollars so that I can breathe easy?

The Aga Khan, whom you must know—because he too is a great capitalist—recently had his platinum jubilee celebrated. I also want my jubilee to be celebrated. You are my very own dear uncle and I can take these liberties with you and you alone, not with Chaudhri Muhammad Ali, the prime minister of Pakistan. Do please organize my jubilee so that I can rest in my grave in peace.

Pakistan, my Pakistan, does not neglect its artists. The trouble is that those who are more deserving than I am are far more in number. Recently, my government announced a pension in perpetuity of five hundred rupees for Khan Bahadur Abdul Rehman Chughtai.[2] The Khan Bahadur, by the grace of God, is a man of property and as such a more deserving case than myself. Similarly, a life stipend has been given to Khan Bahadur Abul Asar Hafiz Jullandhari because he is a man of means as well.

Who knows when my turn will come because I live in a government-allotted house whose rent I cannot pay.

There are other deserving cases. For instance, there is Mian Bashir Ahmed, editor of the monthly *Humayun* and former ambassador to Turkey, Syed Imtiaz Ali Taj, Sheikh Muhammad Ikram, PCS, Fazal Ahmed Karim Fazli, etc. They take precedence over me because

---

[2]Abdul Rehman Chughtai, eminent artist and classicist, who painted in the direct tradition of the great Iranian and Mughal painters. He illustrated the great Urdu poets Ghalib and Iqbal.

they do not need any stipend. In any case, what great deed have I performed that the government should ignore these gentlemen and turn to me? I am only asking because I am your nephew and I want you to organize my jubilee.[3]

I don't have long to live. I know you will be sorry to hear this but you alone are responsible for my brief stay on earth. Had you cared about my health, you would have at least sent Elizabeth Taylor to nurse me. Why are you so indifferent to me? Do you want me to die, or is it something else? It's time you shared this secret with me.

What is not secret is that communism is spreading fast in my country, Pakistan. I tell you sometimes I also want to stick a red feather in my cap and go Red. Is that not a dangerous wish? That was why I advised you to send a delegation of your pin-ups to counter the effects of the Russian goodwill troupe. The rainy season is about to arrive and we people feel very romantic this time of the year. If your delegation were to come now, it would be a capital idea.

Uncle, I have heard the disquieting news about your trade and industry going through a difficult period. You are wise but please listen to my foolish opinion for a minute. This trade and industrial crisis has hit only because you have ended the Korean war. It was a great mistake. What are you now going to do with your tanks, bombers, cannons and guns?

While it is true that you had to end the war because of world opinion, what importance can this opinion have for you when the

---

[3]Manto is being sarcastic. All those he names here were quite well off.

Mian Bashir Ahmed was a retired ambassador who belonged to an old landowning family of Lahore. Syed Imtiaz Ali Taj, playwright and occasional movie-maker, was also quite comfortable financially, while Sheikh Muhammad Ikram, a fine scholar and historian, was a senior civil servant, who enjoyed a host of privileges on account of his official position. Fazal Karim Fazli was in no need of a state stipend either.

All these men were either part of the establishment or well regarded by it. Manto was the eternal outsider and remains one to this day. Nothing has been named after him, and no posthumous honour has been bestowed on him by the state of Pakistan. Some years ago, a postage stamp was issued with his picture on it. This 'lapse' has not since been repeated by the government in any way or form. And yet Manto remains Pakistan's most widely read author and the only one whose name and work are known abroad.

entire world put together is powerless before a single hydrogen bomb! You ended the war in Korea. It was a grave error, but I don't want to labour the point. Why don't you start a war between India and Pakistan? The gains from the Korean war will be nothing compared with the profits from this one. You have your nephew's word.

Just think how beneficial this war would be! All your arms factories would begin to work round the clock. India will buy your arms and so will Pakistan. You will be in clover.

You should also continue the war in Indochina and keep assuring the world that it is a good thing, the French government and the French people be damned. Let them be against this war if they want to be. We should not care what they think. After all, it is our aim to establish peace in the world. True, uncle?

I liked what your Mr Dulles said about the Free World having only one objective: to defeat communism. This is truly the free speech of the hydrogen bomb.

The ignorant say that the western alliance should try to settle the differences that exist between various countries through peaceful means. I ask if differences have ever been resolved without the use of force. The world is full of differences and is there a better way of dealing with them than to declare that unless everyone falls in line they will be instantly destroyed!

Why don't you get Bevan of Britain to shut his mouth? He is your creature and yet he shows you his fangs. The ass is spitting poison against you. Of your Mr Dulles he says the man is unaware of modern ideas, trying as he is to browbeat the world into submission with the hydrogen bomb. What a fool!

Uncle, I really get angry when some British joker thumbs his nose at you. If you were to take my advice, Britain should be wiped off the face of the earth. This little island will only bring trouble to the world. If you don't want to do that, then at least fill in the twenty-mile-wide channel that separates it from Europe. God bless Napoleon Bonaparte and Hitler, both of whom hated this country. Had there been no Britain, there would have been no Bevan and you would not have had to suffer his nonsense.

If truth be told, Britain is going to create a lot of trouble for you in future. It will not let go of you though you would try to get rid of it. In the last war, Germany allied itself with Italy and gained nothing from it. You should learn a lesson from that. Just follow your old principle: cash and carry.

Joining Britain with the continent is one project you should start implementing as soon as you get this letter. Your engineers could do it in a month, I am sure.

I wrote to you this time because I wanted you to celebrate my jubilee because that is something I would really like.

I have been writing for twenty-five years now and you may consider it childish on my part but do please make arrangements for my jubilee.

Since my profession is writing, I should be weighed against Parker 51 fountain pens. The scales I will borrow from the timber depot of Ehsan Danish.[4] I don't know how much a fountain pen weighs. Currently, I weigh a maund and two and a half seers, but on the day of the jubilee, I should be down to a maund. If you keep putting it off, my weight may drop to zero.

It is for you to work out how many Parker 51s one would need to equal a maund. But please hurry.

All is well here, Maulana Bhashani and Mr Suhrawardy are getting healthier by the day but appear to be somewhat annoyed with you. Please send the maulana a real American rosary and Mr Suhrawardy an American camera and they should be all right.[5]

The dancing girls of Hira Mandi convey their regards through the good offices of Shorish Kaashmiri.

Your obedient nephew,

Saadat Hasan Manto

---

[4]Ehsan Danish, Urdu poet who once made a living by selling firewood.

[5]Hussein Shaheed Suhrawardy, eminent Bengali politician and former prime minister of Pakistan. He had a reputation for being fond of dancing, photography and women. Maulana Bhashani was a wily Bengali peasant leader and politician who was always viewed as a rabble rouser and power broker.

LETTER 8

Dear Uncle,
Greetings!

I am sure you have received my seventh letter, but I am still waiting for your reply. Have you made up your mind about sending a goodwill delegation over to counter the Russian cultural troupe that was recently here? You must let me know so that I can put my mind to rest. The local communists are still raving about the Russian success, but the moment they learn from me that my uncle is sending a delegation that will include girls with million-dollar legs and million-dollar looks, they will shut up. There they would be, waiting with their tongues hanging out.

You will be happy to learn that the chief minister of our province, Malik Feroz Khan Noon, has decided to take action. The other day he said in an aside that there was a need to deal with communist conspiracies. This is good news. A beginning has already been made with a police raid on the communist party office. I am writing this letter in celebration so to speak.

Our newspapers say that very soon Red arrests will get under way. The police are said to have prepared a list and, God willing, before long these troublemakers would be in the jug. I would be thrilled if the first man to be nabbed were Comrade Ferozuddin Mansoor. He suffers from asthma and I have heard that asthmatics live long. I think if he were jailed, this time around he would surely croak. Good riddance, I say. Ahmed Nadeem Qasimi would be taken in too. Mian Iftikharuddin has earned no credit by appointing him editor of his newspaper, *Imroze*. The right thing to do would have been to arrest Mian Iftikharuddin, but he is smart. When the police go to arrest him, he will walk out of his palatial home, smile and wave a stay order from the court in their faces. Recently the offices of the *Pakistan Times* and *Imroze* were going to be sealed for non-payment of rent but it didn't happen. Like a conjurer, Mian Iftikharuddin produced a stay order from his bag and flashed it before the disbelieving eyes of the police. One thing is certain. Ahmed Nadeem Qasimi is guilty and must be punished. The man keeps making fun of you in his column under the pen-name 'Panj Darya' or five rivers.[1]

I would suggest that in order to set him straight, we need five or six single American girls whom he will immediately declare to be his sisters, which will make it unnecessary to lock him up. His communism will disappear like a donkey's horns. As soon as they start picking up the Reds, I will let you know. Please make a note of all the services I am performing for you. If you are in a good mood, don't forget to extend a loan of three hundred rupees to me as the last sum of money you sent me has been already spent. And in any case, that act of kindness was two years ago.

I investigated the disappearance of my sixth letter to you and, as I had suspected, it turned out that our communist friends were behind this trick. It was the handiwork of Ahmed Rahi, the same man who wrote that book *Taranjjan* and whom our government gave a prize of five hundred rupees for doing so. He has written some lovely poems in the Punjabi language but what you don't know is that this Ahmed Rahi is a dangerous communist. While other members of the party drink tea out of broken cups in their office, he is a secret beer drinker. As a result, he is getting fat. He is my friend, which was why I asked him to mail that letter, but being a communist, he passed on my letter to the party. I am not as angry as I should be, nor do I have much money these days, but some day I will make him drink so much that he will roll over.

One day the fellow says to me that I should drop my Uncle Sam and start a correspondence with Malenkov who (he said) can also be an uncle. I told him that while it might be so, he could never love me or I him. After all, I know how he treats his real nephews who are utterly devoted to him and who serve him despite their poverty and the rags in which they go about. All they get for it is an occasional letter with a red seal. British uncles were far better than

---

[1]Mian Iftikharuddin founded a group of left-leaning newspapers in Lahore: *The Pakistan Times* in English and *Imroze* in Urdu, as well as the weekly Urdu journal *Lail-au-Nihar*. The Progressive Papers Ltd, as the group was known, were taken over by Ayub Khan and placed under the so-called National Press Trust, a government front group banded together by the regime. Ahmed Nadeem Qasimi was editor of *Imroze* for a while. He also used to write a light column under the pen-name Punj Darya or five rivers.

this Russian uncle and although all that they used to confer by way of reward was titles like 'Sir', 'Khan Bahadur' and 'Khan Sahib', Malenkov doesn't even do that. To convince me, he would have to find a title, even a minor one, for his most faithful nephew, Abdulla Malik. Just think how convenient it would be for him to be sent to jail where he can write his books.

You must remember that I am your greatest devotee. You had me for life when you sent me three hundred rupees. If you were to send me another, I would become your slave for life, unless God who is greater than you makes some arrangement for me whereby I am paid a monthly stipend of five to six hundred rupees. And if He were to arrange for me to wed an Eve, I may no longer be able to keep my promise to you. I hope you admire my frankness. The thing is I dare not open my mouth in the presence of God and Eve.

We are playing host to one prince after another these days. The first one to come was the Shah of Iran, then the Shah of Iraq, then Prince Aly Khan (the former husband of your Rita Hayworth), the Maharaja of Jaipur and currently we have Shah Saud, the King of Saudi Arabia. Let me give you an eyewitness account of his visit. He arrived by air at Karachi with twenty-five of his princes in tow. He was received with full honours. He has fathered many other princes besides, so it is anybody's guess why they are not accompanying him. Perhaps that would have needed two or three additional aircraft. Or maybe they are too young and would rather be in their mothers' laps than in an aircraft. Makes sense because children raised on the milk of their mothers and she-camels cannot be expected to care much for dry Glaxo and Cow & Gate milk.

Uncle, just think about it. Shah Saud has come with twenty-five sons. Only God knows how many daughters he has. May God protect them and him. Do you have anyone in your land of seven freedoms who could boast of so many children? Uncle, this is one of the blessings of our religion of Islam and it's God's bounty. In my humble opinion, you should immediately declare Islam as your state religion. This will result in several benefits. Every married man will be able to take four wives and if, after the exercise of the utmost care, one woman gives birth to four children, each family will produce sixteen children as living proof of the husband's virility and the wife's fertility. Just think of the difference these numbers could make at the time of war. You are a man of experience so I need not labour the point.

I come from Amritsar, which, thanks to Mr Radcliffe, is now part of India.[2] There lived one Hakim Abu Turab who married ten times and had innumerable children. His last marriage was contracted at the age of ninety when his eldest son was seventy-five and the youngest from his latest wife was only two. He died at the age of hundred and twelve in Lahore as a refugee. Some poet versified his year of death with the line: Alas! those buds which withered before flowering!

And this too was on account of the blessings of God and his approved religion of Islam. And if men in your country find it difficult to deal with four wives, you can certainly seek advice and help from Shah Saud by inviting him over. You are a friend of his and I am told you were rather close to his father, whom you had presented with a cavalcade of cars for his harem.

I am sure Shah Saud will keep no secrets from you. Every country, except India and Russia, is taking great interest in our Pakistan these days and this is all due to the kind hand of friendship you have extended to us. We Pakistanis are always prepared to lay down our lives for Islam. There was a time when we were the greatest fans of Mustafa Kamal Pasha and Anwar Pasha in Turkey. When news of Anwar Pasha's death came, we were in mourning. But when we learnt that he was alive after all, we celebrated by decorating our homes with lights. Mustafa Kamal and Anwar were sworn enemies but we knew nothing about it. The Turks had no interest in Indian Muslims. For them, we may as well not have existed. We knew nothing about that either. We just loved them thinking that they were our Islamic brothers. What simpletons we are! We even love a certain scented hair oil because it is sold under the slogan 'prepared by Islamic brothers'. When we rub it into our scalps we feel ourselves in seventh heaven, compared to which the pleasures of paradise pale into insignificance. We are naive but we are good people. May God keep us the way we are until Judgement Day.

I was talking about Shah Saud's visit but became sentimental and started singing Islam's praises. The fact is that we have to praise

---

[2]Sir Cyril Radcliffe, a British judge who was assigned to draw the dividing line in the Punjab (and Bengal) at the time of Independence. The line, drawn arbitrarily and, according to the Pakistani perception, supported by later research, dishonestly, favoured India against Pakistan.

Islam. Is there a Hindu, Christian or Buddhist who can match our performance? That was why I advised you to declare Islam as the state religion of the United States so that you no longer have any need to conquer Japan and cause out-of-wedlock children to be born. Uncle, surely you cannot approve of illegitimate children. I am a Muslim and I swear by God and his Prophet that I hate it from the bottom of my heart. If you must produce children, then Islam offers a simple way of doing so. Get married and procreate to your heart's content. I would say even you should take four wives. If auntie is alive, then take three wives. All you have to do is embrace Islam.

In Pakistan, you can get married to Ishrat Jehan Bibbo as she has experience of several husbands.[3] But to come back to Shah Saud, he has a charming personality. The first thing he did after stepping down from the plane was to embrace Governor General Ghulam Muhammad who comes from Mochi Gate, Lahore. It was a heart-warming spectacle of two Muslim brothers embracing each other. The Muslims of Karachi went hoarse raising slogans at the sight. There were public meetings and marches. There were banquets. In line with centuries-old Islamic tradition, Shah Saud had brought along a box full of gold, which the porters of Karachi had a hard time lifting. He sold this gold in Karachi and gifted one million rupees to Pakistan for the building of a refugee colony to be called Saudabad. Allah be praised.

It has also been rumoured that as further demonstration of his love for Pakistan, Shah Saud wants two of his sons to be married in Pakistan. One hears that in Karachi, Begum Shahnawaz, after having failed to find suitable matches for the princes, phoned Begum Bashir Ahmed in Lahore because, after all, Lahore is Lahore and should have no shortage of 'prince-worthy' girls. One also hears that Begum Bashir Ahmed has co-opted the services of Begum G.A. Khan and Begum Salma Tassaduq Hussain to act as the traditional

[3]Ishrat Jahan, a famous film star who took the screen name Bibbo. She came to Pakistan after Independence but by then she was no longer young enough to play the female lead in Pakistan's fledgling movie industry's presentations, whose number was small. Bibbo had quite a reputation as a 'foxy lady', which is what Manto is really referring to in his light-hearted way.

matchmakers, a function barbers' wives used to perform.[4] They are said to have approached some highly placed families but unfortunately have had no luck. One is told that girls from our upper classes do not like camels. Personally, I think they are making a mistake. Before Pakistan came into being, Saudi Arabia and Indian Muslims had a special link. A young woman from the families of Maulana Daud Ghaznavi and Maulana Ismail Ghaznavi had been admitted to the harem of Shah Saud's father, Abdel Aziz Ibne Saud. You may know that Maulana Ismail Ghaznavi performed Haj thirty-seven times as a result of that whereas one Haj would have sufficed.[5]

Begum Bashir, Begum G.A. Khan and Begum Tassaduq have been unsuccessful in their quest, but I am sure they will in the end find the nightingale they seek. In this Pakistan of ours, two girls will be discovered who would be fit enough for the princes of Hidjaz. In one of my letters, I had written to you something about our ladies of advancing years who wear the briefest of blouses so that they can display their midriffs. This seems to have angered Dr Muhammad Baqar, head of the Persian department of our university, who heaped quite a few civilized words of abuse on me. He said I was to be condemned because I had insulted the womanhood of Pakistan. The devil take him! All I had said was that older women ought not to wear clothes that are too young for them. I am sure were Dr Baqar to read this letter, he would again accuse me of insulting our women. If truth be told, we are basically simple and naive. As for our women, they are like weathercocks; they go in the direction of the prevailing wind.

When the Shah of Iran came here, high-society girls used every trick in the book to look enticing because the Shah was single at the time. He had divorced Fauzia. However, he showed little interest in our women, returned to Iran and married Surriyya Isfandyar. He was followed by Prince Aly who too was single. Our high-society

---

[4]Begum Shahnawaz, Begum G.A. Khan, Begum Bashir Ahmed and Begum Salma Tassaduq Hussain, all came from privileged backgrounds, but they worked hard for many good causes. In the bargain, they were often the butt of jokes, which would be considered sexist today.

[5]Maulana Daud Ghaznavi and Maulana Ismail Ghaznavi from the Ghaznavi family of Lahore, who were well known and well respected for their Islamic learning.

girls left no stone unturned to attract his attention but he only threw cold water over their hopes when he began romancing that Hollywood actress of yours, Gene Tiereney. May God protect your country of seven freedoms! Then came the Shah of Iraq but our single high-society girls were disappointed in him because he was too young. One remarked that he was just a boy and should be out playing. She couldn't understand why he had been burdened with affairs of the state. One older woman, whose midriff was not so exposed, took one look at the Shah and observed, 'He won't be interested in older people; go get someone his age for him.'

And now we have Shah Saud with his twenty-two or twenty-five princes. There was a banquet for him at Government House, Lahore, which was attended by all the marriageable and non-marriageable high-society girls. Smoking was not allowed. The next day, the two dozen princes went shopping in Anarkali and bought hundreds of Pakistani shoes as a mark of goodwill. They will now walk on the sands of the deserts of Arabia in those shoes and leave permanent footprints behind. I am leaving this letter incomplete because I have to go to my publisher to get royalty for my new book. He has been promising it for the last ten days so perhaps today he will pay me ten rupees. If he does, I will mail this letter right away. A flying kiss to Gene Tiereney.

Your obedient nephew,

Saadat Hasan Manto

NINTH AND LAST LETTER TO UNCLE SAM

31 Laxmi Mansion,
Hall Road, Lahore
26 April 1954

Dear Uncle,
All I remember is that my last letter was sort of incomplete. If I can now recall what I wrote, I promise to complete it. My memory has suffered because of drinking local hooch. While drinking is banned

in the Punjab, anyone can obtain a drinking permit by spending twelve rupees and two annas. Five of these rupees go to the doctor as his fee because he has to certify that if the applicant fails to get a drink he will croak.

I remember many years ago you too banned drinking in your country but without bothering with permits. The consequences were not the most salutary. Prohibition created gangsters and bootleggers who almost ran a parallel government. In the end, the law had to be amended and drinking made legal once again.

We are going to have no such luck because our government wants to keep both the mullahs and those who drink happy. It is most interesting that many drinking types are mullahs and many mullahs have a weakness for alcohol. Whatever the case, liquor will continue to sell, so you don't have to worry about me, at least on this score. I may add that you are hard-hearted because despite writing to you several times about the abominable quality of liquor here, it has never occurred to you to send your nephew some decent whisky so that he could be safe from the harmful effects of what he is obliged to drink here. However, I will never raise this subject again. You can send me to hell as long as you continue to give military aid to Pakistan. That will keep me happy.

I am glad you don't use my letters to light your pipe, but read them carefully and pay attention to my advice. Let me now quietly, very quietly advise you so that nobody ever finds out, to come to the aid of the newspaper *Zamindar*. Its cross-eyed and game-legged editor doesn't have brains enough to know how to take your money. Even the founder's son Maulana Akhtar Ali Khan, who has inherited the title Maulana from his father, is a rank amateur when it comes to such things. For instance, recently when Mir Nur Ahmed, former Director of Public Relations, Government of the Punjab, slipped him several thousand rupees so that he would keep his mouth shut, the maulana went right out and bought himself a new American car. He even held a party to announce the acquisition. This was very foolish. He is in jail these days and I pray to God that he stays there so that we do not witness more instances of his stupidity. I am surprised that his son who is managing editor of *Zamindar* these days is also an ass, despite having been given an education.[1]

---

[1]*Zamindar* was founded by the redoubtable journalist, poet and political agitator and activist Maulana Zafar Ali Khan. He was a fiery supporter of

Recently, this Taimur the Lame of this newspaper took it upon himself to get me financial help. Had he not had a game leg, he would have been the Dr Muhammad Mussadaq of Pakistan. When he writes, he takes the entire wide world's burden upon himself. I am sure news has reached you that when Dr Mussadaq's appeal was being heard by Iran's highest court, Zahurul Hassan Dar, who has no peer when it comes to mindless hack writing, said that he did not wish to make any comment because he had full faith in a magic ring given to him by his wife. Once when he was hauled up in a military court, he challenged the prosecution lawyer to a wrestling match. Later he threatened to go on a hunger strike, which, he promised everyone, would kill him within two days. But it did not happen and he is still alive, though he keeps falling unconscious from time to time.

This Pakistani Dr Mussadaq or Zahurul Hassan Dar may not be a doctor but he keeps falling unconscious every now and then, just like him. When that happens, Ali Sufiyan Afaqi and Mansur Ali Khan give him smelling salts (a secret Maulana Zafar Ali Khan recipe) so that he can come to and write the day's diary for the newspaper.[2] Further, Dar is a dyed-in-the-wool journalist and pays no attention to abuse, even abundant abuse. Maybe his secret lies in that magic ring given to him, I very much suspect, by an admirer when he was a boy.

Please send some money to *Zamindar*, but through me, so that I may give some of it to Zahurul Hassan Dar, who is trying to act as my minder, though a well-intentioned one. I normally want fifty rupees a piece, but when he asked me to write one for one of his

---

Muslim causes before Independence. The newspaper was unable to define its role after Independence. Zafar Ali Khan, by now ageing and in poor health, handed over the newspaper to his son Maulana Akhtar Ali Khan. Manto had contempt for the entire lot, including the man he uncharitably calls 'cross-eyed and game-legged'. That man who actually edited the paper was Zahurul Hassan Dar, who belonged to Manto's birthplace, Amrtisar. He was a controvery-loving journalist and pamphleteer. Why Manto disliked him is not clear. Mir Nur Ahmed was a government information official who had a lot of experience in dealing with the press, sometimes using questionable methods, including handouts, to keep it in line.

[2]Mansur Ali Khan was the son of Maulana Akhtar Ali Khan and the grandson of Maulana Zafar Ali Khan.

special numbers, he made it clear that I would be paid no more than twenty rupees. And since he was sure, he said, that I would spend the money on drink, he informed me that he would personally present the cheque. I suppose he wanted to ensure that my family and I remain in his everlasting debt. Perhaps I should be grateful to him for his interest in a wretch like me.

Of all the newspapers here, *Zamindar* is the only one that you can buy with your dollars any time you wish. If Akhtar Ali Khan is released, I would try to make sure that Zahurul Hassan remains the editor. He is not a bad sort really.

If you can, using your influence, get Mir Nur Ahmed reappointed Director of Public Relations. That would be nice because M. Sarfraz is simply not capable of distributing large sums of money among newspapers.[3] It will be better if you send the cash to me and I will hand it out. That way, I will be able not only to impress the *Zamindar* editor but also make sure that your propaganda is carried out effectively under my supervision.

By the way, the journals that your people publish here are all sold in the junk market, which means that the junk dealers are in your debt. Since these journals are printed on good paper, they are excellent for making shopping bags. Do continue the good work because there is a shortage of paper in this country. You may also like to consider buying some of our newspapers that fetch little in the junk market, being printed on poor paper.

Uncle, I have heard disquieting news, though that could well be a rumour circulated by communists. Newspapers have reported that unnatural offences are on the rise in your country. What has happened to those girls with the million-dollar legs? What a shame! But in case the reports are true, please send all your Oscar Wildes here and they would be adequately provided for. We would like to do whatever is asked of us because, after all, you are giving us military aid.

It seems to me that Comrade Sibte Hasan has read that letter I wrote to you and which Ahmed Rahi made off with. He tells me

---

[3]Muhammad Sarfraz, a senior government information official who was later to serve as the first administrator of the forcibly taken over Progressive Papers Ltd, a powerful left-leaning group of newspapers. The *Pakistan Times*, its flagship publication, had Faiz Ahmed Faiz as its first editor.

quite blatantly that whether I admit it or not, I too am a communist. Uncle, I swear to you by your seven freedoms and your dollars that I never was a communist and am not one now. This is all Sibte Hasan's mischief, a very Red mischief aimed at creating a misunderstanding between us. You know very well that I am your most obedient nephew and indebted to you in more ways than one. It is another matter that the three hundred rupees you once sent me were all spent on Gymkhana whisky whose 'qualities' I have enumerated in my earlier letters. I bought no salt with the money so I can claim that I have not eaten your salt, as the phrase goes. You see, the doctors have advised me not to eat salt, but as soon as I am allowed to, I would let you know and you could then send me some pure American salt so that I remain in your everlasting debt.

Let me reassure you once again that I am not a communist. I may become a Qadiani[4] but I will never become a communist because these johnnies have only empty words to hand out, never any money. Although the Qadianis are tight-fisted, being a Pakistani, I do not want any bad blood between the communists and the Qadianis. I do know that after you detonate the hydrogen bomb you would need the services of a prophet which only Mirza Bashiruddin Mahmood can provide.

These days the orthodox Muslims here seem to be much worked up about Sir Zafrulla Khan and are demanding his removal as foreign minister because he is a Qadiani. Personally, I have nothing against him and I do know that he can be most useful to you. It is my advice that you should get him over and I can assure you that he would effectively deal with your country's sexual perversion.

The Iraqi government has announced today that you have agreed to extend military assistance to Islamic countries. It is also said that the assistance will be without conditions. Uncle, were you around, I would have kissed your feet and prayed for your everlasting life. With your heart beginning to soften towards Islamic countries, it is

---

[4]Qadiani. Members of the Jamaat-i-Ahmediyya were and are popularly known as Qadianis (an appellation they resent) since the founder of the movement came from Qadian, now in East Punjab. There was always bad blood between the sect and the mainstream Muslims, which erupted in serious rioting in 1953 all over Punjab. The Qadianis were declared non-Muslims, ironically enough, by the secular-minded government of Zulfikar Ali Bhutto.

only a matter of time before you embrace Islam. Earlier, I have enumerated to you the various virtues of Islam. If auntie is alive, you can still take three wives and I have already persuaded the actress Ishrat Jahan Bibbo to become your wife, but for that to happen you would have to be a bachelor. She is a highly experienced woman in these matters and is not averse to a drink either. Currently, she is married but if I ask her she would happily get rid of her fifth or sixth husband.

Uncle I have heard that your Rita Hayworth is going to Russia. Please try to stop her. When she married Sir Aga Khan's son Prince Aly Khan, I lost no sleep over it but I wouldn't want her in Russia. It is time you pulled this naughty woman's ears. I heard this from Comrade Sibte Hasan who appeared to be proud of what he was telling me. If she does end up going, I would feel belittled, and so would you. Is this mercurial actress going there to marry Malenkov? If that is the case, so then obviously it is one of your political moves. If it is not your move, then her going is both humiliating and dangerous.

Today's newspapers report that Rita is facing charges because of her treatment of Yasmin and another daughter from an earlier marriage (which husband I know not). Both these girls are said to be under the protection of the court and Rita is in Western Florida where the government is busy trying to extern her fourth husband. What is the real story? I asked Ahmed Rahi but he parried my query. However, I am smart enough to gather that it is all a Russian conspiracy. I can't understand your silence on the issue.

My advice would be that you hang Rita's fourth husband who is a musician or sentence him to a life term on the charge that he has stolen nuclear secrets for the Russians. And you may send Rita here forthwith and ask her to entice and marry our Mr Suhrawardy. She may later marry Maulana Bhashani and then, by the grace of God, Sher-e-Bengal Chaudhry Fazle Haq, who is still alive and is the chief minister of East Pakistan. After she has married these three Mr Bigs and got herself duly divorced from them, she can turn to the former prime minister Khwaja Nazimuddin. If I remain alive, she will find me at her service as well, but on the condition that you continue to keep me in funds.

According to your newspapers, our UN ambassador Professor A.S. Bokhari is being offered the post of UN information chief. I had heard that after the easing out of Sir Zafrulla, Bokhari was to be made foreign minister but it seems you want to keep him there permanently.[5]

I know Bokhari well and he is very fond of me, something he makes evident every five years or so. You would only know him as an orator but I know him as a humorist. His essay on Lahore's geography confirms what our elders have always told us: Lahore is Lahore and Bokhari is Bokhari. Please ask him to write a piece called 'America's Geography' so that the whole world would come to know where you are located. It should also be translated into Russian and sent to Uncle Malenkov.

I also write well, but since you know me, the old adage about familiarity breeding contempt once again comes true. Just get me over to your country once and keep me there for two or three months so that I can see for myself what the land of seven freedoms is like. I can assure you that when you read my impressions, you will thrust dollar bills in my mouth.

Japanese scientists have recently discovered that the hydrogen bomb can affect the weather. Recently, you detonated bombs over Marshall Islands that have affected the weather over Japan and though it is the end of April, it is still cold there. I can't understand why these Japs don't like cold weather. We Pakistanis love it. Also, why don't you lob a hydrogen bomb at India so that I can be spared the coming summer, which I hate.

Please ask Rita if she would choose me as her first husband in Pakistan. I will eagerly be waiting for your response.

Your obedient nephew,

Saadat Hasan Manto

---

[5]Bokhari. Professor Ahmed Shah Bokhari, renowned educationist, broadcaster, literary figure and diplomat, whose wit and knowledge of literature were legendary. He served as Pakistan's first ambassador to the United Nations and as undersecretary for public affairs of the United Nations. He was the author of *Patras ke Muzameen*, a classic collection of light and humorous essays.

MANTO ON MANTO

TO MY READERS

Do not think my love will not last
As the dawn is inseparable from the sun
So is my love, which I'll wear
Like a badge on my coffin

—Ghalib

I feel like talking to those who read me, setting aside formalities one observes in introductions and prefaces. Although in my stories, dramas and semi-fictional articles there are things that are strictly personal, to you it is fiction because that is my chosen medium.

My heart is steeped in sorrow today. A strange melancholy has descended on me. Four and a half years ago, when I said goodbye to my second home Bombay, I had felt the same way. I was sad at leaving a place where I had spent so many days of a hard-working life. That piece of land had offered shelter to a family reject and it had said to me, 'You can be happy here on two pennies a day or on ten thousand rupees a day, if you wish. You can also spend your life here as the unhappiest man in the world. You can do what you want. No one will find fault with you. Nor will anyone subject you to moralizing. You alone will have to accomplish the most difficult of tasks and you alone will have to make every important decision of your life. You may live on the footpath or in a magnificent palace; it will not matter in the least to me. You may leave or you may stay, it will make no difference to me. I am where I am and that is where I will remain.'

After living there for twelve years I find myself in Pakistan. I am here because of what I learnt there. If I leave and go elsewhere, I will remain the way I am. I am a walking, talking Bombay. Wherever I happen to be, that is where I will make a world of my own.

I was sad after I left Bombay. I had many friends there, friends of whose friendship I am proud. That was where I got married, where my first child was born, where the second one began the first day of its life. I earned from a few to thousands to hundreds of thousands of rupees there. I loved that city then and I love it today.

I rebelled against the great upheaval that the partition of the country caused. I still feel the same way. However, in the end, I had to accept this monstrous reality, but I did not let myself be overwhelmed by despair. And it was in that sea of blood that I plunged myself to come up with a few pearls of regret at what human beings had done to human beings, at the labour expended by brothers to draw the last drop of blood from their brothers' veins. I gathered the tears which some men had shed because they had been unable to kill their humanity entirely. These were the pearls I brought together in my book *Siyah Haashye*.

I am a human being, the same human being who raped mankind, who indulged in killing and destruction as if that was what constituted man's natural condition. I am the same human being who put human flesh in the shop window, as if it were another item for sale. I am the same human being who attained prophethood, and I am the same human being who dipped his hands in the blood of God's messengers. I bear in my person all those weaknesses and qualities that other human beings have. I felt deeply hurt when some of my contemporaries made fun of my effort, calling me impertinent, a jokemaker, a cynic, a reactionary. A dear friend of mine even said that I had gone through the pockets of dead men and pulled out cigarette butts, rings and other objects. That friend also wrote an open letter, which he could easily have handed over to me personally. He denounced *Siyah Haashye* publicly.

I am only human and I felt angry. In retaliation for the mud that had been thrown at my face, I prepared mud that would have remained stuck on the faces of my critics for a long time, but then I felt that it would be a mistake to repeat what they had done. It is natural for human beings to return an insult with a bigger insult but if insult is answered with silence, it shows wisdom, maturity and forbearance.

I was angry, not because Mr A had misunderstood me but I was angry that Mr A had cast aspersions on me and questioned my good intentions at the instance of a degenerate, foreign-inspired movement. I had been judged on a touchstone to which the only gold was the colour Red.

I was angry. What was wrong with these people, I asked myself.

What kind of progressives were they who were only regressing? Why was this Big Red of theirs rushing headlong into Black Darkness? What was this love of labour that they professed which urged the worker to demand his wages before he had shed any sweat from his brow? How genuine was their struggle against capitalism when they only wanted to arm themselves with that same capital? Hadn't they ended up handing over their favourite weapons, the sickle and the hammer, to their opponents? Where did the modernity of their literary effort lie when they were trying to turn a poem into a machine and a machine into a poem?

I was angry at the manifestoes they issued every second day, at their long-winded resolutions, at their statements, all of which were based on material sent out by Russia's Kremlin through Bombay's Khetwari to McLeod Road, Lahore. Such and such Russian poet had said this and this! Such and such Russian story writer had issued this statement. Such and such Russian intellectual had made this wise observation. That angered me. Why did these people not talk about the land on which they lived and breathed? Had we stopped producing intellectuals that our sterility could now only be cured through Red irradiation?

I was angry that no one was listening to me. After the division of the country, it was a free-for-all. It never occurred to those who were busy grabbing abandoned homes and mills and getting hold of anything of value that after such a great change things would not be what they once were. Old tracks would be turned into highways, or they would simply disappear. No one knew anything for certain. What would be the difference between an alien government and one of our own? One couldn't even make an intelligent guess about that. What kind of environment was going to come into being, no one knew. Will ideas and emotions be allowed to develop along the right lines? What sort of relationship would there be between the state and the individual, and between the state and civil society? There was need to ponder over these questions; we should not have let foreign recipes provide us with the needed answers. Regrettably, our so-called intellectuals behaved impatiently and, blinded by ambition, they poured their raw essence into a cup where it soon started to rot because of lack of care.

The first decision made by these people who considered themselves responsible for literature was that no progressive writer would work for a government publication or write for it. I opposed this and tried to explain to them that this was a mistake, if not something utterly ridiculous. It only betrayed the doubts that the Progressive Writers' Association felt about the lack of resolve of its members. In any case, such a decision should have come from the other side, which I would have declared to be equally ridiculous because every government chooses the option that suits its particular interests.

Our government did take this ridiculous decision, but after a lapse of time, when the progressive writers had already gone hoarse declaring their boycott of the government. Radio broadcasts and the pages of official publications thus became no-go areas for the progressive writers and their ideas. Later some progressives were picked up under the all-purpose state security law. Government is but another name for folly and the series of absurd actions taken to silence the progressive writers, I do not wish to comment on. I am only sorry that Ahmed Nadeem Qasimi and Zaheer Kaashmiri, who are utterly harmless men and whose physical and mental constitution is unsuited to conspiracy, were thrown into jail for no fault of theirs. One is fond of adopting men as brothers, and adopting women as sisters. One can only guess what political significance the government was able to see in this entirely harmless exercise.

Thoughtlessly and in anger, the government sent these people to prison, which amounted to handing them over to a barber who could only disfigure them. Who would be able to tell what creation of God they would become when they are finally released! Would they emerge shaven from head to toe or would they be all hair? Would they be declared holy warriors or martyred leaders? Or would they sell fake herbal cures to passers-by at street corners? Would they vow never to write poetry or pen stories or would they override literature like that old geezer who asked a young man to help him across the river and, once they were at the other bank, refused to get off the young man's shoulders as his thighs closed in around his neck? It is not my intention to insult anyone but had I been jailed, I would have said exactly the same—if not more—about myself because I am very sensitive.

Both the government and the Progressive Writers' Association suffer from an inferiority complex. This was a matter of regret for me in the past and it is a matter of regret for me today. I am sorry for the progressive writers who got themselves involved in politics needlessly and came up with a Kremlin-proposed potion for the patient without bothering to learn anything about his temperament or how his heart beats. The result is evident: everyone is now wailing about literature having stagnated.

My heart is full of sorrow today. Literary magazines, which represented the Progressive Writers' Association, have had to shift their ground repeatedly, as have their contributors. They have had to go back on their old statements, declarations and resolutions to come up with all kinds of excuses in an attempt to regain the cooperation of writers whom they had put on their blacklist and condemned for all times to come.

My heart is full of sorrow today when I find those who had boycotted the government going back on that decision. Why did it not occur to them that the most important struggle a man makes in his life is the struggle to feed himself. Our manliness and courage can make us attempt to reach for the stars and our imagination can make the archangel of God our captive, but no one can escape from the hidden reality of keeping the wolf from the door. There are times when one is constrained to praise a man with money who is a complete rogue and idiot because of one's need. This is the great tragedy of man, but then tragedy is another name for man.

All the anger that was in my heart has now turned into sorrow. I am sad, very sad. What I have seen and what I am now seeing is turning my sadness into despair. My present life is full of hardship. After working day and night, I barely make enough to fulfil my daily needs. The fear that keeps gnawing at me is that were I to die suddenly who will look after my wife and three minor daughters? I may be a writer of obscene stories, a sensationalist, a jokemaker, a reactionary, but I am also the husband of a wife and the father of three girls. If one of them falls ill and I have to beg from door to door so that I can get her treated, it hurts me deeply. I have friends, but they live in even more straitened circumstances than me. If I am unable to come to their help when they need it, I feel deeply hurt. If I see someone praying with his head bowed, as God is my witness, I am deeply saddened. If after my death, the doors of the state radio and libraries are thrown open to my writings, and my stories are given the same elevated status as the poetry of Iqbal, my soul will wander about restlessly. Despite my agitated mental state, I am fully satisfied with the way I have been treated so far. May God protect me from this rot, which will eat away at my bones in my grave.

My heart is full of sorrow today, because I hear those who consider themselves critics declare that literature has become stagnant, that it is in a crisis. Such pronouncements can only be compared to the absurd slogan 'Islam in danger'. Literature has a life of its own, as Islam has its innate vitality. Neither can ever become stagnant and suffer a crisis. The power of the atom was always there, even before it was discovered. And it will always live. If it is misused or not used at all, that wouldn't mean that it has weakened or that it is dead.

Literature is alive with the same vitality, the same glory that it had even before being created. It can never become stagnant or get enfeebled. What we see as literature's stagnation and enfeeblement is actually our own stagnation and enfeeblement.

To identify the reasons for the crisis that we see around us, we should look into our own minds, not at literature. This is not a difficult task. If we stray from the straight road of literature, we should not say that it is the road that has veered away from us. Politics has its own place and it is wrong to press literature into its service, exactly as it would be wrong to use the intricate web of politics to find one's way to literature.

No amount of drum-beating about Soviet literature can turn the dishonest writings that get printed in that country on hundreds of thousands of tons of paper into literature. It most certainly is not literature. Literature has never been anyone's monopoly and it never will be. It is not something that can be contracted out. Those who declare that literature has stagnated or that Islam is in danger are the very same people who used to shout from their housetops not very long ago that the progressive Writers' Association had come to literature's rescue after Partition. They claimed that progressive writers had saved literature by giving their blood to it. It is strange how literature has fallen into jeopardy almost immediately after the arrest of some members of the group.

I feel great sadness today. There was a time when I was considered a progressive, but I was then declared a reactionary. And now, once again, those who had passed the earlier judgement appear willing to admit that I am a progressive. And our government, which pronounced its own judgement over that of others, sees me as a progressive, in other words, a Red, a communist. Sometimes out of exasperation it calls me a pornographer and files a suit against me. The same government also puts out advertisements in its publications declaring Saadat Hasan Manto to be a great writer of this country, a great short-story writer, who has not let his pen rest idle even during the great crisis we recently passed through. My melancholy heart trembles that one day this indecisive government will find itself pleased with me and place a medal on my coffin, which would be a great insult to my commitment to what I believe in.

Since Partition, I have published eight books, the last one, barring two stories, entirely made up of unpublished material. The amount of time it has taken me to write them can be verified from the dates I have appended at the end of each story. I had begun to write the last story in the collection—'Mummy'—when on 16 October 1951 I learnt of Prime Minister Liaquat Ali Khan's murder, which upset me greatly. Next, my middle daughter came down with typhoid, causing me deep anxiety for several days, which is why it took me longer to complete that story.

Saadat Hasan Manto
28 October 1951

A DAY IN COURT

It was on 7 or 8 January 1948 that I arrived in Lahore from Bombay, having stopped in Karachi on my way for a few days. For three months I lived in a daze. Where was I? In Bombay, at my friend Hasan Abbas's home in Karachi or in one of Lahore's restaurants where musical evenings were being held to collect money for the Quaid-e-Azam Relief Fund?

I sat down to write but found my thoughts scattered. Despite my best efforts I could not dissociate India from Pakistan and Pakistan from India. One question repeatedly rose in my mind. Will Pakistani literature be different? If so, then how? Who would inherit what had been written in unpartitioned India? Or will that be partitioned too? Were the basic problems of Indians and Pakistanis not similar? Will Urdu disappear on that side? What form will it take in Pakistan? Will our state be a theocracy? Will allegiance to the state include the right to criticize the government? Now that we were free, will things be different from what they were under the British?

All I could see around me was confusion. Some people were happy because overnight they had become rich, but there was something hollow about this happiness, something told you it wouldn't last. Most people felt ravaged because they had come here without any possessions, having abandoned everything on the other side. Then there were the refugee camps. They had to be seen to be believed, though one heard they were in a much better state now than they were.

In the end, I gave up thinking. All day long, I would loiter around without aim or purpose, listen to others but say nothing myself. The conversations were pointless and empty, marked by raw political

---

This is an account Manto wrote in Lahore on 29 August 1950 of his day in court when he was tried on an obscenity charge for his story 'Thanda Gosht', included in this collection as 'Colder Than Ice'.

argument. However, this aimless loitering did me one good. The dust in my mind began to settle and I started writing light pieces, slowly at first, but quite rapidly after some time. I put them in a collection that was much liked when it was published. I did not feel like writing short stories for some reason. My friend Ahmed Nadeem Qasimi arrived from Peshawar, having at last tired of writing absurd and pointless stuff for Radio Pakistan. He decided to bring out a monthly literary journal from Lahore that was to be called *Naqoosh*. The first story I wrote in Pakistan was for this journal. It was called 'Thanda Gosht'. Qasimi came to see me and I handed him the manuscript. He sat in front of me in a chair and read it from end to end. Then he said apologetically, 'Manto sahib, the story is brilliant, but it is "too hot" for *Naqoosh*.' I quietly took the manuscript from his hand and promised to write something else for him.

He returned the next day. When he walked in, I was writing the last lines of 'Khol Dau' (The Return). Qasimi read the story and I could see he was moved. He published it in the third issue of *Naqoosh*, but the government did not like it as it considered it to be 'against the public peace' and *Naqoosh* was ordered closed for a period of six months. There was much comment in the press about this step, but it had no effect.

After a few days, I gave 'Thanda Gosht' to the editor of *Adab-e-Latif*. The story was calligraphed, proofread and set to appear in the next issue when, at the last moment, they developed cold feet and the magazine appeared without the story. The manuscript was returned to me. (The story was also seen by the editor of the Karachi journal *Naya Daur* but he decided not to use it.) The ban on *Naqoosh* was lifted before the six months were over. I put together some of my stories in a new collection that included both 'Khol Dau' and 'Thanda Gosht'. About this time, Arif Abdul Mateen was appointed editor of a new magazine called *Javed*. He knew about 'Thanda Gosht' and pestered me for permission to publish it. After some hesitation, I asked him to go ahead. It appeared in the March 1949 issue.

Javed was distributed in Pakistan and India through its agents and nothing happened. I was now satisfied that all was well, but I was wrong. One day I heard a rumour that the police had raided the magazine's office and removed all copies of the March issue. The government brought the matter to the attention of the Press Advisory Board, then headed by Faiz Ahmed Faiz, editor of the

Pakistan Times, who was its convener. According to Naseer Anwar who owned *Javed*, Chaudhri Muhammad Hussain[1] of the Punjab Government Press Branch held that the story was 'obscene'.

Faiz said it wasn't but Maulana Akhtar Ali Khan, editor of *Zamindar*, was not to be pacified. He said, 'Such literature will not be allowed to flourish in Pakistan.' For the benefit of F.W. Buston, editor of the *Civil and Military Gazette*, Chaudhri Muhammad Hussain produced a most amusing translation of 'Thanda Gosht' whose theme according to him was: we Muslims are so utterly without a sense of honour that even our dead daughters can be raped by Sikhs.

It was decided that the case would go to court.

After a few days, arrest warrants were issued for Naseer Anwar, Arif Abdul Mateen and myself. The police inspector assigned to arrest us turned out to be a very nice man by the name of Chaudhry Khuda Bux. He hovered around my house for a couple of days but I was always out. One day, he finally found me and said politely, 'Please come to the Civil Lines police station with a friend who can stand bail for you.' He was different from the policemen I had dealt with before.

I went to the police station in the morning with my friend Sheikh Salim who stood my bail. Stage one was over. After a few days, the court issued my summons and a date was set for the hearing. All three of us—Naseer, Arif and I—arrived at the district courts to which I was no stranger as I had appeared there three times in the past on identical charges.

Our counsel, Tassaduq Hussain Khalid, arrived and all of us marched into the court of Mian A.M. Saeed, PCS, Magistrate First Class. At one time, he was a captain in the army, but the gun had been taken away from him and replaced with the scales of justice. As we filed in, he did not look at us but spoke to our counsel. Our bails were confirmed, a new date set and we bowed to him before leaving the court. Arif Abdul Mateen was very nervous. How I wish a member of his communist party had seen him in the state he was in.

We appeared two or three more times and every time the hearing was adjourned. The weather had become unbearably hot but we

---

[1]One of Manto's old torturers who was responsible for at least three of his prosecutions before Independence

had no option but to hang around the court waiting for our names to be called. We were afraid that if we were called and found absent or missing the wrath of the magistrate would descend on us. The counsel suggested to me that we should apply for transfer of the case citing these grounds, but I said to him, 'Forget it, do you think they will serve us sweetmeats in the next court? Let the thing remain where it is.'

I was charged under Section 292 of the Criminal Procedure Code of the Government of India. We were told to submit a list of defence witnesses that we had already prepared with thirty-two names. The magistrate was angry and said, 'I cannot permit this crowd.' When we argued that every witness was important in his own way, he tried to laugh it off. One of the witnesses we had named was Mumtaz Shireen. When the magistrate read her name, he asked sarcastically, 'Who is this Mumtaz Shanti?' Some of the court attendants snickered at this 'joke' but we remained sullen and silent.[2]

After much argument, he agreed to admit fourteen witnesses. Summons were issued. I did not meet any of the witnesses because I wanted each one to express his honest opinion about the story so that I could judge my own position fairly. Those summoned had to drop whatever they were doing, appear early in the morning and hang around till such time as their names were called. I felt bad because these people were being treated as if they too were guilty of wrongdoing.

Sheikh Salim was in a state. He was used to having a drink in his hand from the moment he rose till he went to bed. Now he had nothing to do but yawn all day. In the end, he decided that he was not going to stand this torture any longer and began to come armed with a small bottle of whisky tucked in his pocket. He would take a swig from it from time to time. He had absolutely nothing to do with literature and would ask others, 'What is this obscenity bit? I haven't read Manto's story but it cannot be obscene because Manto is an artist.'

The first three witnesses—Abid Ali Abid, Professor Ahmed Saeed of Dyal Singh College, Lahore, and Khalifa Abdul Hakim—appeared one after the other during one hearing and since the magistrate had to take down their lengthy statements in long hand, he was in a

[2]Mumtaz Shireen was the famous writer and the other woman, a famous actress of her time.

temper. More than once, he said, 'I am a magistrate, not a scribe.'

At one point, the magistrate noticed a tin of cigarettes in my hand. He was furious. 'This is not your private home; this is a court of law.' When I said as humbly as I could, 'But, sir, I am not smoking,' he screamed, 'Keep quiet and put that tin into your pocket.' As soon as I had done that, he picked up his own tin of cigarettes where it lay on his table, pulled out a cigarette and began to smoke while I watched from the dock.

At the next hearing, Tassaduq Hussain Khalid did not appear and we were given an adjournment. He did not appear at the next hearing either because his son was said to be returning from England that day and he had to go to Karachi to receive him. We were in trouble. I asked the magistrate to give us another date as we were without a counsel, but he refused and the hearing got under way.

I come from a family of lawyers and judges and decided to plead my own case. Dr Saeedullah, the psychologist, appeared as a witness and I helped him record his statement but the magistrate kept interrupting us repeatedly. 'You can't say this, you can't say that . . .' I ignored him. Dr Saeedullah was barely halfway through when four smartly turned out young lawyer walked into the court. One of them whispered in my ear, 'Manto sahib, can we defend you?' 'Yes, you can,' I replied. When the lawyer who had a finely trimmed moustache took my place, the magistrate said, 'Who are you?' The young man smiled. 'I am his lawyer, am I not, Manto sahib?' I nodded and the proceedings were resumed. The magistrate did not like it at all and asked after some time, addressing the four lawyers,[3] 'Why are all of you butting in?' 'Because we are representing the accused, are we not, Manto sahib?' they asked. I nodded.

The four lawyers later told me that they had heard in the bar room of the Lahore High Court that Manto was conducting his defence himself and they had rushed out to help me. When I thanked them, Sheikh Khurshid Ahmed said, 'No need to thank us, but we

---

[3]The four young lawyers were Sheikh Khurshid Ahmed, later to become Pakistan's law minister; Mazhar-ul-Haq, later judge of the Lahore High Court; Sardar Muhammad Iqbal, later chief justice of the Lahore High Court; and Ijaz Muhammad Khan. The witnesses were Faiz Ahmed Faiz, the famous poet, Sufi Ghulam Mustafa Tabussum and Dr I. Latif, both eminent professors of Persian and psychology.

do deserve some praise because neither Sardar Iqbal nor I have read the story.'

After seven defence witnesses had been examined, Sheikh Khurshid applied for permission to summon the rest but was refused. Instead, four prosecution witnesses were produced. They were Maulana Tajwar Najibabadi, Shorish Kaashmiri, Abu Saeed Bazmi and Dr Muhammad Din Taseer.[4] With that the proceedings stood concluded and we were told that the court would announce the judgement on 16 January 1950, although we had heard Mian A.M. Saeed pronounce the judgement several times during the hearings. Khurshid was confident that it could be no worse than a fine. The last statement to be recorded was mine, after which the magistrate was pleased to observe, 'This statement in itself is enough to convict the accused.'

On 16 January, Sheikh Salim began to drink first thing in the morning, and heavily too, because he had a bad feeling about what lay in store. Naseer Anwar was indifferent as was his style, but Arif Abdul Mateen was as dry-mouthed as he had been on the first day. I arrived at the court with five hundred rupees in my pocket. Sheikh Salim was already there and feeling somewhat fortified with a half bottle of whisky in his pocket. He looked restless though and kept saying, 'Manto sahib, there's nothing to worry; it is all going to turn out all right in the end.' I merely smiled.

The magistrate arrived in court but appeared to give no indication that he was going to deliver the judgement any time soon. We waited outside, drinking water and waiting to be called in. Someone whispered in my ear that the judgement was ready but the magistrate wanted to make some last-minute changes. Someone else reported that the magistrate hadn't looked at any case since morning and was sitting in his chamber. One person said the man looked on edge. In short, there were all kinds of stories.

Then somebody brought the news that one of the sentences in the judgement read '. . . and sentence him to undergo . . .' written against my name. He said the others would be merely fined. I wondered how long the sentence would be. One month, two, or

[4]The first was a noted conservative scholar, while the second and third witnesses were well-known journalists with right-wing views. Dr Taseer was Faiz's brother-in-law and principal of the famous Islamia College, Lahore.

just a few days? When I talked to Sheikh Khurshid, who had already prepared all necessary papers in case a bail application had to be placed before the court, he said, 'Don't you worry, it can be no more than ten to twelve days but of course he could always refuse to accept the bail application.'

I told Sheikh Salim what Khurshid had said and that really upset him but he recovered soon to announce, 'Not a thing to worry about. I will come to the jail in a taxi, money can do anything. You will have no problem in case you are sent in. I know how to deal with these things. Tell you what, take a large drink, here you are.'

'Not now,' I said, 'but in the evening.' 'I will get it for you in the jail too,' Sheikh Salim promised as I began to laugh. At one o'clock we bought food from a street vendor and ate while we sat on the grass in front of Government College. Sheikh Salim was now drinking without a break and coming up with the most novel schemes of how he would take care of me in jail. Mushtaq Ahmed, a friend of mine, had brought along a rich friend of his by the name of Sharif, who was to stand bail for me if it came to that. We were all bored and we were all waiting. Sheikh Salim was getting emotional about the fact that someone else had been asked to be around to stand bail when he, Sheikh Salim, was there. He was also worried that in case I was sent to jail, the entire evening would be ruined.

At 5.30 p.m. there was a spurt of activity and we filed into court, led by Sheikh Khurshid. There sat Mian A.M. Saeed, holding a pen between his teeth. Sheikh Khurshid looked worried and I felt my heart pounding. Sheikh Salim's face had gone pale and Arif was running his tongue over his parched lips. Naseer Anwar looked utterly unconcerned but that was the way he was. There were press reporters present, I noticed. The magistrate shuffled through his papers, cleared his throat, retrieved the pen from between his teeth, dipped it into an inkpot, scribbled a word here and a word there and announced calmly that Saadat Hasan Manto had been sentenced to three months' rigorous imprisonment and a fine of three hundred rupees or another twenty-one days in jail if he failed to pay. The other two were fined three hundred rupees each or twenty-one days in jail in case they failed to pay.

I stepped forward to pay the fine as Sheikh Khurshid placed my bail application in front of the magistrate, who said, 'If I accept this application, then the entire purpose of the sentencing is lost.'

Sheikh Khurshid argued that in case my appeal in a higher court was successful, how would I ever be compensated for the time I was being told to spend in prison. Finally, he agreed to take the bail but with the utmost reluctance.

There was the question of Naseer Anwar's fine as he did not have any money. Sheikh Salim, who was roaring drunk by now, stepped forward and stated, 'I stand bail for him.' My heart began to beat faster as I was afraid that if the magistrate so much as suspected that Salim was drunk, he would throw him into the clinker. Who would bail him out then? Since I did not want to watch what I thought was inevitable, I walked out of the courtroom. After some time, Sheikh Salim appeared, walking unsteadily. He lumbered forward, threw his arms around me and broke down. 'God has saved my brother,' he wailed. Then he pulled out the bottle from his pocket, drank what was left of it and declared, 'Let's get out of here before the liquor stores pull their shutters down.'

On 28 January 1950, I filed an appeal against the judgement in the court of Mehrul Haq, sessions judge, Lahore. He transferred the case to the additional sessions judge, P.N. Joshua, on the ground that he knew my family and many of its members, being a native of Amritsar like me. Mr Joshua sent the file back because he said he did not know Urdu well enough. In the end, the appeal landed in the court of Enayatullah Khan, additional sessions judge, where we appeared. The first thing he said to our counsel was that since it was the first such case he was hearing, he would like to study it in greater detail and, therefore, was putting off the hearing for a month.

My counsel, Sheikh Khurshid, was happy because he would have time to prepare himself when the case was heard on 10 July, but he was uneasy about the judge. 'He is the wrong type. He is narrow-minded and he has a beard. He also fasts and the rest of it.' I told him that if we lost, we would go to the high court. The day of the hearing arrived and I felt anxious. At home, everyone was praying for success. The judge had set aside four hours for arguments but I was afraid he would be hostile like Mian A.M. Saeed. We presented ourselves at the court first thing in the morning and heard the judge tell my counsel, Sheikh Khurshid, 'I am sorry but you will have to wait for about half an hour as there are a few small things I need to sort out.'

We left the courtroom. Arif was very quiet. Khurshid had brought along a large number of thick law books and was looking through the references he had marked. Naseer Anwar had spread his handkerchief on the grass and was sitting on it contentedly humming a Kashmiri song perhaps. We were called in about forty-five minutes later. We entered the courtroom and bowed to the judge. He acknowledged it with a slight movement of his head. We were walking towards the corner reserved for the appellants when he said in a low voice, 'Kindly be seated.' First I thought he was addressing someone else but was pleasantly surprised when I realized that he had meant us. Before the arguments began, he said, 'I have studied the case with great care and you should be rest assured that there would be no difficulties. I have looked at the subordinate court's opinion and the evidence. I have also read the story "Thanda Gosht" with the utmost attention.'

After about half an hour of intricate legal formalities and arguments, the judge smiled and said, 'If I sentence Saadat Hasan Manto, he will go around telling everyone that he was sentenced by a man with a beard.' Then he said a few things about the judgement under appeal and stopped abruptly to ask if we had paid the fines. When we said we had, he announced, 'You are all acquitted and your fines will be refunded.'

MANTO ON MANTO

A great deal has been said and written about Manto up till now, little of it in his favour and much of it against him. No one in his right mind will be able to form an opinion about Manto if those writings were to be placed in front of him. As I sit down to write this, I realize how difficult it is to express my views about Manto; but in a way, it is not so difficult because I have had the privilege of knowing Manto. The truth is that I am his doppelganger.

I have no objection to whatever has been so far written about this man, but I do know that none of it is quite in line with reality. Some people see him as the devil himself, while others call him a bald angel. But let me first make sure that the fellow is not listening—I suppose it is all right because I have just remembered that this is his drinking hour. He is in the habit of drinking his bitter syrup after six every evening.

We were born together and I suppose we will die together. But it may also come to pass that Saadat Hasan may die and Manto may not. That thought really bothers me because I have always done my best to keep our friendship. Now if he were to die and I do not, it would be like being left with an eggshell that has been emptied of its yellow and white.

I do not wish to go into details but frankly speaking, I have never seen a 'one-two' man like Manto in my entire life. Were he to be added up, the result would be three. He knows a great deal about triangles but as far as I know his trinity is yet to find completion. Only the most perceptive readers can follow these hints.

While I have known Manto since the day he was born, both of us having come into this world on 11 May 1912, he has always tried to be like a tortoise, who, once he withdraws his head and

---

Manto wrote this very Mantoesque sketch about himself not long before his death.

neck into his shell, is difficult to find, no matter how hard you try. Since I am his doppelganger, I have studied every single one of his tricks.

Now let me tell you who this ass turned into a storywriter is. Critics write long, learned articles about him to show off their knowledge, lacing them with references to Schopenhauer, Freud, Hegel, Nietzsche and Marx, but they remain miles away from reality.

Manto's short-story writing is the result of a clash between two factors. His father (may he rest in heaven) was extremely harsh and his mother had a very tender heart. You can yourself imagine in what shape this grain of wheat would have emerged after being meshed between these two stone grinders.

Let me now turn to his school days. He was very intelligent and very naughty. In those days, he was no taller than three and a half feet. He was the last son of his father, and while he had the love of his parents, three of his much older brothers were studying in England. He had never had the opportunity of meeting them because they were his half-brothers. He wanted them to meet him and to treat him as elder brothers treat younger brothers, but this treatment only came his way after he had become famous as a great story writer.

Let's now talk about his story writing. He is a first-class fraud. His first story was called 'Tamasha' which was about the Jallianwala Bagh tragedy. He did not publish it under his own name because he was afraid of being arrested by the police if he did.

The restless person that he was, he now set his heart on getting a higher education, having failed his entrance examination to a bachelor's degree twice before passing it, but in the third division. It will surprise you to know that he failed his Urdu paper. Now when people say that he is a great Urdu writer, I can only laugh because even now he does not know Urdu. He runs after words as a man with a net chases butterflies without catching them. That is why there is a paucity of beautiful words in his writing. He likes to wield a stick, but it needs to be pointed out that he has borne with great equanimity every blow struck across his neck.

The manner in which he wields his stick is not of the crude kind, which rustic folk are known for; he is an artist and he brings great finesse to the act. He is the sort of person who does not walk on a straight road, but on a tightly strung rope. People expect him to fall any moment but he has so far not fallen. It is possible that he may one day fall, and fall on his face, never to get up. But I do know that when he is dying, he will tell people that he fell because he wanted to overcome the disappointment that a fall brings.

I have often said to him that Manto is a fraud of the first order. An additional proof of that is his oft-expressed claim that he does not think a short story; it is the short story that thinks him. But that too is a fraud. I know that when he has to write a story, he is like a hen about to lay an egg, with the difference that he does not lay this egg hidden from view but right in front of everyone. His friends and his three daughters continue to create the racket that they do, but there he sits in his chair with his legs up, laying his eggs, which cluck away to turn into stories. His wife is tired of him and often tells him to stop his story writing and open a store. However, the store that Manto has opened in his mind has more goods than any general store can carry. However, it has sometimes occurred to him that if he ever opens a store, it may turn into a cold storage where all his thoughts and ideas will freeze.

I am writing this article and afraid at the same time that Manto will be annoyed with me. Anything that he does can be tolerated but not his annoyance. When he is annoyed, he is the devil himself, although only for a few minutes. God protect us from that. When he is to write a story, he fusses a lot, but I know why: because I am his doppelganger and I know that it is all a fraud. He himself said once that countless stories lie in his pocket, but the fact is that when he has to write a story, he thinks about it the night before, though nothing comes to him. He will get up at five in the morning and try to extract a story from the day's newspapers. But it does not work; so he goes to the bathroom where he tries to cool his turbulent head with water so that he can think. When this does not work, he starts to argue with his wife without any reason. When that does not work either, he walks out of the house to buy betel leaf. The betel leaf continues to rest on his table and he still finds himself without a subject. In the end, by way of revenge, he will pick up a pen or a pencil and inscribe the numbers 786 on top of the page and whatever comes to his mind then becomes the starting point of a story.

'Babu Gopi Nath', 'Toba Tek Singh', 'Hattak', 'Mummy', 'Mozail' were all written through this fraudulent method.

It is strange that people consider him irreligious and a pornographer, although I would concede that to some extent he does fall into these categories. He takes up profound themes and he employs words which can be considered objectionable, but I do know that whenever he has written something, he has begun it with the numbers 786 which mean Bismillah or 'I begin in the name of God'. A man who does not believe in God becomes a believer on paper. That is the paper-Manto, somewhat like those almonds with paper-thin skins that you can crack open with your fingers. It is another matter that he is the kind of person whom even an iron hammer cannot crack open.

Let me now come to Manto's personality and do so by conferring some titles on him. He is a thief, a liar, a cheat and a man who likes to hold forth before others. Taking advantage of his wife's preoccupation, he has stolen hundreds of rupees from her. On occasions, he has brought her eight hundred rupees, and with his spying eye made note of where she keeps the money. The next day, one of the green bills is found missing. When she discovers the loss, it is the poor servants who get it in the neck.

Although it is said of Manto that he speaks the truth, I am not prepared to buy that. He is a first-rate liar. In the beginning, his lies used to work at home because they always had that special Manto touch. Later, it was found out that whatever he had told his wife about something or the other was a lie. Manto's lies are told with economy, but the trouble is that the family has come to believe that whatever he says is a lie, like the beauty spot a woman makes on her cheek with antimony.

He is illiterate, considering that he has never read Marx, nor any of Freud's books. Hegel he knows only by name, and the same goes for Havelock Ellis. The funny thing is that all the critics say that he is influenced by these thinkers. As far as I know, Manto is not impressed by anyone. He says those who try to teach him are all fools. No one should be told what to do; people should learn what to do without being told.

By trying to understand things by himself, he has become something beyond anyone's comprehension. Sometimes he talks such nonsense that I begin to laugh. I can tell you with full responsibility that Manto, who has been tried on obscenity charges many times, is a very neat and fussy person. At the same time, I would like to add that he fusses far too much, constantly dusting himself, as it were.

MANTO'S EPITAPH

Here lies Saadat Hasan Manto. With him lie buried all the arts and mysteries of short-story writing . . . Under tons of earth he lies, wondering who of the two is the greater short-story writer: God or he.

Manto wrote his own epitaph but it does not appear on his grave in Lahore because of his family's fears that it would enrage the orthodox and the clergy.

APPENDIXES

APPENDIX 1

UNCLE MANTO

by Hamid Jalal

There is no such person as Uncle Manto in my everyday vocabulary and if someone were suddenly to ask me about him I would not immediately know that he was referring to my youngest maternal uncle. I call him Saadat Mamajan, for we speak to each other in Punjabi. That is the language he normally speaks at home, except with his children, whom he is bringing up on Urdu, his medium of literary expression. He finds it a great strain to have long conversations in Urdu and he avoids this, almost as he does writing in Punjabi.

As my relationship with him implies, I need not be a Manto. In fact, I am not one. For Uncle Manto, this may come as a shock even though he has very generously conceded that all his likeable relatives cannot be Mantos. He can understand, and perhaps even forgive, my not being a Manto, but my openly declaring that I am not one—well, I suppose that is my own funeral!

The fact is that even if I had been a Manto, I would not have used the family name, for it now belongs less to the family and more to the person who has already made it so well known in Urdu literature. In the years to come, the name Manto is likely to be converted into an adjective to describe a literary trend or personality. It is on the latter aspect that I feel qualified to throw some light. My main problem, however, is to distinguish and differentiate between Saadat Hasan and Manto, for Saadat Hasan Manto is really a split personality. Saadat Hasan was born in Sambrala (now part of East Punjab) on the 11 May 1912 and he himself gave birth to Manto as he neared the end of his school days.

This piece was written during Manto's lifetime by his nephew Hamid Jalal, and includes an epitaph he added after Manto's death.

It is not possible for me to set the exact date on which the Manto aspect of his personality began to assert itself, but perhaps I would not be too wide of the mark if I narrated an incident to show how it must have first manifested itself. He was not yet out of his teens, when Master Khuda Bukhsh created a sensation in London, driving his car blindfolded through Piccadilly Circus. Shortly afterwards, there appeared in Amritsar a fire-walker, who claimed to be Master Khuda Bukhsh's tutor. His name, I think, was Allah Rakha. Thousands flocked every day to see him walk unscathed across a shallow ditch full of glowing coals. One day, he went a step further: he announced that anyone who had faith in him and God could also follow his bare feet across the red-hot ditch without any ill effects. The crowd took one look at the tiny flames, quickly painting the coal red, and shrank back as if Master Allah Rakha would force them to follow him. He repeated his invitation but the crowd held back in hushed silence.

Then a young man stepped forward. He seemed to have waited only to make sure that no one else would make the attempt. As the crowd began to murmur, the lanky youngster, at Master Allah Rakha's bidding, took off his shoes and socks and rolled up his trouser bottoms. 'Draw in your toes and recite the Kalima . . . Follow me.' The crowd had hardly got over its surprise when Master Allah Rakha and the youngster completed their journey over the burning coals. While the amazed youngster examined his feet for the non-existent burns and blisters, the crowd began to clap.

That was Saadat Hasan Manto's first public ovation. It was rather an unfortunate beginning of a public career, for Uncle Manto has been walking on fire ever since. He has had his share of public ovation, and a very big share it has been, but he has not always escaped the natural effects of fire. His public, however, seem to think that this is a part of the act and they watch with indifference while he makes half-hearted attempts to fight the flames that threaten to envelop him. I describe his attempts as half-hearted, because Uncle Manto seems to believe that fire-walking is a part of his public career as writer and personality. Perhaps, subconsciously, he feels that he will have no public ovation, if he does not indulge in feats that are as abnormal and dangerous as fire-walking.

I could even say that this subconscious fear is the key to his personality, but what holds me back is the fact that his personality has a very large number of facets and each calls for a separate unlocking device. A painstaking psychoanalyst could, perhaps, isolate, distinguish and list the various aspects of Uncle Manto's personality but for me that task is very difficult. When I look back on my association with him, I feel that I am looking into a kaleidoscope: his literary activities, home life and behaviour as a dipsomaniac forming the three sides of the mirror prism and our common experiences representing the tiny fragments of coloured glass that form a new pattern every time the base is rotated.

To give a complete picture of Uncle Manto in this sketch is as impossible a task as copying out all the patterns that a kaleidoscope can produce. All I can do is slowly turn the Manto kaleidoscope and describe and interpret the various personality patterns that are formed on the screen of my mind.

One such image that readily takes shape dates back to the days of his fire-walking exploit. I can see him in his study, at his writing table, which is dominated by a huge brass motorcar-shaped inkpot. He whispers to me and I go out, to return some time later, after his usual group of cronies has assembled for its daily sitting. He introduces me to a couple of new friends whom I have not met before, explains that I have just arrived from Lahore and anxiously inquires whether any further news has reached Lahore about the Taj Mahal. Not yet quite ten, but having been properly briefed some minutes earlier, I reply, with all the gravity I can muster, 'Yes, the news is correct. Everybody in Lahore says that the Taj has been sold to the Americans.' Uncle Manto and some of his more intimate friends pounce upon this statement of mine and convince a gullible newcomer to their fold that the rumour they have mentioned to him earlier is correct . . . the Taj Mahal has been sold by the British to the Americans, who are rushing special equipment to Agra to remove the monument to New York. By next day, several bazaars in Amritsar are abuzz with this rumour, while Uncle Manto sits back in his study and chuckles.

In those days, Uncle Manto revelled in such rumour-mongering, and every rumour spread by him showed a creative mind at work. As a sort of sideline, he went about asking his friends to believe that his fountain pen was carved out of a donkey's horn and things of that kind. He was the leader of a young group of intellectuals of Amritsar and prescribed for them several new phrases and conversational styles so that they could distinguish themselves from the general body of students.

Two of his expressions, which have gained wide currency these last twenty years or so, are his use of the words 'fraud' and 'kabab'. Today, a large number of people use the word 'fraud' as if it belonged to the Urdu or Punjabi languages, and so far as Uncle Manto is concerned, he uses the word not to describe an act but a personality. If anyone lets him down or annoys him, he has, to use Uncle Manto's expression, made a 'kabab' of him. The originality of his idiom was confusing for the outsider. If he wanted to know what a person thought about his shirt or fountain pen, he would ask, 'What is your button about this shirt?' or 'What is your nib about this pen?' The underlying reason, of course, was the urge to be different, to be independent of all traditions, to owe nothing to anybody; in short, to be nothing but Manto.

As I visited Amritsar only occasionally, I could not watch this race from close quarters. In fact, even if I had lived in Amritsar or Uncle Manto had visited Lahore more often, the difference in our ages would have made it difficult for me to know all about his activities. Then he left for Bombay and the gulf between us widened. It took several years for us to meet again. The occasion was his visit to Lahore in December 1940, when his first book of short stories, *Manto ke Afsane*, was being published. I heard him giving directions regarding the dust cover, which was to be dominated by a portrait sketch of his, showing him with his shirt collar open and head thrown back in an attitude of defiance and arrogance. 'Let it be drawn in such a way,' he told the publisher, 'that it should provoke people to abuse me.'

I cannot say whether he said this to overawe his publisher or whether that was his view of the relationship that should exist between an author and his reader. Personally, I think, the remark was not made deliberately and I doubt if Uncle Manto even remembers having made it, but it provides an important clue to his personality. His first objective, perhaps, was to impress upon the publisher the fact that, in dealing with Manto, he should discard his standards for normal persons. What is more important, it revealed Uncle Manto's aim to make his personality a part of his writings, because his study of literature must have convinced him that generally what matters is not what is said, but who says it. He had before him examples of writers like Oscar Wilde and George Bernard Shaw, who won as much fame or should I say notoriety for their personalities as for their literary output. Uncle Manto was, perhaps, the first modern Urdu writer to have his picture on the dust cover of his book, as if to say, 'I am as much the author of the personality of Manto as of his writings'.

I doubt if anyone abused him, as he wanted, merely by looking at the dust cover of his book—which, incidentally, was designed by M. Ismail, the well-known film star—though later on this desire of his must have been more than fulfilled. Actually, Saadat Hasan himself, that is to say, when he was still himself, must have abused his creation as roundly as anyone else. The responsibility for the creation was his, but while he had imagined himself a Pygmalion, his handiwork had followed in the footsteps of Mr Hyde or Frankenstein.

This monster, for in this context I can call him nothing else, has been on the rampage for several years now. Attempts to tame him have not been very successful and this is mainly due to his absolute inability to resist alcohol. To illustrate this, I will narrate an incident that involves no more than a few drops of whisky . . .

In August 1953, Uncle Manto was removed to the Mayo Hospital suffering from acute jaundice. The doctor soon discovered that he actually had cirrhosis of the liver from which affliction hardly one in a thousand recovers. I was in Murree at that time and, on the day I was to return, I received a telegram saying that his condition was grave. On arriving at Rawalpindi, I telephoned Lahore and was informed that the doctors had given up the fight, that I would be too late and that he had been asking for me. Although I had been expecting some such end during the last few years, the news that it was now in sight came as a big shock. The fact that he had been asking for me made it all the more poignant, for it filled me with the realization, that along with Manto, my Saadat Mamajan of the good old days also lay dying. It left me benumbed and helpless. The train journey by night seemed so futile, for the doctors had given him only a couple of hours more.

The reader will perhaps be wondering how many more words I am going to use to describe an incident involving a few drops of alcohol. Well, I am afraid that will have to wait, while I mention some other aspects of Uncle Manto's personality, the more lovable ones, which come naturally to a person in an obituarist frame of mind.

I remember a train journey we had taken together from Lahore. He was going to Bombay while I was to accompany him up to

Delhi only. His luggage contained no less than a dozen pairs of sandals and gold embroidered jootis, which he always bought on his visits to Lahore and gave most of them away to his friends in the film industry. Footwear has always been an obsession with him. He not only wore the most expensive shoes, sandals and jootis himself, he loved giving them away. They always formed a topic of conversation for us. Whenever I went to Bombay, I knew that he would come to the railway station to receive me in a new pair of shoes. I noticed them the moment we met, but a discussion on them was always postponed until we were in a taxi or gharry, where he would cross his legs and bring the shoes more prominently into the picture. He has never worn heavy shoes, for his feet are slim and almost effeminate. I do not remember having ever bought sandals for myself; every summer under some pretext or the other a pair or two are passed on to me. This continued even during the days when Uncle Manto was in acute financial difficulties, days when nothing mattered except alcohol. At times it seemed to me that next to alcohol, footwear was his main interest in life. The last pair of sandals that I got from him was in exchange for a couple of razor blades.

I have always found him short of razor blades, because they are not difficult to buy. Tell him that a certain article or commodity has gone underground and his eyes will light up and he will have taken up the challenge and started making rounds of the black market. When I mention this characteristic of his, I am referring to his Bombay days, where he always had lots of money and I think the more exorbitant the price he had to pay, the greater the satisfaction he derived. When gold-and silver-capped Parker and Sheaffer pens first came to India during the last war, Uncle Manto was a prolific buyer. He paid up to one hundred and fifty rupees for these models. He must have bought about ten of them and with the exception of one, which he kept for himself, he gave all of them away. It was their novelty rather than utility that attracted him, for he seldom used them. To write radio-plays or film scenarios, he always uses his Urdu typewriter, which is a slower process but it gives him time to think, while for short stories and other articles, he prefers a soft pencil which can help his hand keep pace with his thoughts. I have seen him write a complete short story in one sitting, in a room full of noisy children playing games, and calling upon him to give rulings on disputed points, and also at the same time taking part in the general conversation of others who may be visitors or members of his family.

Why did he have to drink himself to death? That was the question that repeated itself to me as I travelled to Lahore that night. Instead of feeling sorry for him, I felt angry with him. It was unfair of him to have done so. It had all along been a fight between his love for his family and the magnetism of alcohol, and alcohol had won hands down. In the last few weeks I had suspected him toying with the idea of suicide, either because it was the easiest way out or because he wanted to fill the family with remorse for having given him up as a hopeless case. I was certain that I would be too late, for I had been told last night that he was already unconscious and in an oxygen tent.

It would be a defeat also for that astrologer in Bombay who had predicted a very long life for Uncle Manto but who had very correctly foretold bad times ahead. That was in 1946, when Uncle Manto was at the peak of his lucrative film career. The rot had set in almost immediately afterwards with a slump in the film industry, and on migration to Lahore after Partition, his condition worsened. The astrologer had warned Uncle Manto that his ketu or something like that was about to slip into a bad orbit and that he would have seven lean years before all would be well with him again. I now read a new meaning into the astrologer's words. Perhaps he had meant that Uncle Manto would have a long life as a literary figure, while his seven-year bad period would come to an end with physical death.

I arrived at the hospital, bracing myself for the worst. I was met by a cluster of red-eyed relatives who told me that he was still alive. I could not ask any questions, for there was a lump in my throat. I went into the ward and immediately stopped at the foot of his bed, which was nearest to the door. I shall never forget what I saw.

On the bed was a skeleton of a man and all that I could see of his face, partially covered with shaving lather, was a pair of very prominent eyes, yellowed with jaundice. Yes, I said 'shaving lather', and the person leaning over him was no doctor's assistant either. He was the hospital barber and he was trying to hear what the patient was saying in his very feeble voice. With a great effort, Uncle Manto took a trembling bony hand up to his chin and moved his fingers across it. The barber then understood him. 'Sahib says it is not smooth enough,' he explained to us as he reached for his shaving brush. I went up to Uncle Manto, not knowing whether he might not have lived another few hours was an anti-climax. It was almost like the ending of a Manto short story.

I met the doctors but they just shook their heads and said that the case was hopeless. They held on to this view for another two weeks in spite of the daily improvement shown by Uncle Manto. Statistics, they said, were against him, to say nothing of the various blood test reports. Being such a hopeless case, the doctors did not at once completely stop his whisky. His system was too used to it and they allowed him a few drops two or three times a day.

A day or two after my arrival from Murree, there was a mild sensation when a glass of diluted whisky disappeared from a side table near Uncle Manto's bed. Had it been thrown away by mistake or had one of the hospital attendants drained it off? No one knew. Uncle Manto was beyond suspicion. Most of the time he lay in a coma and when he was conscious he could not even support a cigarette placed in his mouth. When the time came for his afternoon quota, he managed with his feeble gestures to attract attention and whisper a reminder. The attendant who bent down to hear what he was saying caught a faint smell of whisky coming from Uncle Manto. It was with great difficulty that he was made to confess that he had already had the drink. We asked him who had given it to him and learnt to our astonishment that he, whose fingers could not hold a cigarette for more than a few seconds, had raised himself on his elbow, picked up the glass, which a careless nurse had left there before time, and after finishing it had replaced it on the table.

It showed amazing will power but it also showed that his fight was not against the disease: it was *for* it. The doctors were in despair, for the deterioration in his condition a few days earlier had followed a successful attempt by his bottle friends to smuggle in some whisky for him. The doctors now took a drastic step. They completely stopped his whisky.

This had just the effect I had anticipated. He started getting hallucinations. This had happened once before, too. He had got up at the dead of night and started seeing things and talking about them. He had frightened us all, for it seemed as if he had lost his mind. When I came on the scene, he was insisting that his wife fry the huge fish that an Anglo-Pakistani neighbour had just sent him. On seeing me, he took my arm and we both walked out of the flat. He began shouting the name of the Anglo-Pakistani and it was with great difficulty that I dragged him back into the house. For the first few minutes I did not quite know how to deal with the situation and just mumbled a few answers to his questions. He was talking in the most terribly normal manner possible. The only thing wrong was the subject matter of his conversation. He wanted me to accompany him to another neighbour's house, where he said some singing girls were performing. He wanted to hear their Punjabi song which he repeated as he 'heard' it.

Banking on his intelligence, I took a risk. I abruptly told him that he was in the grip of hallucinations, that the Anglo-Pakistani neighbour who he thought had just given him the fish had been transferred from Lahore over six months ago, that no one was singing anywhere in the vicinity and that the only sounds in the stillness of the night were our voices. After a moment's silence, he said, 'Then I suppose there are no sparrows fluttering their wings in that corner either?'

'No,' was my reply.

'The voice of the singing girl is still coming through . . . I'll write down the song.' He did so for about a minute.

'We can hear no such song,' I remarked.

He asked his wife and some other members of the family who had come to the sitting room whether they heard the song. They all said 'no'. He stopped writing, but insisted that he could still hear the song. Gradually he began to distinguish reality from imagination, and just before he reluctantly went to bed, he said to me, 'I am very sorry about that fish. It was a good fish.'

I do not quite remember what had caused the hallucinations, but I think it was because he had suddenly given up both drink and food. At the hospital the attack was worse and it lasted almost a week. Most of the time he imagined himself to be in Bombay, where he had spent the happiest period of his life. Every day I would tell him that he was in Lahore, but he found that hard to believe. Perhaps, he did not want to believe it, for his stay in Lahore since Partition had been an unhappy one. His hallucinations moved in strange grooves. One day he read out to me an imaginary news item from a newspaper: 'Reports have been received of a successful police raid on liquor shops. The police arrested six empty bottles, twenty-two playing cards and a dancing girl.' I interpreted this as a denunciation by him, in his hallucinatory state, of the killjoys around him.

He had come through the more dangerous part of his illness with courage and fortitude, but as he grew better he became peevish. He wanted to do all sorts of things that were forbidden: he demanded tabooed food and drink that would have killed him in a few hours and he wanted to walk, which the doctors said he should not even think of attempting before another month or so. But the urge to walk was irresistible; he wanted to electrify the ward with his feat, he wanted to prove that Manto could do it. He made a clandestine attempt but it was as if he had stepped into a red-hot ditch with legs of butter. They just melted away and he was lucky to escape with minor injuries when his bony frame struck the concrete floor.

This was but one result of his obstinacy. A twenty-four-hour watch had to be kept on him. There was no knowing what he might do. His eyes and mind all the time seemed to be searching for a glowing coal on which he could step bare-footed. His attitude during his peevish moods was of a person who by getting well was doing a good turn to his doctors and relatives. This attitude sometimes made me rather bitter towards him, something that surprised scores of his friends and fans who came to see him daily. Some of them wanted him to shift to some other bed, for it was in the same bed that Akhtar Shirani, the poet, had died some years earlier, while others did not like the ward itself, for Uncle Manto's old friend Abdul Bari, the well-known historian, had also breathed his last here. My bitterness was mainly due to the apprehension that all this fight for his life would be in vain if he took to the bottle again. I hoped against hope that he would not, but his so-called friends took only a couple of months to convince him that he never had cirrhosis or he would never have recovered and Uncle Manto was at the bottle again.

I found out the very day he had his first drink after his recovery, although he denied it vehemently. This also is a peculiar habit of his. He cannot hide the effects of even a peg of whisky or gin but he deludes himself into thinking that he can hold his drink well. Any reference to this physical disability of his hurts his vanity. I wish he would realize that alcohol is damaging him in more ways than one. I would say it has ravaged his personality far more than his health.

Hardly ten years ago his home was one of the happiest I have ever known. One hardly noticed what one ate at his dining table, for the main attraction was his witty conversation and the happy laughter of the family and friends gathered around it. He always had guests in his modest little flat in Bombay. What brought them there was his unobtrusive hospitality. If ever the guests outnumbered the beds, Uncle Manto was always the first to spread out his bedding on the floor. Sometimes he even ran short of floor space and he never hesitated to sleep on the old, creaking planks of the narrow passage leading to the lavatory. He never made a show of his sacrifice, not to mention anything about the inconvenience caused to his uncomplaining wife. The whole thing was managed in such a manner that the arrangement was accepted by all as natural.

I personally felt the first impact of his new personality at the dining table. He usually drank in the evenings and became unpleasant and aggressive in his conversation during dinner. Almost every evening we had sharp arguments over trifles and lost our tempers. I was unreasonable perhaps, because even under the influence of drink I expected him to behave normally. Whenever I visited Bombay, I came to dread the evenings, for I knew I would not be able to tolerate the alcohol-powered personality masquerading as Uncle Manto. The only way out was not to meet him in the evenings and that is what I did.

Since Partition we have been living in almost the same house, my first-floor flat being connected with his on the ground floor. His resistance to drink weakened and the proximity of a bar made it possible for him to drink throughout the day. His favourite route, which he thought was secret, was through the bathroom. Several times a day he would proceed to the bathroom, bolt it noisily from inside, turn on the tap, quietly open the other door leading out of the flat, rush to the bar through the back lane, have a quick gin and return the same way. Once on his return, he immediately began to talk about the tactical genius of General Rommel and I could not help imagining the German commander in full uniform, riding a tank through the streets of Cairo on a secret reconnaissance before the El Alamein battle!

Later, with the coming of prohibition the bar closed, but the bathroom still remained important in his alcoholic life. He usually hid the bottle there and went in every fifteen or thirty minutes to have a nip. Once I saw the bottle behind the commode. It filled me with pity, for when sober nothing is more important to Uncle Manto than hygiene. He is known for his snow-white starched kurta and pajama; his handwriting is neat and clean; he never types unless he has thoroughly cleaned his typewriter; he never writes on cheap or smudgy paper; and he never eats off a plate that is not spotless nor drinks from a glass that is not as clean. He would rather wash them himself. For such a person to drink straight from a bottle hidden behind a leaky flush commode is possible only when the compulsion is too forceful to resist.

Under such circumstances we stopped seeing each other even during the day and sometimes it was weeks before we came across one another. I was, of course, aware of his activities, most of which would have caused any normal person to boil with rage. He would be most irresponsible and unreasonable. He could not sleep at all during the nights and had to take a swig at the bottle every half hour or so. Sometimes, his hazily made calculations would be wrong and in the middle of the night he would find himself without any drink. Then the ordeal would begin for the family. One by one, all of us would wake up to hear him shouting accusations at his wife, whom he suspected of having located the bottle and reducing its contents by pouring them down the sink.

Sometimes he would run out of cigarettes and he would keep on shouting for his servant every ten minutes, asking him to go to the bazaar and get him a packet. The servant's report, after his first attempt, that no shop was open would have no effect on him; he would repeat his command at regular intervals, until through sheer exhaustion he would doze off or fall into a sort of coma.

In the quiet night his almost incoherent shouting sounded terrible. At first, all the family used to gather in his flat and persuade him to go to sleep but this was given up as these persuasions had no effect on him. His nocturnal shouting and storming continued and as usual woke up his family and mine, but none of us left our beds any longer. We lay awake, our hearts pounding, not speaking a word, but with the same thoughts in our minds. When would his ordeal and ours end? I cannot speak for others, but I know that for me the ordeal will never end. Even when he was in hospital, any shout in the night was enough to wake me up and agitate me.

I have often wondered whether it is normal for a writer's family to pay such a price for his literary eminence. Uncle Manto knows all about his weaknesses and once he came up with an excuse, which some others may offer on his behalf. He said that in order to write he must undergo various experiences, however unpleasant and painful they might be. He may be right to a certain extent, but he would find it difficult to list more than a dozen stories written by him under the influence of liquor. The fact is that he can write only when he is sober. I am aware of certain stories written by him during his 'lost weekends' but their quality is such that he now even denies their authorship. Why then must he drink?

Ask him the question and he will love to discuss it with you. He will probably even ask for help to fight the evil, readily offer himself for psychoanalysis and supply all the information required by his friends to make amateurish attempts to find out the causes and suggest remedies for his dipsomania. He will flatter and encourage them by agreeing with their conclusions and accepting their interpretations and make them feel that they are the first to treat his case scientifically and sympathetically. All the while he will be making regular trips to the hidden bottle, coming back to encourage his friends to continue their psychoanalytical efforts, and growing progressively unsteadier with every new promise that he would give up drinking forever. After their departure, I suppose, he chuckles to himself as he did the day the bazaars of Amritsar buzzed with the rumour about the Taj Mahal.

Only once in his life—as far as I can remember—did Uncle Manto make a serious attempt to give up drinking. His condition was daily growing worse when his wife told him about my suggestion that he be taken for treatment to the Alcoholic Ward of the Punjab Mental Hospital. The next day, much to my surprise, I heard him call my name as I passed his room. I went in and found him in bed, his face turned away towards the wall to prevent me from seeing the real state he was in. He said, 'I am prepared to go to the hospital . . . please make the arrangements.'

I made an appointment for him the very next day, but he disappeared some time before we were due to leave for the hospital and did not reappear until several hours later. He had not baulked at the last minute. The reason was quite different. He had heard that the superintendent's fee was thirty-two rupees and had gone out to raise the amount. During his palmy days in Bombay, consulting the most expensive doctor, who charged sixty-four rupees for consultation alone, was almost a hobby with him. He once even took his servant to one such doctor with the intention of paying the full fee. For the doctor the situation was novel; his clients were usually millionaires who probably never even sent their poorer relations to him. He took only thirty-two rupees, half his normal fee.

Thirty-two rupees! That amount had not stood between him and the doctor. In those days, he was still particular about whom he borrowed from. He got the money somehow and was admitted to the hospital, had a very difficult time for the first few days and came out after six weeks. He was effectively cured and did not drink again for about eight months. During that period he wrote almost a book a month; at times the rate was a story a day. Then he relapsed and the attack was worse than before. He was drunk all the time and since he was in that state he could not write. His earnings dropped to zero.

Uncle Manto then started on a course which distressed the family even more than his addiction to the bottle. He began borrowing money indiscriminately. The amount or the person never mattered. He touched relatives, friends, neighbours and I would say even strangers, for he could not resist borrowing even from fans who came only to pay their respects to him. He was almost on a never-ending binge during 1952 and up to August 1953, when he was removed to hospital for cirrhosis of the liver. During that period, we once took him to the mental hospital by force but he refused to cooperate and the hospital authorities had to let him go home after a couple of days, for under the rules of their institution they could not treat any sane person against his will. Uncle Manto was very bitter towards the family after that. But then in those days he hardly knew what he was doing.

I remember those days as vividly as a nightmare. His eldest daughter fell seriously ill and I noted with dismay that this made not the slightest impression on him. His drinking had never before been as bad as this. He has always professed great love for his children and has shown it in many ways. For instance, he has never failed to rally in time for Pakistan Day celebrations. Like most other intellectuals, he cannot make a flag of his patriotism and flutter it from his housetop, but he wants his children to do so. He has always sobered up for Pakistan Day, bought buntings and with the help of the delighted children put up the little flags all over the front of his flat and mine. The last time a daughter of his fell ill, he had nursed her himself and dedicated a book to her.

When his eldest daughter was down with typhoid, he must have been vaguely aware of the fact that there was little money in the house and that the treatment was bound to be expensive. That evening he borrowed money in the name of his daughter but when he came home it was with a bottle of whisky rather than the vital medicines. It was alcohol's most important victory to date. He must have been full of remorse and self-condemnation, for he tried to make up by demonstrating his love for the stricken child. In spite of his wife's protests he sat unsteadily on the bed, his long hair falling all over his face, and tried to lift the child on to his lap and overwhelm her with paternal affection. When his wife dragged him away from the bed, he was enraged; he was determined to exercise his parental right even if it meant resorting to violence. Before he could do so, my wife—who was witness—unexpectedly lost her temper, probably for the first time in her mild-mannered life. That came as a terrible shock to Uncle Manto. He sobered down immediately and quietly went away to his room.

Next morning we found him extremely weak, for he had again given up drinking. There was sunshine again in the Manto home and everyone basked in it, hoping to make it permanent. Vitamin tablets and tonics appeared on his bedside table. Another periodical cycle began in Uncle Manto's life and soon he was pottering about the house, having the broken chairs mended, selling empty bottles and old newspapers—an old hobby of his—fixing a swing for the children, making a huge bird-house and stocking it with lovebirds, hiring carpenters and masons to repair various things and parts of the house, making sofa sets for the children with empty cigarette cartons and taking full part in discussions on all domestic and family matters.

In these discussions, Uncle Manto always reveals himself as conservative and almost a reactionary on issues like women's education and mixed social gatherings. Whenever he expresses his views on these matters I cannot help identifying him with a character he has had in mind for over ten years but has not yet written about him. The character is a goonda, who is the terror of the town and has a hand in almost every murder, robbery, abduction and assault, but no sooner does he enter the mohalla in which he lives than a transformation takes place. He no longer walks erect, his eyes are on the ground, the children call out to him to play with them and he obliges, the elders have but to command and their wishes are fulfilled, he does not look at women but if he hears that anyone has dared even to smile at a girl in his mohalla, God help the Majnu!

But the sunshine in the Manto home does not last long. No sooner has his strength been built up, which the family hopes he will use to resist alcohol, than he succumbs to temptation again.

Usually the cause of these relapses are his companions. I have deliberately not used the word 'friends' because there is a dividing line between his real friends and the pretenders. His real friends now always remain in the background because they do not approve of his drinking and because they are free and frank with him about other matters as well. He prefers to have around him companions who can assure him at frequent intervals that he is a great writer and a great personality, whom even cirrhosis could not touch. They have had a very bad influence on him. With them, he is always the centre of attraction and he can snub or insult them as he pleases. He must have undivided attention even if he has to stand up on his chair to demand it.

One evening, after the Pakistan cricket team had returned from its tour of India, Uncle Manto heard that some of the team members, including Waqar Hasan and Mahmood Hussain, had come to call on me. Although he was in a condition in which he never came to my flat, he turned up to meet the cricketers. He was introduced, after which he sat along with several others listening to what the cricketers had to say about their India tour. But how long could Uncle Manto take a back seat? I use the term in a figurative sense, for he was actually sitting in a chair in the inner ring, in which the cricketers also sat. Hardly five minutes after his arrival, he slipped down from his chair, sat on the carpet in the centre of the room, stopped Mahmood Hussain in the middle of a sentence and said, 'I know all fast bowlers are frauds. Come on, demonstrate to me how you bump the ball.' Waqar Hasan also had to show to Uncle Manto how he played some of his 'fraud strokes'. The rest of the evening was dominated by Uncle Manto; the other fans did not get a chance to have a word with the Test cricketers.

Why this desire to focus the spotlight on himself? I have only one explanation for it. In the last few years, he has lost much prestige at home and among his relatives and friends. This has hurt him more than he would ever admit. He is hungry for love and affection, and when he does not get it, he falls back on drawing attention to himself. It is a poor substitute but it is better than being ignored altogether. For the family and his true friends, I would say that they want to return the love and affection he has given them ungrudgingly and unselfishly in his happier days; all they want is a chance, a chance to return it to the right personality. His attitude seems to be,

'Love Saadat Hasan; forgive and forget Manto.' This is not unacceptable, only experience has shown that Manto usually leads Saadat Hasan by the nose.

Also, Uncle Manto has all along been aware of the ramifications of his self-made personality. I came to know this in rather interesting circumstances. I was in Bombay and was invited by Ashok Kumar and Savak Vacha of Bombay Talkies to give my views on a screenplay Uncle Manto was writing for them. It was a powerful story, but the role tailored for Ashok Kumar, who was to be the hero, was completely overshadowed by another personality, an alcoholic and a sadist. I vigorously advocated reducing the importance of this character, but Uncle Manto was adamant. During the discussion, he happened to leave the room for a few moments and Ashok Kumar at once whispered to me, 'What are you doing, don't you know he is to act that himself?' But that did not stop me from saying what I wanted to. I was as frank and harsh as I have been in this article, which Uncle Manto read as it was being written, page by page, without a single protest. Ultimately, in that discussion, Uncle Manto said that he wanted to act the role himself because he had based the character on himself. In the screenplay, that character was killed by his own mother.

The only meaning I can read into this is the realization that the only person who can end the dangerous trend in the Manto personality is its creator, Saadat Hasan himself. Some of his fans may fear that this would mean the end of his literary career. I do not agree. In fact, I think such a change would lead to the widening of his canvas. The family, particularly his wife, would not be very sorry even if he had to change his profession. So far as they are concerned he might as well be a carpenter. Before the snobs and highbrows cry sacrilege, I would hasten to add that I agree with the family. Appreciating literature is one thing, producing it for bread and butter is quite another, particularly in a country where a best-selling writer like Uncle Manto hardly gets more than fifty rupees for a short story.

Uncle Manto has earned more money in the field of literature than any other Urdu writer of his time. Unlike most others, he is entirely dependent on his pen for his living. The secret of Uncle Manto's success is his effective coordination as author and salesman. Both occupations are strenuous, taxing his mind and sapping his vitality. In Uncle Manto's case the strain is continuous. He perhaps first stuck to liquor as a tonic to revitalize him. This started a vicious circle. His way of living has always been expensive; he loved to engage taxis when buses could have served the purpose, and whatever he bought was of the best quality: clothes, pens, paper, cigarettes, shoes, neckties, railway accommodation and medical advice. All was well so long as the film companies paid him handsomely for his screenplays and scenarios, but then came the slump in the Indian film industry and his migration to Pakistan. To earn more he had to write more, to write more he felt he must have more of his self-prescribed tonic, but the more he drank the less he wrote, the less he wrote the more worried he became, the more worried he became, the more he drank to forget his worries.

That is the nature of the whirlpool in which Uncle Manto now finds himself, struggling hard to prevent himself from being drawn deeper into the vortex.

He is no longer happy, for unlike the fire-walking exploit there is now no applause and, what is worse, on touching his feet, he finds that after all these years, blisters have now made their appearance. But he is now struggling hard for existence, both physical and spiritual.

Occasionally the struggle is weakened by a relapse caused by a bottle thrown into the whirlpool by unwise friends, but it is firmer and more consistent than it was before his last and almost fatal visit to the hospital.

To restore his family's confidence in him, he has done several things to keep himself in check and break out of the vicious circle and, perhaps, force his ketu into a more auspicious orbit. He has signed away all his rights in his writings, past, present and future. All accounts are now in his wife's name. He cannot now borrow even a rupee from any publisher, unless his wife signs the receipt.

But his wife is still not reconciled to literature. She has had to pay too heavy a price for Uncle Manto's success and notoriety. If Uncle Manto has suffered in the cause of literature, she has suffered more. It was not surprising, therefore, for me to learn of her concern, genuine and grave, on hearing that I too had literary pretensions and was developing into a writer. She said to my wife, her younger sister, 'I hope this is not true, pray that he may never be a writer or you'll regret it all your life.'

POSTSCRIPT

(*Uncle Manto died on the 18 January 1955, about six months after the publication of the above article.*)

I have often wondered what I would say to Uncle Manto if he returned home from his grave in Miani Sahib. I am certain I would overlook the miracle of resurrection and say to him, 'Of all the irresponsible things you ever did, the most irresponsible was your death.'

I was at the cricket stadium in Bahawalpur, helping Bobby Talyar Khan with the running commentary on the second India–Pakistan Test, when I received a phone call from Lahore. 'Saadat Hasan Manto died this morning,' I was told. I was not immediately overwhelmed with grief. My first reaction was of anger. I was very angry. How could he do this to his family? But that is not what I said. When I spoke, my voice was full of concern. 'Where did he die?' I asked. 'At home,' was the reply. I was relieved, for I was afraid he might have died suddenly anywhere else . . . in a tonga, a restaurant, a publisher's office, a film studio . . .

As I returned to my seat, my colleagues in the commentators' box made signs to me, wanting to know what had happened. I picked up my writing pad and scribbled: 'The Umpire has at last given Saadat Manto out. He died this morning.' Uncle Manto had survived many appeals. Now his impatient and erratic innings had come to an end. Had he been a cricketer he could never have been a steady and careful batsman like Hanif Mohammad, whom he wanted to see in action in Lahore in the third Test. This I learnt on my return home, twenty-four hours after his death. In fact, that was one of his last two wishes. The evening before he died, he had said to some of his friends in a restaurant, 'Let Hamid Lala come home. I'll go with him to see Hanif in the Test match.'

His second wish was to write about the tragic death of a lonely young woman whose nude body was found on a roadside in Gujarat. According to the newspaper reports published that day, she and her little baby had died of exposure after she had been kidnapped from a waiting room of a bus terminal, ravished by over half a dozen brutes and allowed to run out of their den, without a stitch of clothing, into the freezing wintery night. This report had moved Uncle Manto very deeply. The same evening he had met some people from Gujarat, who I am told gave him some more information about the tragedy. This must have excited him no end, and if I can reconstruct that evening, it must have resulted in his having more than his normal quota of alcohol. That proved fatal. Shortly after he returned home, late in the evening, he vomited blood. My six-year-old son, who happened to be near him, pointed out the streaks of blood, but Uncle Manto said, 'No, that is paan spittle . . . and don't you tell anyone about it.' After that he had his normal dinner and went to bed. No one in the family suspected that anything was wrong, for my son had kept Uncle Manto's secret. Perhaps Uncle Manto himself thought that it was nothing serious. Normally, he tried to keep the family in the dark about such relapses because it meant the inevitable advice: stop drinking.

It was in the early hours of the morning that he woke up his wife and told her that he was in terrible pain and that he had lost much blood. His liver must have disintegrated. When his wife found that she could not cope with the situation herself, she woke up other members of the family. Then the fight began to save his life. Because of his numerous recoveries no one thought, at that stage, that he had only a few hours more to live. The fact, however, was that the Umpire had started raising his finger the moment Uncle Manto had first vomited that evening.

From what I have heard of Uncle Manto's last hours, I think he himself did not know that this was the absolute end, until an hour or so after the doctor had given him some injections. He did not rally as he always did after his treatment. His pulse continued to be bad and the pain increased. He lost more blood. In the morning the doctor suggested that Uncle Manto be taken to the hospital.

Uncle Manto was quite conscious. When he heard about the hospital, he protested, 'It's too late now . . . don't shift me about. Let this disgraceful life end . . . let me die here in peace.'

This was too much for some of the womenfolk. They started sobbing. This made him very angry. 'I don't want anyone to cry,' he said, irritably, as he hid his face under the quilt. This was the real Manto. The man who had always lived his life in full view of others did not want anyone to see him die.

His whole behaviour showed that he was angry, perhaps with himself or with alcohol that was bringing about his premature death.

Only once or twice before the ambulance arrived did he take the quilt away from his face. He said, 'I'm feeling very cold, colder than I will be in my grave—get more quilts.' He paused and with a strange gleam in his eyes, he added, 'In my coat pocket there are three rupees eight annas, give them and some more money to someone . . . and get me some whisky . . .' He insisted and to placate him a quarter bottle was brought for him. He looked at the bottle with a strange feeling of satisfaction.

'Warm up a peg or so,' he said, and he shuddered as the spasms of pain grew more intense.

There was no self-pity in his eyes. He knew he was dying but not once did he become sentimental. He did not ask for his children or anyone else. He never believed in last looks or last words. For persons like him the dividing line between life and death was very thin, and that is as it should be, for his soul had already been transferred from his body to his books. There he is assured of immortality; there he will go on living, laughing, loving. On his deathbed, Uncle Manto did not call for anything except whisky. Long ago he had recognized whisky as his mortal enemy and he had come to regard it as synonymous with Death over which there can be no physical victory. As every man is powerless before Death, so Uncle Manto was before Whisky.

But it was his nature to defy everything, even Death. He also hated defeat, even at the hands of Death. That was the reason he wanted to die alone, unobserved—undefeated! A lesser man would have tried to stage-manage his death—for various reasons: for posterity to write and talk about, for his relatives and friends to say that, though he had lived a life they did not approve of, he had died repentant and a good man. But Uncle Manto was no hypocrite. He resisted the temptation. His only dramatic gesture was his asking for whisky. This was stage-managing his death scene, but only for the benefit of the main actor. He alone understood the significance of the gesture.

Had I been present, I feel certain, he would have given me a hint of what was in his mind. That would not have been difficult. All he would have had to do would have been to say, 'Remember the story of the man and the snake?' I would have nodded my head and given him a last drink of whisky. That sentence would have made everything clear. His reference would have been to a man, who despite the warning of his friends kept a deadly poisonous snake as his pet, and who on being fatally bitten by the snake, caught the reptile and bit off its head.

Just as the ambulance arrived, he again asked for his drink. A spoonful was put to his lips, but he hardly swallowed a drop; the rest dribbled out of his mouth as he collapsed. That was the first time he had lost consciousness. In that state he was carried to the ambulance.

On arrival at the hospital, the doctors stepped into the ambulance to examine him. They found him dead. He had died on the way without regaining consciousness.

APPENDIX 2

MANTO FAMILY CONVERSATIONS

Nasira Iqbal: Saadat came home one day and announced with great pride that he was going to be writing for the school magazine. Our mother said nothing but our father was extremely cross and forbade him from any such indulgence. He said it was totally wrong. He was told not to write anything, but only to concentrate on his school books. Our father would always cite the example of his three oldest sons [all half-brothers of Nasira and Saadat] who, he would say, were brilliant. He wanted Saadat to be able to match their performance. Writing was not to be permitted to him. Therefore, Saadat never wrote anything as long as he was around his father. He started writing later. My mother always encouraged people to do what they wanted. One day Saadat wrote a story and announced that he was going to send it to a high-class magazine. Our cousins and other members of the family all lived on the same street [Koocha Vakeelaan, Amritsar]. He said he was going to send it to *Humayun* [a leading literary magazine of the time from Lahore]. Everyone was a bit taken aback. 'This is your first effort and you want to send it to *Humayun*!' they all exclaimed. 'Yes, I will,' Saadat replied.

A couple of days later, he came in looking very down. Our mother noticed immediately that something was wrong, so she asked him if he had had a fight with someone. 'No,' he replied, 'I didn't have a fight, but when I was walking past the houses of our elder sister and our uncle, they all came out and made fun of me, saying, "Look, there goes the writer."' Our mother told him not to pay any attention to that but to write what he wanted and to send it where he pleased.

Manto's three daughters, Nighat, Nuzhat and Nusrat, his sister Nasira Iqbal and Zakia Jalal, his wife's sister, talk about Manto, Lahore, April 1990.

Nighat: We were very young but I remember that we would all jump on his bed first thing in the morning and he would make us sit on his stomach and talk to us and play games with us.

Nasira Iqbal: Once all three girls caught measles. All night long, Saadat sat next to the middle daughter's cot, watching over her anxiously. 'Like me, she is restless, so I'll keep an eye on her,' he said. His wife, Safia, and I were attending to the other two.

Nusrat: I am the third and the youngest sister. I was a delicate child and so my father was never cross with me. And when he was cross, he would shout at my middle sister, Nuzhat, but it used to scare me nevertheless. My father used to call me Jujia Jee.

Nasira Iqbal: He loved Nuzhat a lot. He used to say, 'She is my real daughter.'

Nuzhat: Indeed, because I am very much like him in temperament. He must have seen something of himself in me.

Zakia Jalal: I was the youngest sister of his wife and he was always joking that the wife's sister is half-owner of the house and everything in it. 'If all you sisters decided to exert that right, I would find myself living on the footpath,' he would say. He was a very affectionate person.

Nusrat: Our mother used to tell us what good taste he had in things. He was very fond of buying expensive pens, and the paper he would write on would always be of very fine quality.

Nuzhat: Yes, that's right. He was always buying well-made shoes. We had one of his old pairs in the house but I don't know what happened to it.

Nighat: Our mother had very simple habits. Our father would help her do her hair, iron her clothes and cook. He liked to cook. His speciality was pakoras.

Zakia Jalal: I remember in Bombay during the war when things were scarce and only to be had on the black market, he would look for the rarest kind and bring them home. My sister Safia would complain. 'Why do you waste so much money on these trifles?' she would say. But he was fond of things that were hard to come by, special things.

Nighat: Later in Pakistan there was so much hardship.

Zakia Jalal: He saw wonderful times in Bombay

Nuzhat: Yes, in Bombay when the phone would ring, he would answer, 'One two,' not Manto. Just imagine, he had a phone in those days.

Nighat: He would joke on the phone. 'One two,' he would say and when the other party would answer, he would say, 'This is actually one-two's father on the line.'

Nuzhat: We are told that one day he repeatedly kept receiving phone calls from someone who thought he, Manto, was a stock exchange broker. 'Dispose of it,' Manto finally told the caller in exasperation. Later, when he was asked why he had done that, he answered, 'Whoever it was, he'll either have been wrecked or made.'

Nusrat: It is only now that we have begun to receive some royalty from his work. For thirty-five years, we received not a penny from his publishers. For the first time, Sang-e-Meel Publishers, Lahore, have given the family some money. We miss our mother today. She suffered a lot.

Zakia Jalal: We all used to live together in the same house. Everything was pooled and shared. We used to eat together.

Nighat: Our aunt (*pointing to Nasira Iqbal*) used to live with us as well.

Nasira Iqbal: After my husband died, Saadat brought me to live with him. He told me, 'You don't want to grow old alone while your daughter is growing up. Come and live here with us.'

Zakia Jalal: His only weakness was drinking. As a human being, he was very sensitive, very sincere. There was no difference between his exterior and his interior.

Nuzhat: I remember when we would return home from school, he would be waiting with a plateful of pomegranate seeds. Children from the neighbourhood would be invited to join.

Nighat: And in the playground in front of the house, he would arrange kabbadi matches.

Nuzhat: Since we lived together, there were always fights among us children, especially between Shahid and me [Hamid and Zakia Jalal's son, now married to Nusrat, Manto's youngest daughter]. Our father would tell him, 'Go upstairs because you two are always fighting.' Then he would add, 'This Shahid is a cry baby. Send him upstairs.'

(*Translated from Urdu and Punjabi by Khalid Hasan*)

APPENDIX 3

FRIENDS OF MANTO REMINISCE ABOUT HIM

A. Hamid: Qasimi sahib, when did you meet Manto?

Ahmed Nadeem Qasimi: We met much later but our correspondence began in 1937. My first short story, 'Begunah', was published in *Rooman*, a magazine edited by Akhtar Shirani. Manto, having read it, wrote to Shirani, asking to be put in touch with the author. Shirani passed on the letter to me and I wrote back to Manto, which was how our correspondence began. We met in Delhi when Manto called me over for an assignment he had found for me, just to help me supplement my meagre income. It was to write the dialogues and lyrics for *Dharam Patni*, a movie being made by a Maharashtrian writer. Manto travelled from Bombay to Delhi and I came from Multan. We met in Chowri Bazaar, which was Delhi's red-light district. Our meeting took place in the office of an English movie magazine, which was located there, edited by one Kirpa Ram. We spent the night in that office and in the morning we moved to New Delhi where I got down to work on my assignment.

Hamid: You met in Bombay later?

Qasimi: No, I never went to Bombay. We always met in Delhi. Manto had joined All India Radio and I travelled five or six times to Delhi to see him. I also used to stay with him.

Hamid: He used to sit in Noon Meem Raashed's room, who was director of programmes. I first saw Manto there. He had another person with him by the name of Chander Kant.

Qasimi: Manto never got along with Raashed. I don't know how you saw him in his room.

This conversation among Ahmed Nadeem Qasimi, Abdulla Malik, Ahmed Rahi and A. Hamid was recorded in April 1990 at Lahore.

Hamid: I was staying at Raashed's home.

Qasimi: When Raashed passed by, Manto would say, 'O Raashed, do you know the basic steps of ballroom dancing?' And Raashed would answer that he did not. 'Then why have you written that poem which begins: "I am a fugitive from life, hold me in your arms, my dance partner."' He was always teasing Krishen Chander as well.

Hamid: When I went to All India Radio, I saw Manto in Raashed's room. He was writing his radio plays at the time, later published in the collection *Janazey.*

Qasimi: You must have seen him, but I have a story. A radio official came to Manto and asked him if he had completed the play he was supposed to have written. The official wanted the name of the play for an announcement. Manto told him, 'Call it *Kabootri.*' He later wrote a play by that name. He had an Urdu typewriter that he worked with, using the touch system. He was the first Urdu writer to use a typewriter.

Rahi: However, when Upindar Nath Ashk bought one, Manto sold his.

Hamid (*to Abdulla Malik*): Did you meet Manto in Bombay?

Malik: No, I had met him earlier, in 1938 or 1939, at the house of Bari Alig, who used to live in Anarkali, Lahore. We were one day drinking beer, Hassan Abbas, Bari Alig, Manto and I, when Rajindra Singh Bedi walked in. He said he did not much care for beer. 'Then what are you doing here with us?' Manto shot back.

Rahi: But Bedi used to smoke.

Malik: That he started to do later. I want to say that the rebel in Manto was so dominant that he wanted to smash every established institution. At the time, Iqbal was a formidable influence. That evening while we were drinking beer, Manto suggested to Bari that we all go to Hira Mandi and later visit Iqbal's tomb and ask him, 'You rascal, while you were alive, you frequented Hira Mandi, and even after your death, you haven't let go of the place.'

That was Manto. Always the rebel. The Russian literature he had read had also influenced him deeply. But more than anything, it was Bari Alig who was the biggest influence on Manto. It was Bari who first introduced socialist literature to India. He was popularly known as 'Bari, the socialist writer'.

I met Manto often in 1943 when I was a full-timer with the Indian Communist Party. I travelled to Bombay to attend the first party congress and was asked to join the party weekly newspaper, *Qaumi Jang*. I was staying in the Byculla quarter of the city in a flat with the painter Shakir Ali, Ali Sardar Jaffrey and Sajjad Zaheer. So there I was, a Punjabi, thrown in with three UP-walas. Manto also lived in the area, just about five minutes from our flat. When he came to know that I had arrived in Bombay, one day he popped in and said to me right in front of my flatmates, 'What are you doing with these three rascals? They will neither give you anything to eat nor do you any good. Come, get up and I'll take you home and give you some breakfast.' As long as I lived there, I used to go to Manto's house every morning for breakfast.

Hamid: Was Manto writing for movies in those days and for the movie magazine *Musawwar*?

Malik: Yes, but I must tell a story. One day, I was in the party office working when he walked in. I took him to the reception room where he told me that something important had brought him to our office. He wanted to know if I had any literature on the psychology of love-making while bombs were falling. The Japanese had recently bombed the Bengal port of Chittagong. I replied that I knew nothing about it but promised to keep my eyes open in case I ran into something. But it was the rebel in Manto who was very strong, the overpowering element in his personality.

Rahi: Yes, that's true. I remember once he asked me, 'Can anyone tell me what really took place when Adam and Eve met for the first time?'

Malik: Qasimi sahib, Manto's story 'Naya Qanoon' was a big hit with the Progressive Writers' Movement before Independence, but what was it that led to the break between Manto and the progressive writers after Independence?

Qasimi: It was not political, nor was it personal. After all, inside the movement, there were friends of Manto like me. Then there were people like you. What actually happened was that the Progressive Writers' Association fell a victim to extremism. Anyone who did not completely fall in line with the manifesto of the association was declared 'non-progressive'. The result was that a man like Manto, who was a true progressive in my opinion—and indeed of others—was boycotted. So was Qurratulain Hyder. And many others, all leading, noteworthy writers. This did us great damage. A year or eighteen months later I, as general secretary of the association, recanted the earlier resolution. It was officially rescinded at the general conference of the Progressive Writers' Association held at Karachi. However, because of that hiatus lasting nearly two years, we were the losers. We lost a writer like Manto.

Another point I would like to make is about the oft-brandished charge that Manto's writing was obscene. I have always believed that he was a man of singular courage who, while living in this hypocritical society, spoke for the rights of helpless and persecuted women through the medium of fiction. There were many forces, mainly religious men like Maulana Abdul Maid Daryabadi, who carried on a relentless campaign of vilification against Manto. Many cases were instituted against him. I was involved in a couple of them as editor. We were ultimately acquitted.

Malik: Was it not always Chaudhri Muhammad Hussain, who was Javid Iqbal's guardian, who instituted all the cases against Manto in the Punjab? Every case charging him with obscenity was brought against him in the Punjab, without exception. Isn't that correct?

Qasimi: Yes, that is correct. All of them in the Punjab. Abdul Majid Daryabadi could not have had the guts to take us to court. He only used to denounce Manto in his magazine. Manto was forced to travel all the way from Bombay to Lahore every time there was a hearing. That he found most upsetting. But it was always good for the Lahore writers to have Manto come to the city.

Hamid: Rahi sahib, tell us about Manto's last days in Lahore. His days at *Savera*.

Rahi: No, he used to frequent the *Savera* office when he first arrived in Pakistan, not in his last days. And I think we can date the start of Manto's woes from that point on. Soon after his arrival, he was given an assignment by Masood Pervez, who was making a film called *Beli*. Manto wrote the story and the dialogue and was given five thousand rupees, which was a reasonable sum of money in those days. He never found any work after that. He would be paid twenty to twenty-five rupees for a story. It would take him two to three hours in the morning to complete one. He would then go out, sell it, emptied of everything and knowing that he would have to do the same thing the next day and the next day. He couldn't live on twenty to twenty-five rupees a day. He would often ask his publishers, Chaudhry Rashid and Chaudhry Nazir, to give him an office, a place where he could work from morning till evening. That office he never got and his life became irregular. He had always had a routine in the old days. He would go to his office in the morning, work all day and be ready for the evening. This was his routine at *Musawwar* in Bombay, at Filmistan and at Imperial Film Company. In the evening, he would drink according to his requirements or mood, eat, go to bed and start the next day by going to work first thing in the morning.

In Pakistan, none of that was available. The result was that he began to indulge in excesses. His drinking became heavy and he was always assailed by anxiety. Some people took advantage of that and turned him into a kind of beggar. But that was not the real Manto, who was a man of great self-respect, who always came to the help of others. For us in those days, five to ten rupees used to be enough and he would see to it that we got that money. Qasimi has spoken about Manto summoning him to Delhi so he could be helped. But here people began to use Manto. They would say to him, 'Go and ask so and so for money. He dare not say no to you.' And those people, all hangers-on, would cling to Manto like leeches. In his last days, I was not around him, having joined the movies, so he was surrounded by such people.

In my opinion, Manto began to die the day he set foot in Pakistan.

(*Translated from Urdu and Punjabi by Khalid Hasan*)